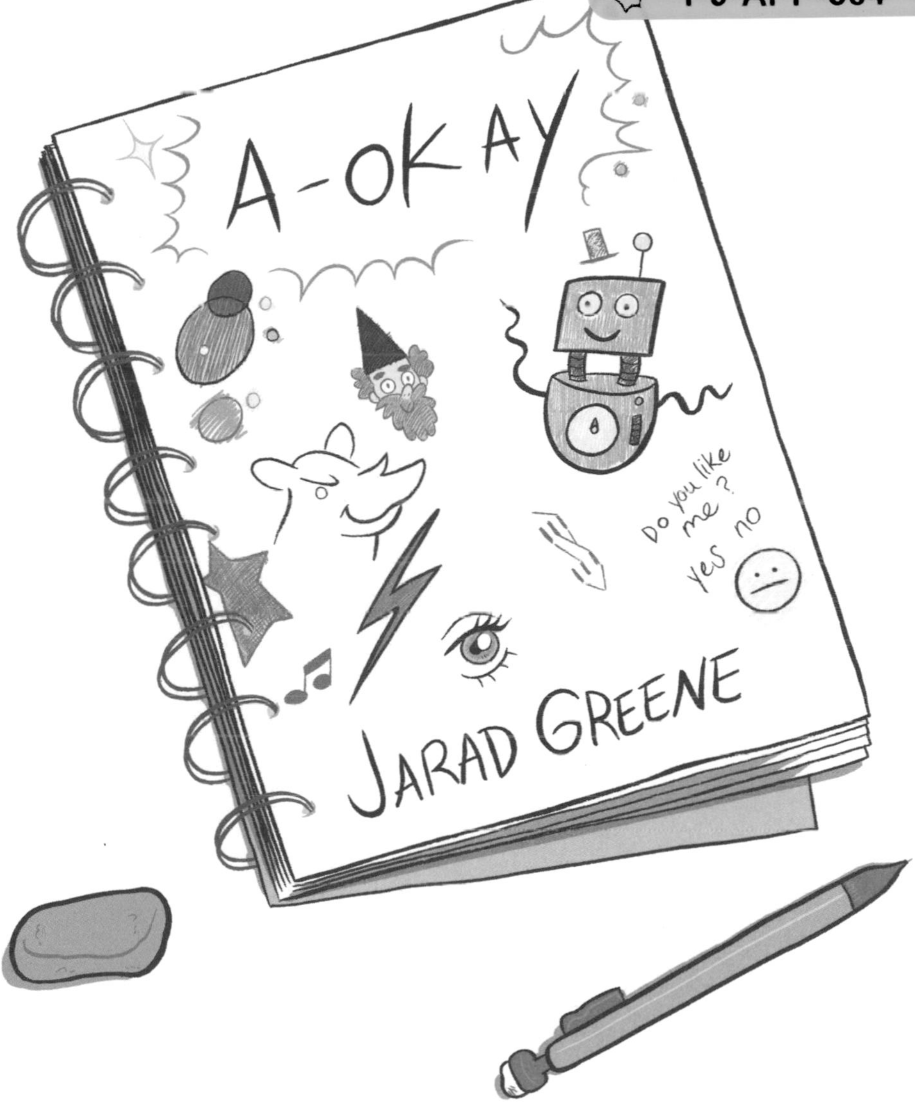
A-OKAY
Do you like me?
yes no
JARAD GREENE

HARPER alley
An Imprint of HarperCollinsPublishers

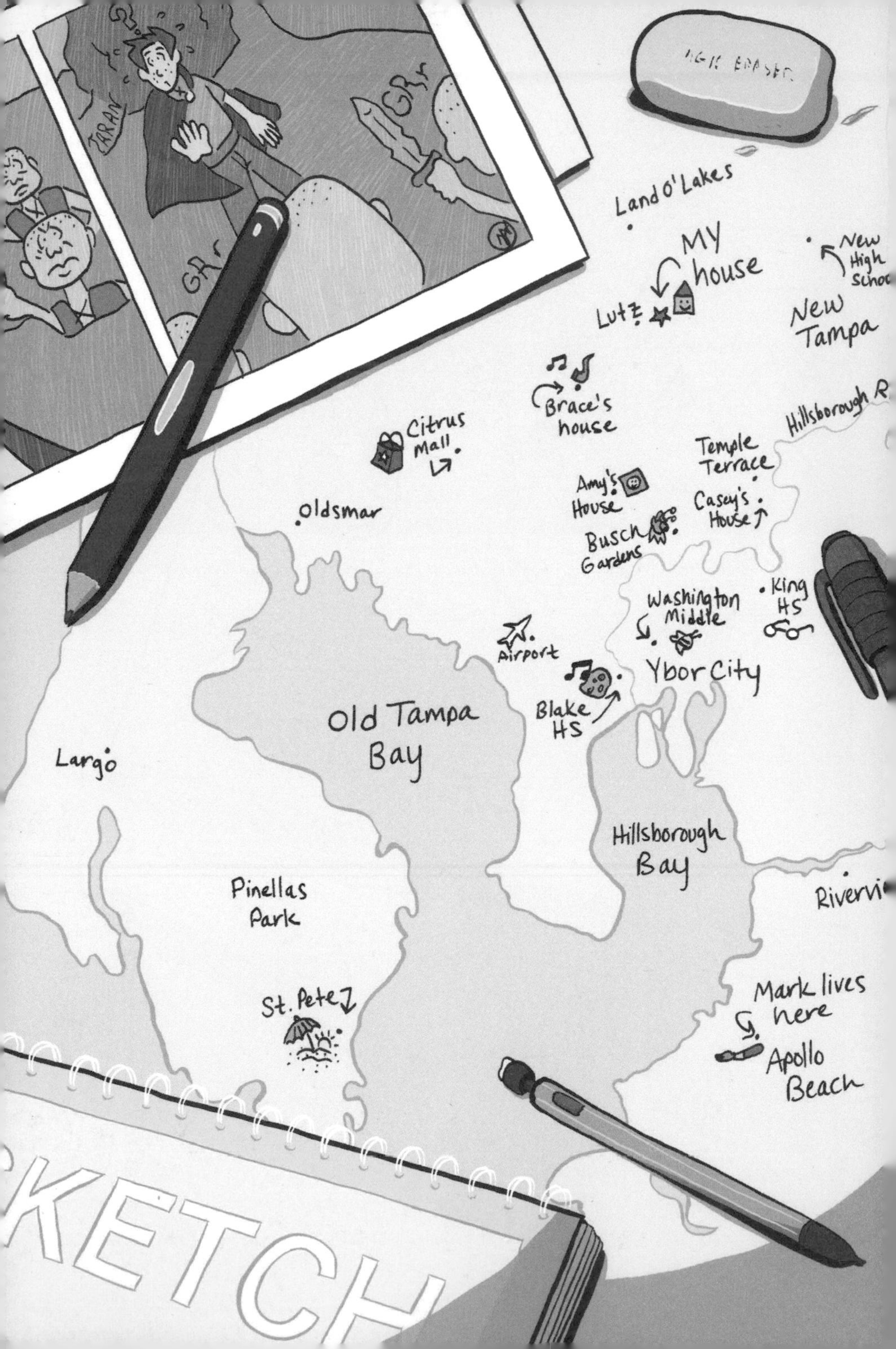

TARAN
GRr
GRr
Land O' Lakes
My house
New High
Lutz
New Tampa
Brace's house
Citrus Mall
Hillsborough R
Temple Terrace
Amy's House
Casey's House
Oldsmar
Busch Gardens
Washington Middle
King HS
Airport
Ybor City
Blake HS
Old Tampa Bay
Largo
Hillsborough Bay
Pinellas Park
St. Pete
Mark lives here
Apollo Beach
KETCH

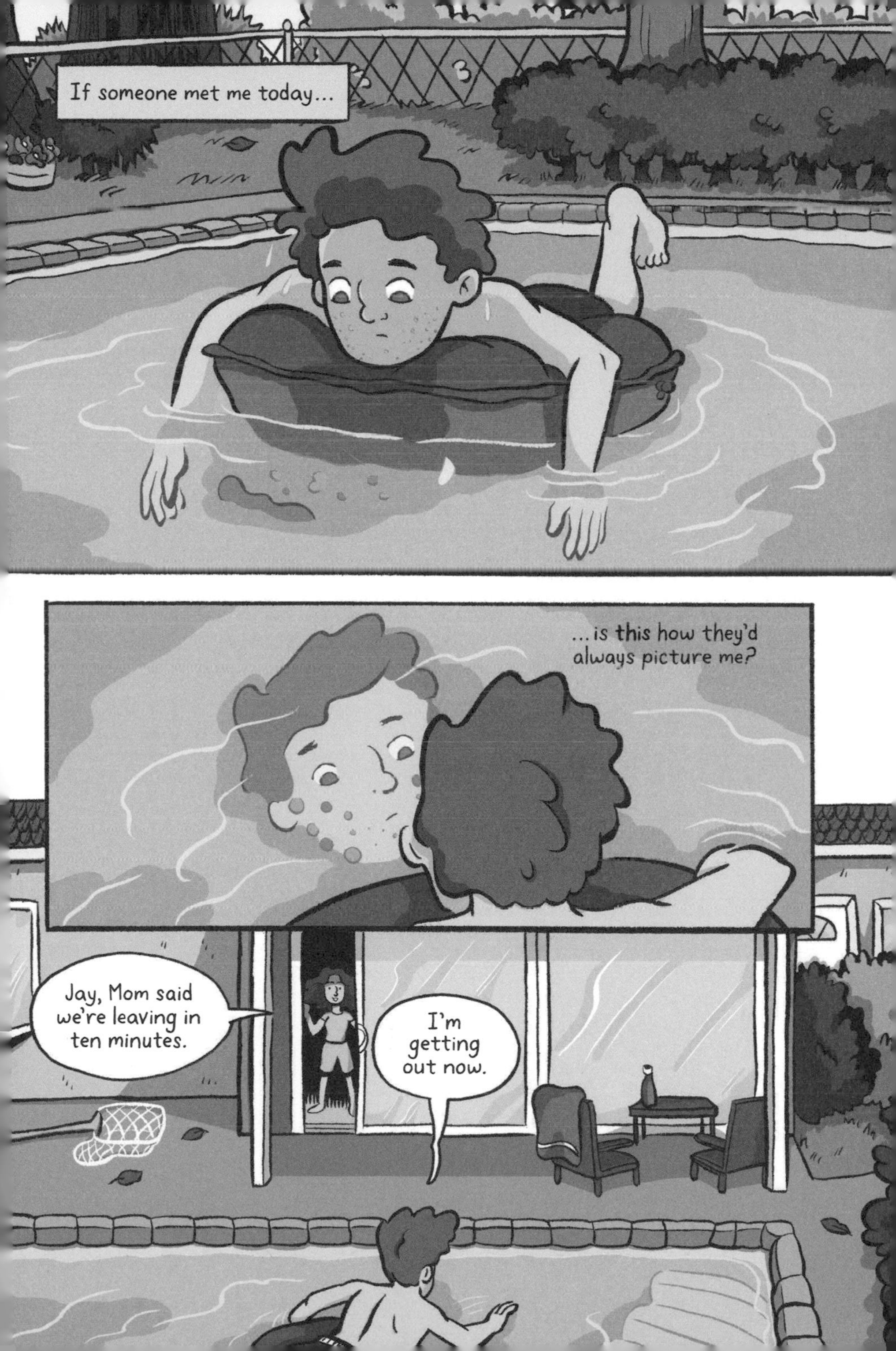
If someone met me today...
...is this how they'd always picture me?
Jay, Mom said we're leaving in ten minutes.
I'm getting out now.

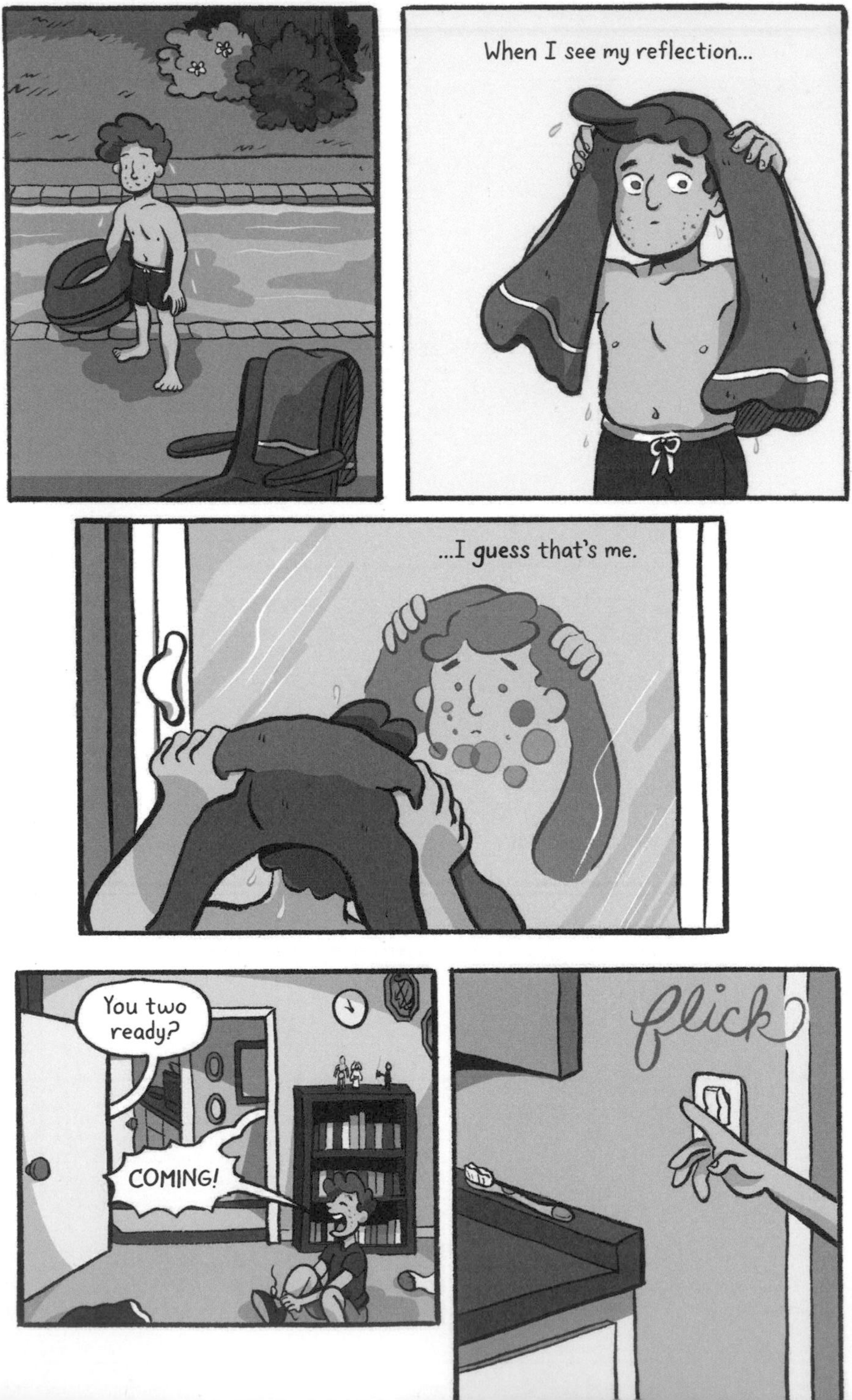

When I see my reflection...
...I guess that's me.
You two ready?
COMING!
flick

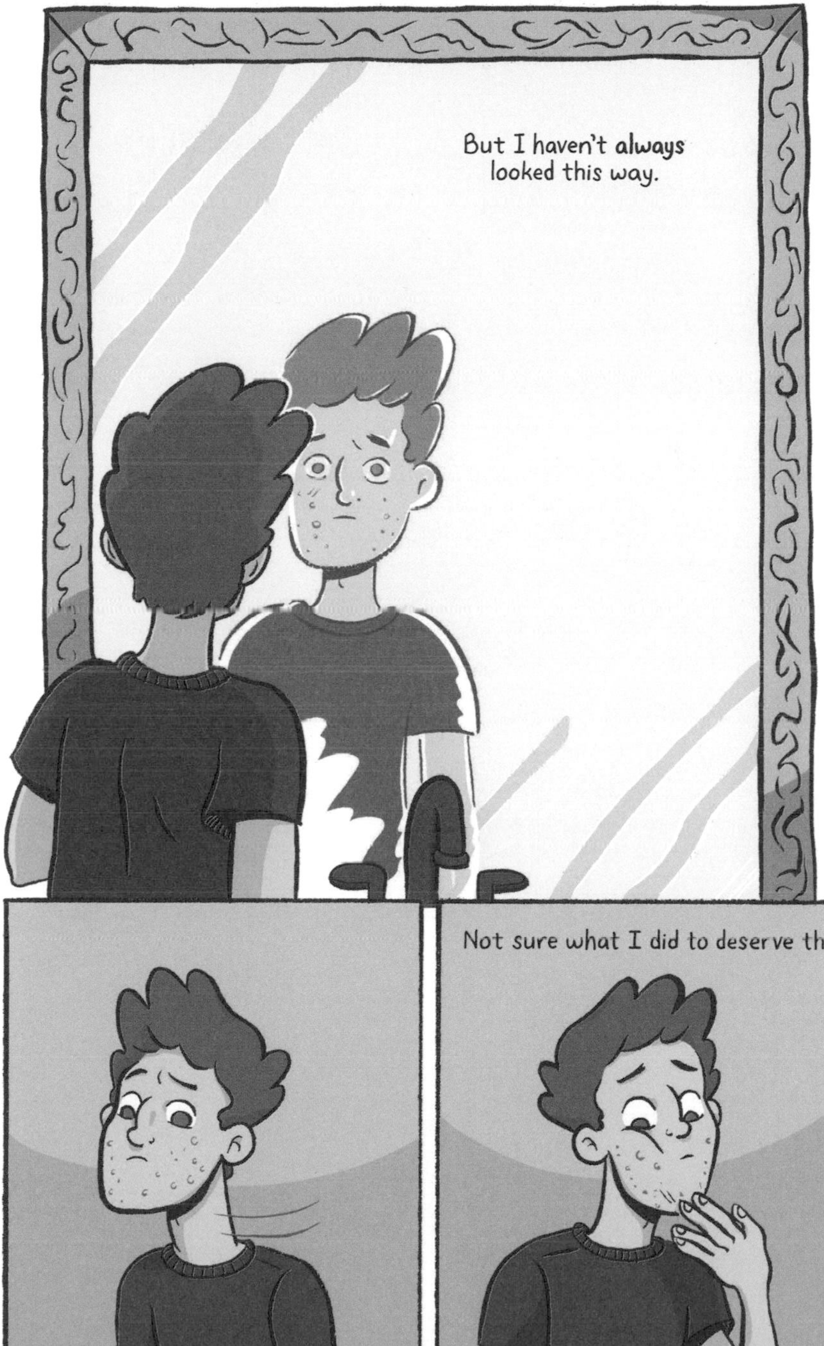
But I haven't always looked this way.
Not sure what I did to deserve this.

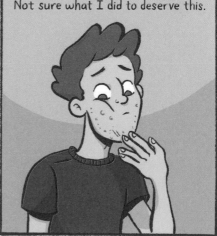

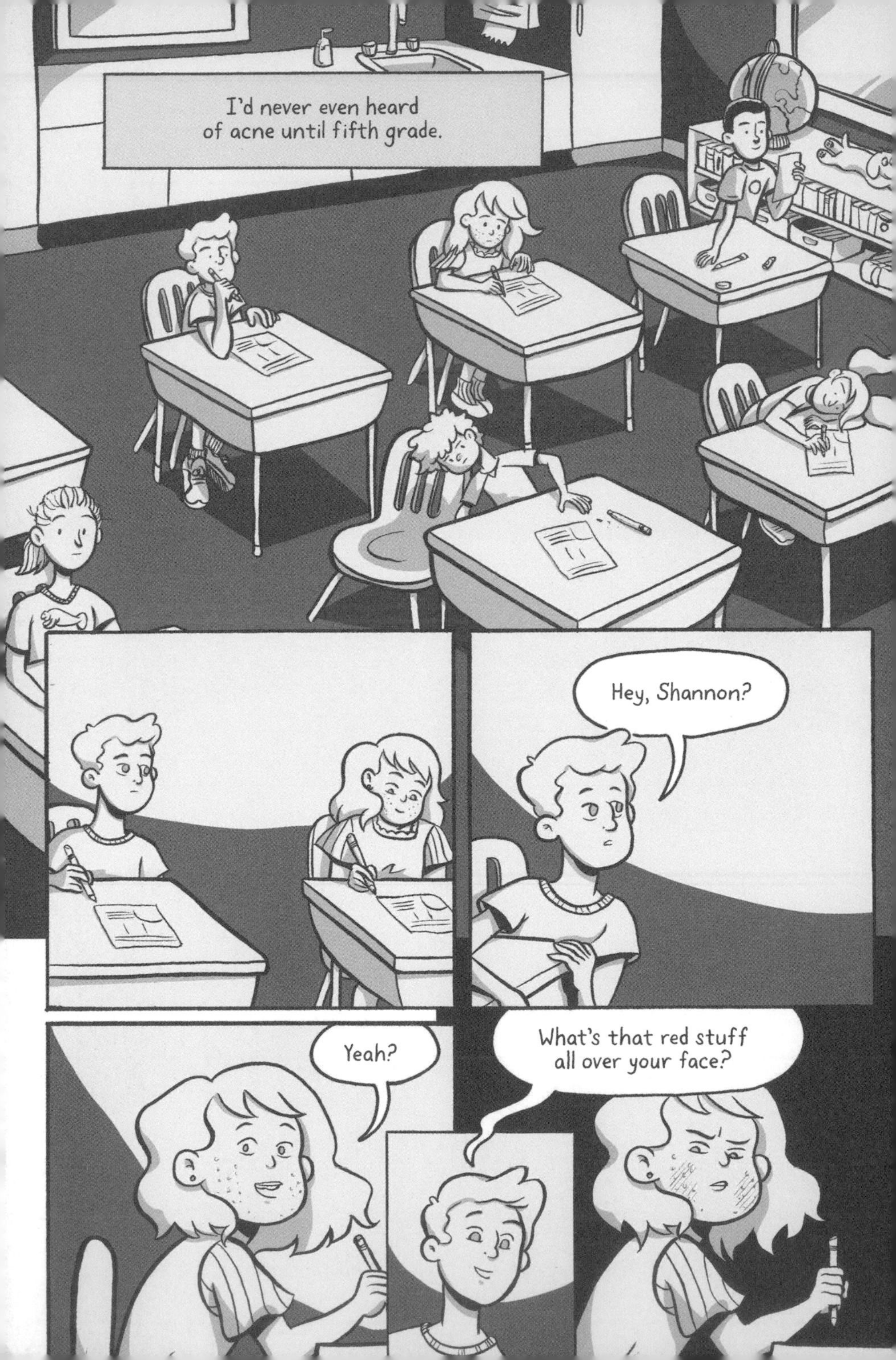
I'd never even heard of acne until fifth grade.
Hey, Shannon?
Yeah?
What's that red stuff all over your face?

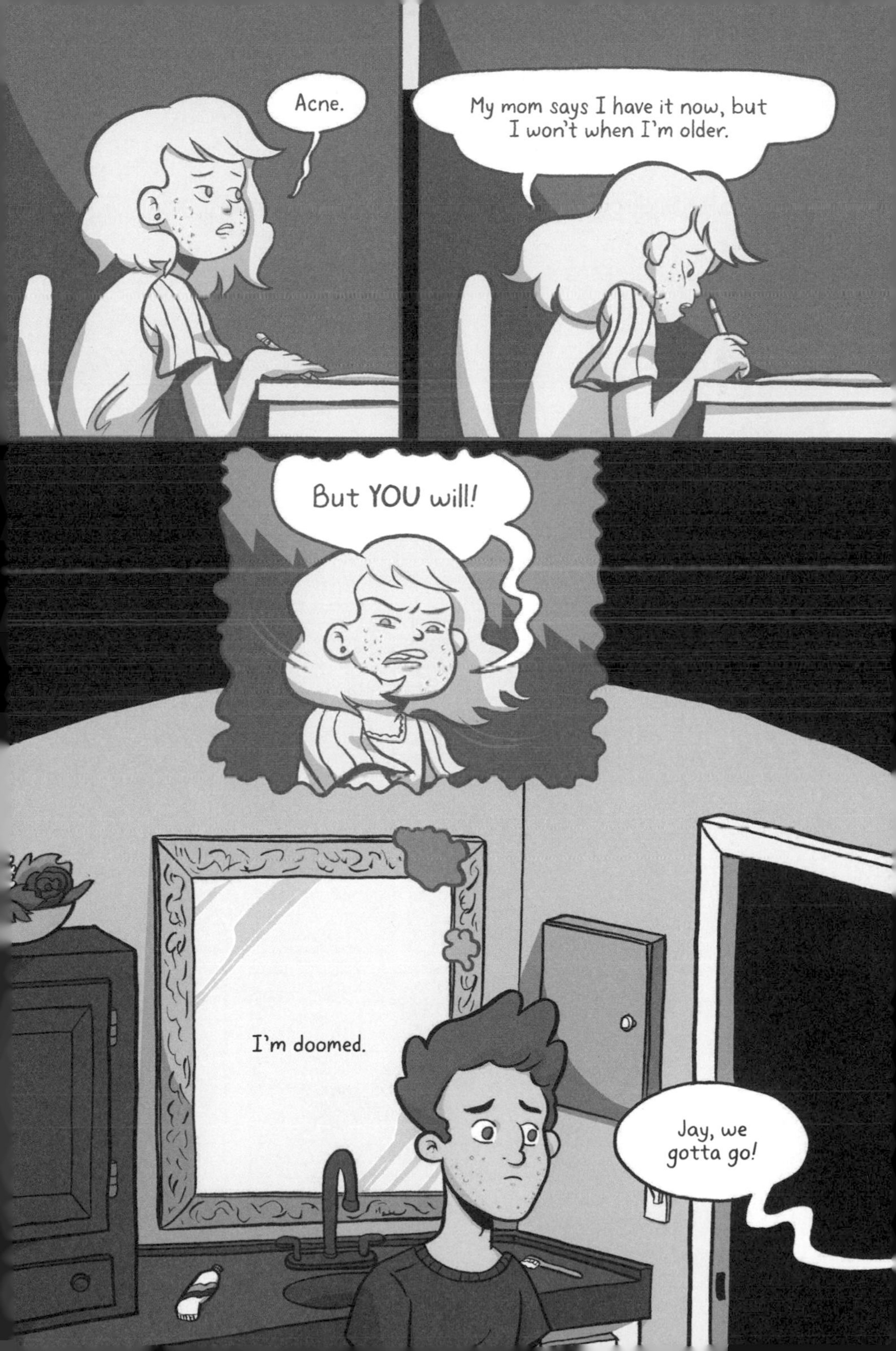
Acne.
My mom says I have it now, but I won't when I'm older.
But YOU will!
I'm doomed.
Jay, we gotta go!

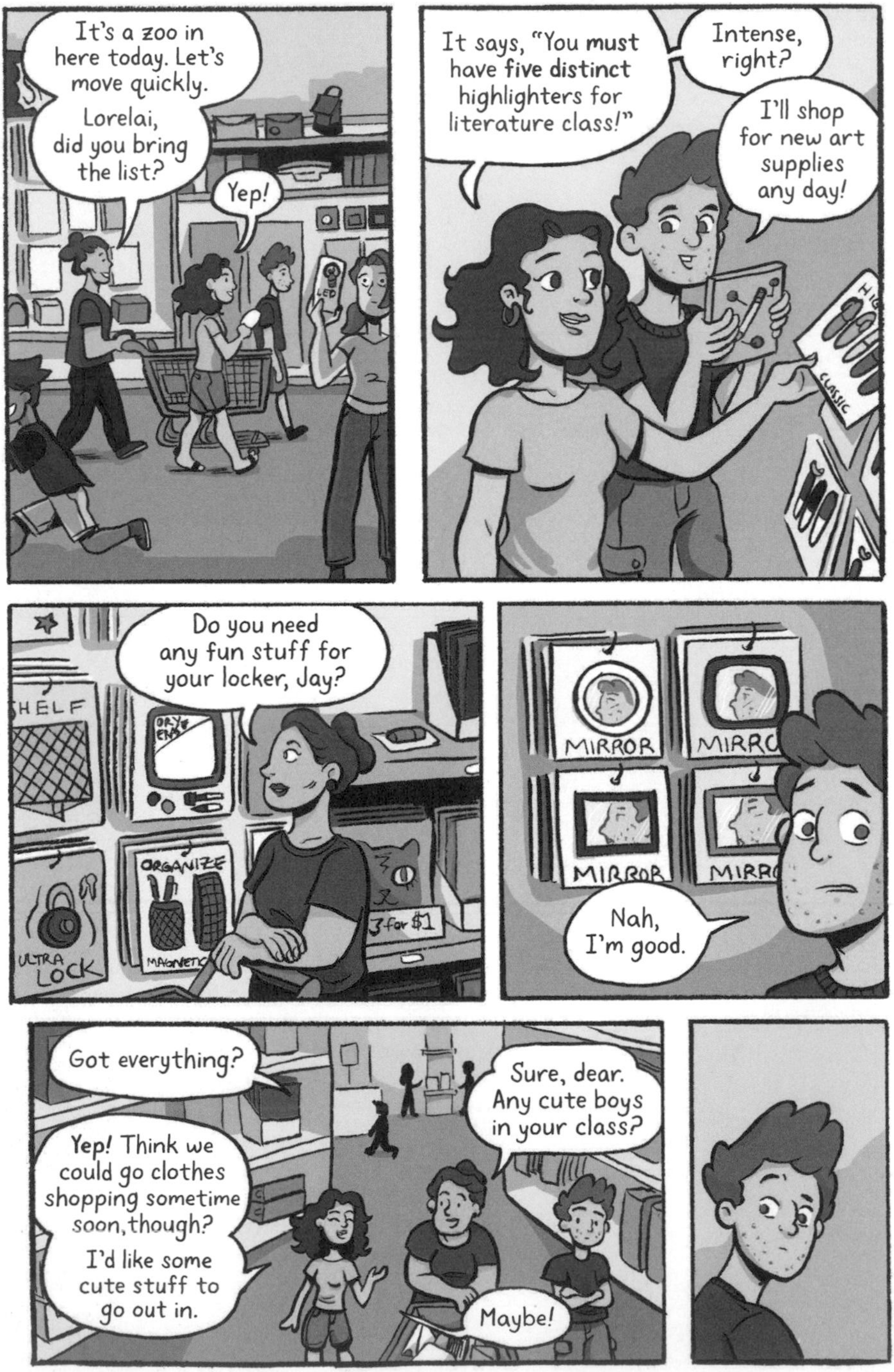
It's a zoo in here today. Let's move quickly.
Lorelai, did you bring the list?
Yep!
LED
It says, "You **must** have **five distinct** highlighters for literature class!"
Intense, right?
I'll shop for new art supplies any day!
CLASSIC
Do you need any fun stuff for your locker, Jay?
ORGANIZE
ULTRA LOCK
3 for $1
MIRROR
MIRROR
Nah, I'm good.
Got everything?
Sure, dear. Any cute boys in your class?
Yep! Think we could go clothes shopping sometime soon, though?
I'd like some cute stuff to go out in.
Maybe!

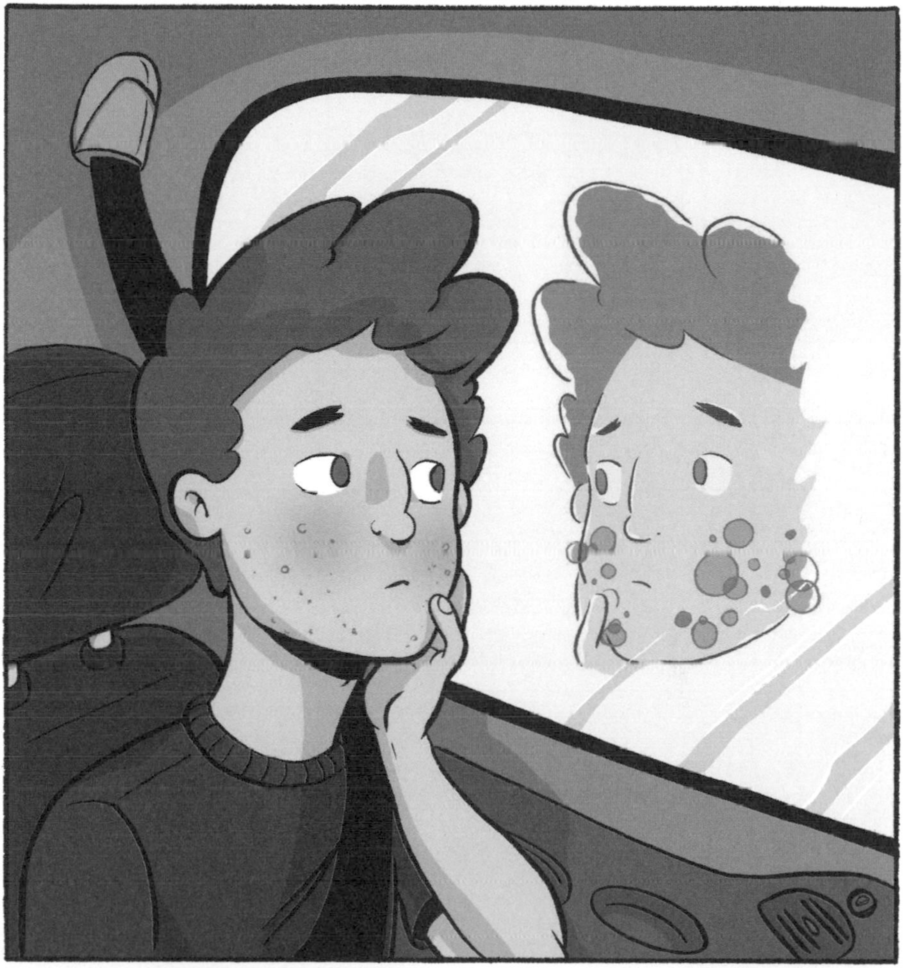

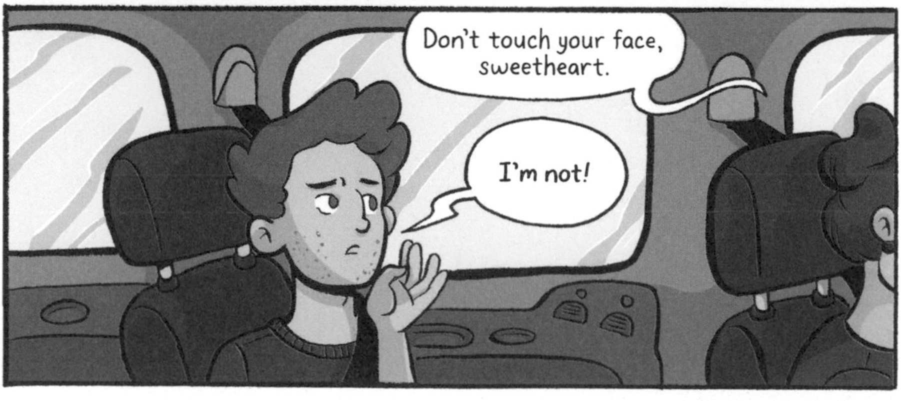
Don't touch your face, sweetheart.
I'm not!

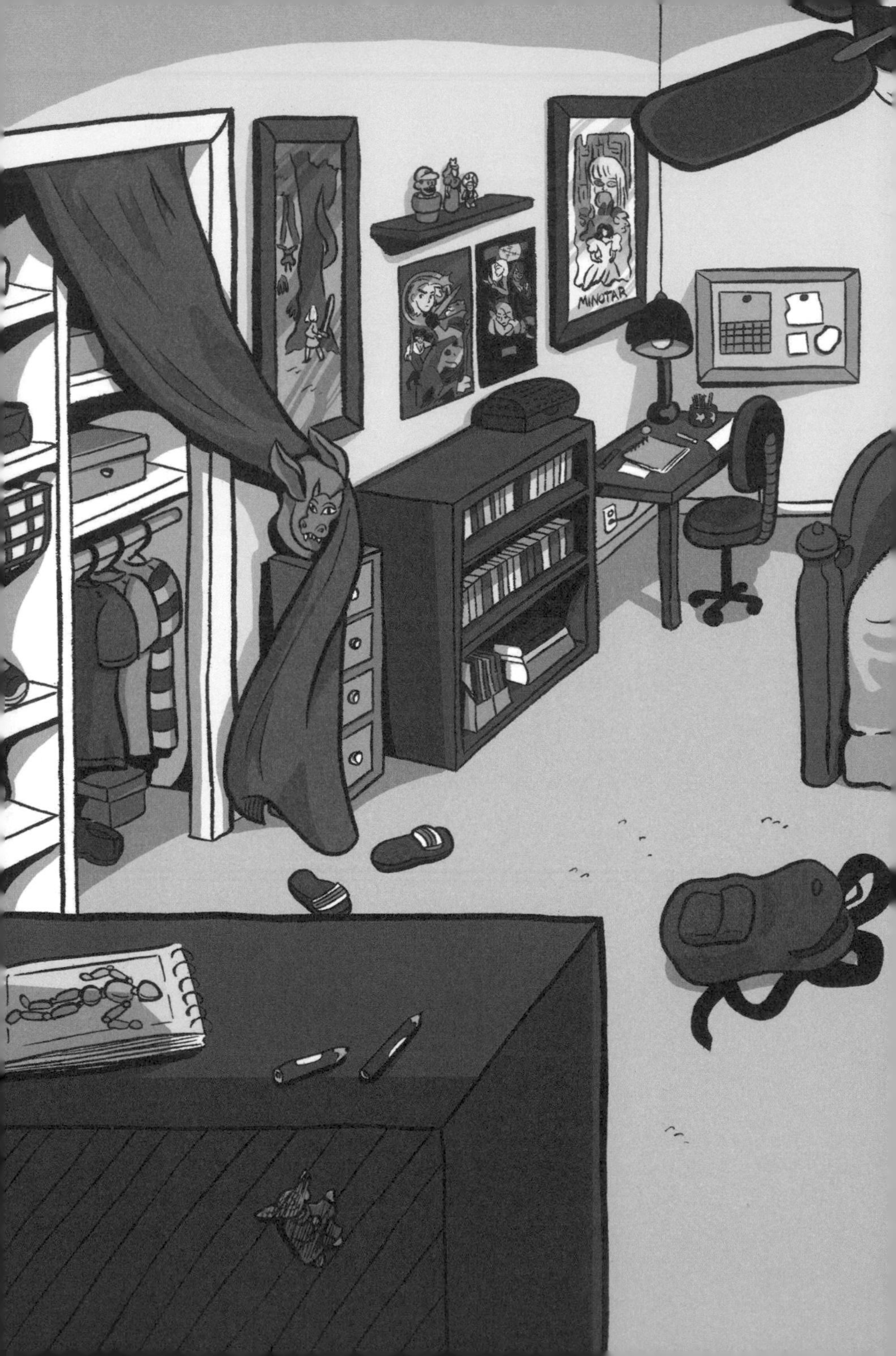
MINOTAR

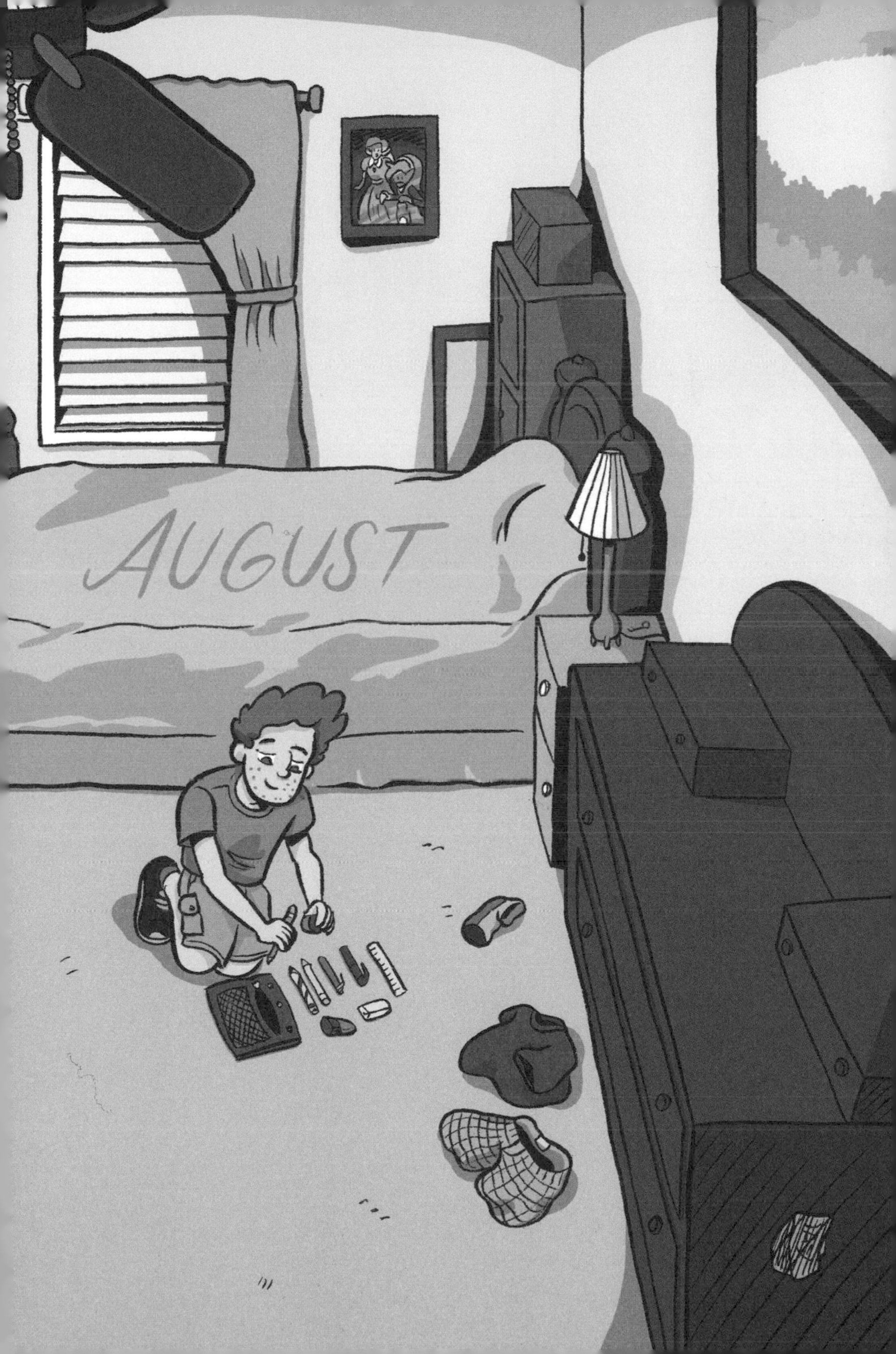
AUGUST

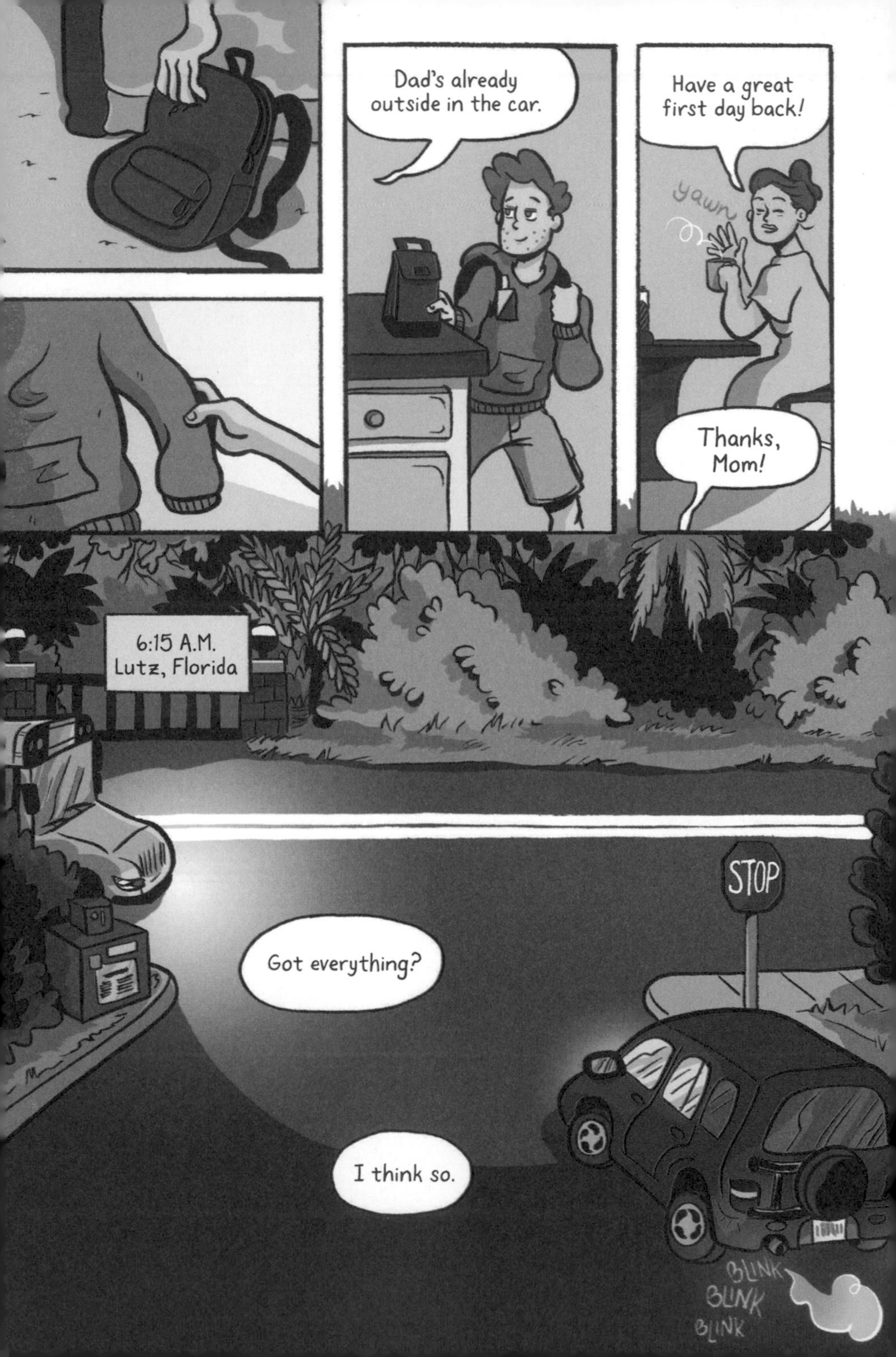
Dad's already outside in the car.
Have a great first day back!
yawn
Thanks, Mom!
6:15 A.M. Lutz, Florida
STOP
Got everything?
I think so.
BLINK
BLINK
BLINK

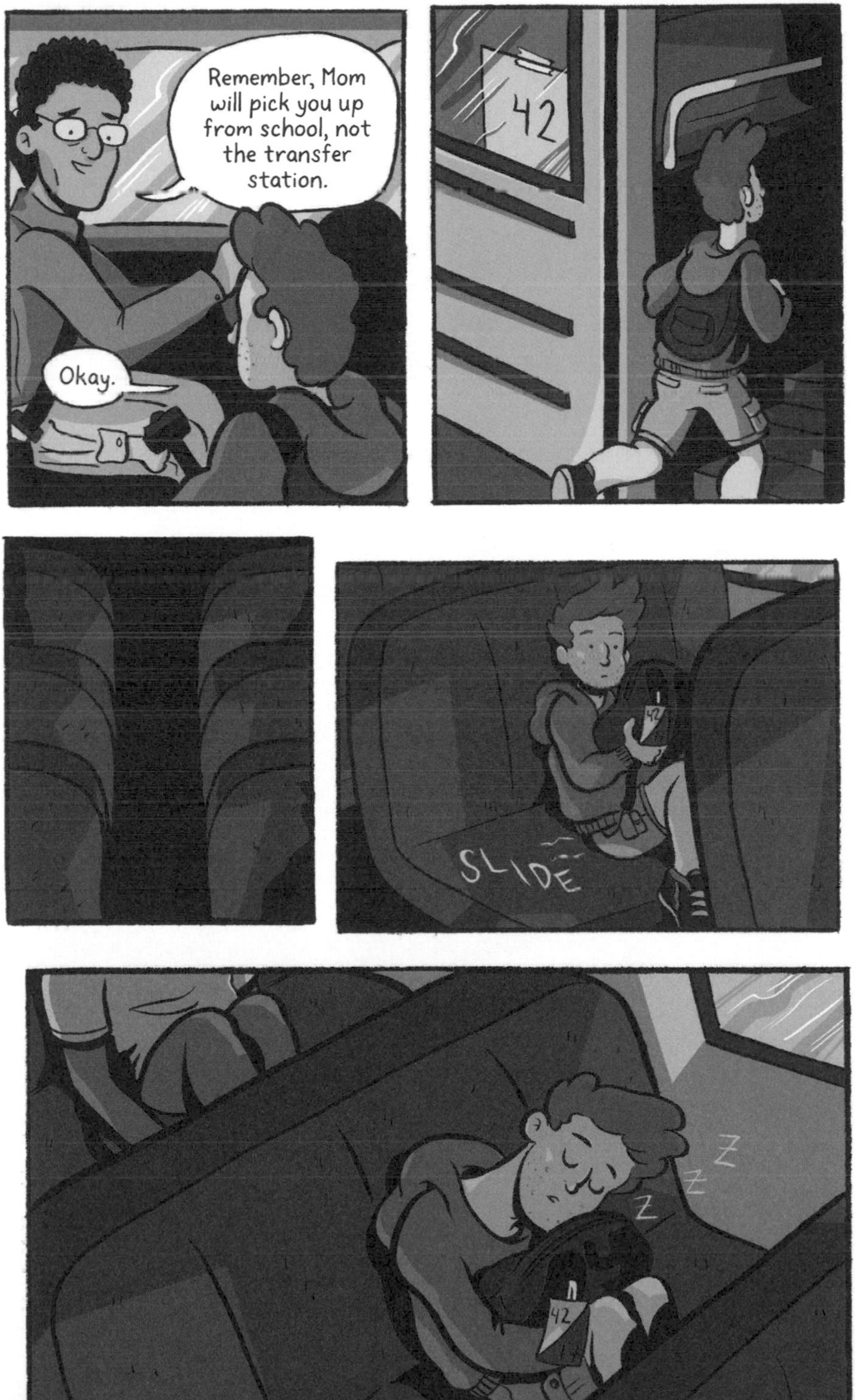
Remember, Mom will pick you up from school, not the transfer station.
Okay.
42
42
SLIDE
42
Z
Z
Z

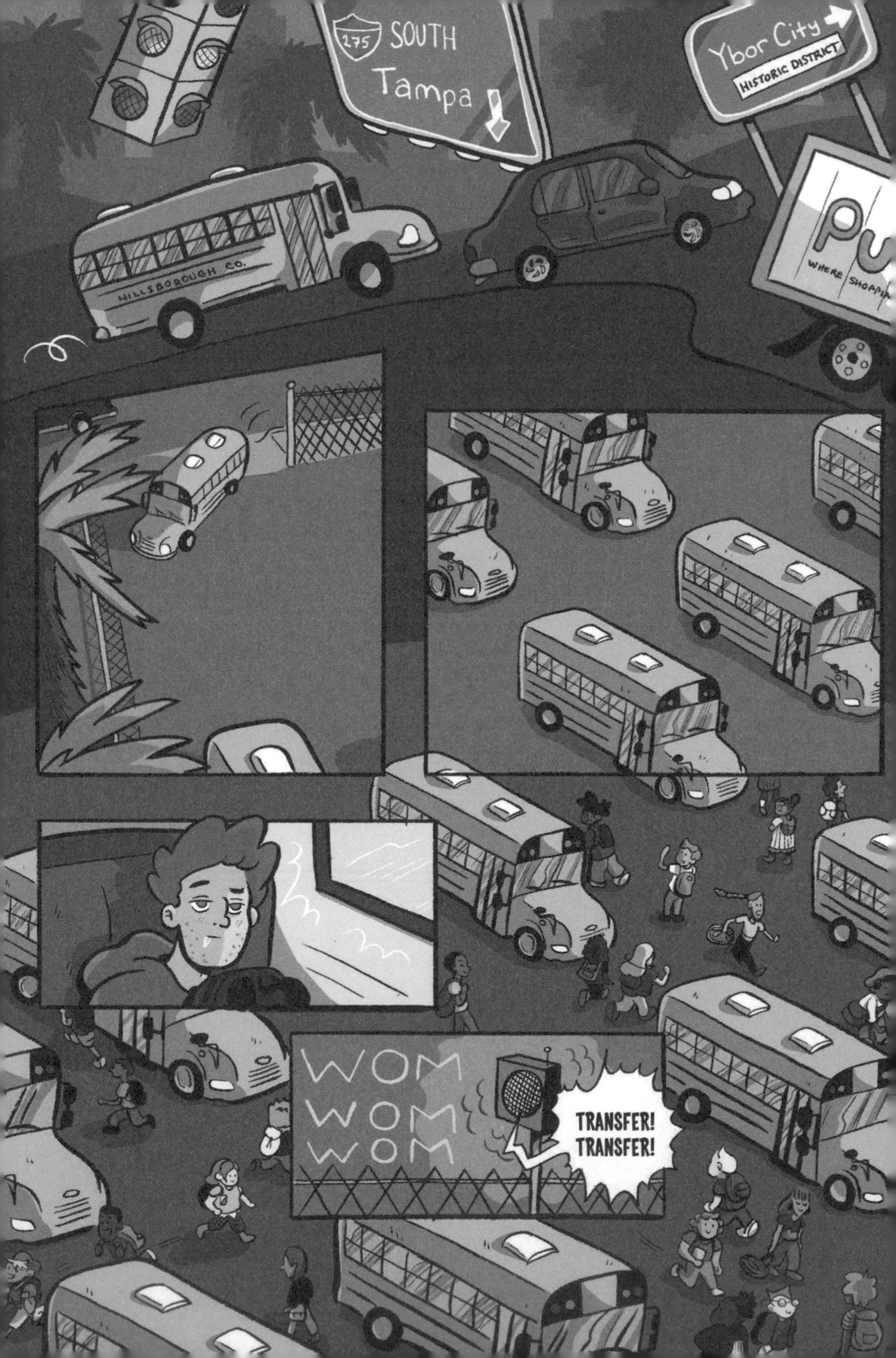
275 SOUTH
Tampa
Ybor City
HISTORIC DISTRICT
HILLSBOROUGH CO.
WHERE SHOPPI
WOM
WOM
WOM
TRANSFER!
TRANSFER!

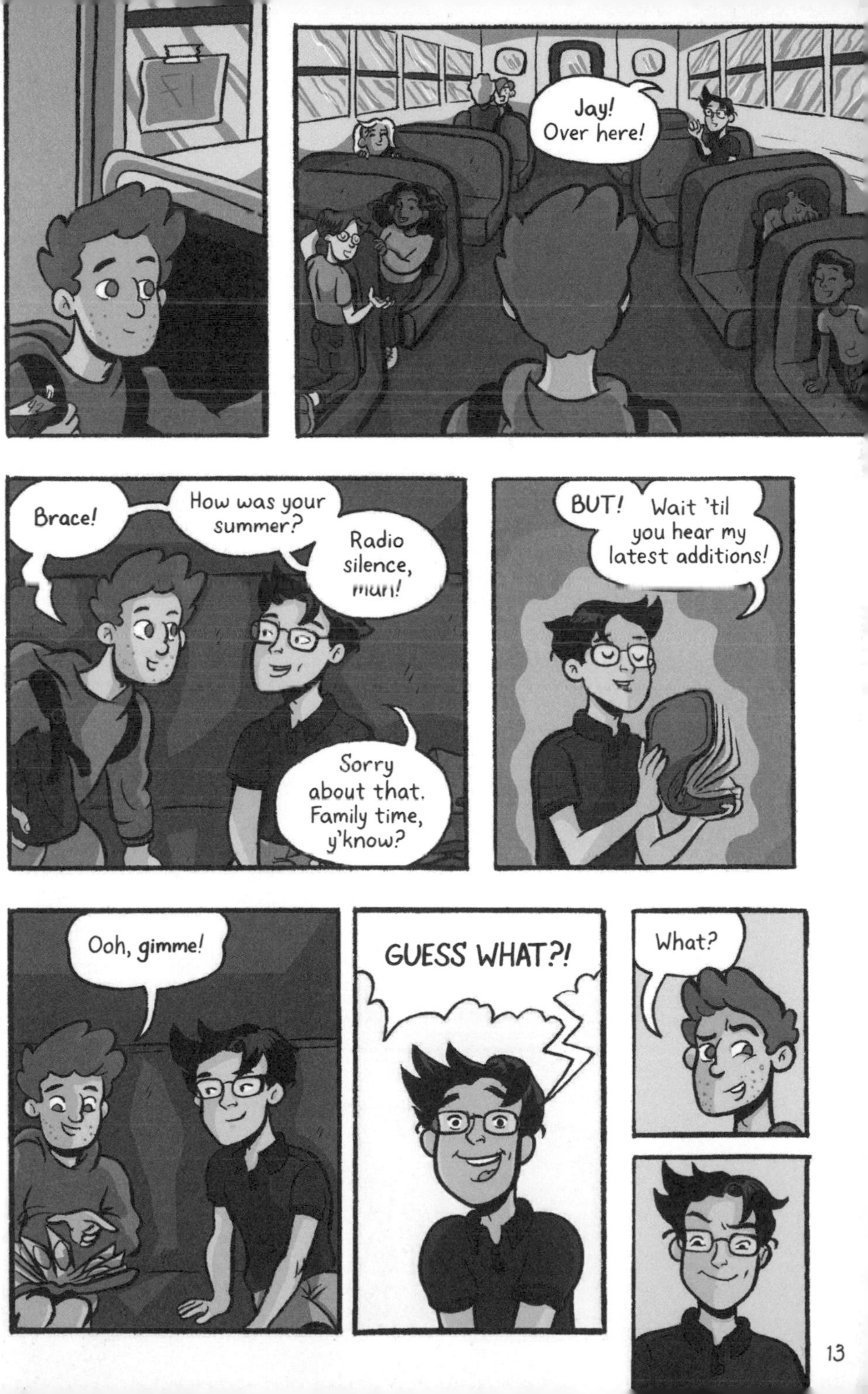
Jay! Over here!
Brace!
How was your summer?
Radio silence, man!
Sorry about that. Family time, y'know?
BUT! Wait 'til you hear my latest additions!
Ooh, gimme!
GUESS WHAT?!
What?

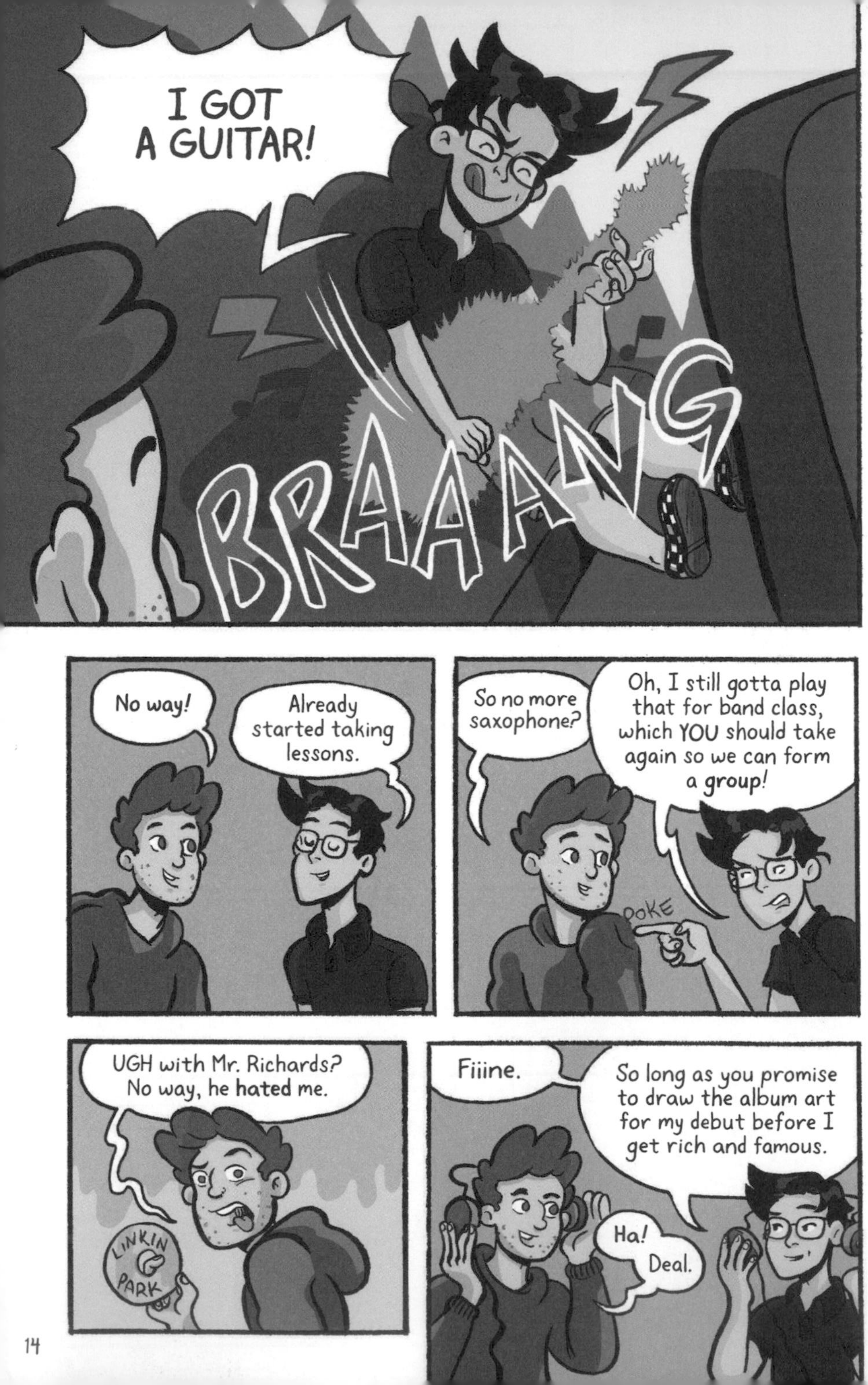
I GOT A GUITAR!
BRAAANG
No way!
Already started taking lessons.
So no more saxophone?
Oh, I still gotta play that for band class, which YOU should take again so we can form a group!
POKE
UGH with Mr. Richards? No way, he hated me.
LINKIN PARK
Fiiine.
So long as you promise to draw the album art for my debut before I get rich and famous.
Ha! Deal.

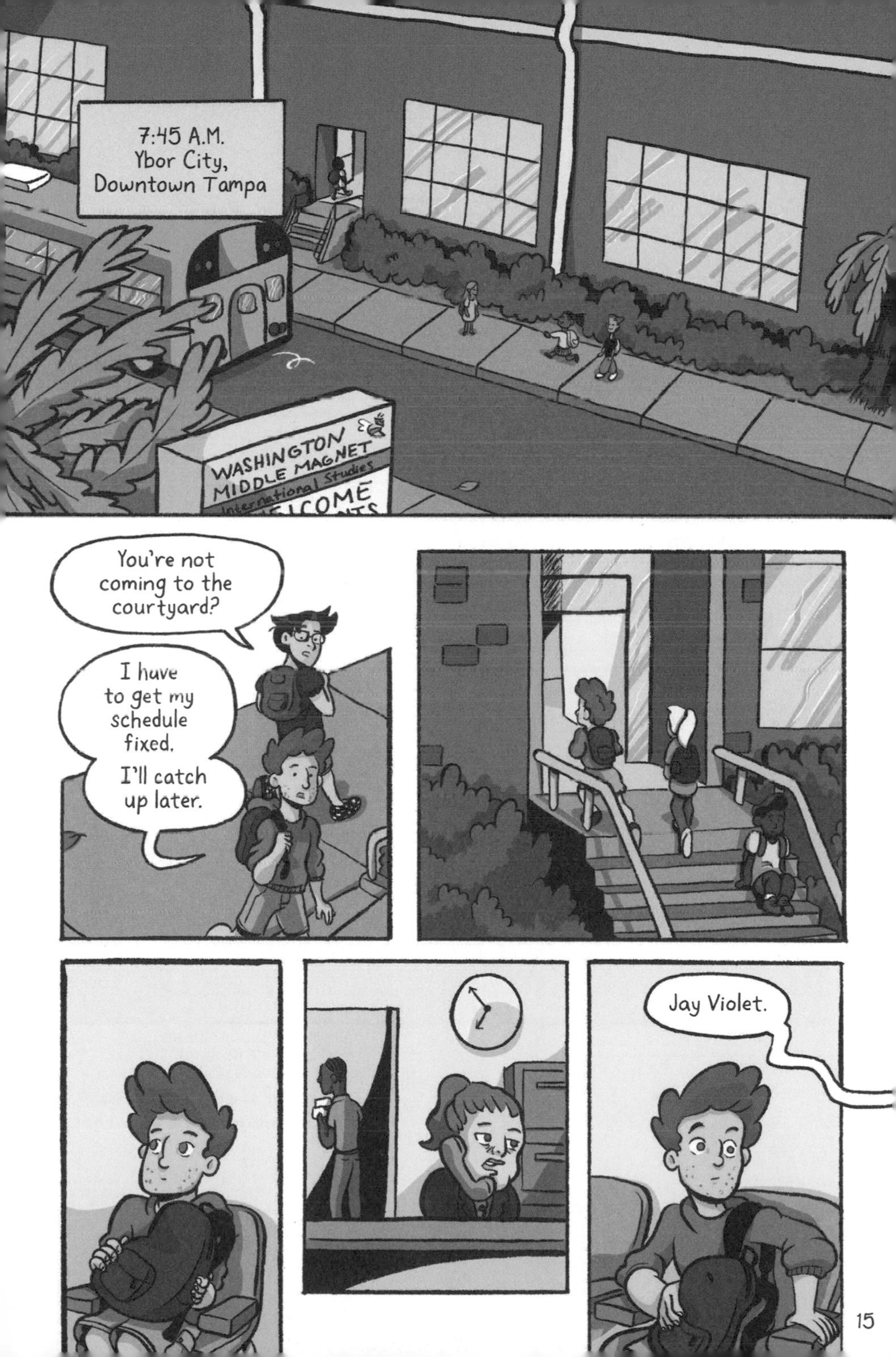

7:45 A.M.
Ybor City,
Downtown Tampa
WASHINGTON
MIDDLE MAGNET
International Studies
You're not coming to the courtyard?
I have to get my schedule fixed.
I'll catch up later.
Jay Violet.

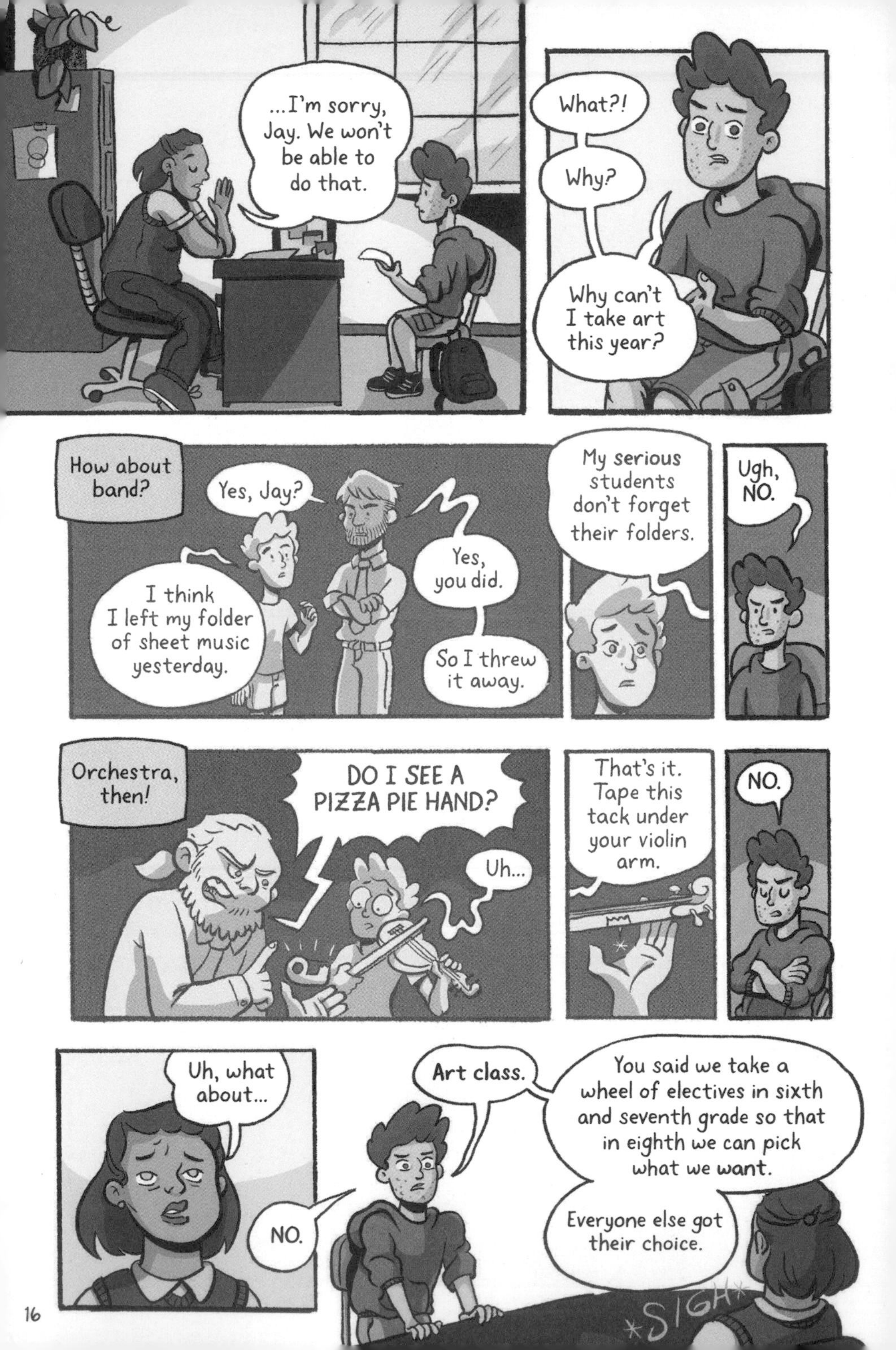
...I'm sorry, Jay. We won't be able to do that.
What?!
Why?
Why can't I take art this year?
How about band?
Yes, Jay?
I think I left my folder of sheet music yesterday.
Yes, you did.
So I threw it away.
My serious students don't forget their folders.
Ugh, NO.
Orchestra, then!
DO I SEE A PIZZA PIE HAND?
Uh...
That's it. Tape this tack under your violin arm.
NO.
Uh, what about...
NO.
Art class.
You said we take a wheel of electives in sixth and seventh grade so that in eighth we can pick what we want.
Everyone else got their choice.
SIGH

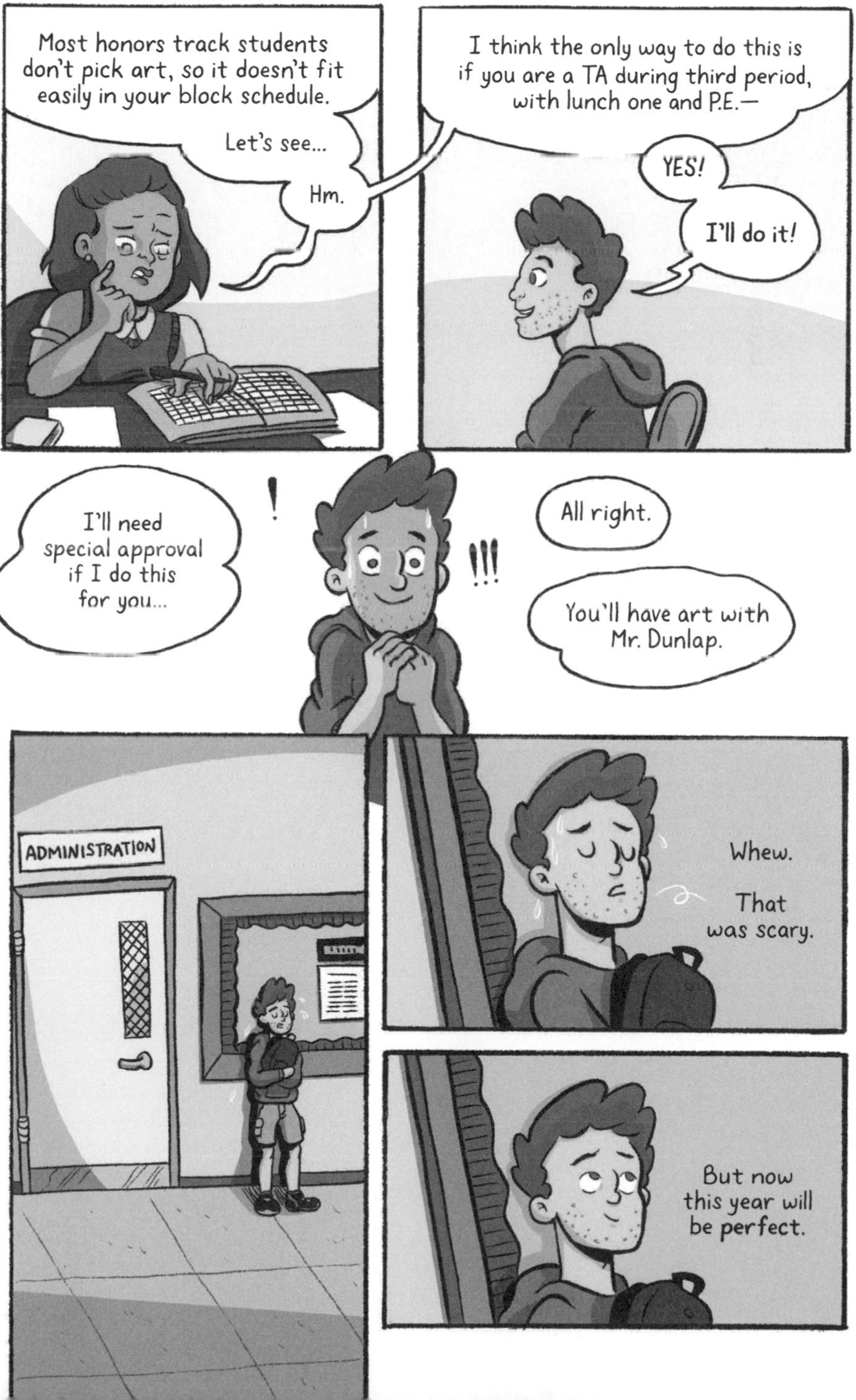

Most honors track students don't pick art, so it doesn't fit easily in your block schedule.
Let's see...
Hm.
I think the only way to do this is if you are a TA during third period, with lunch one and P.E.—
YES!
I'll do it!
I'll need special approval if I do this for you...
!
!!!
All right.
You'll have art with Mr. Dunlap.
ADMINISTRATION
Whew.
That was scary.
But now this year will be perfect.

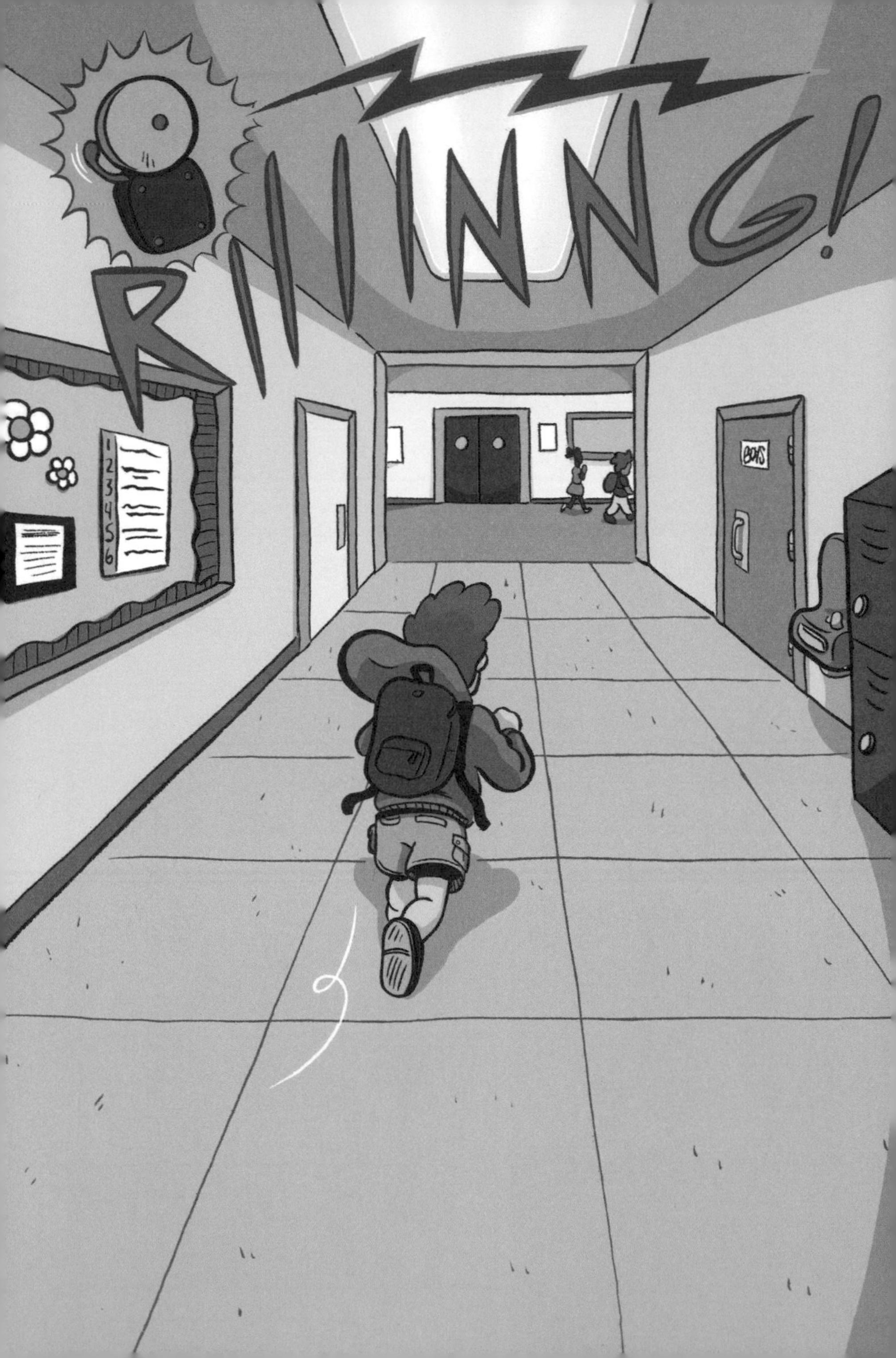
RIIINNG!
1
2
3
4
5
6
BOYS

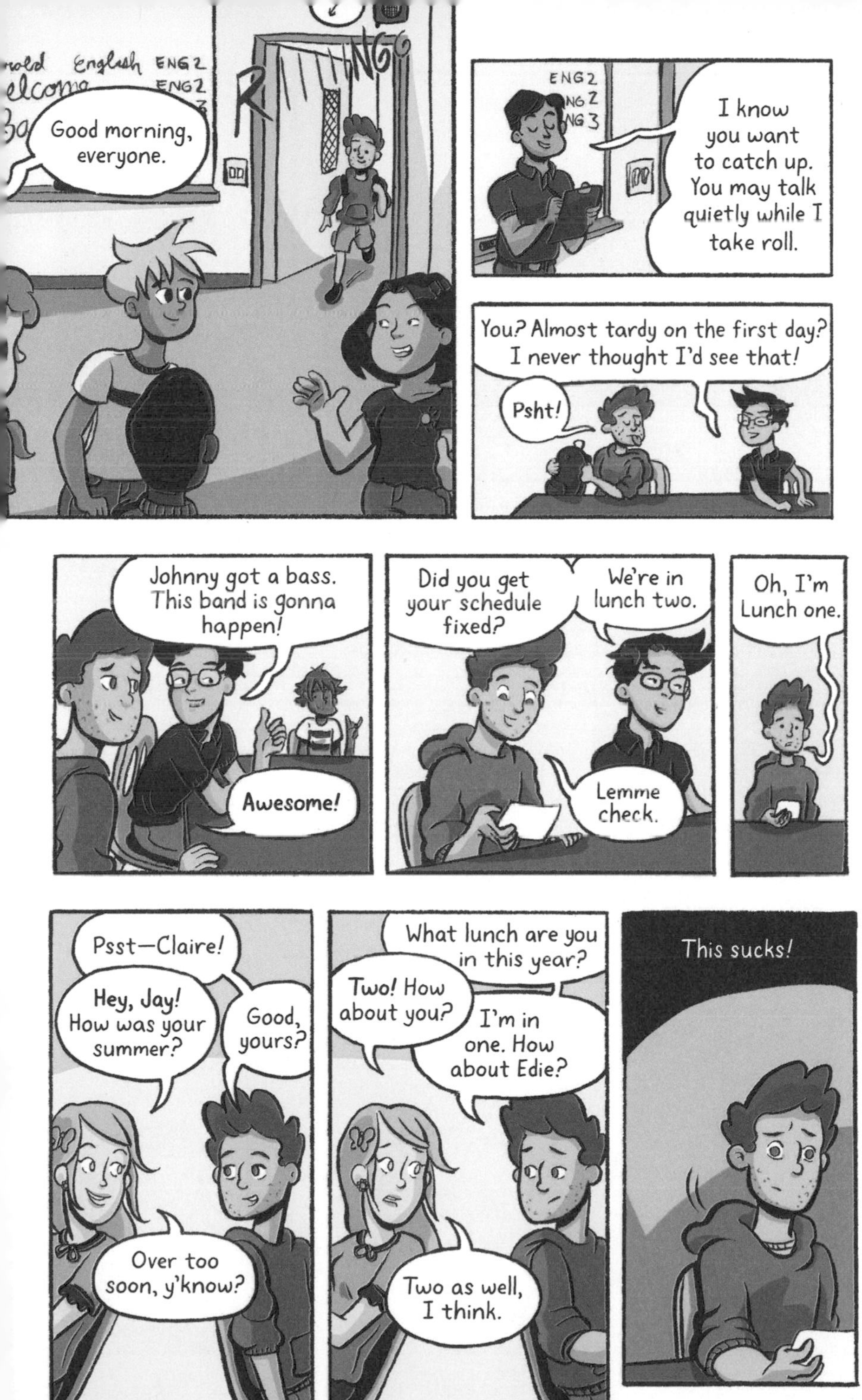
English ENG 2
ENG 2
Good morning, everyone.
I know you want to catch up. You may talk quietly while I take roll.
You? Almost tardy on the first day? I never thought I'd see that!
Psht!
Johnny got a bass. This band is gonna happen!
Awesome!
Did you get your schedule fixed?
We're in lunch two.
Lemme check.
Oh, I'm Lunch one.
Psst—Claire!
Hey, Jay! How was your summer?
Good, yours?
Over too soon, y'know?
What lunch are you in this year?
Two! How about you?
I'm in one. How about Edie?
Two as well, I think.
This sucks!

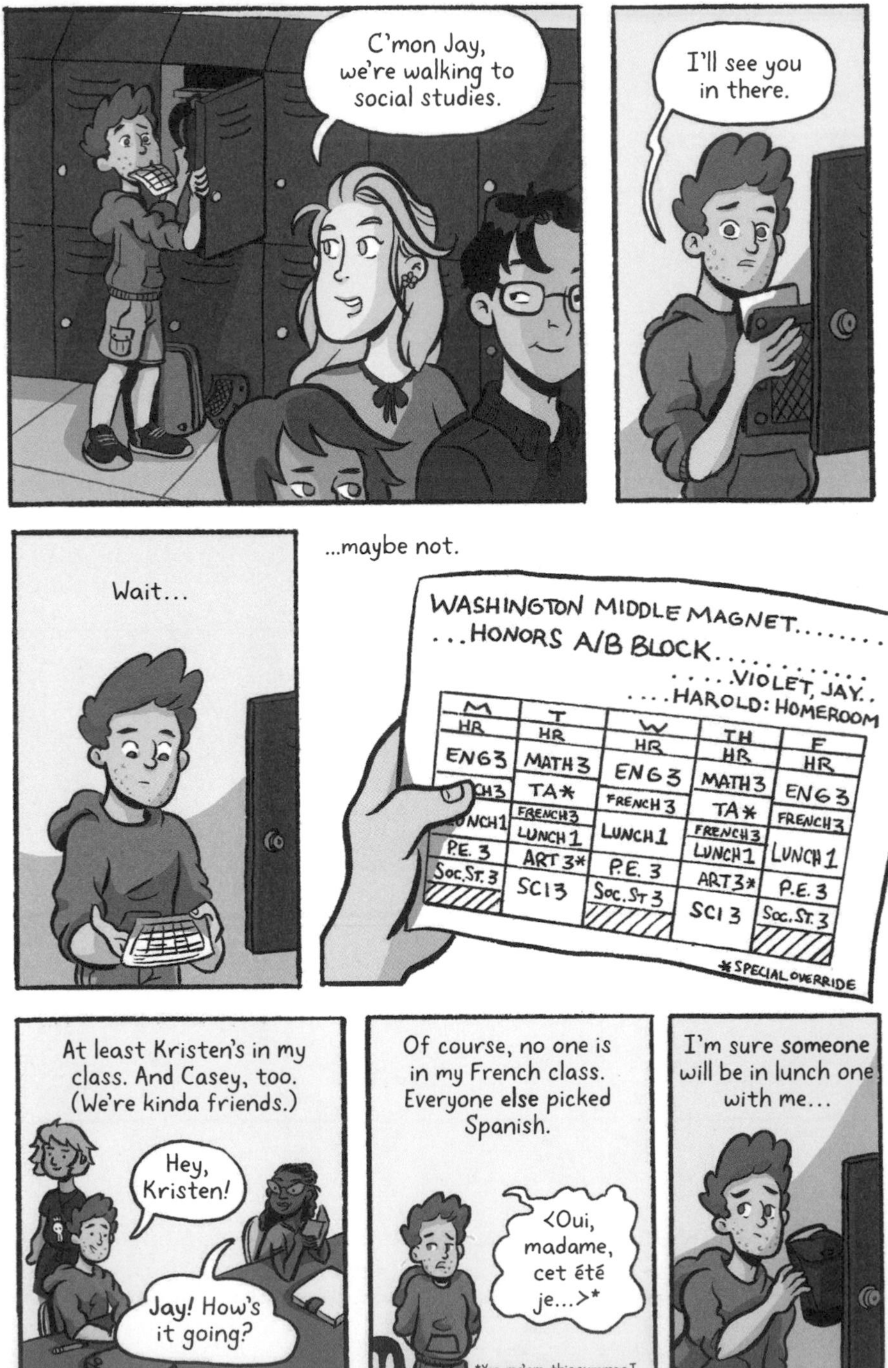
C'mon Jay, we're walking to social studies.
I'll see you in there.
Wait...
...maybe not.
WASHINGTON MIDDLE MAGNET........
...HONORS A/B BLOCK.............
.....VIOLET, JAY..
....HAROLD: HOMEROOM
M T W TH F
HR HR HR HR HR
ENG3 MATH3 ENG3 MATH3 ENG3
TA* FRENCH3 TA* FRENCH3
FRENCH3 LUNCH1 FRENCH3
LUNCH1 LUNCH1 LUNCH1
P.E. 3 ART 3* P.E. 3 ART3* P.E. 3
Soc.St. 3 SCI3 Soc.St 3 SCI 3 Soc.St. 3
*SPECIAL OVERRIDE
At least Kristen's in my class. And Casey, too. (We're kinda friends.)
Hey, Kristen!
Jay! How's it going?
Of course, no one is in my French class. Everyone else picked Spanish.
<Oui, madame, cet été je...>*
*Yes, ma'am, this summer I...
I'm sure someone will be in lunch one with me...

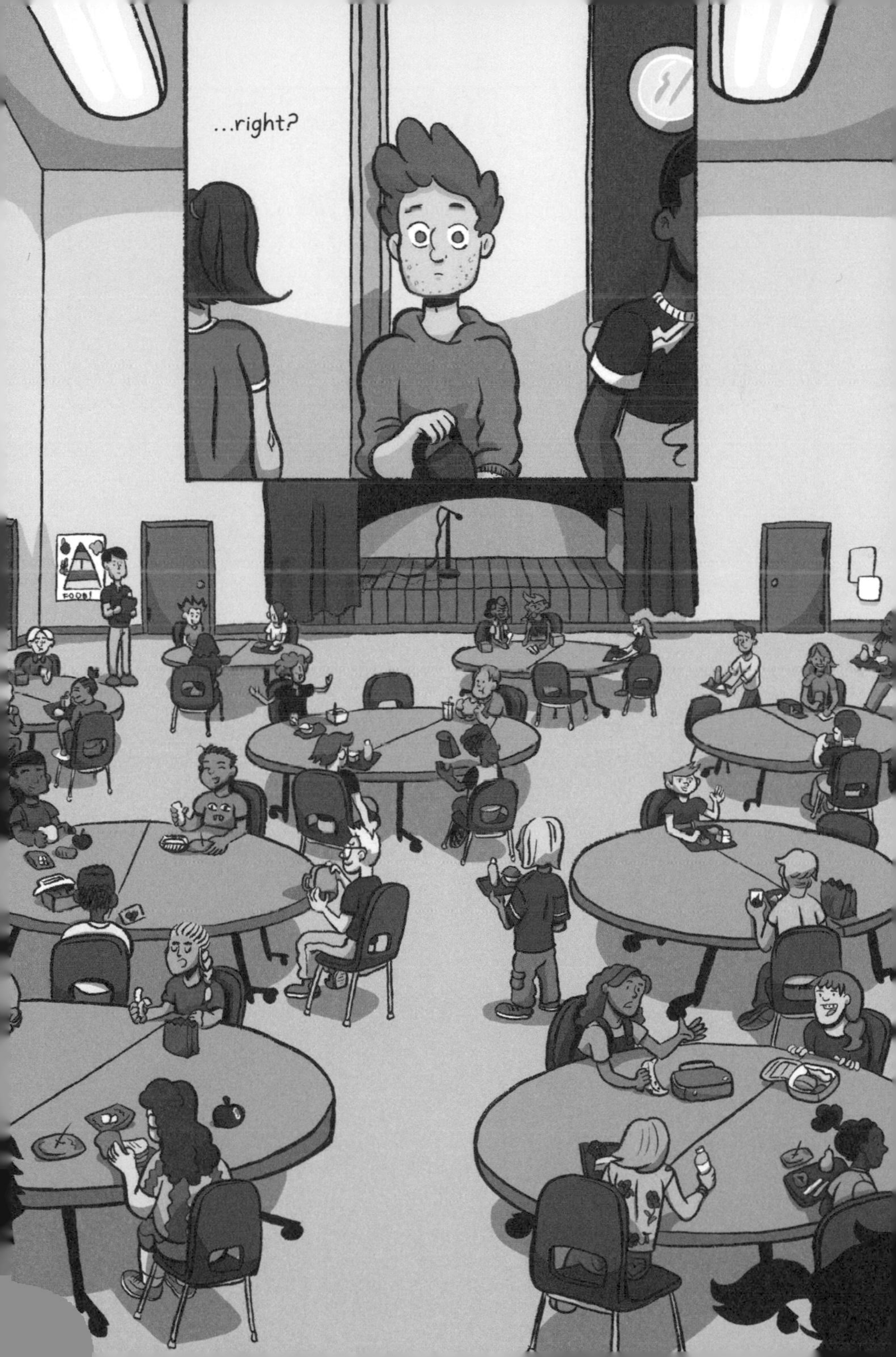
...right?
FOOD!

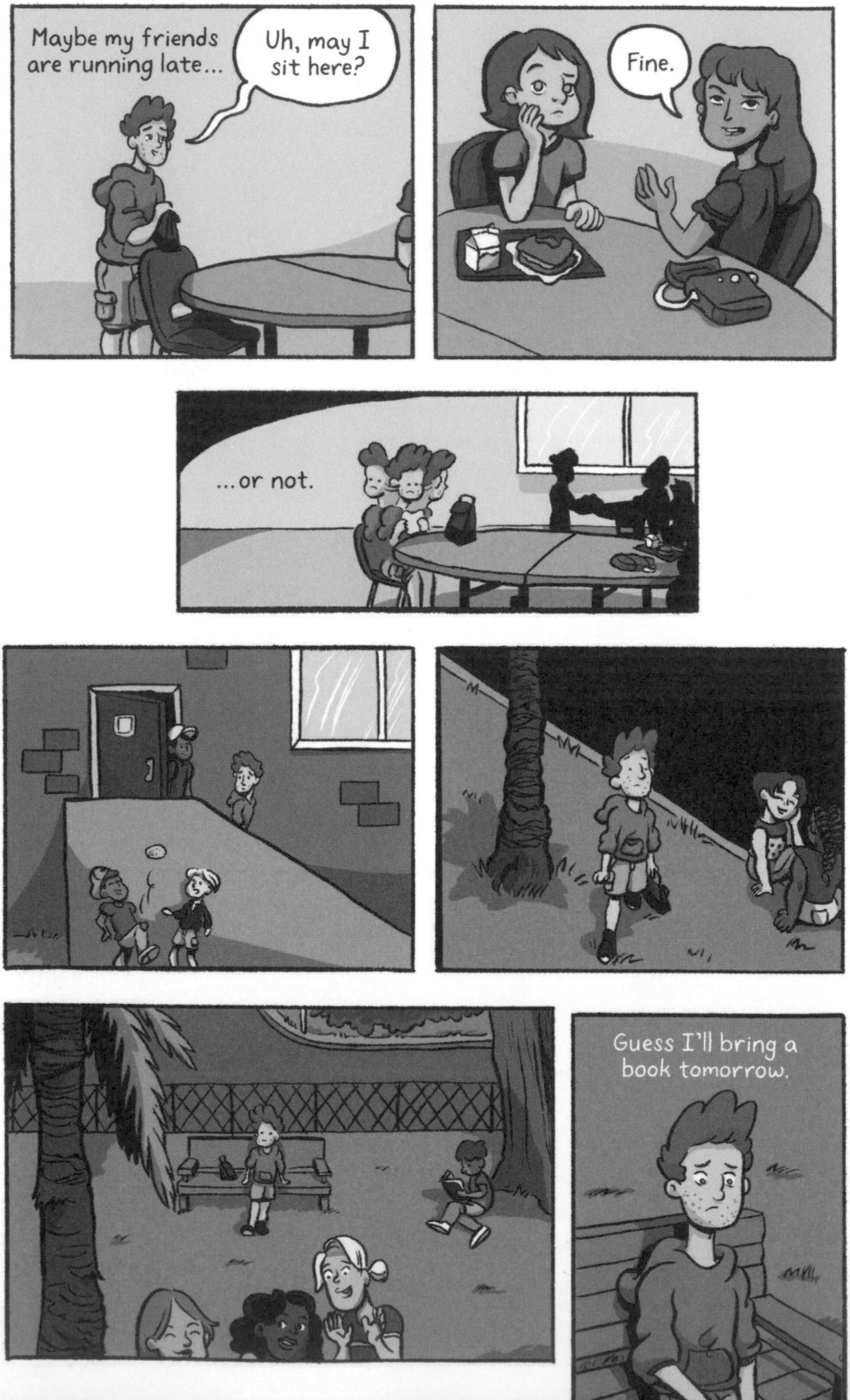
Maybe my friends are running late...
Uh, may I sit here?
Fine.
...or not.
Guess I'll bring a book tomorrow.

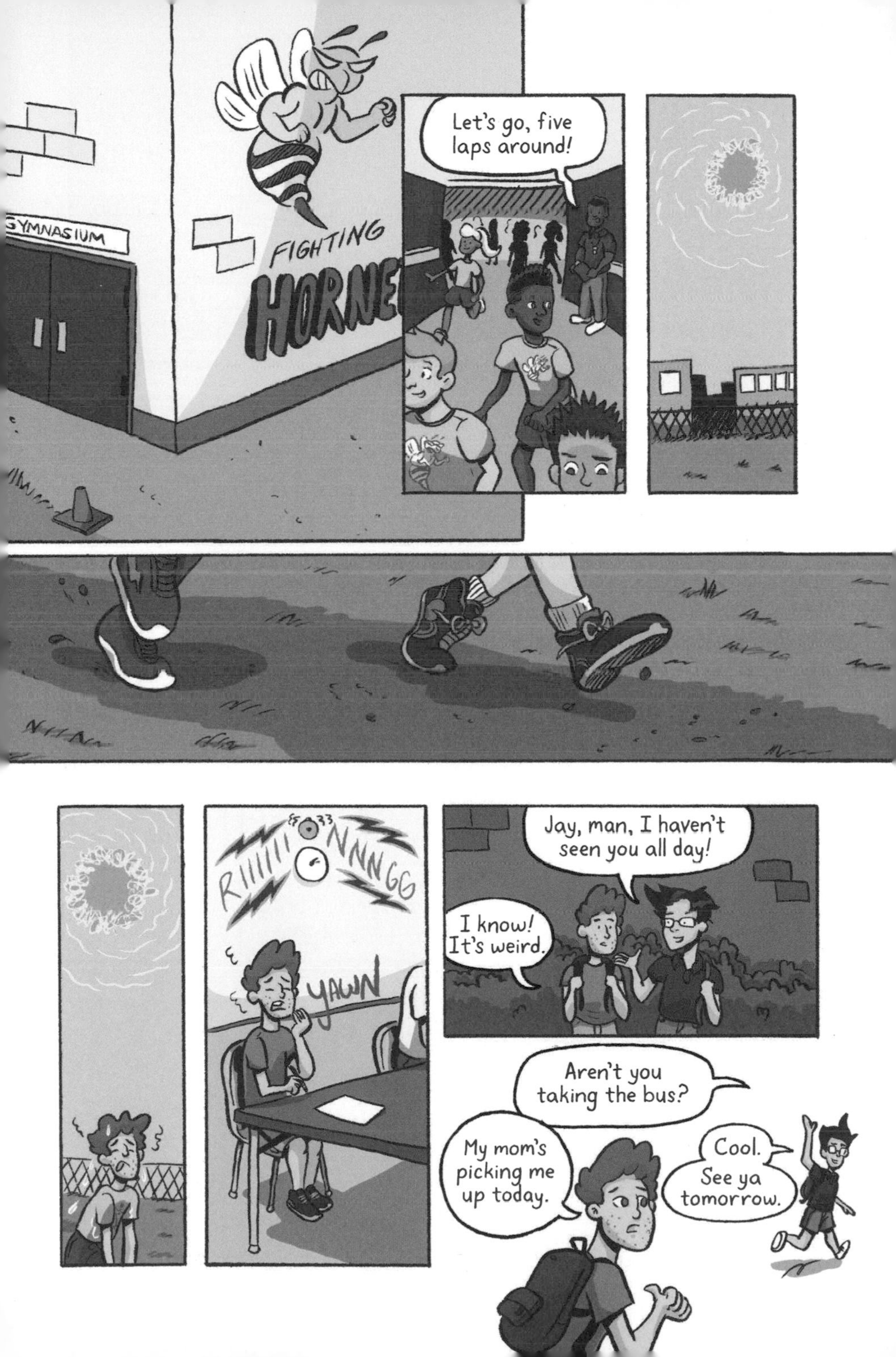
GYMNASIUM
FIGHTING
HORNE
Let's go, five laps around!
RIIIIIINNNGG
YAWN
Jay, man, I haven't seen you all day!
I know! It's weird.
Aren't you taking the bus?
My mom's picking me up today.
Cool. See ya tomorrow.

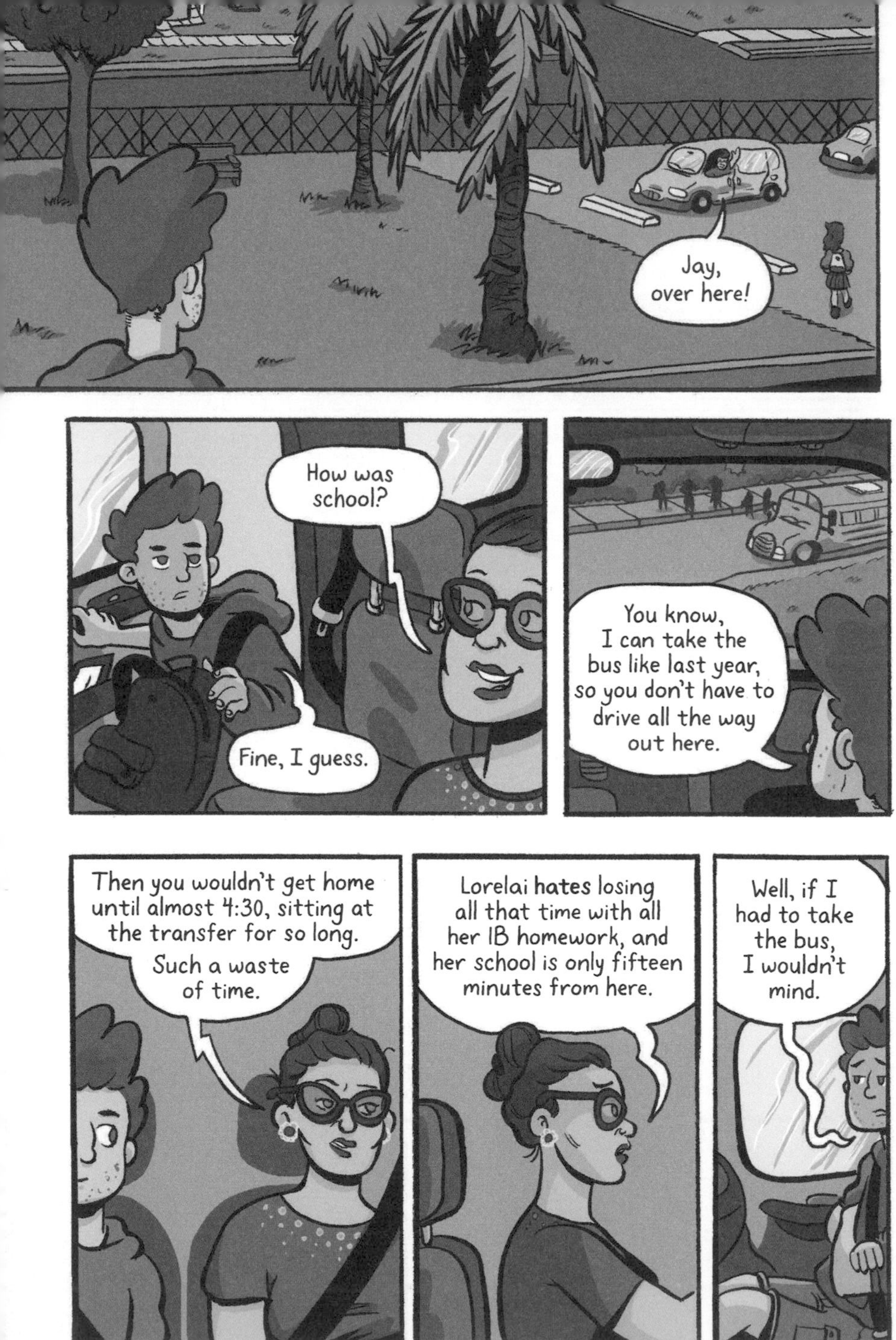

Jay, over here!
How was school?
Fine, I guess.
You know, I can take the bus like last year, so you don't have to drive all the way out here.
Then you wouldn't get home until almost 4:30, sitting at the transfer for so long.
Such a waste of time.
Lorelai **hates** losing all that time with all her IB homework, and her school is only fifteen minutes from here.
Well, if I had to take the bus, I wouldn't mind.

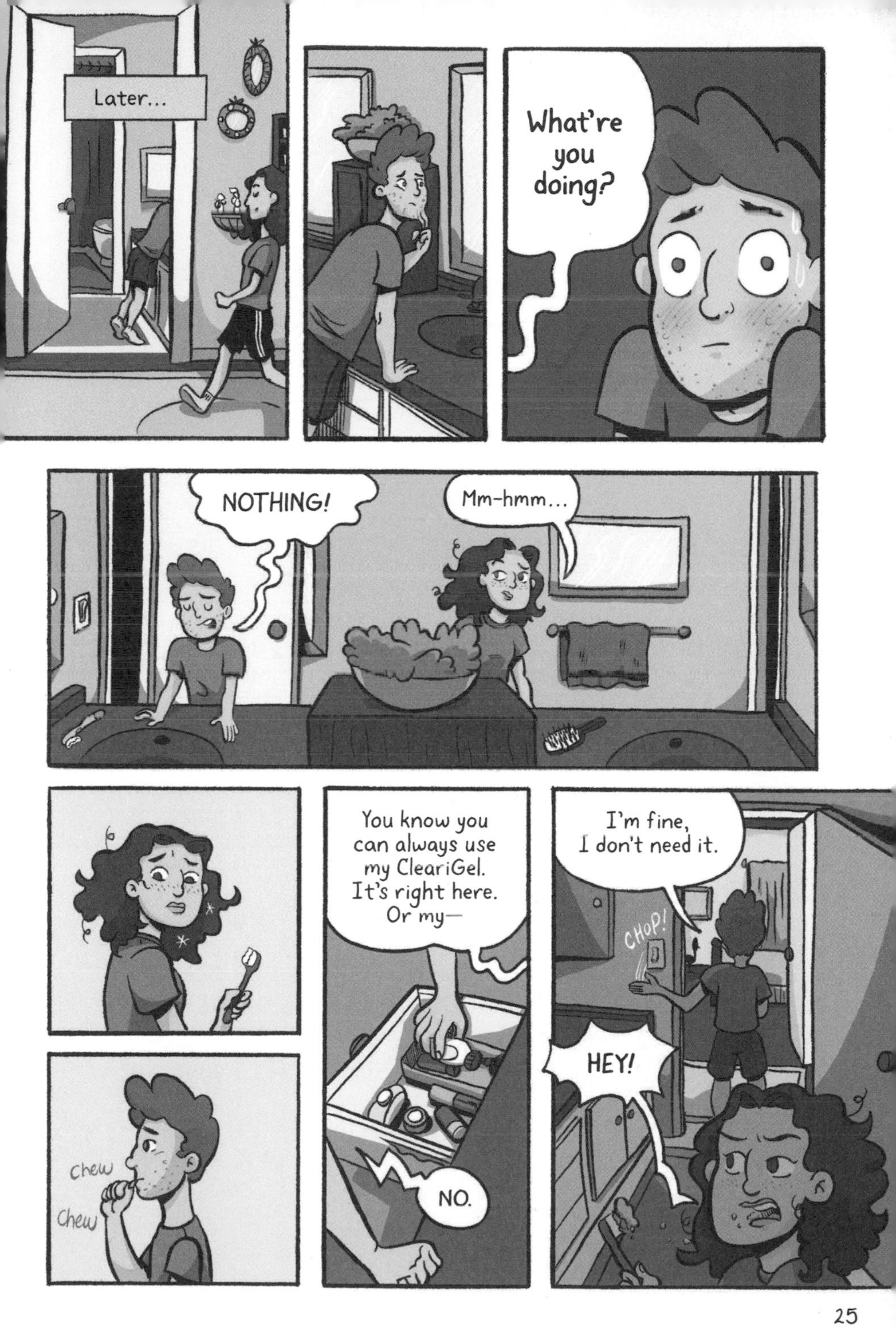
Later...
What're you doing?
NOTHING!
Mm-hmm...
You know you can always use my CleariGel. It's right here. Or my—
NO.
chew
chew
I'm fine, I don't need it.
CHOP!
HEY!

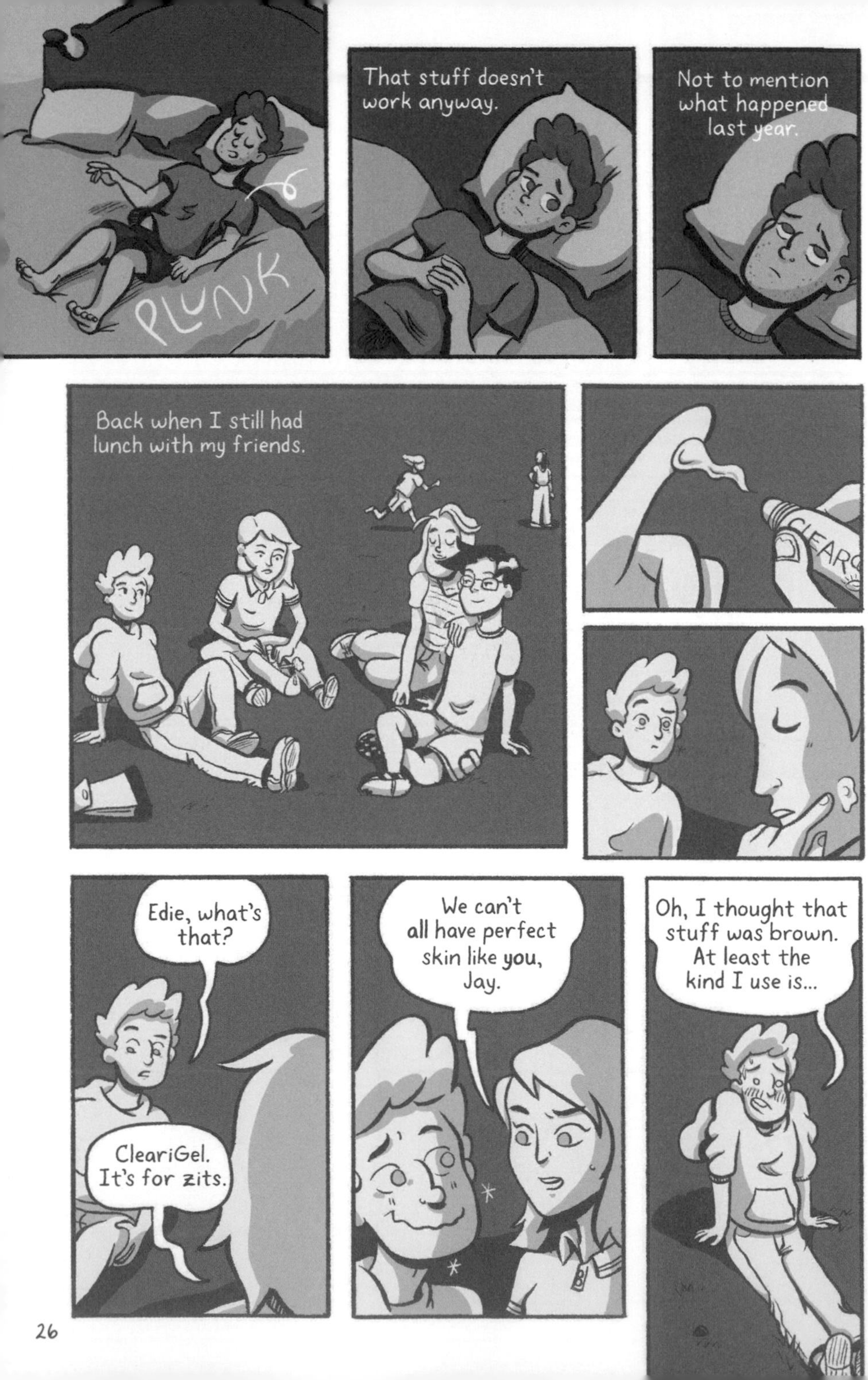
PLUNK
That stuff doesn't work anyway.
Not to mention what happened last year.
Back when I still had lunch with my friends.
Edie, what's that?
ClеariGel. It's for zits.
We can't all have perfect skin like **you**, Jay.
Oh, I thought that stuff was brown. At least the kind I use is...

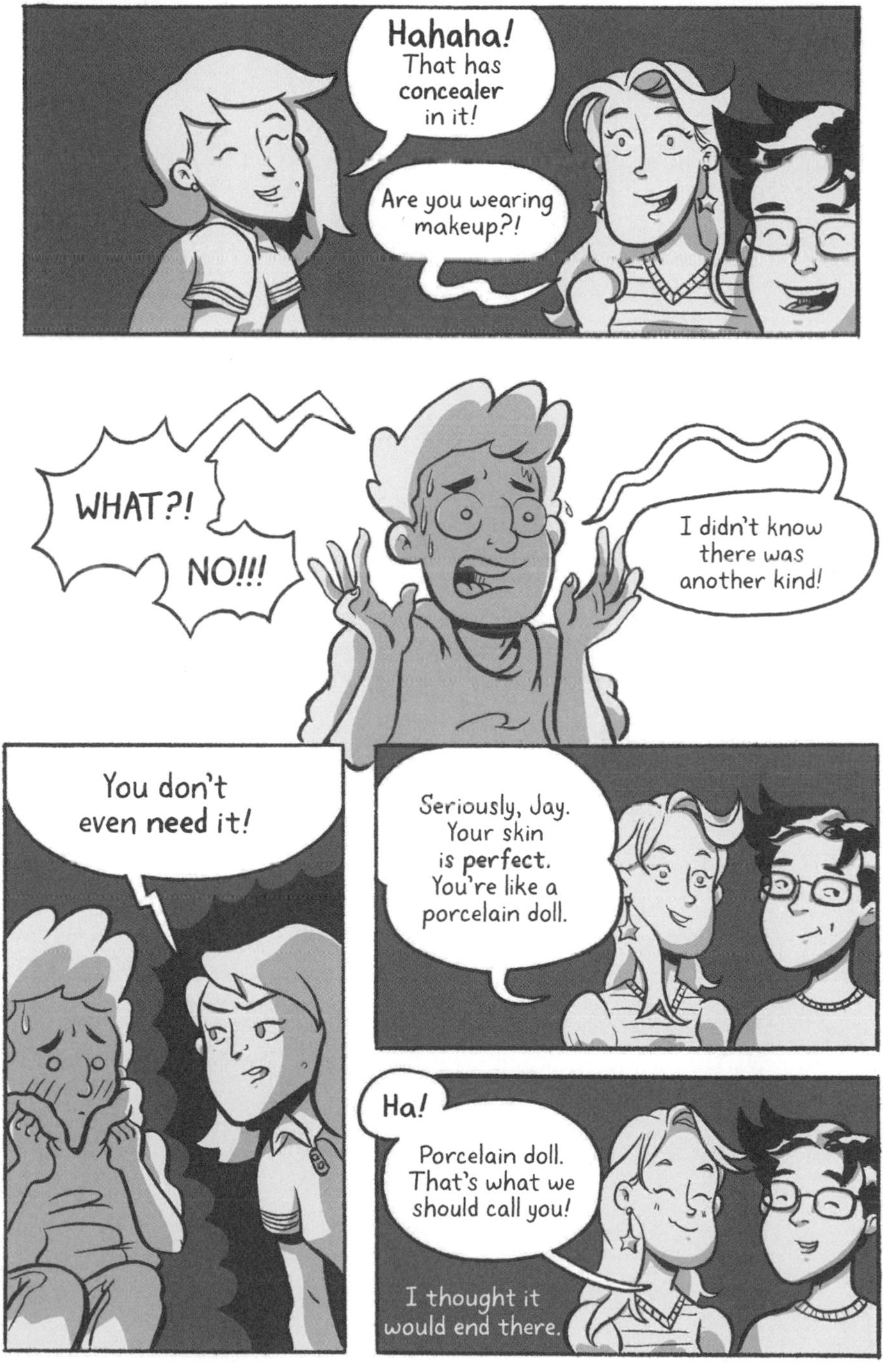
Hahaha! That has concealer in it!
Are you wearing makeup?!
WHAT?!
NO!!!
I didn't know there was another kind!
You don't even need it!
Seriously, Jay. Your skin is perfect. You're like a porcelain doll.
Ha!
Porcelain doll. That's what we should call you!
I thought it would end there.

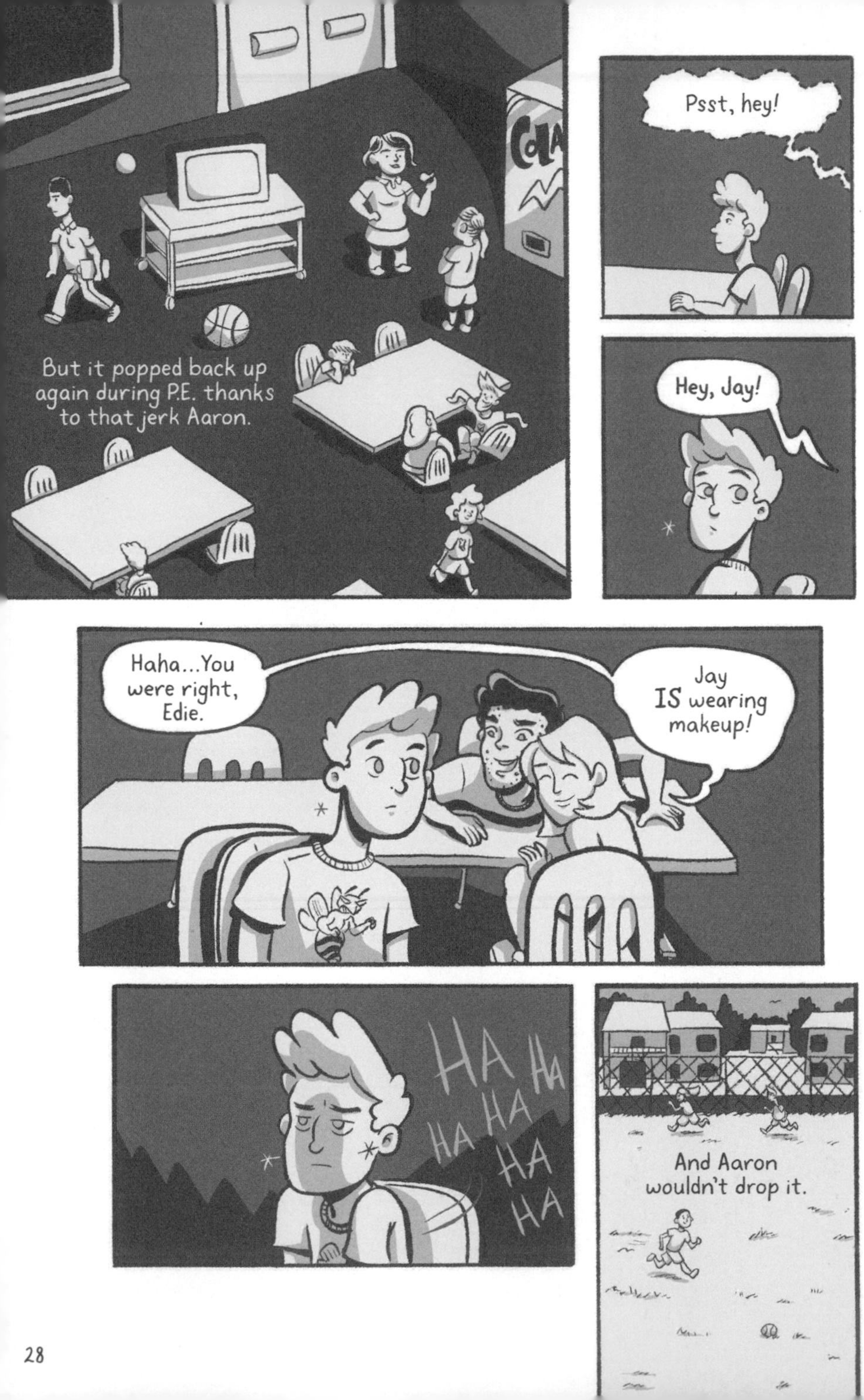

But it popped back up again during P.E. thanks to that jerk Aaron.
Psst, hey!
Hey, Jay!
Haha...You were right, Edie.
Jay IS wearing makeup!
HA HA HA HA HA HA HA
And Aaron wouldn't drop it.

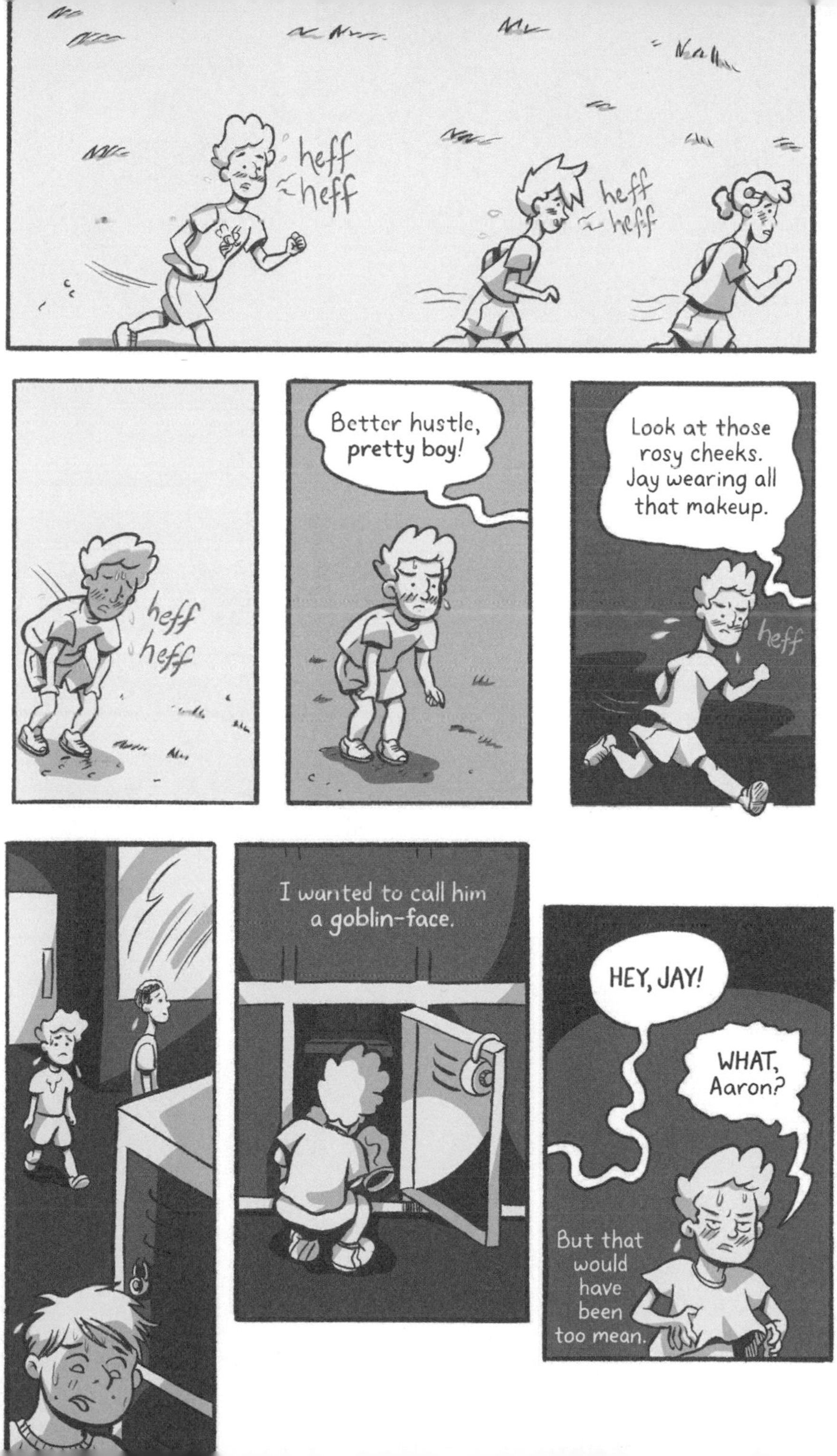
heff heff
heff heff
heff heff
Better hustle, pretty boy!
Look at those rosy cheeks. Jay wearing all that makeup.
heff
I wanted to call him a goblin-face.
HEY, JAY!
WHAT, Aaron?
But that would have been too mean.

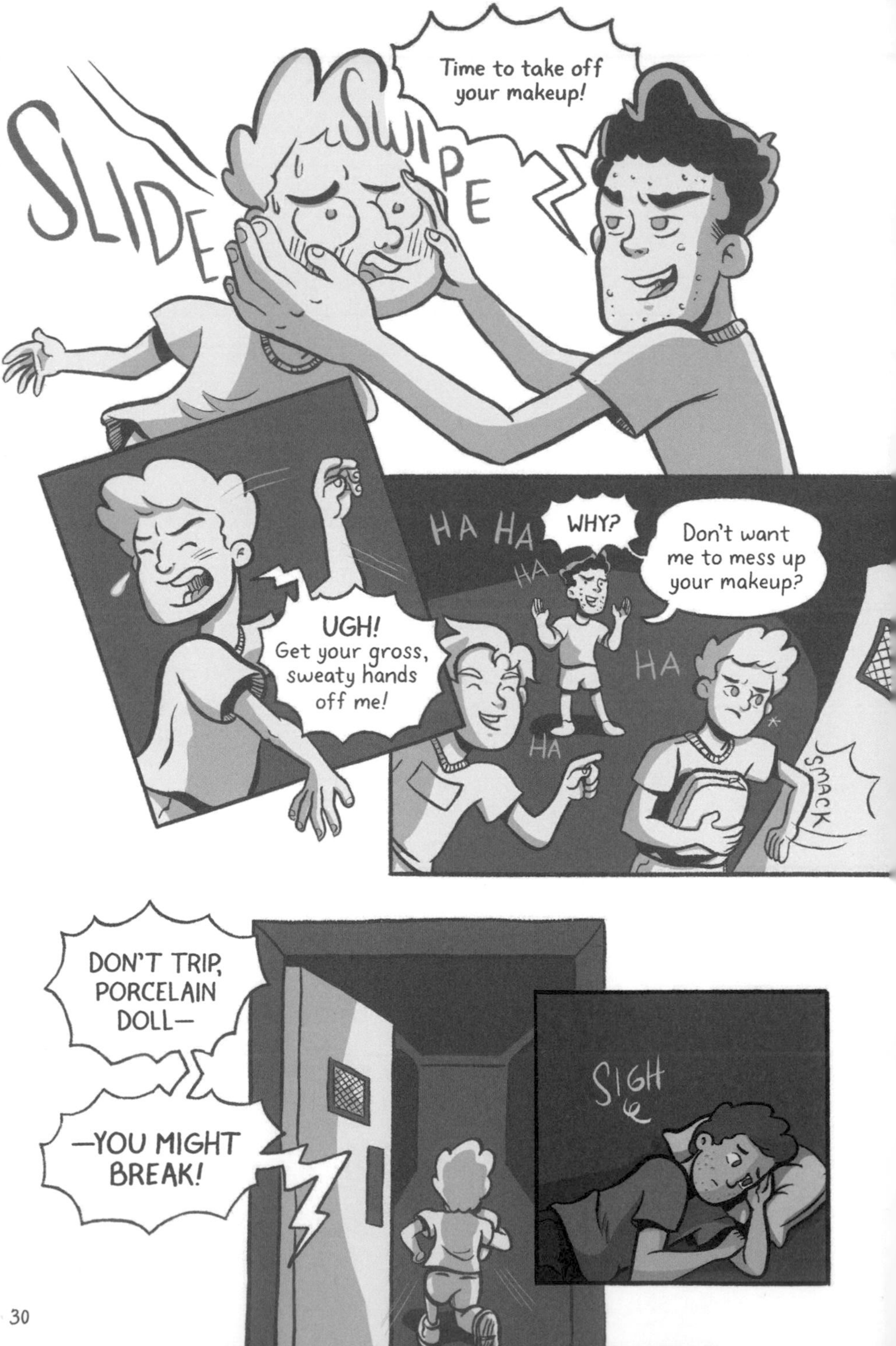
Time to take off your makeup!
SLIDE
SWIPE
UGH! Get your gross, sweaty hands off me!
HA HA
WHY?
HA
Don't want me to mess up your makeup?
HA
HA
SMACK
DON'T TRIP, PORCELAIN DOLL—
—YOU MIGHT BREAK!
SIGH

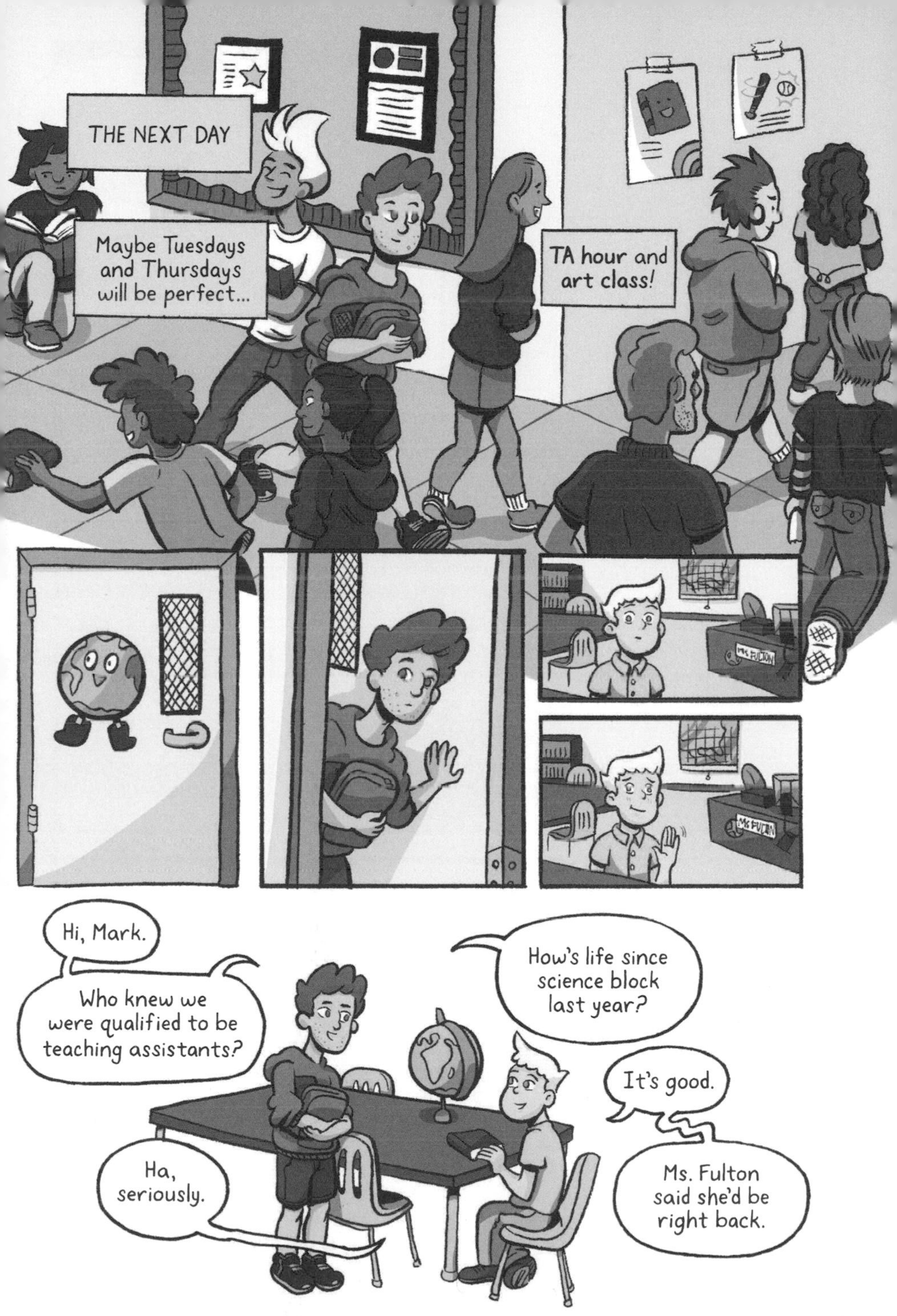
THE NEXT DAY
Maybe Tuesdays and Thursdays will be perfect...
TA hour and art class!
MS. FULTON
MS. FULTON
Hi, Mark.
Who knew we were qualified to be teaching assistants?
How's life since science block last year?
It's good.
Ms. Fulton said she'd be right back.
Ha, seriously.

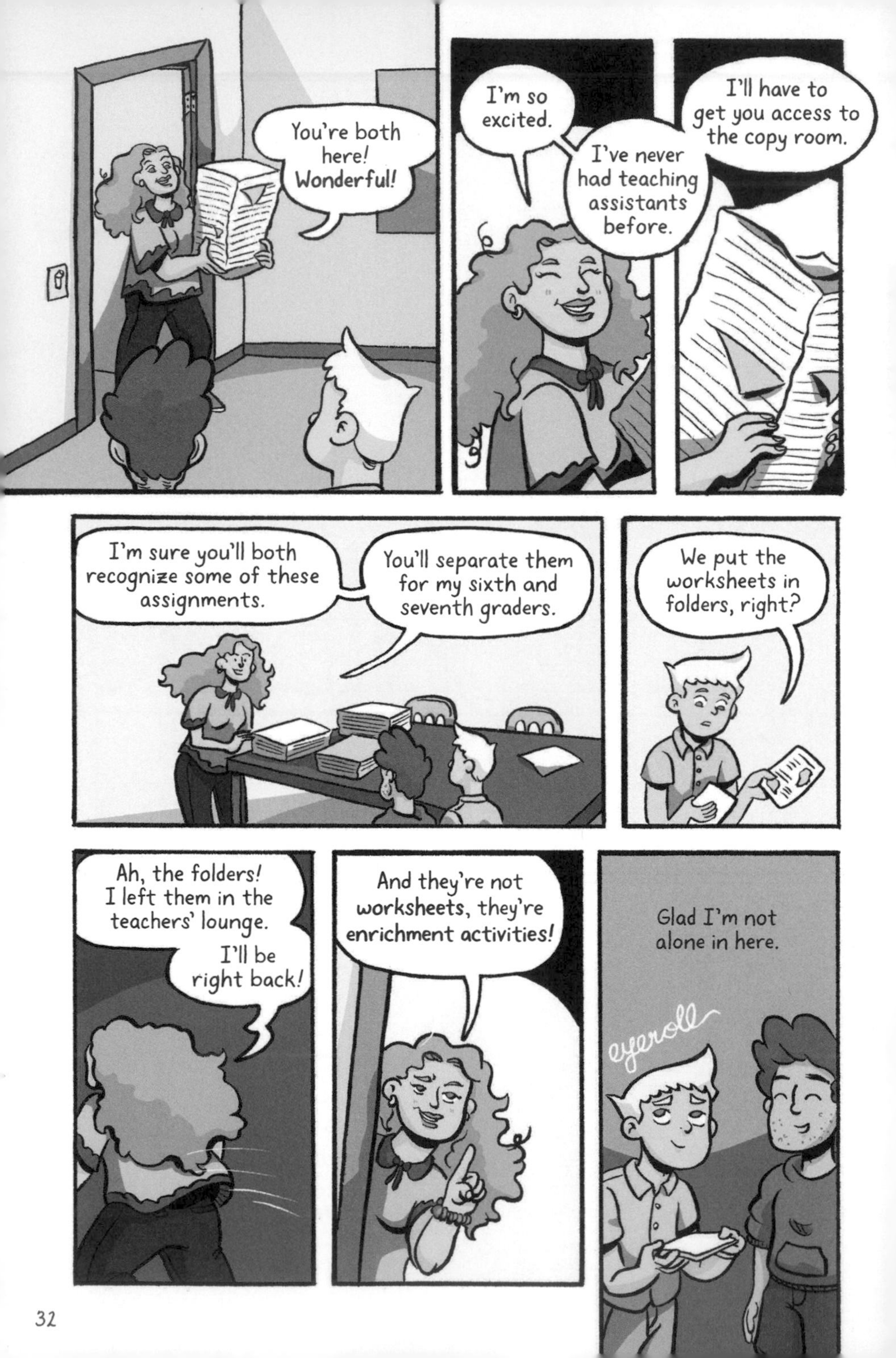
You're both here! Wonderful!
I'm so excited.
I've never had teaching assistants before.
I'll have to get you access to the copy room.
I'm sure you'll both recognize some of these assignments.
You'll separate them for my sixth and seventh graders.
We put the worksheets in folders, right?
Ah, the folders! I left them in the teachers' lounge.
I'll be right back!
And they're not worksheets, they're enrichment activities!
Glad I'm not alone in here.
eyeroll

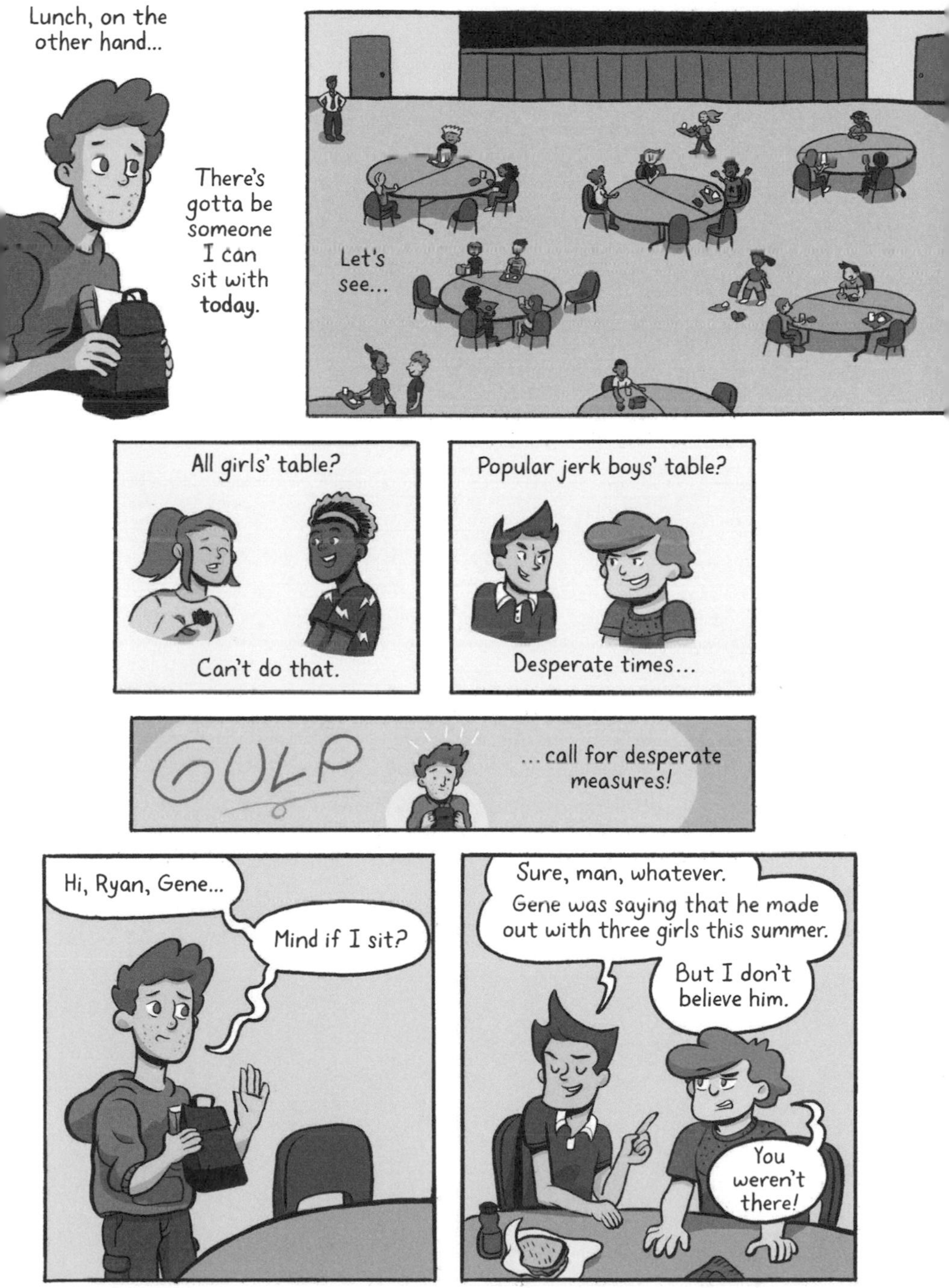

Lunch, on the other hand...
There's gotta be someone I can sit with today.
Let's see...
All girls' table?
Can't do that.
Popular jerk boys' table?
Desperate times...
GULP
...call for desperate measures!
Hi, Ryan, Gene...
Mind if I sit?
Sure, man, whatever.
Gene was saying that he made out with three girls this summer.
But I don't believe him.
You weren't there!

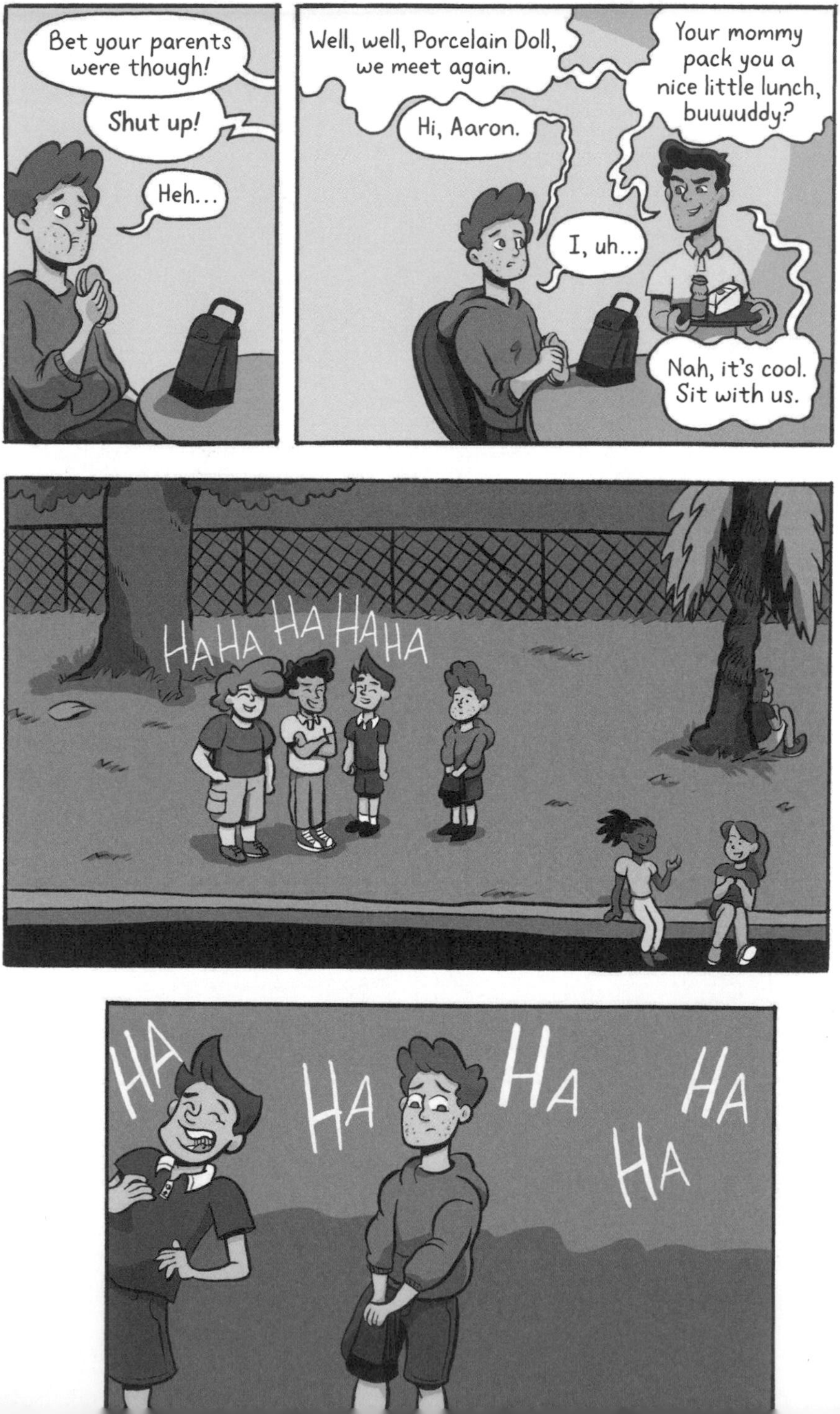

Bet your parents were though!
Shut up!
Heh...
Well, well, Porcelain Doll, we meet again.
Hi, Aaron.
Your mommy pack you a nice little lunch, buuuuddy?
I, uh...
Nah, it's cool. Sit with us.
HAHA HA HAHA
HA
HA
HA
HA
HA

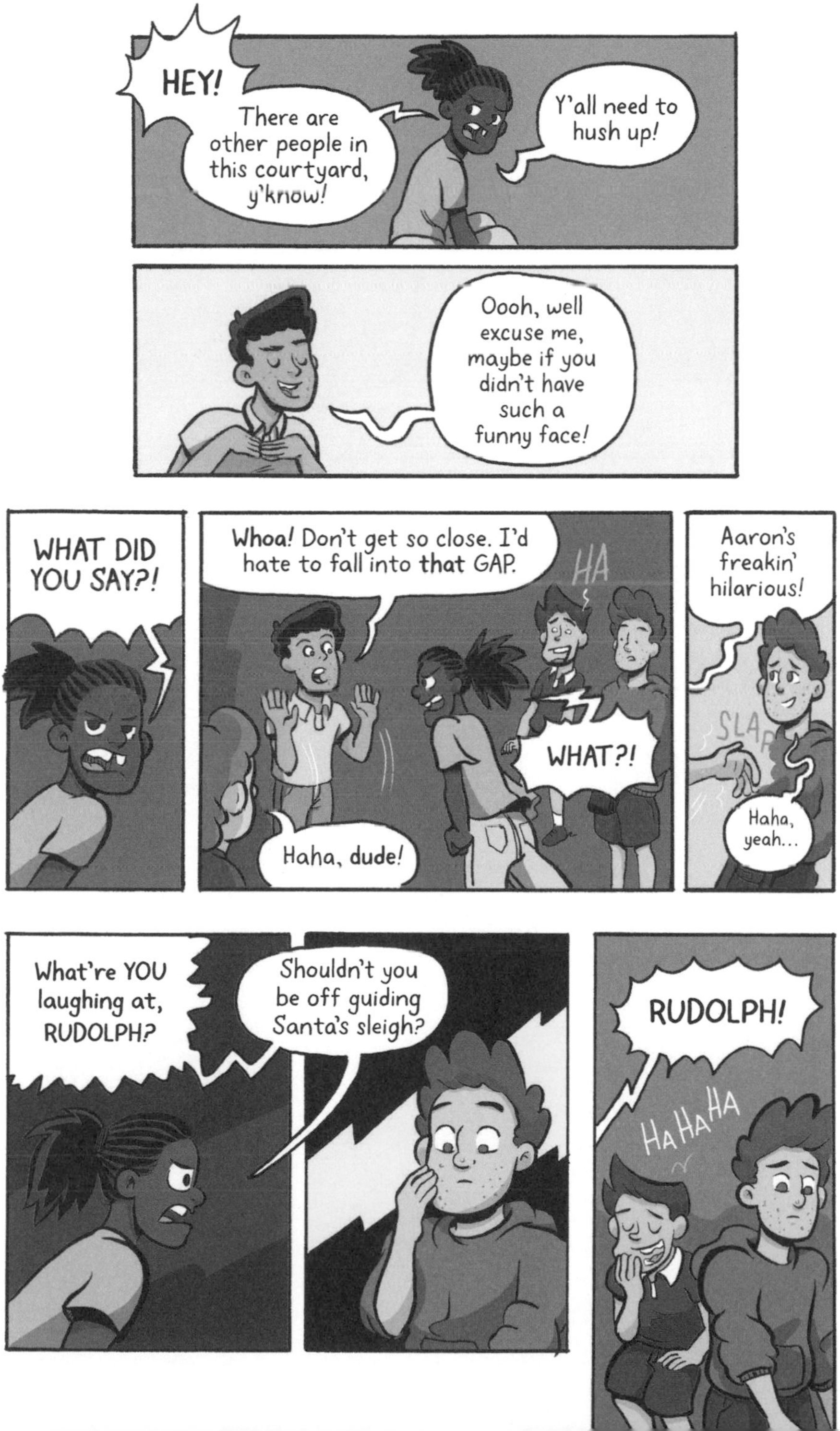
HEY!
There are other people in this courtyard, y'know!
Y'all need to hush up!
Oooh, well excuse me, maybe if you didn't have such a funny face!
WHAT DID YOU SAY?!
Whoa! Don't get so close. I'd hate to fall into that GAP.
HA
WHAT?!
Haha, dude!
Aaron's freakin' hilarious!
SLAP
Haha, yeah...
What're YOU laughing at, RUDOLPH?
Shouldn't you be off guiding Santa's sleigh?
RUDOLPH!
HA HA HA

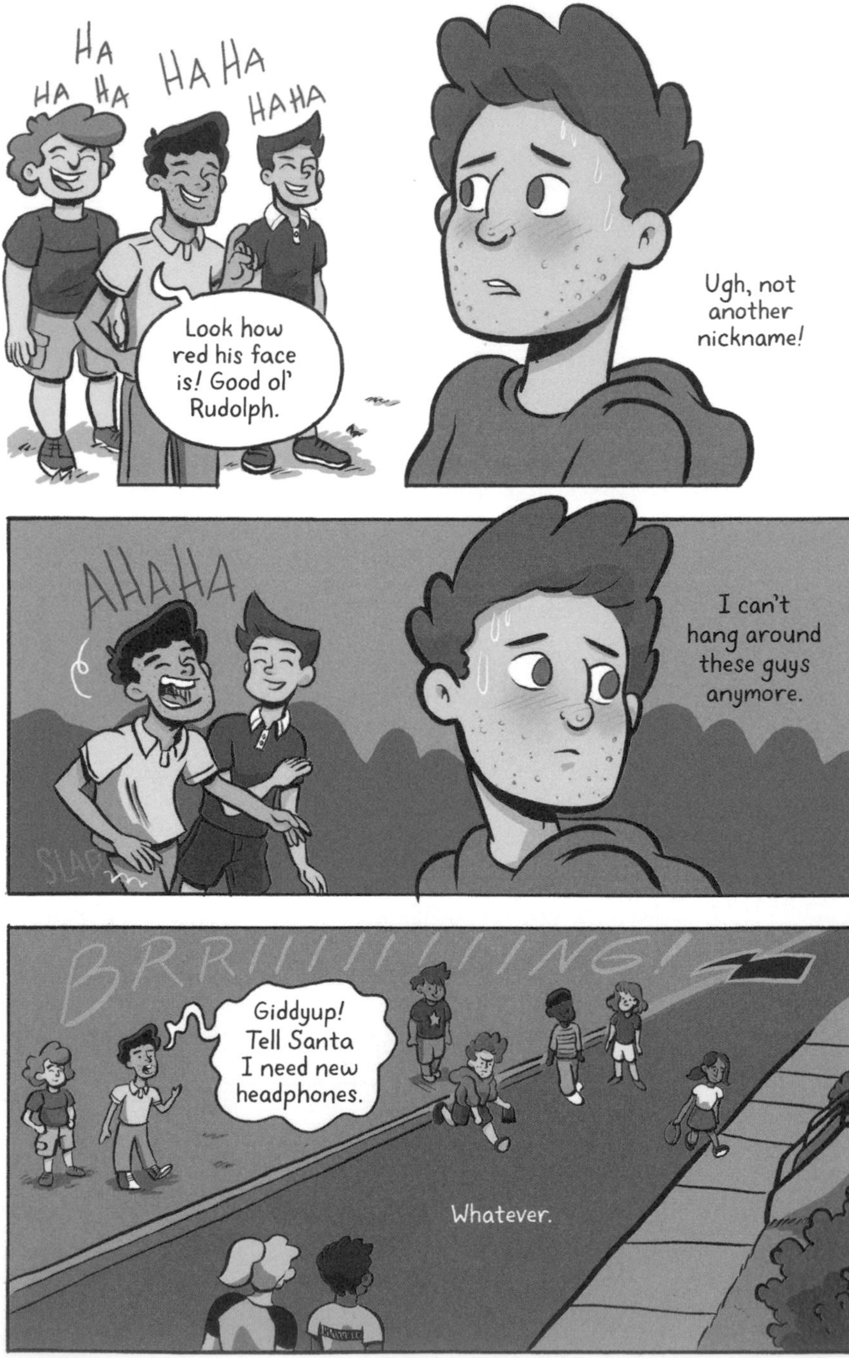
HA HA HA HA HA HAHA
Look how red his face is! Good ol' Rudolph.
Ugh, not another nickname!
AHAHA
SLAP
I can't hang around these guys anymore.
BRRIIIIIING!
Giddyup! Tell Santa I need new headphones.
Whatever.

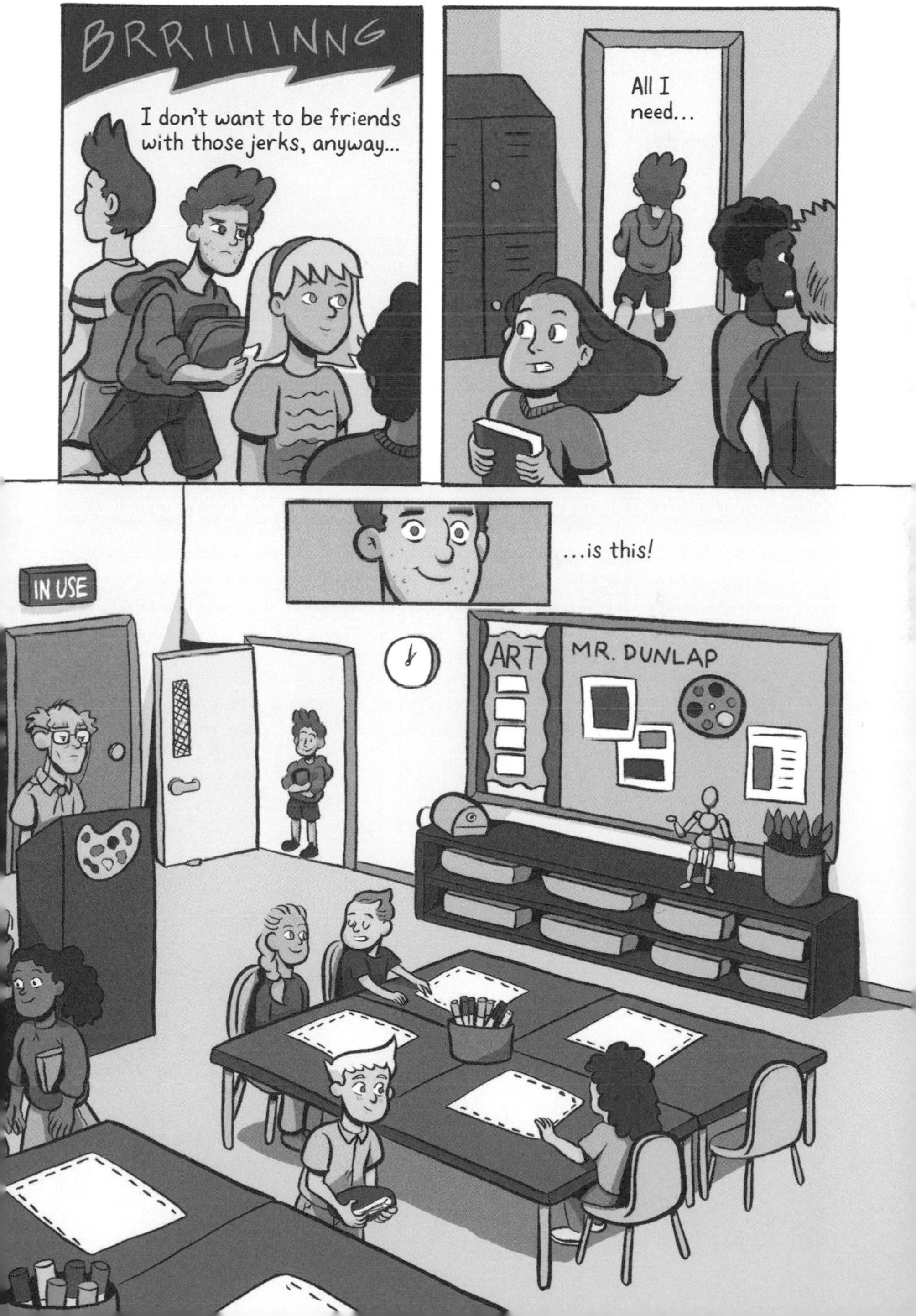
BRRIIIINNG
I don't want to be friends with those jerks, anyway...
All I need...
...is this!
IN USE
ART
MR. DUNLAP

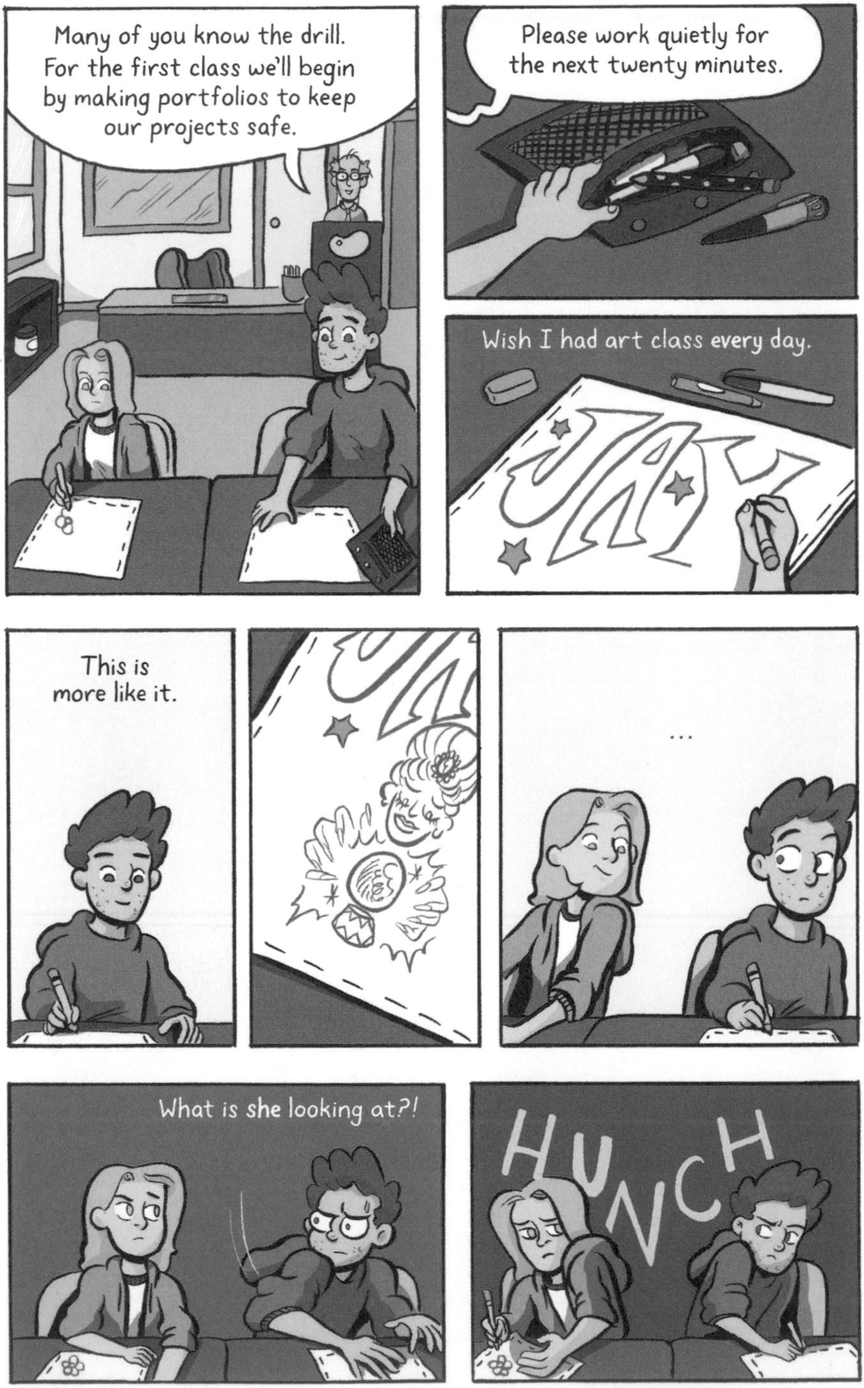
Many of you know the drill. For the first class we'll begin by making portfolios to keep our projects safe.
Please work quietly for the next twenty minutes.
Wish I had art class every day.
JAY
This is more like it.
...
What is she looking at?!
HUNCH

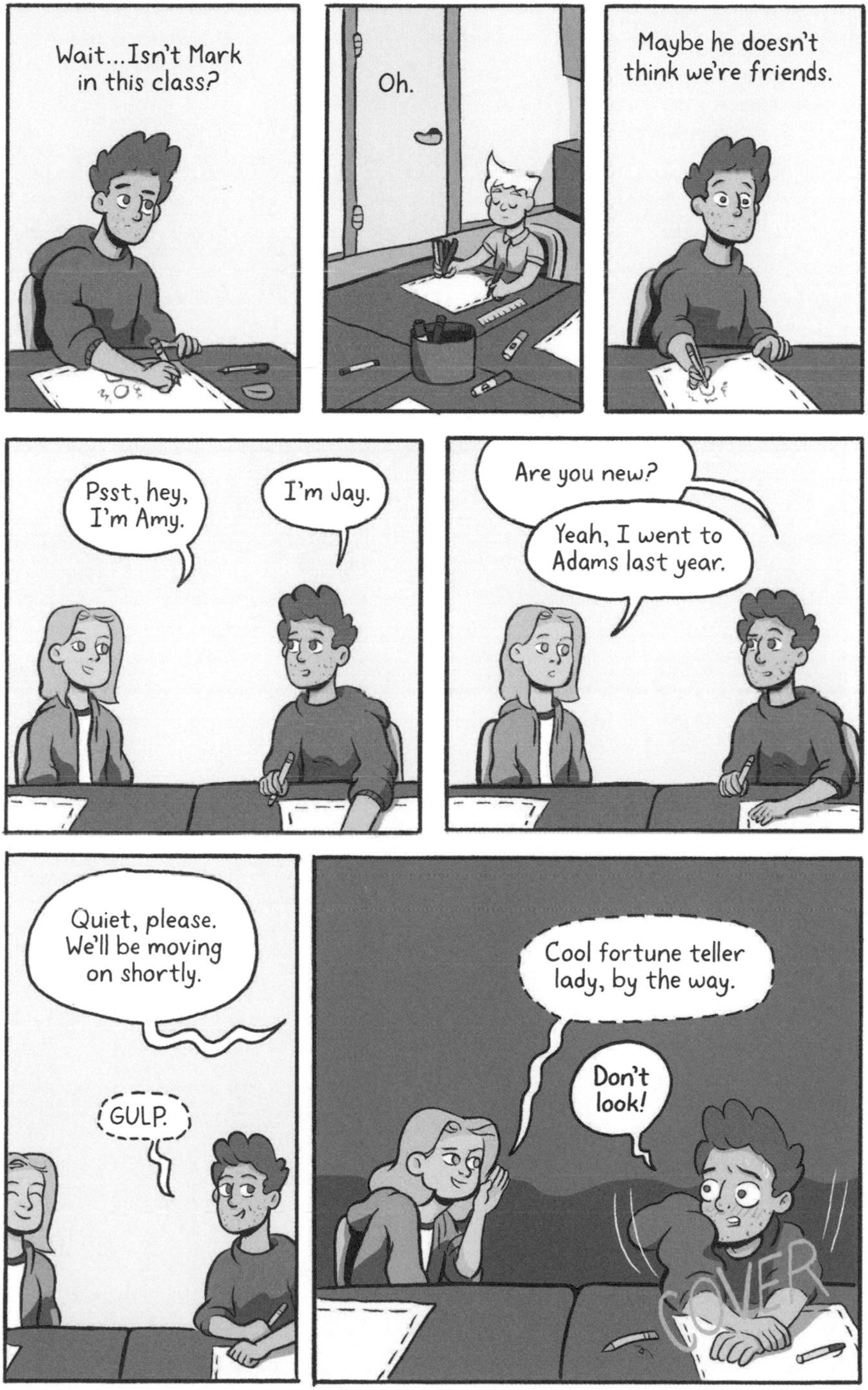

Wait...Isn't Mark in this class?
Oh.
Maybe he doesn't think we're friends.
Psst, hey, I'm Amy.
I'm Jay.
Are you new?
Yeah, I went to Adams last year.
Quiet, please. We'll be moving on shortly.
GULP.
Cool fortune teller lady, by the way.
Don't look!
COVER

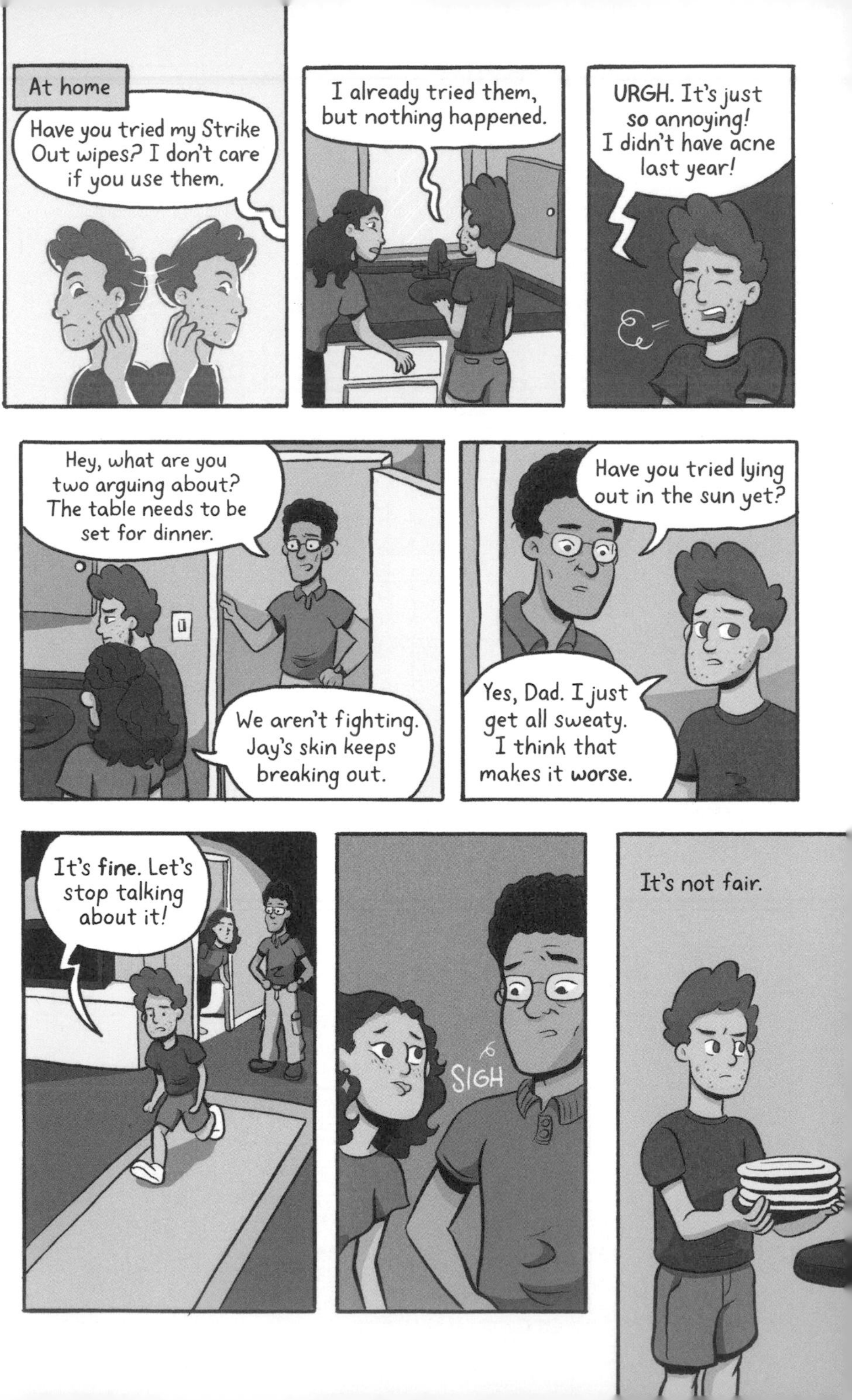
At home
Have you tried my Strike Out wipes? I don't care if you use them.
I already tried them, but nothing happened.
URGH. It's just so annoying! I didn't have acne last year!
Hey, what are you two arguing about? The table needs to be set for dinner.
We aren't fighting. Jay's skin keeps breaking out.
Have you tried lying out in the sun yet?
Yes, Dad. I just get all sweaty. I think that makes it worse.
It's fine. Let's stop talking about it!
SIGH
It's not fair.

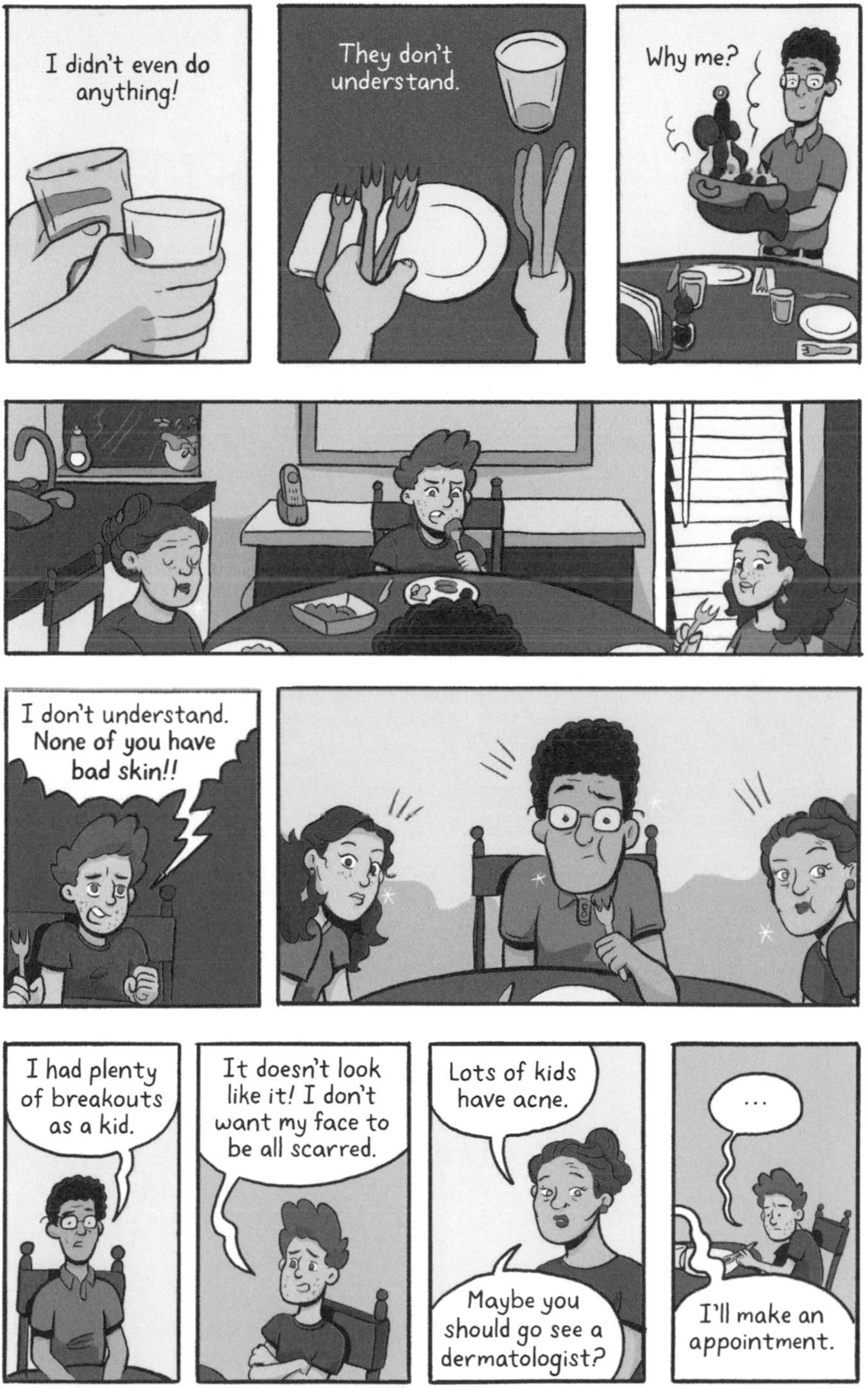
I didn't even do anything!
They don't understand.
Why me?
I don't understand. None of you have bad skin!!
I had plenty of breakouts as a kid.
It doesn't look like it! I don't want my face to be all scarred.
Lots of kids have acne.
Maybe you should go see a dermatologist?
...
I'll make an appointment.

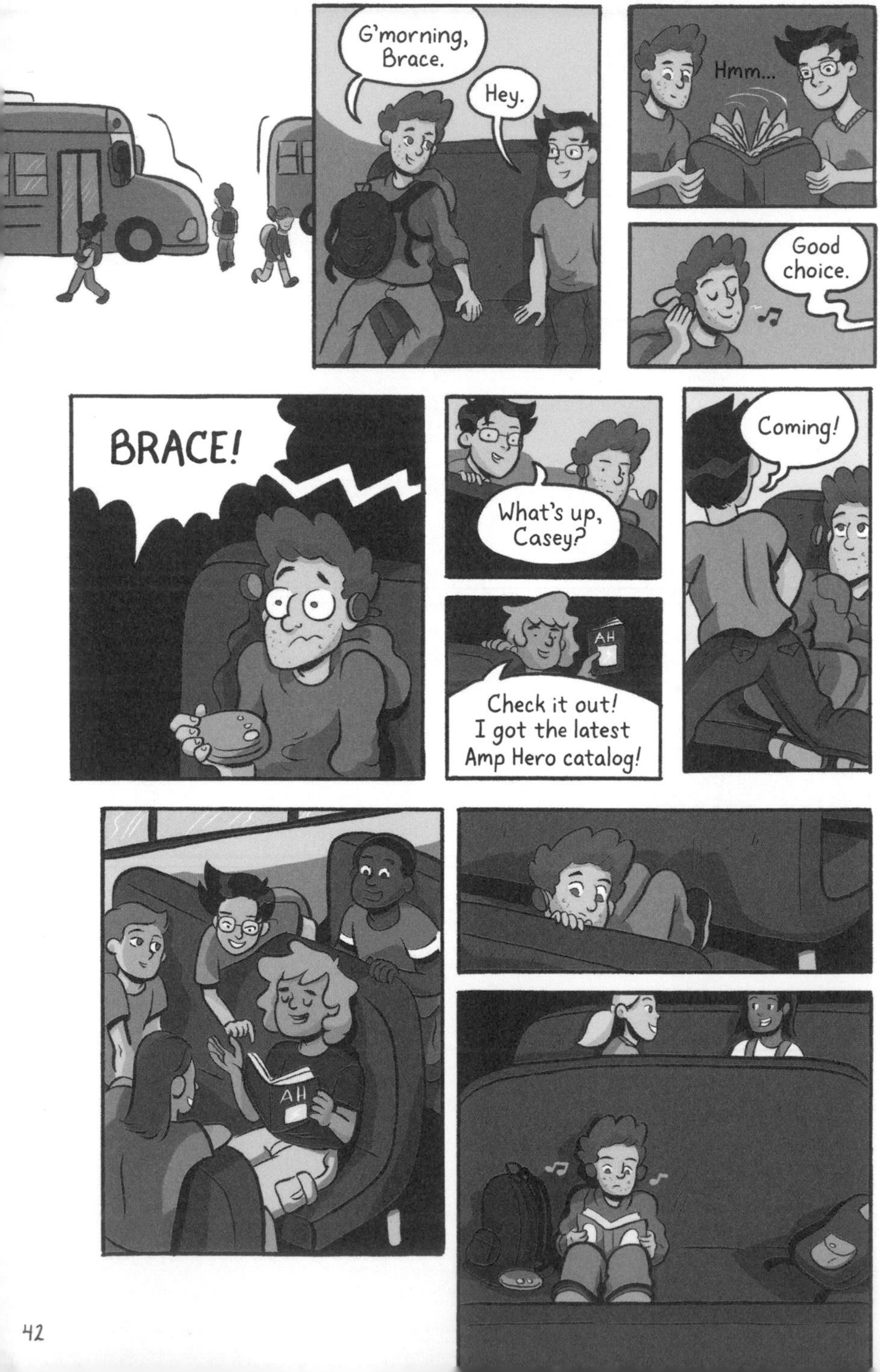
G'morning, Brace.
Hey.
Hmm...
Good choice.
BRACE!
What's up, Casey?
Check it out! I got the latest Amp Hero catalog!
Coming!
AH
AH

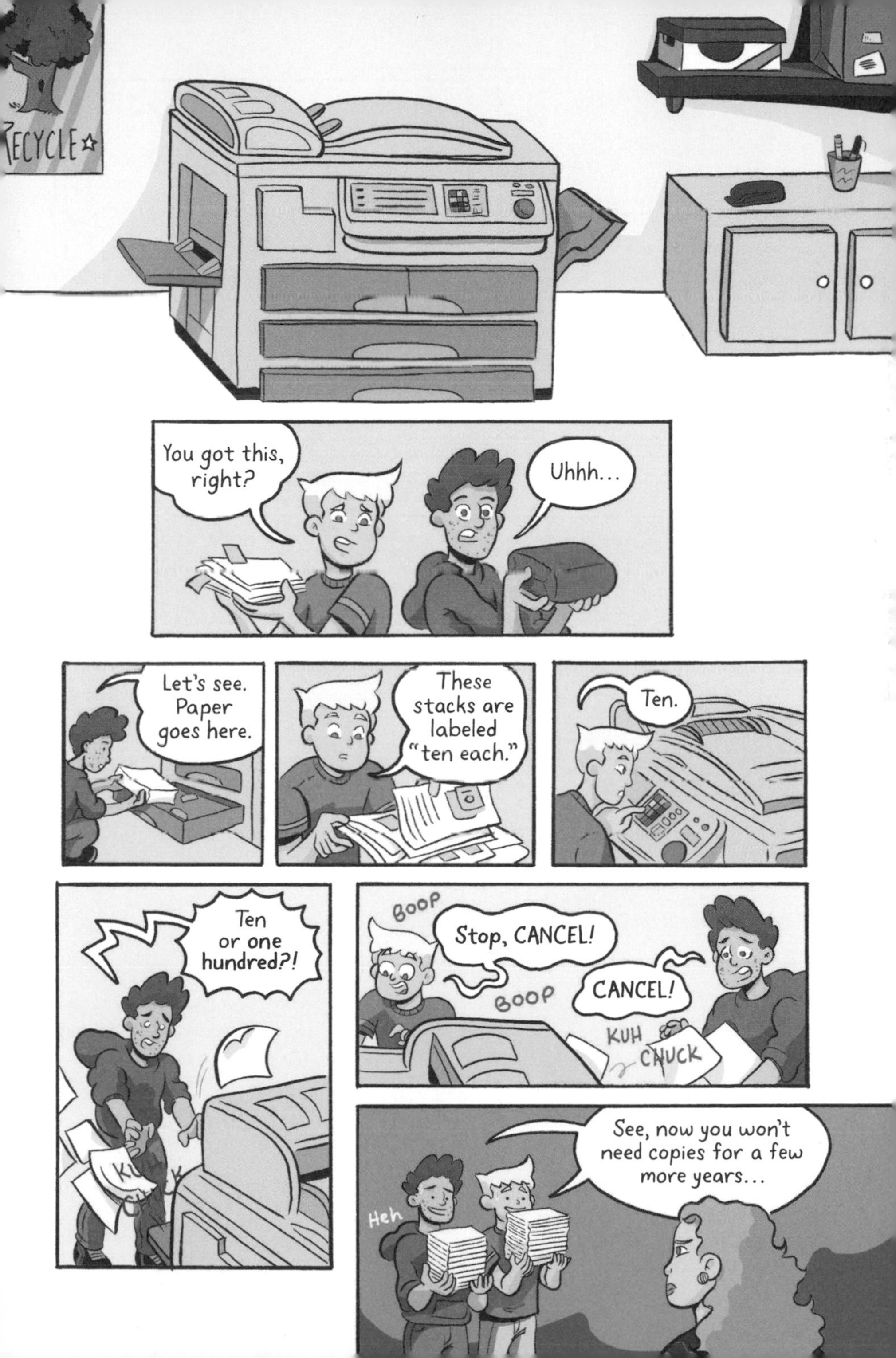
RECYCLE
You got this, right?
Uhhh...
Let's see. Paper goes here.
These stacks are labeled "ten each."
Ten.
Ten or one hundred?!
BOOP
Stop, CANCEL!
BOOP
CANCEL!
KUH CHUCK
Heh
See, now you won't need copies for a few more years...

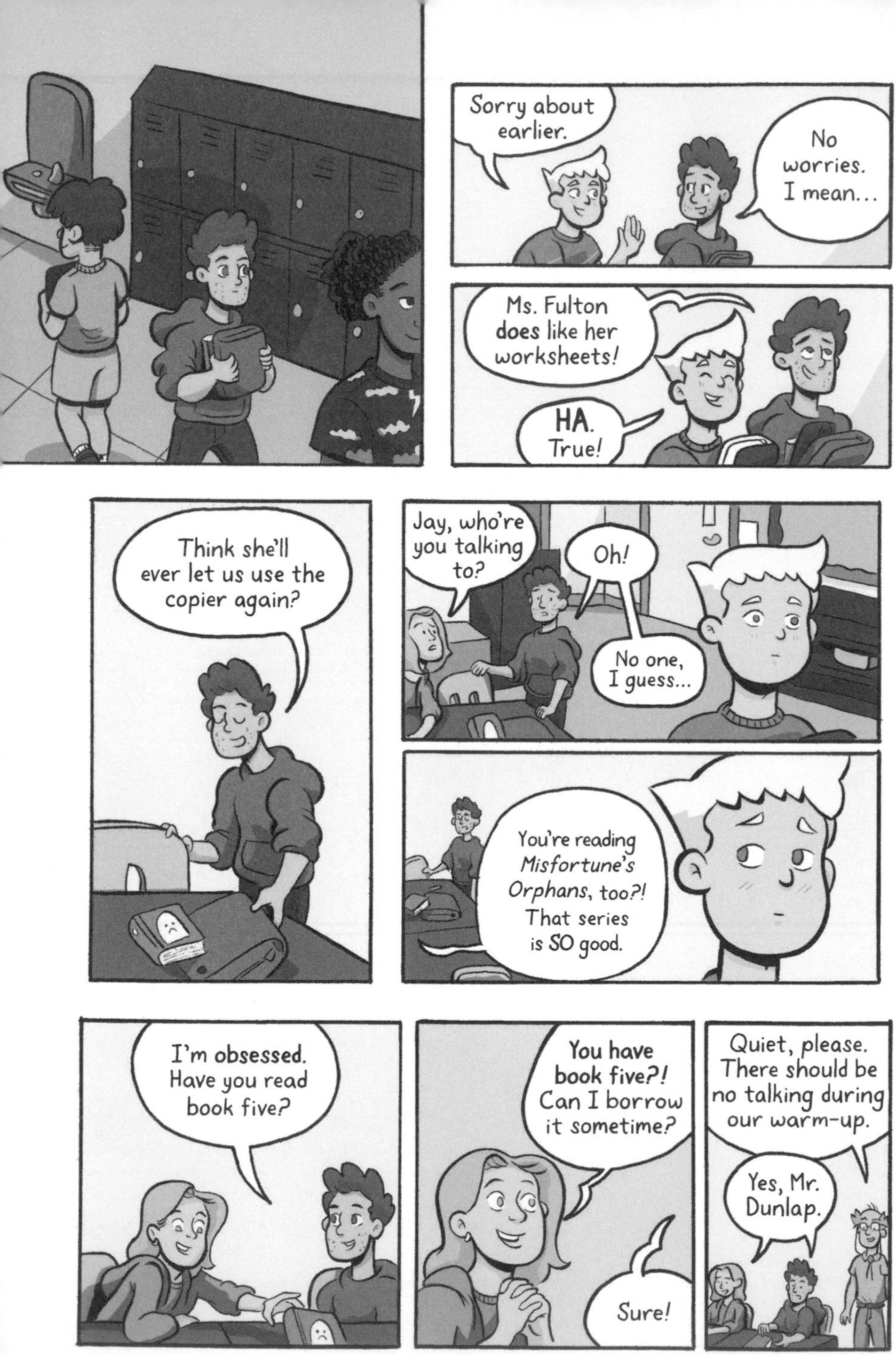
Sorry about earlier.
No worries. I mean...
Ms. Fulton **does** like her worksheets!
HA. True!
Think she'll ever let us use the copier again?
Jay, who're you talking to?
Oh!
No one, I guess...
You're reading *Misfortune's Orphans*, too?! That series is SO good.
I'm **obsessed.** Have you read book five?
You have book five?! Can I borrow it sometime?
Sure!
Quiet, please. There should be no talking during our warm-up.
Yes, Mr. Dunlap.

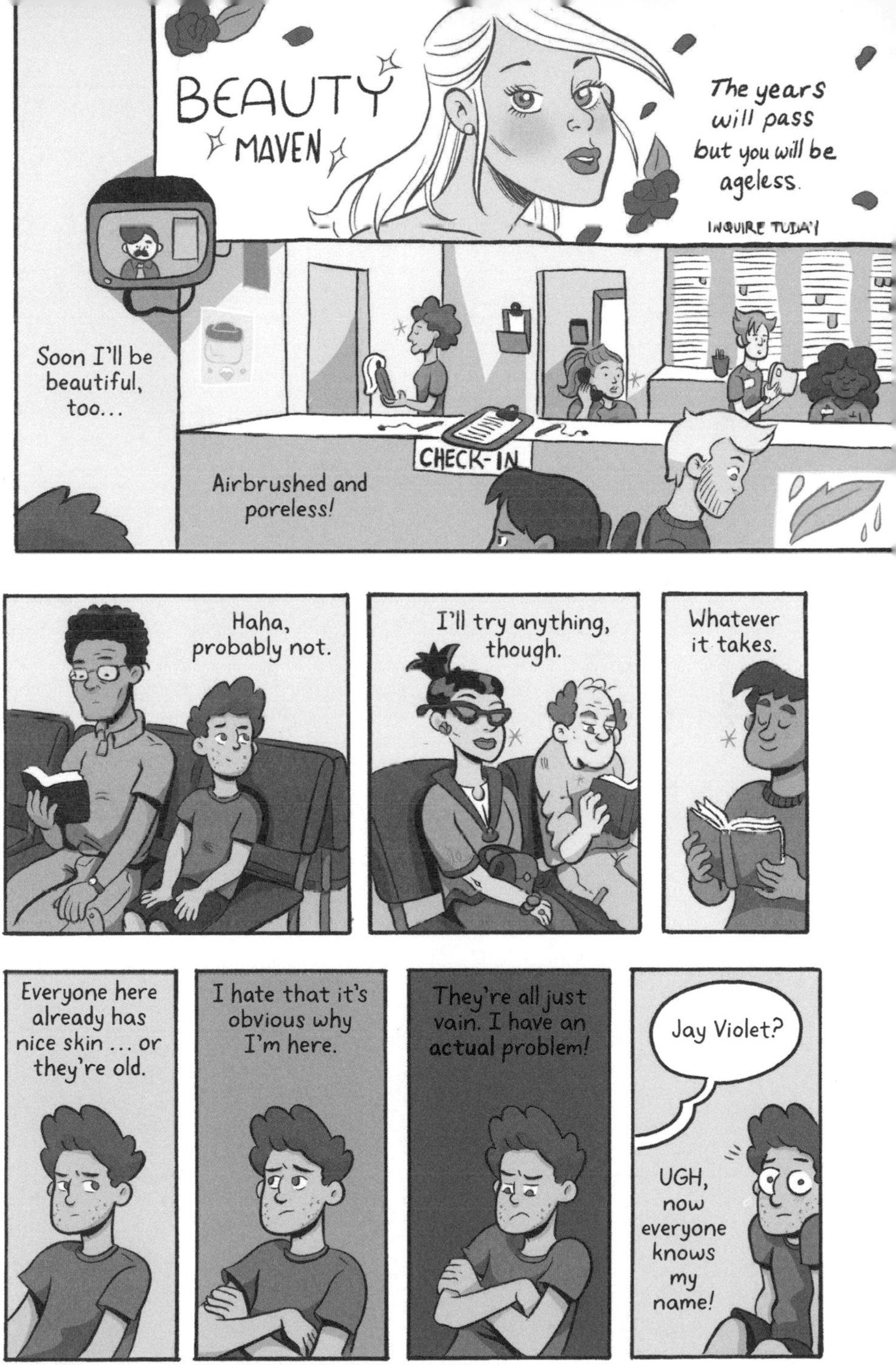
BEAUTY
MAVEN
The years will pass but you will be ageless.
INQUIRE TODAY
Soon I'll be beautiful, too...
CHECK-IN
Airbrushed and poreless!
Haha, probably not.
I'll try anything, though.
Whatever it takes.
Everyone here already has nice skin ... or they're old.
I hate that it's obvious why I'm here.
They're all just vain. I have an actual problem!
Jay Violet?
UGH, now everyone knows my name!

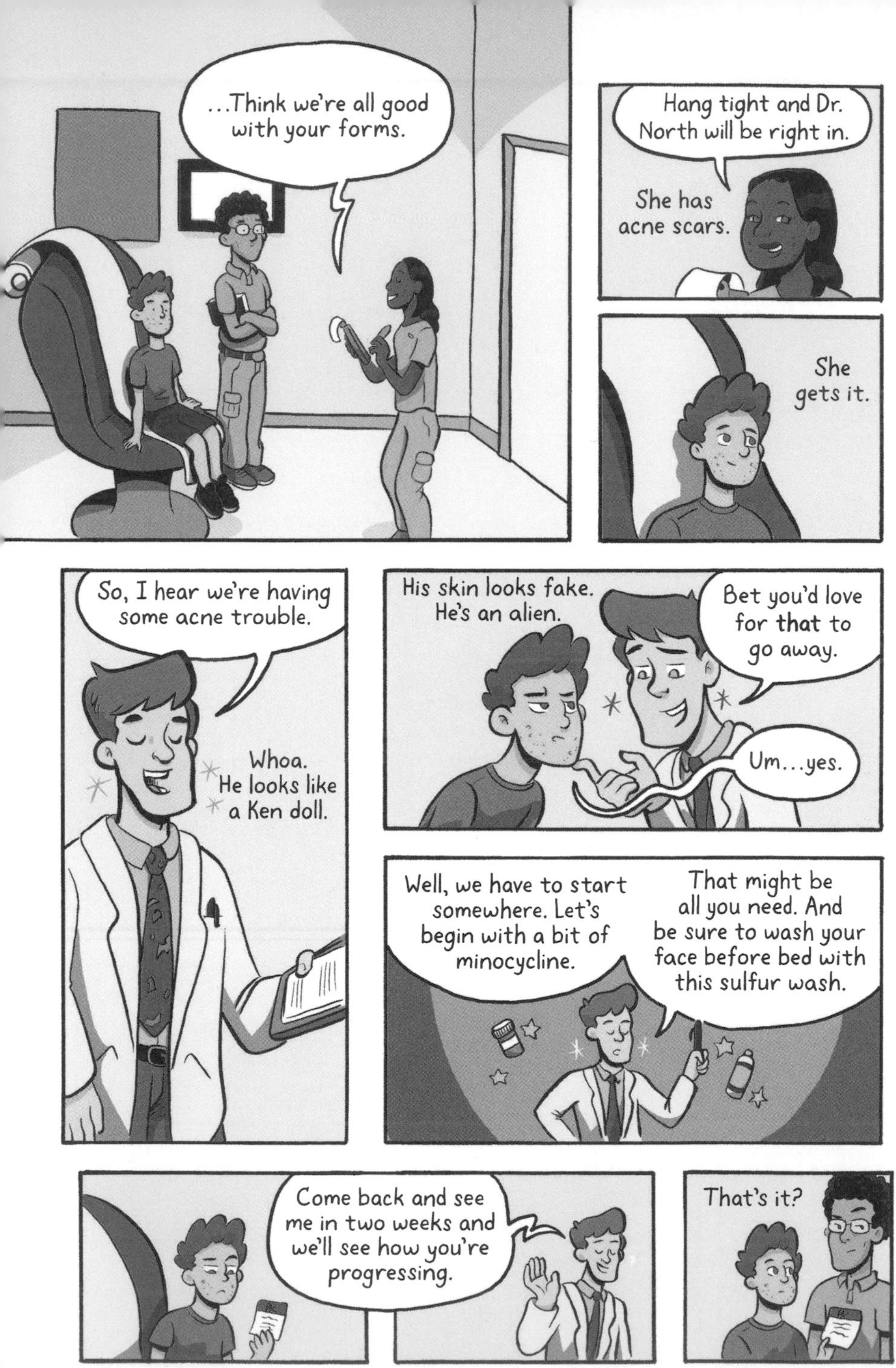

...Think we're all good with your forms.
Hang tight and Dr. North will be right in.
She has acne scars.
She gets it.
So, I hear we're having some acne trouble.
Whoa. He looks like a Ken doll.
His skin looks fake. He's an alien.
Bet you'd love for **that** to go away.
Um...yes.
Well, we have to start somewhere. Let's begin with a bit of minocycline.
That might be all you need. And be sure to wash your face before bed with this sulfur wash.
Come back and see me in two weeks and we'll see how you're progressing.
That's it?

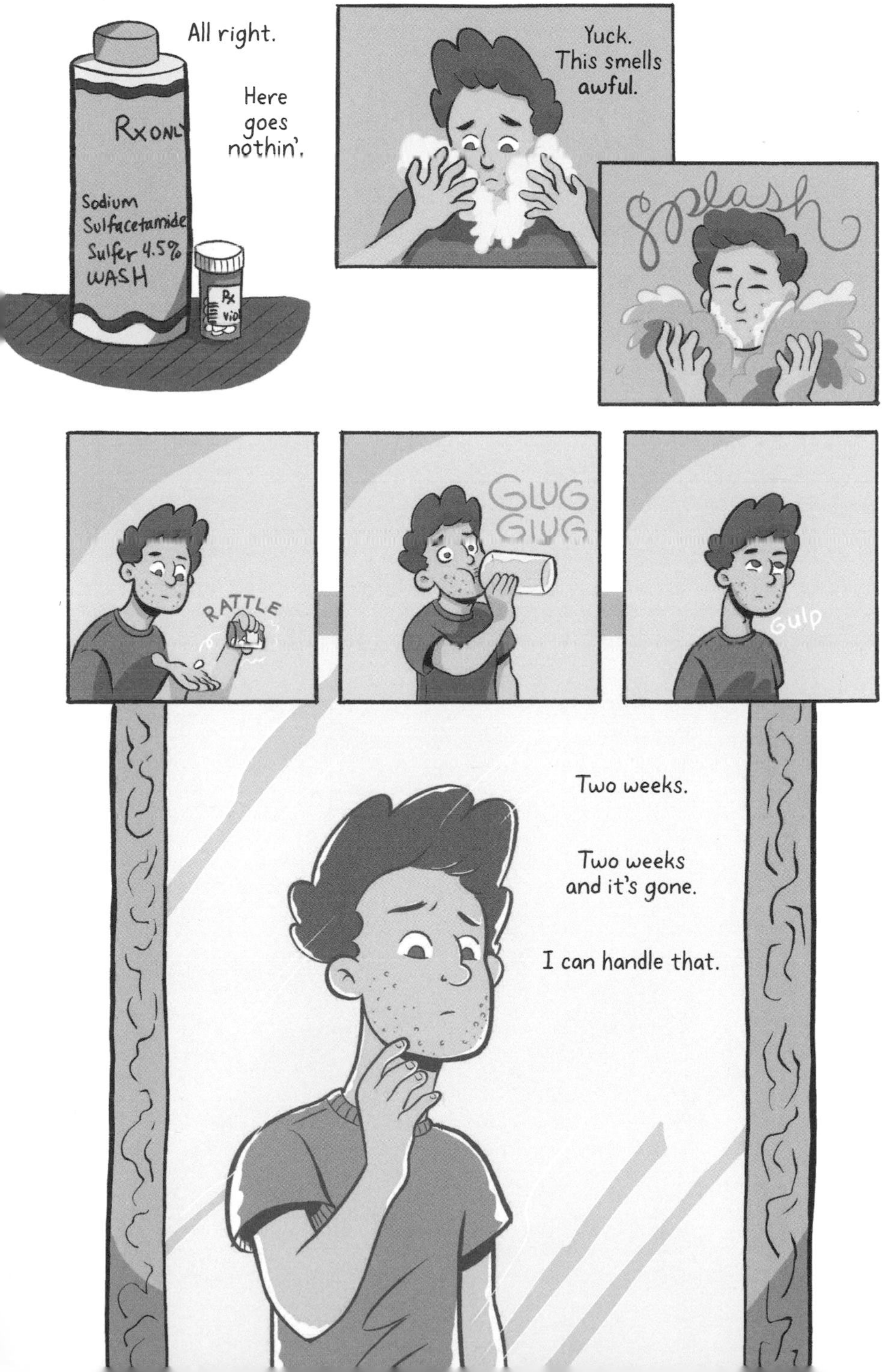
All right.
Here goes nothin'.
Rx ONLY
Sodium Sulfacetamide Sulfer 4.5% WASH
Yuck. This smells awful.
splash
RATTLE
GLUG GLUG
GULP
Two weeks.
Two weeks and it's gone.
I can handle that.

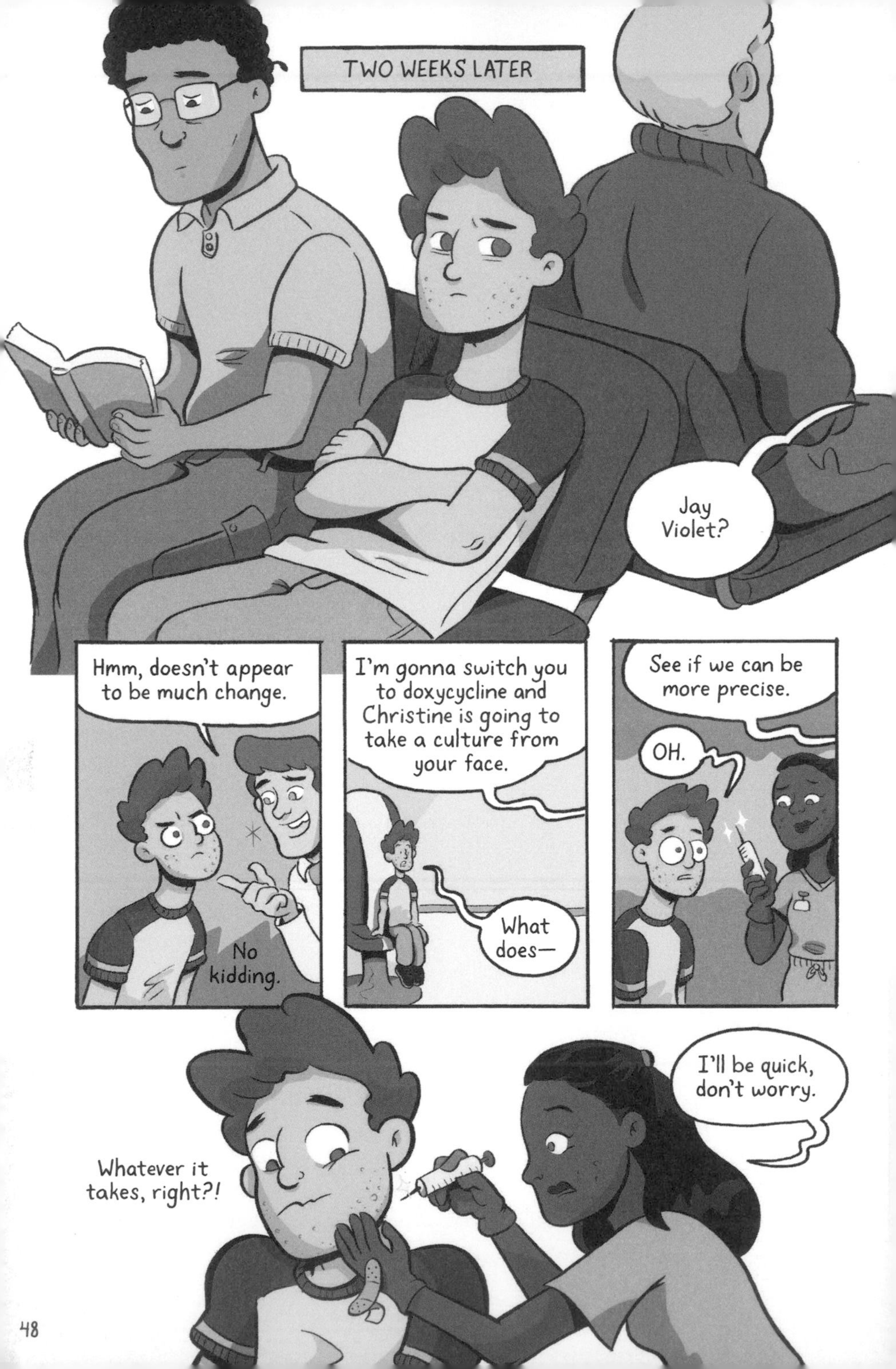
TWO WEEKS LATER
Jay Violet?
Hmm, doesn't appear to be much change.
No kidding.
I'm gonna switch you to doxycycline and Christine is going to take a culture from your face.
What does—
See if we can be more precise.
OH.
I'll be quick, don't worry.
Whatever it takes, right?!

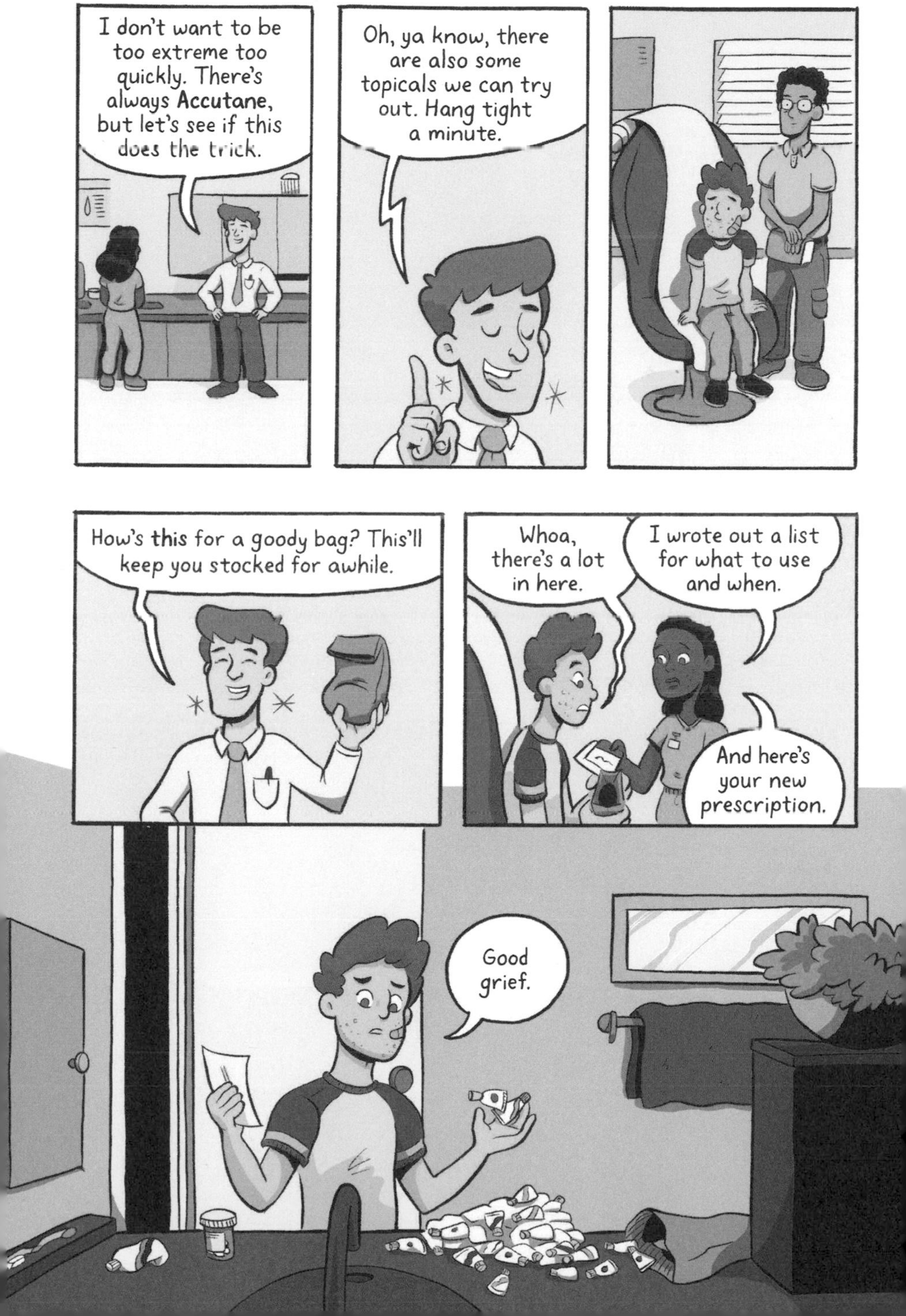
I don't want to be too extreme too quickly. There's always **Accutane**, but let's see if this does the trick.
Oh, ya know, there are also some topicals we can try out. Hang tight a minute.
How's **this** for a goody bag? This'll keep you stocked for awhile.
Whoa, there's a lot in here.
I wrote out a list for what to use and when.
And here's your new prescription.
Good grief.

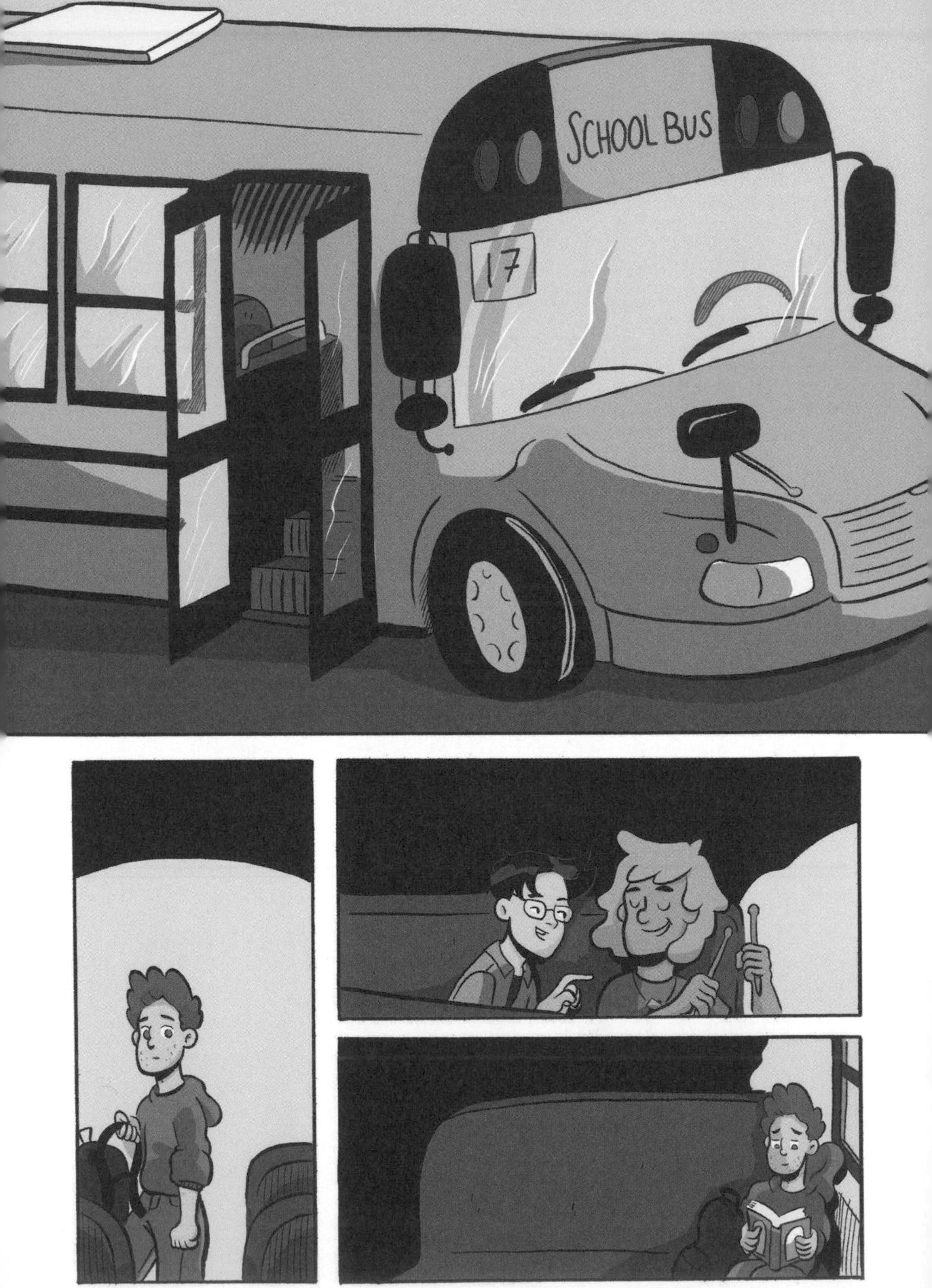
SCHOOL BUS
17

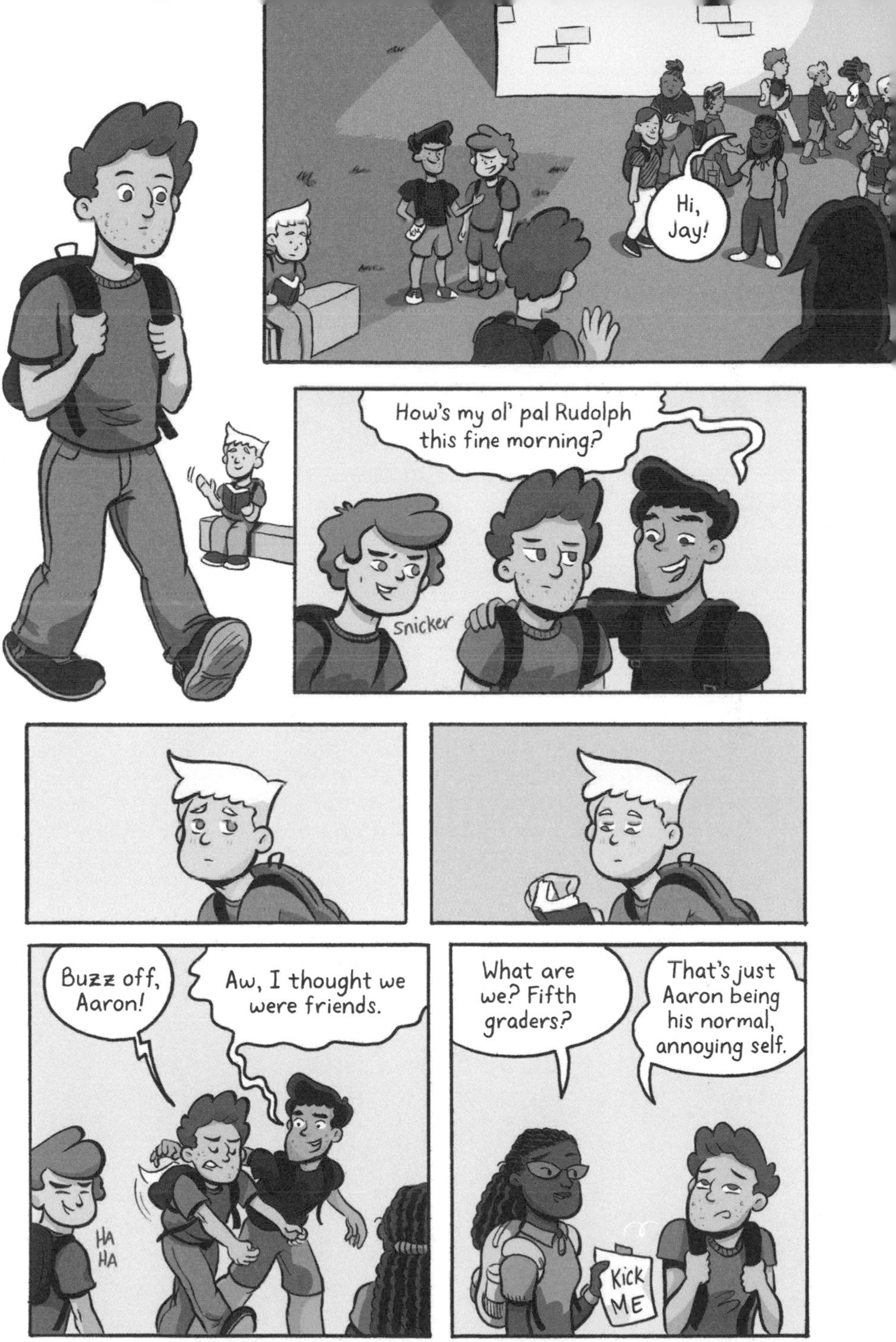
Hi, Jay!
How's my ol' pal Rudolph this fine morning?
snicker
Buzz off, Aaron!
Aw, I thought we were friends.
HA HA
What are we? Fifth graders?
That's just Aaron being his normal, annoying self.
KICK ME

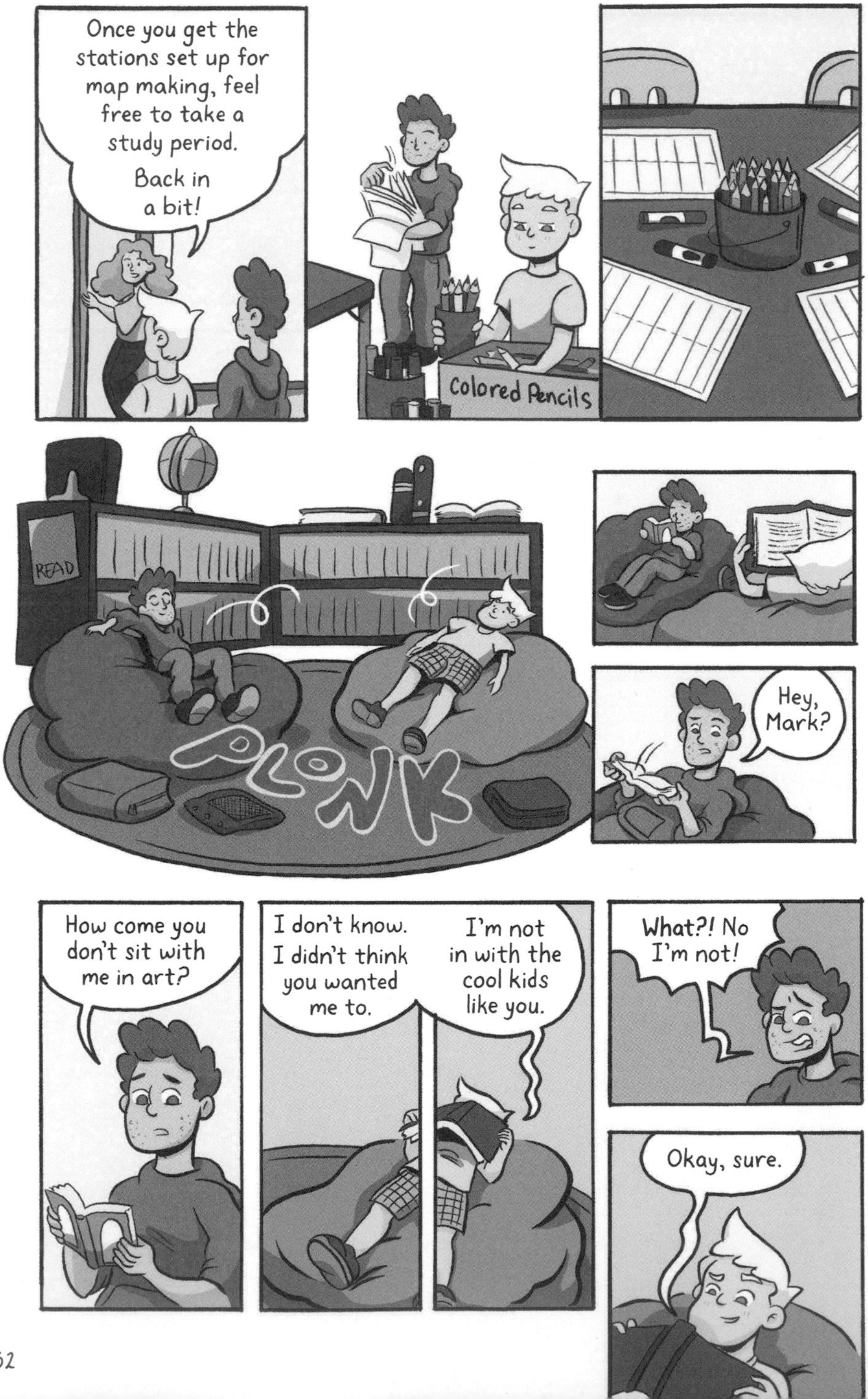

Once you get the stations set up for map making, feel free to take a study period.
Back in a bit!
Colored Pencils
READ
PLONK
Hey, Mark?
How come you don't sit with me in art?
I don't know. I didn't think you wanted me to.
I'm not in with the cool kids like you.
What?! No I'm not!
Okay, sure.

"In with the cool kids?!"

Psht, no way!

I'm not **mean** like them...

S'il vous plait, regardez ça.

...am I?

I did laugh about that girl's teeth...

No.

They tease **me**, too!

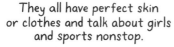

They all have perfect skin or clothes and talk about girls and sports nonstop.

We're **not** the same.

We don't even **look** like we'd be friends.

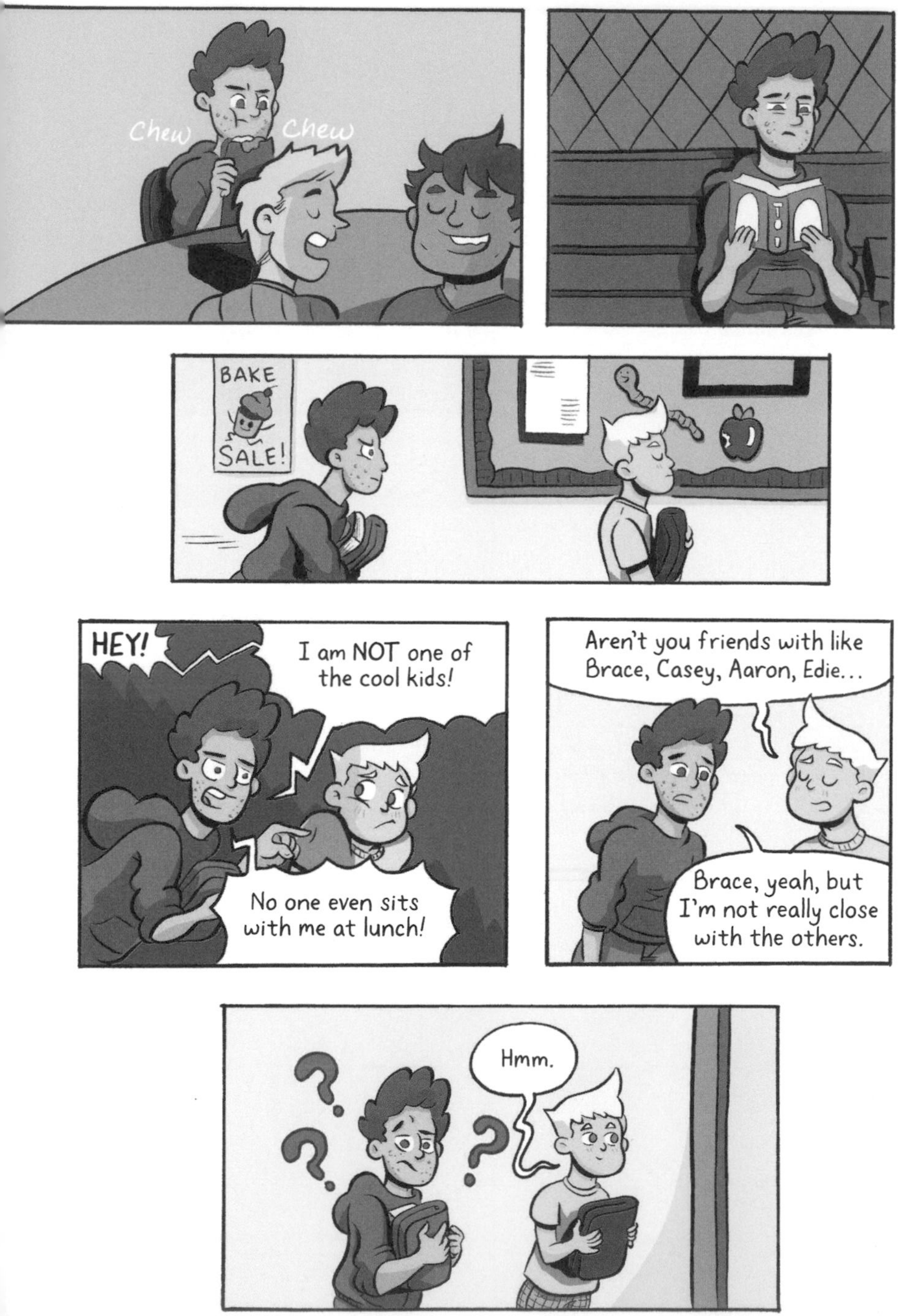
Chew
Chew
BAKE SALE!
HEY!
I am NOT one of the cool kids!
No one even sits with me at lunch!
Aren't you friends with like Brace, Casey, Aaron, Edie…
Brace, yeah, but I'm not really close with the others.
Hmm.

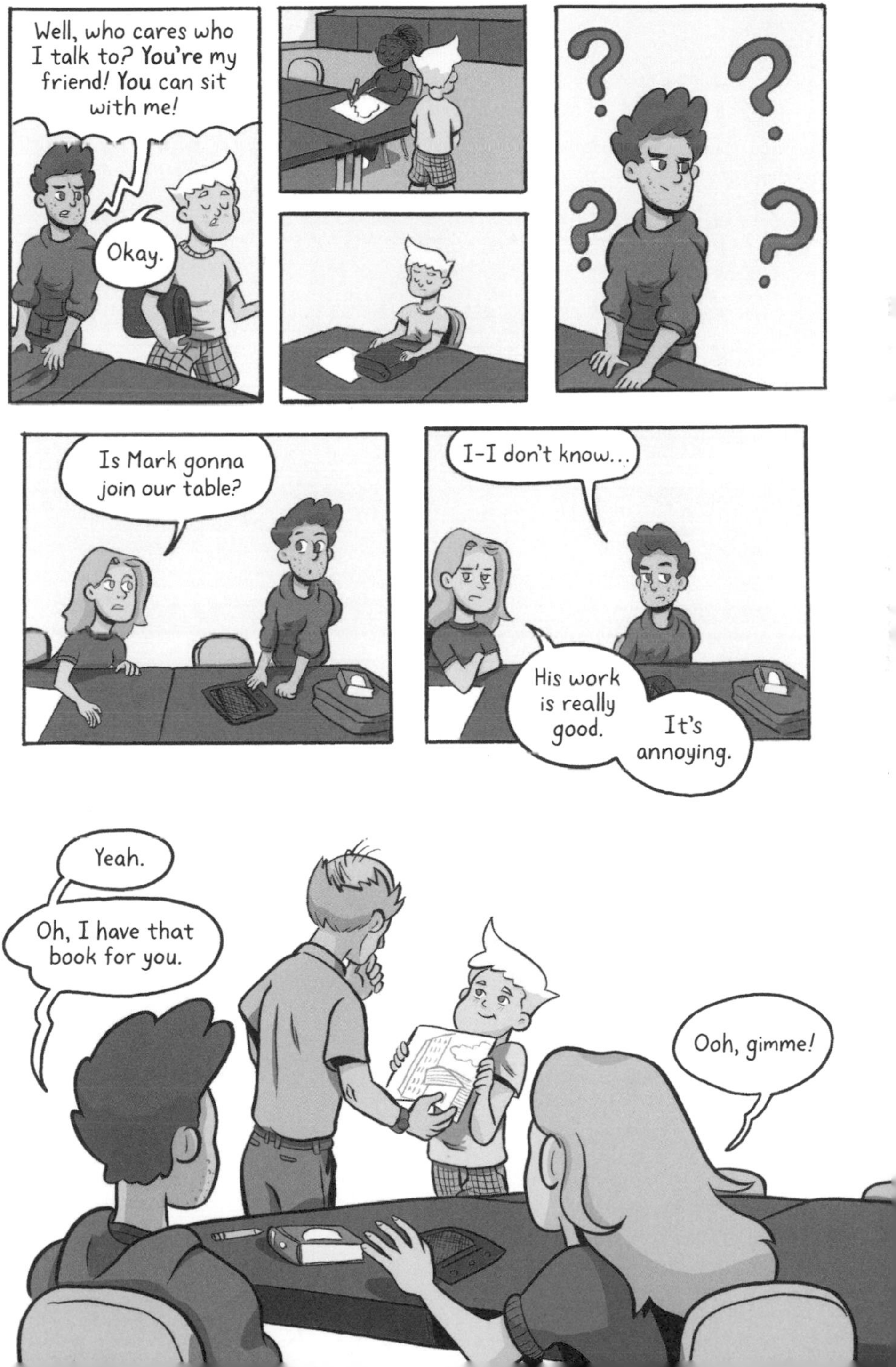
Well, who cares who I talk to? You're my friend! You can sit with me!
Okay.
Is Mark gonna join our table?
I-I don't know...
His work is really good.
It's annoying.
Yeah.
Oh, I have that book for you.
Ooh, gimme!

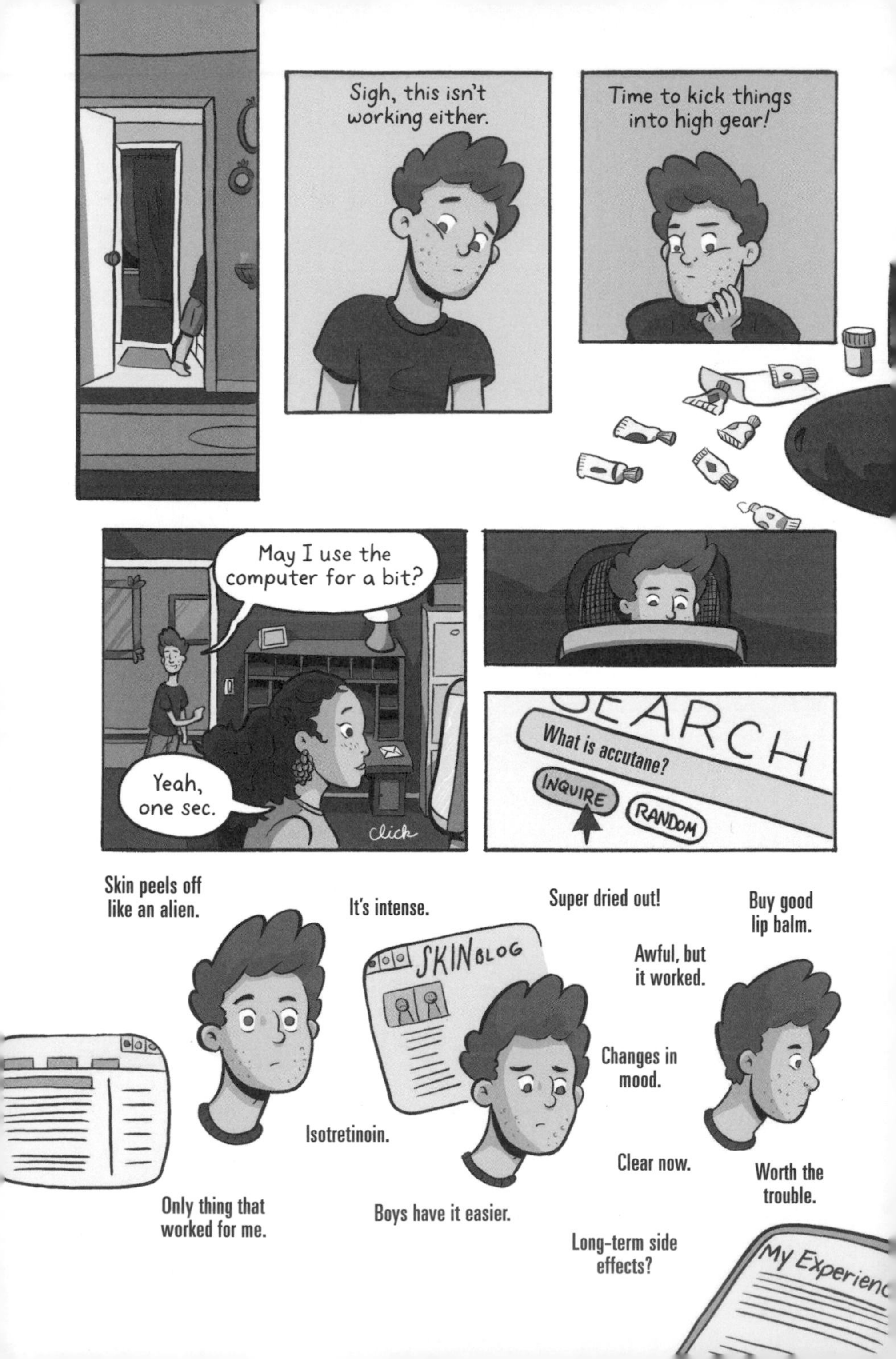
Sigh, this isn't working either.
Time to kick things into high gear!
May I use the computer for a bit?
Yeah, one sec.
click
SEARCH
What is accutane?
INQUIRE
RANDOM
Skin peels off like an alien.
It's intense.
Super dried out!
Buy good lip balm.
SKIN BLOG
Awful, but it worked.
Changes in mood.
Isotretinoin.
Clear now.
Worth the trouble.
Only thing that worked for me.
Boys have it easier.
Long-term side effects?
My Experienc

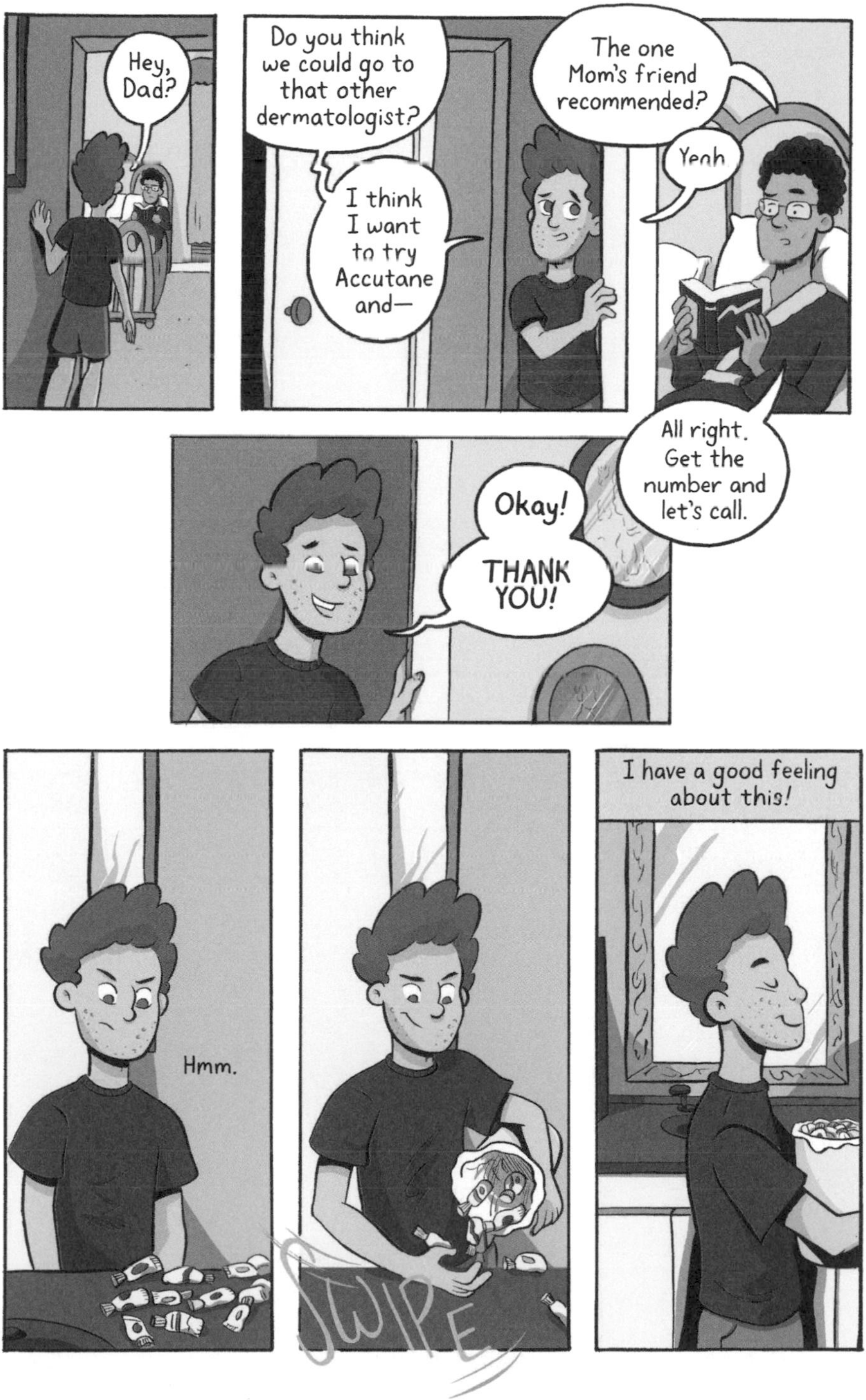
Hey, Dad?
Do you think we could go to that other dermatologist?
I think I want to try Accutane and—
The one Mom's friend recommended?
Yeah.
All right. Get the number and let's call.
Okay!
THANK YOU!
Hmm.
SWIPE
I have a good feeling about this!

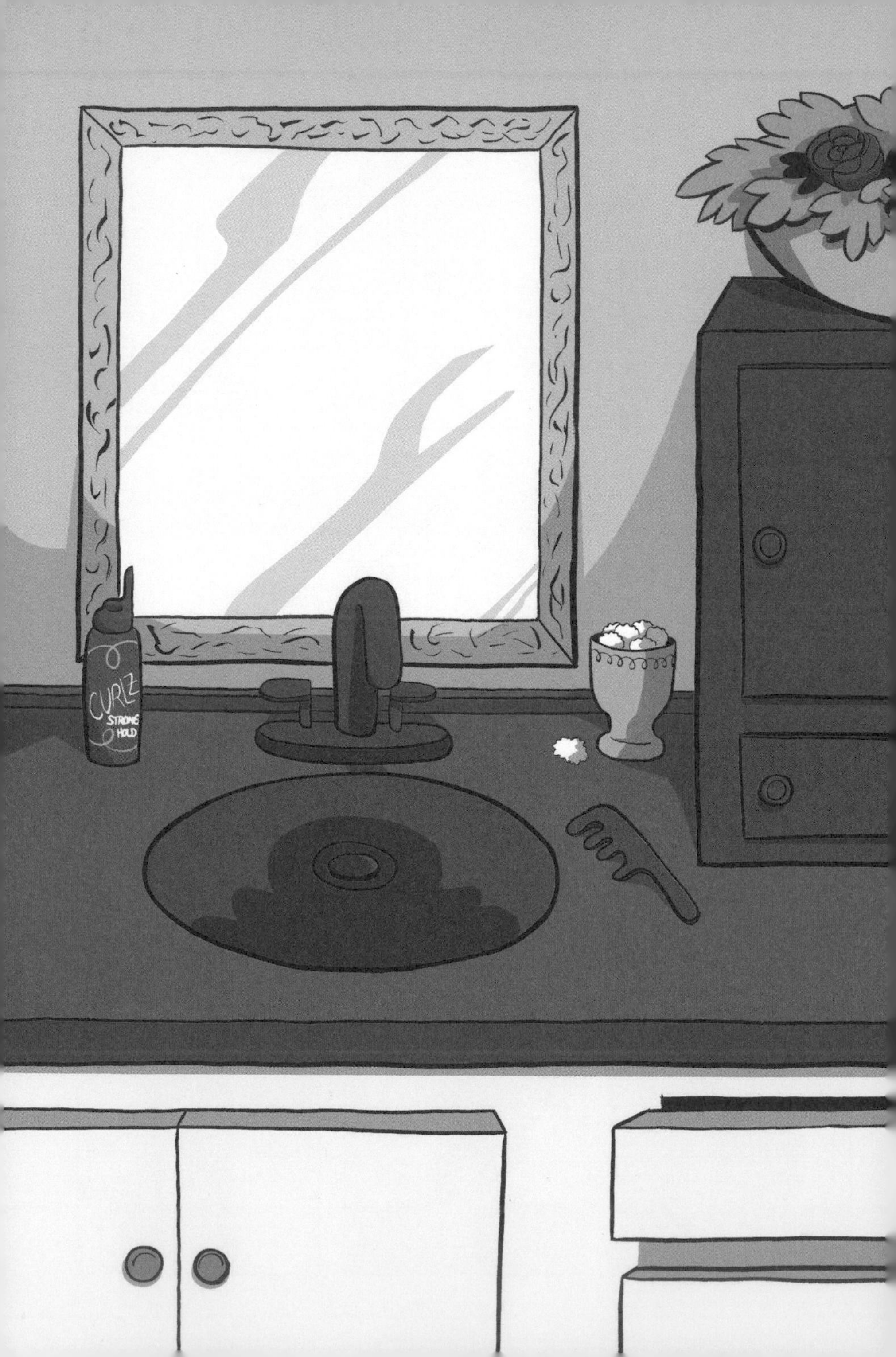
CURLZ
STRONG HOLD

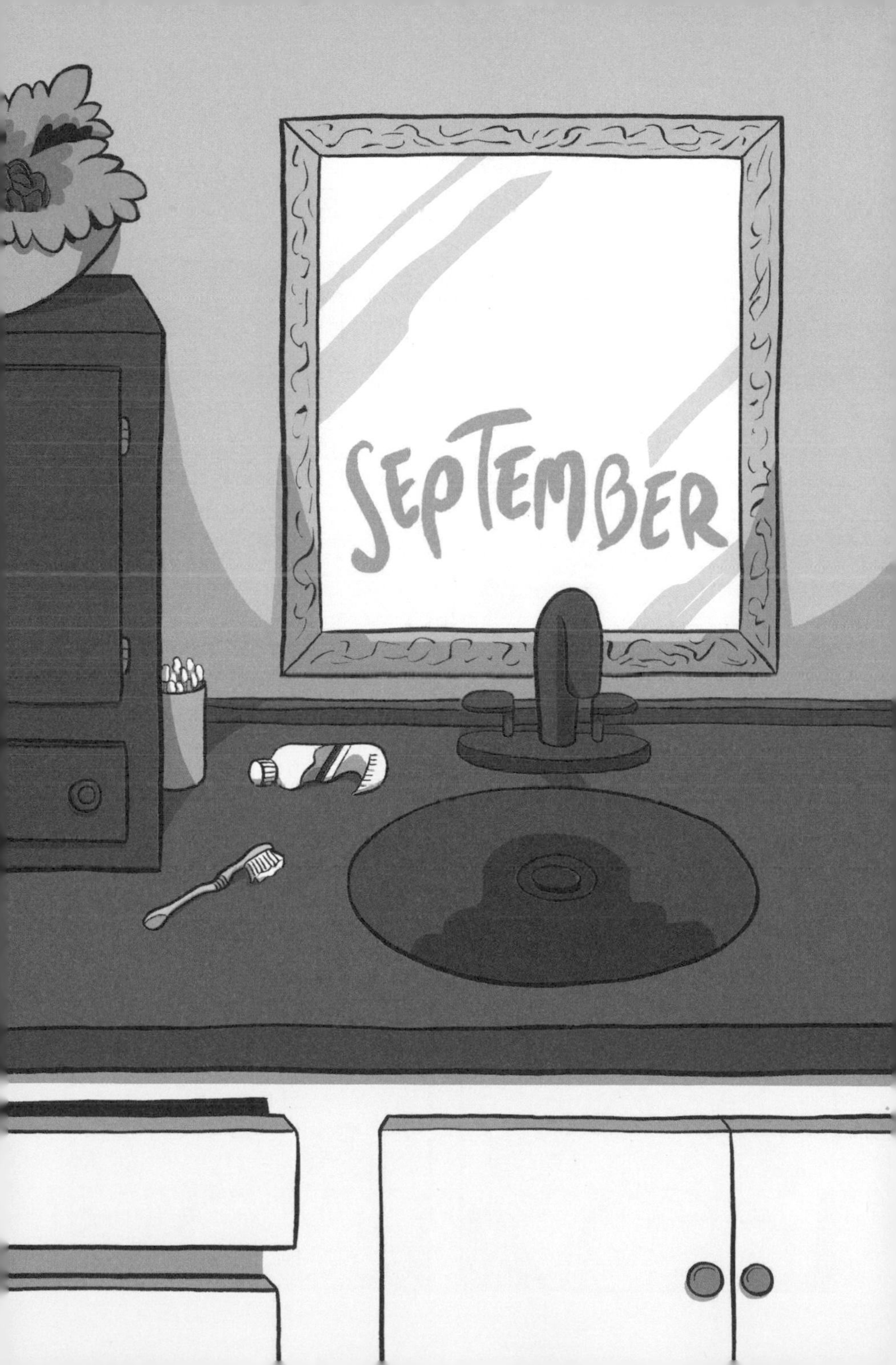
SEPTEMBER

What did Mom's friend say about Dr. Laski?

That he was "odd but really good."

BAY SKIN CLINIC

Jay?

Yes.

Let's take a look.

Hmm.

Okay.

Okay.

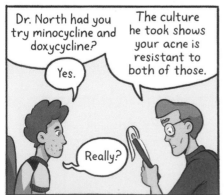

Dr. North had you try minocycline and doxycycline?

Yes.

The culture he took shows your acne is resistant to both of those.

Really?

And you used all these topicals?

Yes.

Notice any improvements?

Not really.

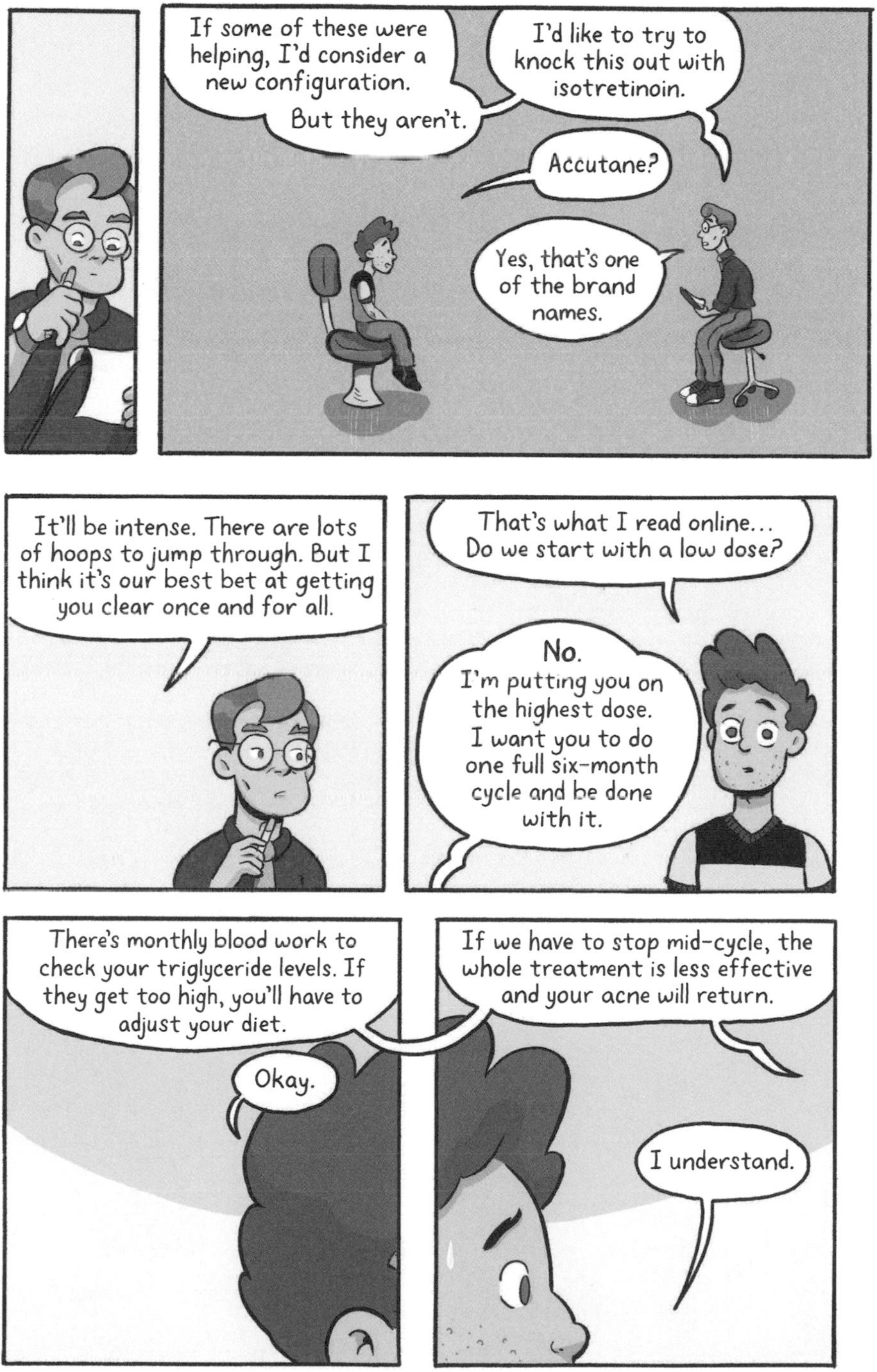
If some of these were helping, I'd consider a new configuration.
But they aren't.
I'd like to try to knock this out with isotretinoin.
Accutane?
Yes, that's one of the brand names.
It'll be intense. There are lots of hoops to jump through. But I think it's our best bet at getting you clear once and for all.
That's what I read online... Do we start with a low dose?
No.
I'm putting you on the highest dose. I want you to do one full six-month cycle and be done with it.
There's monthly blood work to check your triglyceride levels. If they get too high, you'll have to adjust your diet.
Okay.
If we have to stop mid-cycle, the whole treatment is less effective and your acne will return.
I understand.

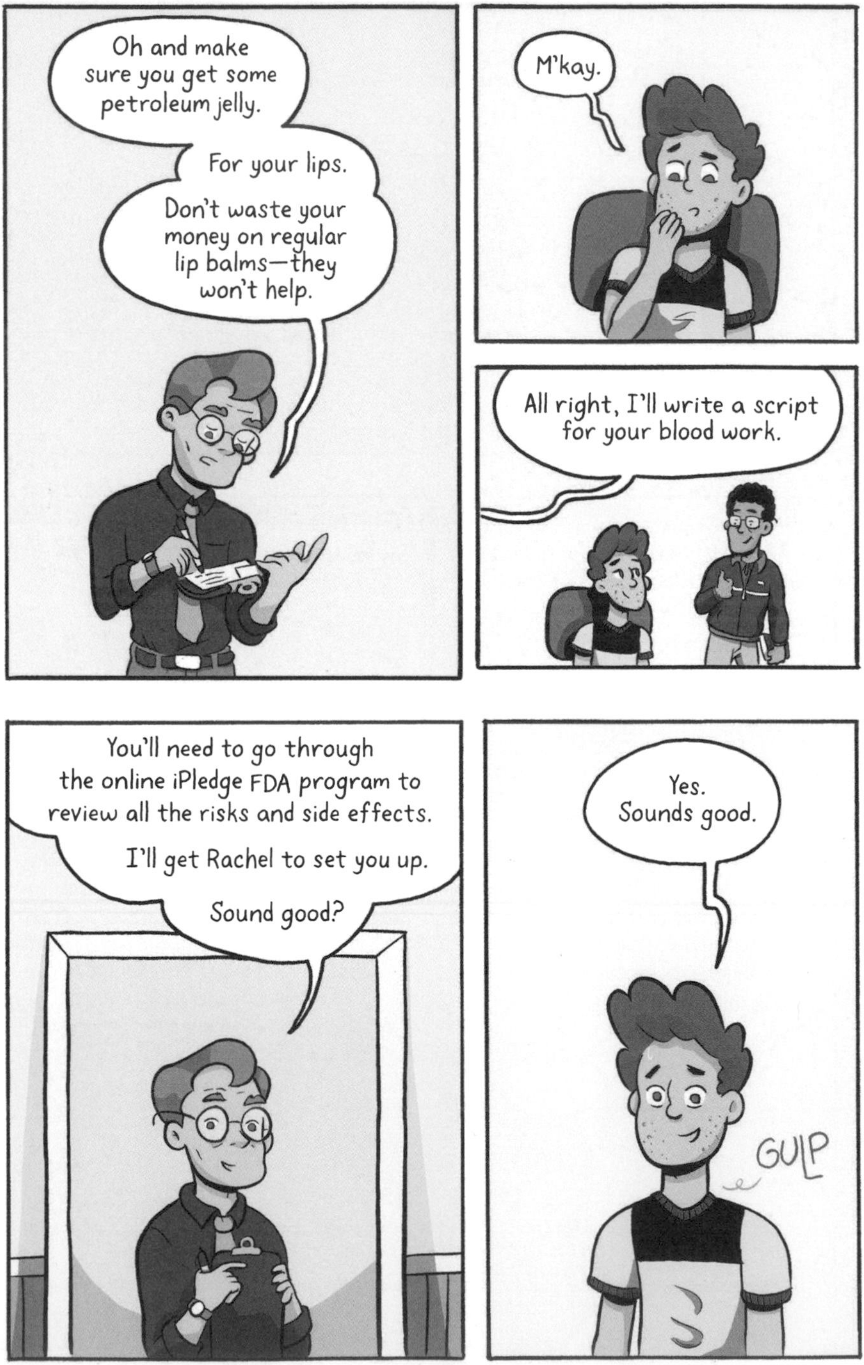
Oh and make sure you get some petroleum jelly.
For your lips.
Don't waste your money on regular lip balms—they won't help.
M'kay.
All right, I'll write a script for your blood work.
You'll need to go through the online iPledge FDA program to review all the risks and side effects.
I'll get Rachel to set you up.
Sound good?
Yes. Sounds good.
GULP

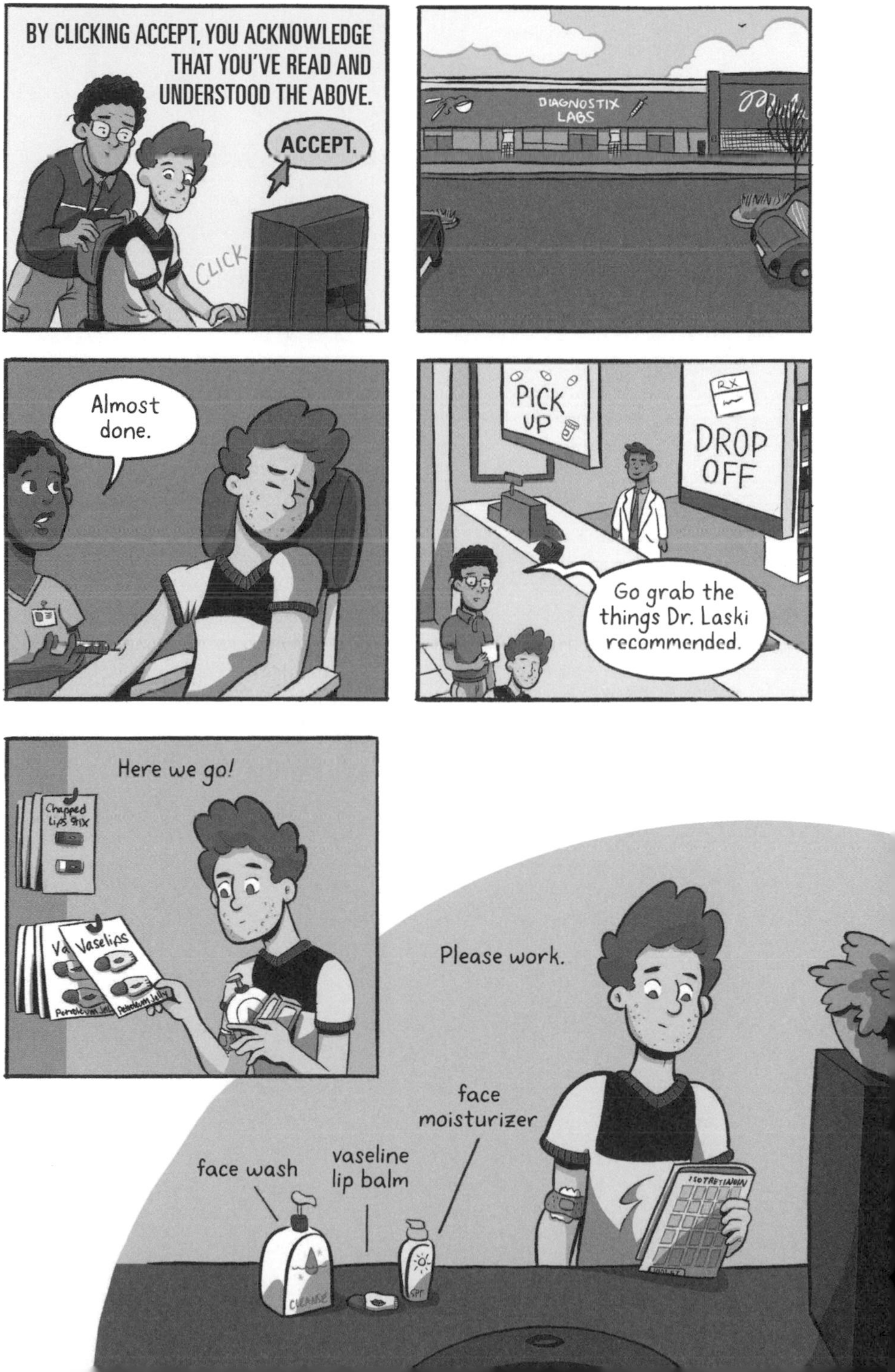
BY CLICKING ACCEPT, YOU ACKNOWLEDGE THAT YOU'VE READ AND UNDERSTOOD THE ABOVE.
ACCEPT.
CLICK
DIAGNOSTIX LABS
Almost done.
PICK UP
RX
DROP OFF
Go grab the things Dr. Laski recommended.
Here we go!
Chapped Lips Stix
Vaselips
Petroleum Jelly
Please work.
face wash
vaseline lip balm
face moisturizer
CLEANSE
SPF
ISOTRETINOIN

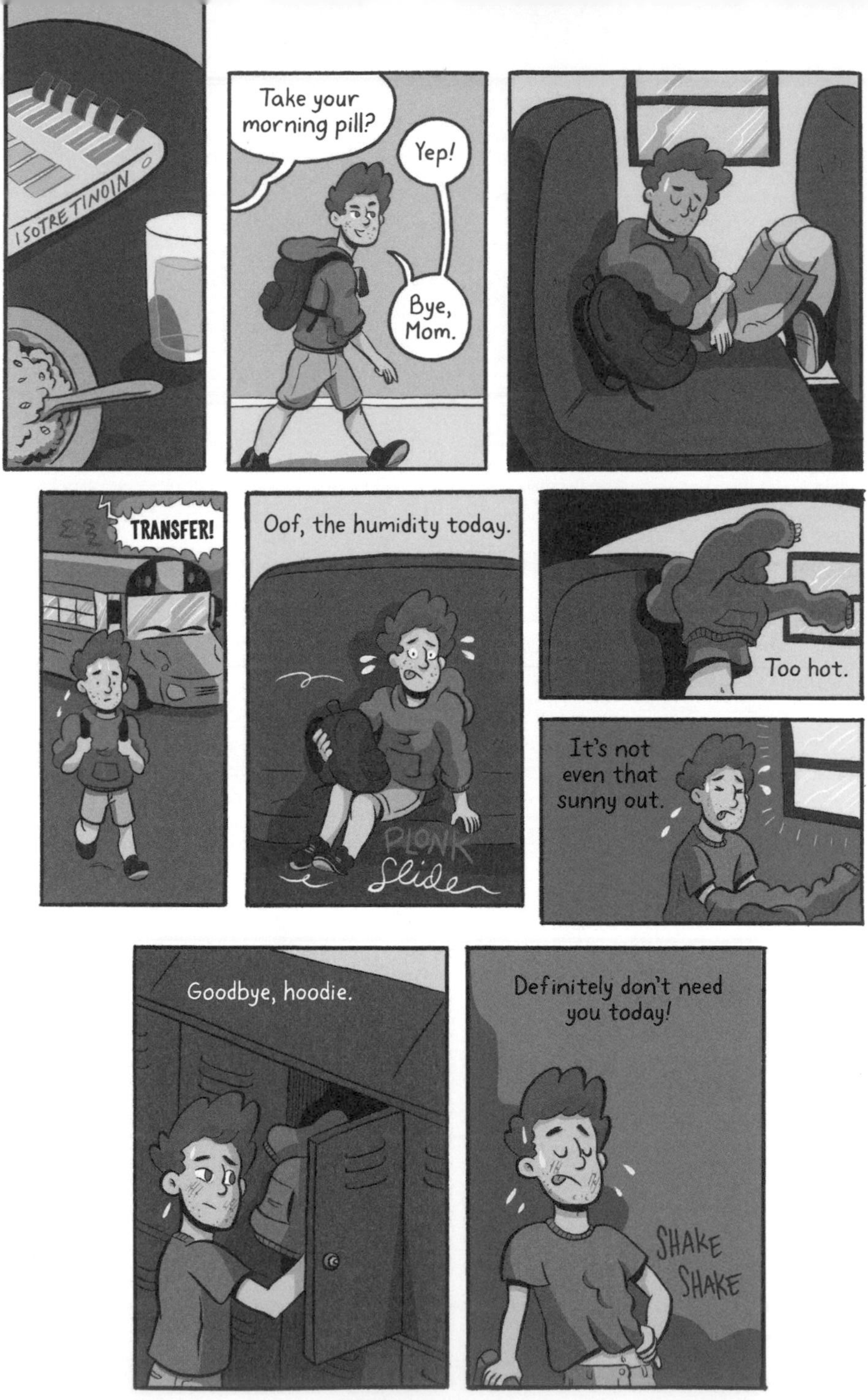
ISOTRETINOIN
Take your morning pill?
Yep!
Bye, Mom.
TRANSFER!
Oof, the humidity today.
PLONK
Slide
Too hot.
It's not even that sunny out.
Goodbye, hoodie.
Definitely don't need you today!
SHAKE
SHAKE

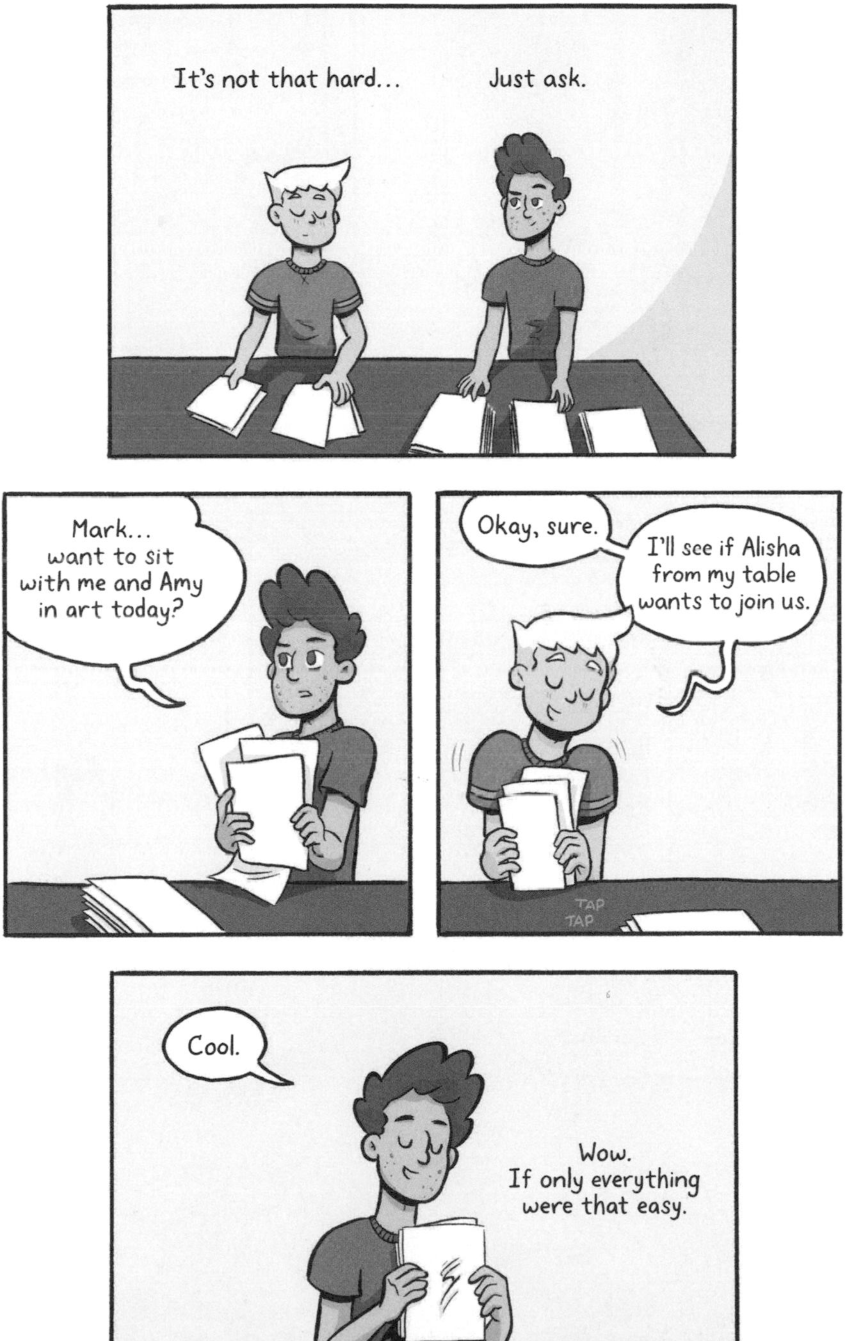
It's not that hard...
Just ask.
Mark... want to sit with me and Amy in art today?
Okay, sure.
I'll see if Alisha from my table wants to join us.
TAP TAP
Cool.
Wow. If only everything were that easy.

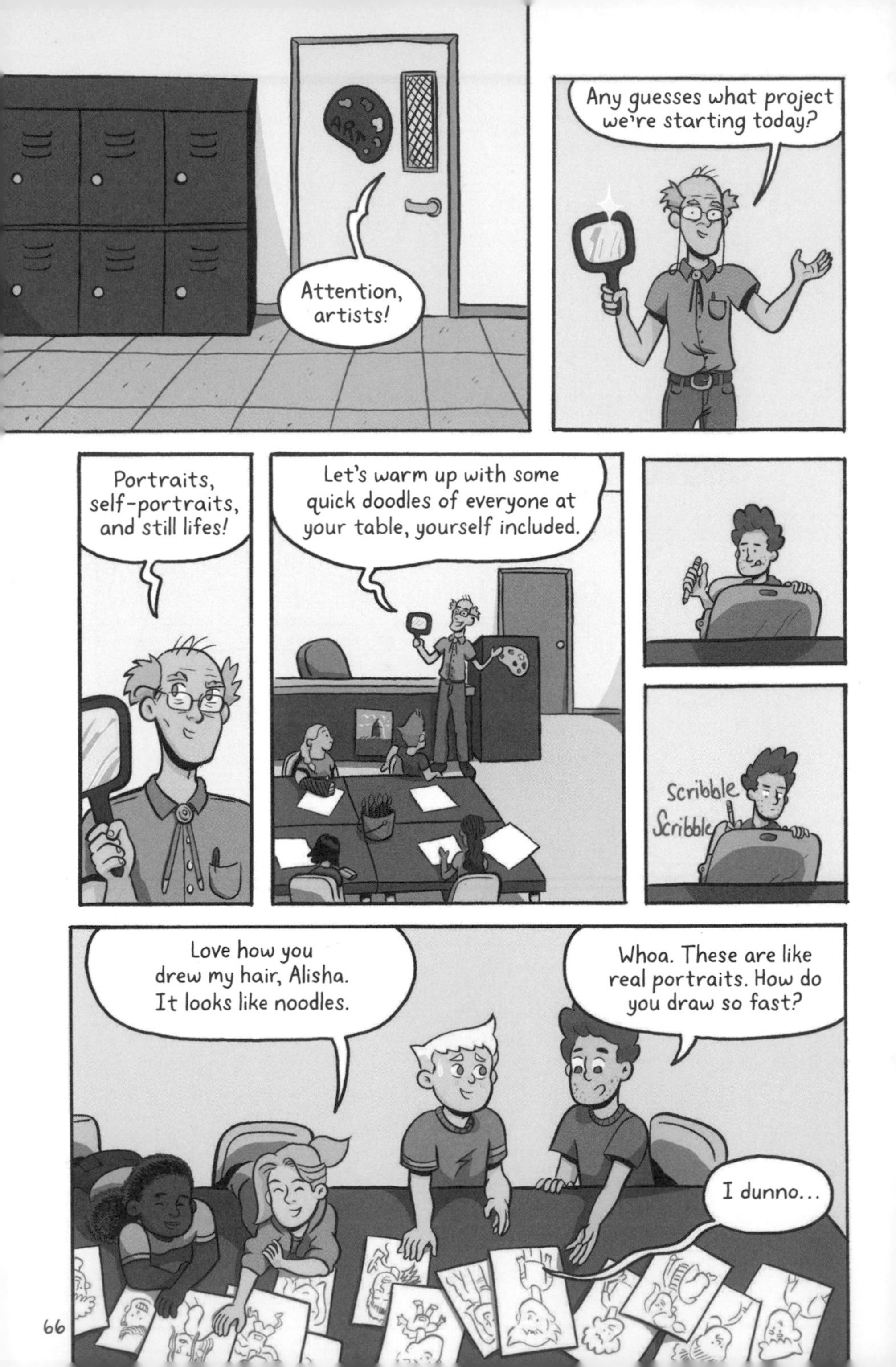
ART
Attention, artists!
Any guesses what project we're starting today?
Portraits, self-portraits, and still lifes!
Let's warm up with some quick doodles of everyone at your table, yourself included.
Scribble
Scribble
Love how you drew my hair, Alisha. It looks like noodles.
Whoa. These are like real portraits. How do you draw so fast?
I dunno...

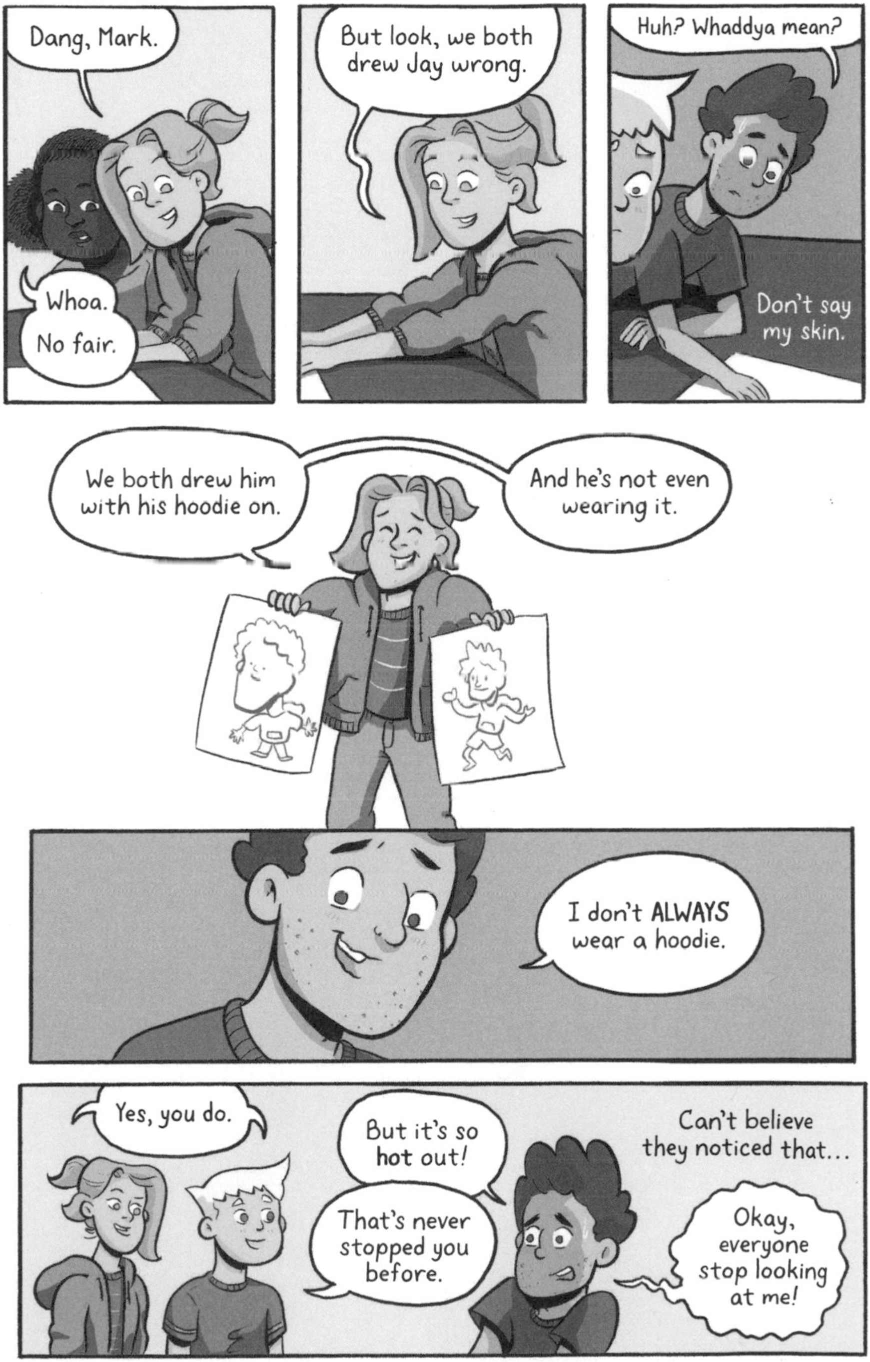
Dang, Mark.
Whoa.
No fair.
But look, we both drew Jay wrong.
Huh? Whaddya mean?
Don't say my skin.
We both drew him with his hoodie on.
And he's not even wearing it.
I don't **ALWAYS** wear a hoodie.
Yes, you do.
But it's so **hot** out!
That's never stopped you before.
Can't believe they noticed that...
Okay, everyone stop looking at me!

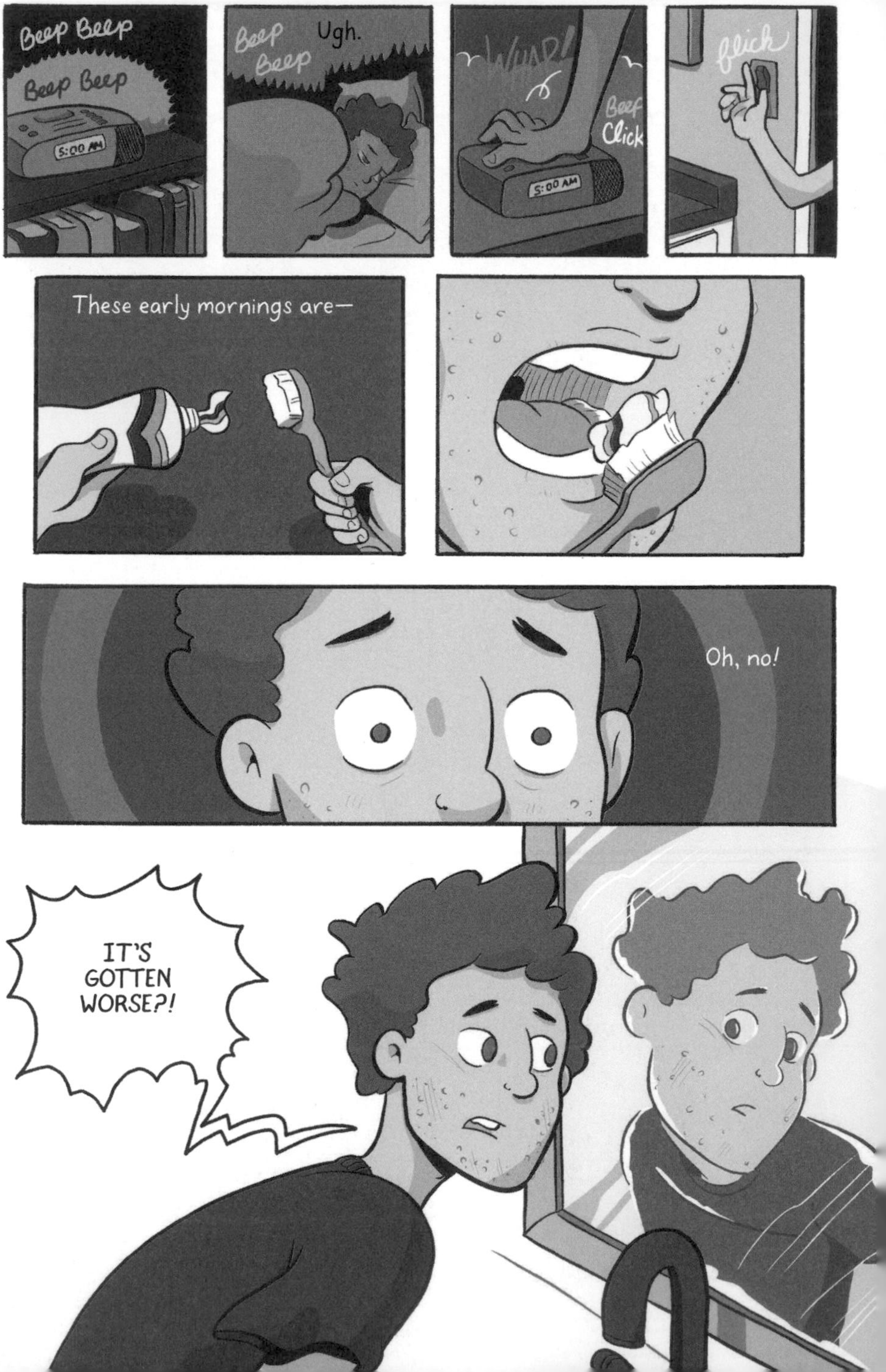
Beep Beep
Beep Beep
5:00 AM
Beep Beep
Ugh.
WHAP!
Beep
Click
5:00 AM
flick
These early mornings are—
Oh, no!
IT'S GOTTEN WORSE?!

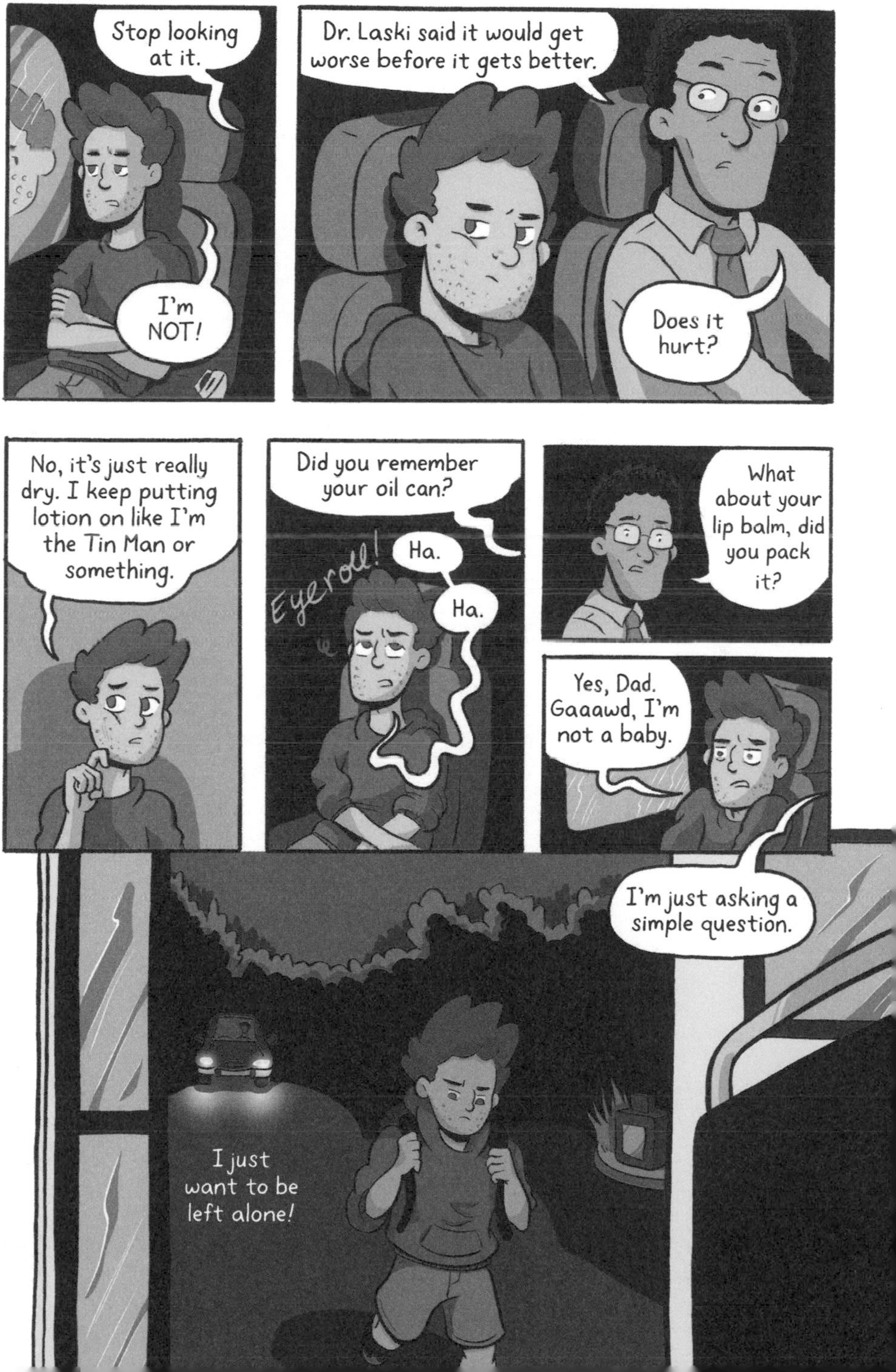
Stop looking at it.
I'm NOT!
Dr. Laski said it would get worse before it gets better.
Does it hurt?
No, it's just really dry. I keep putting lotion on like I'm the Tin Man or something.
Did you remember your oil can?
Eyeroll!
Ha.
Ha.
What about your lip balm, did you pack it?
Yes, Dad. Gaaawd, I'm not a baby.
I'm just asking a simple question.
I just want to be left alone!

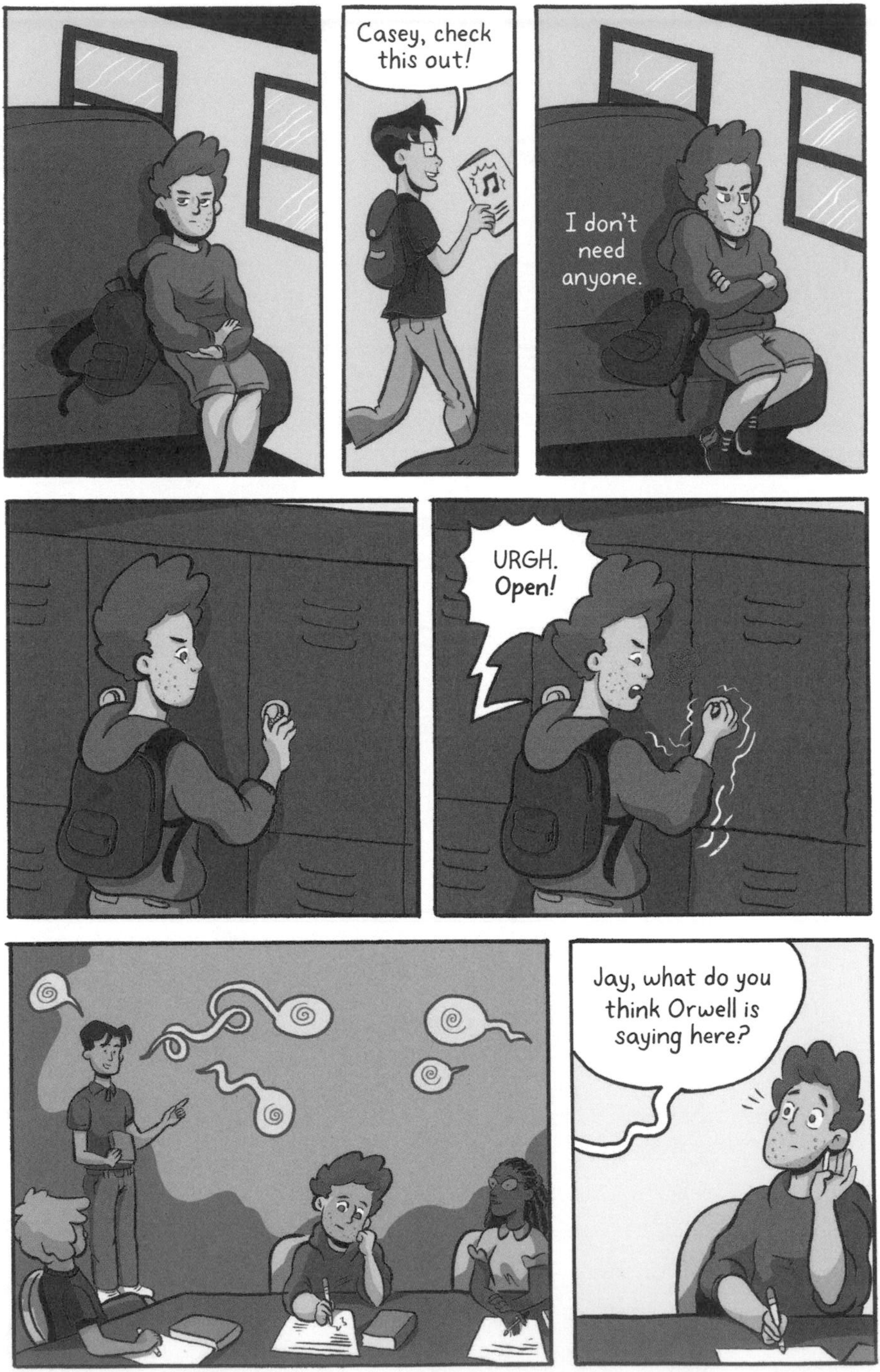
Casey, check this out!
I don't need anyone.
URGH. Open!
Jay, what do you think Orwell is saying here?

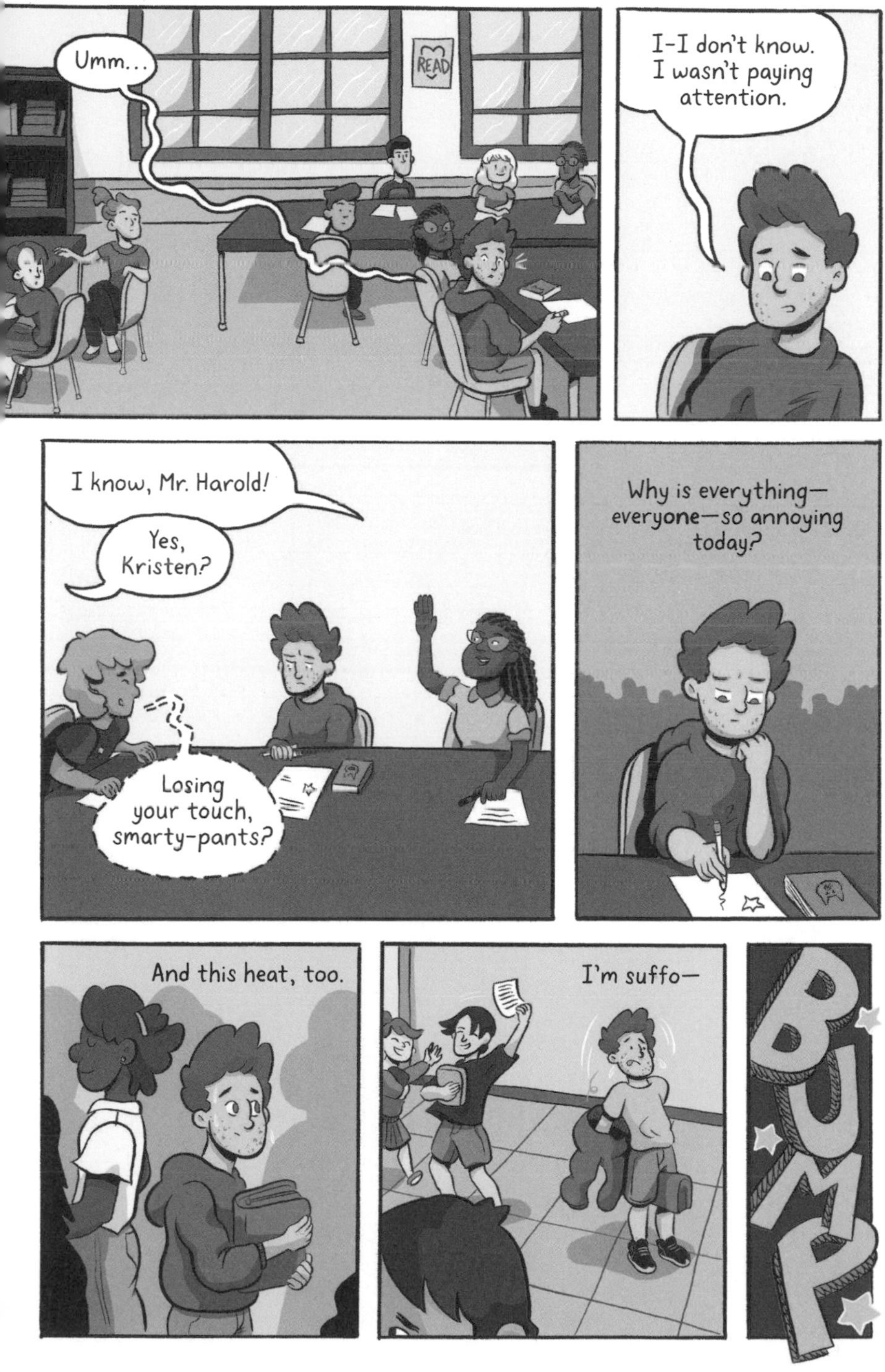
Umm...
READ
I-I don't know. I wasn't paying attention.
I know, Mr. Harold!
Yes, Kristen?
Losing your touch, smarty-pants?
Why is everything—everyone—so annoying today?
And this heat, too.
I'm suffo—
BUMP

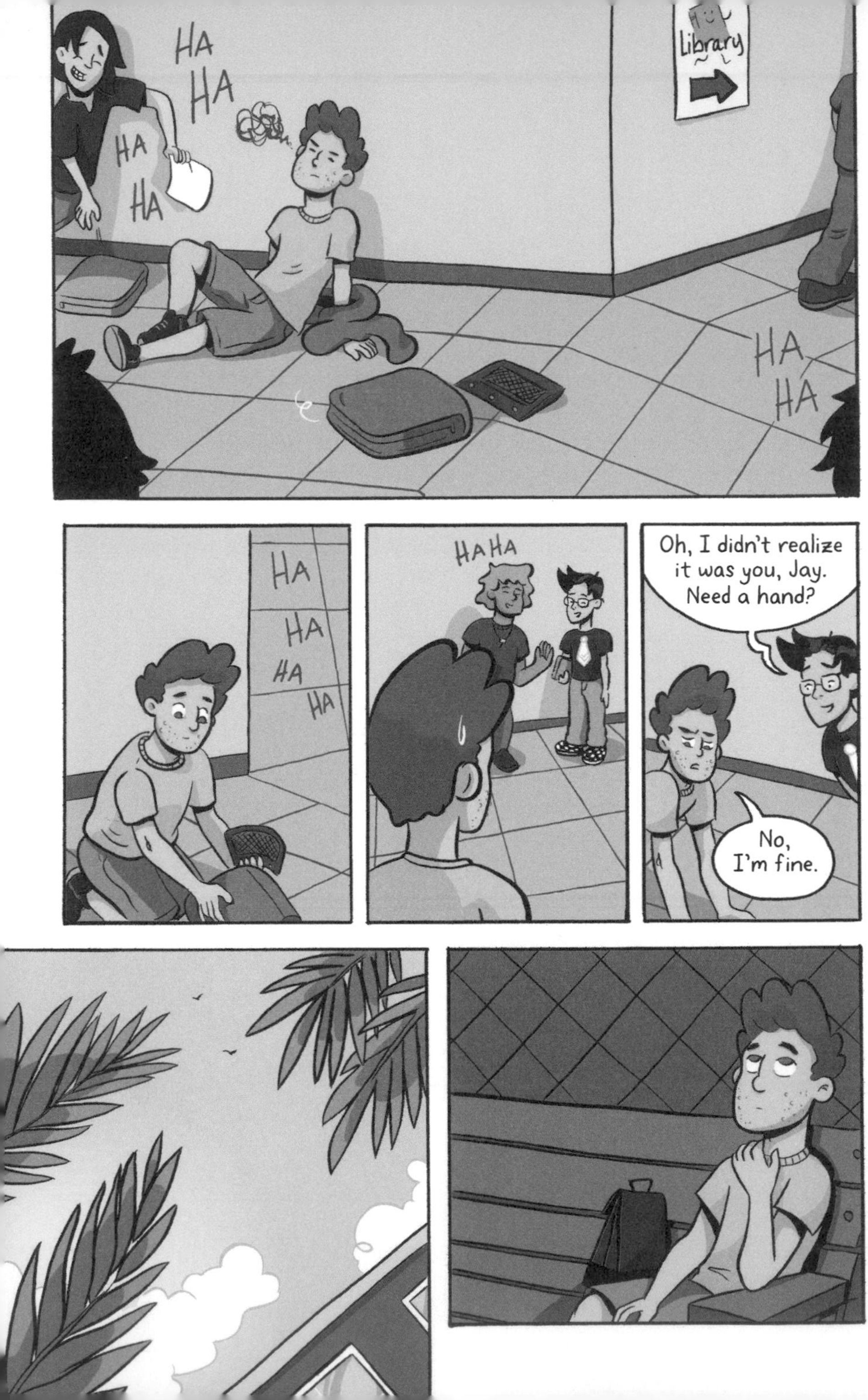
Library
HA
HA
HA
HA
HA
HA
HA
HA
HA
HA
HAHA
Oh, I didn't realize it was you, Jay. Need a hand?
No, I'm fine.

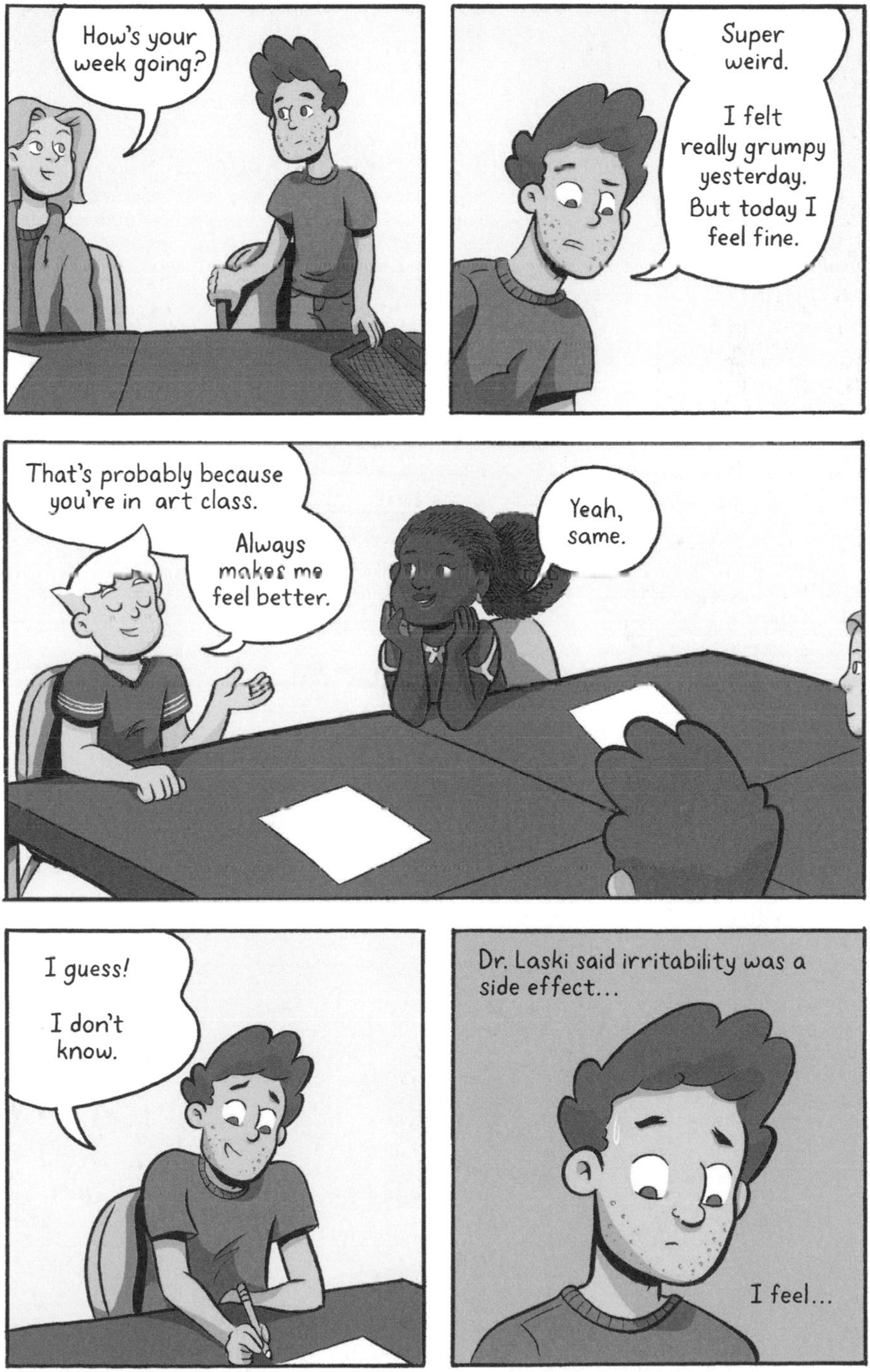
How's your week going?
Super weird.
I felt really grumpy yesterday. But today I feel fine.
That's probably because you're in art class.
Always makes me feel better.
Yeah, same.
I guess!
I don't know.
Dr. Laski said irritability was a side effect...
I feel...

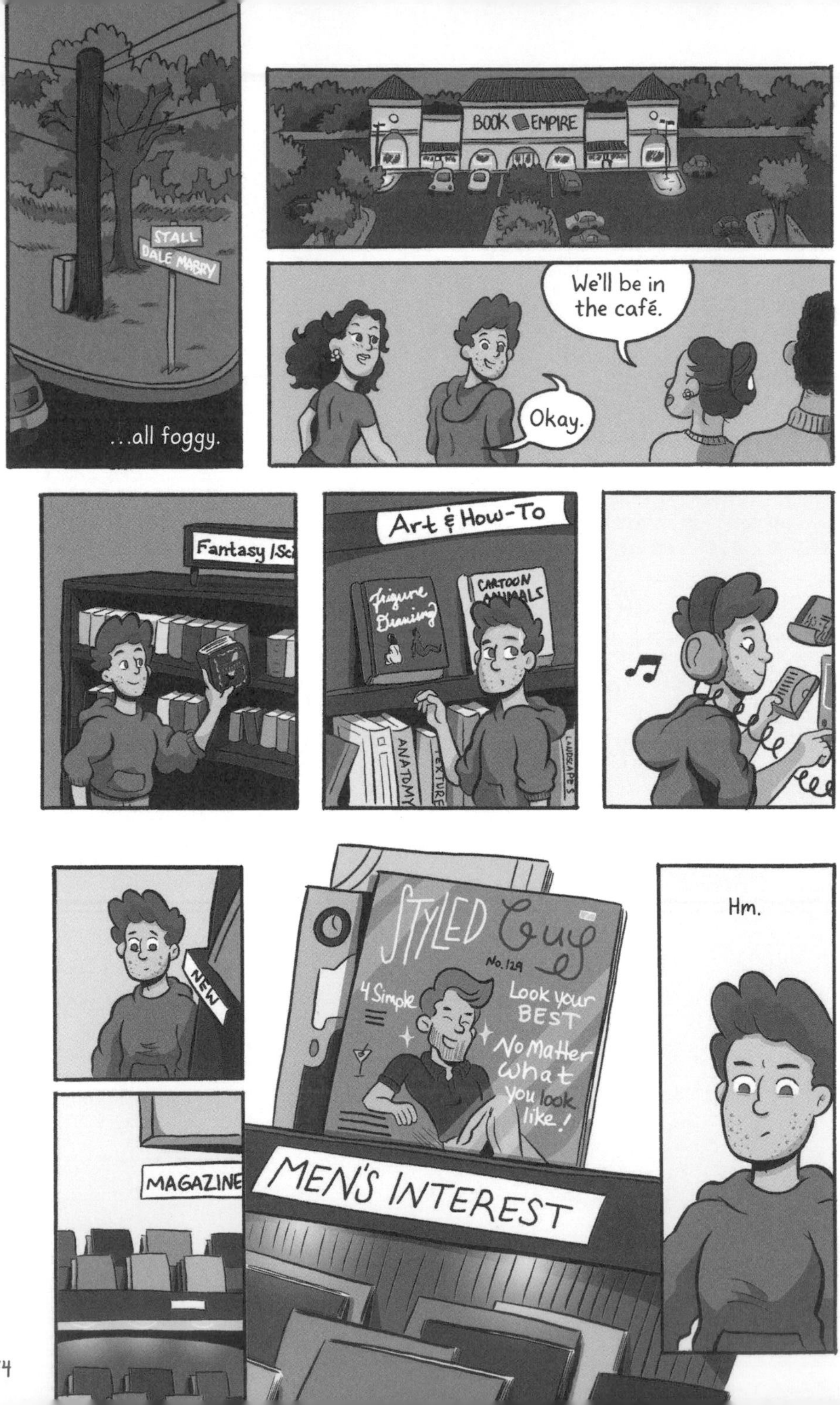
STALL
DALE MABRY
...all foggy.
BOOK EMPIRE
We'll be in the café.
Okay.
Fantasy /Sci
Art & How-To
Figure Drawing
CARTOON ANIMALS
ANATOMY
TEXTURE
LANDSCAPES
NEW
MAGAZINE
Styled Guy
No. 129
4 Simple
Look your BEST
No Matter what you look like!
MEN'S INTEREST
Hm.

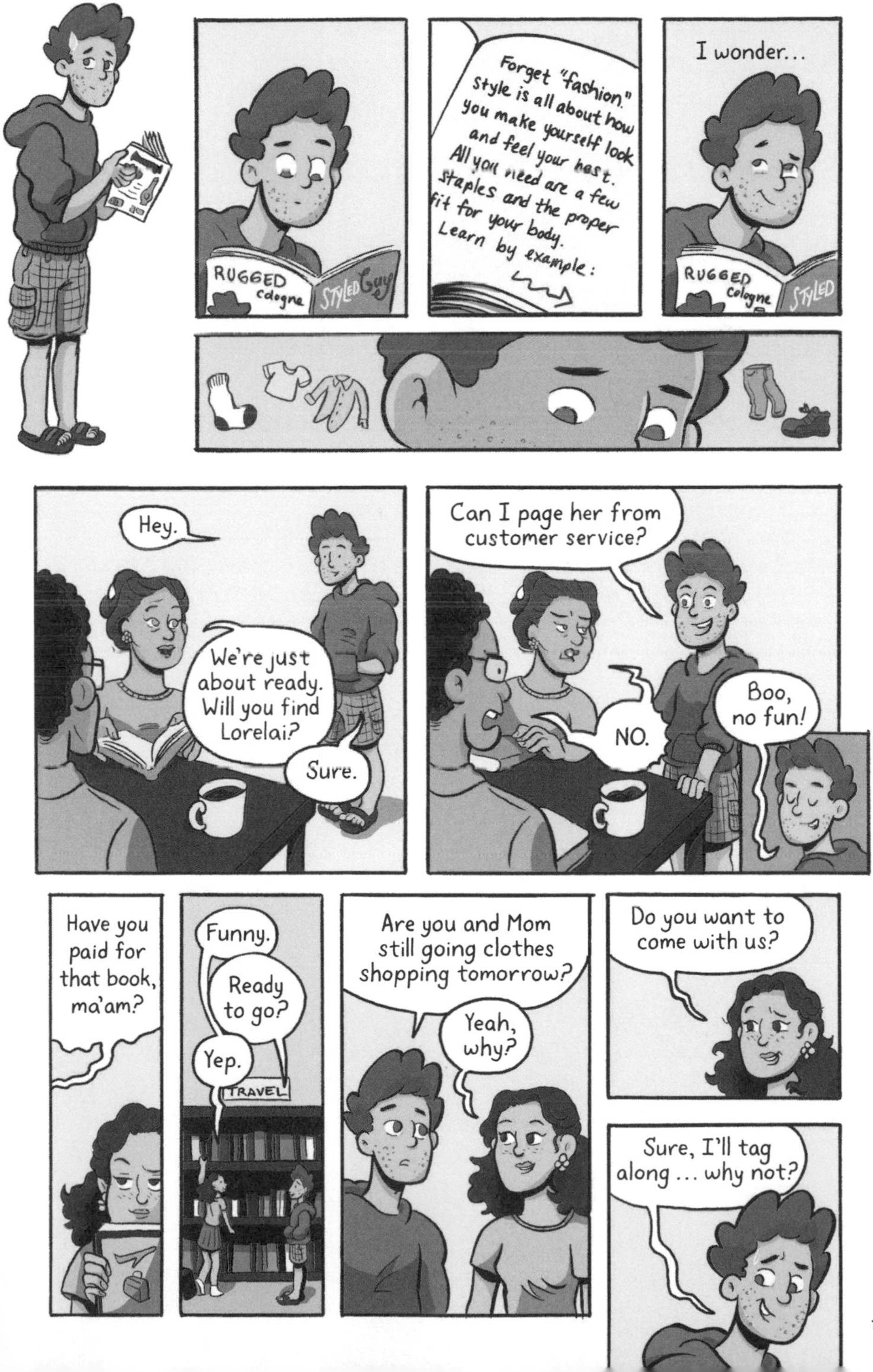
RUGGED cologne
STYLED Guy
Forget "fashion."
Style is all about how you make yourself look and feel your best.
All you need are a few staples and the proper fit for your body.
Learn by example:
I wonder...
RUGGED Cologne
STYLED
Hey.
We're just about ready. Will you find Lorelai?
Sure.
Can I page her from customer service?
NO.
Boo, no fun!
Have you paid for that book, ma'am?
Funny.
Ready to go?
Yep.
TRAVEL
Are you and Mom still going clothes shopping tomorrow?
Yeah, why?
Do you want to come with us?
Sure, I'll tag along ... why not?

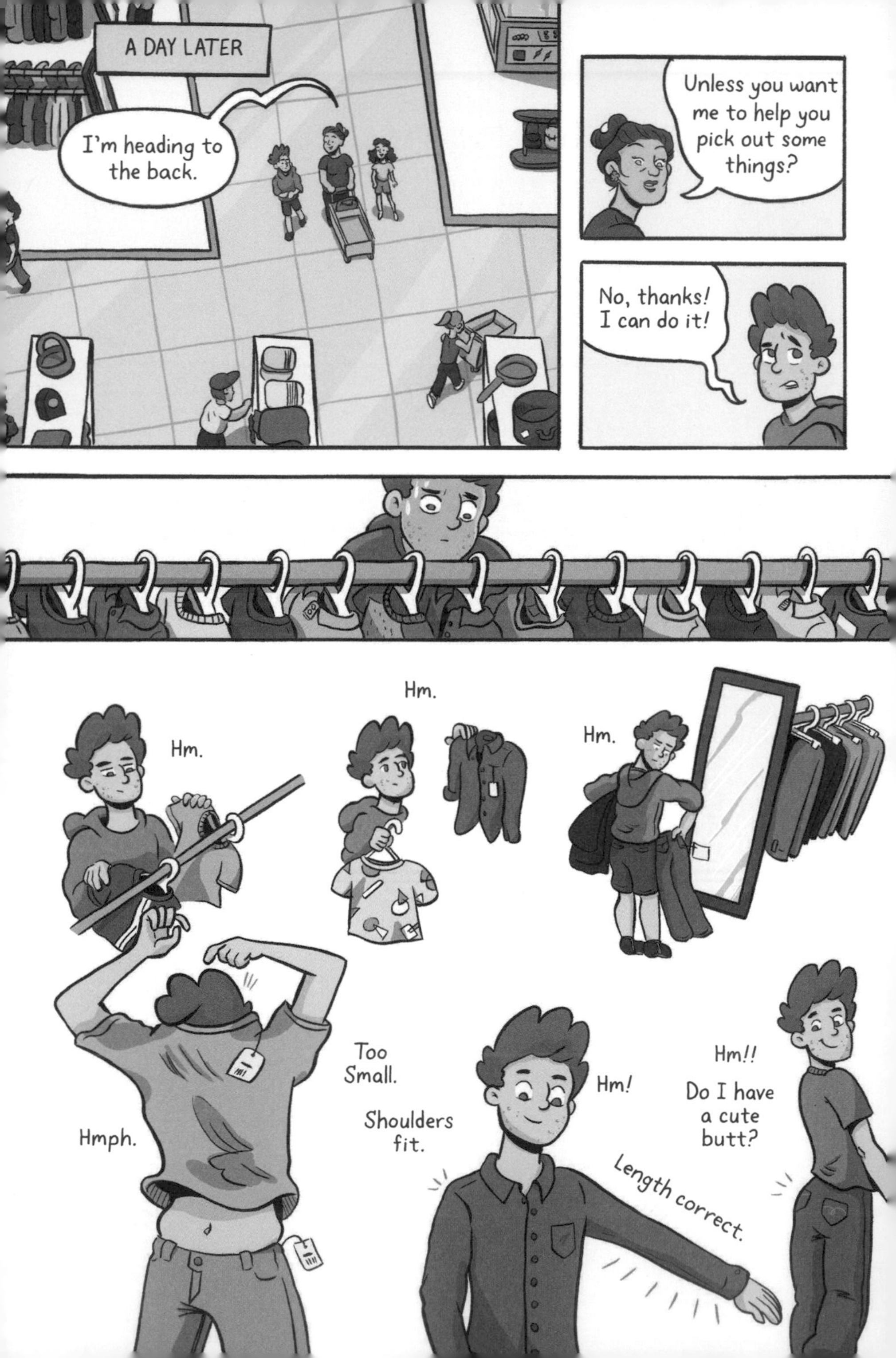
A DAY LATER
I'm heading to the back.
Unless you want me to help you pick out some things?
No, thanks! I can do it!
Hm.
Hm.
Hm.
Hmph.
Too Small.
Shoulders fit.
Hm!
Length correct.
Hm!!
Do I have a cute butt?

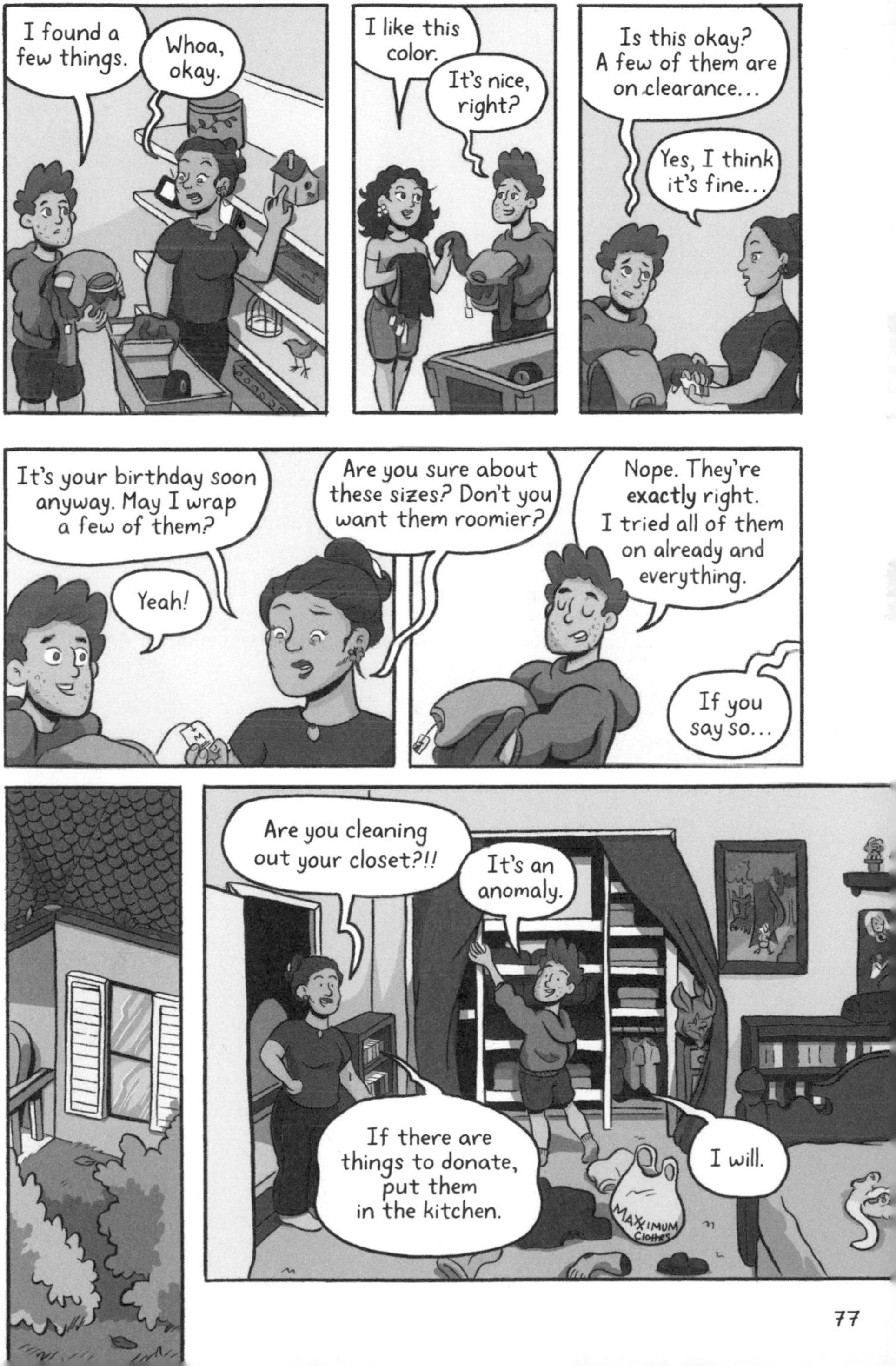
I found a few things.
Whoa, okay.
I like this color.
It's nice, right?
Is this okay? A few of them are on clearance...
Yes, I think it's fine...
It's your birthday soon anyway. May I wrap a few of them?
Yeah!
Are you sure about these sizes? Don't you want them roomier?
Nope. They're **exactly** right. I tried all of them on already and everything.
If you say so...
Are you cleaning out your closet?!!
It's an anomaly.
If there are things to donate, put them in the kitchen.
I will.
MAXXIMUM Clothes

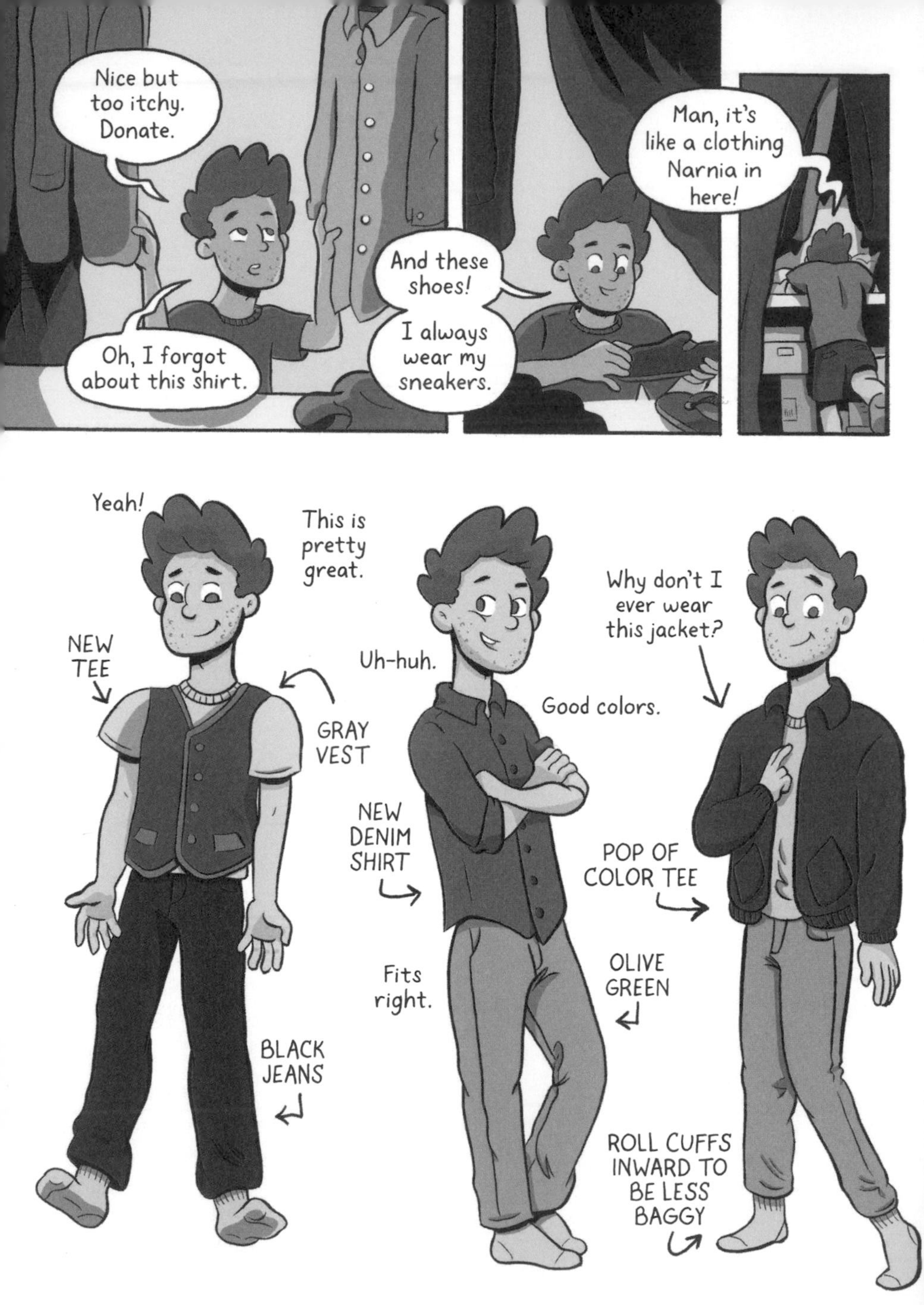
Nice but too itchy. Donate.
Oh, I forgot about this shirt.
And these shoes!
I always wear my sneakers.
Man, it's like a clothing Narnia in here!
Yeah!
This is pretty great.
NEW TEE
GRAY VEST
BLACK JEANS
Uh-huh.
Good colors.
NEW DENIM SHIRT
Fits right.
OLIVE GREEN
Why don't I ever wear this jacket?
POP OF COLOR TEE
ROLL CUFFS INWARD TO BE LESS BAGGY

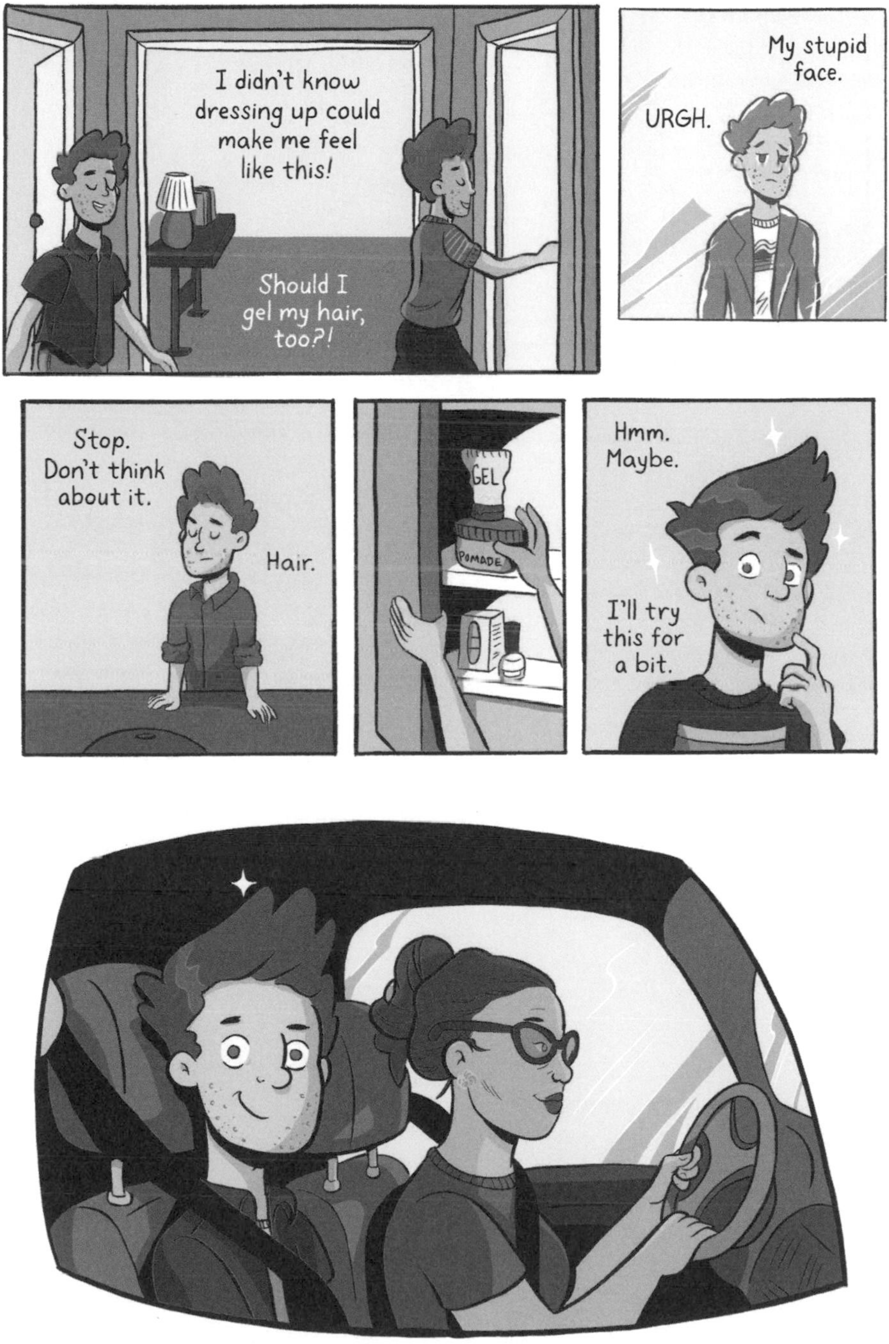
I didn't know dressing up could make me feel like this!
Should I gel my hair, too?!
My stupid face.
URGH.
Stop. Don't think about it.
Hair.
GEL
POMADE
Hmm. Maybe.
I'll try this for a bit.

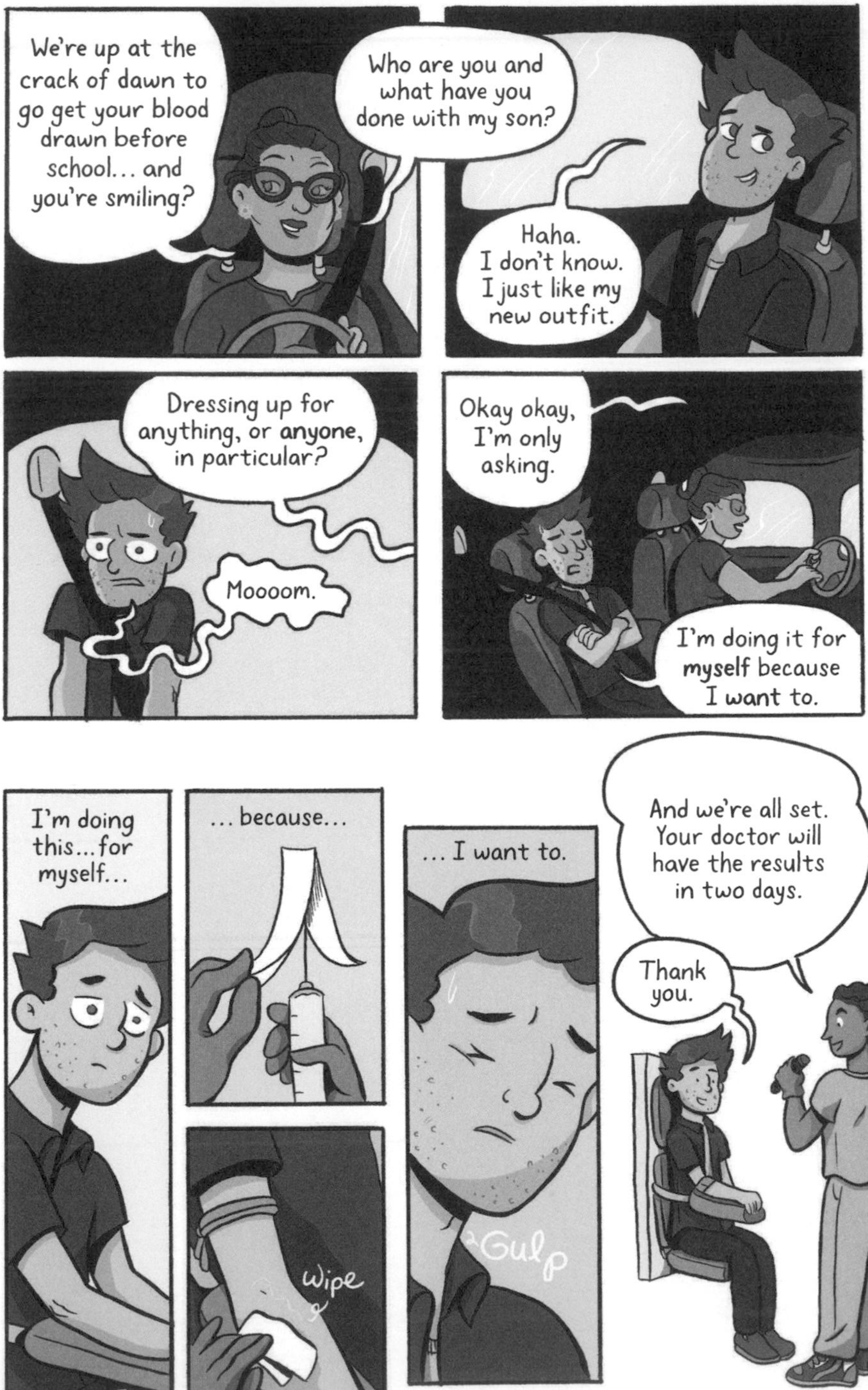
We're up at the crack of dawn to go get your blood drawn before school... and you're smiling?
Who are you and what have you done with my son?
Haha. I don't know. I just like my new outfit.
Dressing up for anything, or **anyone**, in particular?
Moooom.
Okay okay, I'm only asking.
I'm doing it for **myself** because I **want** to.
I'm doing this... for myself...
... because...
Wipe
... I want to.
Gulp
And we're all set. Your doctor will have the results in two days.
Thank you.

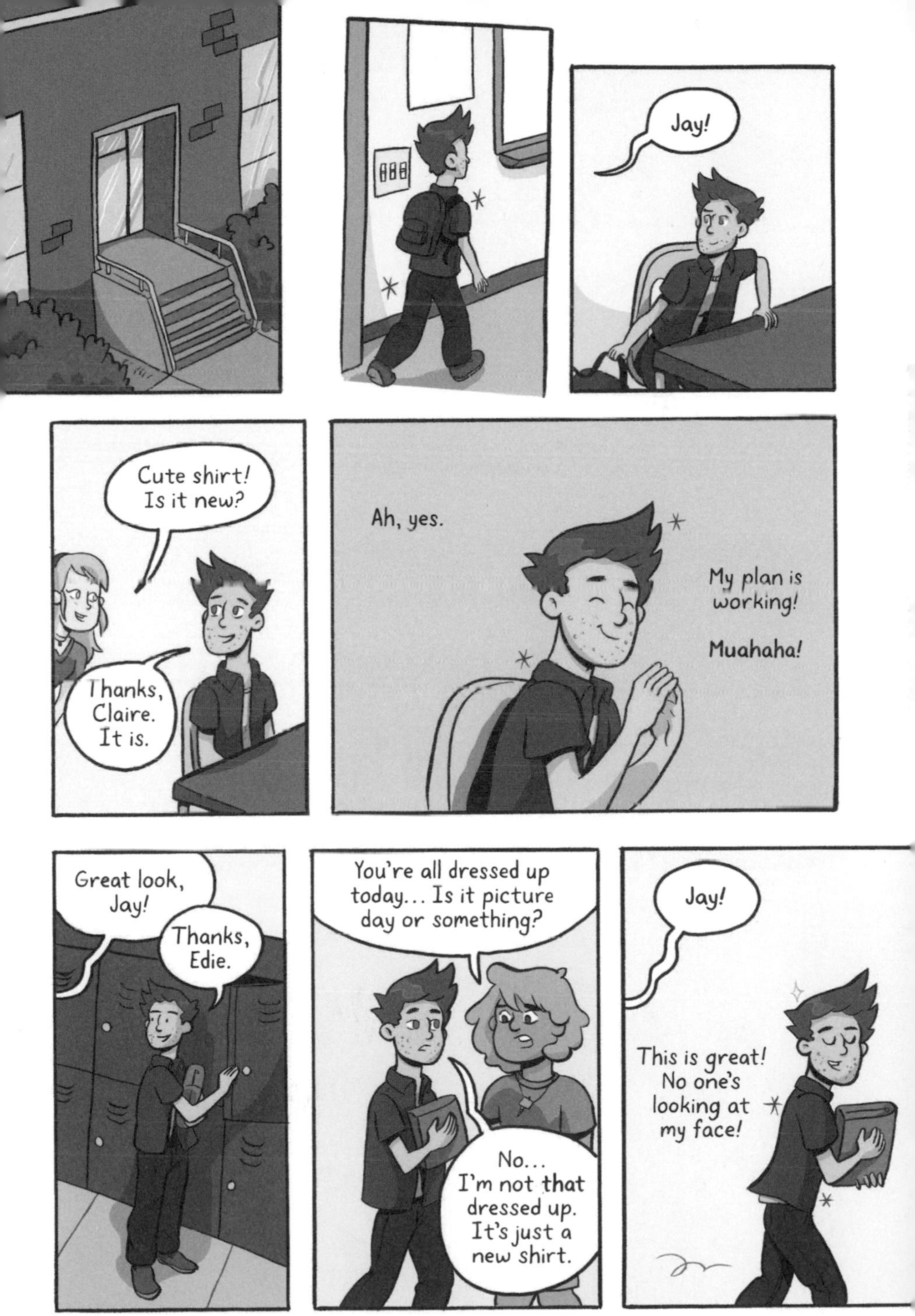
Jay!
Cute shirt! Is it new?
Thanks, Claire. It is.
Ah, yes.
My plan is working!
Muahaha!
Great look, Jay!
Thanks, Edie.
You're all dressed up today... Is it picture day or something?
No... I'm not that dressed up. It's just a new shirt.
Jay!
This is great! No one's looking at my face!

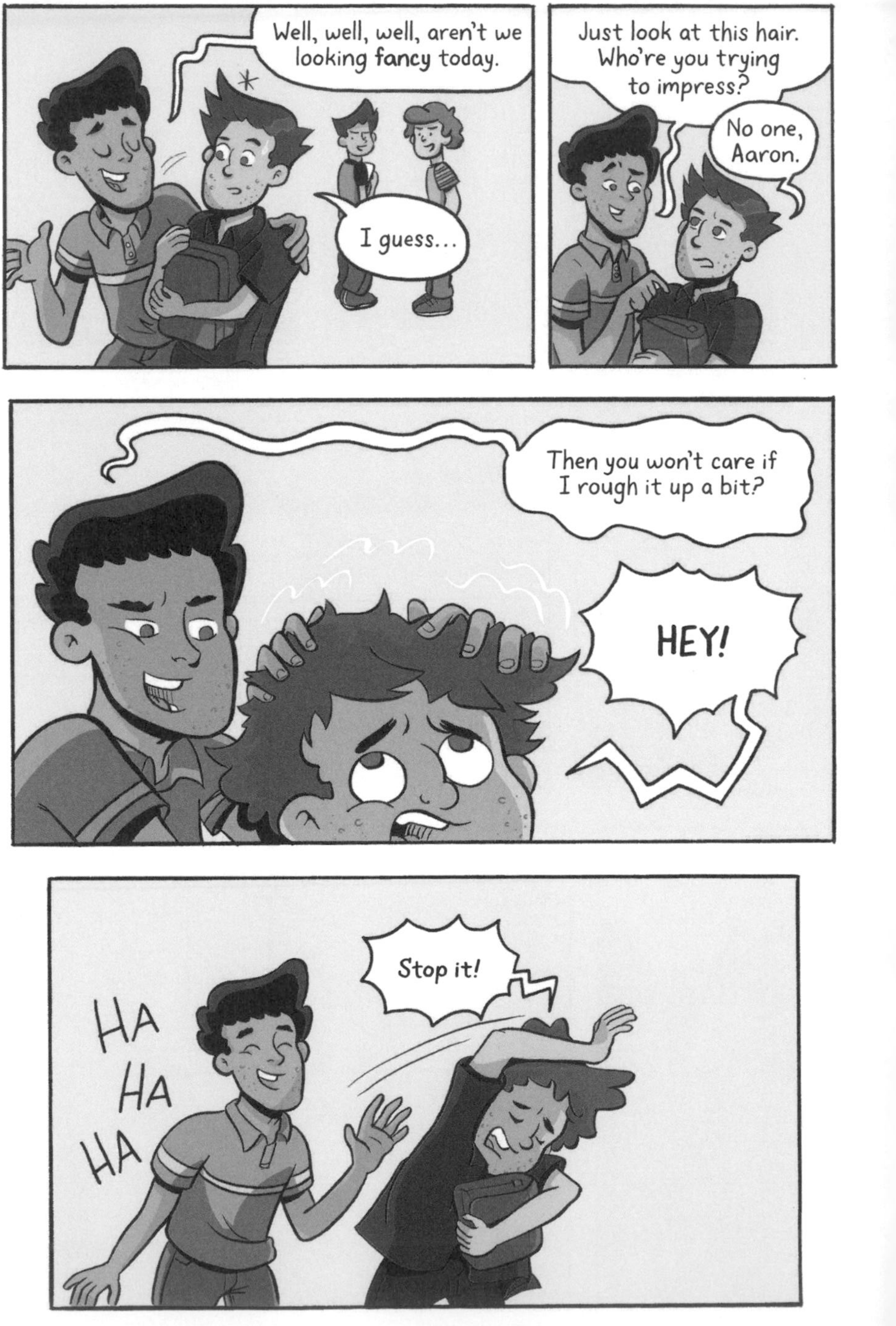
Well, well, well, aren't we looking fancy today.
I guess...
Just look at this hair. Who're you trying to impress?
No one, Aaron.
Then you won't care if I rough it up a bit?
HEY!
Stop it!
HA HA HA

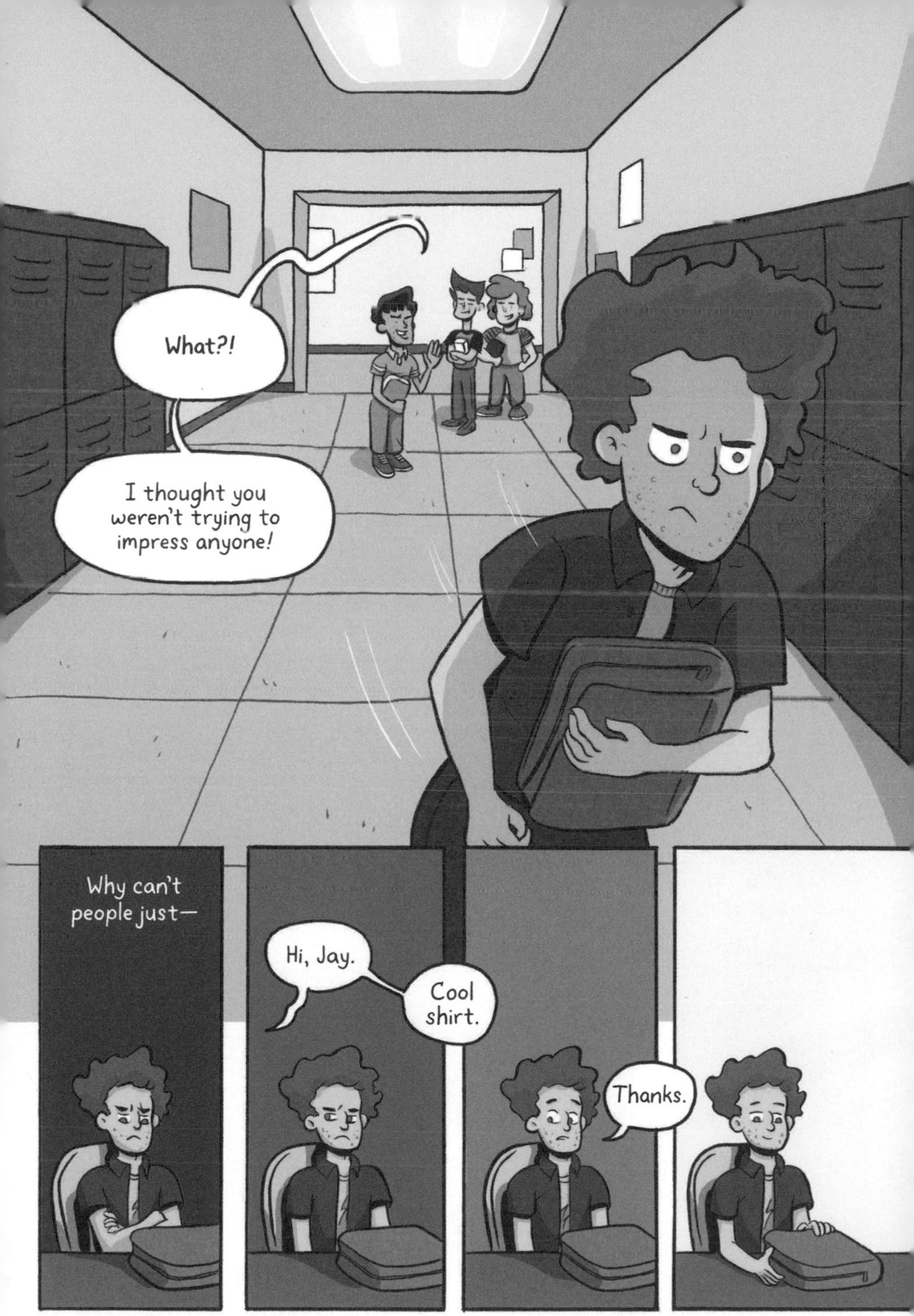
What?!
I thought you weren't trying to impress anyone!
Why can't people just—
Hi, Jay.
Cool shirt.
Thanks.

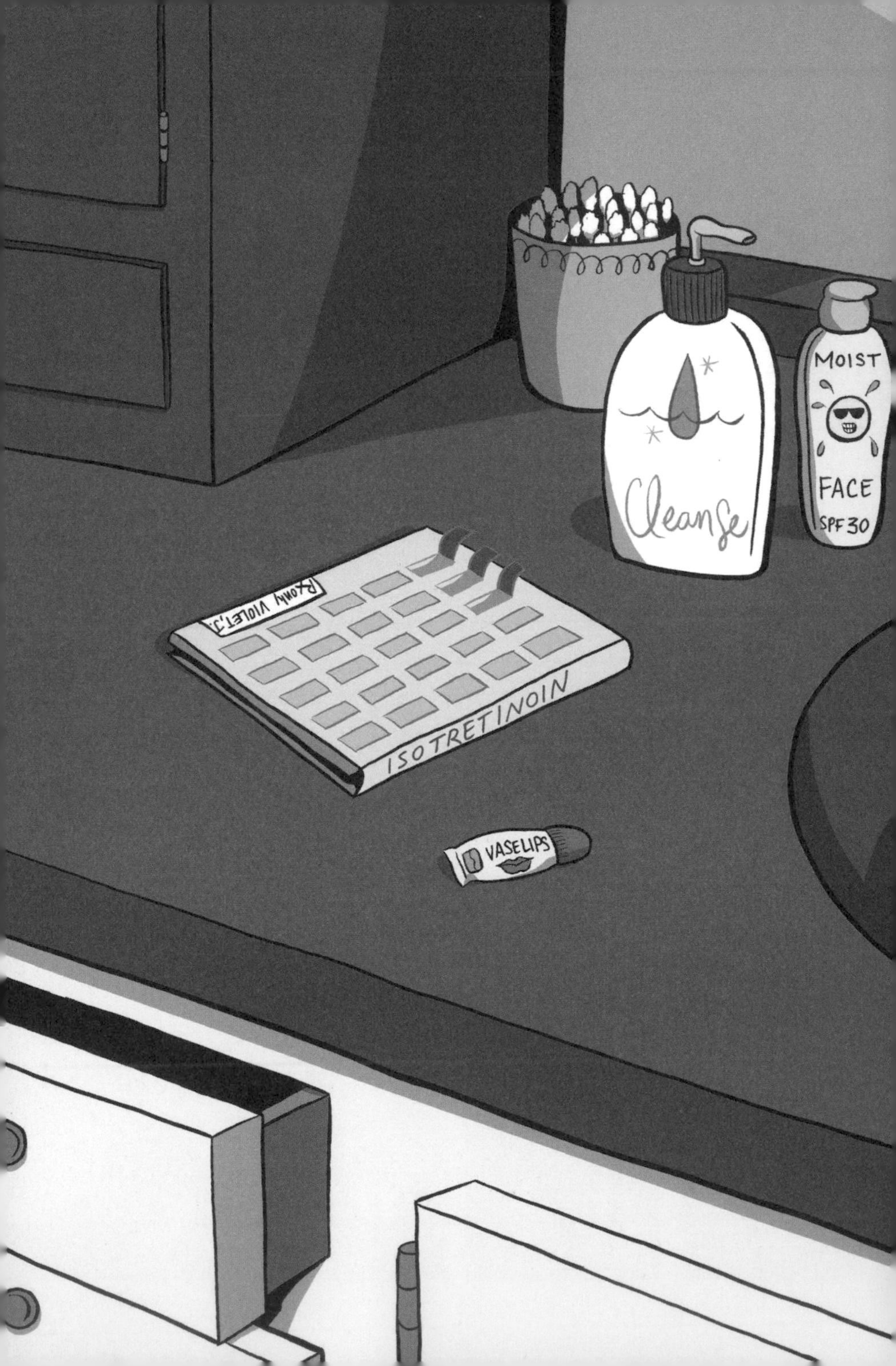
Rx only VIOLET J.
ISOTRETINOIN
Cleanse
MOIST
FACE
SPF 30
VASELIPS

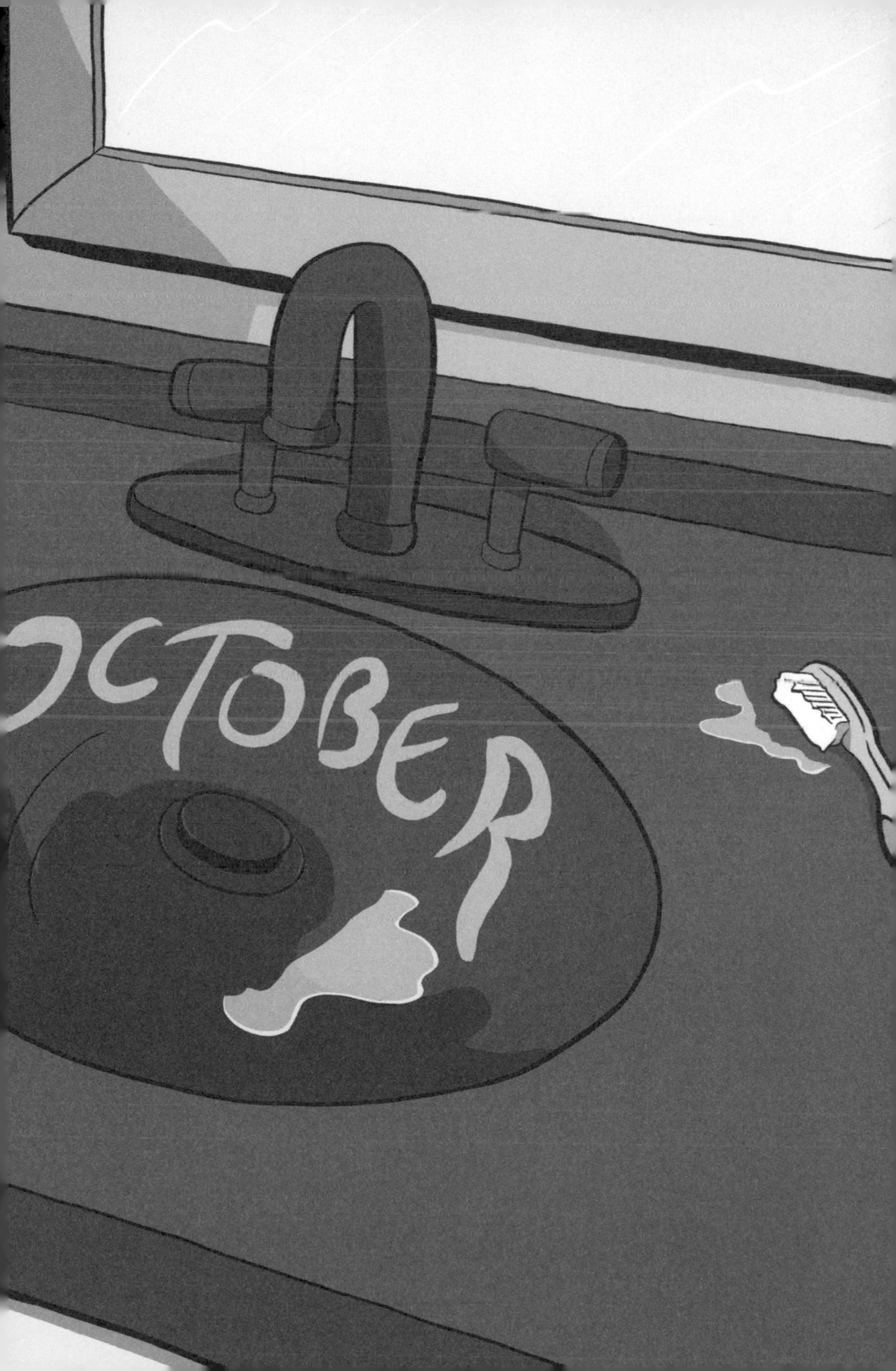
OCTOBER

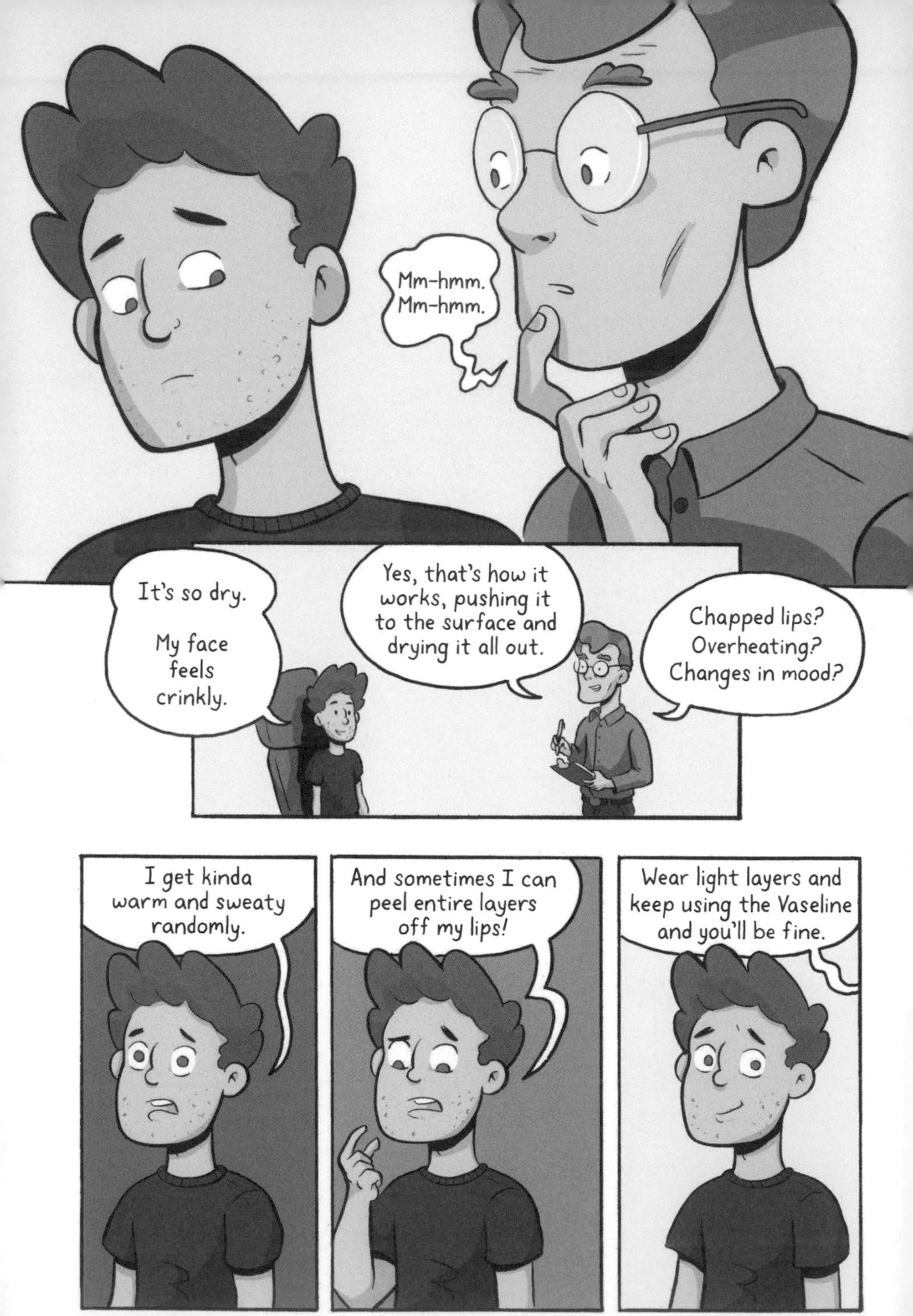
Mm-hmm.
Mm-hmm.
It's so dry.
My face feels crinkly.
Yes, that's how it works, pushing it to the surface and drying it all out.
Chapped lips? Overheating? Changes in mood?
I get kinda warm and sweaty randomly.
And sometimes I can peel entire layers off my lips!
Wear light layers and keep using the Vaseline and you'll be fine.

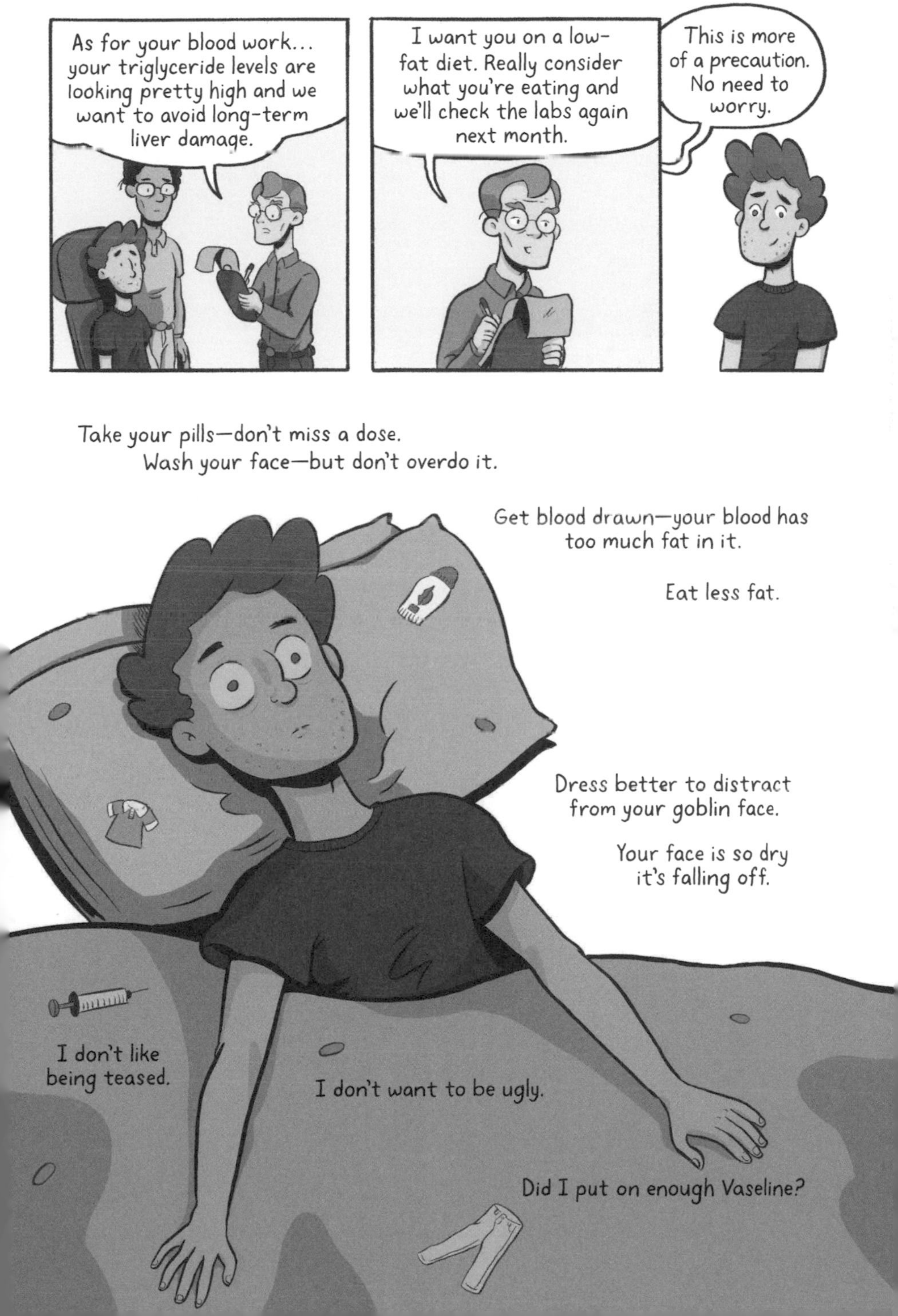

As for your blood work... your triglyceride levels are looking pretty high and we want to avoid long-term liver damage.
I want you on a low-fat diet. Really consider what you're eating and we'll check the labs again next month.
This is more of a precaution. No need to worry.
Take your pills—don't miss a dose.
Wash your face—but don't overdo it.
Get blood drawn—your blood has too much fat in it.
Eat less fat.
Dress better to distract from your goblin face.
Your face is so dry it's falling off.
I don't like being teased.
I don't want to be ugly.
Did I put on enough Vaseline?

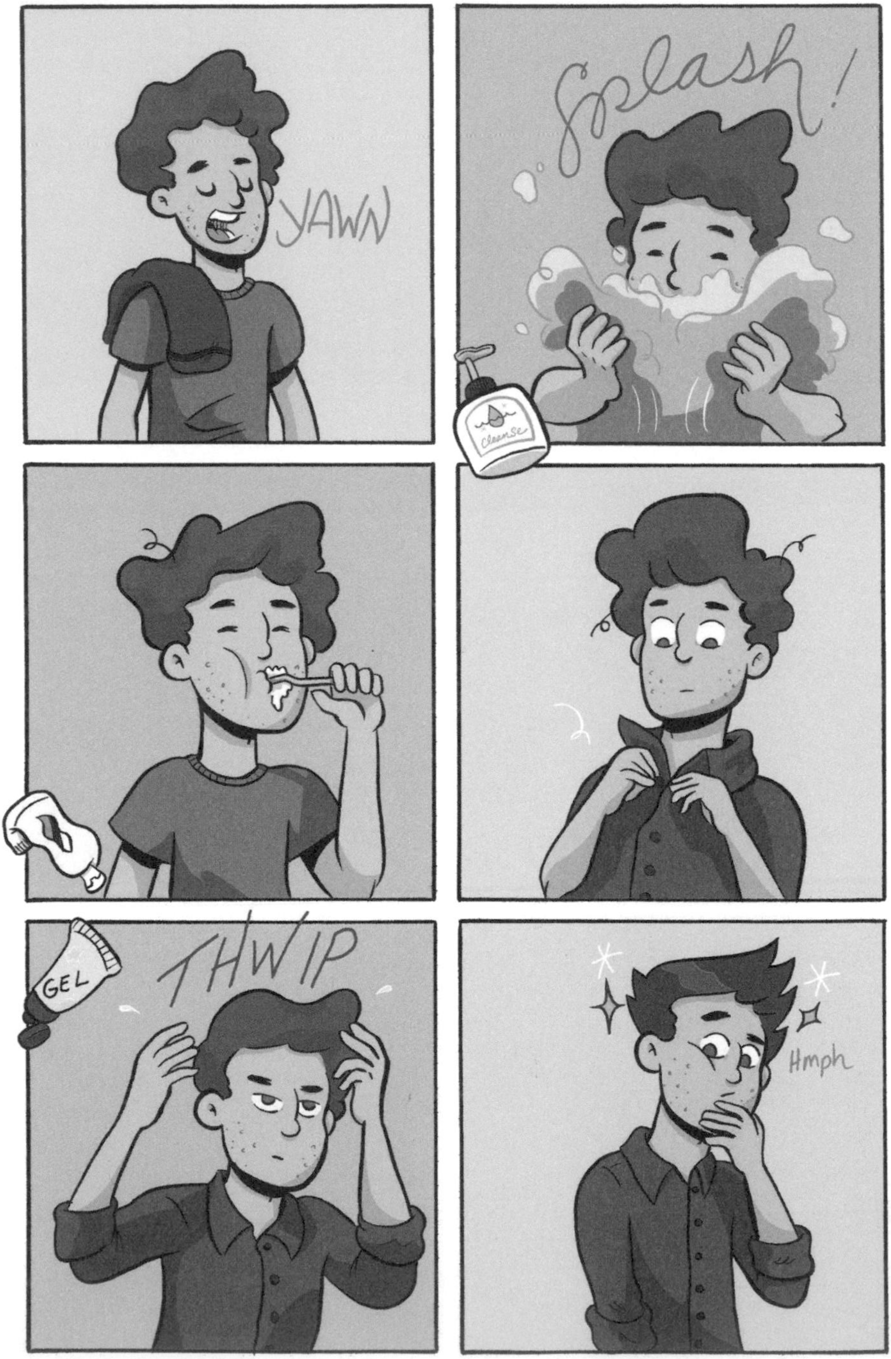
YAWN
splash!
cleanse
GEL
THWIP
Hmph

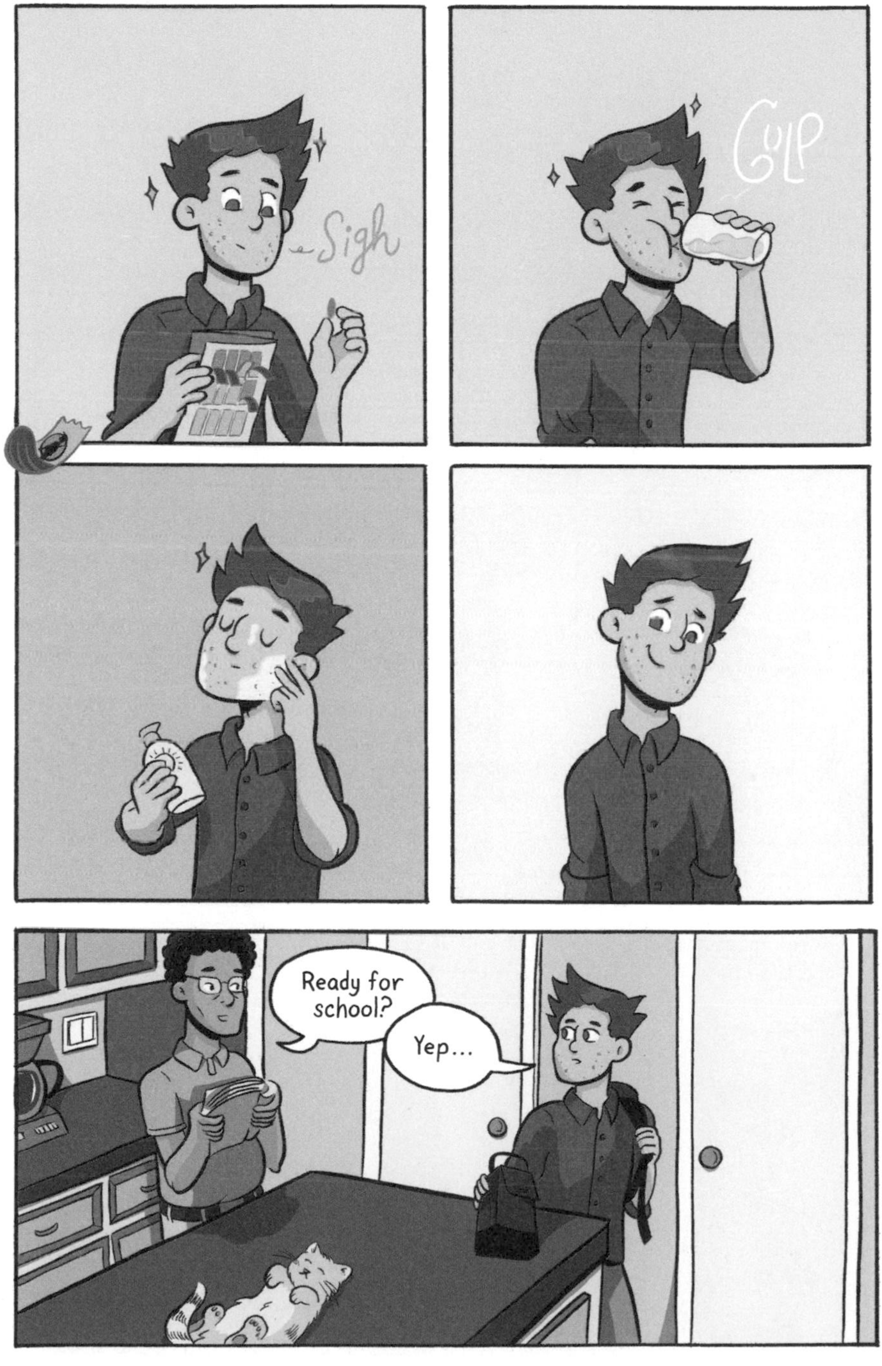
Sigh
GULP
Ready for school?
Yep...

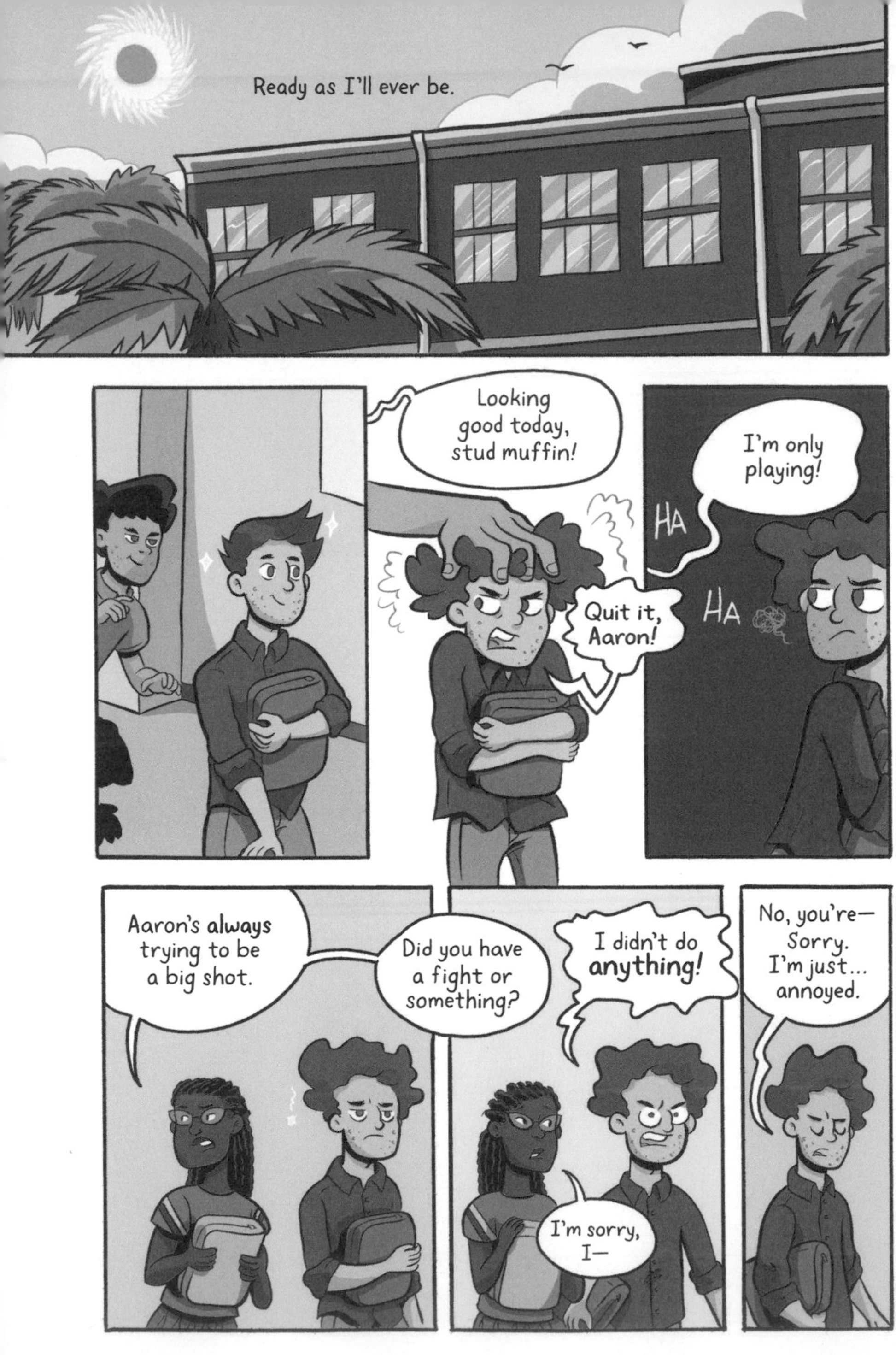
Ready as I'll ever be.
Looking good today, stud muffin!
Quit it, Aaron!
I'm only playing!
HA
HA
Aaron's **always** trying to be a big shot.
Did you have a fight or something?
I didn't do **anything**!
I'm sorry, I—
No, you're— Sorry. I'm just... annoyed.

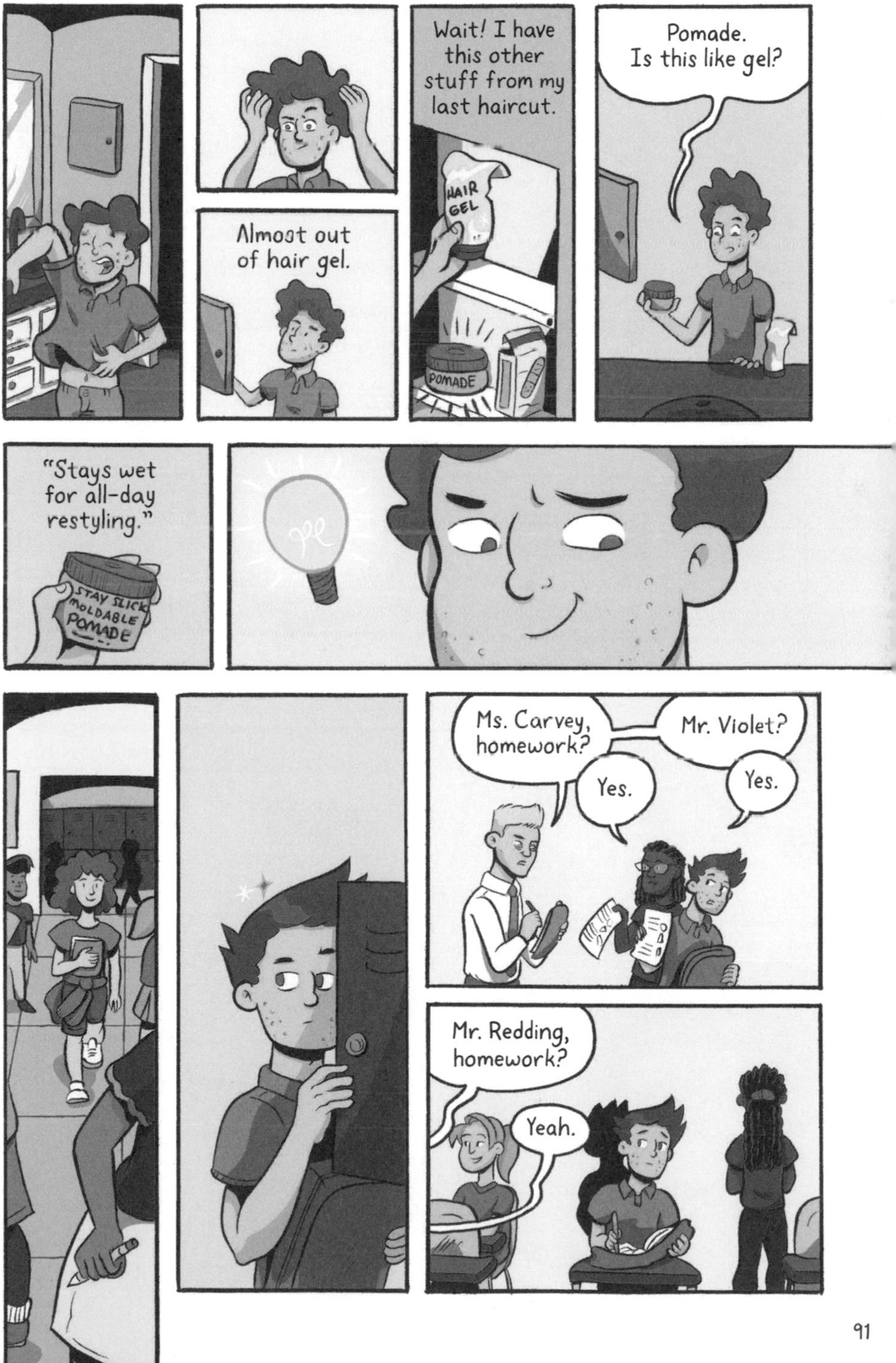
Almost out of hair gel.
Wait! I have this other stuff from my last haircut.
HAIR GEL
POMADE
Pomade. Is this like gel?
"Stays wet for all-day restyling."
STAY SLICK MOLDABLE POMADE
Ms. Carvey, homework?
Yes.
Mr. Violet?
Yes.
Mr. Redding, homework?
Yeah.

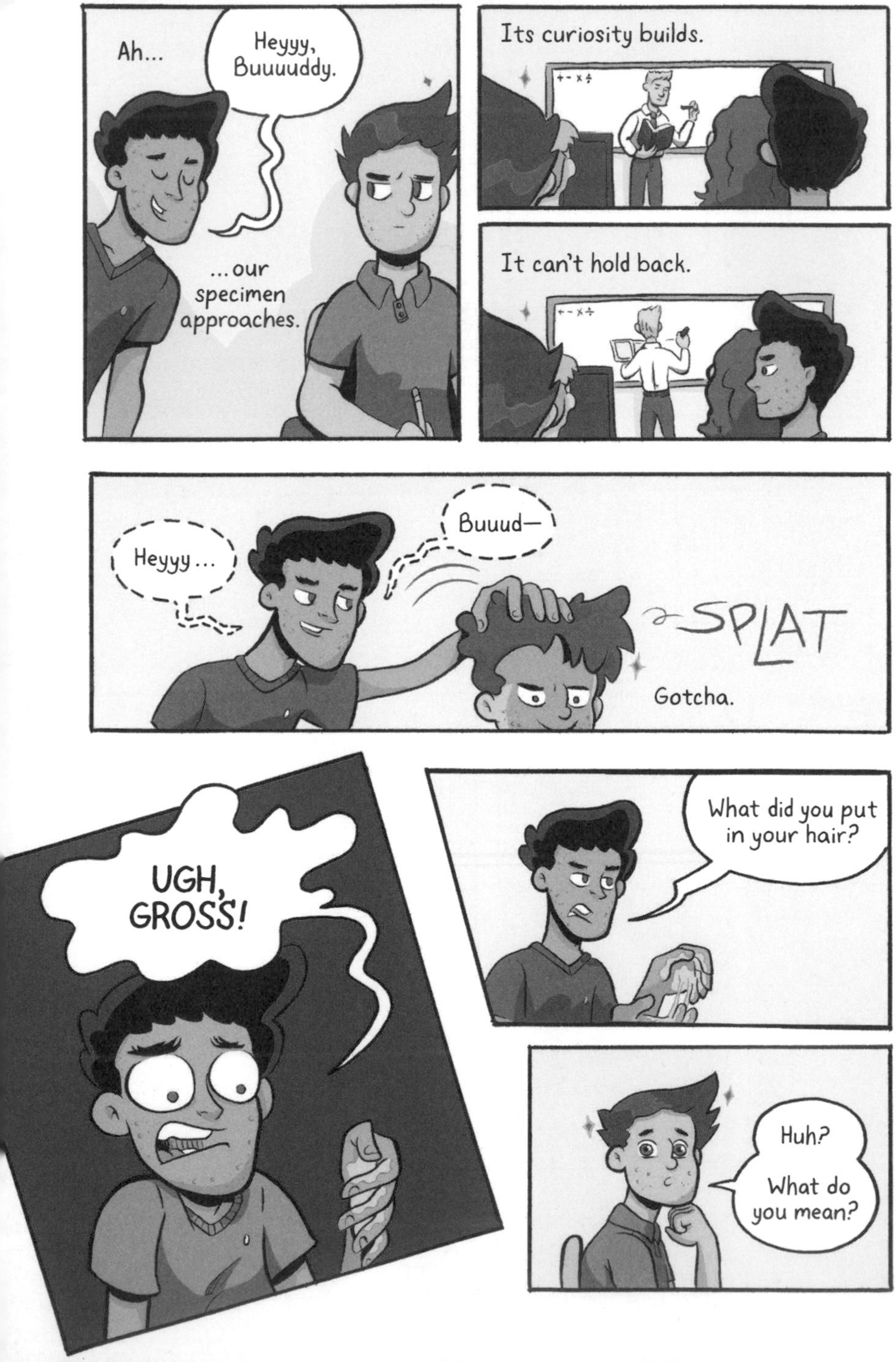
Ah...
Heyyy, Buuuuddy.
...our specimen approaches.
Its curiosity builds.
It can't hold back.
Heyyy...
Buuud—
SPLAT
Gotcha.
UGH, GROSS!
What did you put in your hair?
Huh?
What do you mean?

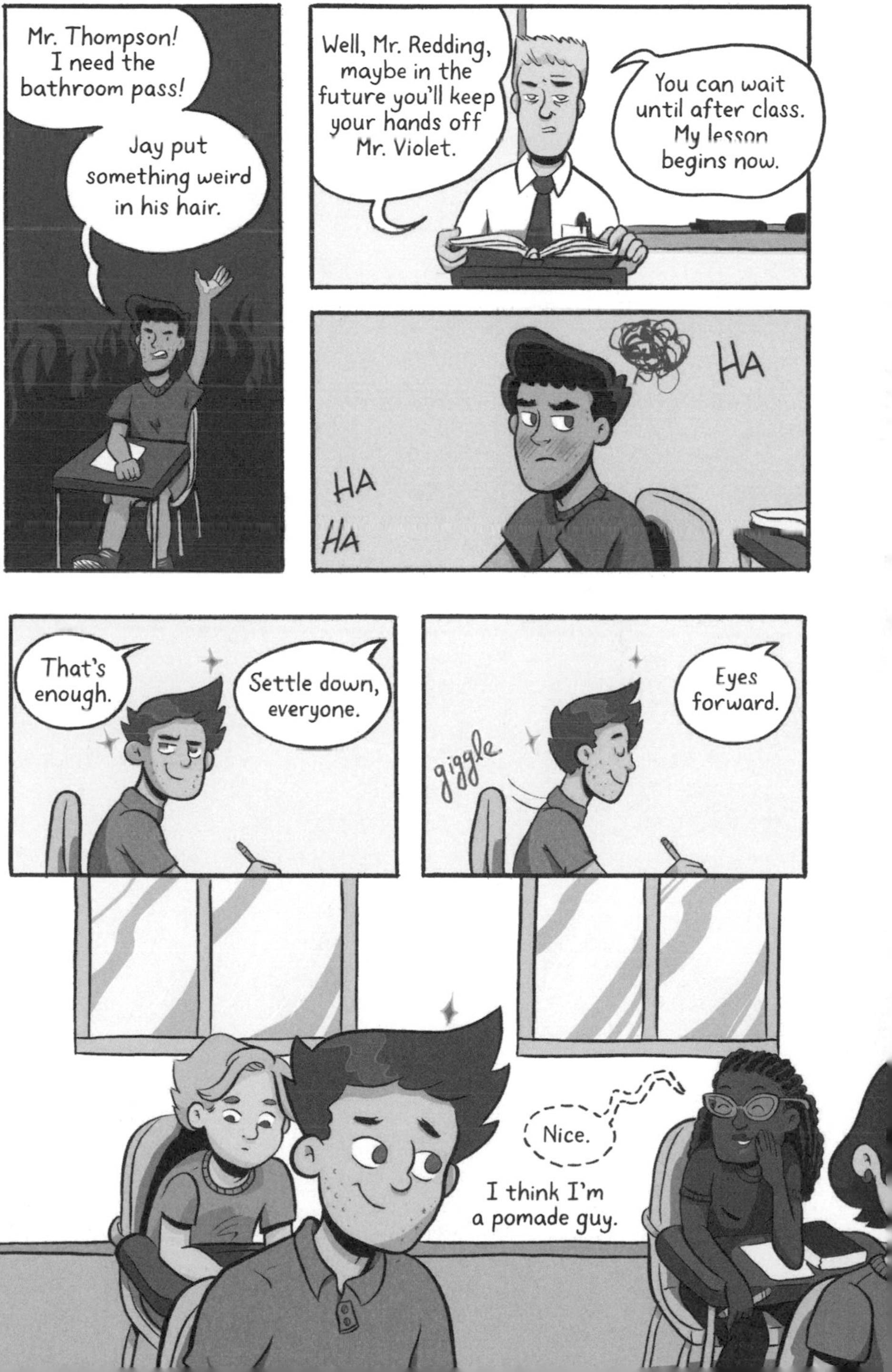
Mr. Thompson! I need the bathroom pass!
Jay put something weird in his hair.
Well, Mr. Redding, maybe in the future you'll keep your hands off Mr. Violet.
You can wait until after class. My lesson begins now.
HA
HA
HA
That's enough.
Settle down, everyone.
giggle
Eyes forward.
Nice.
I think I'm a pomade guy.

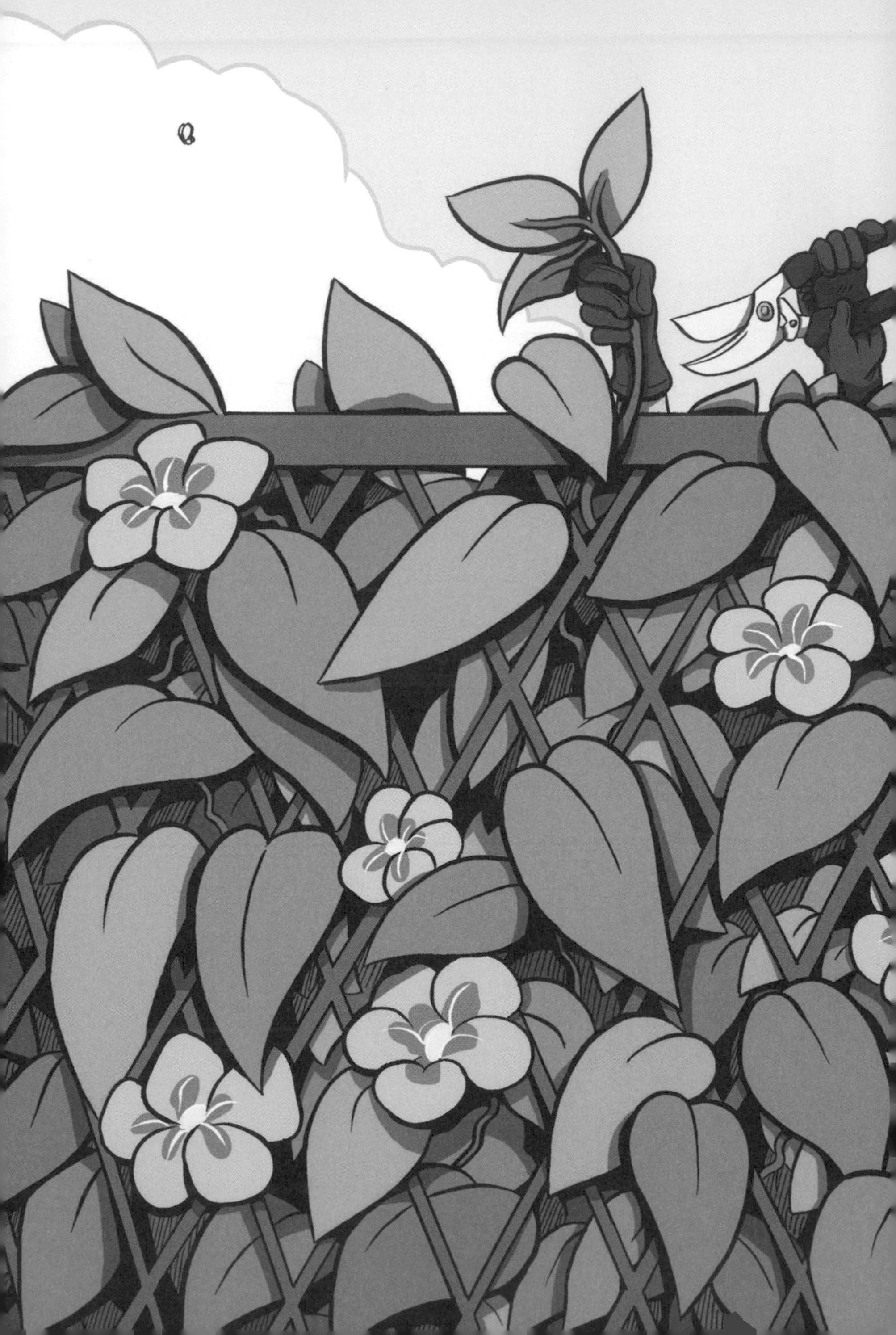

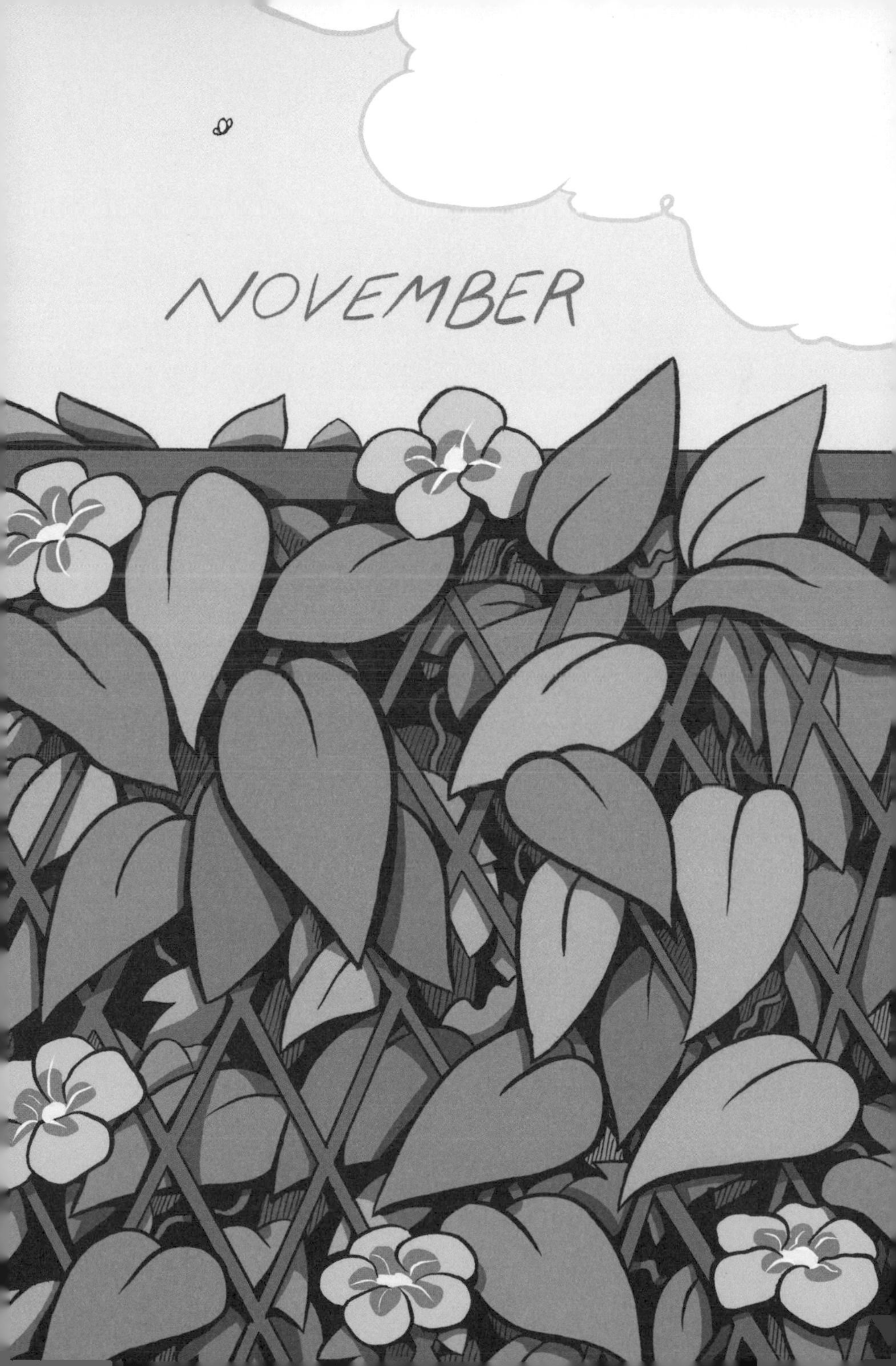
NOVEMBER

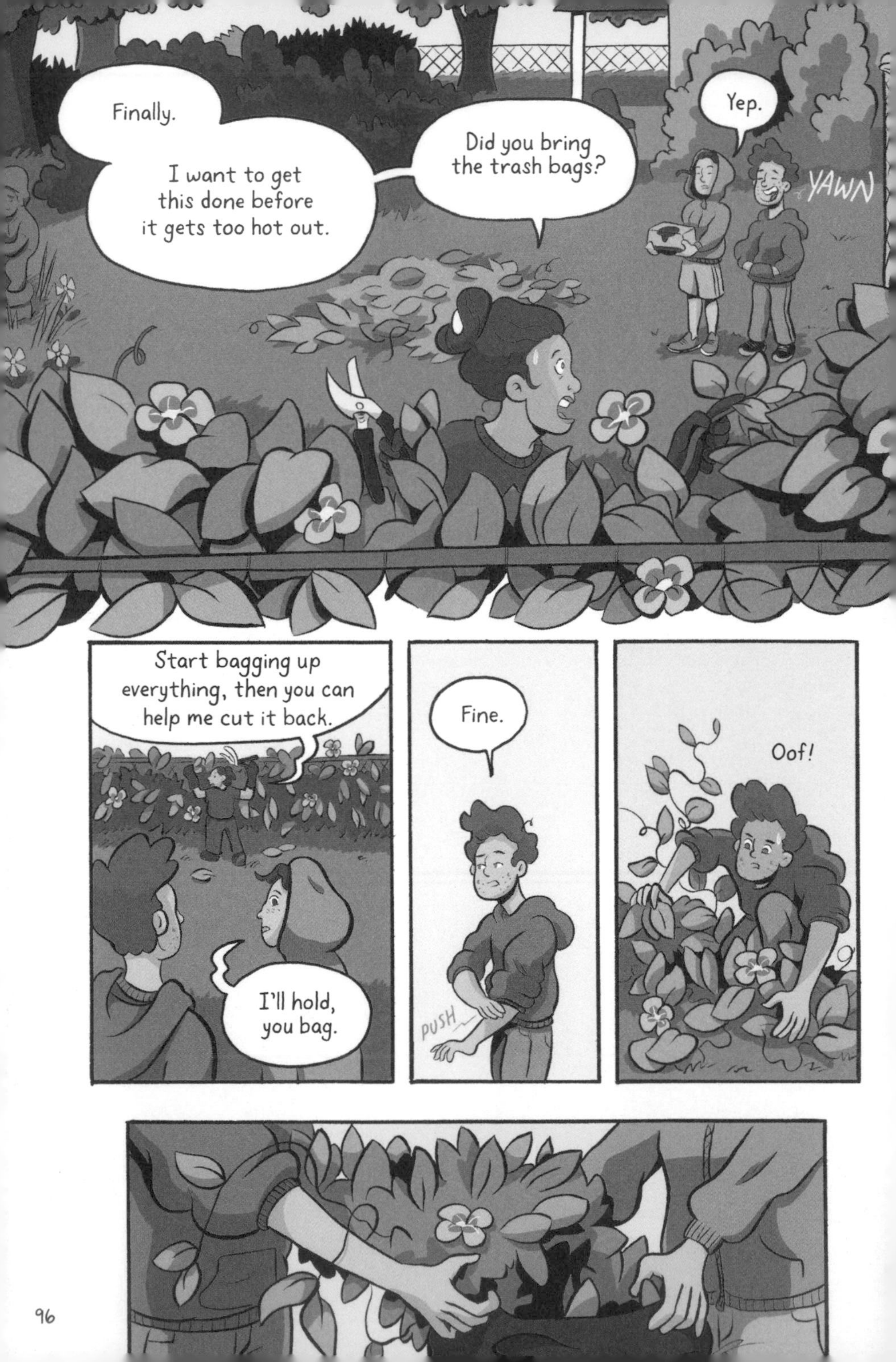
Finally.
I want to get this done before it gets too hot out.
Did you bring the trash bags?
Yep.
YAWN
Start bagging up everything, then you can help me cut it back.
I'll hold, you bag.
Fine.
PUSH
Oof!

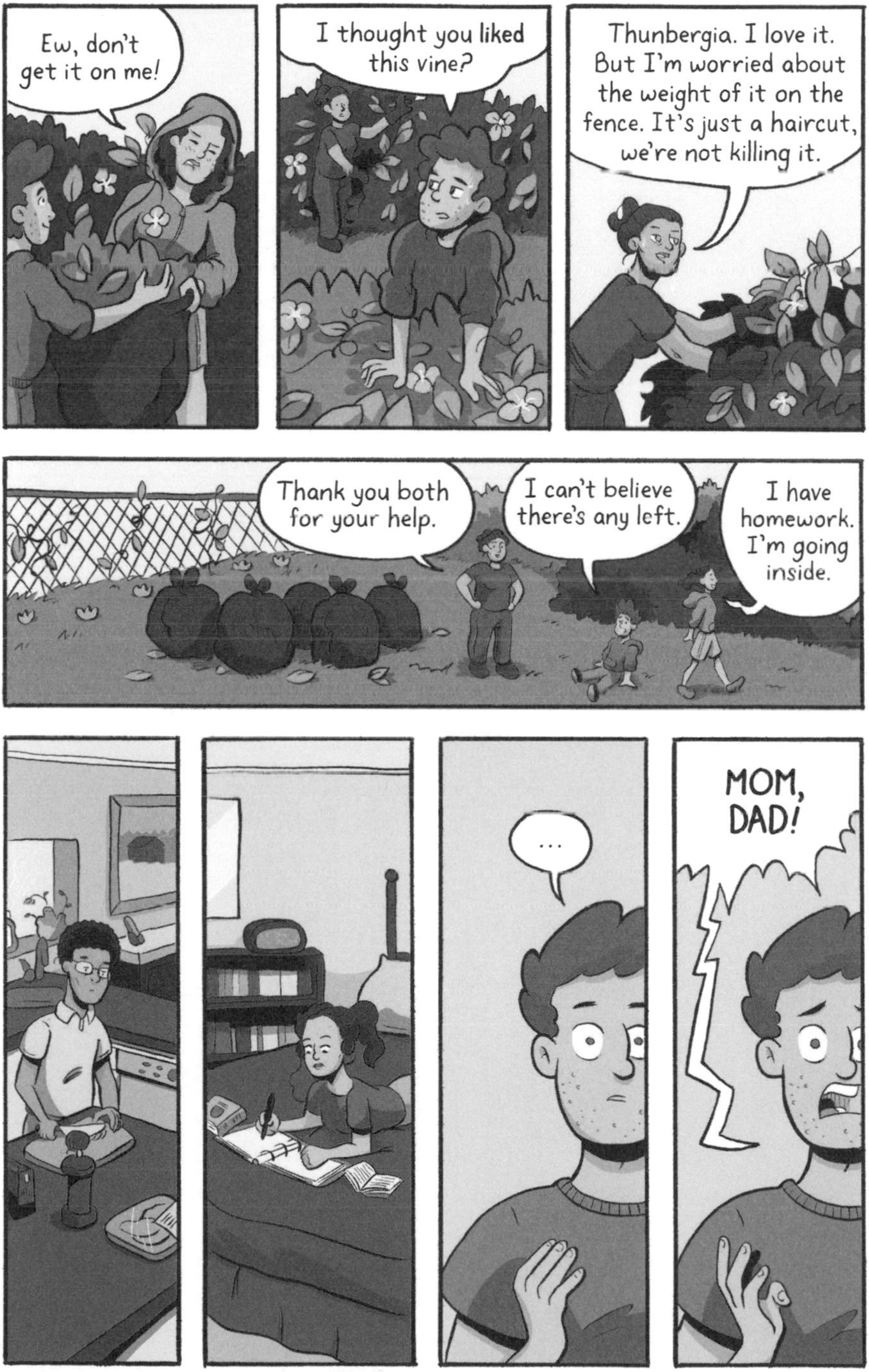
Ew, don't get it on me!
I thought you liked this vine?
Thunbergia. I love it. But I'm worried about the weight of it on the fence. It's just a haircut, we're not killing it.
Thank you both for your help.
I can't believe there's any left.
I have homework. I'm going inside.
...
MOM, DAD!

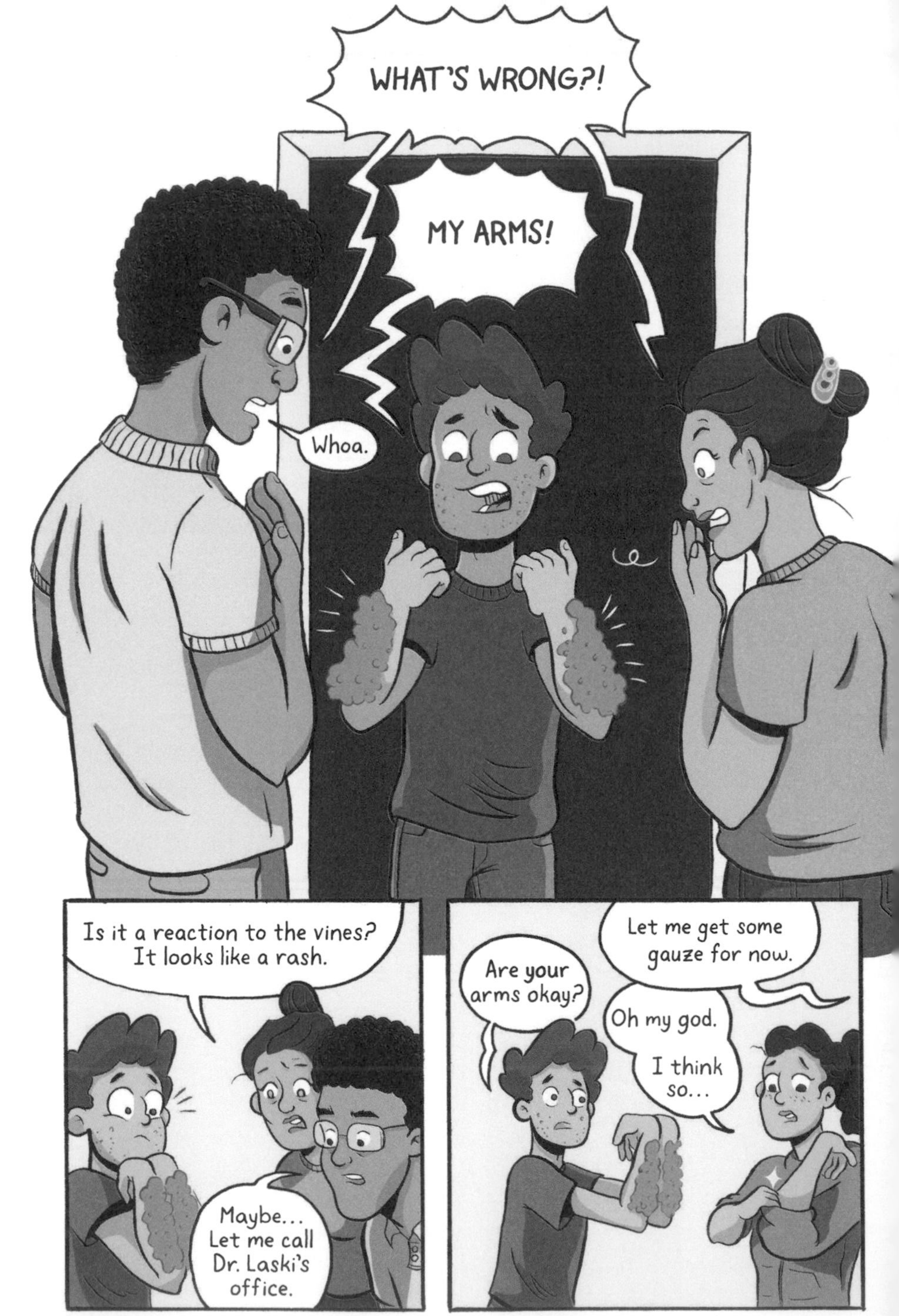
WHAT'S WRONG?!
MY ARMS!
Whoa.
Is it a reaction to the vines? It looks like a rash.
Maybe... Let me call Dr. Laski's office.
Let me get some gauze for now.
Are your arms okay?
Oh my god.
I think so...

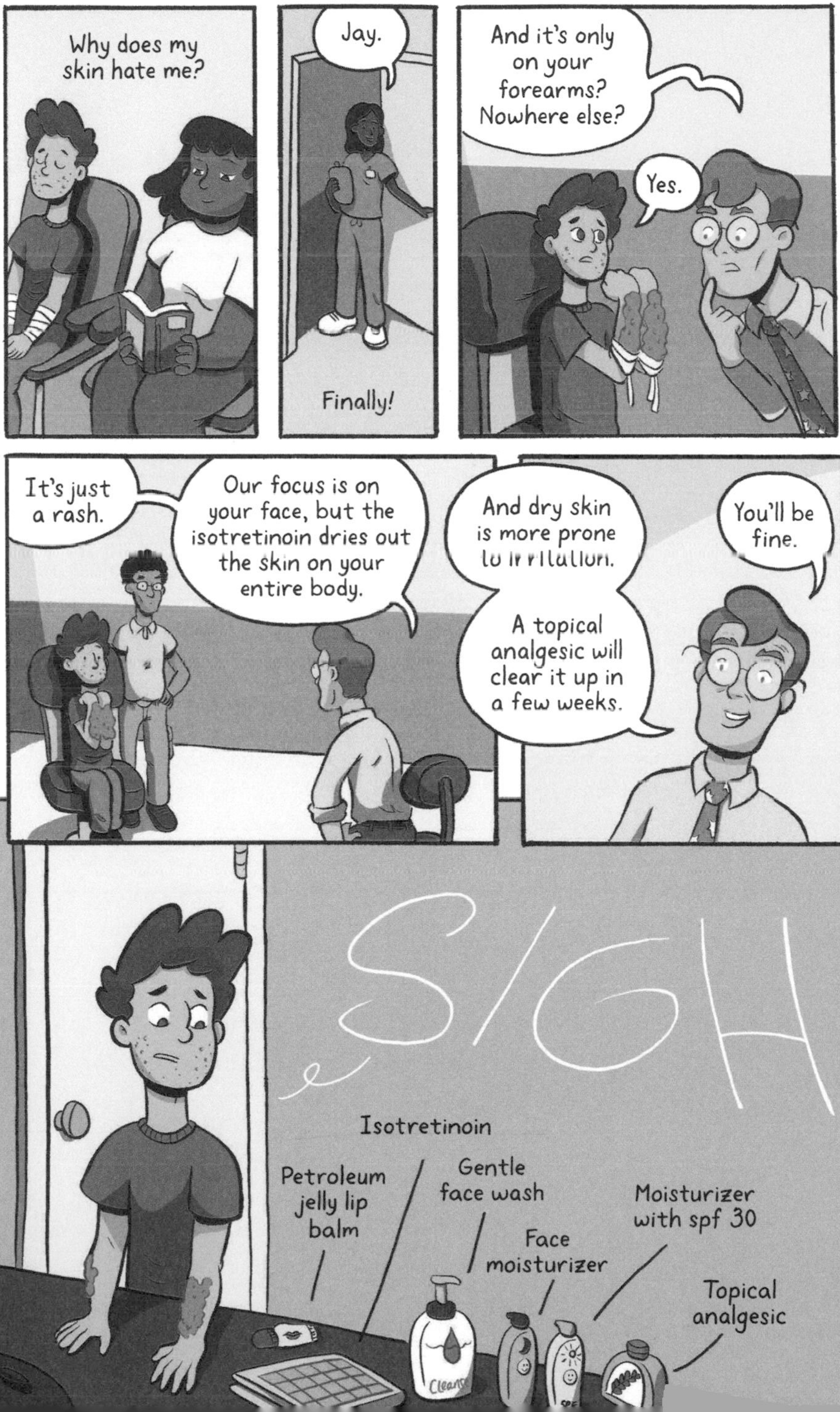
Why does my skin hate me?
Jay.
Finally!
And it's only on your forearms? Nowhere else?
Yes.
It's just a rash.
Our focus is on your face, but the isotretinoin dries out the skin on your entire body.
And dry skin is more prone to irritation.
A topical analgesic will clear it up in a few weeks.
You'll be fine.
SIGH
Isotretinoin
Petroleum jelly lip balm
Gentle face wash
Face moisturizer
Moisturizer with spf 30
Topical analgesic

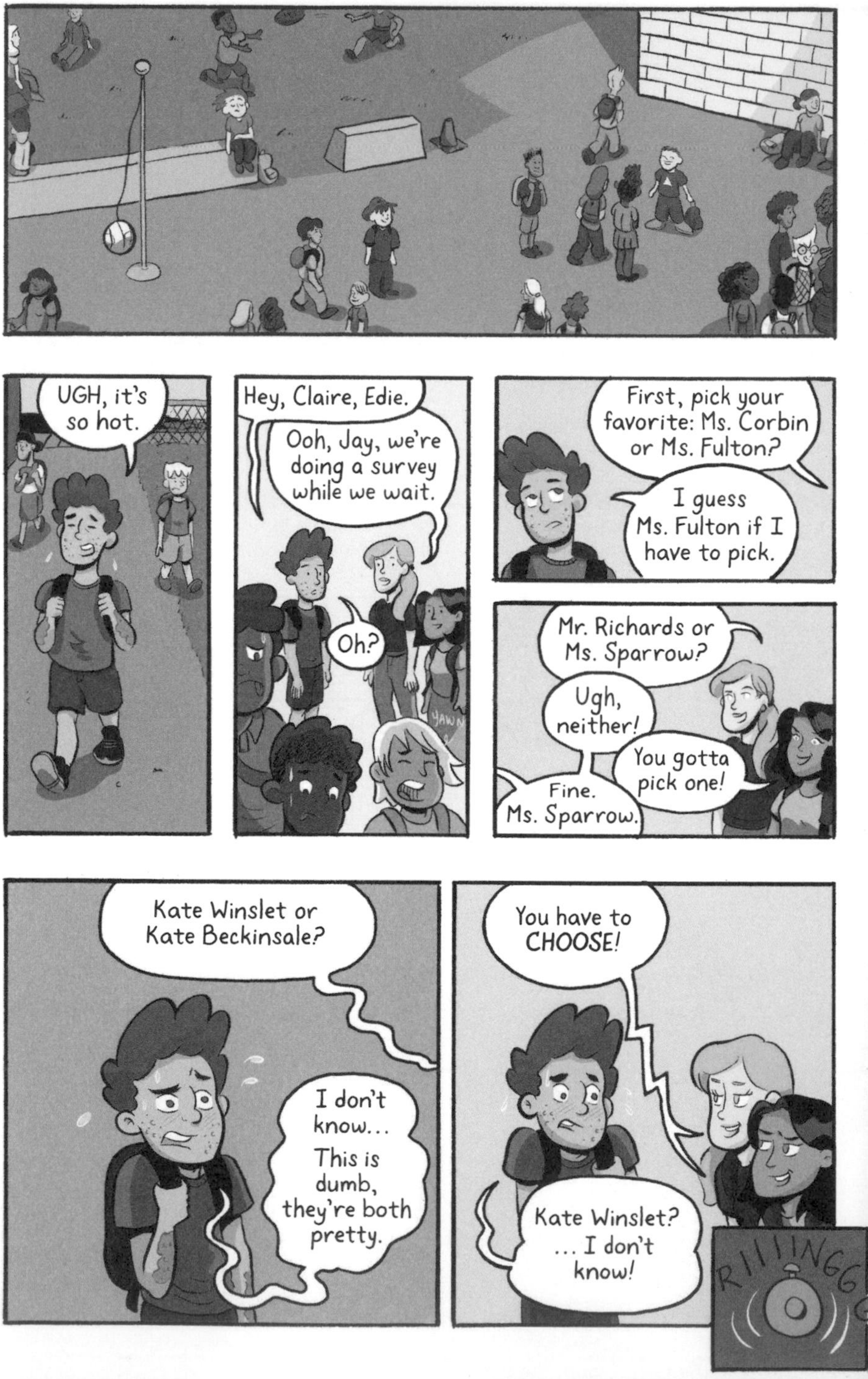
UGH, it's so hot.
Hey, Claire, Edie.
Ooh, Jay, we're doing a survey while we wait.
Oh?
First, pick your favorite: Ms. Corbin or Ms. Fulton?
I guess Ms. Fulton if I have to pick.
Mr. Richards or Ms. Sparrow?
Ugh, neither!
You gotta pick one!
Fine. Ms. Sparrow.
Kate Winslet or Kate Beckinsale?
I don't know...
This is dumb, they're both pretty.
You have to CHOOSE!
Kate Winslet? ... I don't know!
RIIIINGGG

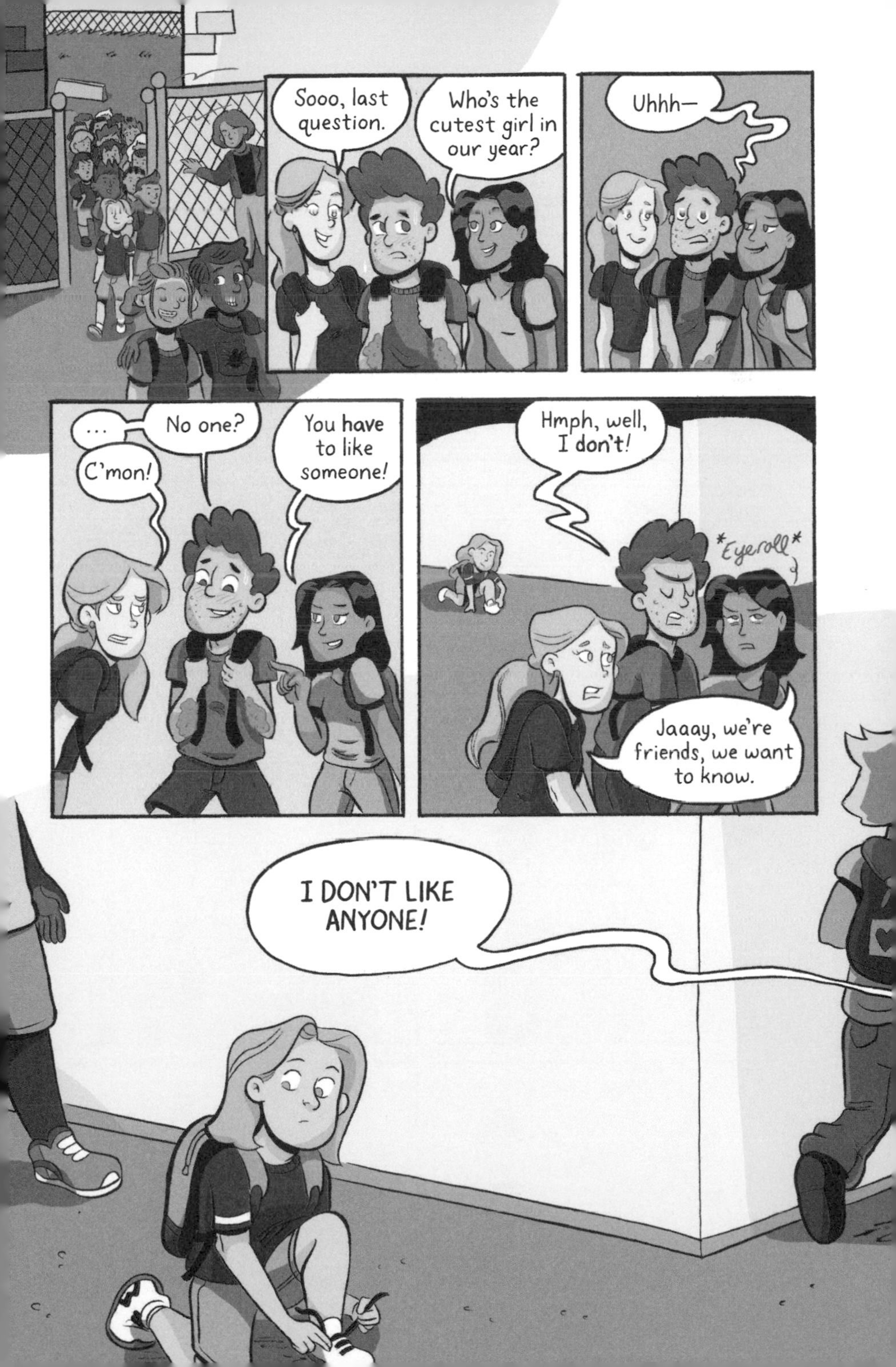
Sooo, last question.
Who's the cutest girl in our year?
Uhhh—
...
No one?
C'mon!
You have to like someone!
Hmph, well, I don't!
Eyeroll
Jaaay, we're friends, we want to know.
I DON'T LIKE ANYONE!

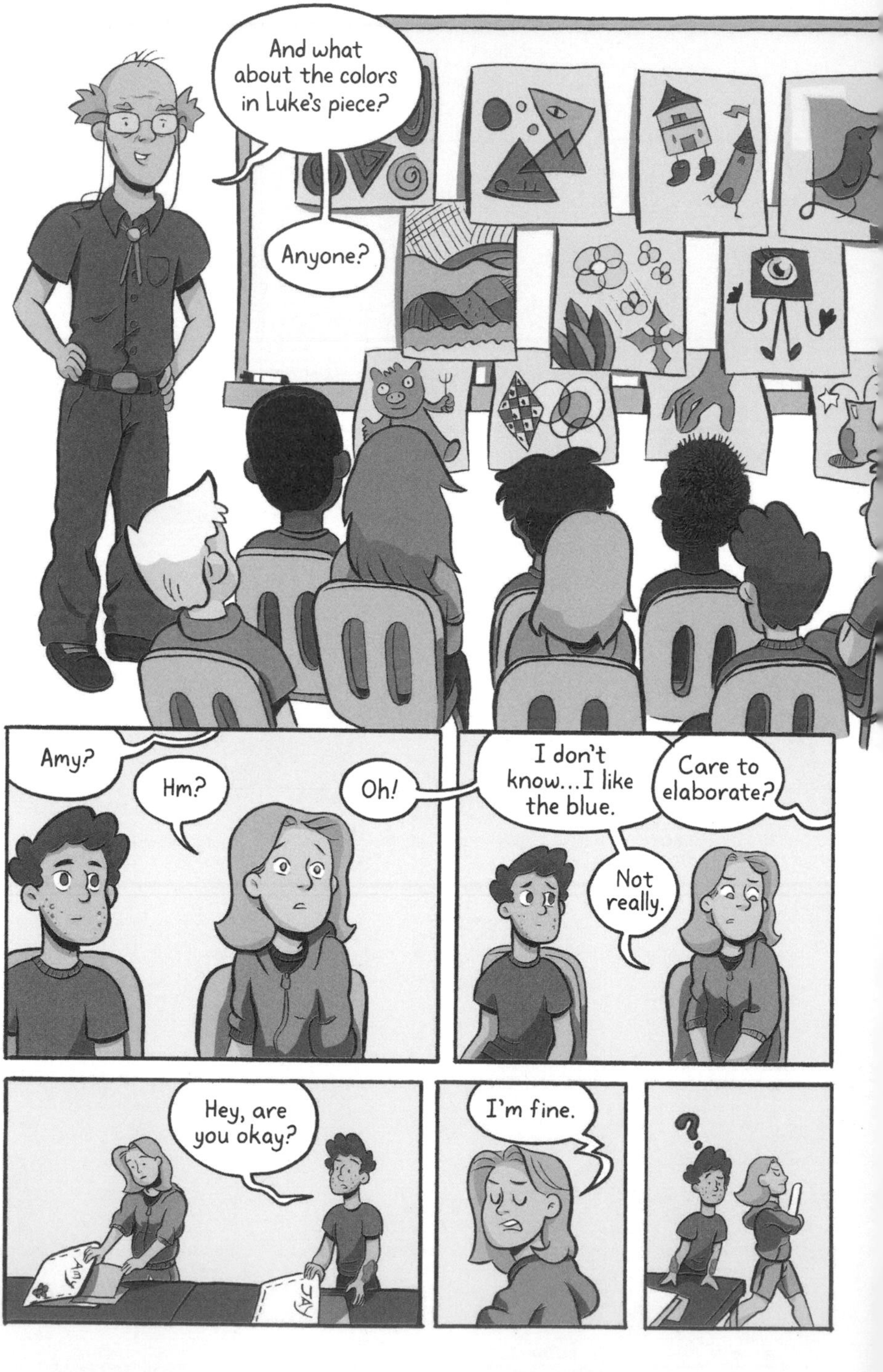
And what about the colors in Luke's piece?
Anyone?
Amy?
Hm?
Oh!
I don't know...I like the blue.
Care to elaborate?
Not really.
Hey, are you okay?
JAY
I'm fine.
?

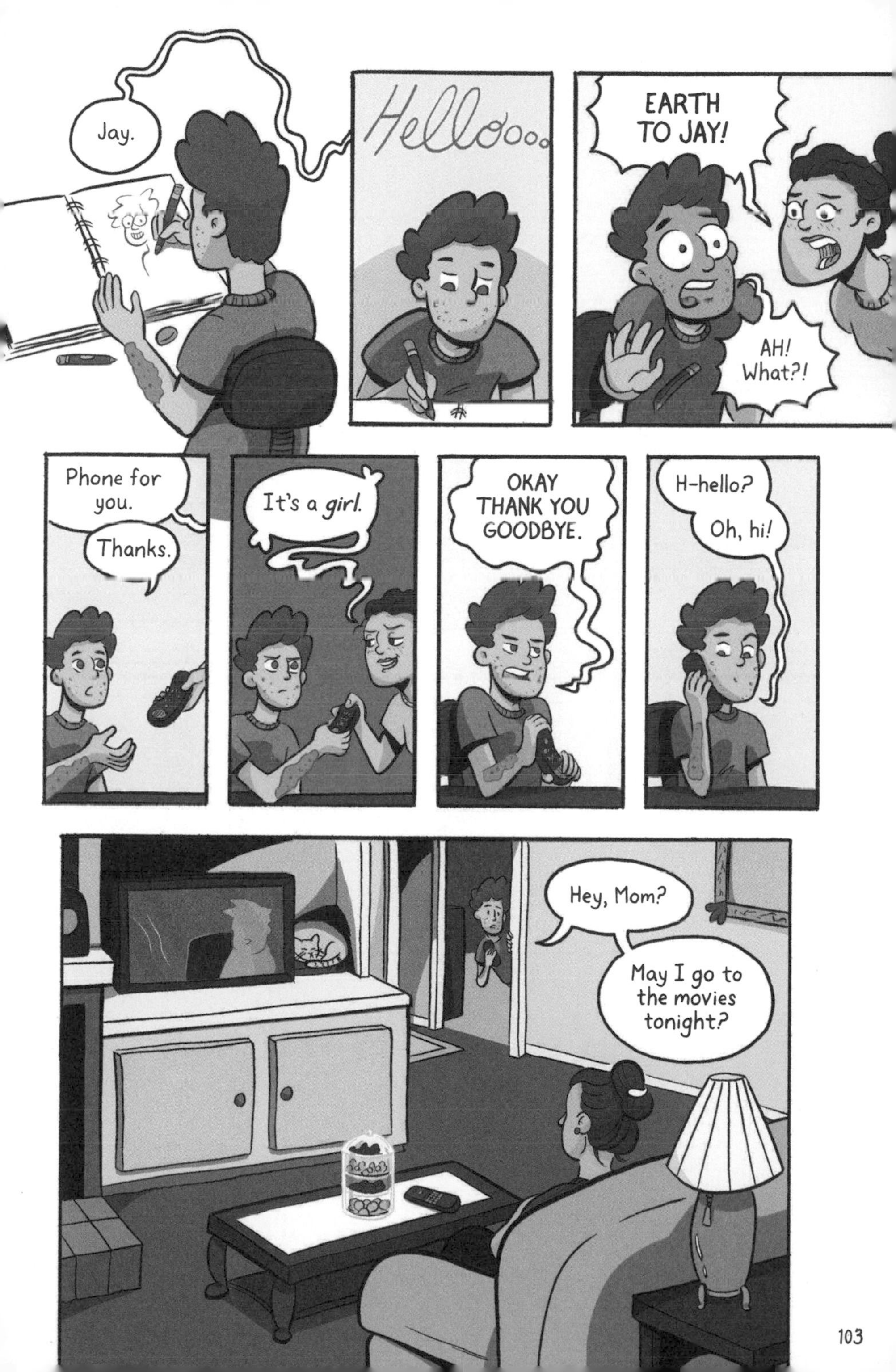
Jay.
Helloooo..
EARTH TO JAY!
AH! What?!
Phone for you.
Thanks.
It's a *girl*.
OKAY THANK YOU GOODBYE.
H-hello?
Oh, hi!
Hey, Mom?
May I go to the movies tonight?

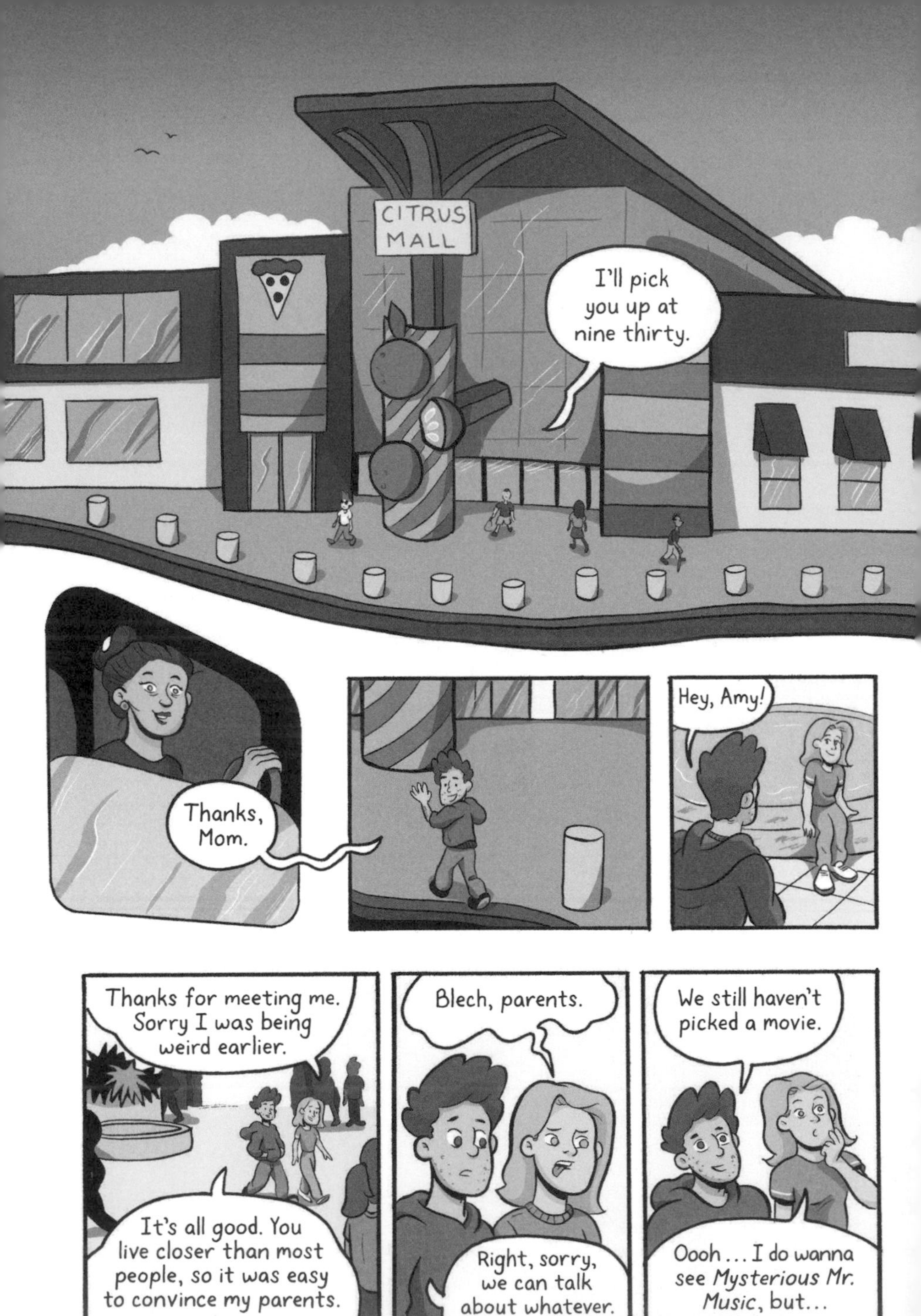
CITRUS MALL
I'll pick you up at nine thirty.
Thanks, Mom.
Hey, Amy!
Thanks for meeting me. Sorry I was being weird earlier.
It's all good. You live closer than most people, so it was easy to convince my parents.
Blech, parents.
Right, sorry, we can talk about whatever.
We still haven't picked a movie.
Oooh . . . I do wanna see *Mysterious Mr. Music*, but . . .

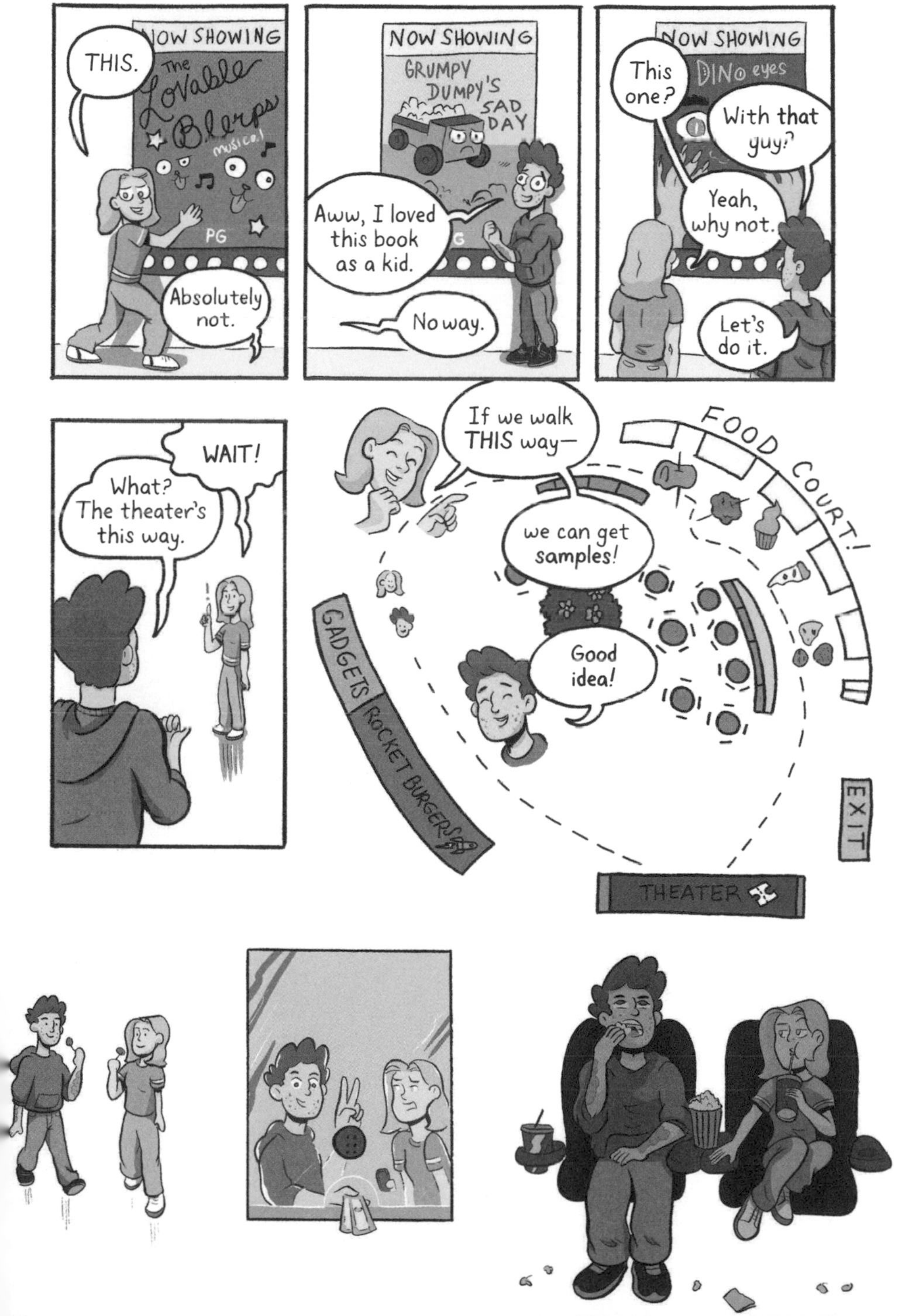
NOW SHOWING
THIS.
The Lovable Blerps
musical!
PG
Absolutely not.
NOW SHOWING
GRUMPY DUMPY'S SAD DAY
Aww, I loved this book as a kid.
No way.
NOW SHOWING
DINO eyes
This one?
With that guy?
Yeah, why not.
Let's do it.
WAIT!
What? The theater's this way.
If we walk THIS way—
we can get samples!
Good idea!
FOOD COURT!
GADGETS
ROCKET BURGERS
EXIT
THEATER

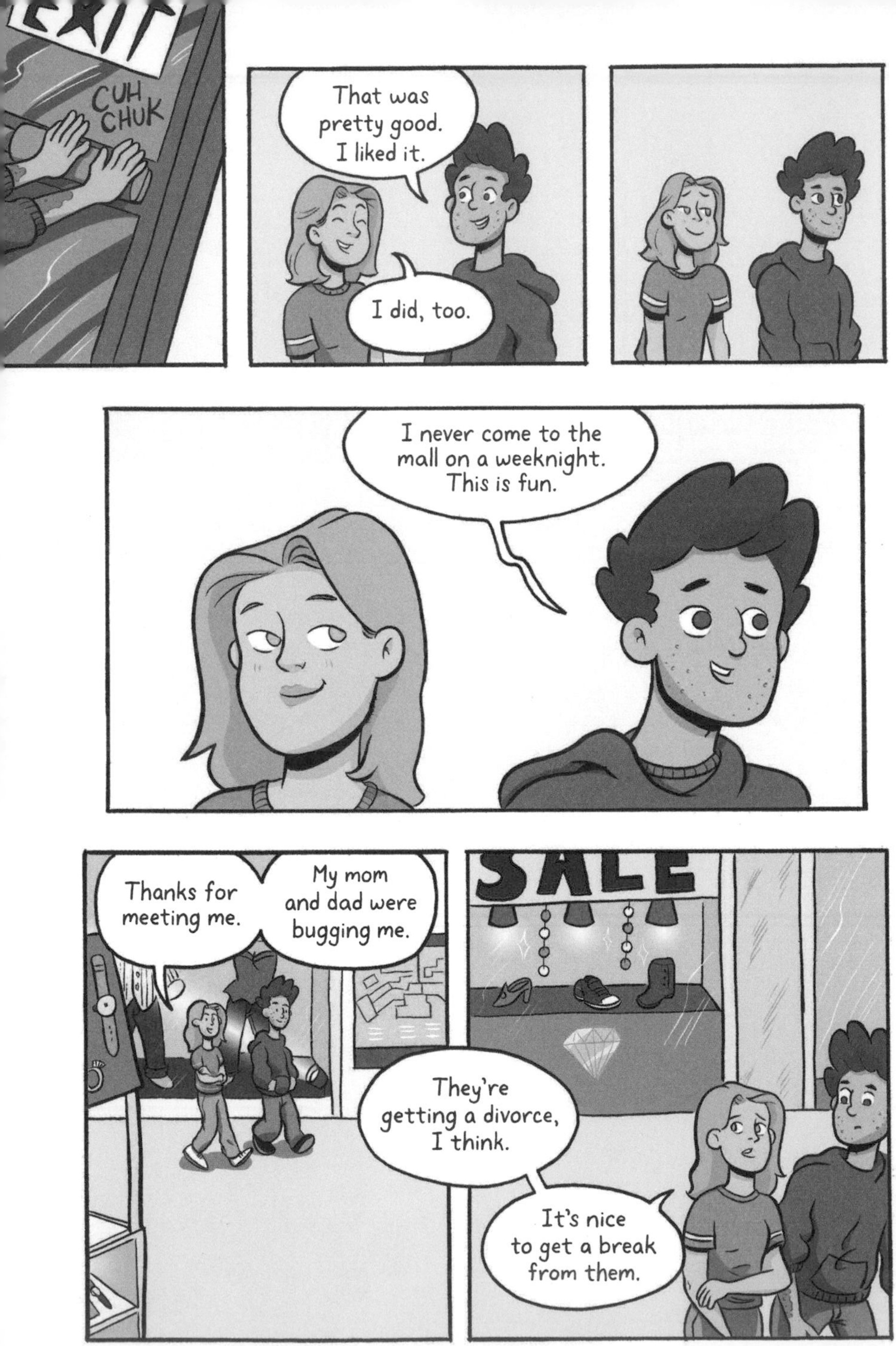
EXIT
CUH CHUK
That was pretty good. I liked it.
I did, too.
I never come to the mall on a weeknight. This is fun.
Thanks for meeting me.
My mom and dad were bugging me.
SALE
They're getting a divorce, I think.
It's nice to get a break from them.

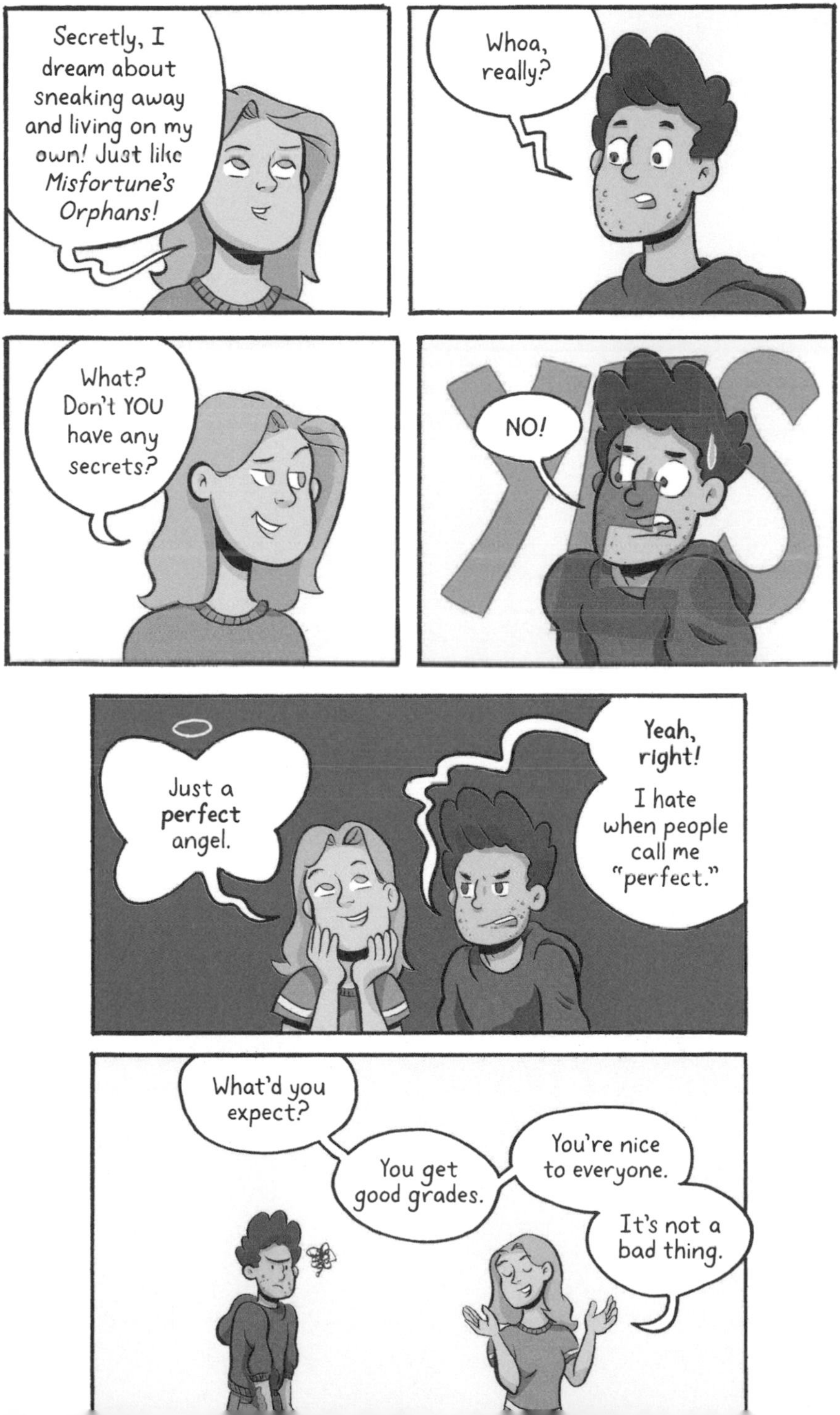
Secretly, I dream about sneaking away and living on my own! Just like *Misfortune's Orphans!*
Whoa, really?
What? Don't YOU have any secrets?
NO!
YES
Just a **perfect** angel.
Yeah, right!
I hate when people call me "perfect."
What'd you expect?
You get good grades.
You're nice to everyone.
It's not a bad thing.

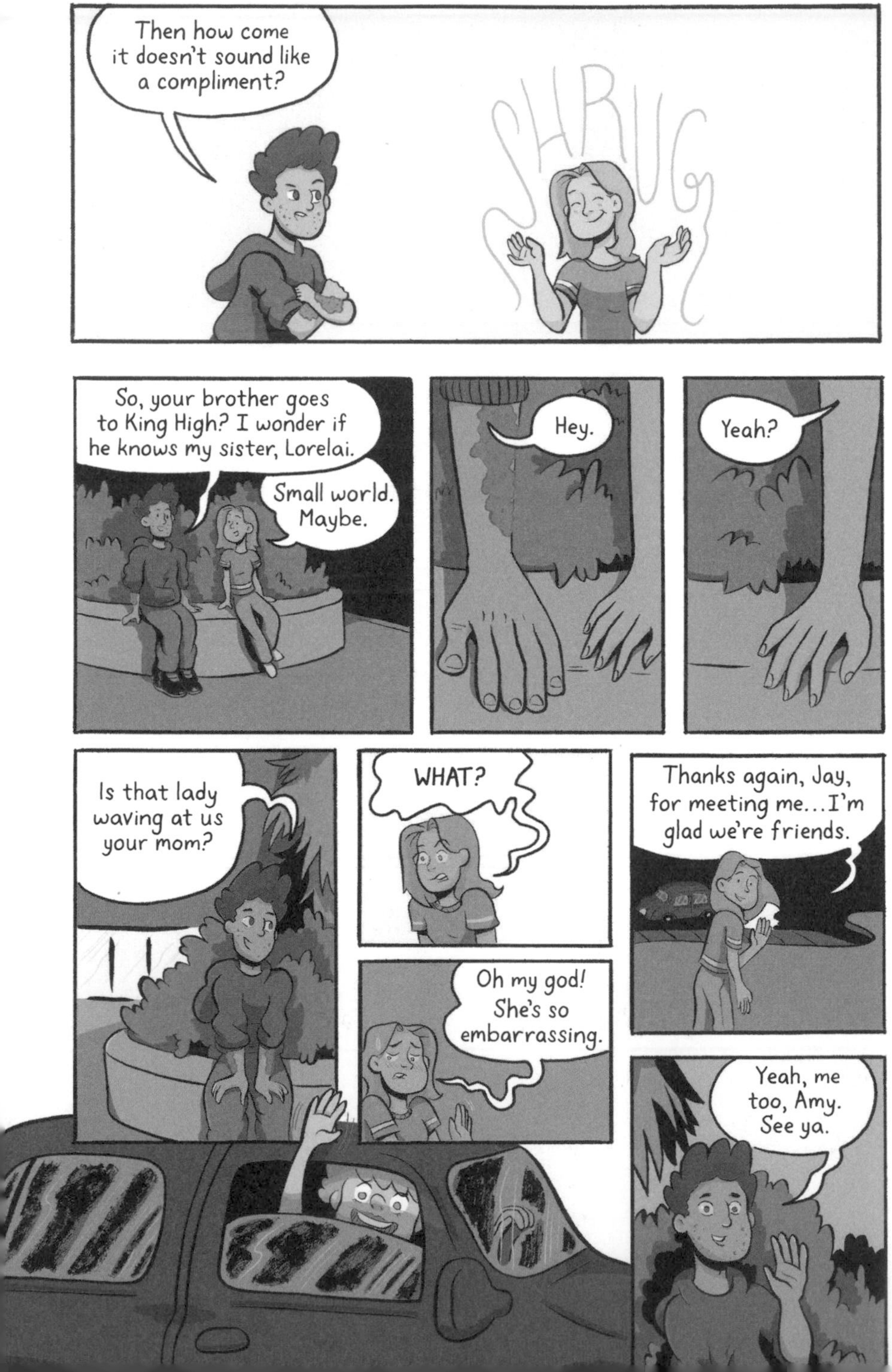
Then how come it doesn't sound like a compliment?
SHRUG
So, your brother goes to King High? I wonder if he knows my sister, Lorelai.
Small world. Maybe.
Hey.
Yeah?
Is that lady waving at us your mom?
WHAT?
Oh my god! She's so embarrassing.
Thanks again, Jay, for meeting me...I'm glad we're friends.
Yeah, me too, Amy. See ya.

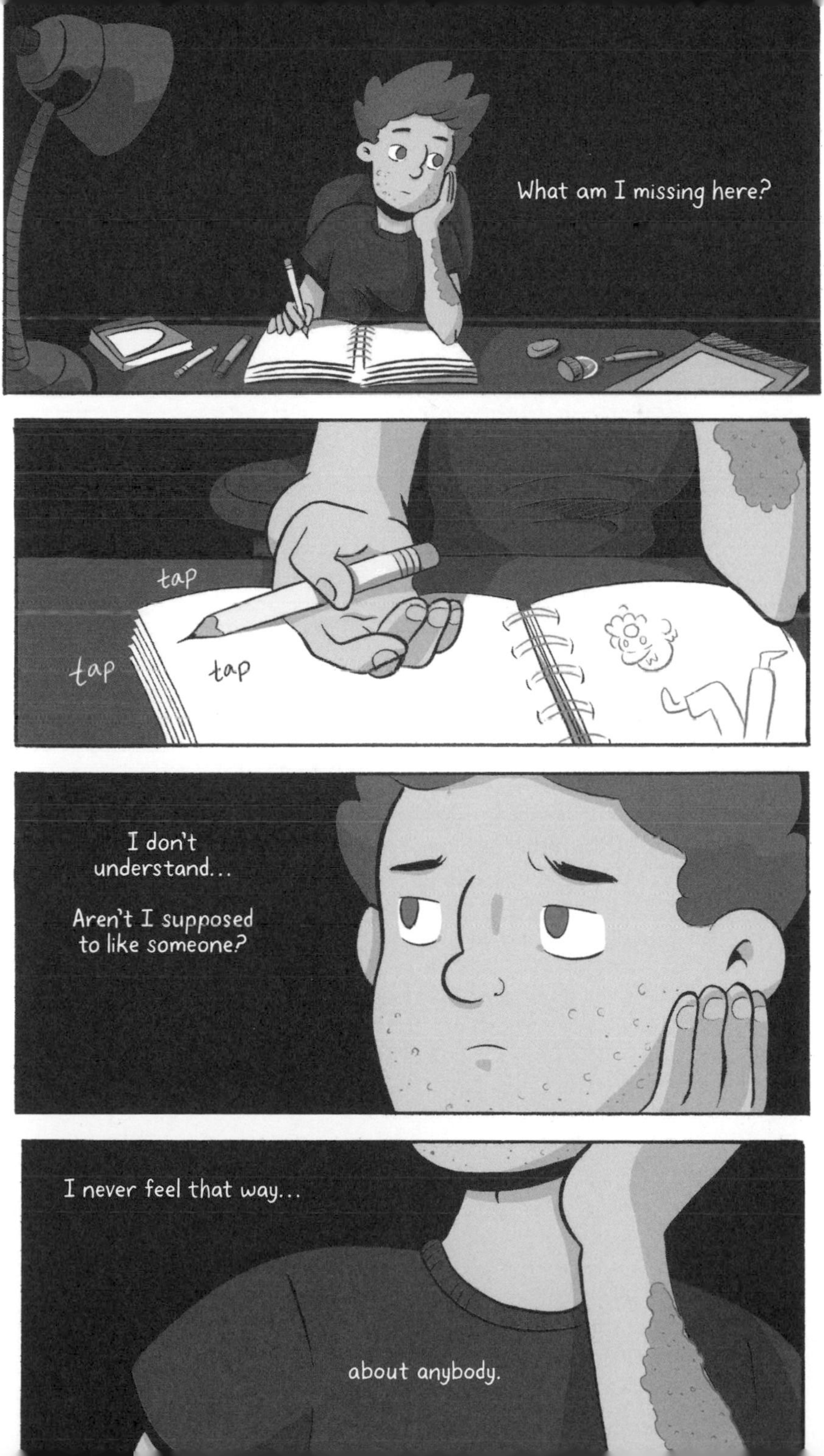
What am I missing here?
tap
tap
tap
I don't understand...
Aren't I supposed to like someone?
I never feel that way...
about anybody.

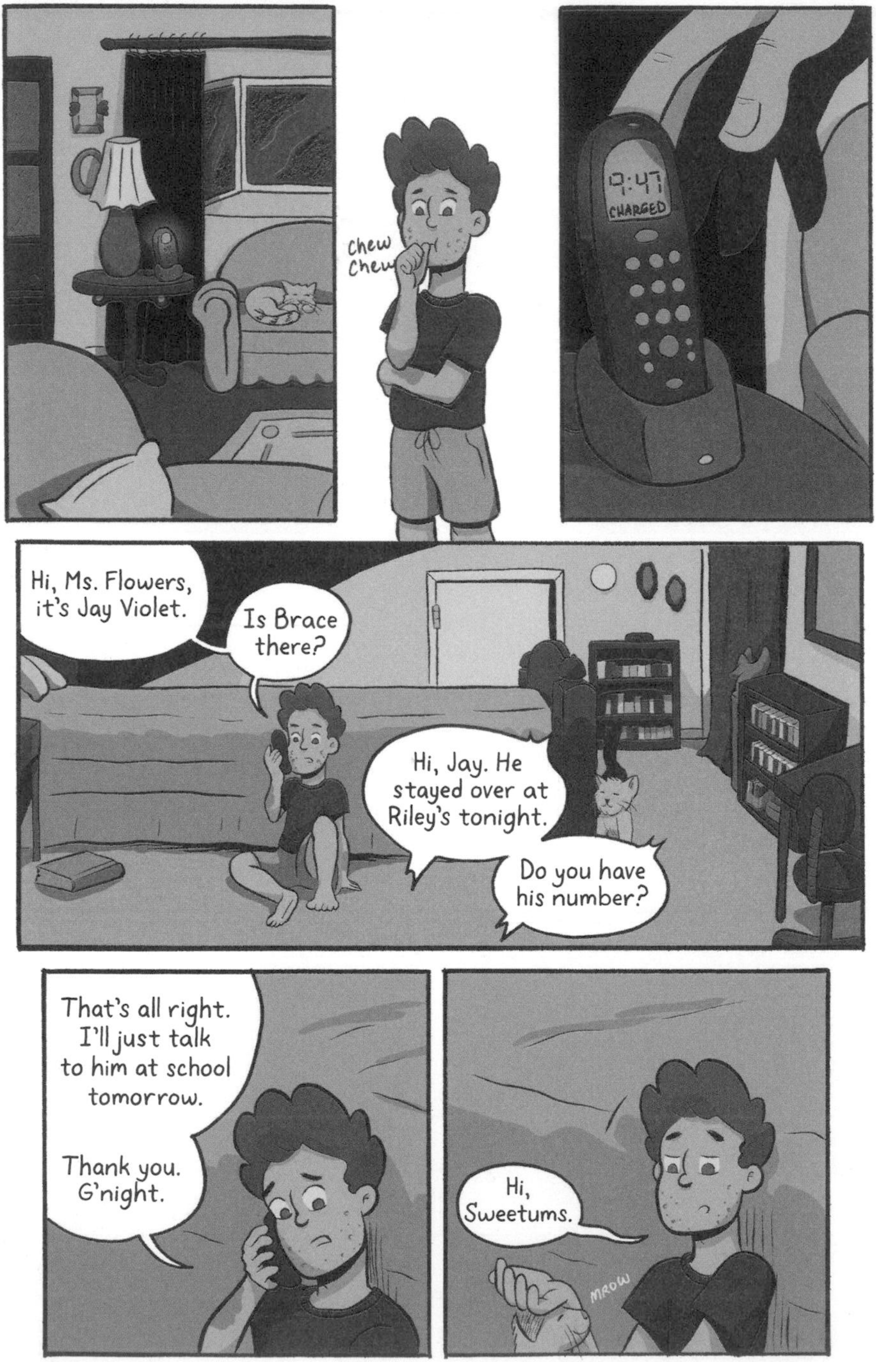

Chew
Chew
9:47
CHARGED
Hi, Ms. Flowers, it's Jay Violet.
Is Brace there?
Hi, Jay. He stayed over at Riley's tonight.
Do you have his number?
That's all right. I'll just talk to him at school tomorrow.
Thank you. G'night.
Hi, Sweetums.
MROW

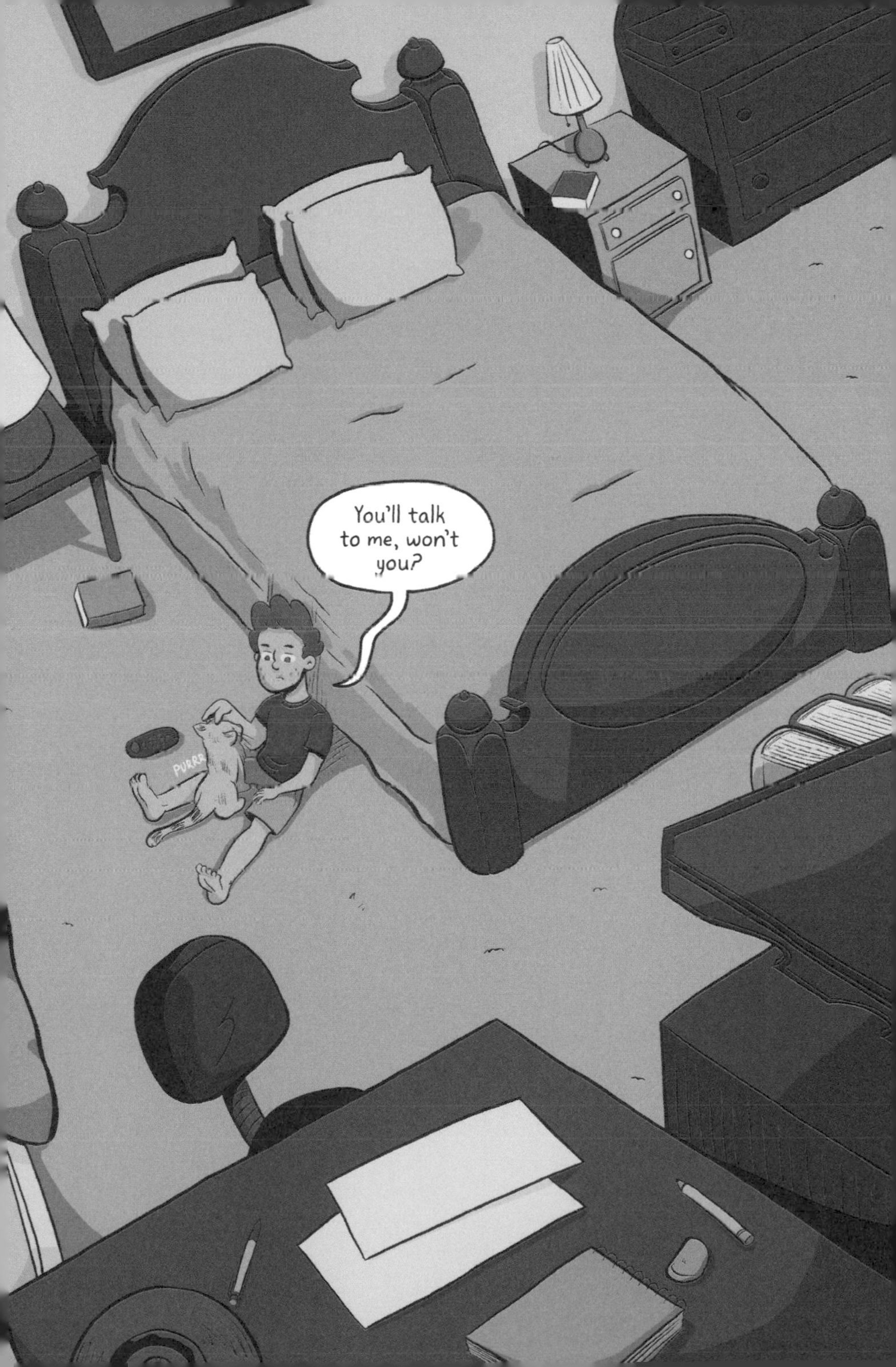
You'll talk to me, won't you?
PURRR

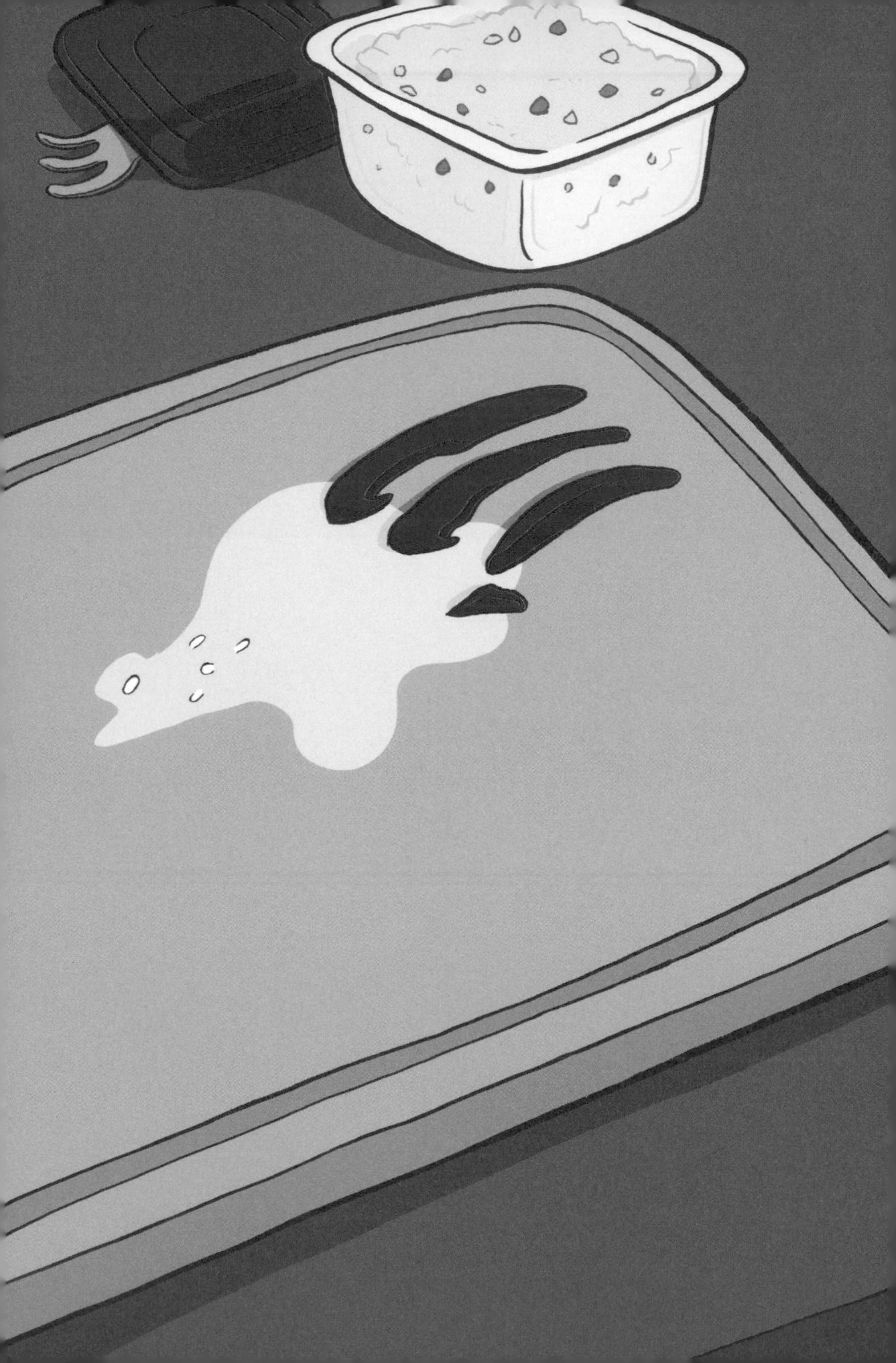

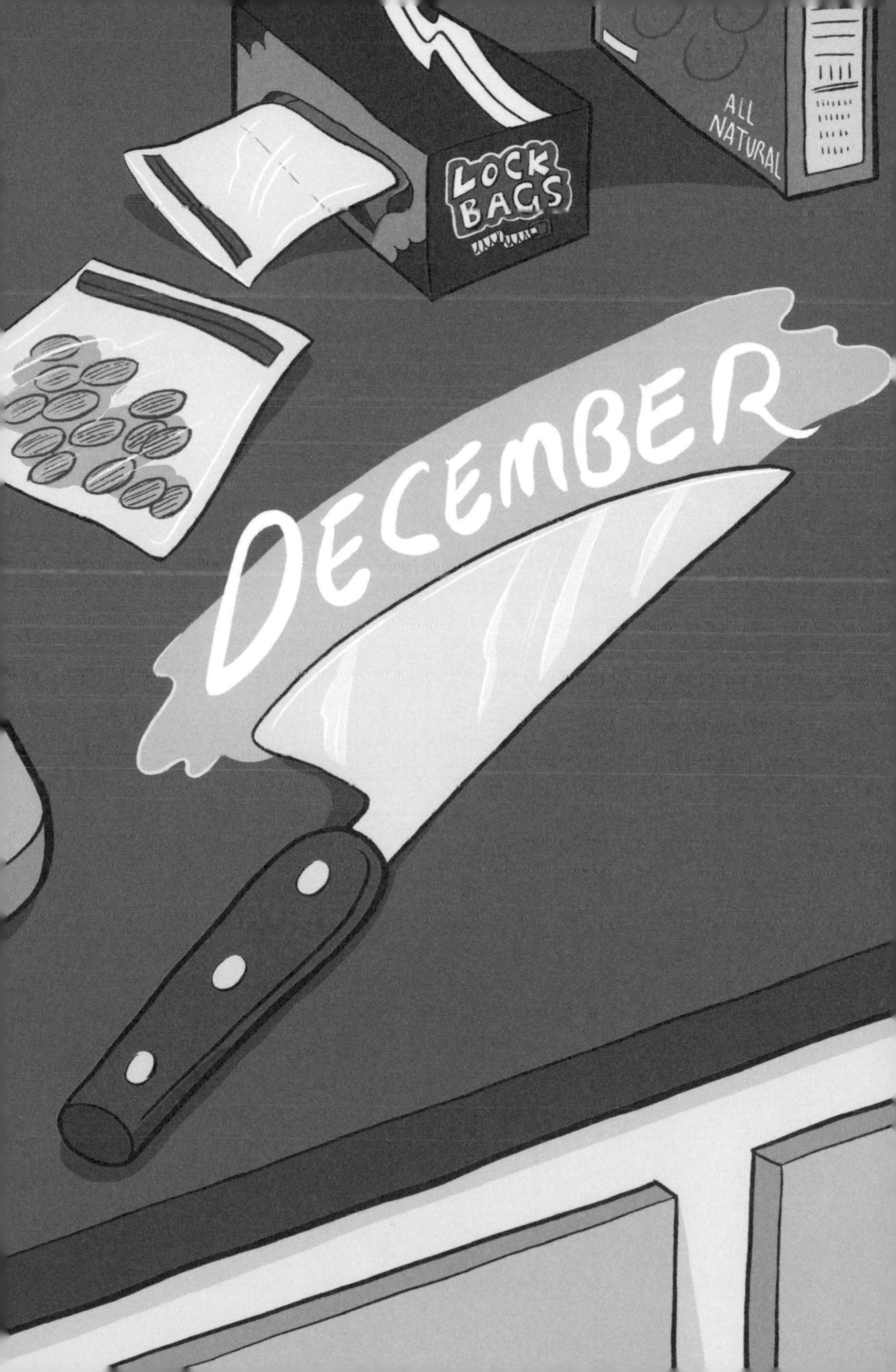
LOCK BAGS
ALL NATURAL
DECEMBER

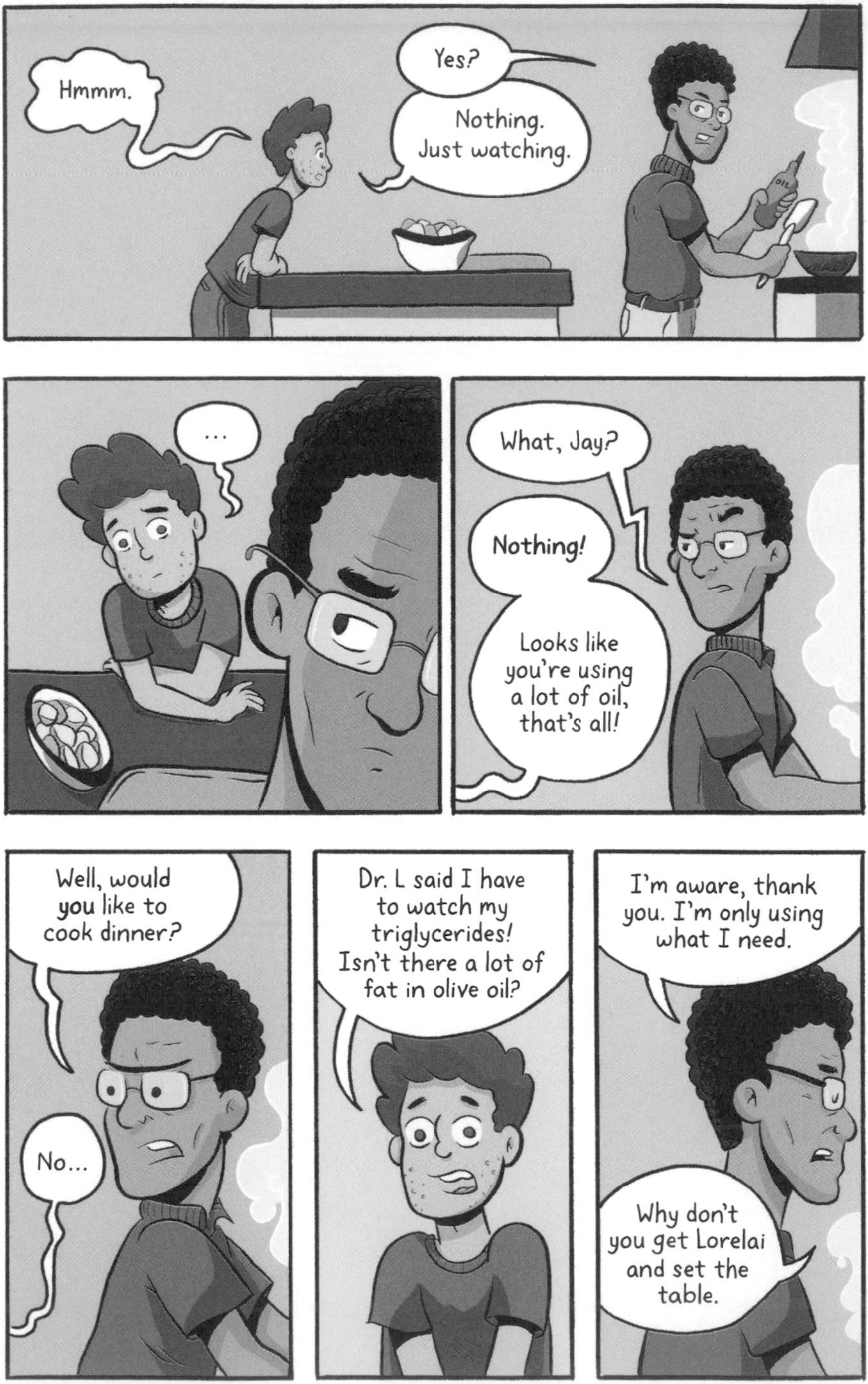
Hmmm.
Yes?
Nothing. Just watching.
...
What, Jay?
Nothing!
Looks like you're using a lot of oil, that's all!
Well, would **you** like to cook dinner?
No...
Dr. L said I have to watch my triglycerides! Isn't there a lot of fat in olive oil?
I'm aware, thank you. I'm only using what I need.
Why don't you get Lorelai and set the table.

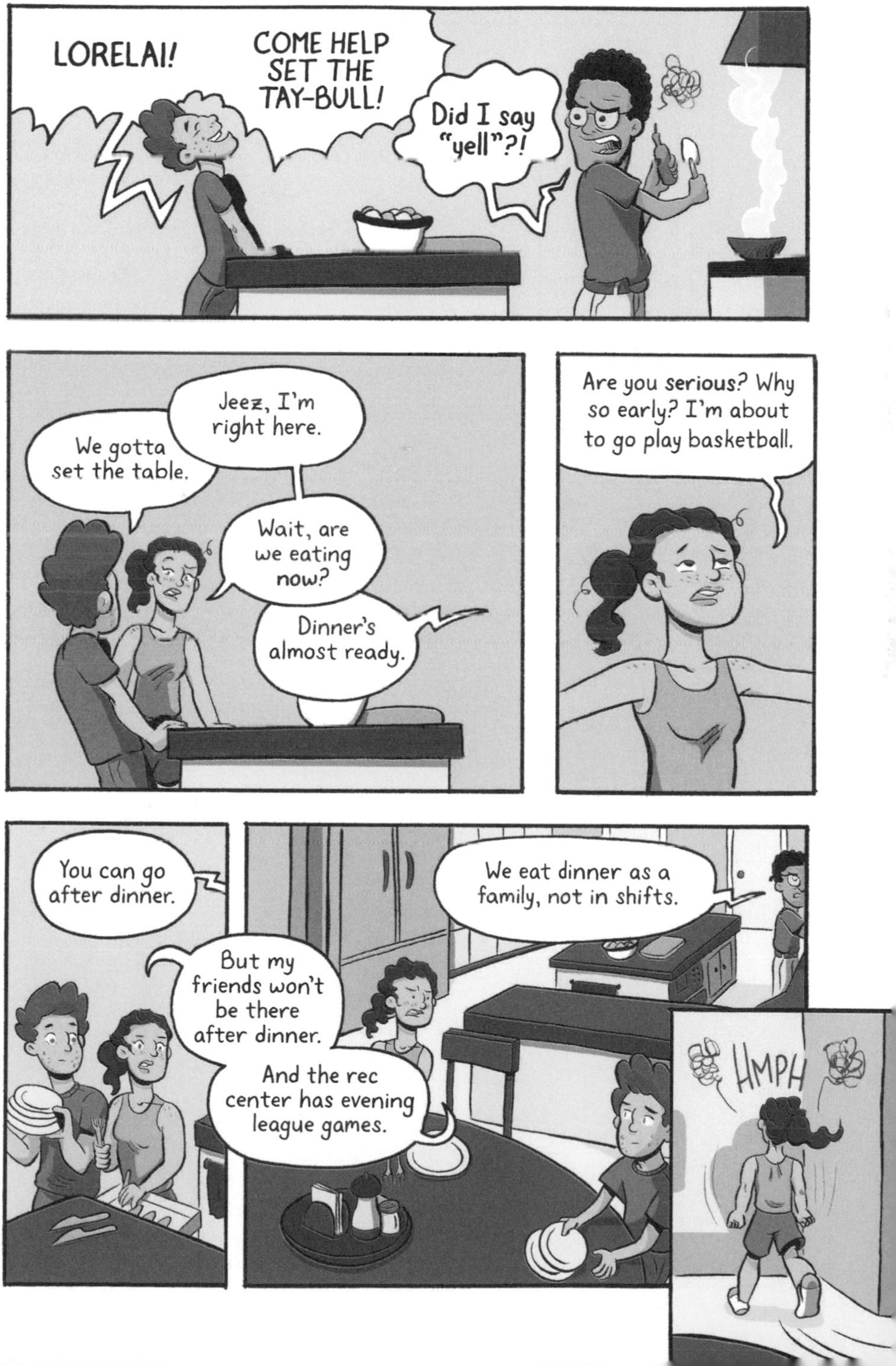
LORELAI!
COME HELP SET THE TAY-BULL!
Did I say "yell"?!
We gotta set the table.
Jeez, I'm right here.
Wait, are we eating now?
Dinner's almost ready.
Are you serious? Why so early? I'm about to go play basketball.
You can go after dinner.
We eat dinner as a family, not in shifts.
But my friends won't be there after dinner.
And the rec center has evening league games.
HMPH

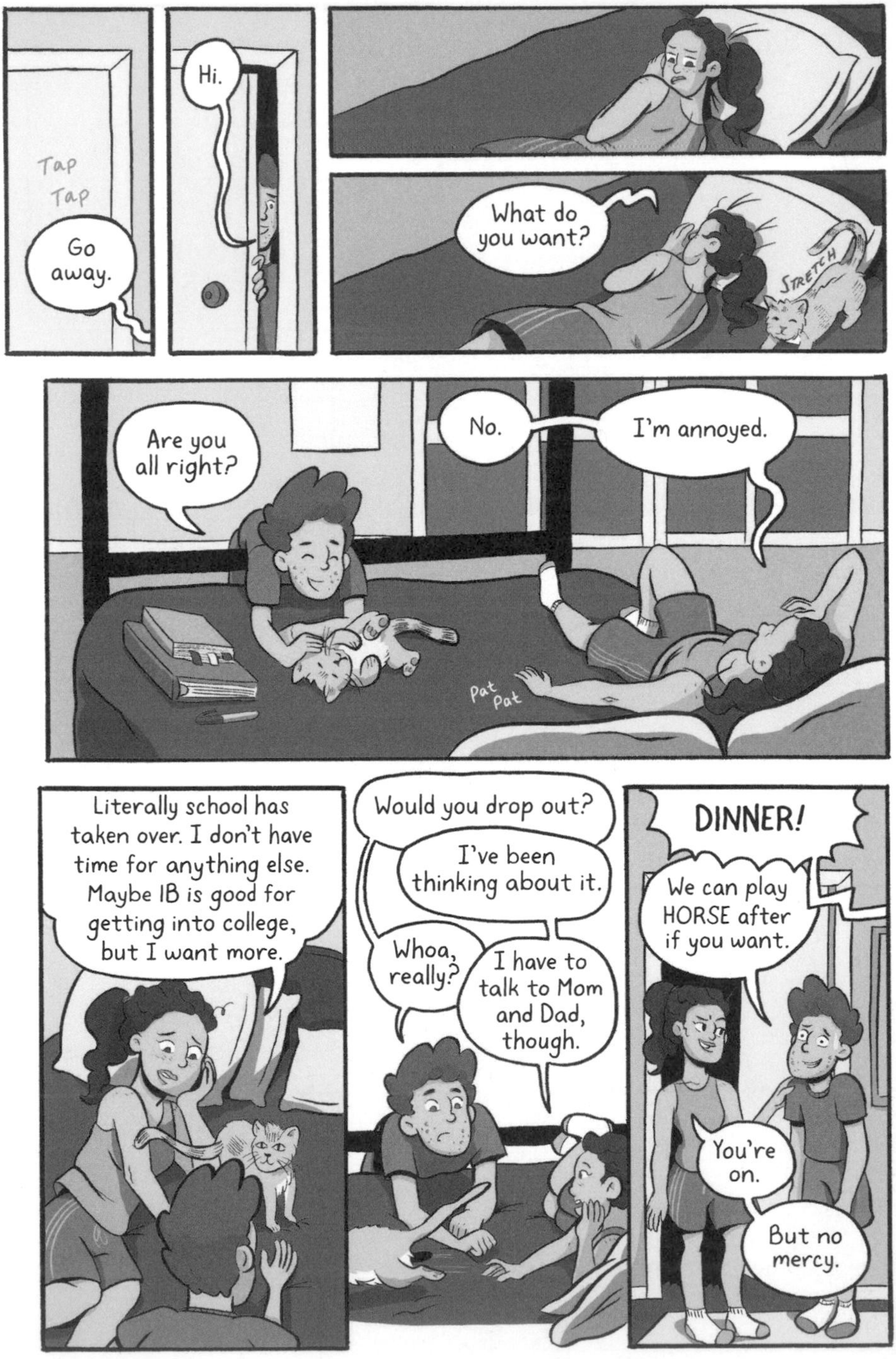

Tap
Tap
Go away.
Hi.
What do you want?
STRETCH
Are you all right?
No.
I'm annoyed.
Pat
Pat
Literally school has taken over. I don't have time for anything else. Maybe IB is good for getting into college, but I want more.
Would you drop out?
I've been thinking about it.
Whoa, really?
I have to talk to Mom and Dad, though.
DINNER!
We can play HORSE after if you want.
You're on.
But no mercy.

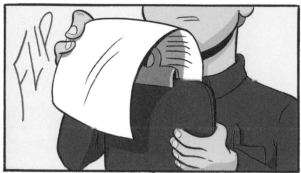

It's not what I wanted to see. Your triglycerides are elevated. No cause for concern, though.

It's only month three. You really need to be diligent about your diet.

I don't want to stop the cycle, but if we can't get these down, I'll have to.

And I'd hate to impede the progress I'm seeing.

Let's knock this out!

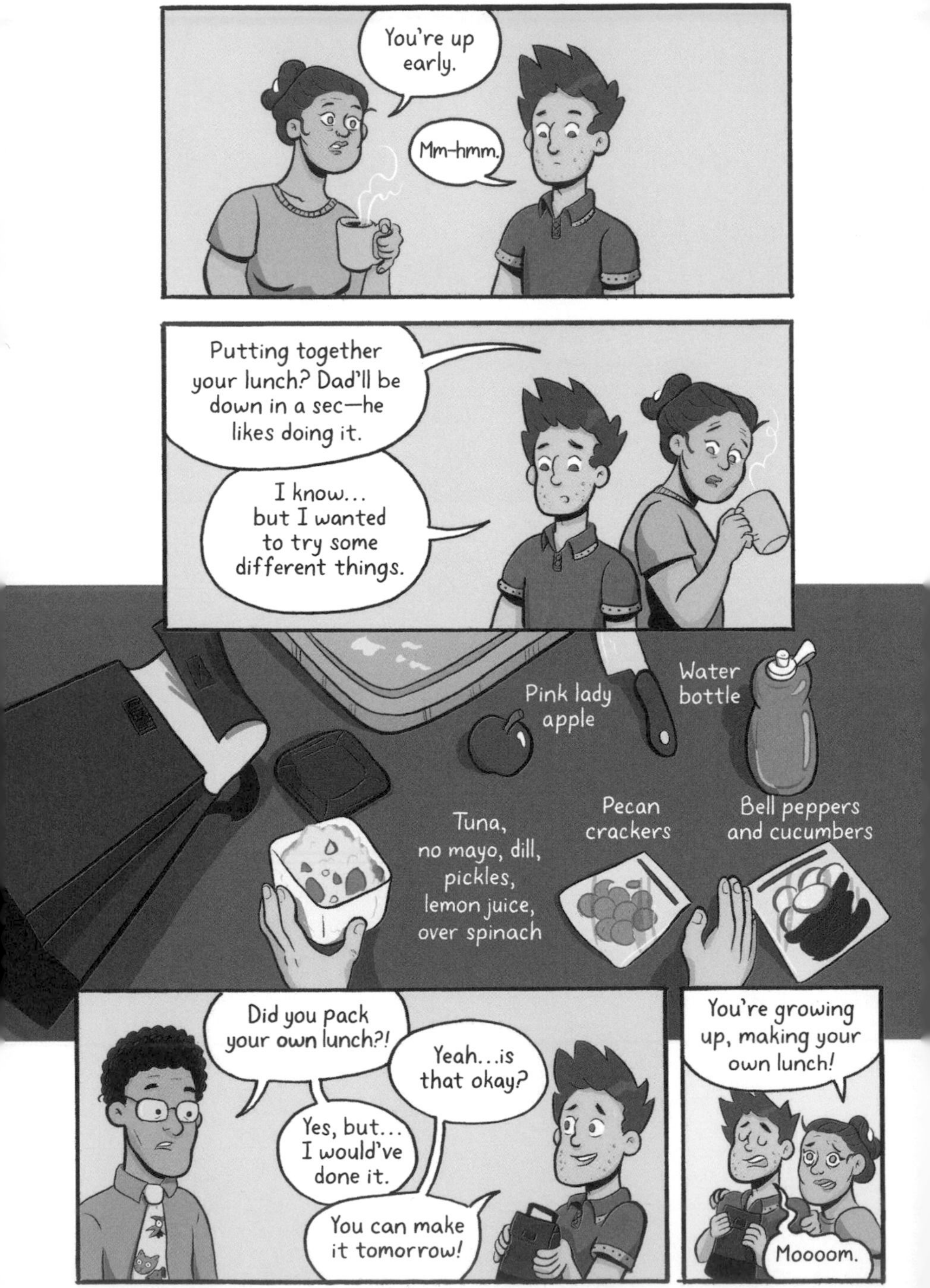

You're up early.
Mm-hmm.
Putting together your lunch? Dad'll be down in a sec—he likes doing it.
I know... but I wanted to try some different things.
Pink lady apple
Water bottle
Tuna, no mayo, dill, pickles, lemon juice, over spinach
Pecan crackers
Bell peppers and cucumbers
Did you pack your own lunch?!
Yeah...is that okay?
Yes, but... I would've done it.
You can make it tomorrow!
You're growing up, making your own lunch!
Moooom.

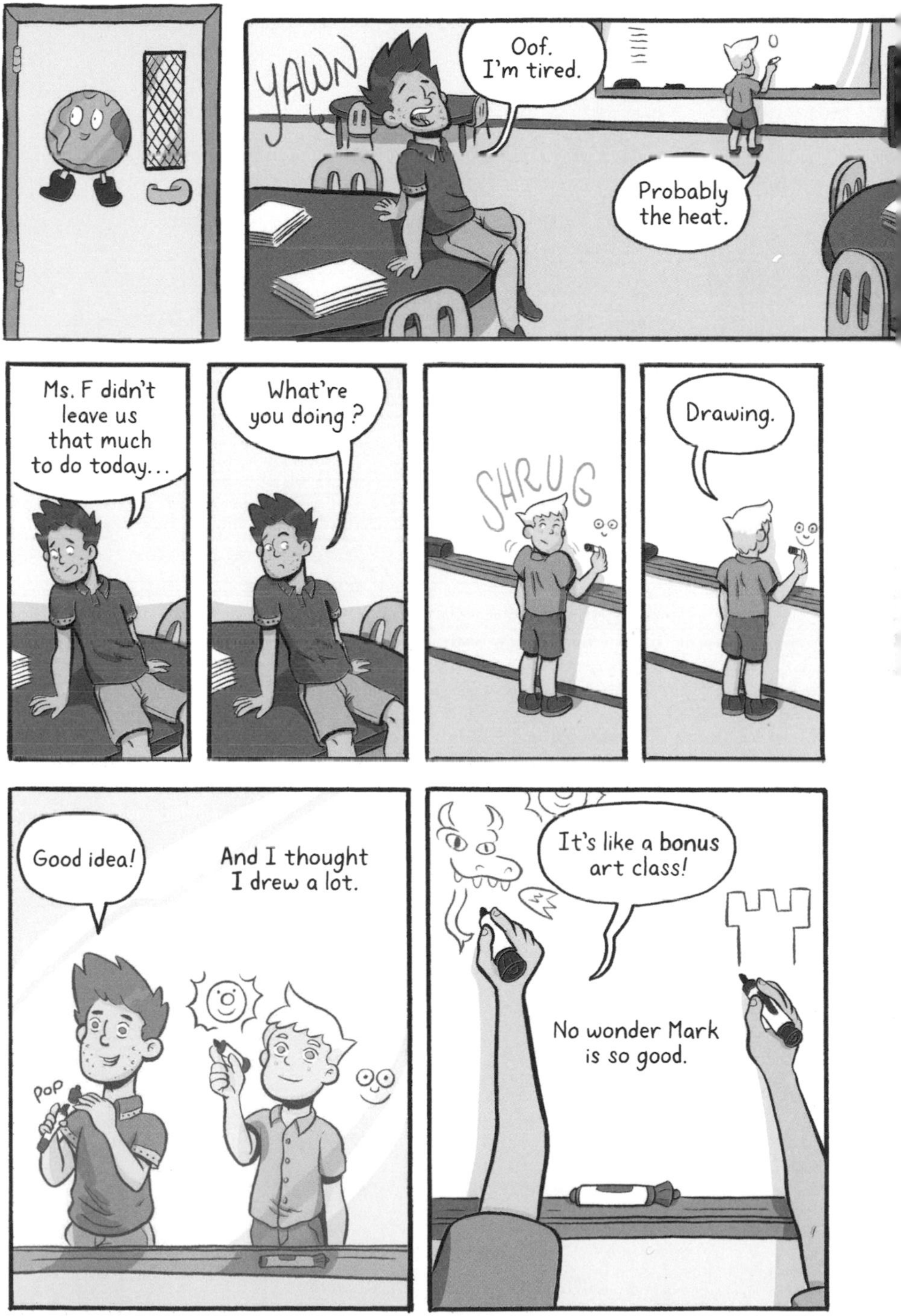
YAWN
Oof. I'm tired.
Probably the heat.
Ms. F didn't leave us that much to do today...
What're you doing?
SHRUG
Drawing.
Good idea!
And I thought I drew a lot.
POP
It's like a bonus art class!
No wonder Mark is so good.

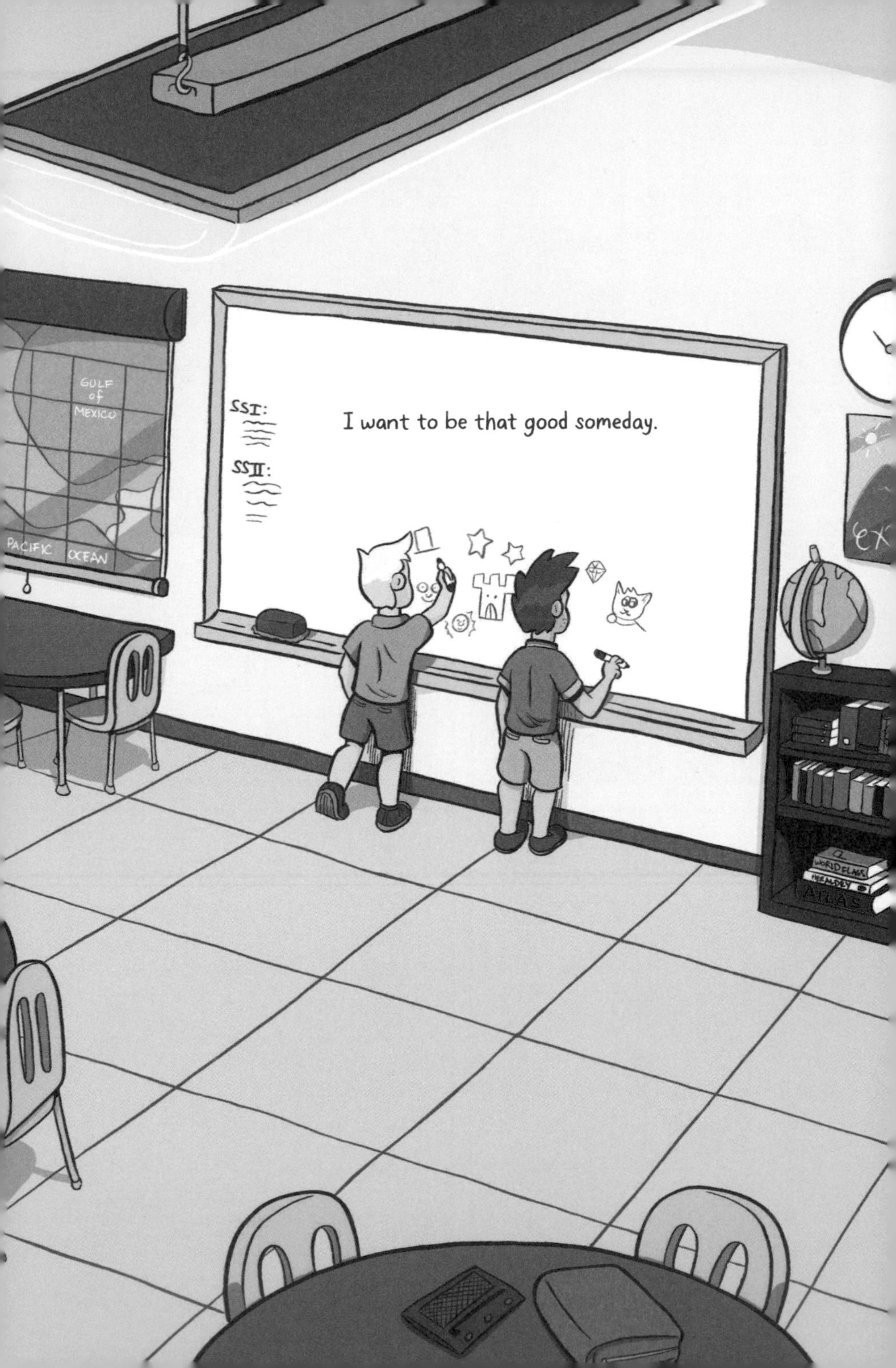
I want to be that good someday.
SSI:
SSII:
GULF of MEXICO
PACIFIC OCEAN
WORLD FLAGS
ATLAS

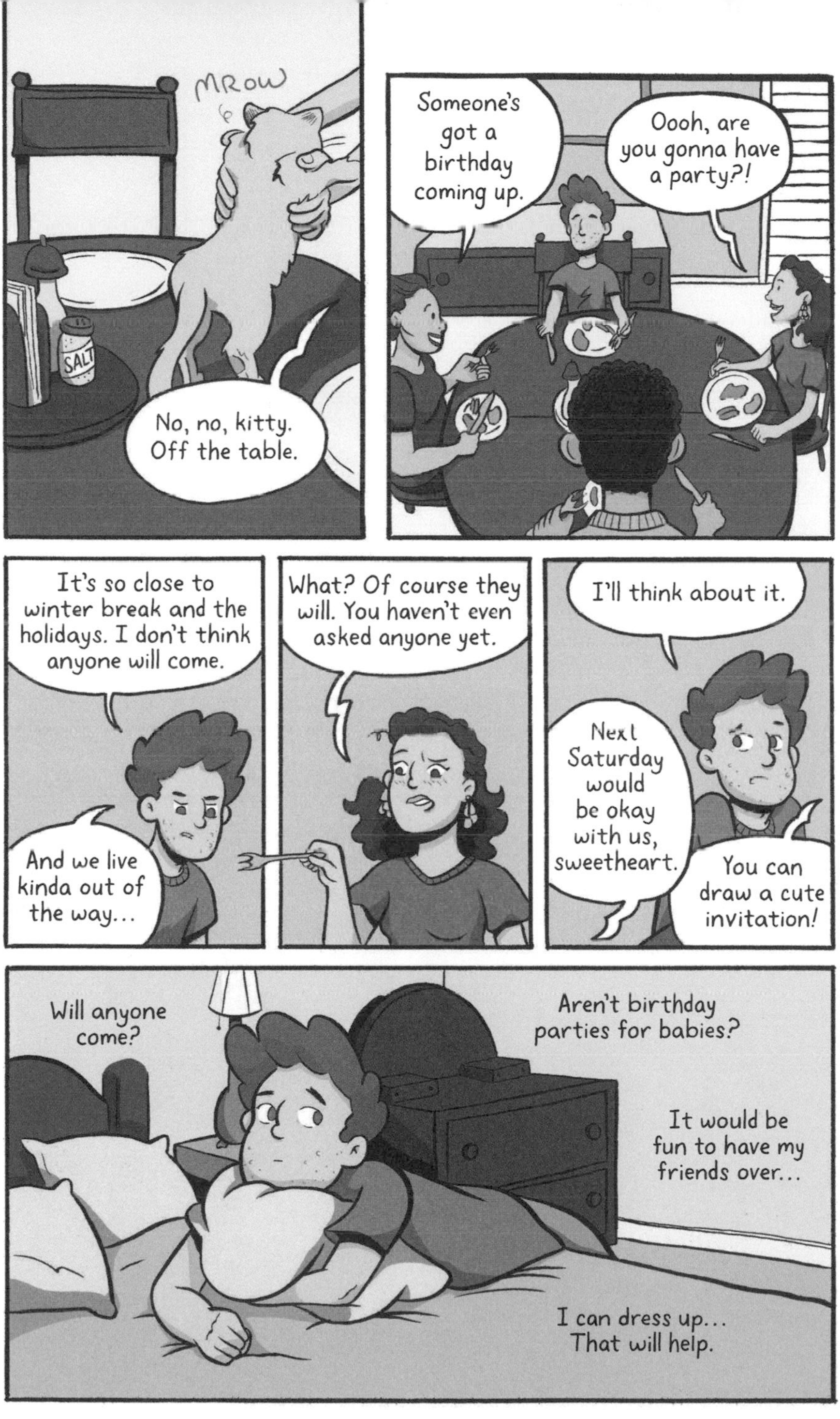
MROW
No, no, kitty. Off the table.
Someone's got a birthday coming up.
Oooh, are you gonna have a party?!
It's so close to winter break and the holidays. I don't think anyone will come.
And we live kinda out of the way...
What? Of course they will. You haven't even asked anyone yet.
I'll think about it.
Next Saturday would be okay with us, sweetheart.
You can draw a cute invitation!
Will anyone come?
Aren't birthday parties for babies?
It would be fun to have my friends over...
I can dress up... That will help.

Couple of legs...

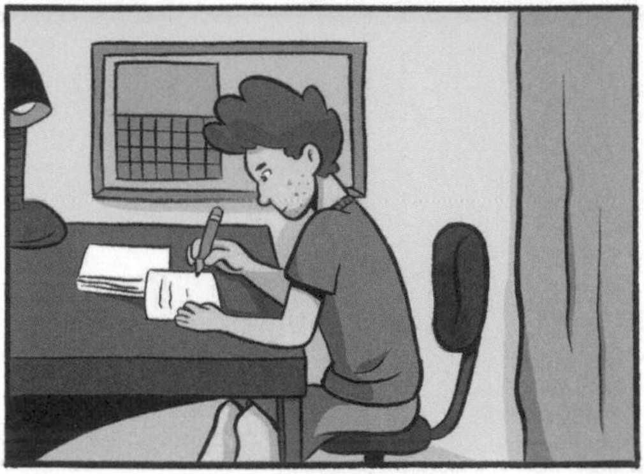

and a little face here...

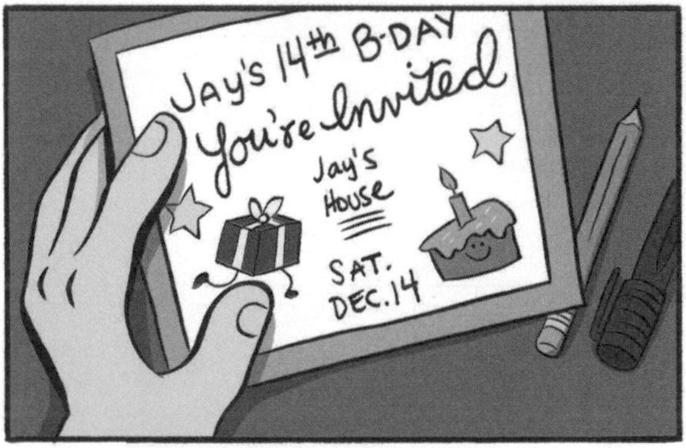
Jay's 14th B-DAY
You're Invited
Jay's HOUSE
SAT. DEC. 14

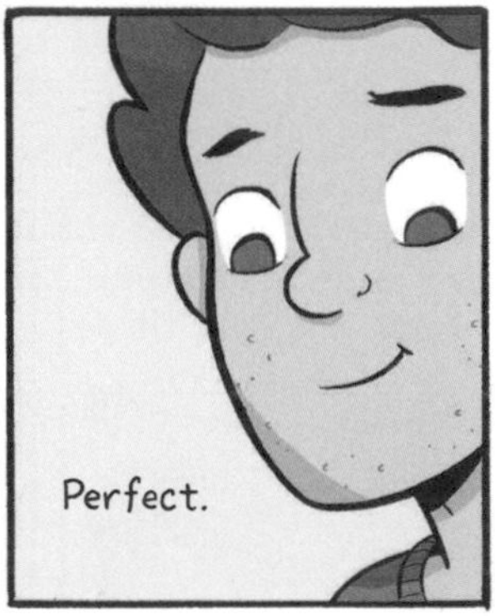
Perfect.

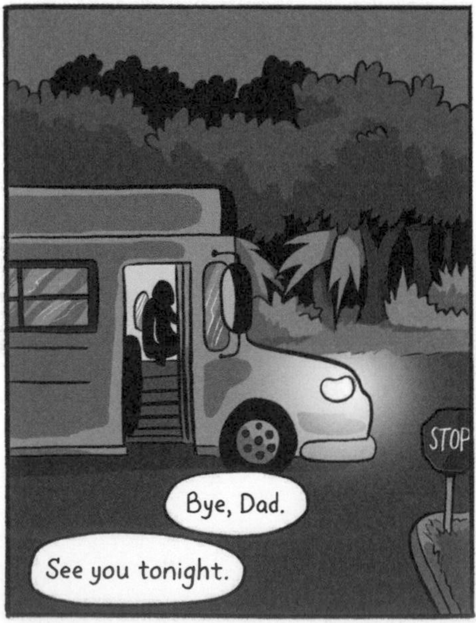
STOP
Bye, Dad.
See you tonight.

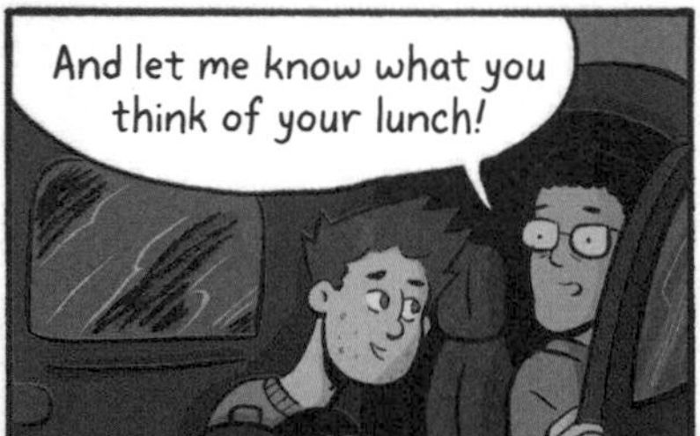
And let me know what you think of your lunch!

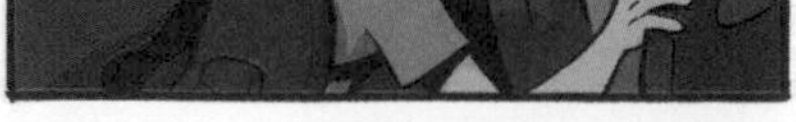
I will. Byyyye.

Guess what, Jay?

What?

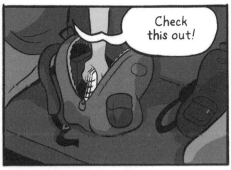

Check this out!

Riley made it after our practice.

Whoa.

Is that the band name?

Brace and I used to brainstorm band names together...

Last year.

It's kinda silly, Brace, but I like it!

Why didn't he ask me?

I would've drawn it for the band.

Yeah, it's rad!

I should've redrawn the cake. It's too dorky.

I'm having a party next weekend for my birthday.

Awesome! I'll be there.

Casey!

You gotta see this!

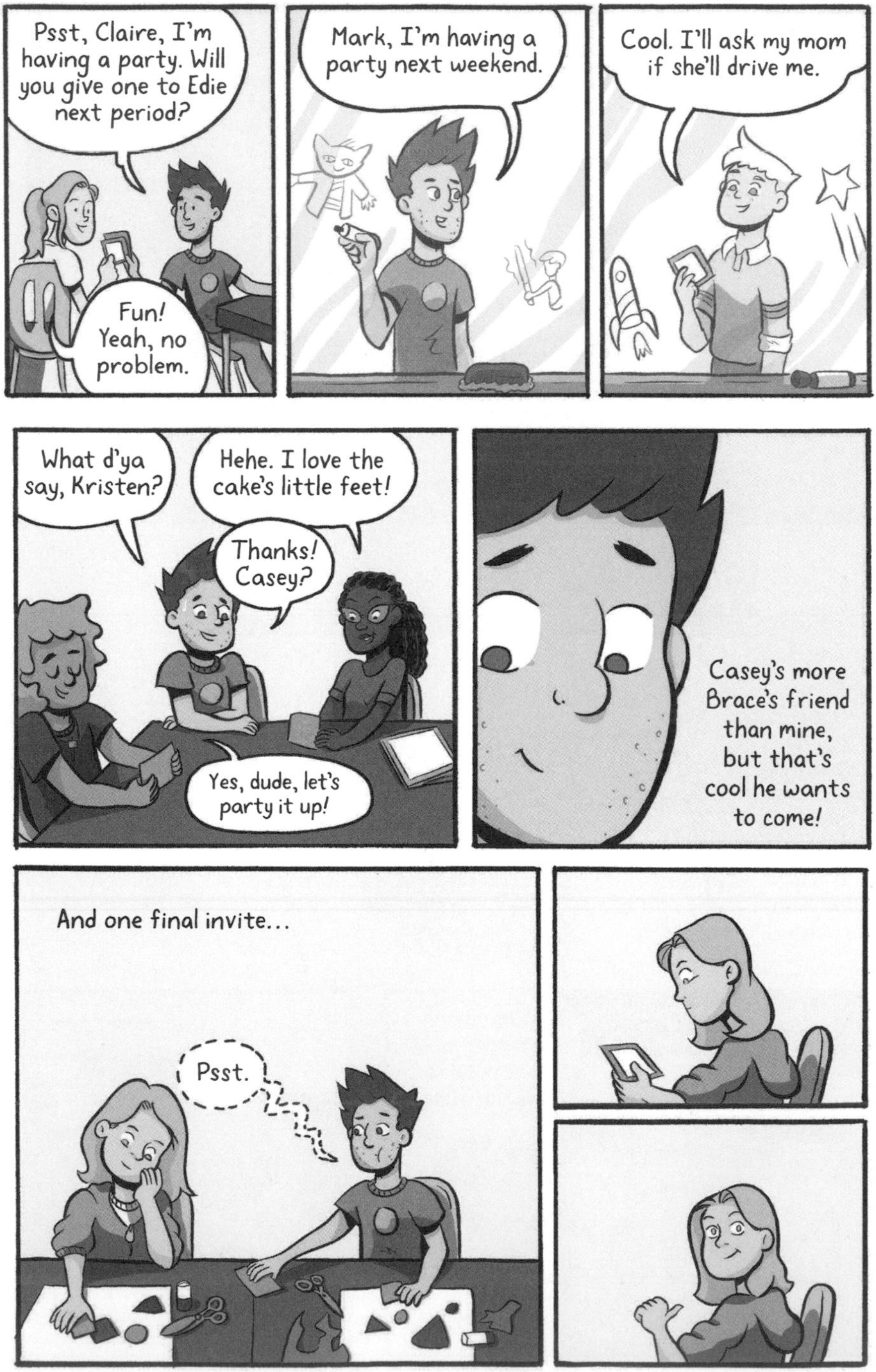
Psst, Claire, I'm having a party. Will you give one to Edie next period?
Fun! Yeah, no problem.
Mark, I'm having a party next weekend.
Cool. I'll ask my mom if she'll drive me.
What d'ya say, Kristen?
Hehe. I love the cake's little feet!
Thanks! Casey?
Yes, dude, let's party it up!
Casey's more Brace's friend than mine, but that's cool he wants to come!
And one final invite...
Psst.

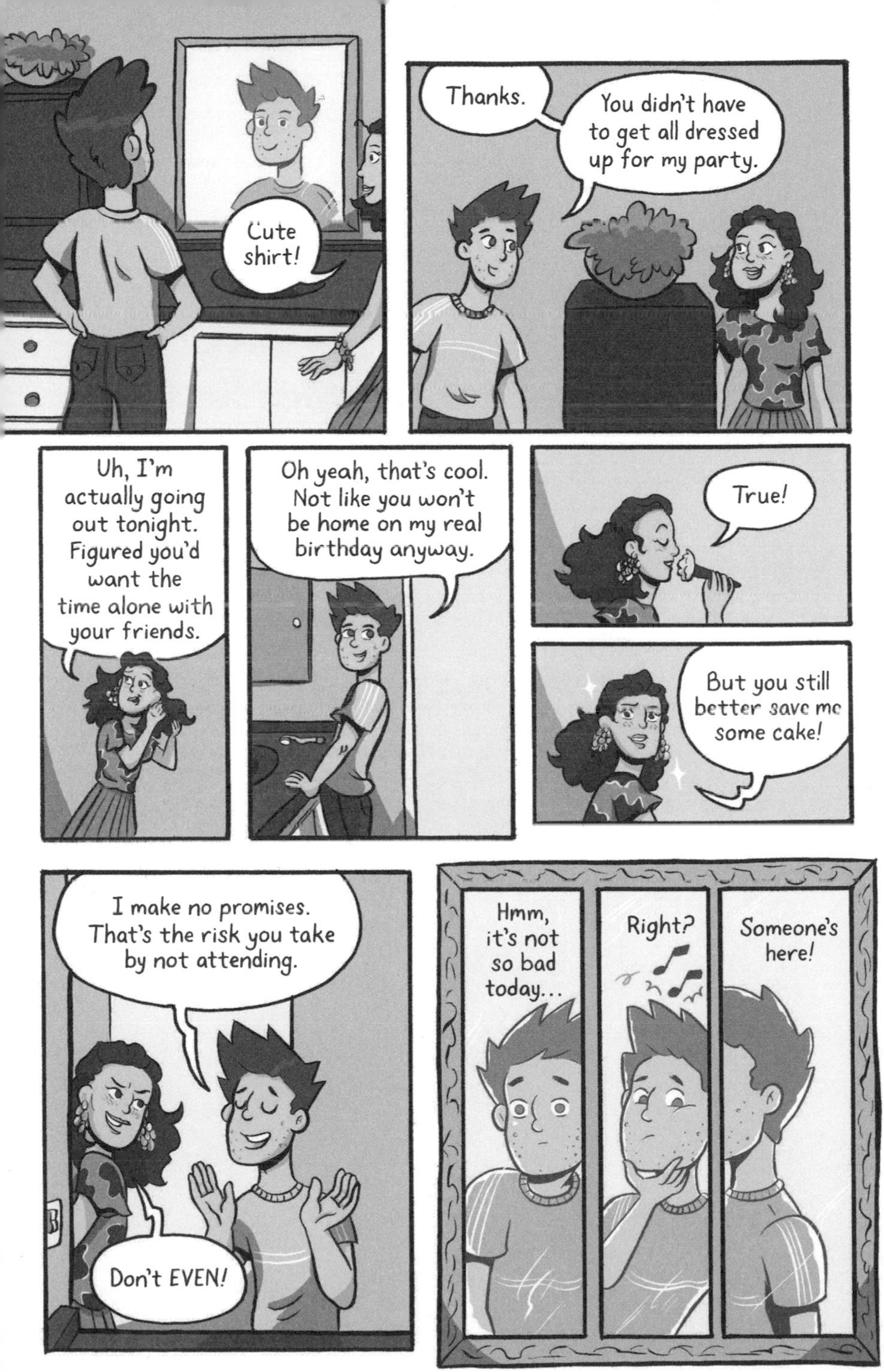
Cute shirt!
Thanks.
You didn't have to get all dressed up for my party.
Uh, I'm actually going out tonight. Figured you'd want the time alone with your friends.
Oh yeah, that's cool. Not like you won't be home on my real birthday anyway.
True!
But you still better save me some cake!
I make no promises. That's the risk you take by not attending.
Don't EVEN!
Hmm, it's not so bad today...
Right?
Someone's here!

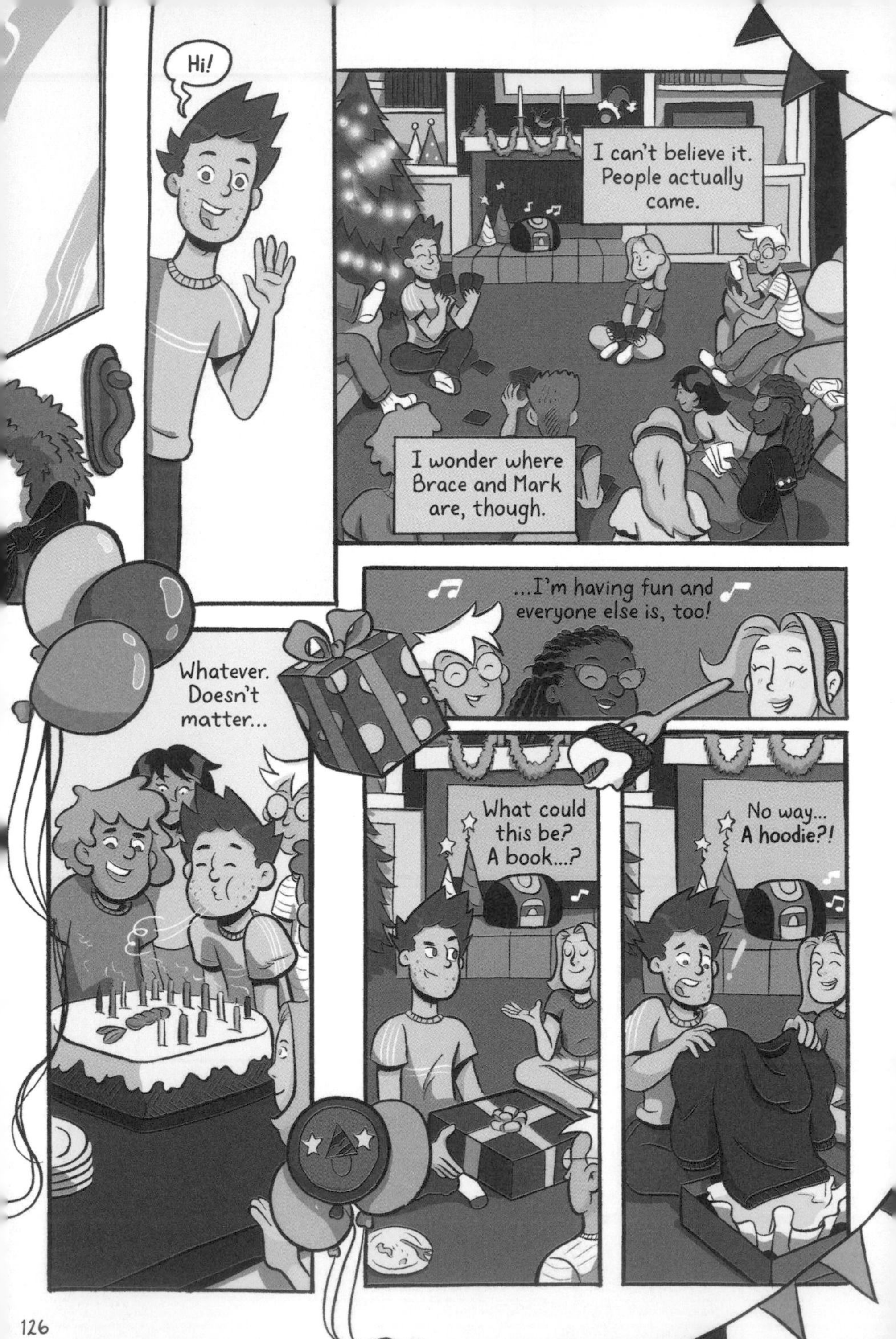
Hi!
I can't believe it. People actually came.
I wonder where Brace and Mark are, though.
...I'm having fun and everyone else is, too!
Whatever. Doesn't matter...
What could this be? A book...?
No way... A hoodie?!

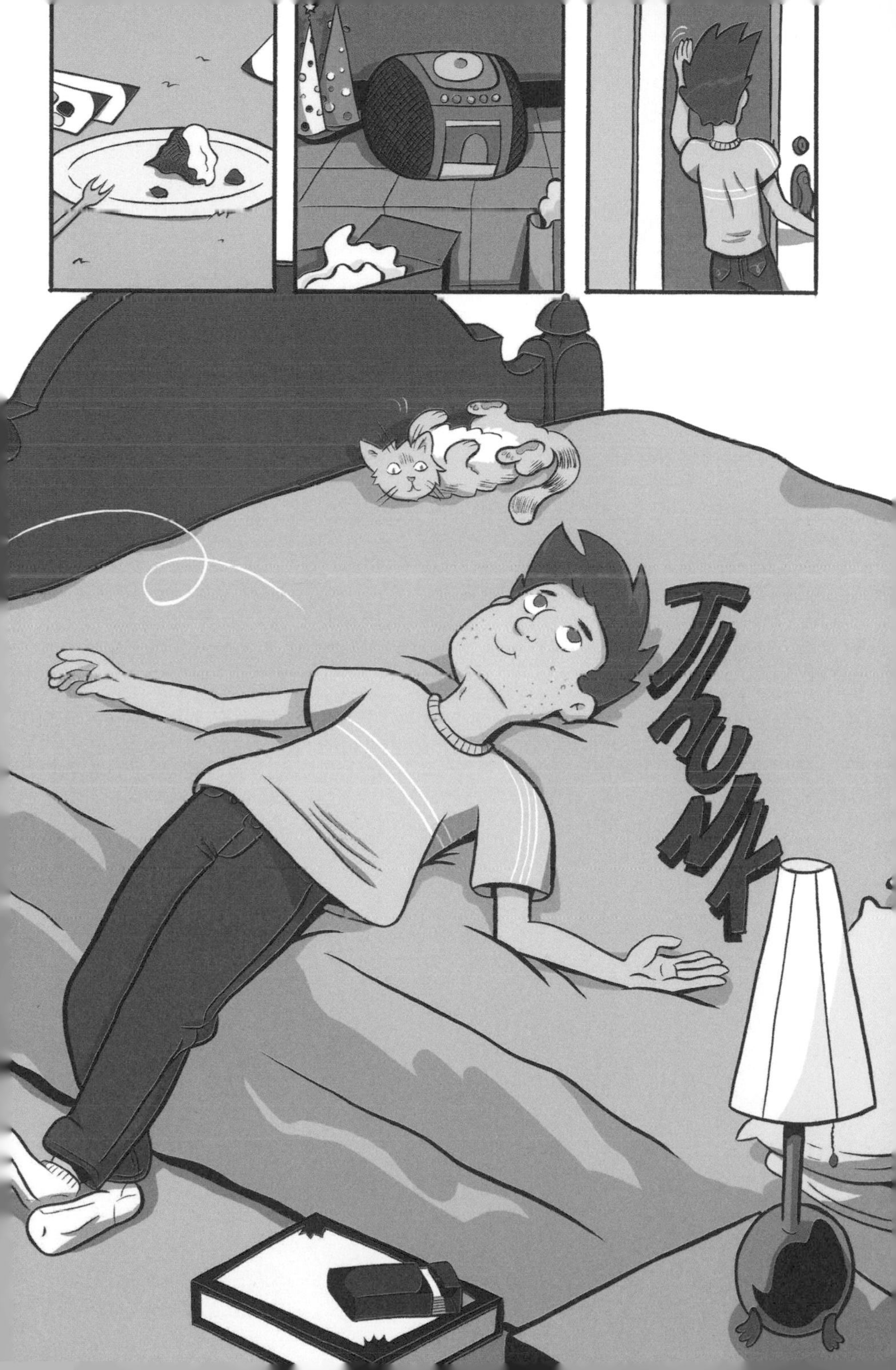
THUNK

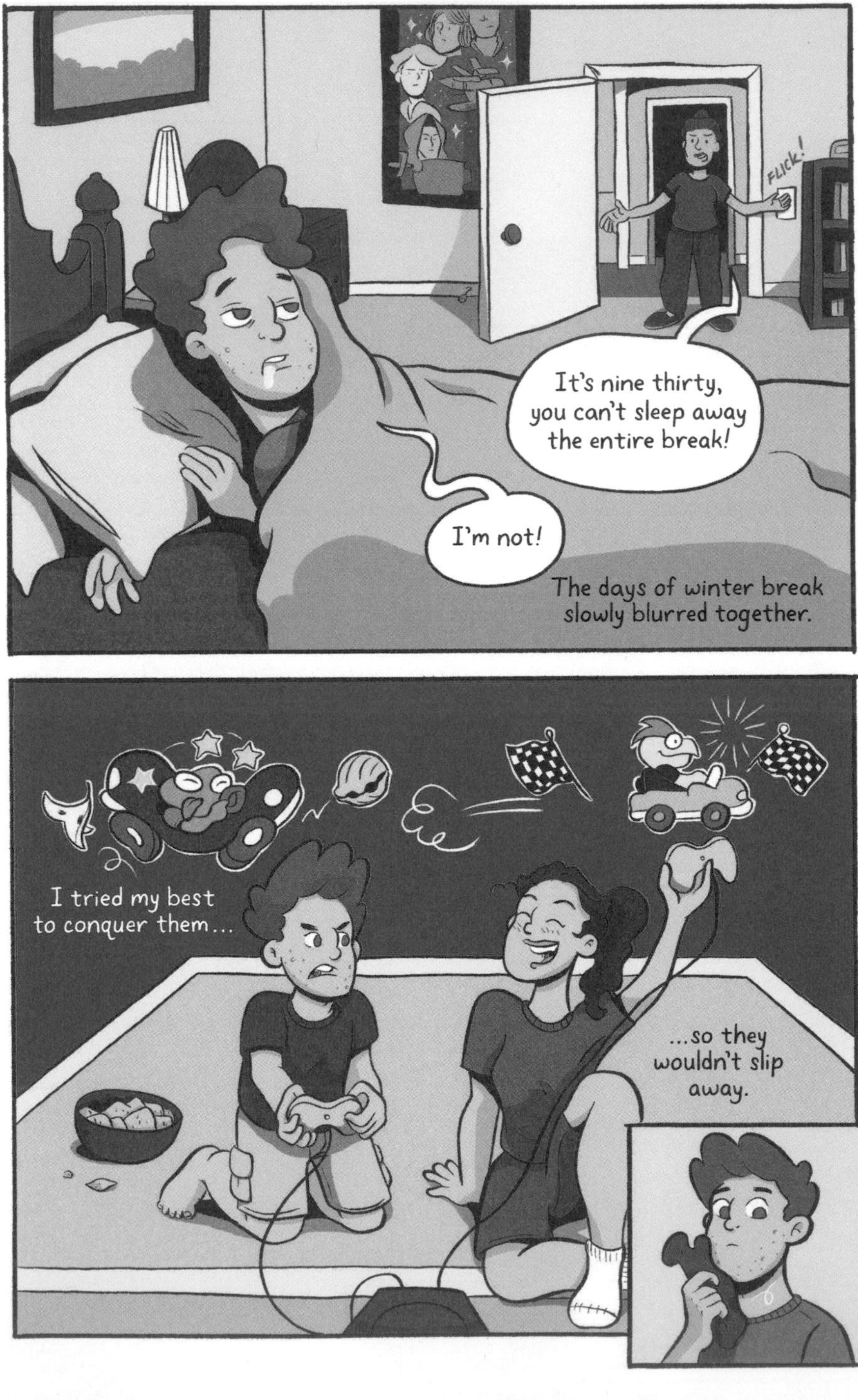
FLICK!
It's nine thirty, you can't sleep away the entire break!
I'm not!
The days of winter break slowly blurred together.
I tried my best to conquer them...
...so they wouldn't slip away.

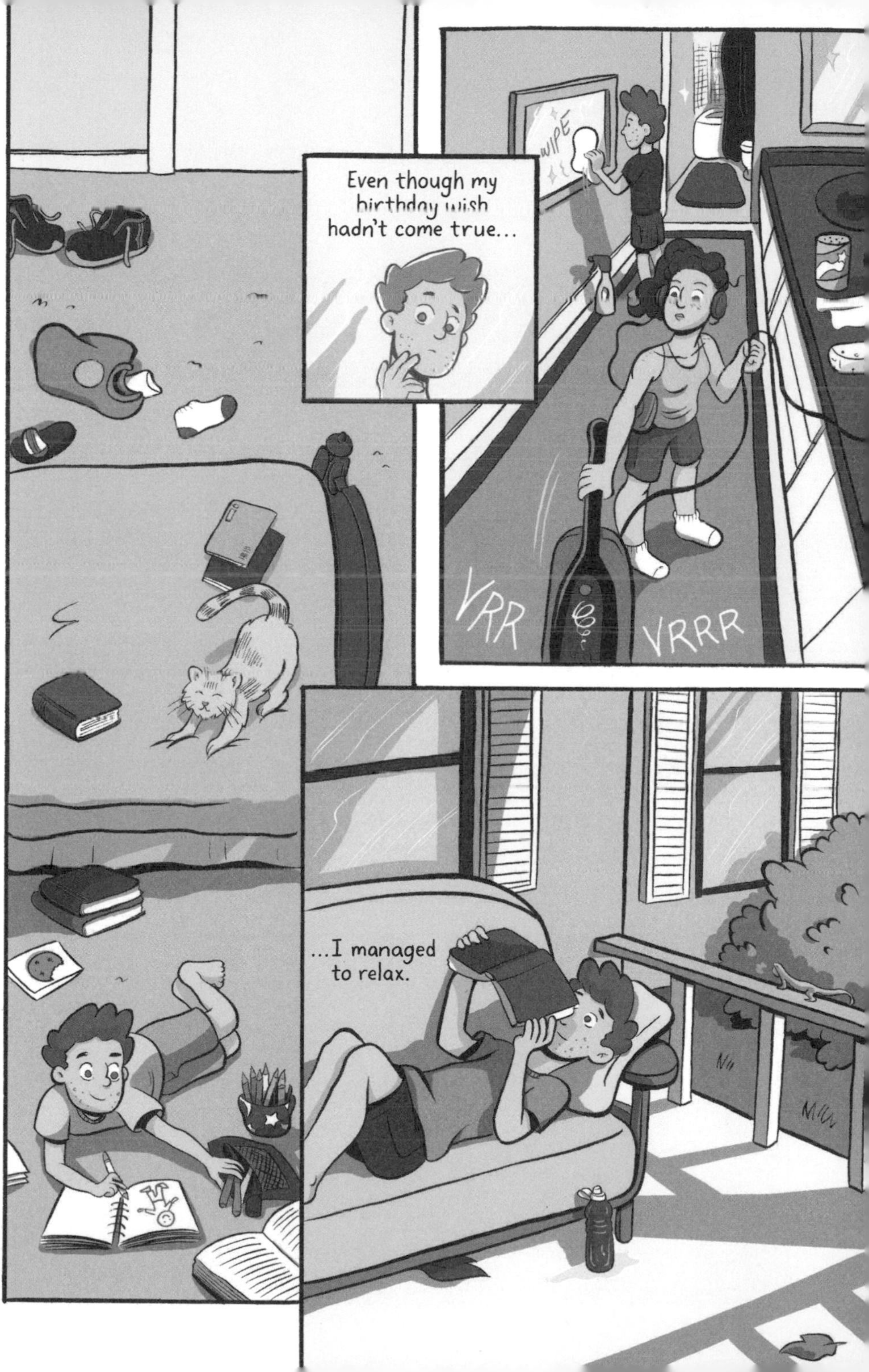

Even though my birthday wish hadn't come true...
WIPE
VRR
VRRR
...I managed to relax.

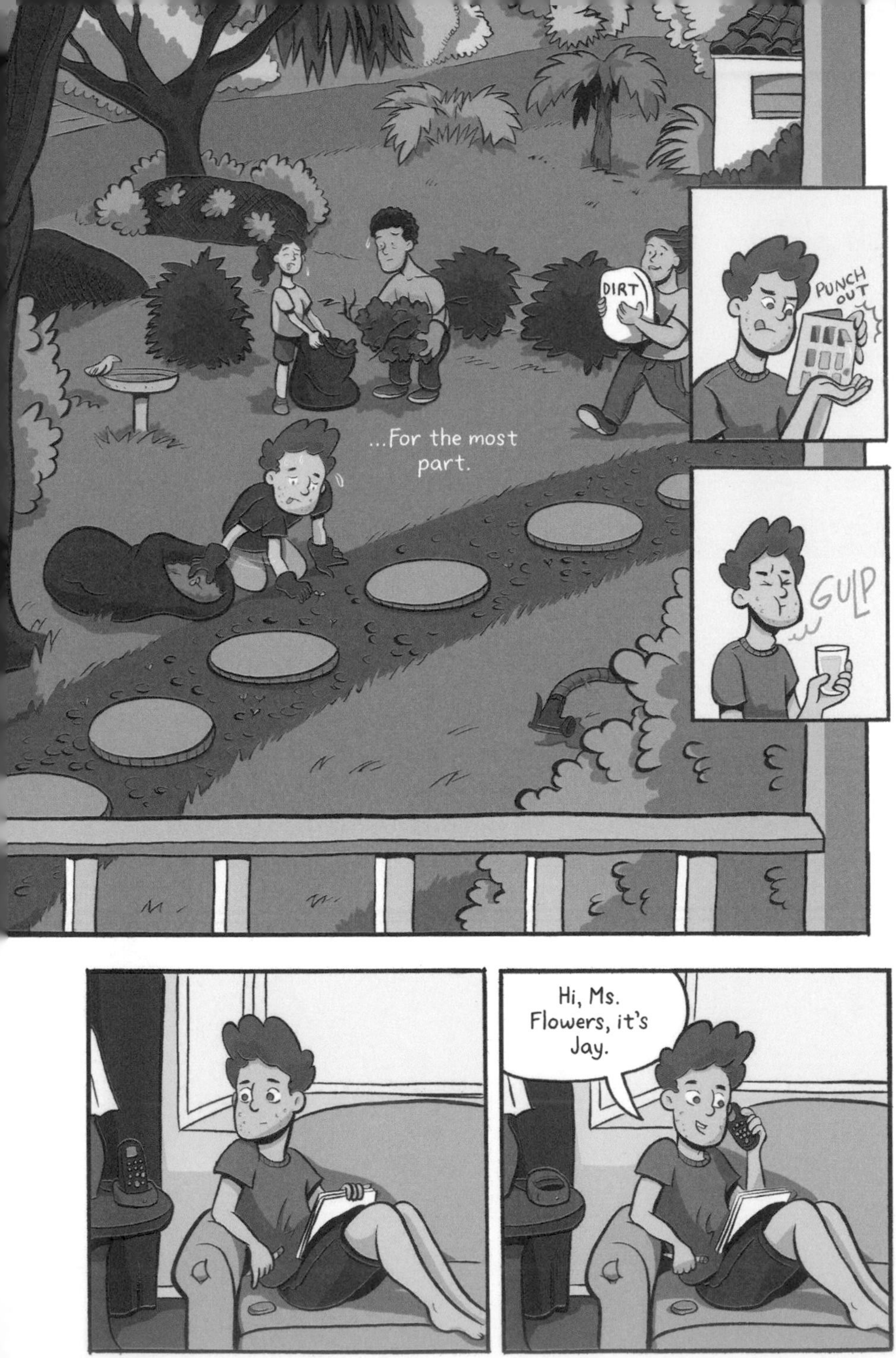
DIRT
...For the most part.
PUNCH OUT
GULP
Hi, Ms. Flowers, it's Jay.

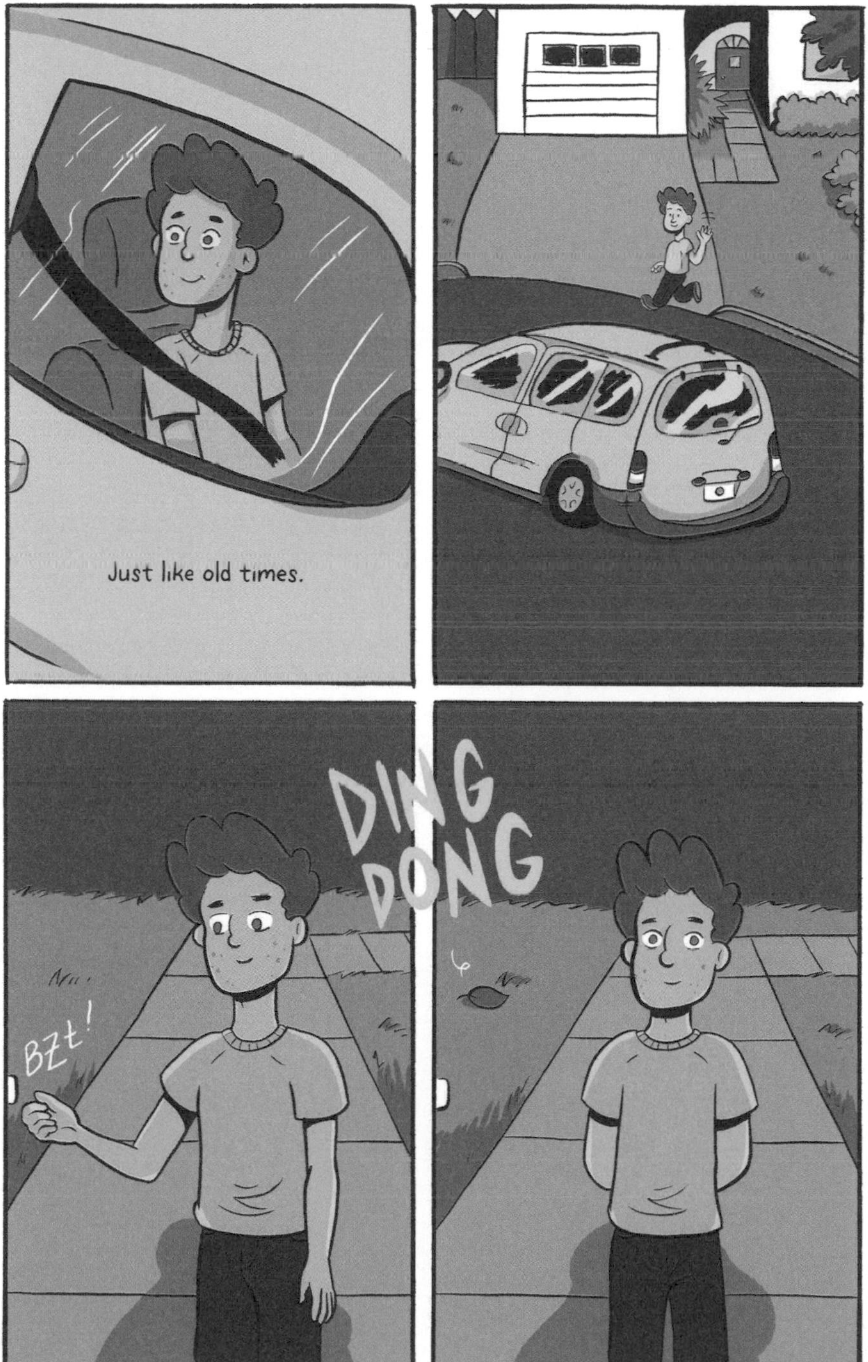
Just like old times.
BZt!
DING
DONG

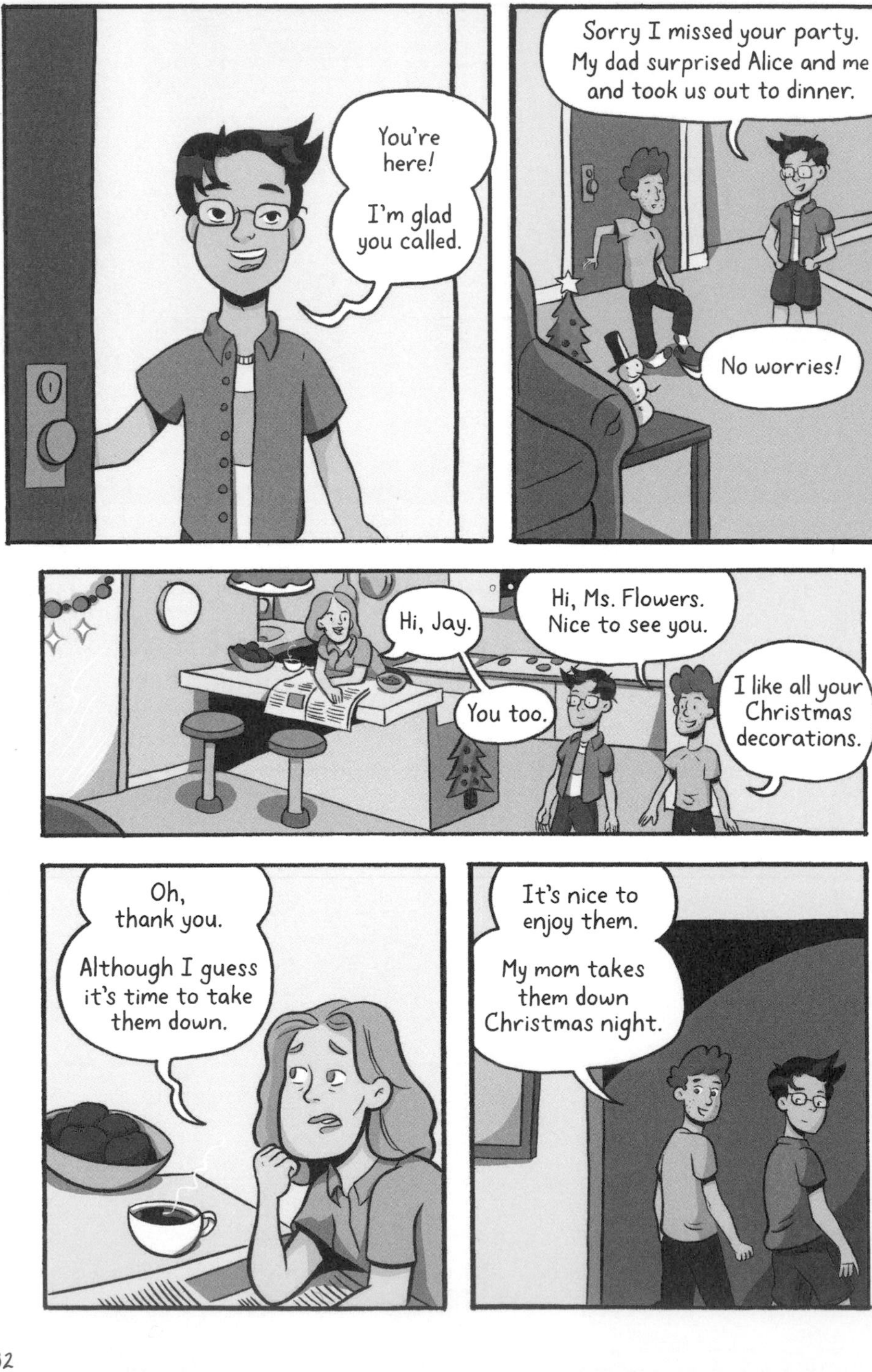
You're here!
I'm glad you called.
Sorry I missed your party. My dad surprised Alice and me and took us out to dinner.
No worries!
Hi, Ms. Flowers. Nice to see you.
Hi, Jay.
You too.
I like all your Christmas decorations.
Oh, thank you.
Although I guess it's time to take them down.
It's nice to enjoy them.
My mom takes them down Christmas night.

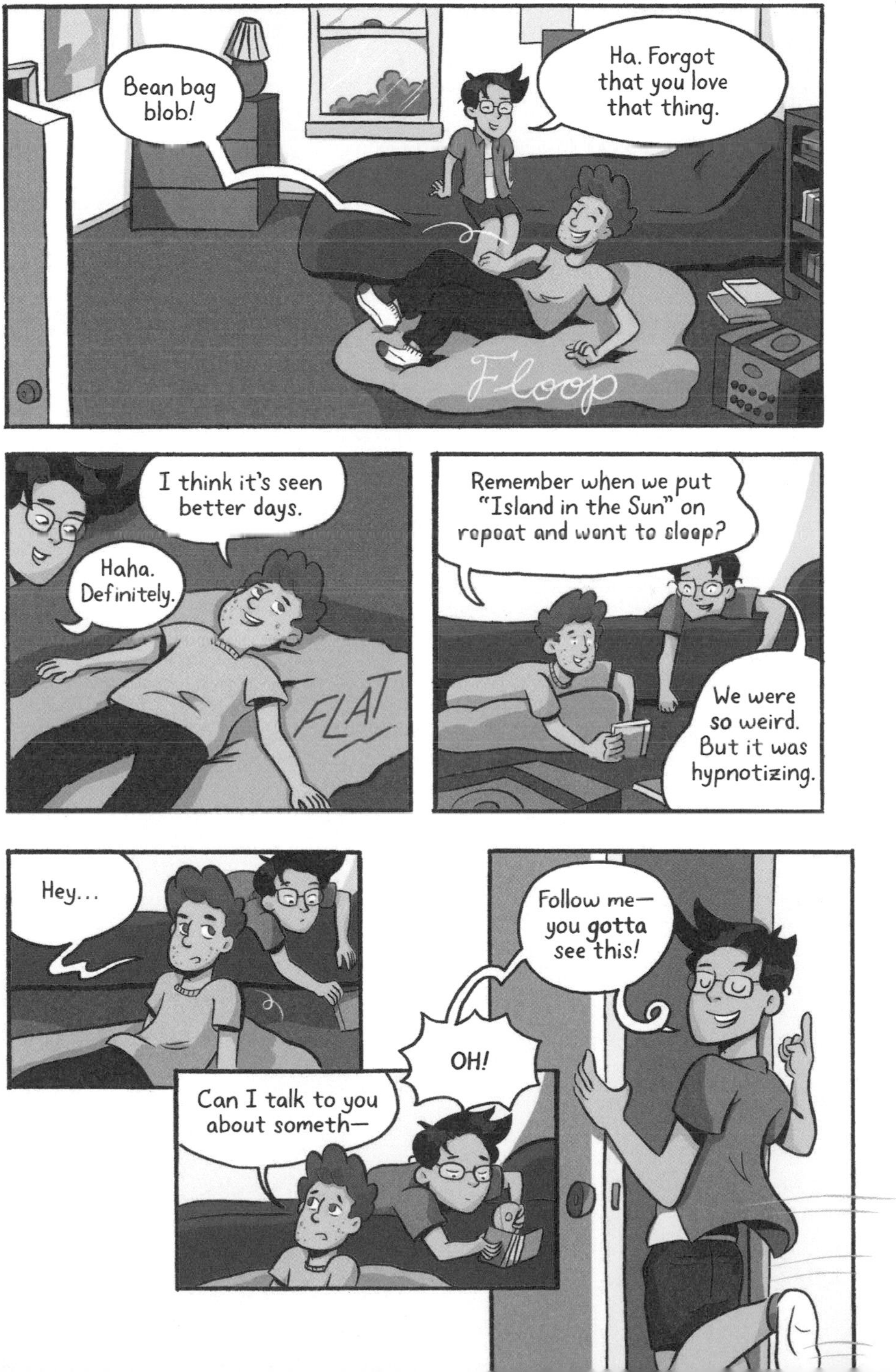
Bean bag blob!
Ha. Forgot that you love that thing.
Floop
I think it's seen better days.
Haha. Definitely.
FLAT
Remember when we put "Island in the Sun" on repeat and went to sleep?
We were so weird. But it was hypnotizing.
Hey...
Can I talk to you about someth—
OH!
Follow me—you **gotta** see this!

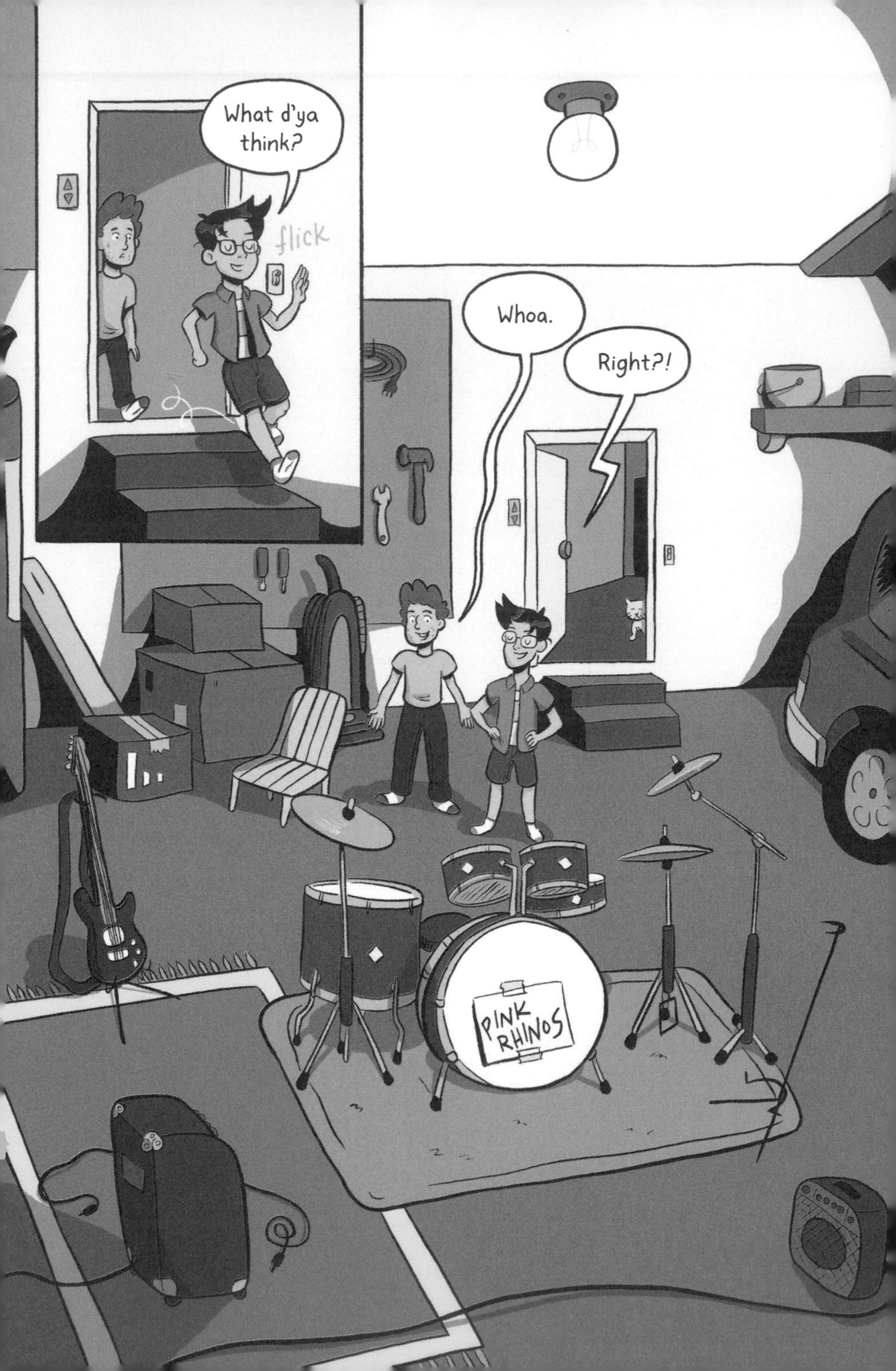
What d'ya think?
flick
Whoa.
Right?!
PINK RHINOS

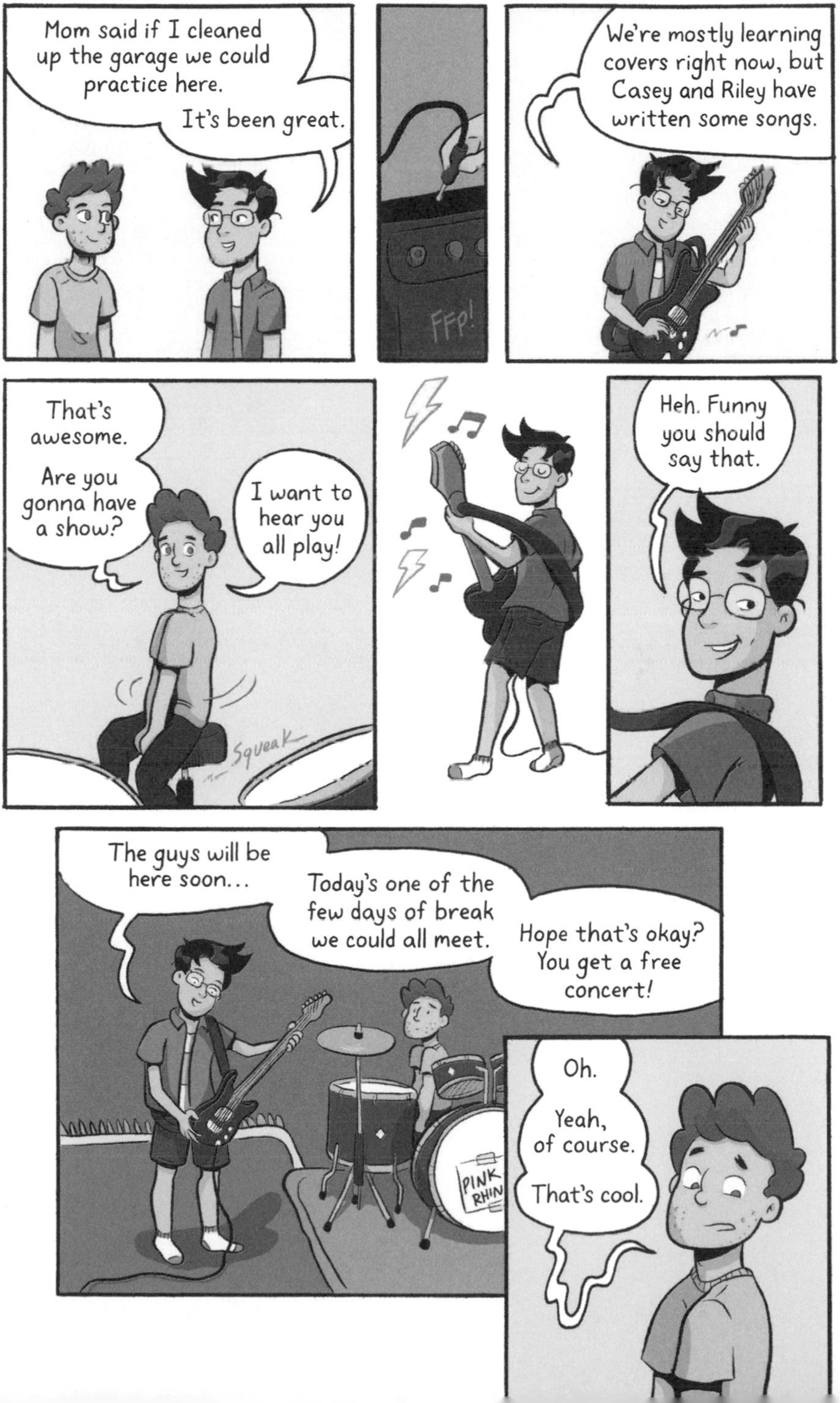
Mom said if I cleaned up the garage we could practice here.
It's been great.
FFP!
We're mostly learning covers right now, but Casey and Riley have written some songs.
That's awesome.
Are you gonna have a show?
I want to hear you all play!
Squeak
Heh. Funny you should say that.
The guys will be here soon...
Today's one of the few days of break we could all meet.
Hope that's okay? You get a free concert!
PINK RHIN
Oh.
Yeah, of course.
That's cool.

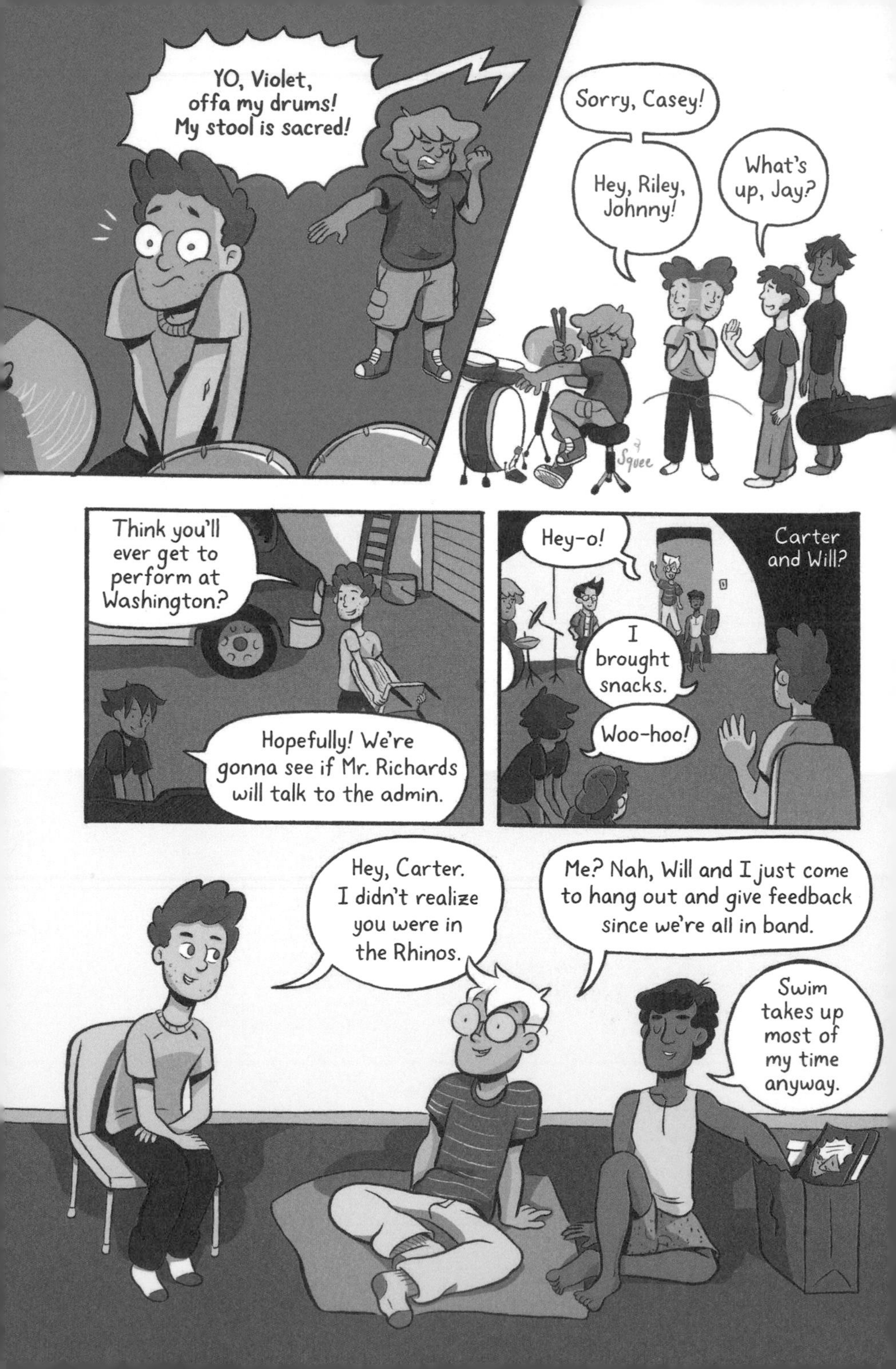
YO, Violet, offa my drums! My stool is sacred!
Sorry, Casey!
Hey, Riley, Johnny!
What's up, Jay?
Squee
Think you'll ever get to perform at Washington?
Hopefully! We're gonna see if Mr. Richards will talk to the admin.
Hey-o!
Carter and Will?
I brought snacks.
Woo-hoo!
Hey, Carter. I didn't realize you were in the Rhinos.
Me? Nah, Will and I just come to hang out and give feedback since we're all in band.
Swim takes up most of my time anyway.

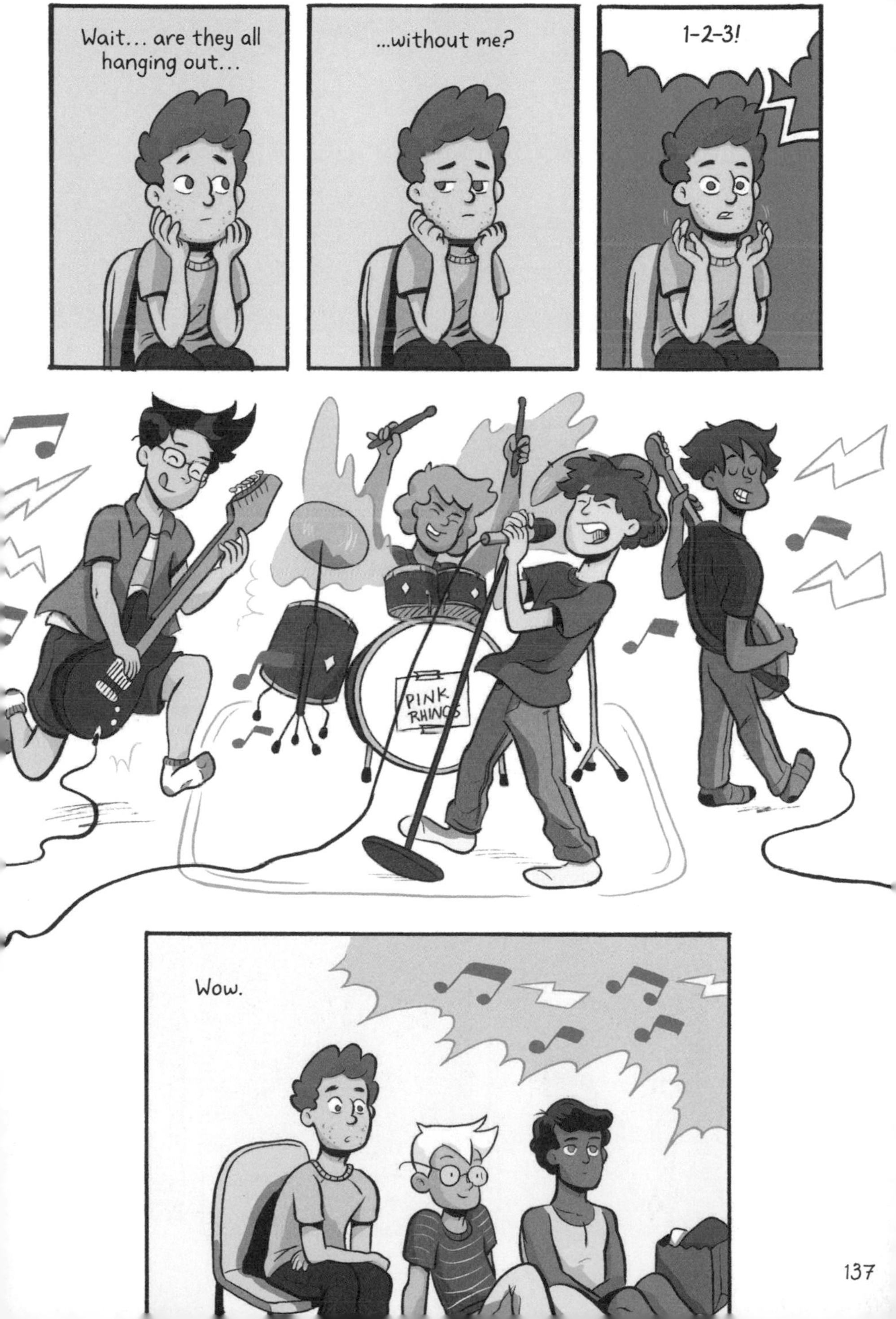
Wait... are they all hanging out...
...without me?
1-2-3!
PINK RHINOS
Wow.

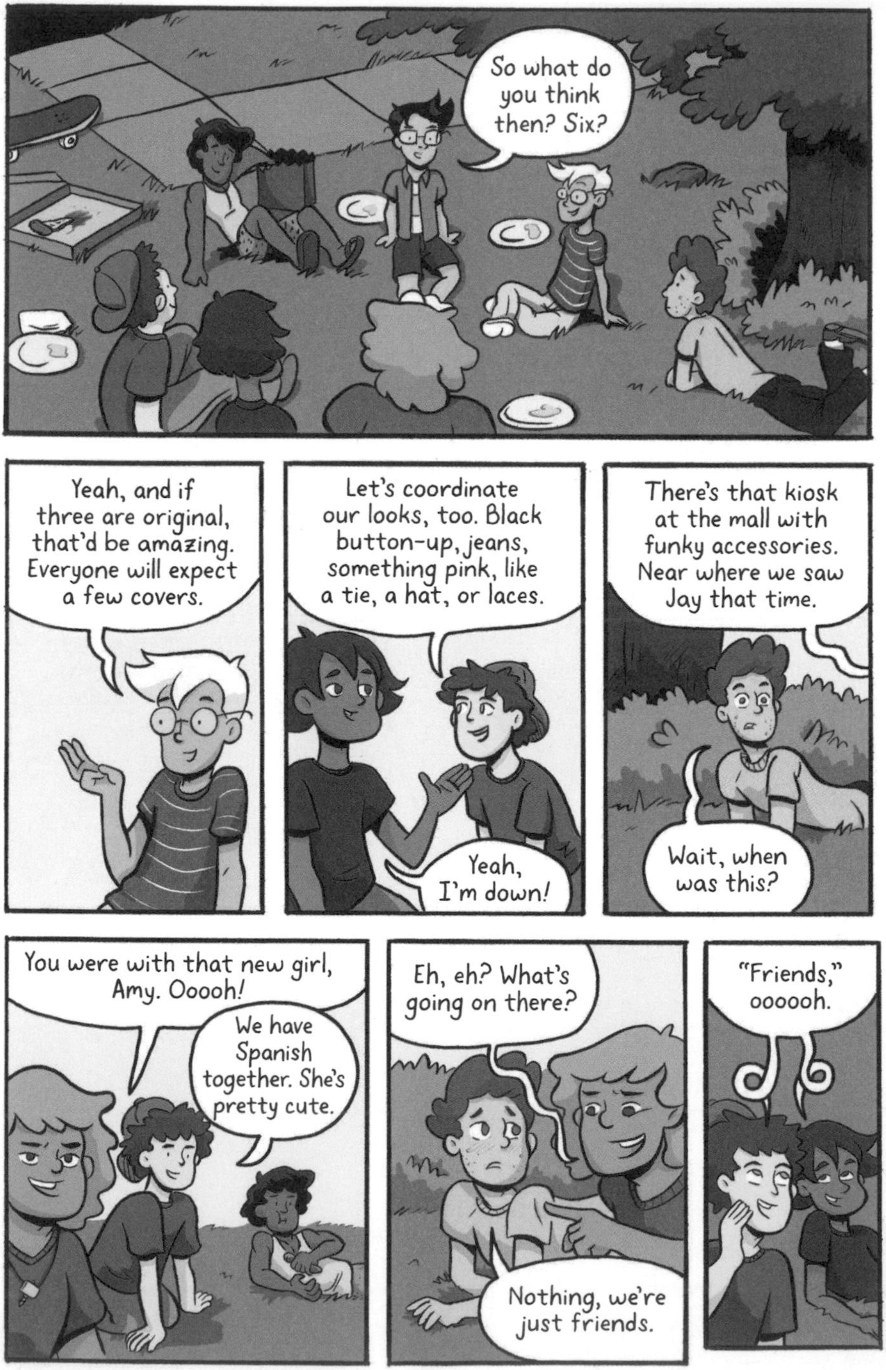
So what do you think then? Six?
Yeah, and if three are original, that'd be amazing. Everyone will expect a few covers.
Let's coordinate our looks, too. Black button-up, jeans, something pink, like a tie, a hat, or laces.
Yeah, I'm down!
There's that kiosk at the mall with funky accessories. Near where we saw Jay that time.
Wait, when was this?
You were with that new girl, Amy. Ooooh!
We have Spanish together. She's pretty cute.
Eh, eh? What's going on there?
Nothing, we're just friends.
"Friends," oooooh.

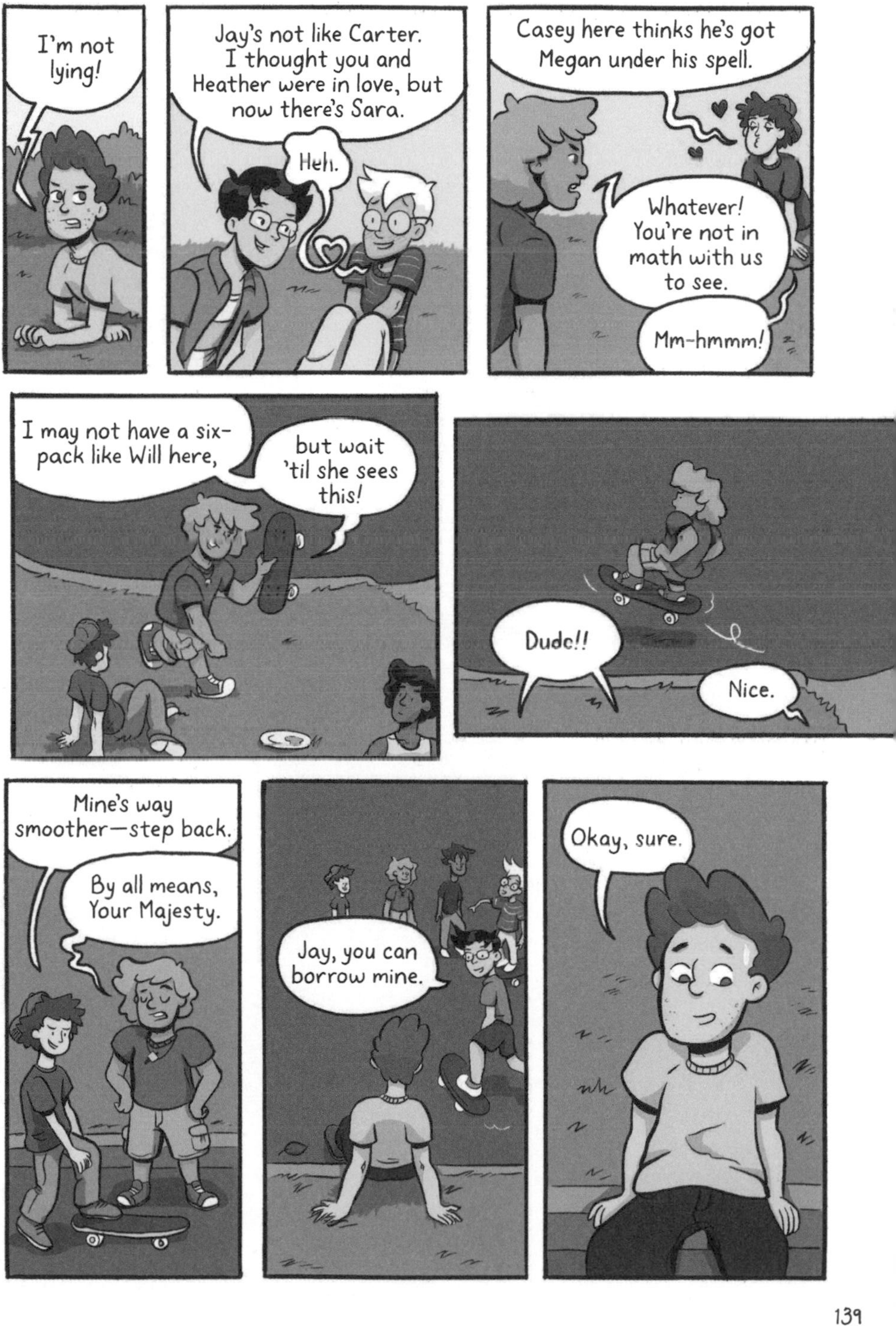
I'm not lying!
Jay's not like Carter. I thought you and Heather were in love, but now there's Sara.
Heh.
Casey here thinks he's got Megan under his spell.
Whatever! You're not in math with us to see.
Mm-hmmm!
I may not have a six-pack like Will here,
but wait 'til she sees this!
Dude!!
Nice.
Mine's way smoother—step back.
By all means, Your Majesty.
Jay, you can borrow mine.
Okay, sure.

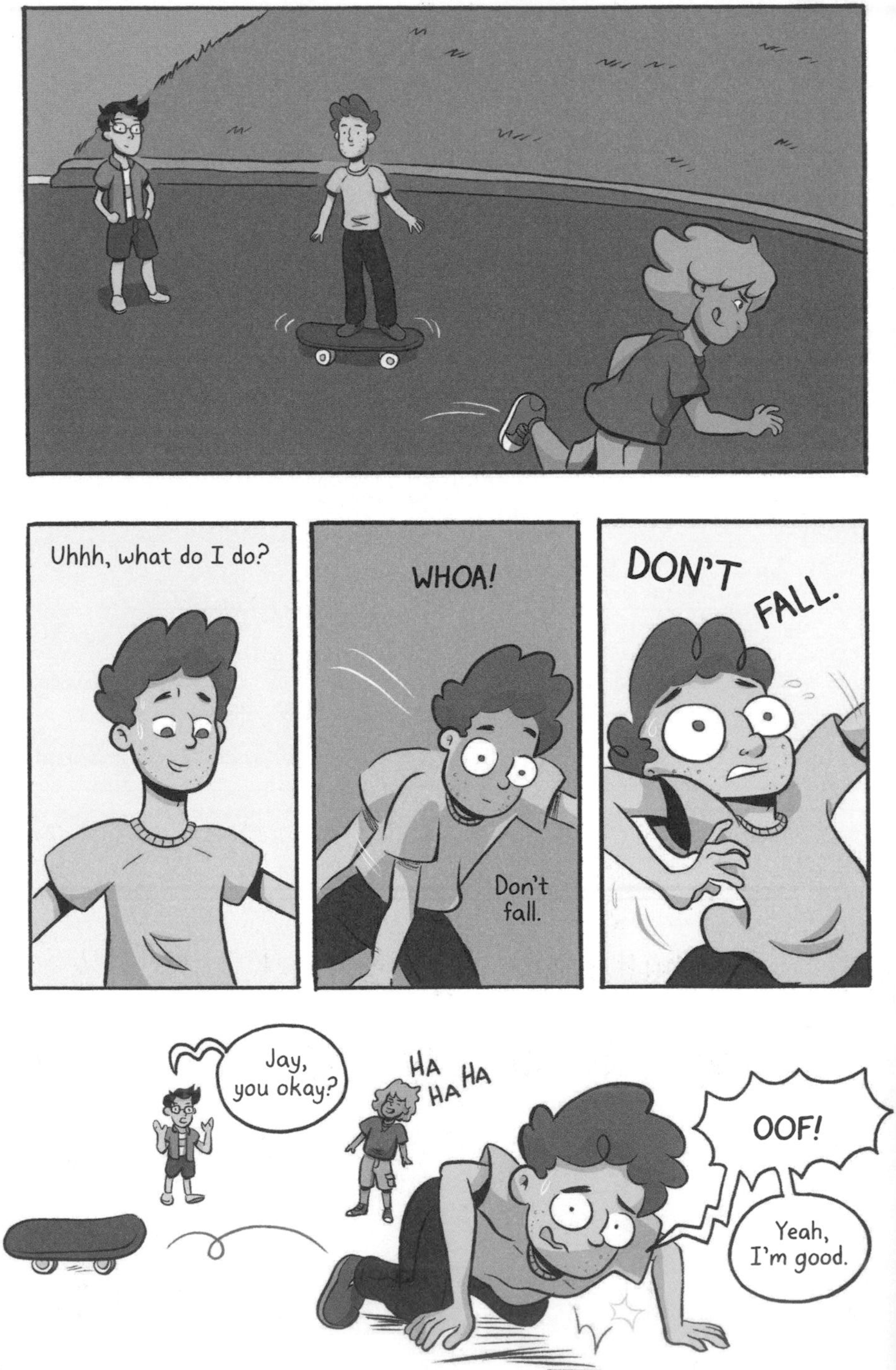
Uhhh, what do I do?
WHOA!
Don't fall.
DON'T FALL.
Jay, you okay?
HA HA HA
OOF!
Yeah, I'm good.

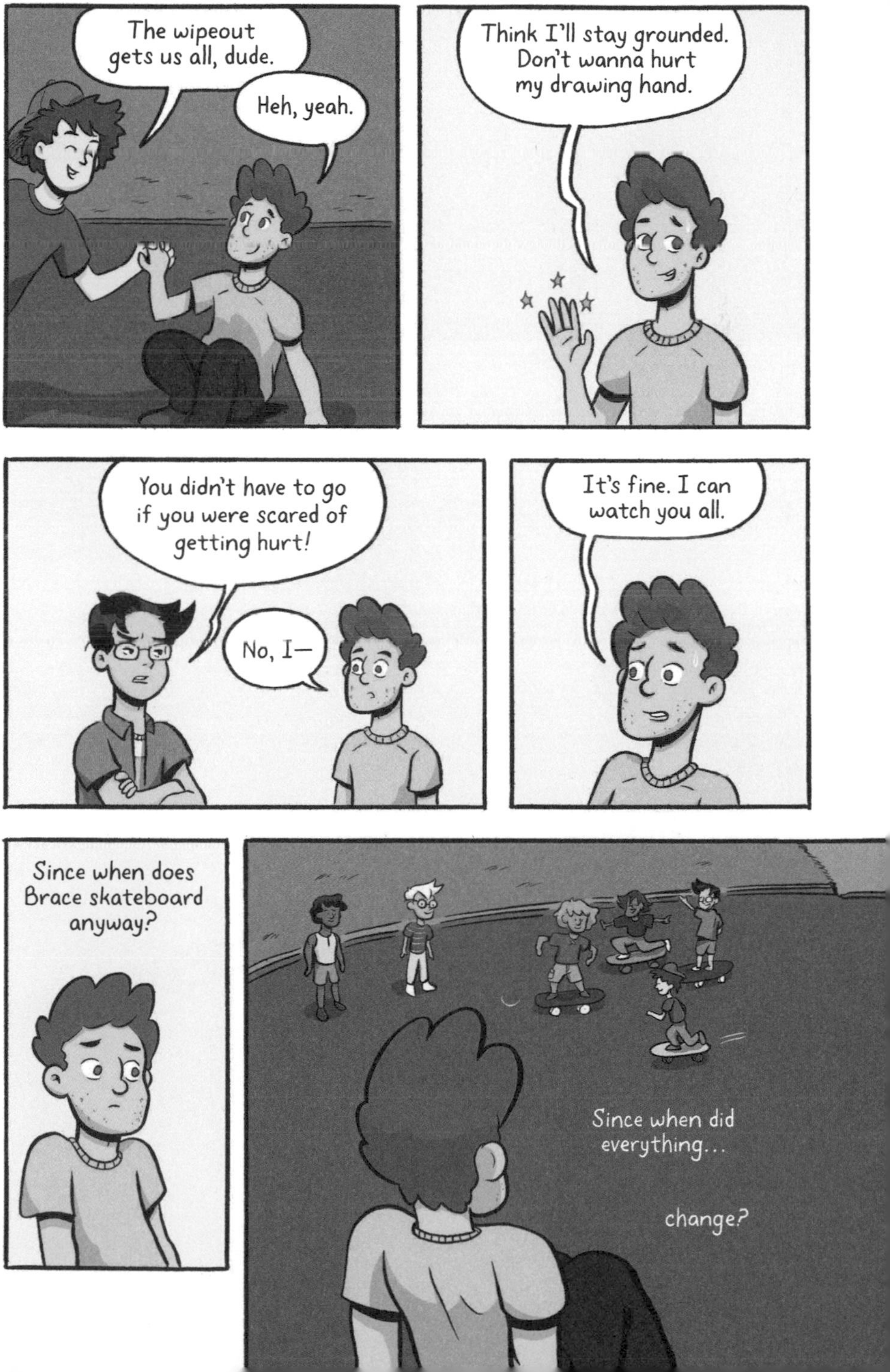
The wipeout gets us all, dude.
Heh, yeah.
Think I'll stay grounded. Don't wanna hurt my drawing hand.
You didn't have to go if you were scared of getting hurt!
No, I—
It's fine. I can watch you all.
Since when does Brace skateboard anyway?
Since when did everything…
change?

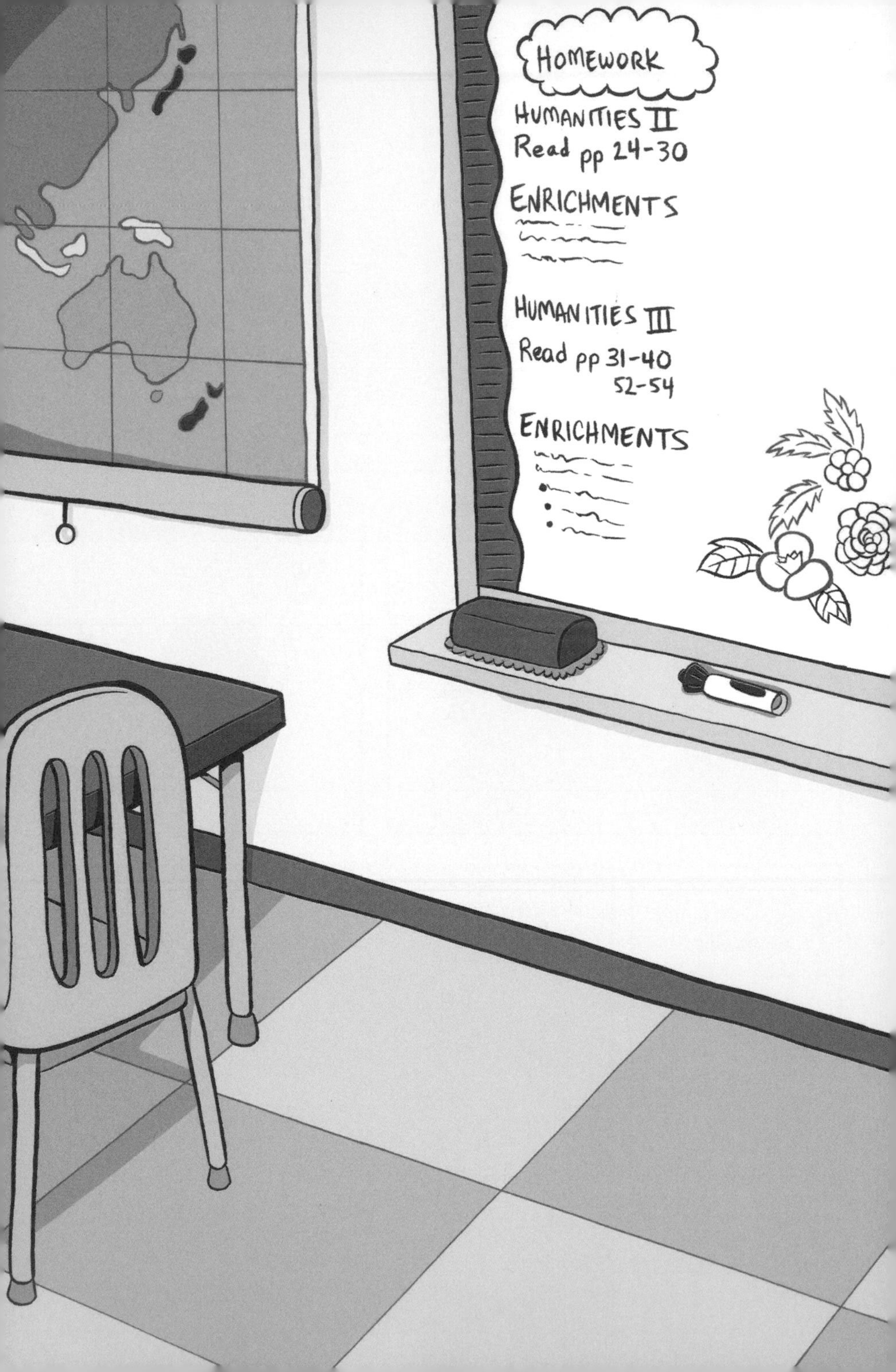
HOMEWORK
HUMANITIES II
Read pp 24-30
ENRICHMENTS
HUMANITIES III
Read pp 31-40
52-54
ENRICHMENTS

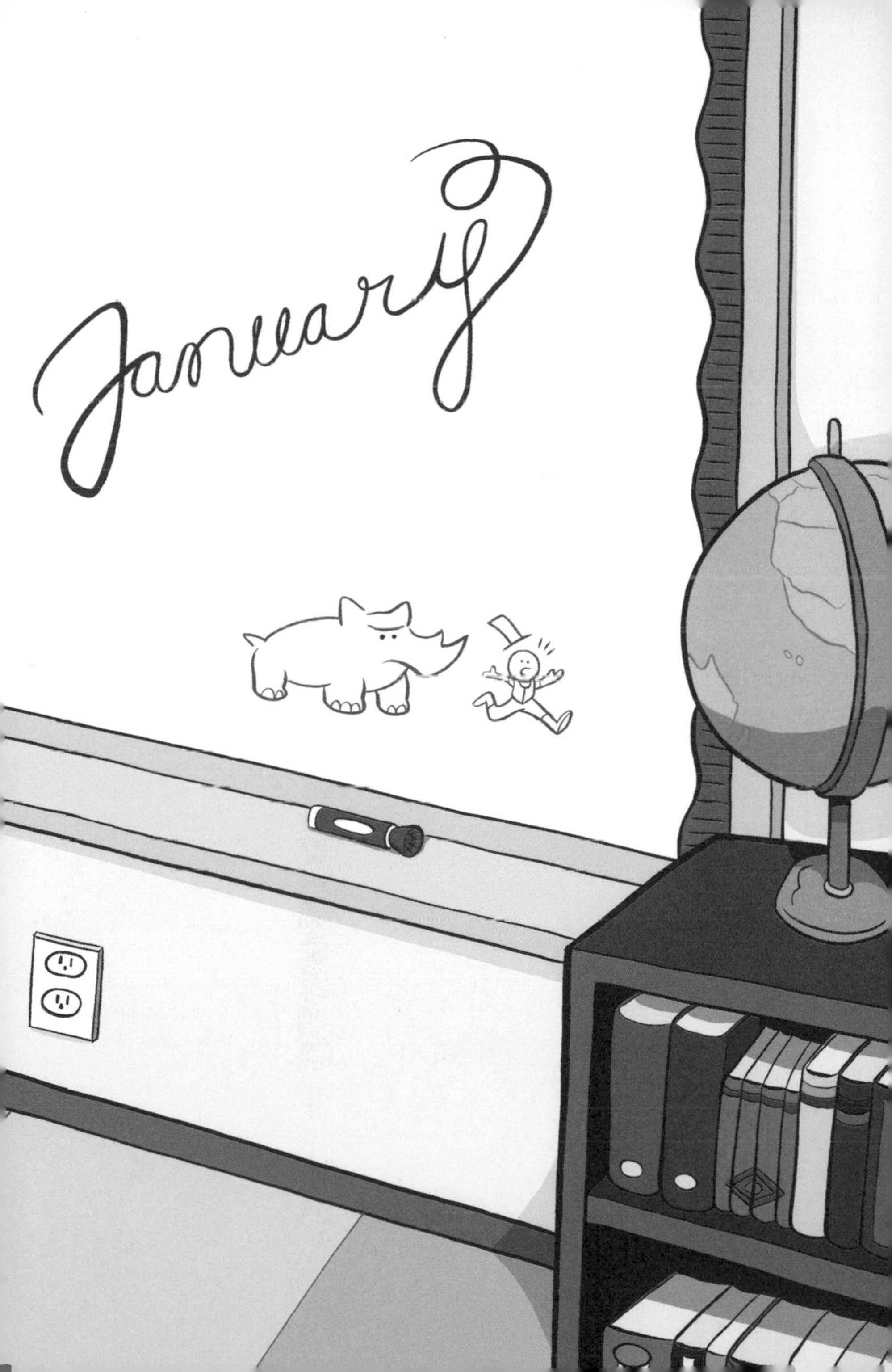
January

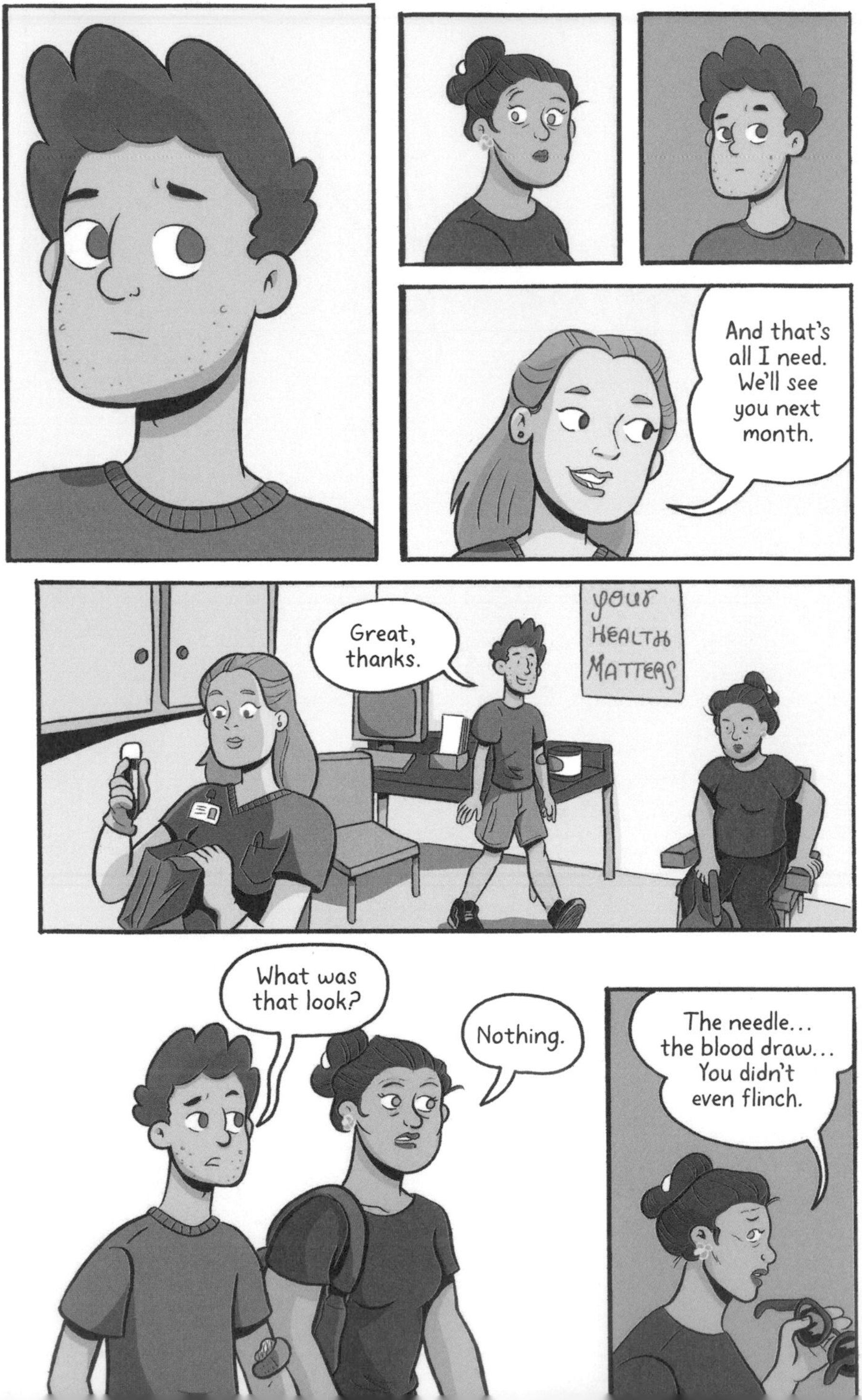
And that's all I need. We'll see you next month.
Great, thanks.
your HEALTH MATTERS
What was that look?
Nothing.
The needle... the blood draw... You didn't even flinch.

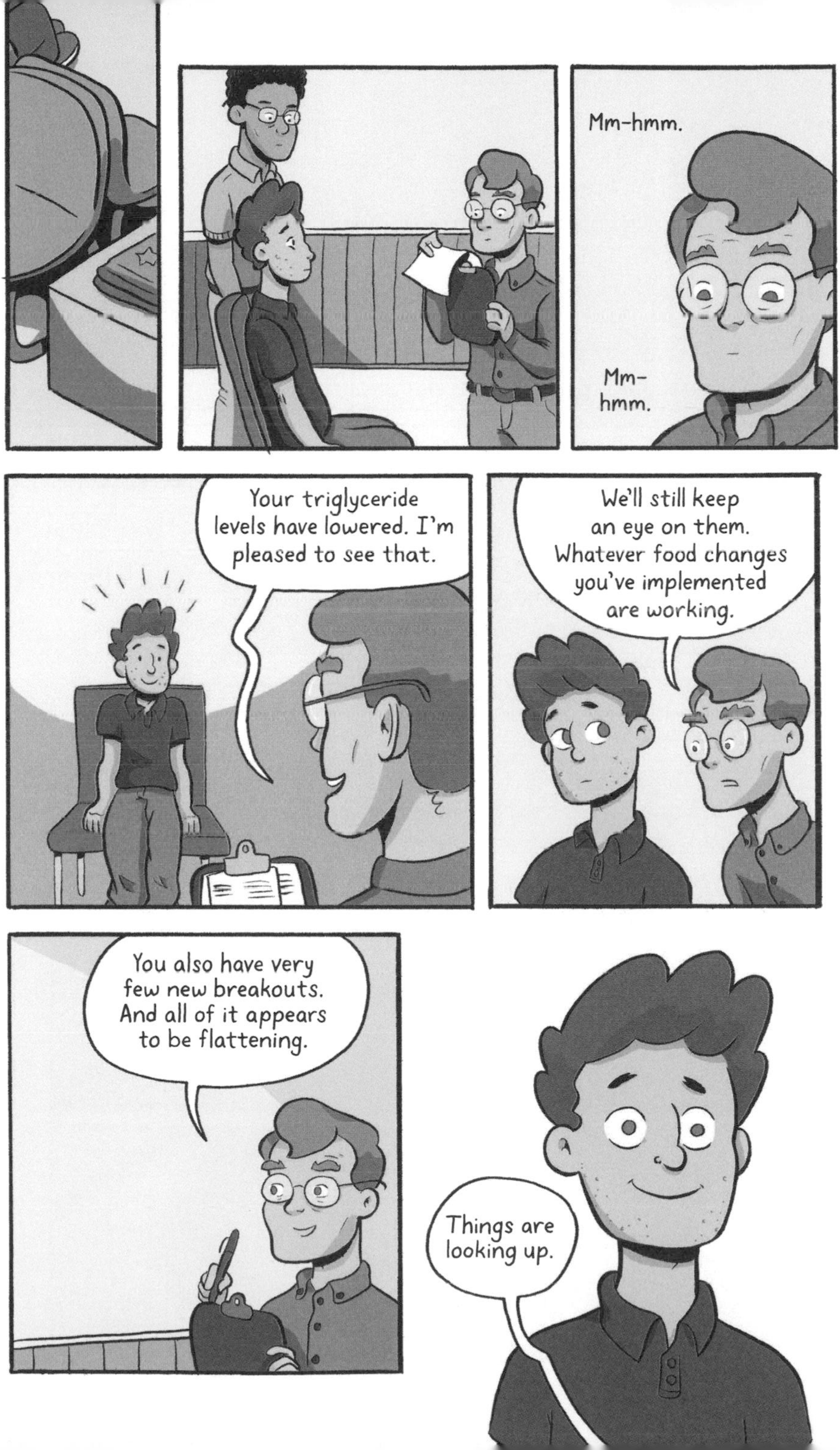
Mm-hmm.
Mm-hmm.
Your triglyceride levels have lowered. I'm pleased to see that.
We'll still keep an eye on them. Whatever food changes you've implemented are working.
You also have very few new breakouts. And all of it appears to be flattening.
Things are looking up.

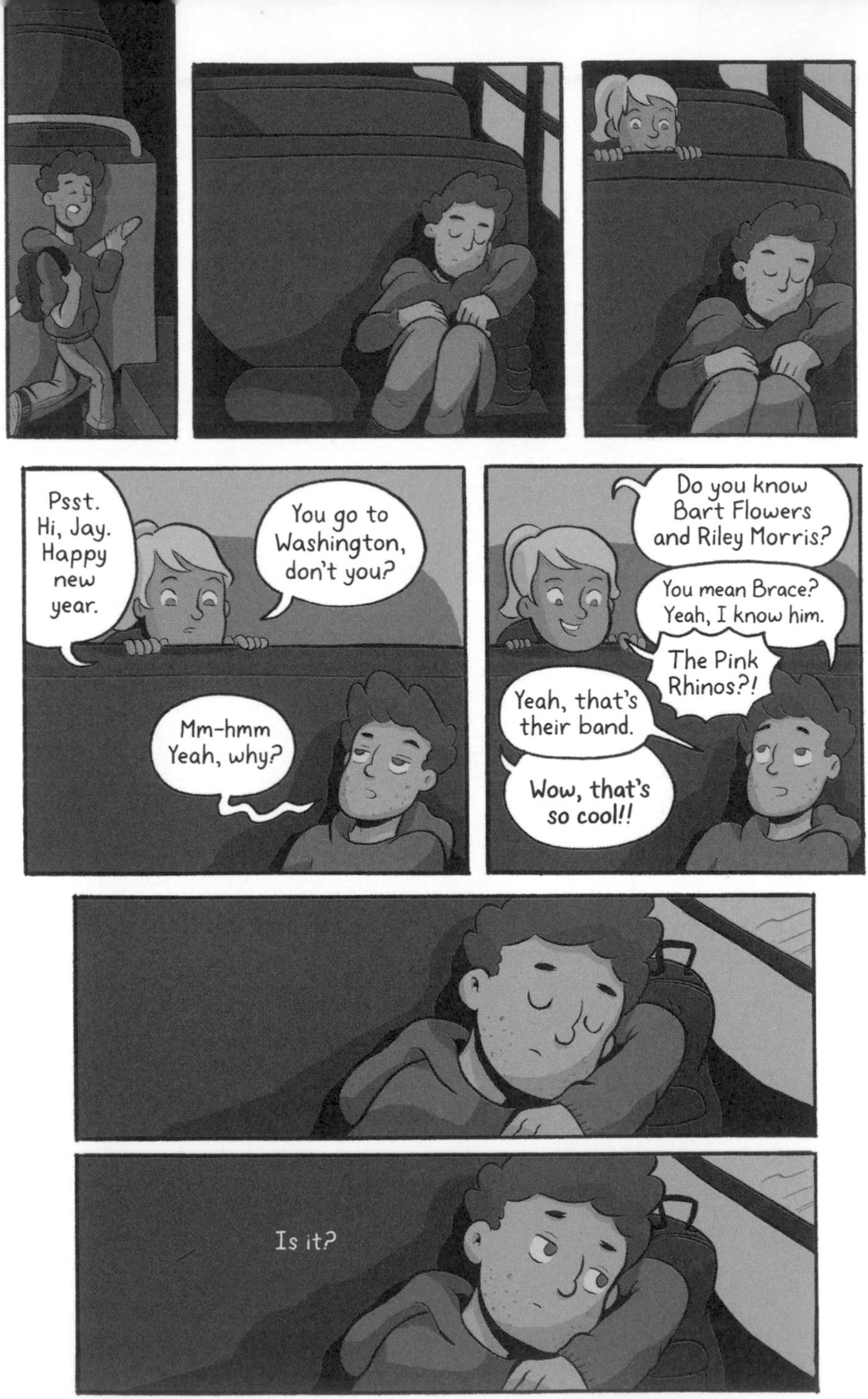
Psst.
Hi, Jay.
Happy
new
year.
You go to
Washington,
don't you?
Mm-hmm
Yeah, why?
Do you know
Bart Flowers
and Riley Morris?
You mean Brace?
Yeah, I know him.
The Pink
Rhinos?!
Yeah, that's
their band.
Wow, that's
so cool!!
Is it?

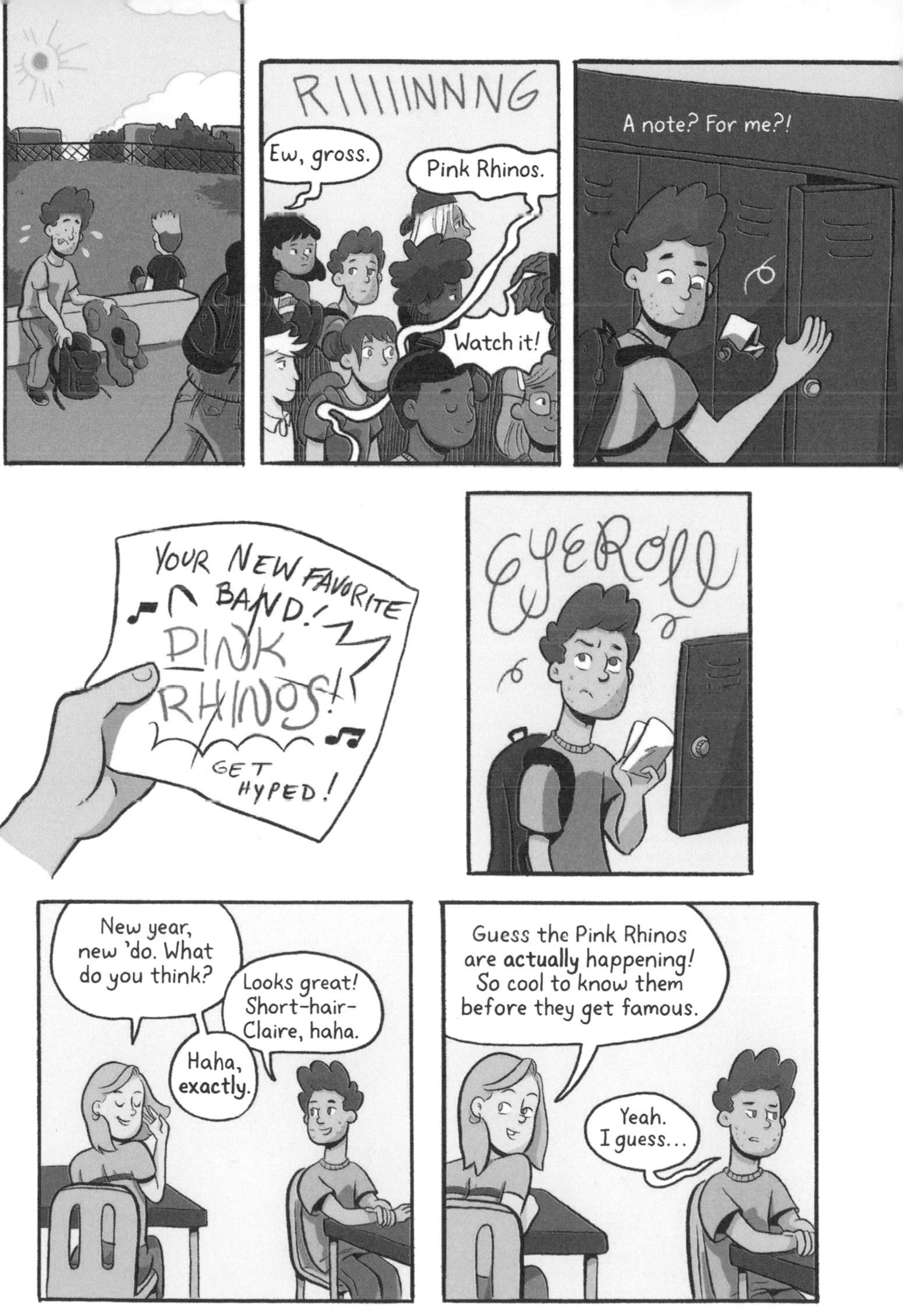
RIIIIINNNG
Ew, gross.
Pink Rhinos.
Watch it!
A note? For me?!
YOUR NEW FAVORITE BAND! PINK RHINOS! GET HYPED!
EYEROLL
New year, new 'do. What do you think?
Looks great! Short-hair-Claire, haha.
Haha, exactly.
Guess the Pink Rhinos are actually happening! So cool to know them before they get famous.
Yeah. I guess...

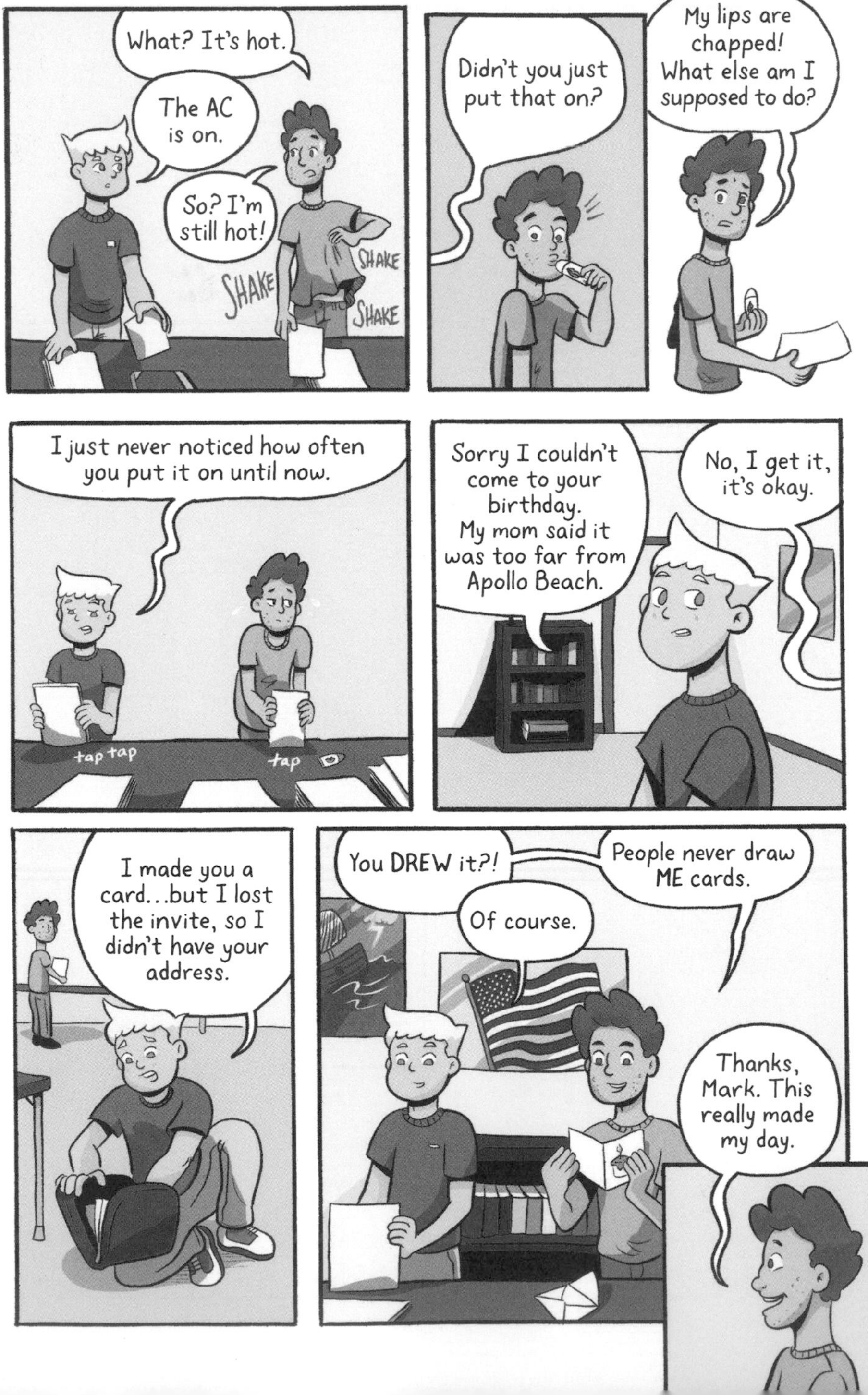
What? It's hot.
The AC is on.
So? I'm still hot!
SHAKE
SHAKE
SHAKE
Didn't you just put that on?
My lips are chapped! What else am I supposed to do?
I just never noticed how often you put it on until now.
tap tap
tap
Sorry I couldn't come to your birthday. My mom said it was too far from Apollo Beach.
No, I get it, it's okay.
I made you a card...but I lost the invite, so I didn't have your address.
You DREW it?!
Of course.
People never draw ME cards.
Thanks, Mark. This really made my day.

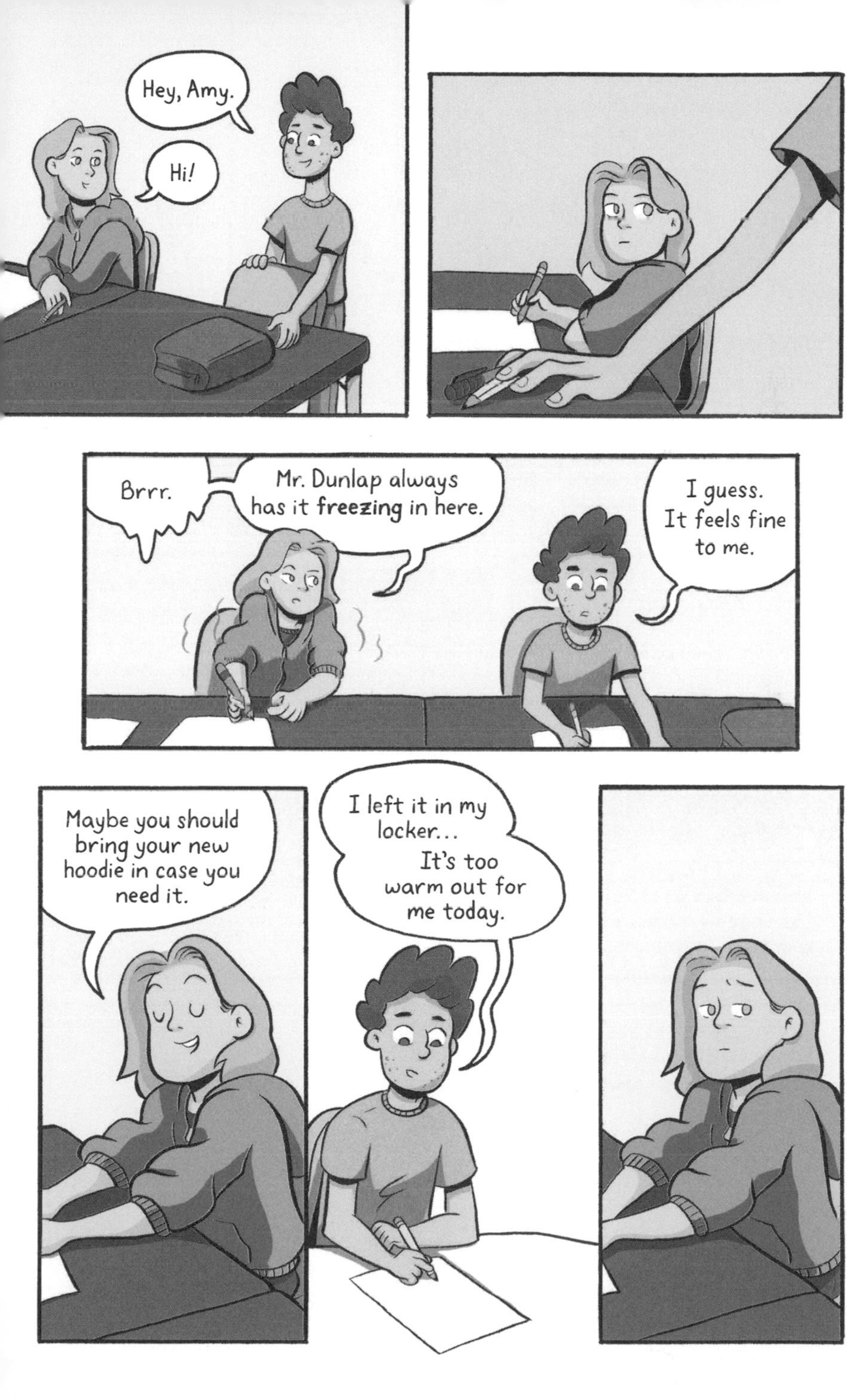
Hey, Amy.
Hi!
Brrr.
Mr. Dunlap always has it freezing in here.
I guess. It feels fine to me.
Maybe you should bring your new hoodie in case you need it.
I left it in my locker...
It's too warm out for me today.

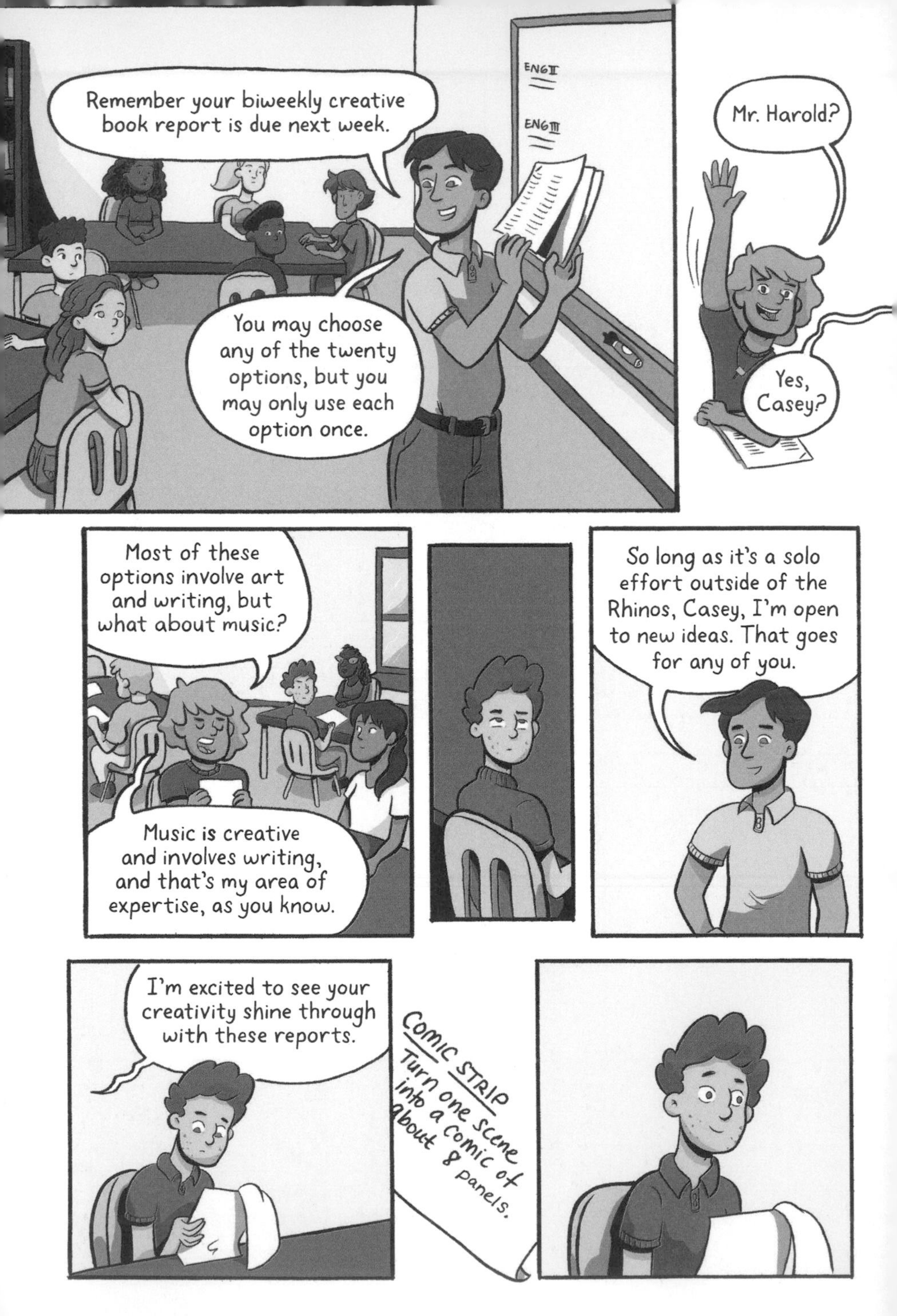
Remember your biweekly creative book report is due next week.
You may choose any of the twenty options, but you may only use each option once.
ENG II
ENG III
Mr. Harold?
Yes, Casey?
Most of these options involve art and writing, but what about music?
Music is creative and involves writing, and that's my area of expertise, as you know.
So long as it's a solo effort outside of the Rhinos, Casey, I'm open to new ideas. That goes for any of you.
I'm excited to see your creativity shine through with these reports.
COMIC STRIP
Turn one scene into a comic of about 8 panels.

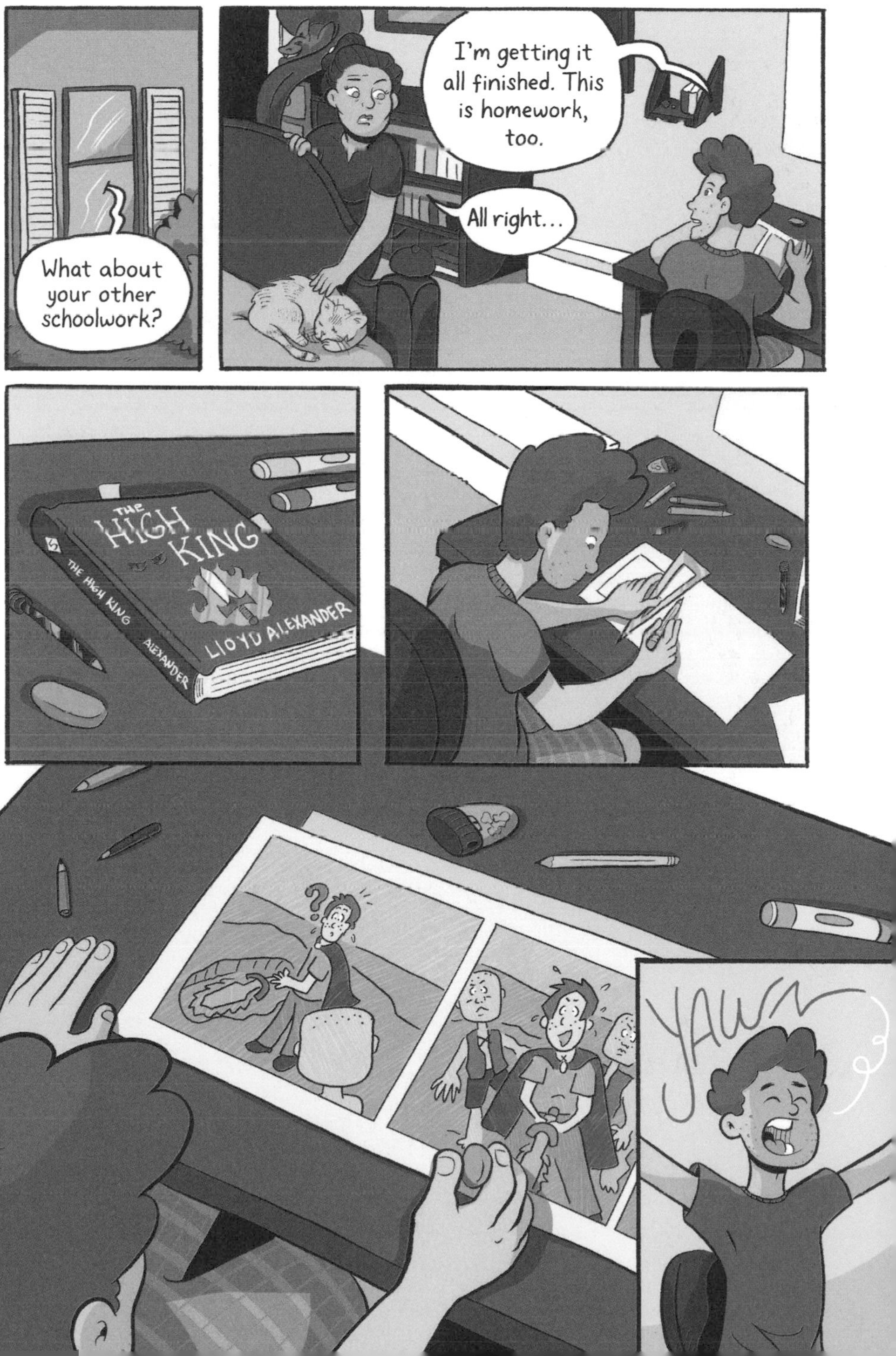
What about your other schoolwork?
I'm getting it all finished. This is homework, too.
All right...
THE HIGH KING
LLOYD ALEXANDER
THE HIGH KING
ALEXANDER
YAWN

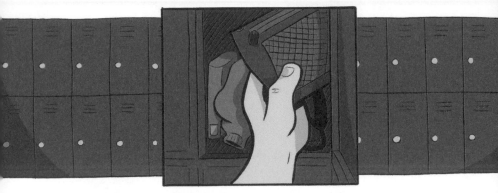

Hi, Jay.

Hey, Riley.

Yeah, man. Friday works for me.

Sweet. Brace, Casey, and Will are down, too. Just some chill hang time.

KUH CHUK

Can your mom give me a ride to the mall?

Yep. I got you.

No music, no skateboarding? Count me in.

Asseyez-vous, Monsieur Violet.

Pardon, Madame Ehrlich.

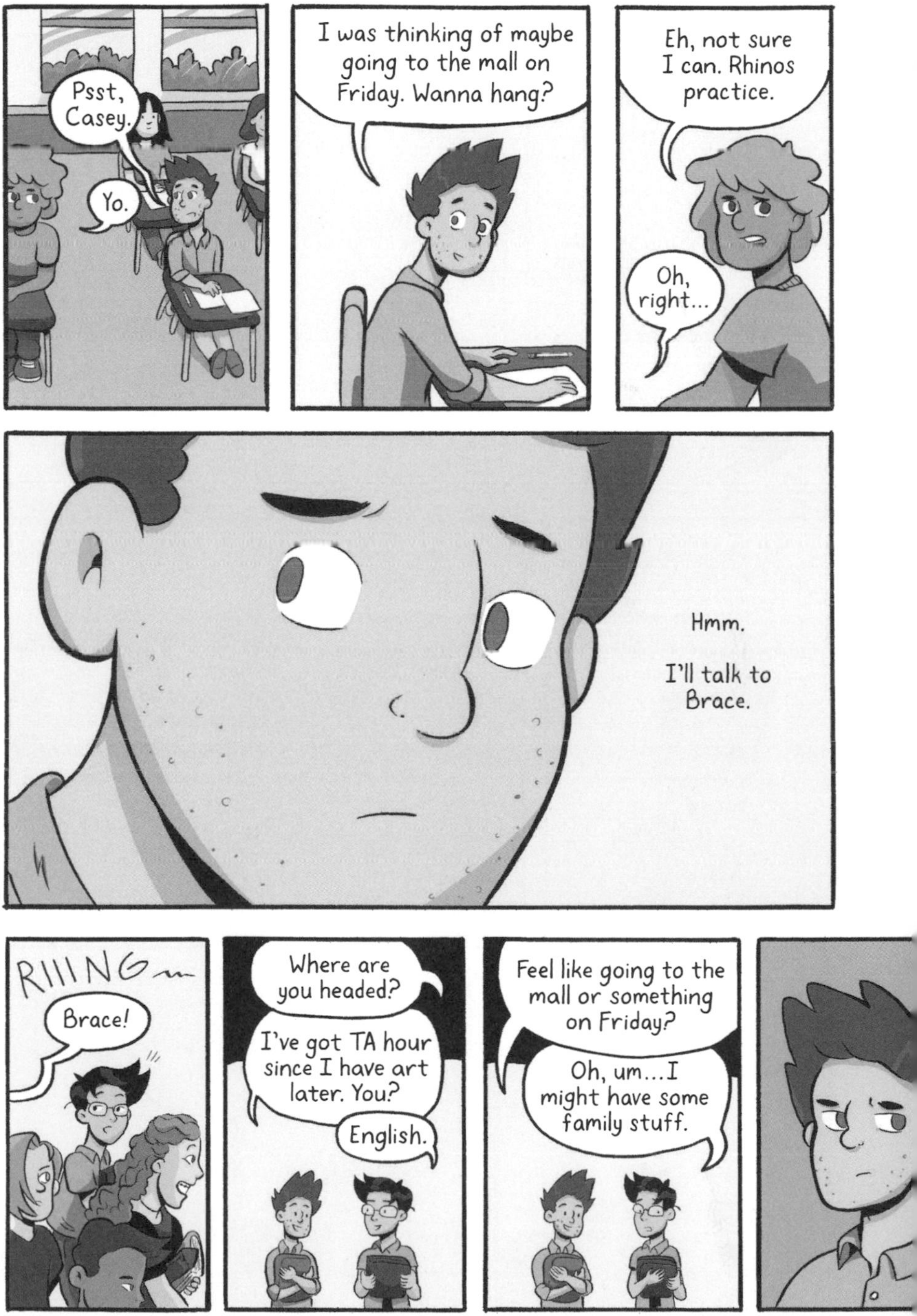
Psst, Casey.
Yo.
I was thinking of maybe going to the mall on Friday. Wanna hang?
Eh, not sure I can. Rhinos practice.
Oh, right...
Hmm.
I'll talk to Brace.
RIIING
Brace!
Where are you headed?
I've got TA hour since I have art later. You?
English.
Feel like going to the mall or something on Friday?
Oh, um...I might have some family stuff.

Thought you might just be hanging out with the Rhinos again...

...well, yeah, kinda.

And I can't come? Why not? I hung out with you all before.

You're not really part of the group...

Carter and Will aren't even in the band!

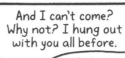 

They're different. They're **cool**.

You and I hung out all **the time** last year.

That was **different**.

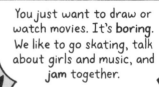

You just want to draw or watch movies. It's **boring**. We like to go skating, talk about girls and music, and **jam** together.

Why don't you hang out with that weirdo, Mark, who never talks to anyone?

That's not true, he talks a lot. Just maybe not to jerks like you who think being in a band makes you **better** than everyone.

Whatever, Jay!

Stop trying to fit in where you **don't** belong.

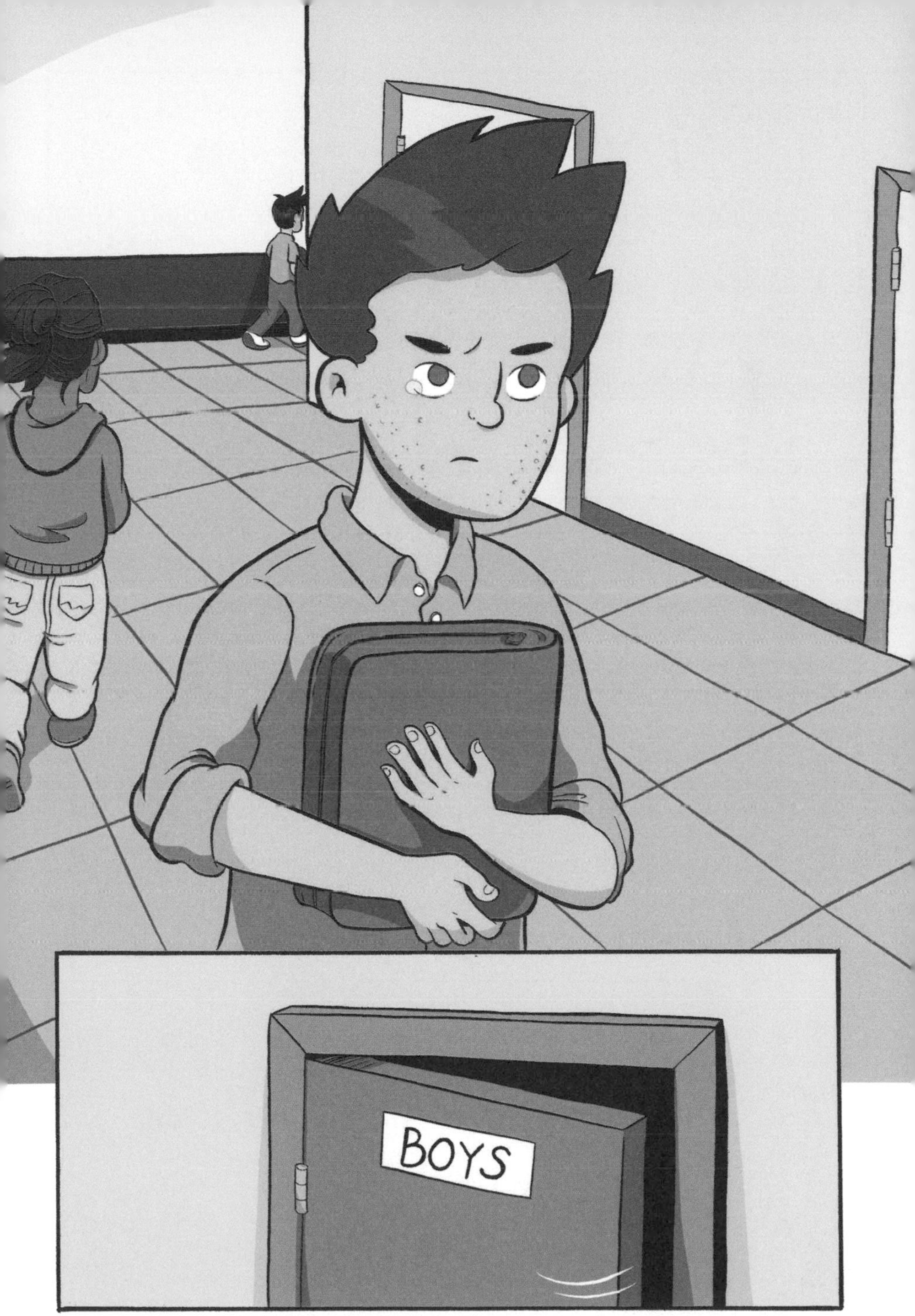
BOYS

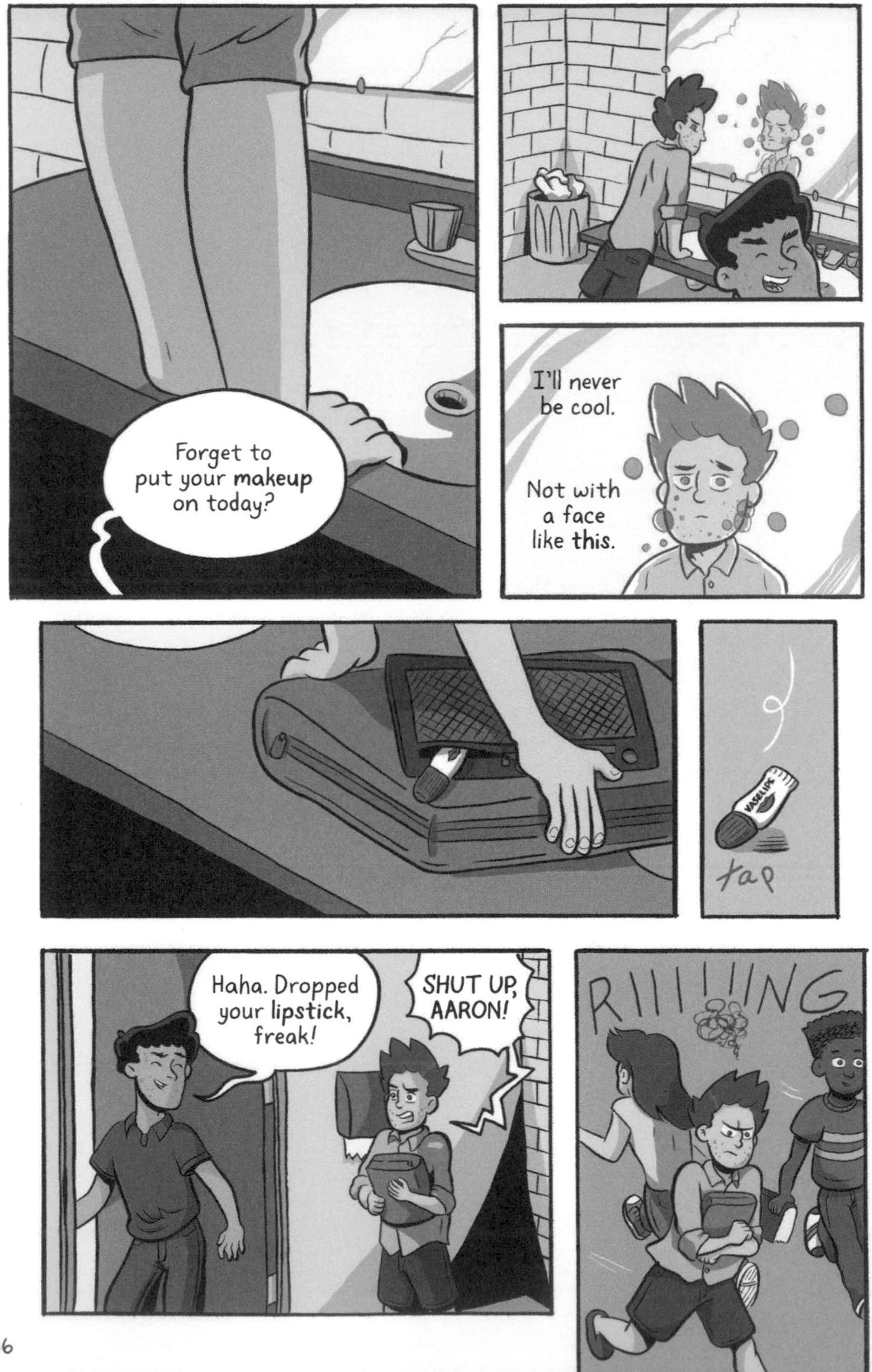
Forget to put your makeup on today?
I'll never be cool.
Not with a face like this.
VASELIPS
tap
Haha. Dropped your lipstick, freak!
SHUT UP, AARON!
RIIIIING

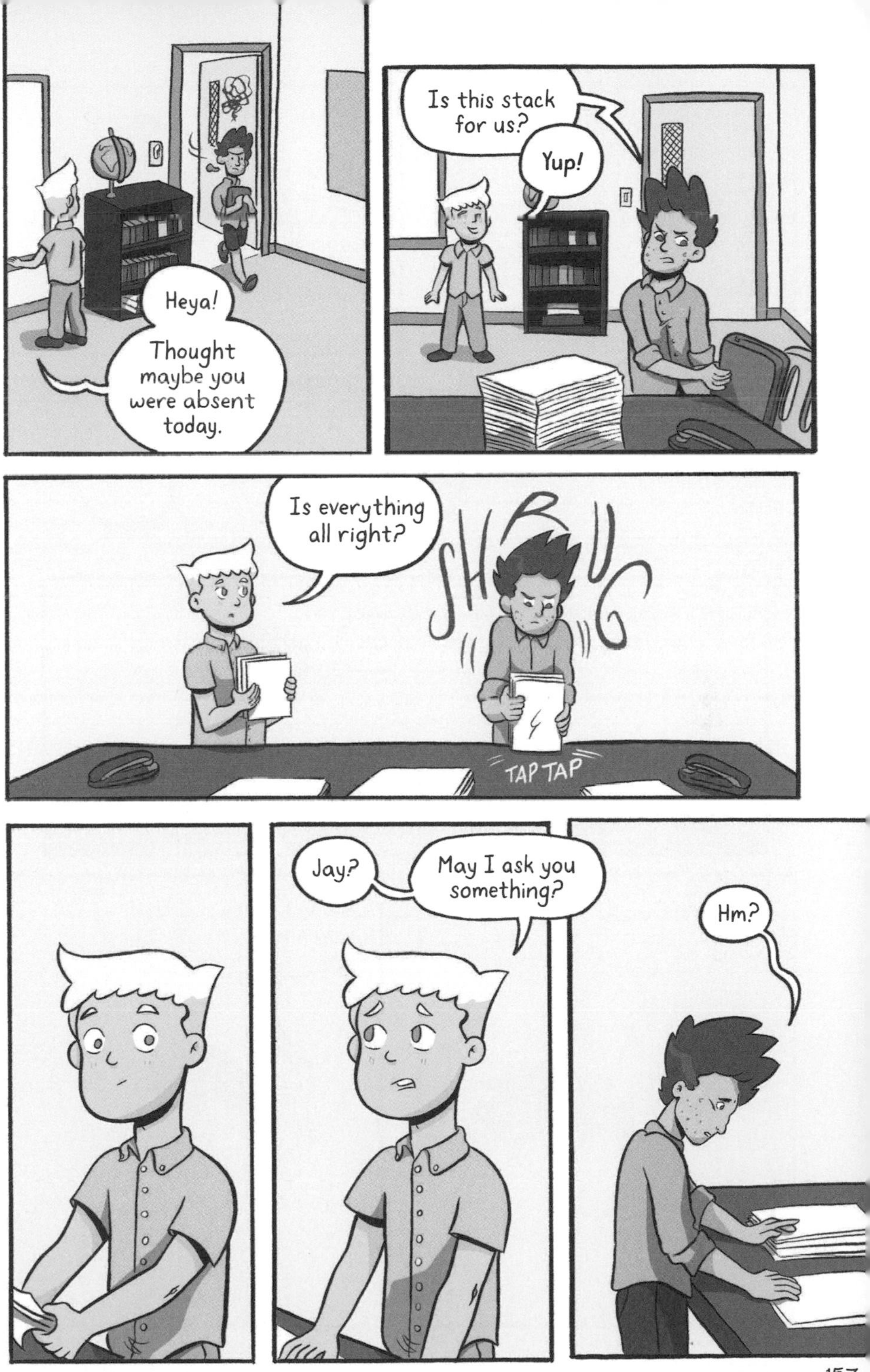
Heya!
Thought maybe you were absent today.
Is this stack for us?
Yup!
Is everything all right?
SHRUG
TAP TAP
Jay?
May I ask you something?
Hm?

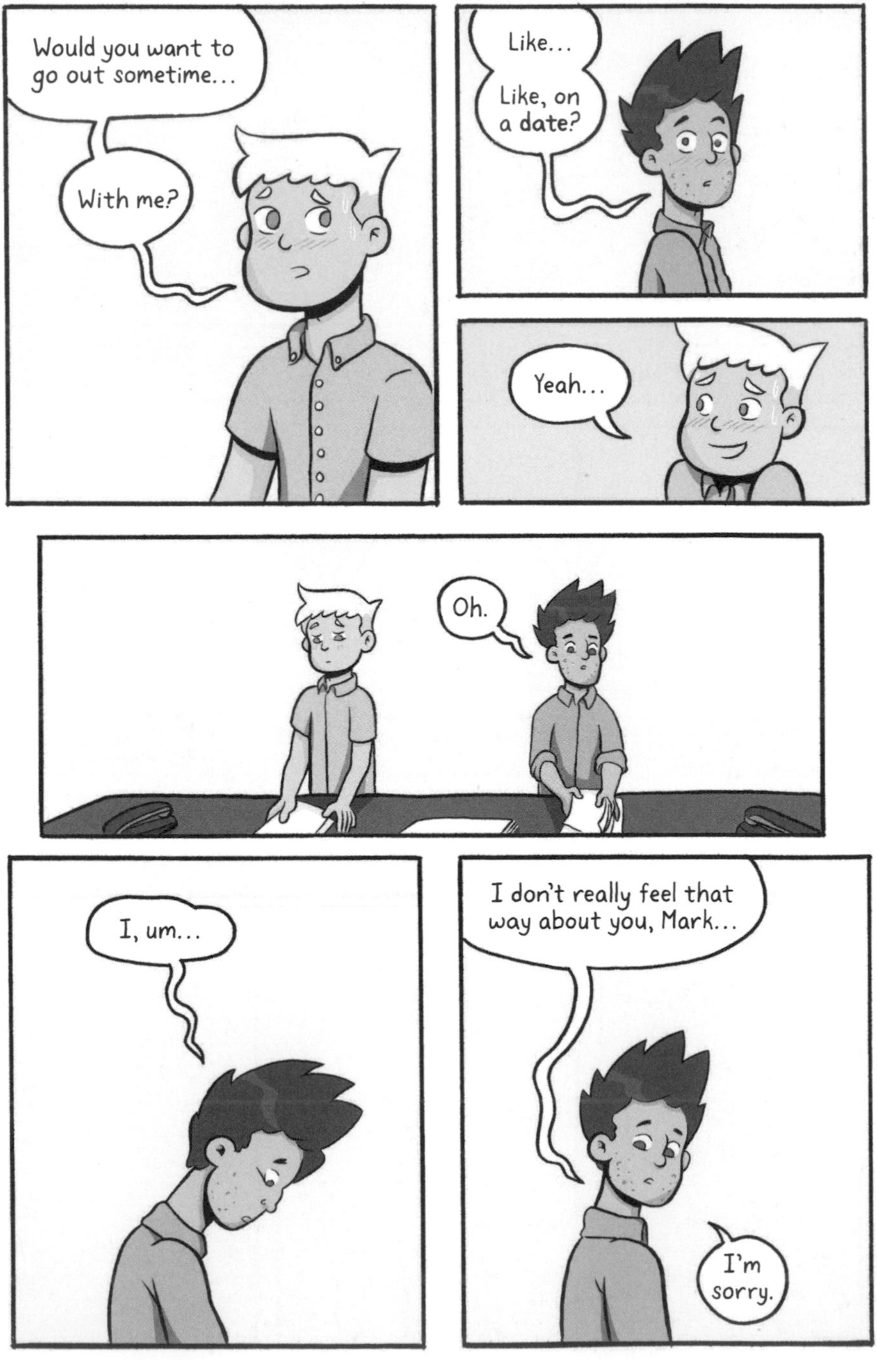
Would you want to go out sometime...
With me?
Like...
Like, on a date?
Yeah...
Oh.
I, um...
I don't really feel that way about you, Mark...
I'm sorry.

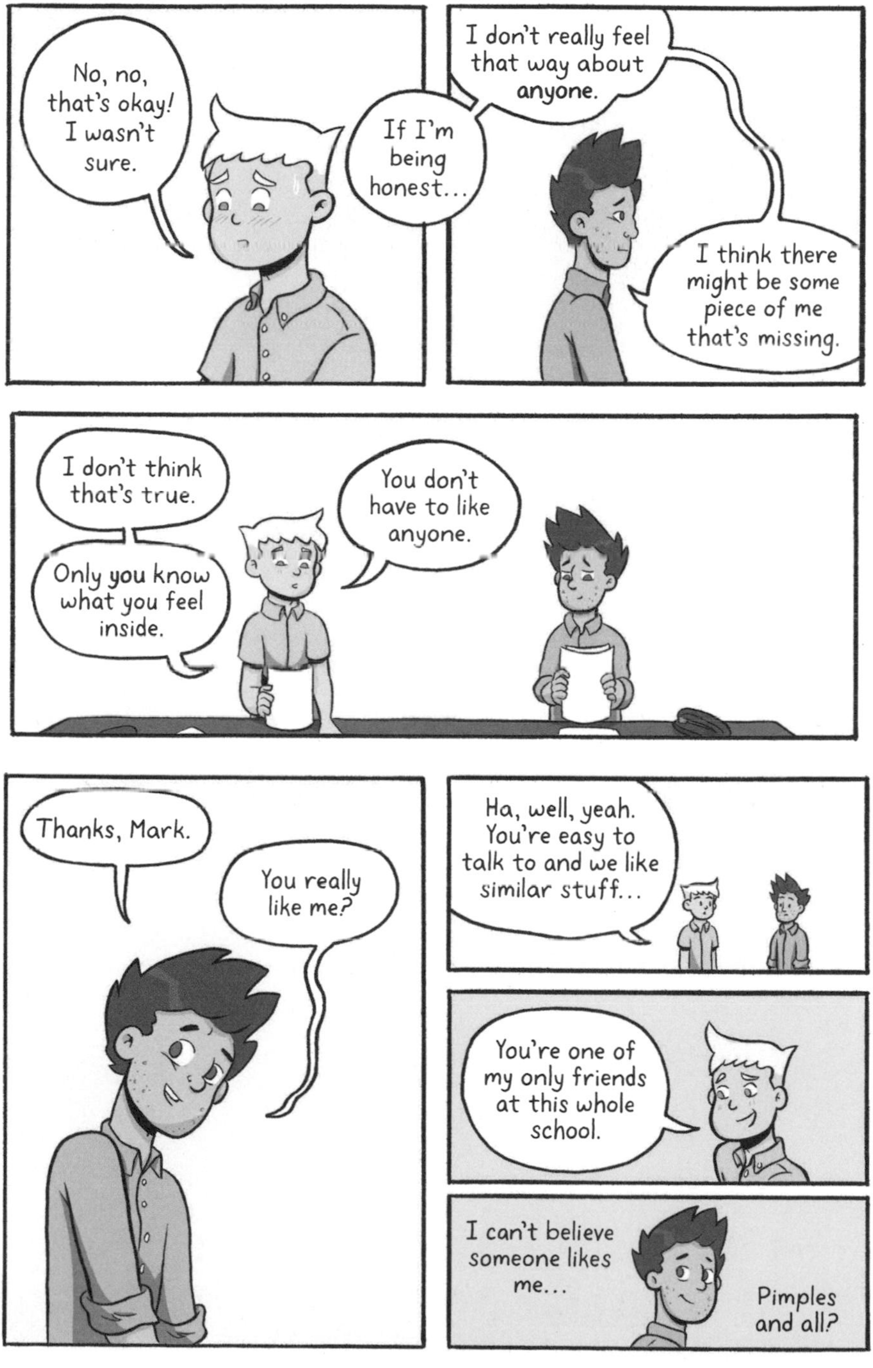
No, no, that's okay! I wasn't sure.
If I'm being honest...
I don't really feel that way about **anyone**.
I think there might be some piece of me that's missing.
I don't think that's true.
Only **you** know what you feel inside.
You don't have to like anyone.
Thanks, Mark.
You really like me?
Ha, well, yeah. You're easy to talk to and we like similar stuff...
You're one of my only friends at this whole school.
I can't believe someone likes me...
Pimples and all?

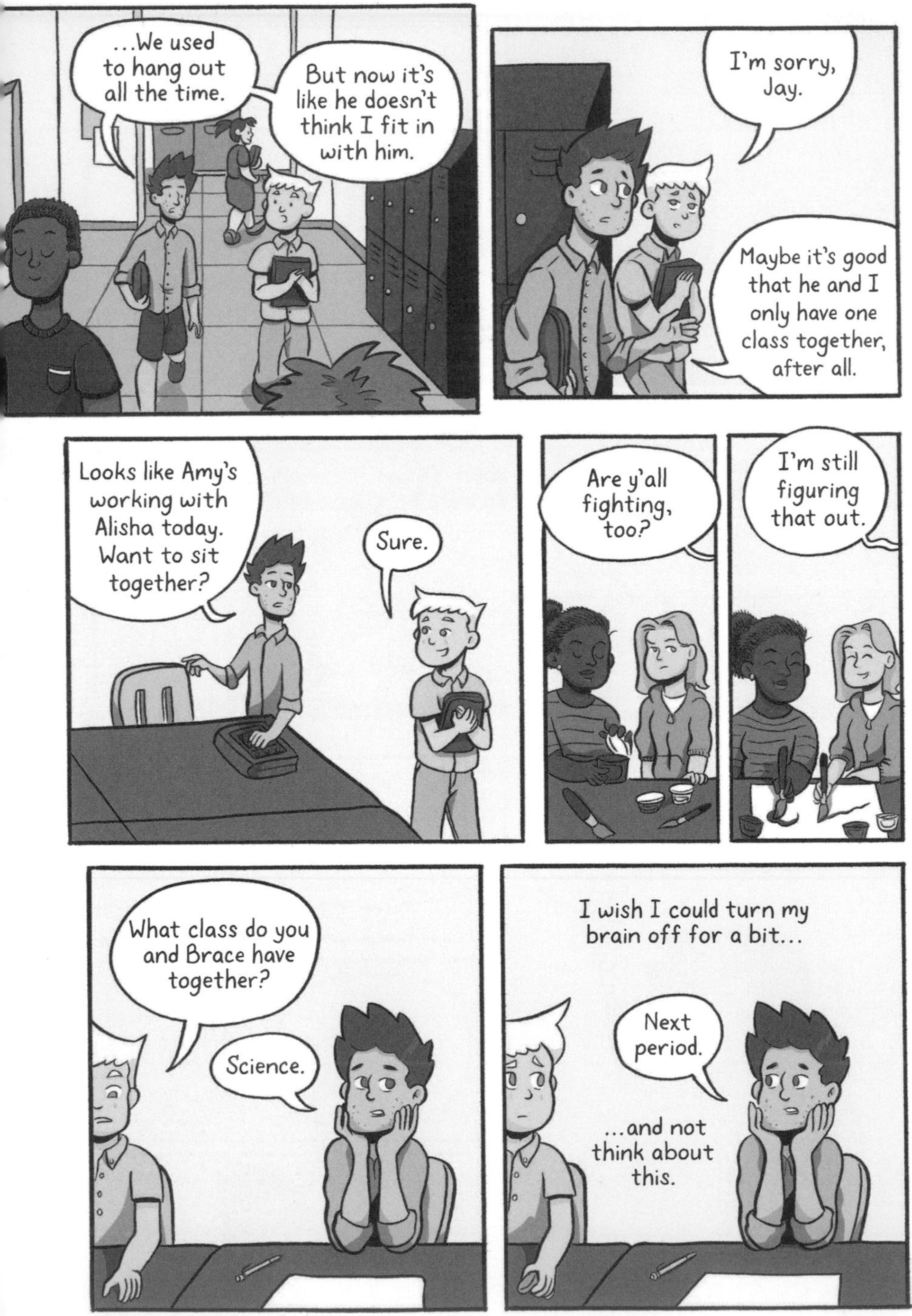
...We used to hang out all the time.
But now it's like he doesn't think I fit in with him.
I'm sorry, Jay.
Maybe it's good that he and I only have one class together, after all.
Looks like Amy's working with Alisha today. Want to sit together?
Sure.
Are y'all fighting, too?
I'm still figuring that out.
What class do you and Brace have together?
Science.
I wish I could turn my brain off for a bit...
Next period.
...and not think about this.

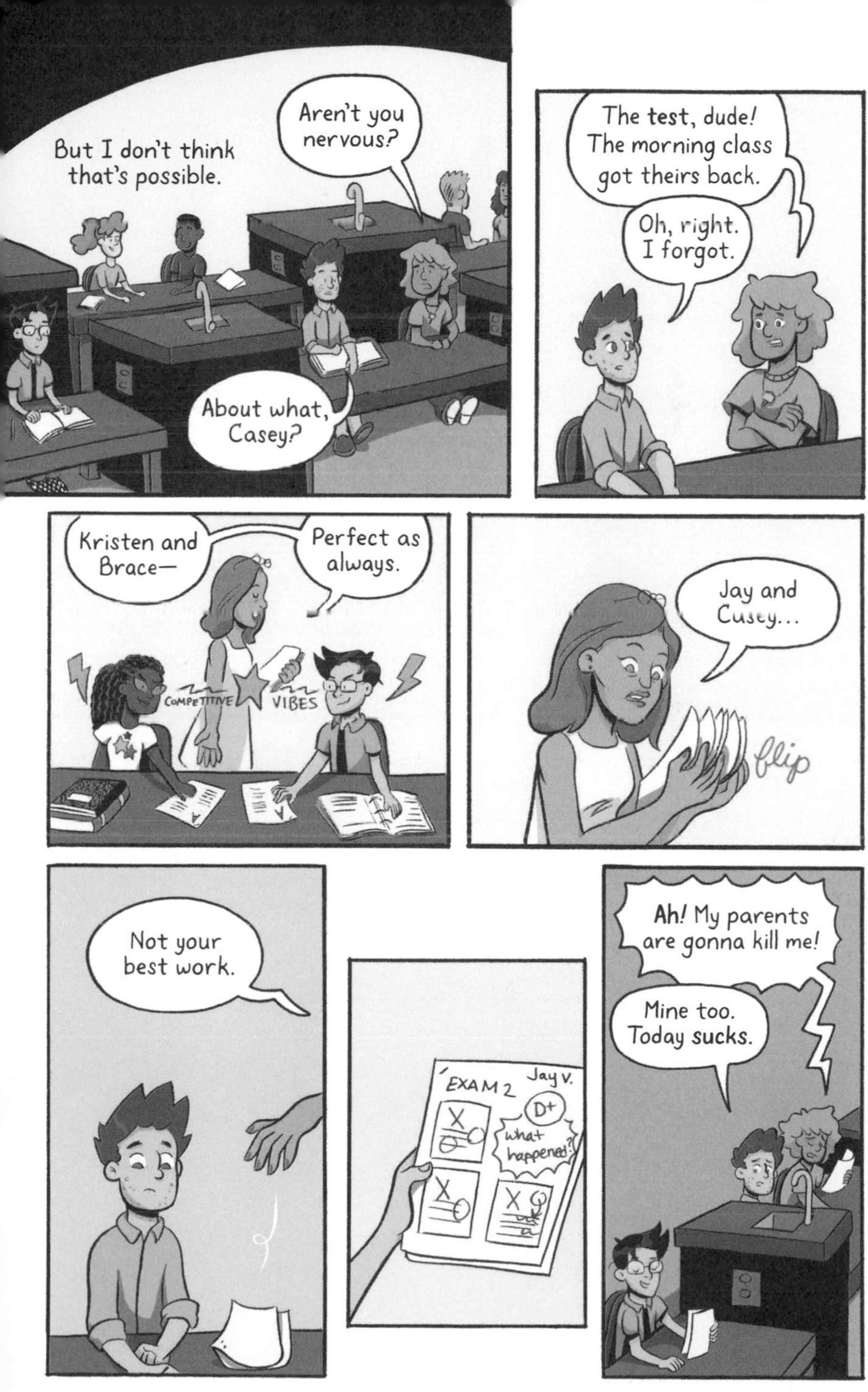
But I don't think that's possible.
Aren't you nervous?
About what, Casey?
The test, dude! The morning class got theirs back.
Oh, right. I forgot.
Kristen and Brace—
Perfect as always.
COMPETITIVE
VIBES
Jay and Casey...
flip
Not your best work.
EXAM 2
Jay V.
D+
what happened?
Ah! My parents are gonna kill me!
Mine too. Today sucks.

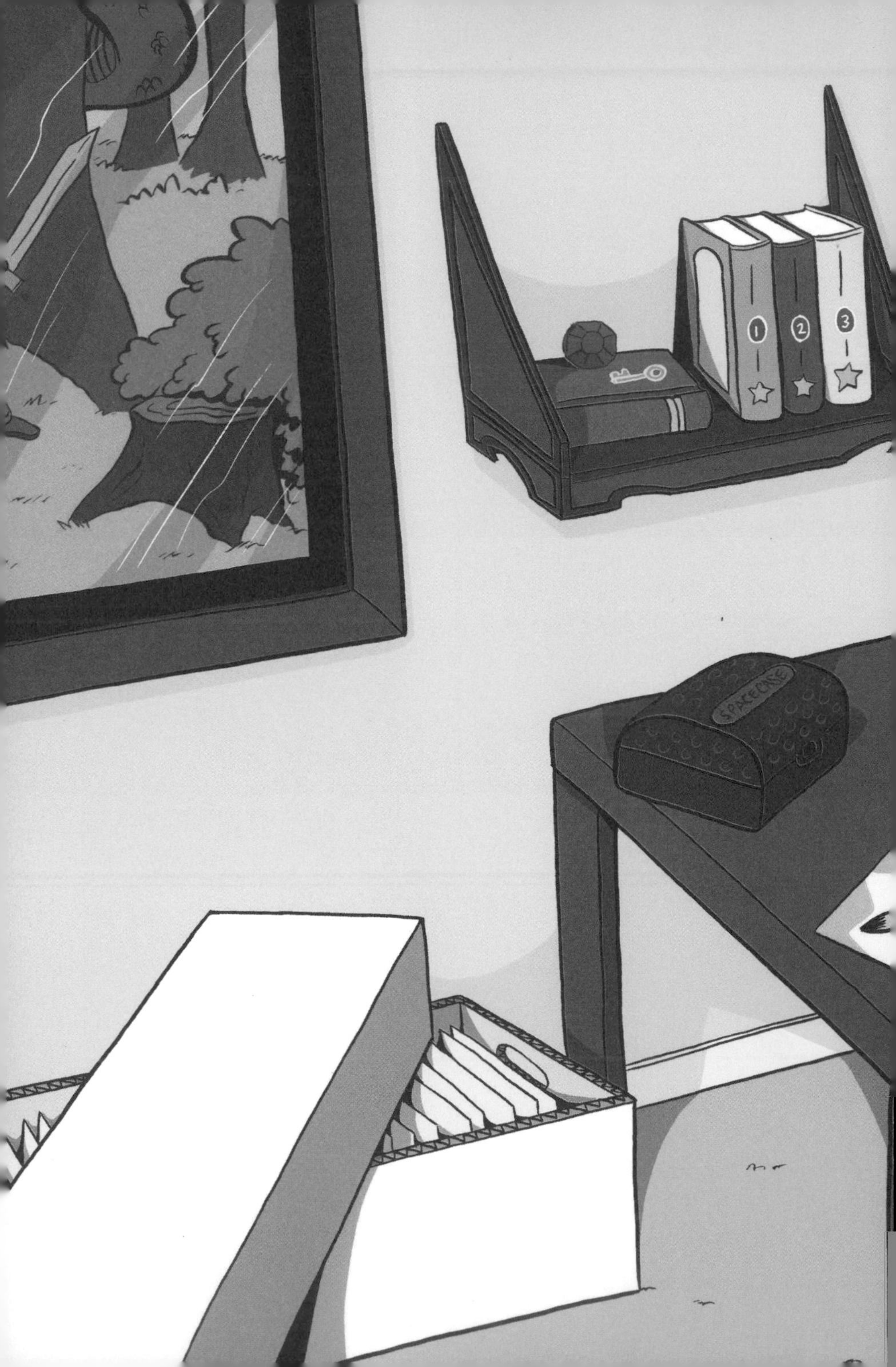
1
2
3
SPACECASE

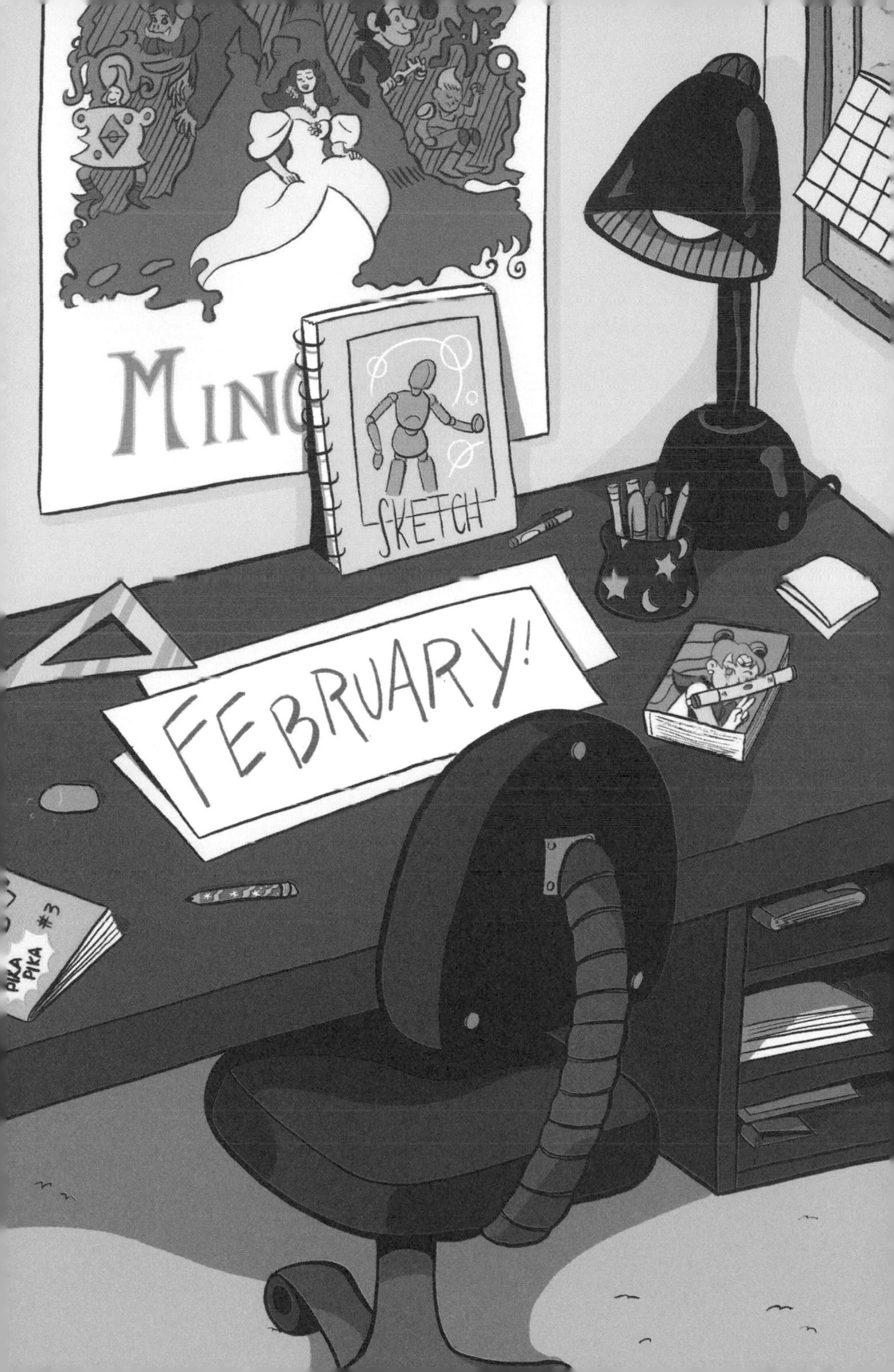
MINC
SKETCH
FEBRUARY!
PIKA PIKA
#3

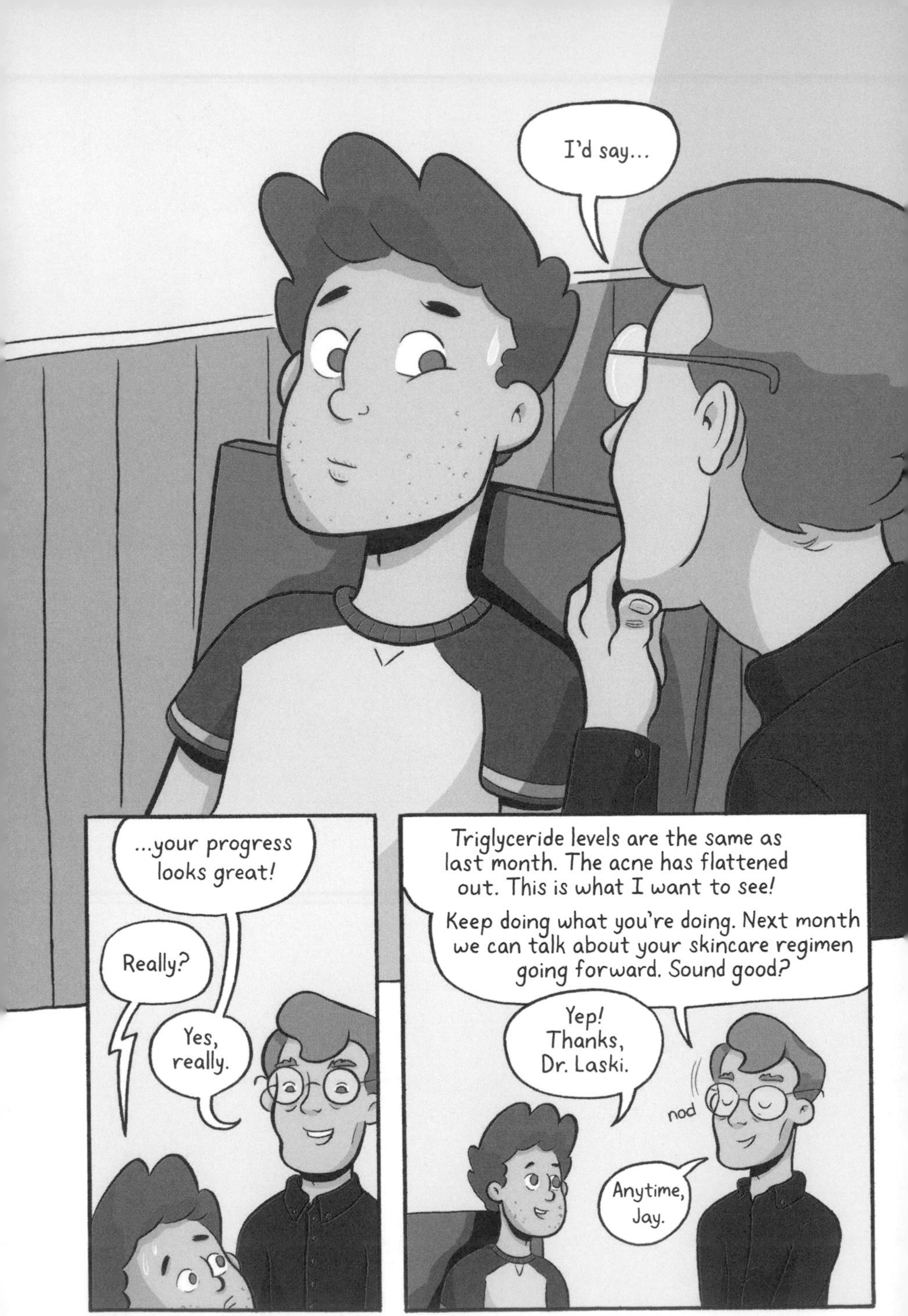
I'd say...
...your progress looks great!
Really?
Yes, really.
Triglyceride levels are the same as last month. The acne has flattened out. This is what I want to see!
Keep doing what you're doing. Next month we can talk about your skincare regimen going forward. Sound good?
Yep! Thanks, Dr. Laski.
nod
Anytime, Jay.

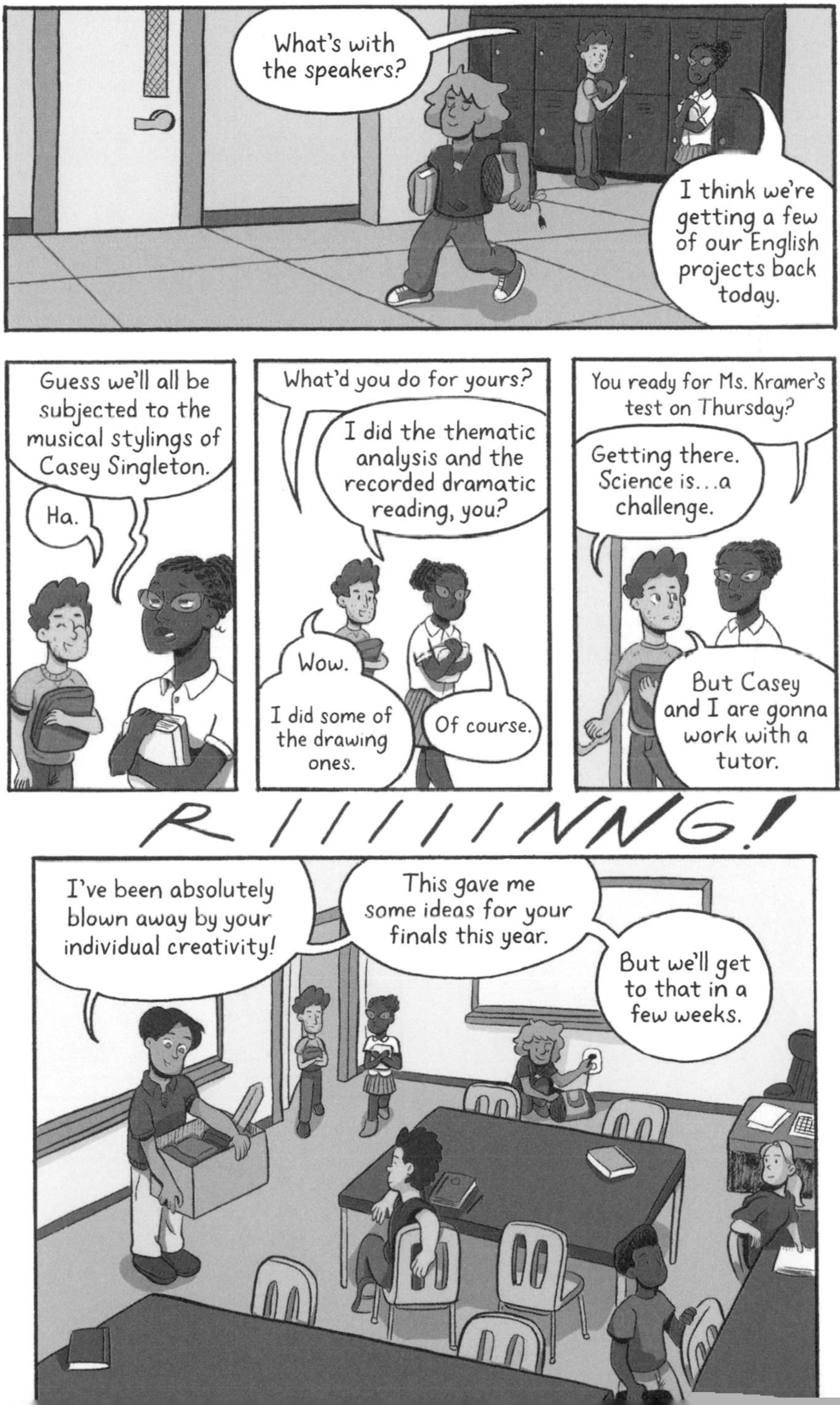
What's with the speakers?
I think we're getting a few of our English projects back today.
Guess we'll all be subjected to the musical stylings of Casey Singleton.
Ha.
What'd you do for yours?
I did the thematic analysis and the recorded dramatic reading, you?
Wow.
I did some of the drawing ones.
Of course.
You ready for Ms. Kramer's test on Thursday?
Getting there. Science is...a challenge.
But Casey and I are gonna work with a tutor.
RIIIIINNG!
I've been absolutely blown away by your individual creativity!
This gave me some ideas for your finals this year.
But we'll get to that in a few weeks.

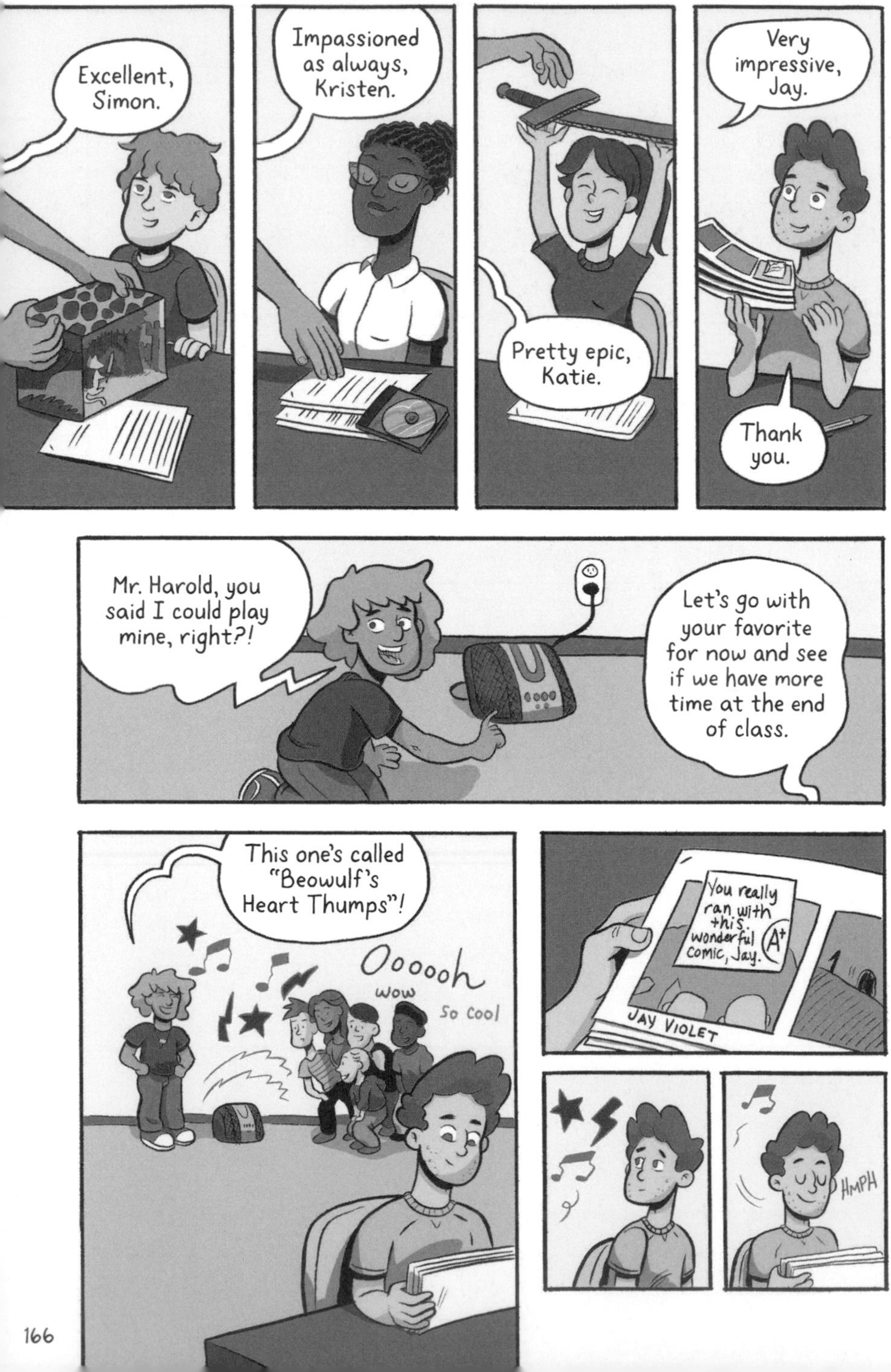
Excellent, Simon.
Impassioned as always, Kristen.
Pretty epic, Katie.
Very impressive, Jay.
Thank you.
Mr. Harold, you said I could play mine, right?!
Let's go with your favorite for now and see if we have more time at the end of class.
This one's called "Beowulf's Heart Thumps"!
Oooooh
wow
so cool
You really ran with this. wonderful comic, Jay. A+
JAY VIOLET
HMPH

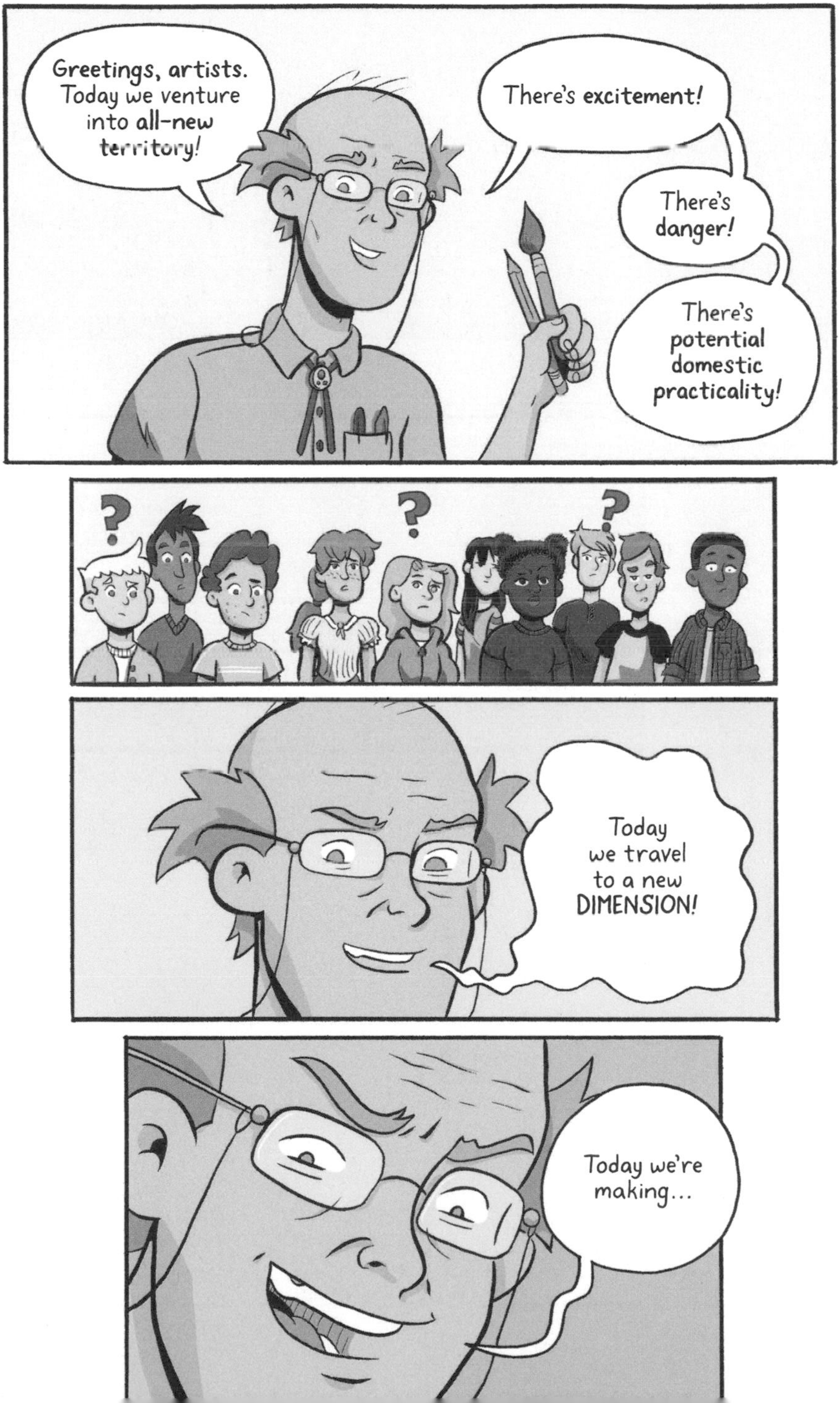
Greetings, artists. Today we venture into all-new territory!
There's excitement!
There's danger!
There's potential domestic practicality!
Today we travel to a new DIMENSION!
Today we're making...

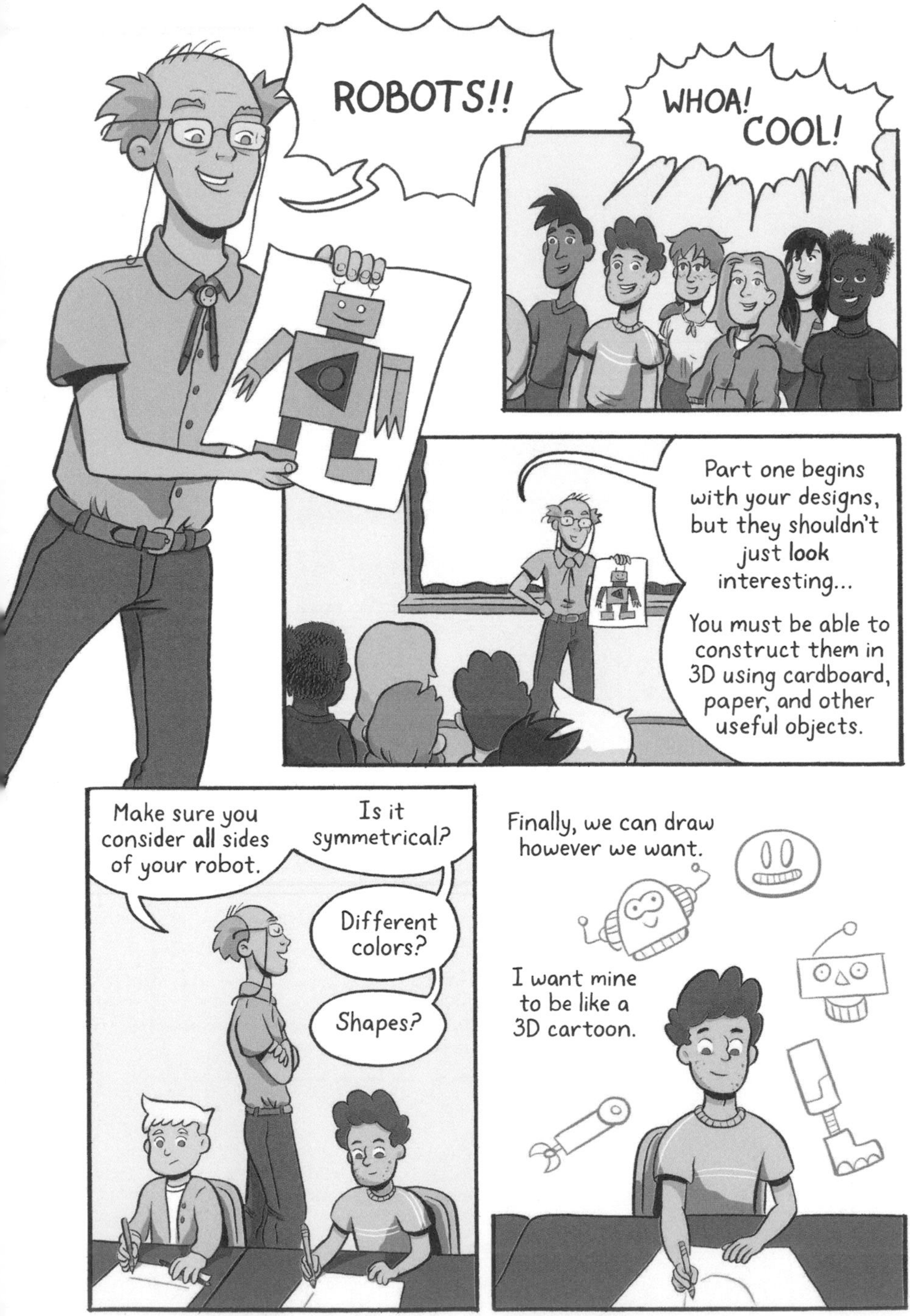
ROBOTS!!
WHOA! COOL!
Part one begins with your designs, but they shouldn't just **look** interesting...
You must be able to construct them in 3D using cardboard, paper, and other useful objects.
Make sure you consider **all** sides of your robot.
Is it symmetrical?
Different colors?
Shapes?
Finally, we can draw however we want.
I want mine to be like a 3D cartoon.

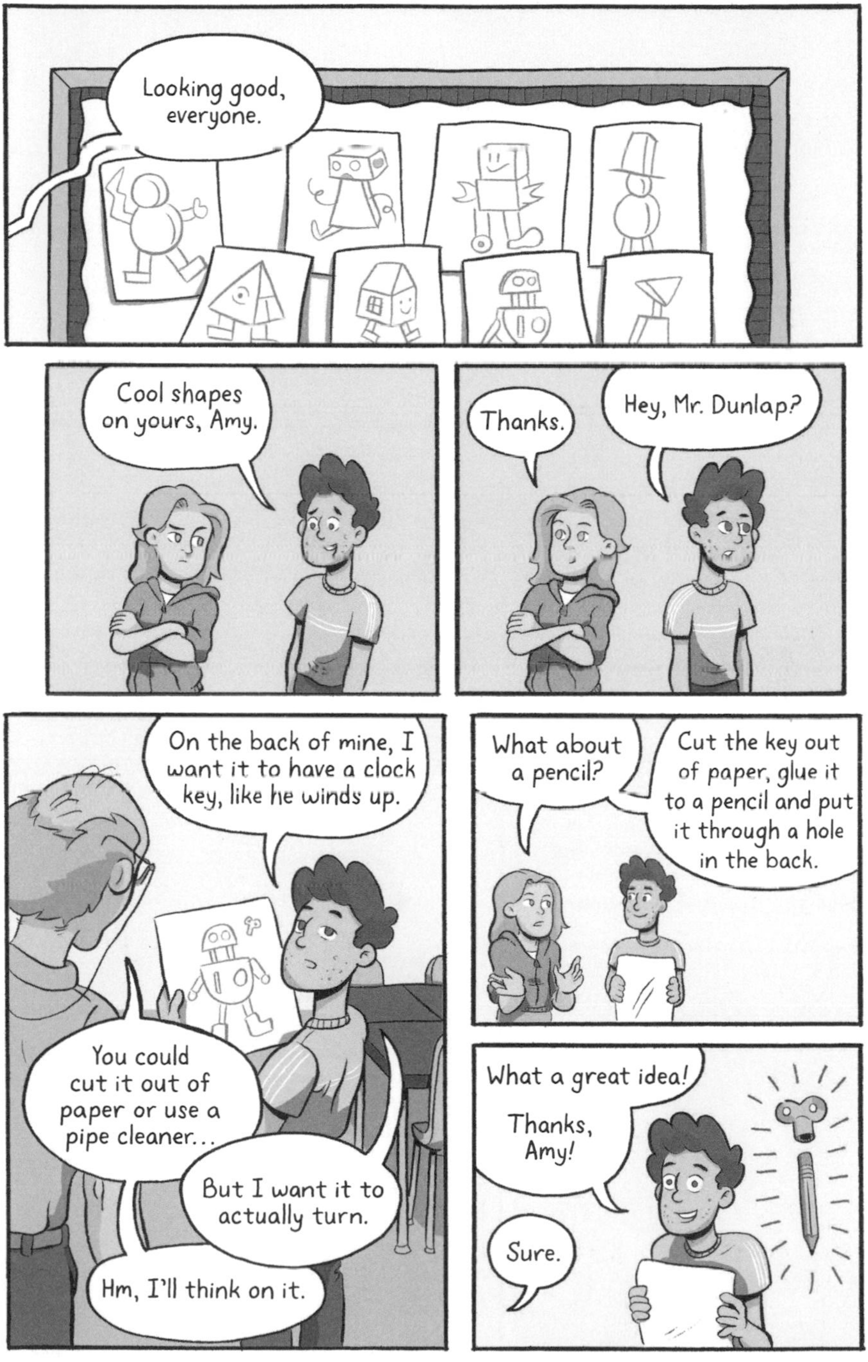

Looking good, everyone.
Cool shapes on yours, Amy.
Thanks.
Hey, Mr. Dunlap?
On the back of mine, I want it to have a clock key, like he winds up.
You could cut it out of paper or use a pipe cleaner...
But I want it to actually turn.
Hm, I'll think on it.
What about a pencil?
Cut the key out of paper, glue it to a pencil and put it through a hole in the back.
What a great idea!
Thanks, Amy!
Sure.

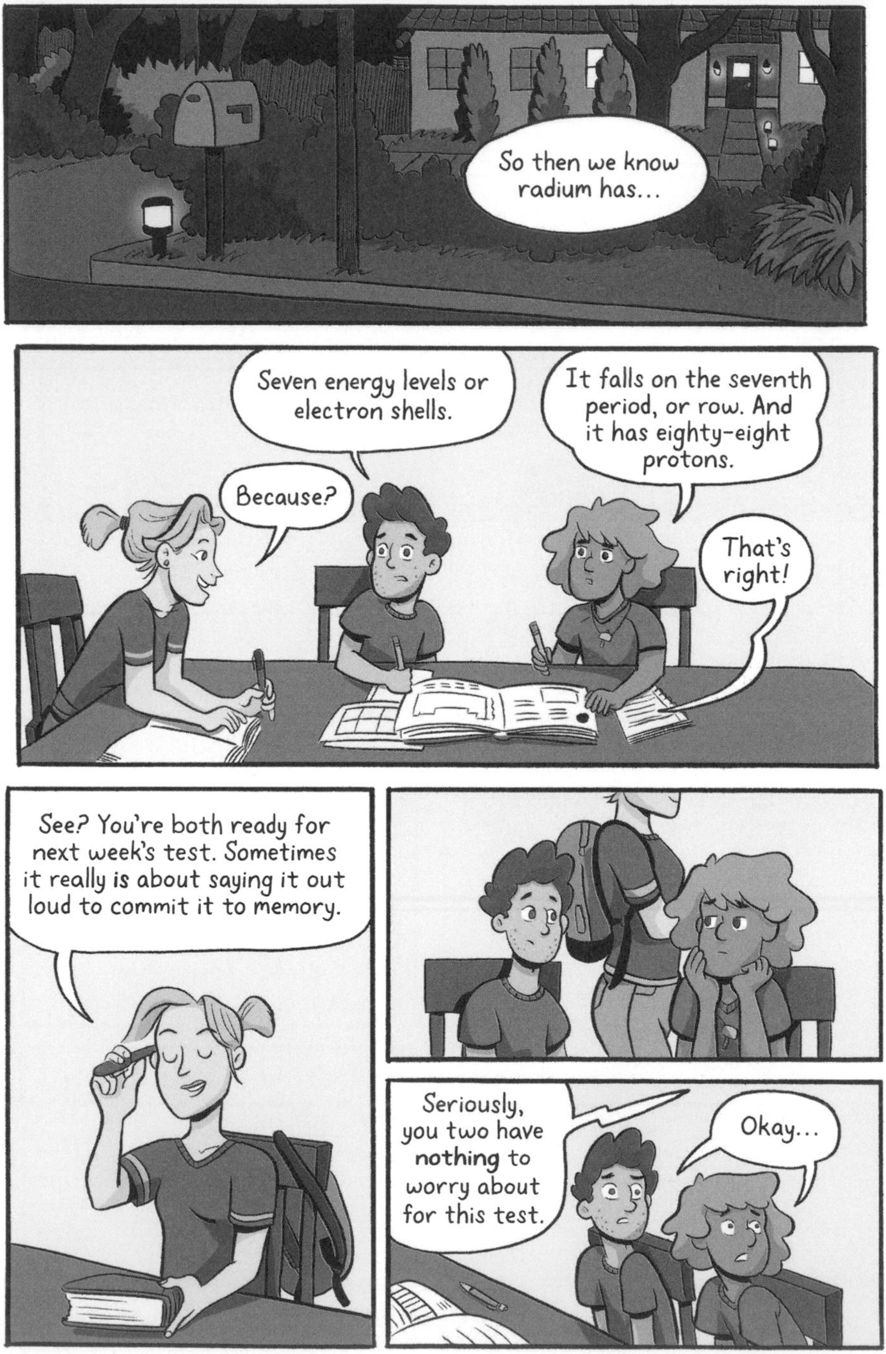
So then we know radium has...
Because?
Seven energy levels or electron shells.
It falls on the seventh period, or row. And it has eighty-eight protons.
That's right!
See? You're both ready for next week's test. Sometimes it really **is** about saying it out loud to commit it to memory.
Seriously, you two have **nothing** to worry about for this test.
Okay...

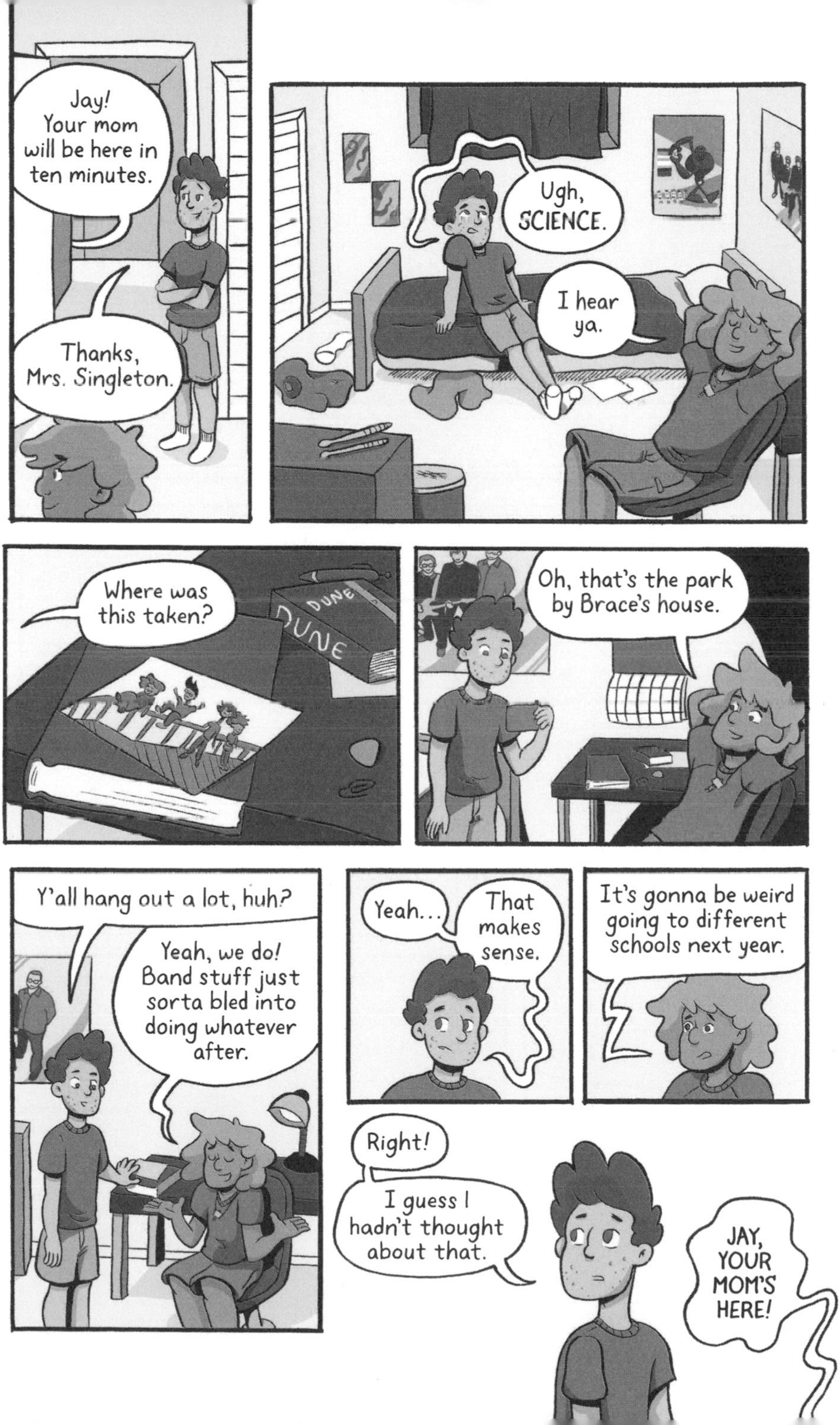

Jay! Your mom will be here in ten minutes.
Thanks, Mrs. Singleton.
Ugh, SCIENCE.
I hear ya.
Where was this taken?
DUNE
DUNE
Oh, that's the park by Brace's house.
Y'all hang out a lot, huh?
Yeah, we do! Band stuff just sorta bled into doing whatever after.
Yeah...
That makes sense.
It's gonna be weird going to different schools next year.
Right!
I guess I hadn't thought about that.
JAY, YOUR MOM'S HERE!

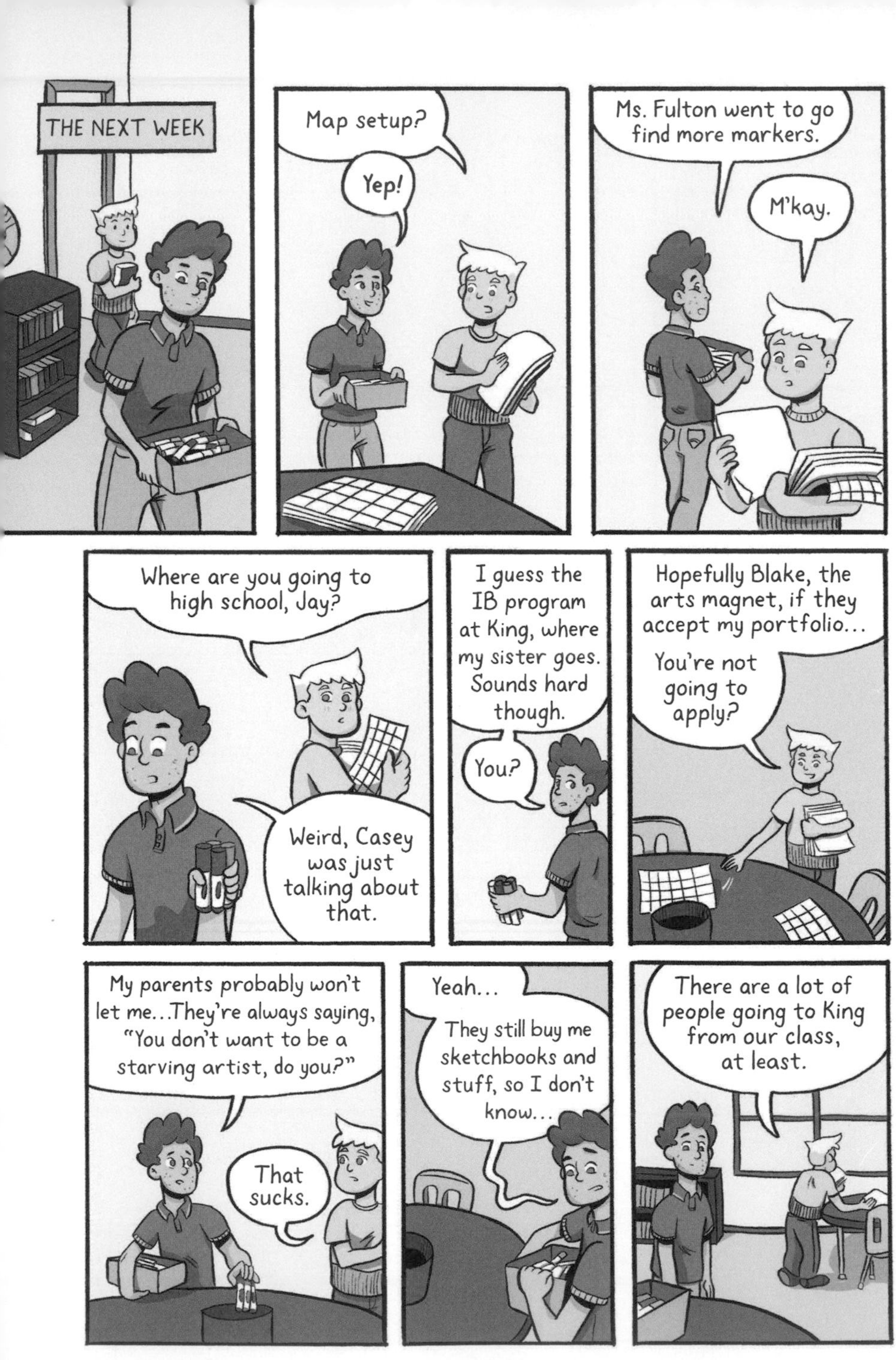
THE NEXT WEEK
Map setup?
Yep!
Ms. Fulton went to go find more markers.
M'kay.
Where are you going to high school, Jay?
Weird, Casey was just talking about that.
I guess the IB program at King, where my sister goes. Sounds hard though.
You?
Hopefully Blake, the arts magnet, if they accept my portfolio...
You're not going to apply?
My parents probably won't let me...They're always saying, "You don't want to be a starving artist, do you?"
That sucks.
Yeah...
They still buy me sketchbooks and stuff, so I don't know...
There are a lot of people going to King from our class, at least.

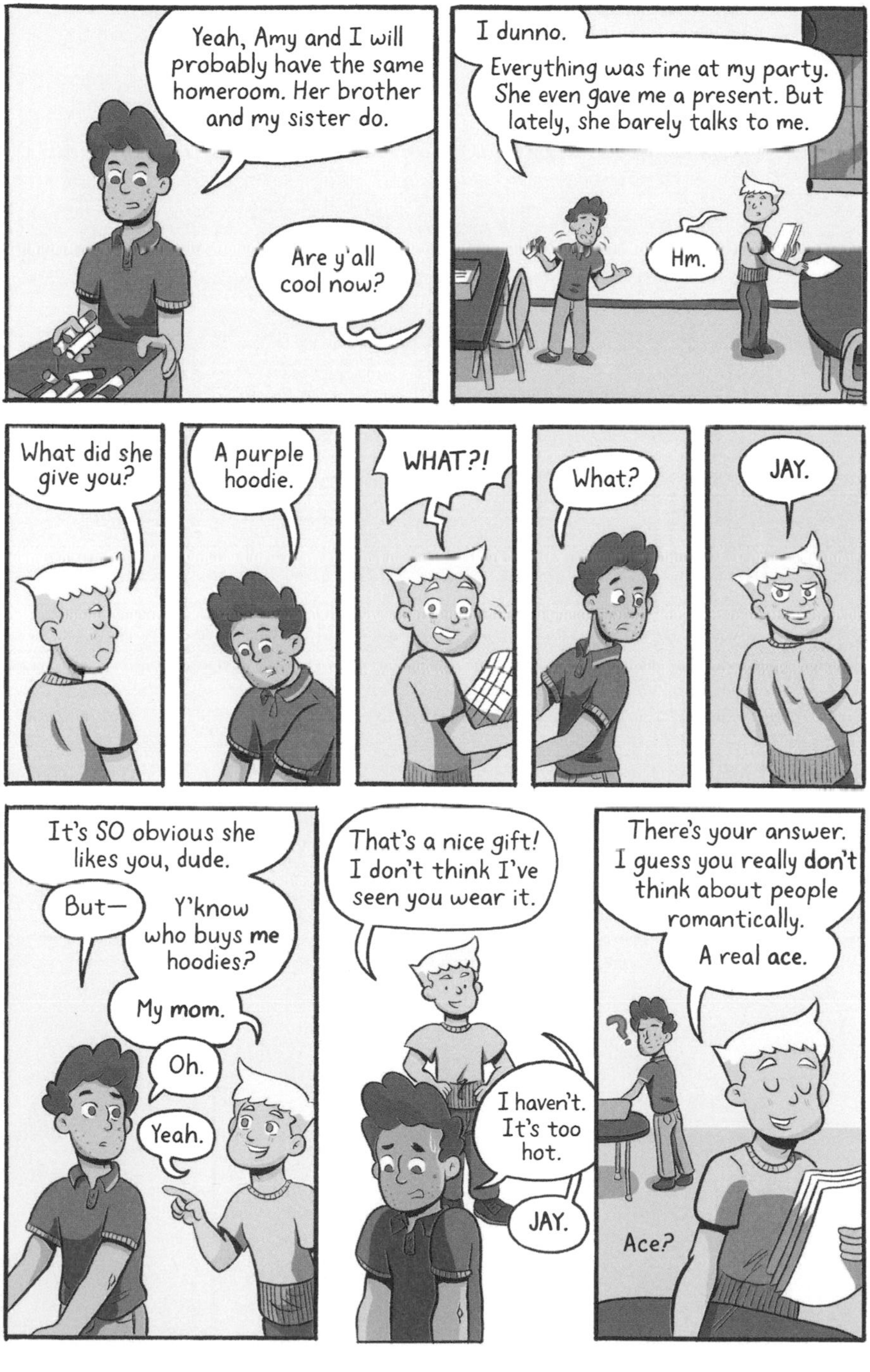
Yeah, Amy and I will probably have the same homeroom. Her brother and my sister do.
Are y'all cool now?
I dunno.
Everything was fine at my party. She even gave me a present. But lately, she barely talks to me.
Hm.
What did she give you?
A purple hoodie.
WHAT?!
What?
JAY.
It's SO obvious she likes you, dude.
But—
Y'know who buys **me** hoodies?
My **mom**.
Oh.
Yeah.
That's a nice gift! I don't think I've seen you wear it.
I haven't. It's too hot.
JAY.
There's your answer. I guess you really **don't** think about people romantically.
A real **ace**.
?
Ace?

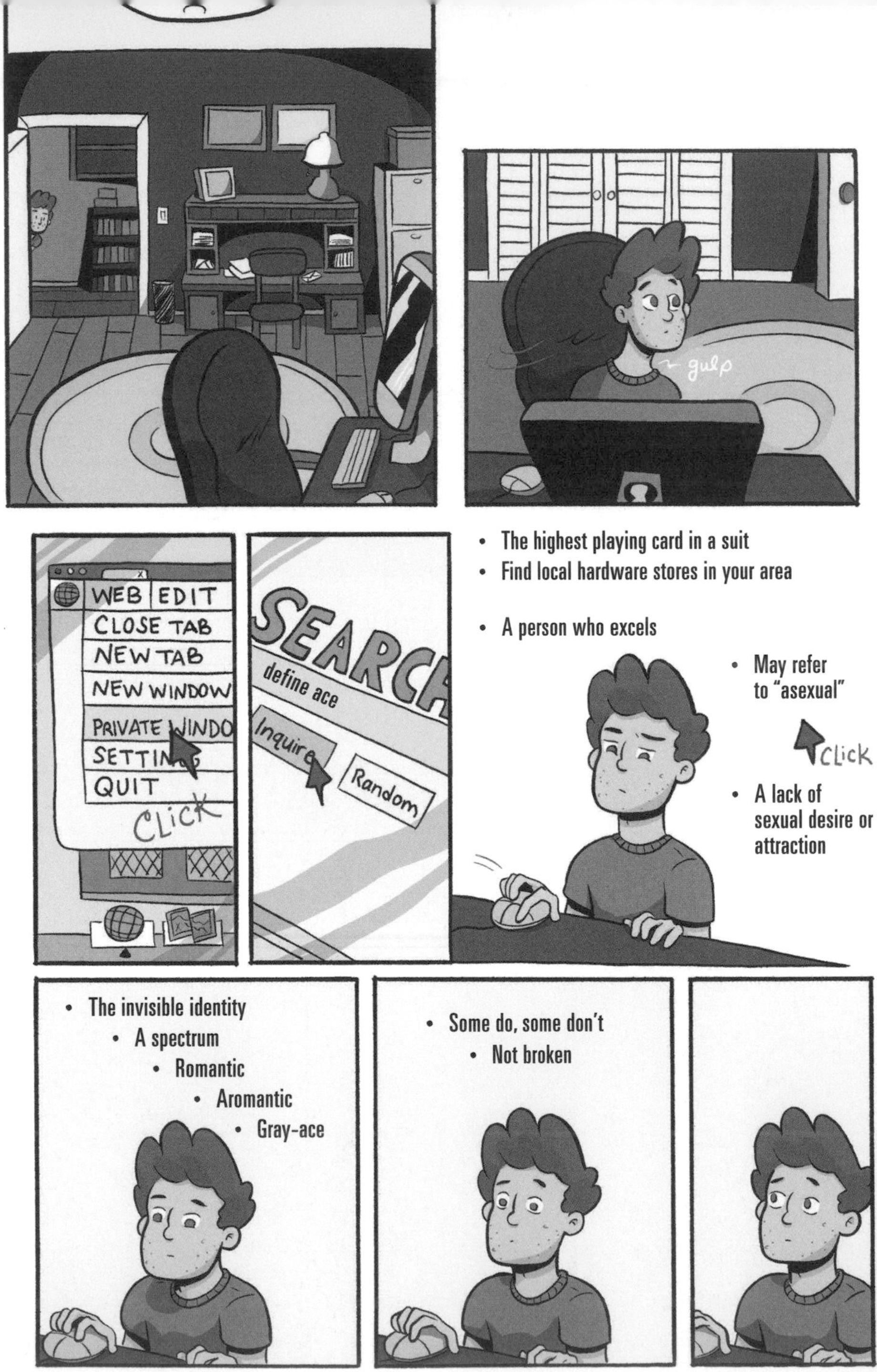
gulp
WEB EDIT
CLOSE TAB
NEW TAB
NEW WINDOW
PRIVATE WINDO
SETTING
QUIT
CLICK
SEARCH
define ace
Inquire
Random
• The highest playing card in a suit
• Find local hardware stores in your area
• A person who excels
• May refer to "asexual"
CLICK
• A lack of sexual desire or attraction
• The invisible identity
• A spectrum
• Romantic
• Aromantic
• Gray-ace
• Some do, some don't
• Not broken

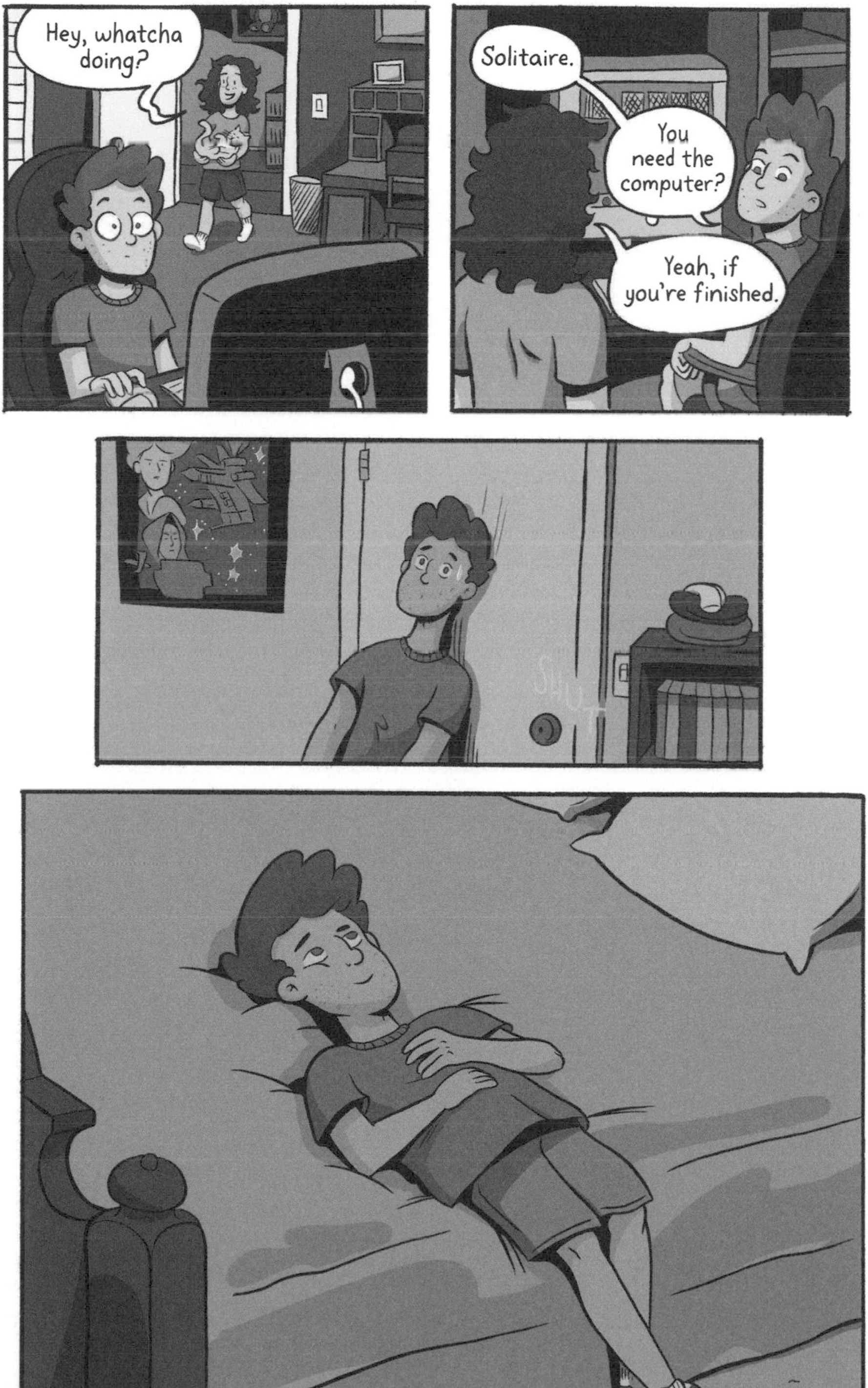
Hey, whatcha doing?
Solitaire.
You need the computer?
Yeah, if you're finished.
SHUT

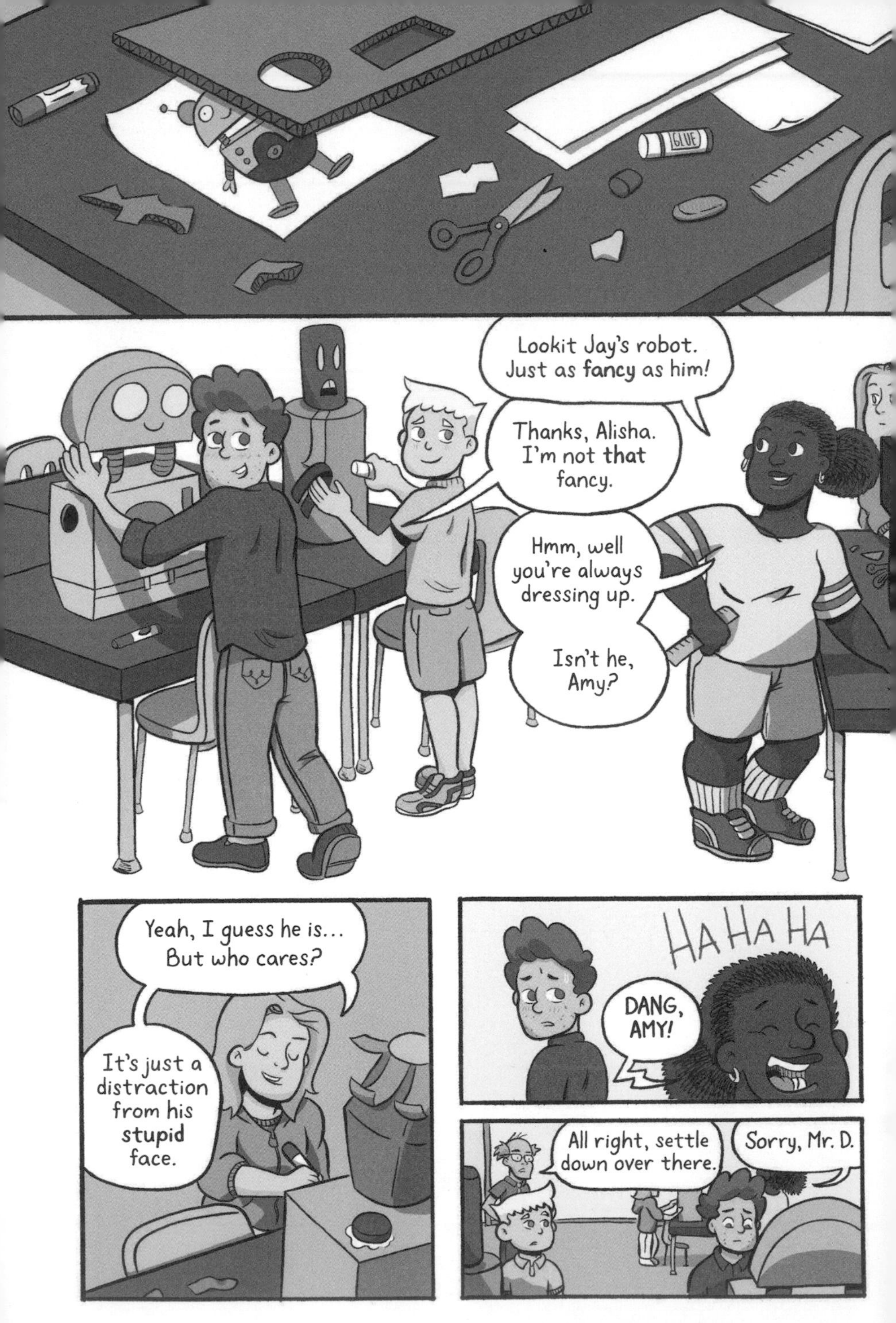
GLUE
Lookit Jay's robot. Just as fancy as him!
Thanks, Alisha. I'm not that fancy.
Hmm, well you're always dressing up.
Isn't he, Amy?
Yeah, I guess he is... But who cares?
It's just a distraction from his stupid face.
HA HA HA
DANG, AMY!
All right, settle down over there.
Sorry, Mr. D.

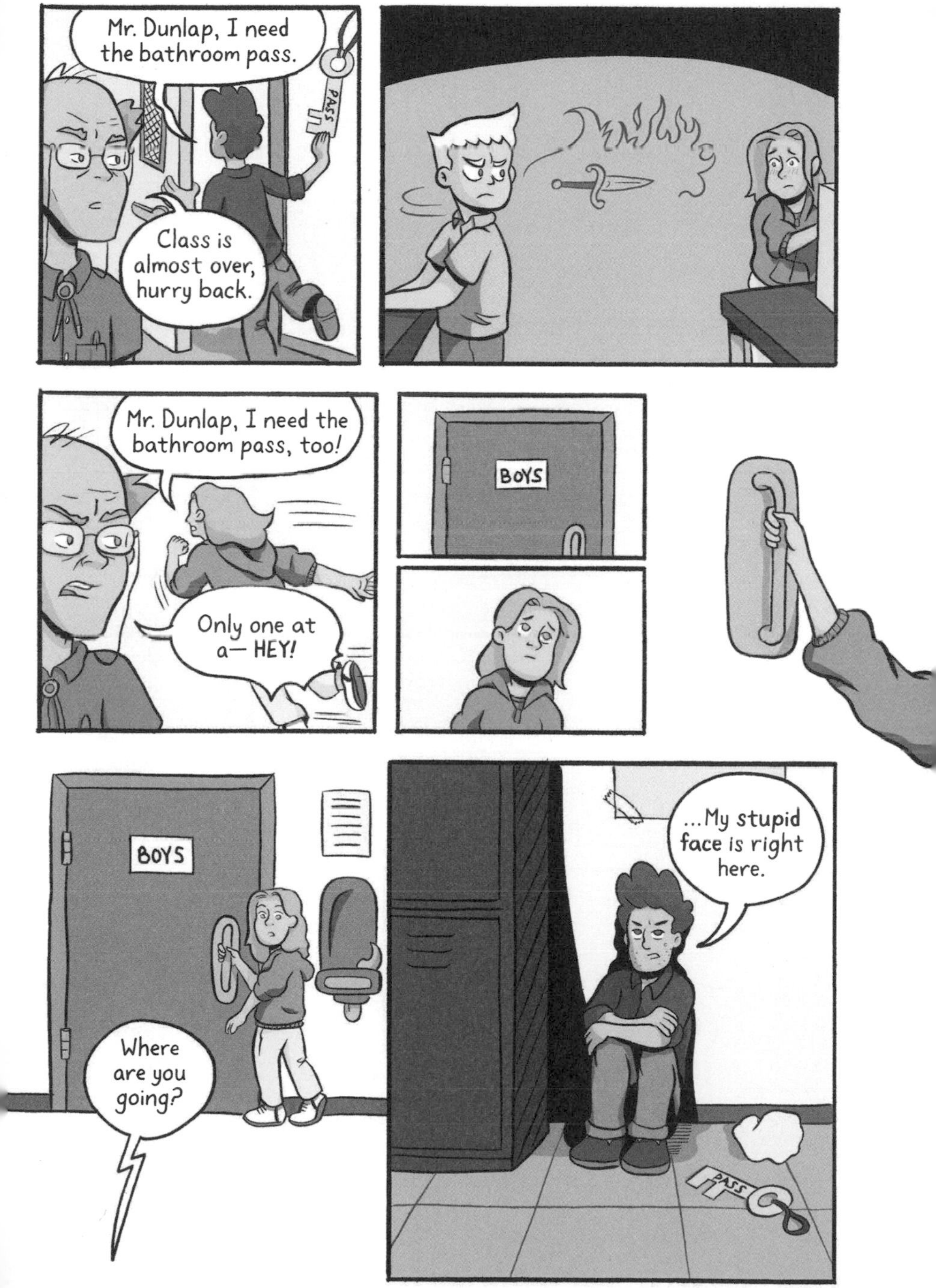

Mr. Dunlap, I need the bathroom pass.
PASS
Class is almost over, hurry back.
Mr. Dunlap, I need the bathroom pass, too!
Only one at a— HEY!
BOYS
BOYS
Where are you going?
...My stupid face is right here.
PASS

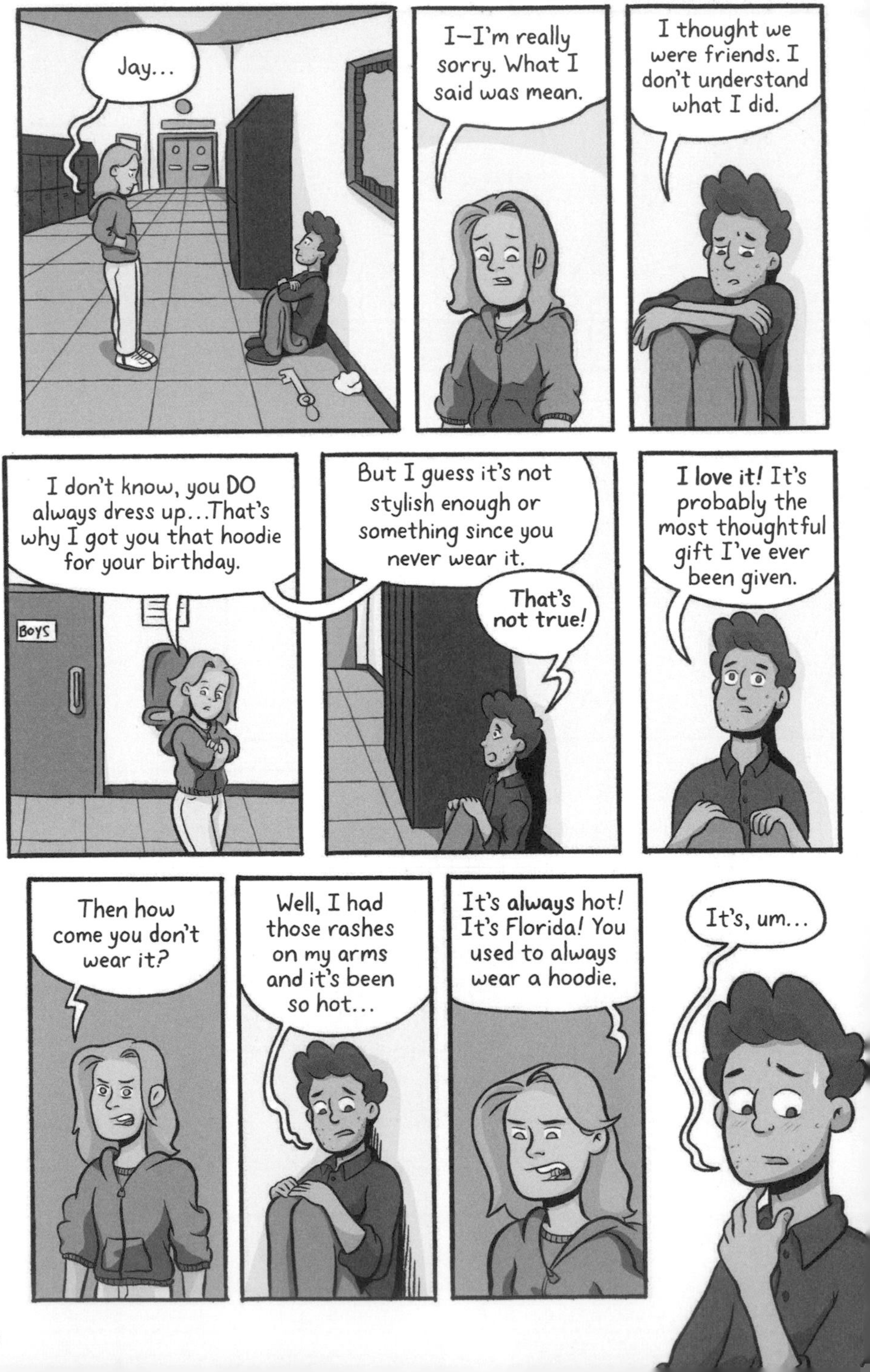
Jay...
I—I'm really sorry. What I said was mean.
I thought we were friends. I don't understand what I did.
I don't know, you DO always dress up...That's why I got you that hoodie for your birthday.
BOYS
But I guess it's not stylish enough or something since you never wear it.
That's not true!
I love it! It's probably the most thoughtful gift I've ever been given.
Then how come you don't wear it?
Well, I had those rashes on my arms and it's been so hot...
It's always hot! It's Florida! You used to always wear a hoodie.
It's, um...

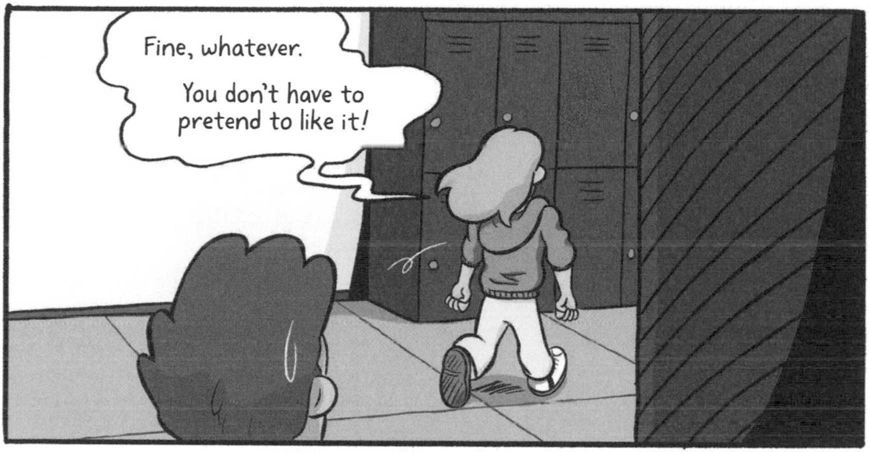
Fine, whatever.
You don't have to pretend to like it!

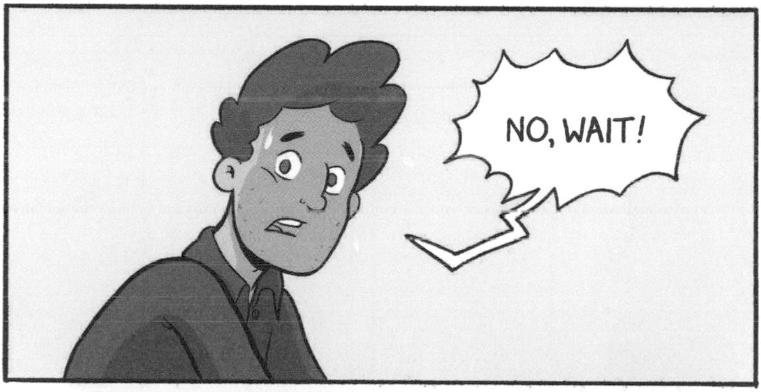
NO, WAIT!

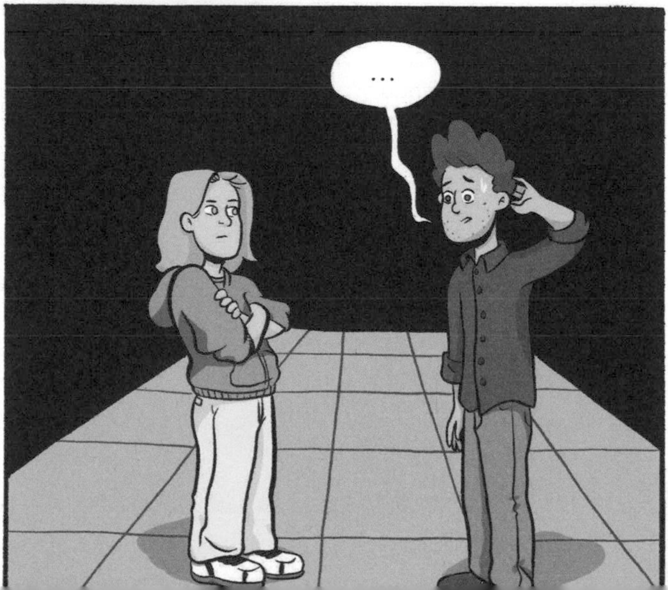
...

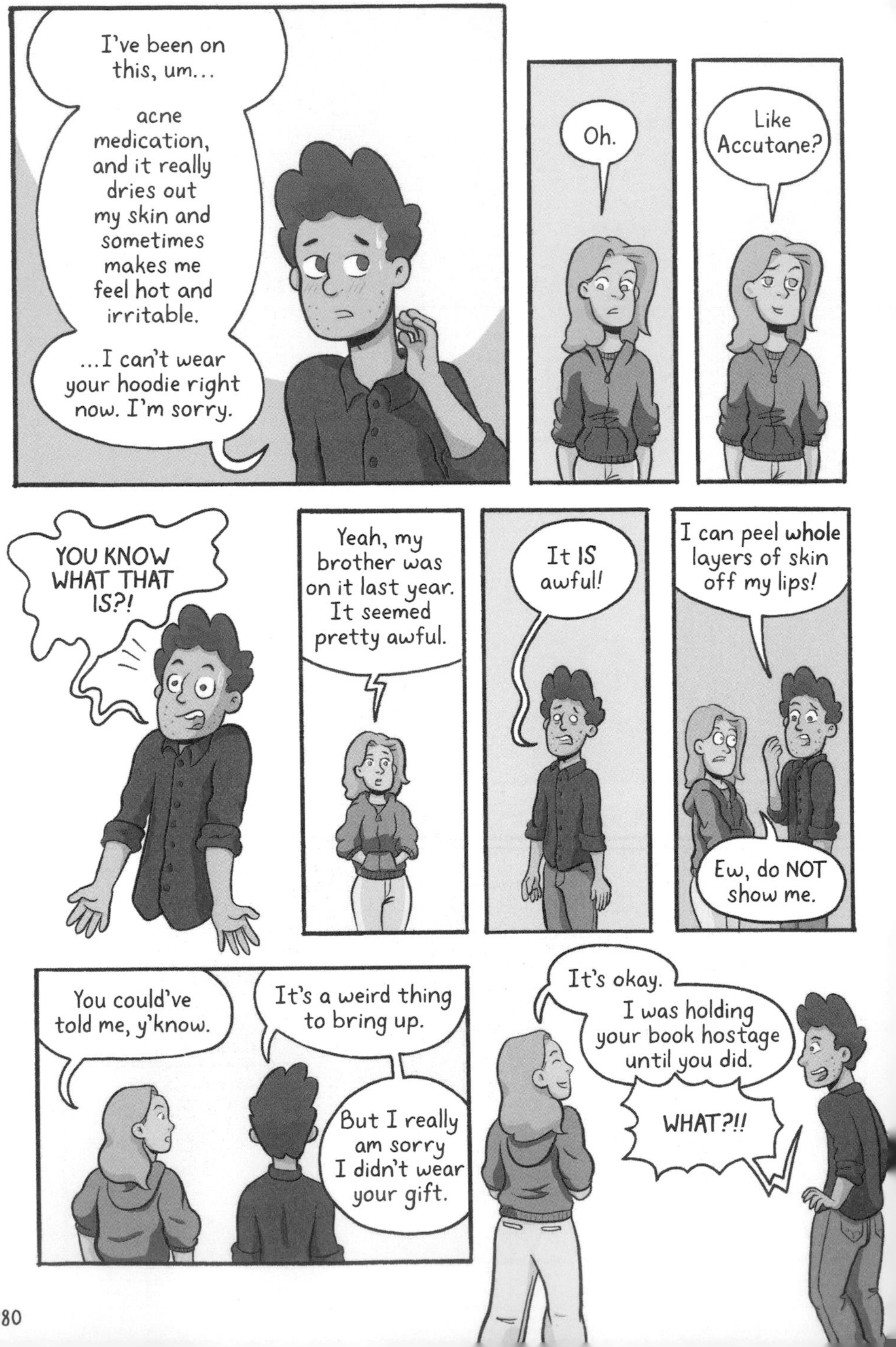
I've been on this, um...
acne medication, and it really dries out my skin and sometimes makes me feel hot and irritable.
...I can't wear your hoodie right now. I'm sorry.
Oh.
Like Accutane?
YOU KNOW WHAT THAT IS?!
Yeah, my brother was on it last year. It seemed pretty awful.
It IS awful!
I can peel **whole** layers of skin off my lips!
Ew, do NOT show me.
You could've told me, y'know.
It's a weird thing to bring up.
But I really am sorry I didn't wear your gift.
It's okay.
I was holding your book hostage until you did.
WHAT?!!

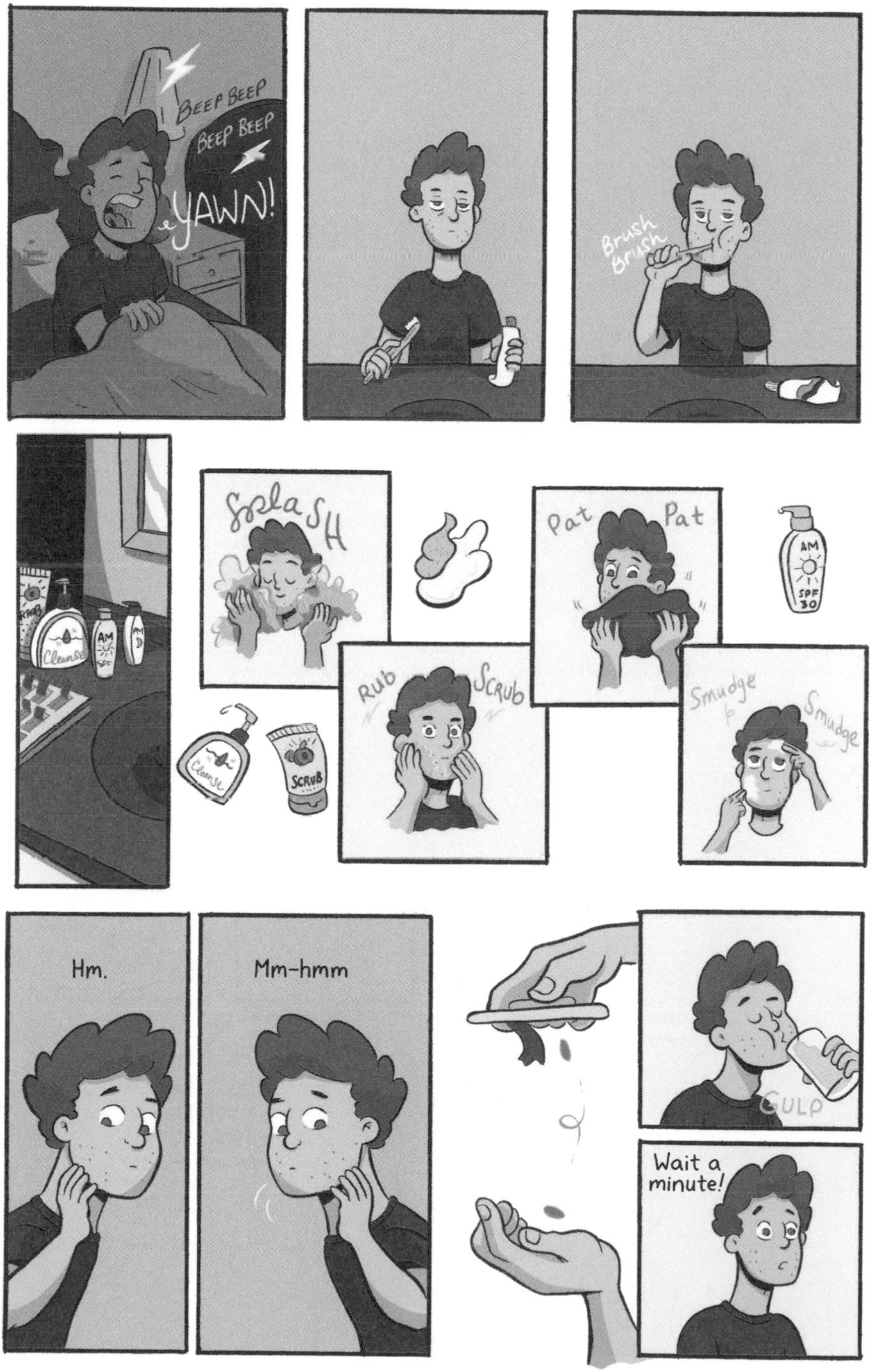
BEEP BEEP
BEEP BEEP
YAWN!
Brush
Brush
SPLASH
Pat
Pat
AM
SPF 30
Rub
SCRUB
Smudge
Smudge
Cleanse
SCRUB
Hm.
Mm-hmm
GULP
Wait a minute!

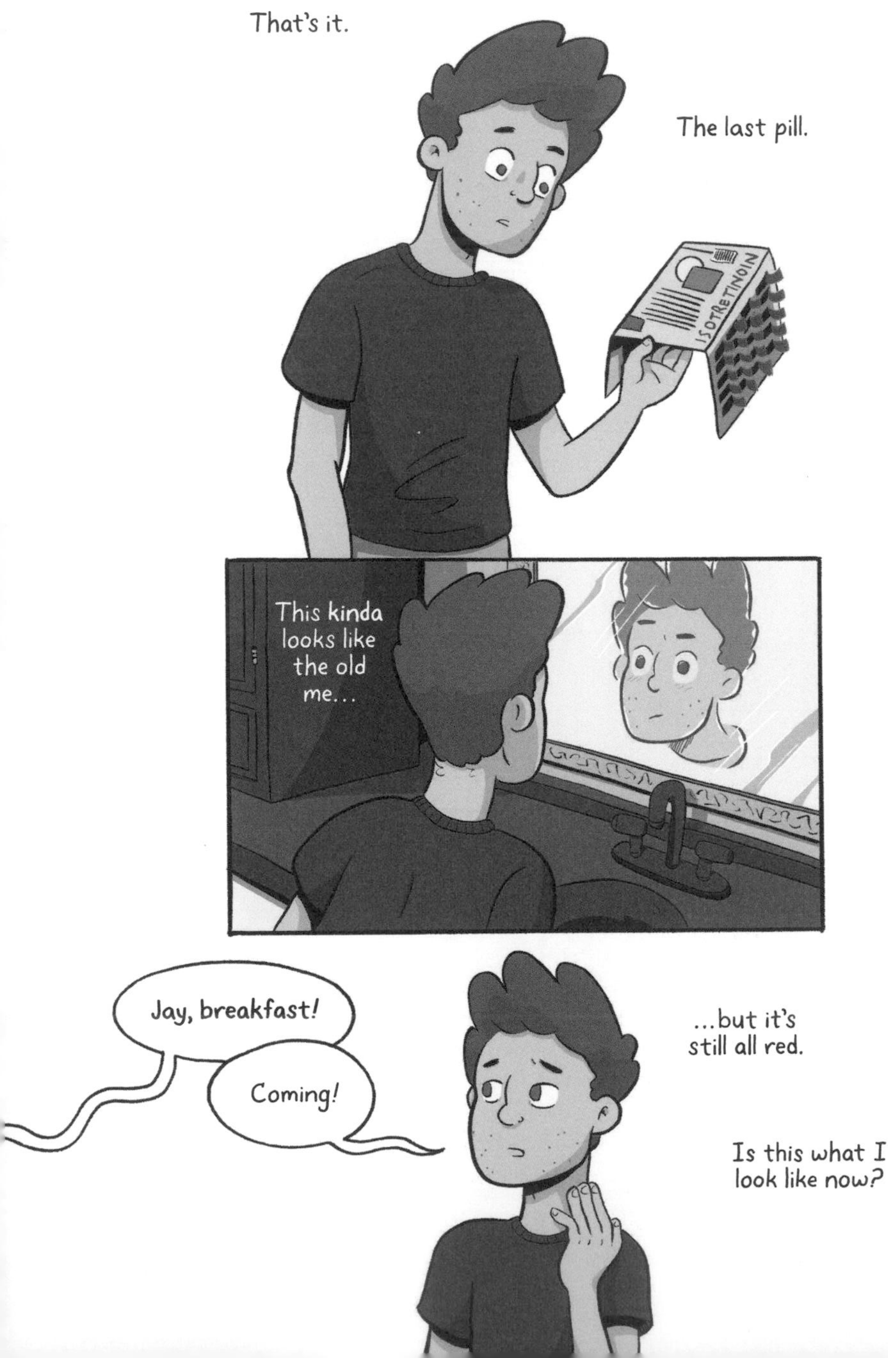
That's it.
The last pill.
ISOTRETINOIN
This kinda looks like the old me...
...but it's still all red.
Jay, breakfast!
Coming!
Is this what I look like now?

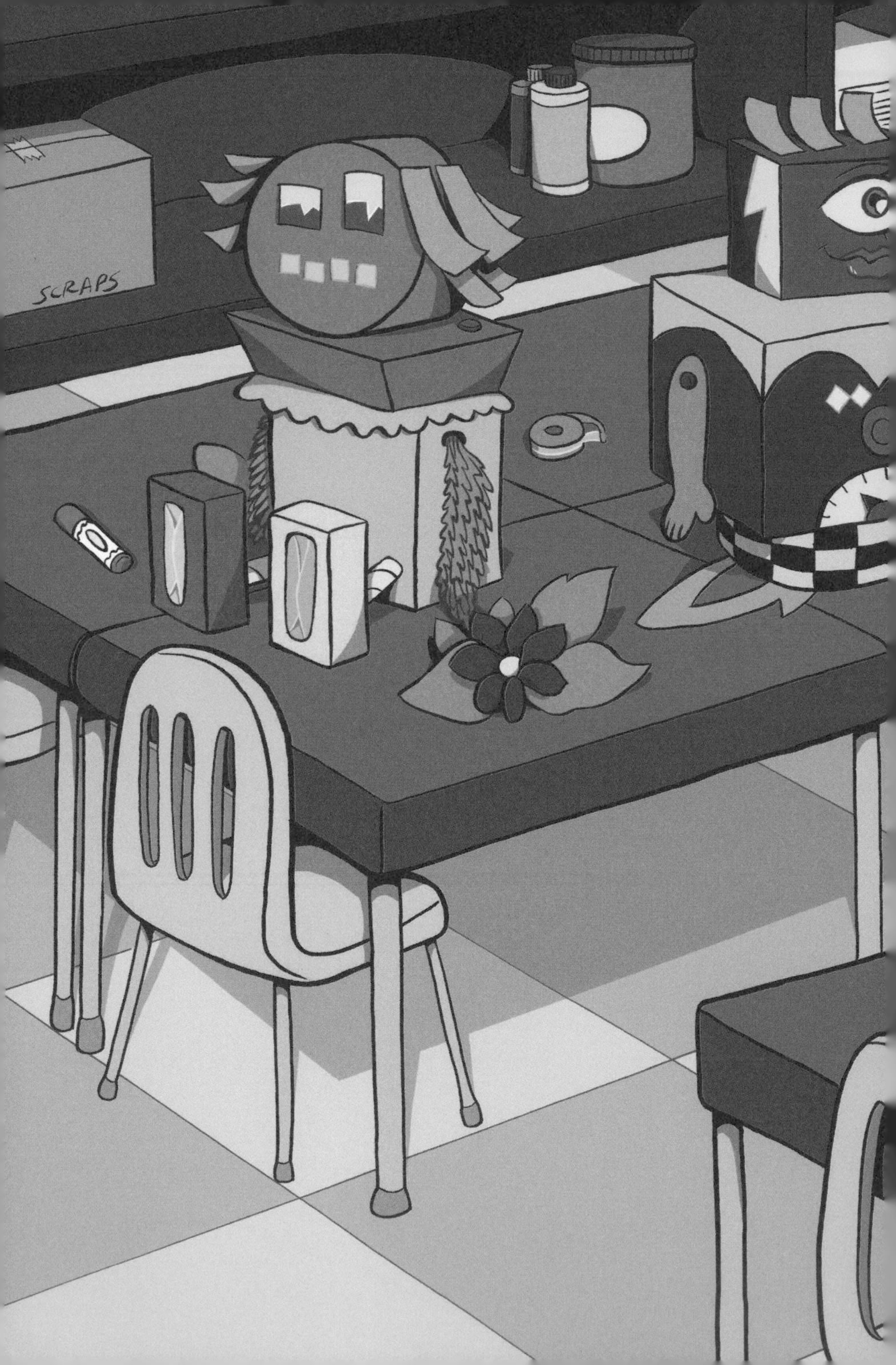
SCRAPS

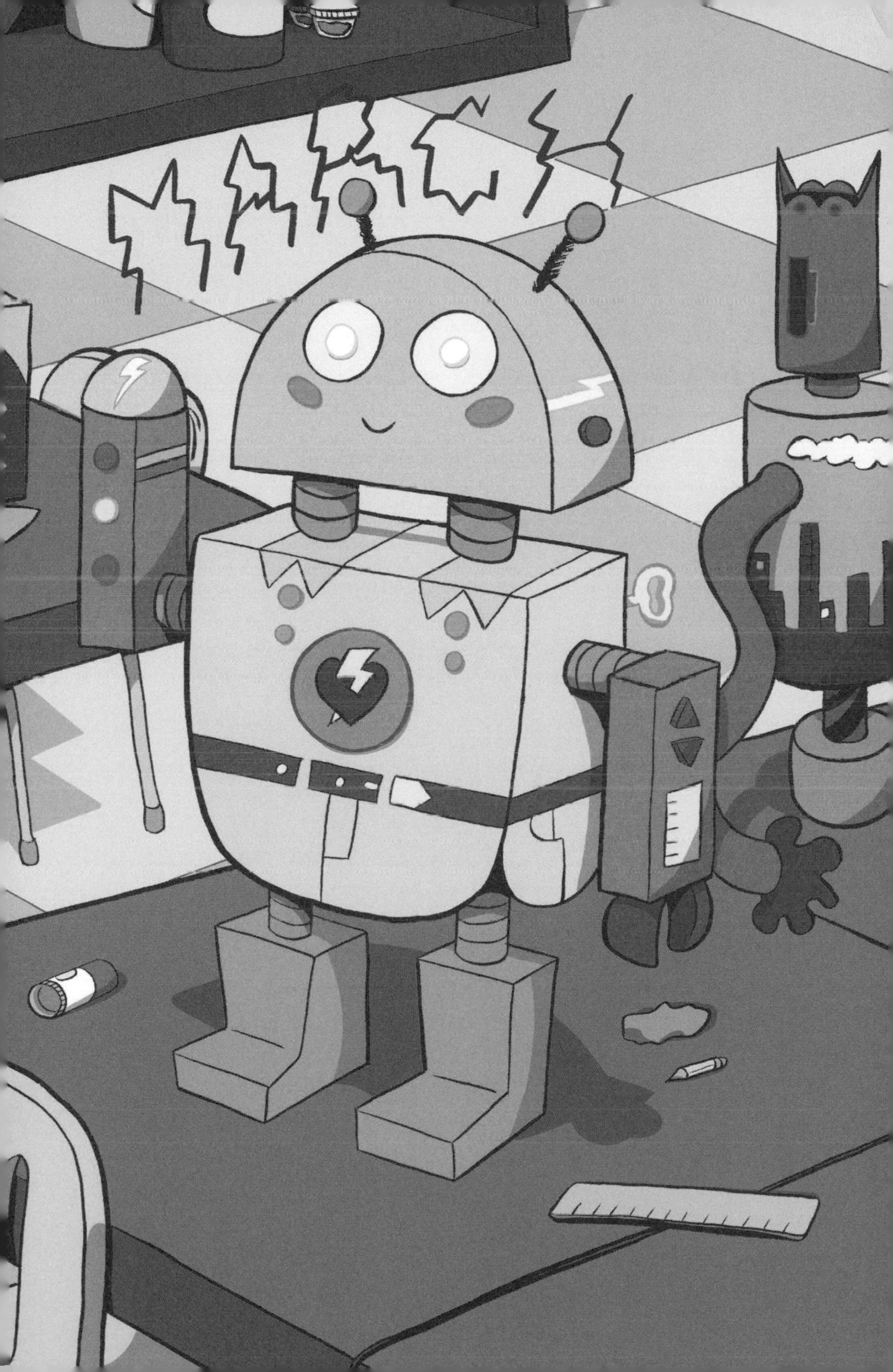

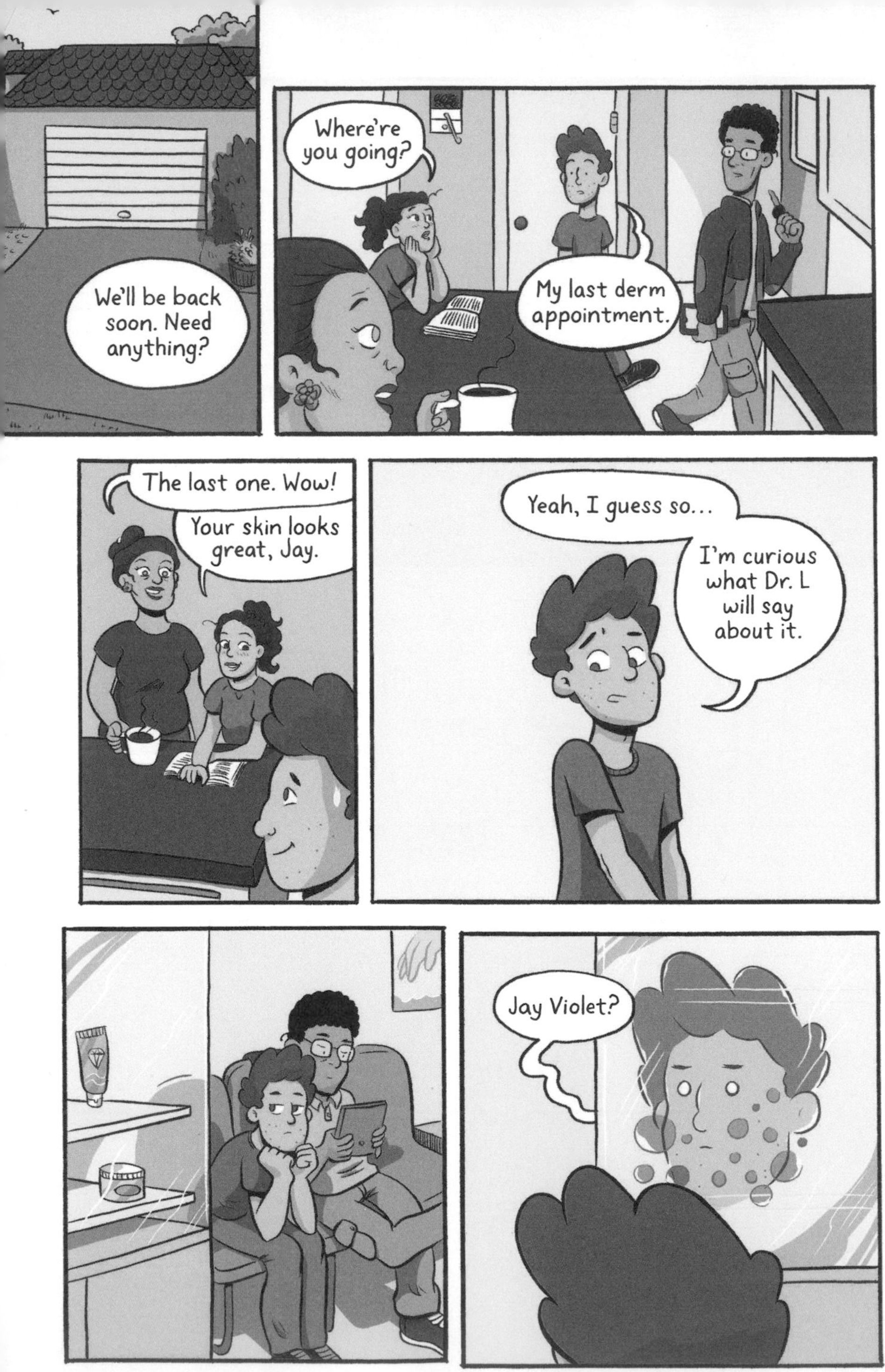
We'll be back soon. Need anything?
Where're you going?
My last derm appointment.
The last one. Wow!
Your skin looks great, Jay.
Yeah, I guess so...
I'm curious what Dr. L will say about it.
Jay Violet?

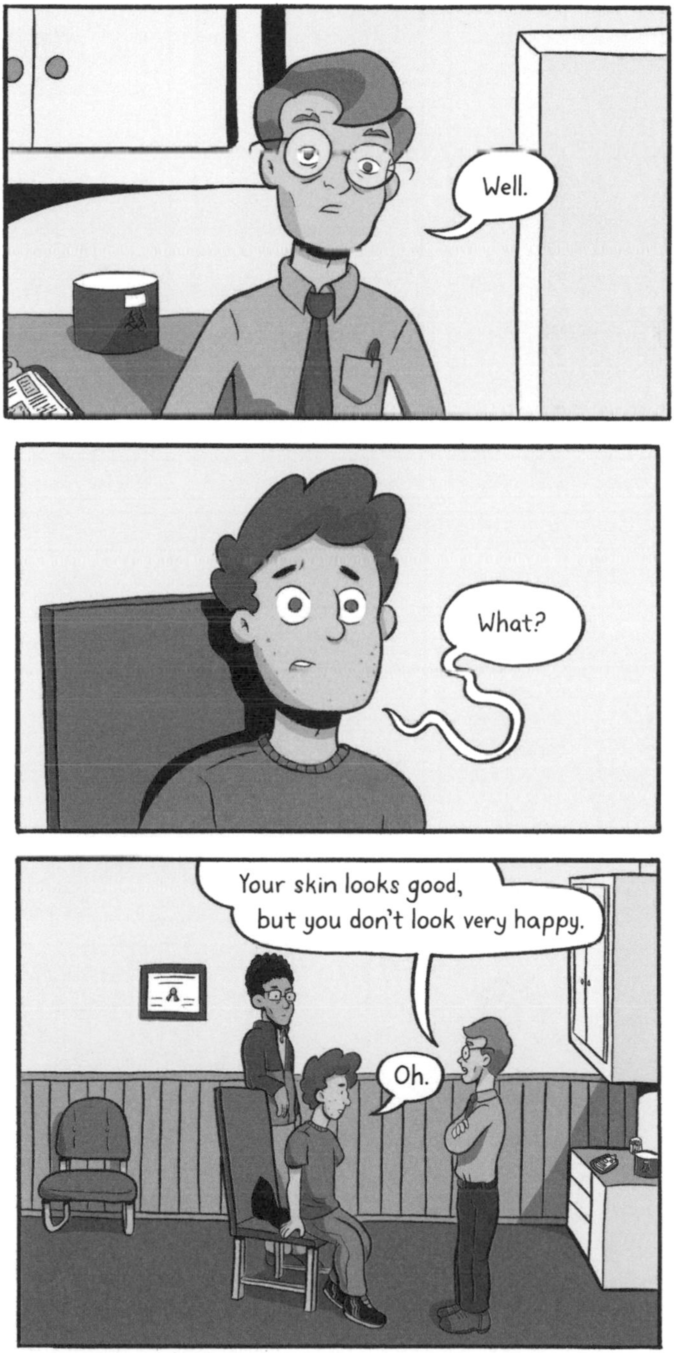
Well.
What?
Your skin looks good, but you don't look very happy.
Oh.

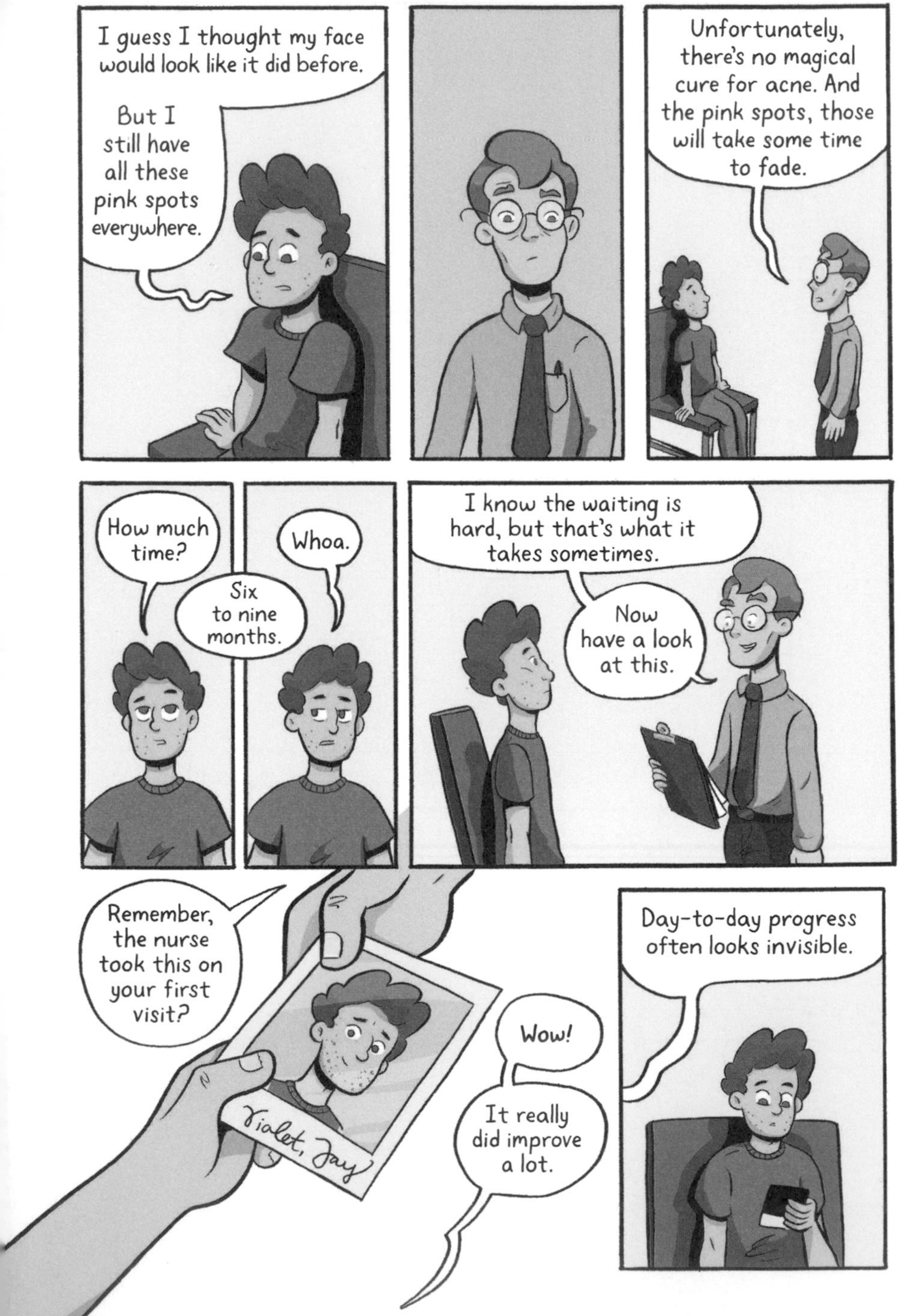
I guess I thought my face would look like it did before.
But I still have all these pink spots everywhere.
Unfortunately, there's no magical cure for acne. And the pink spots, those will take some time to fade.
How much time?
Six to nine months.
Whoa.
I know the waiting is hard, but that's what it takes sometimes.
Now have a look at this.
Remember, the nurse took this on your first visit?
Vialet, Jay
Wow!
It really did improve a lot.
Day-to-day progress often looks invisible.

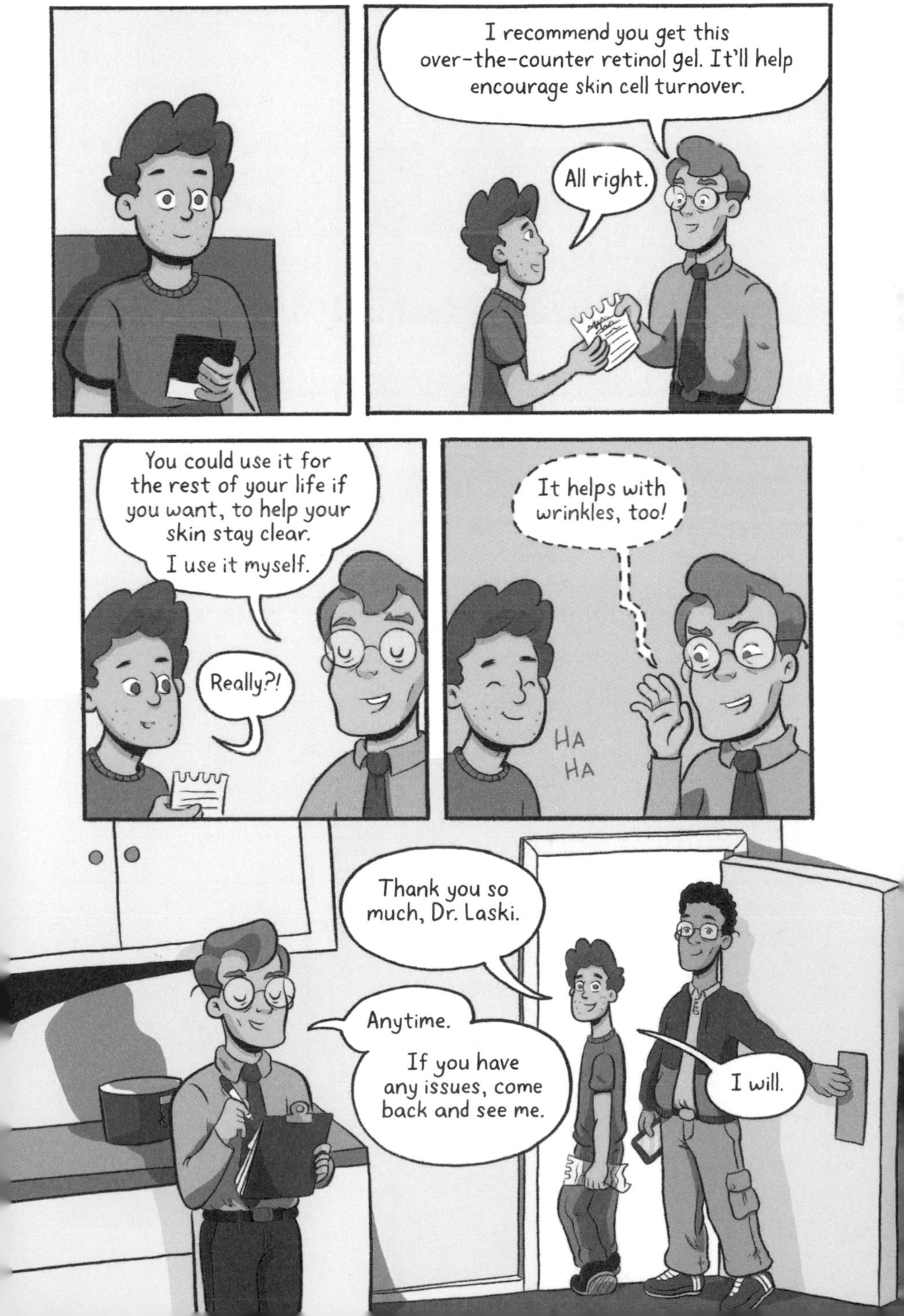
I recommend you get this over-the-counter retinol gel. It'll help encourage skin cell turnover.
All right.
You could use it for the rest of your life if you want, to help your skin stay clear.
I use it myself.
Really?!
It helps with wrinkles, too!
HA HA
Thank you so much, Dr. Laski.
Anytime.
If you have any issues, come back and see me.
I will.

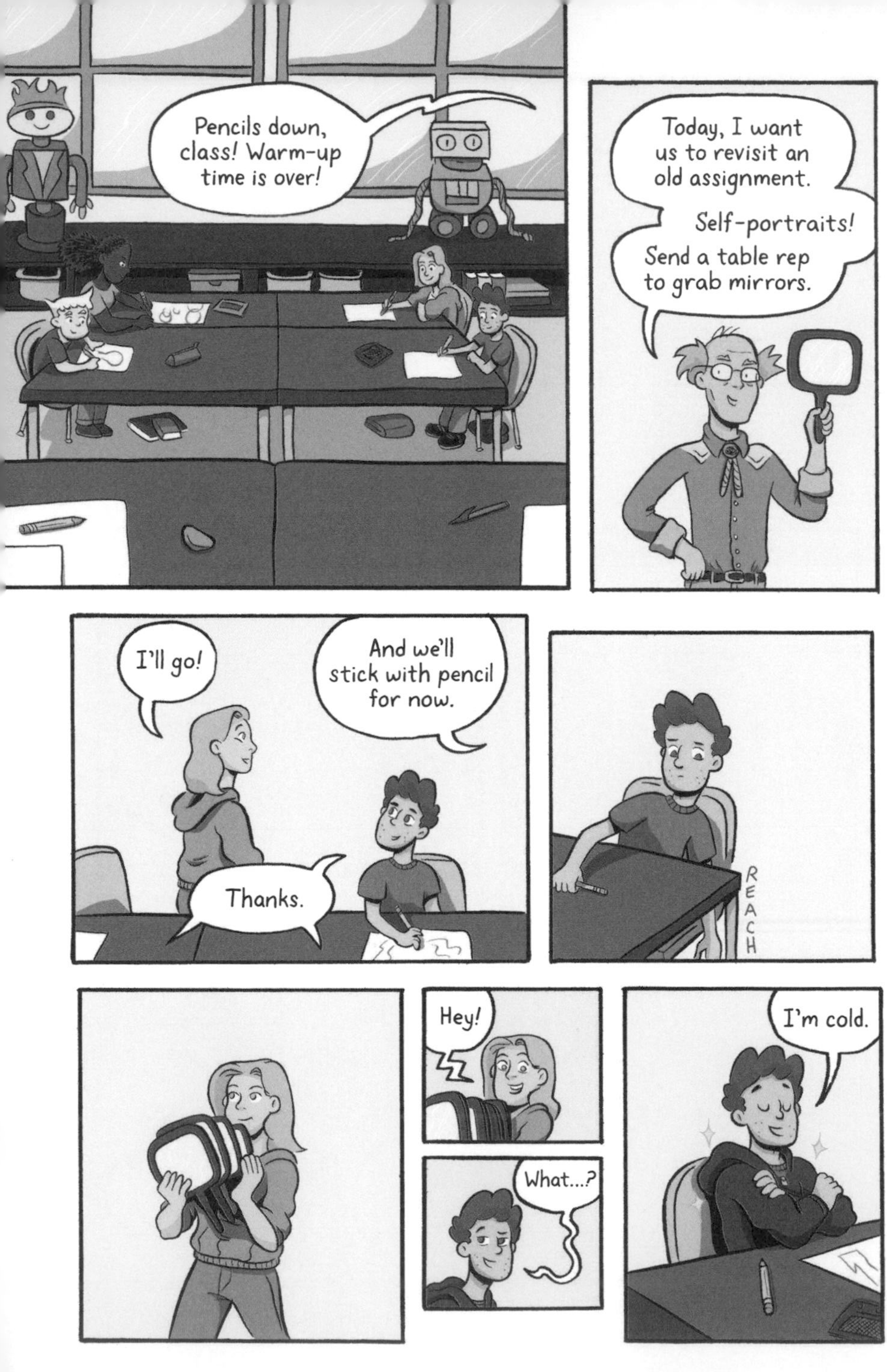
Pencils down, class! Warm-up time is over!
Today, I want us to revisit an old assignment.
Self-portraits!
Send a table rep to grab mirrors.
I'll go!
And we'll stick with pencil for now.
Thanks.
REACH
Hey!
What...?
I'm cold.

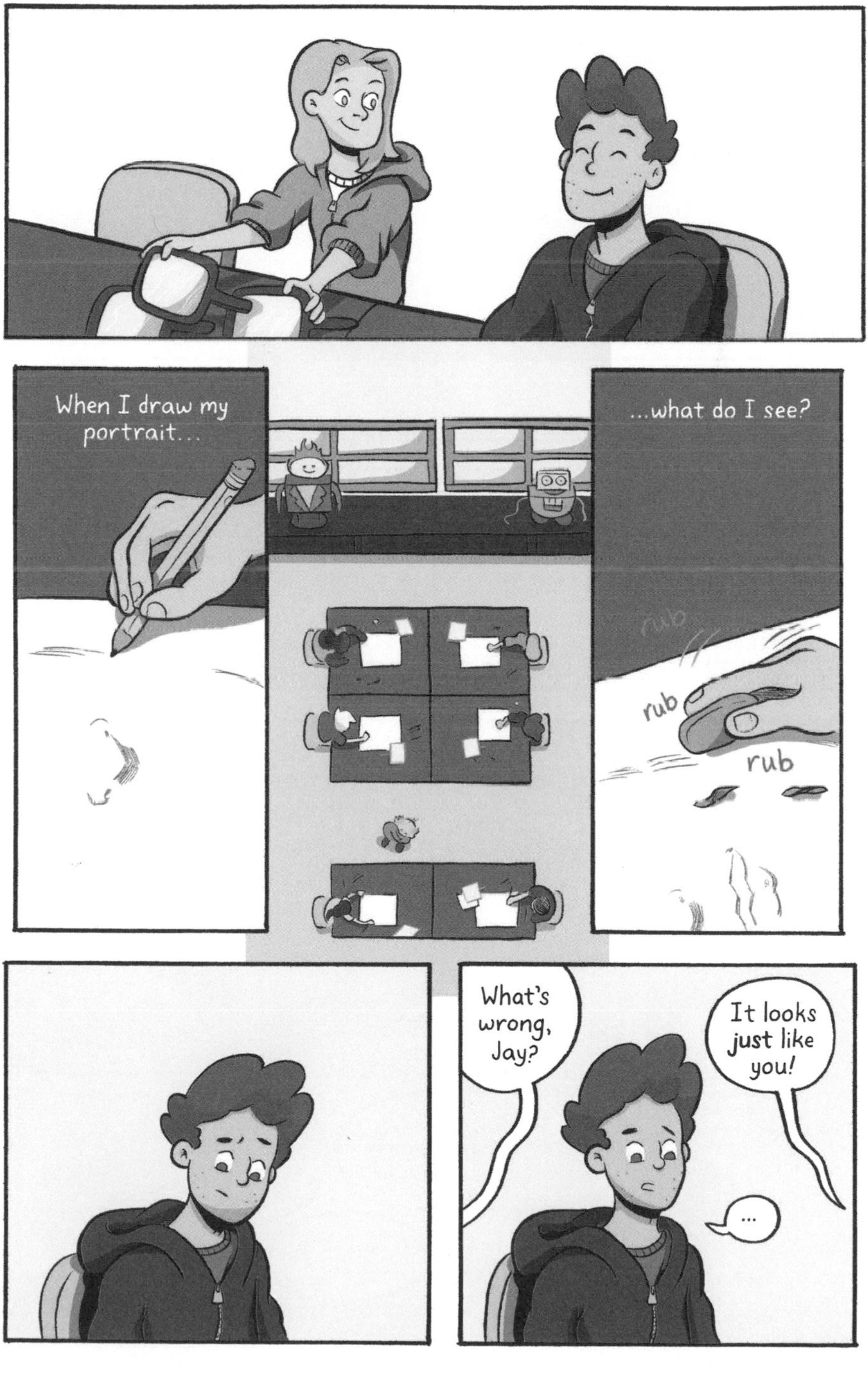
When I draw my portrait...
...what do I see?
rub
rub
rub
What's wrong, Jay?
It looks just like you!
...

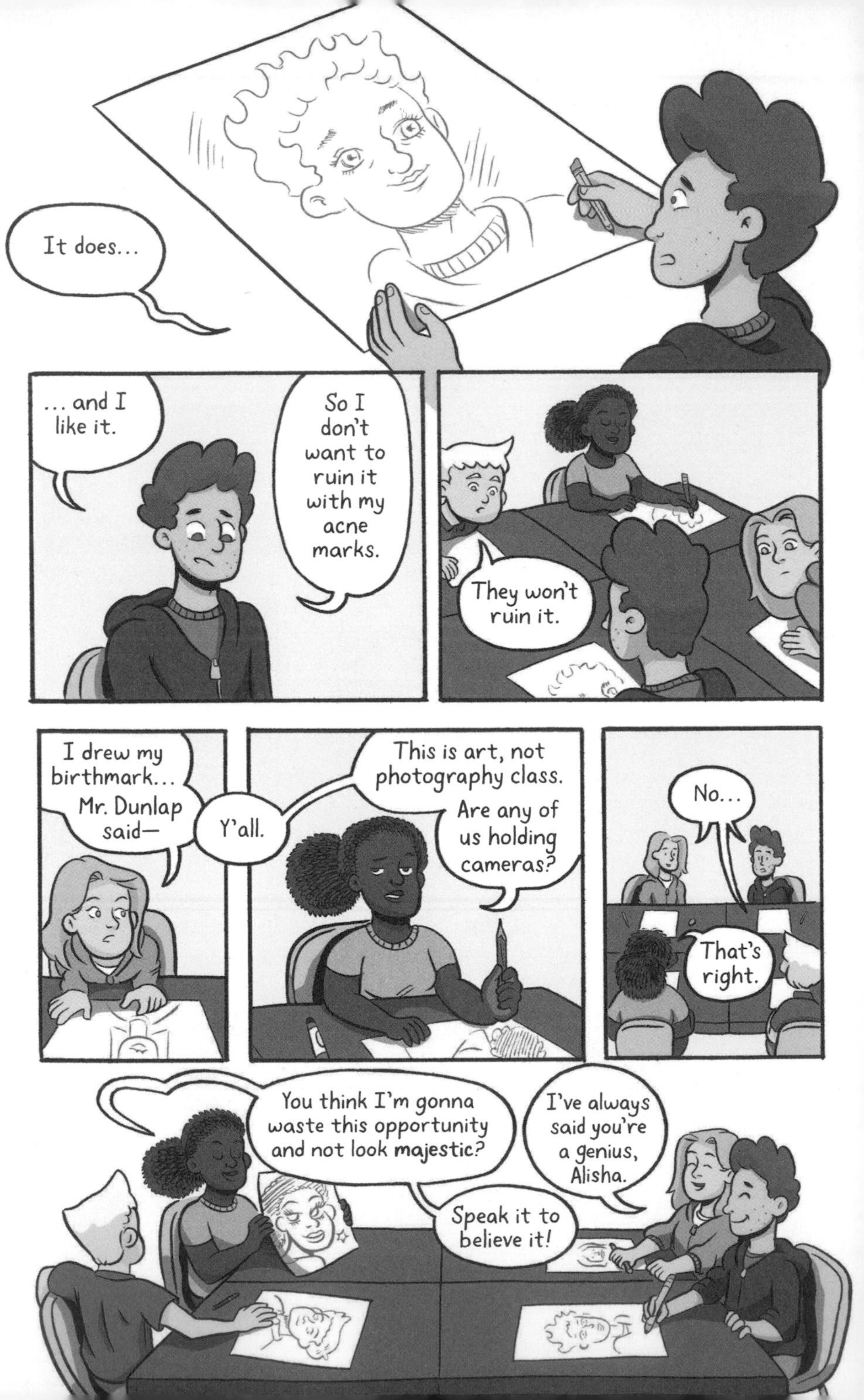
It does...
... and I like it.
So I don't want to ruin it with my acne marks.
They won't ruin it.
I drew my birthmark... Mr. Dunlap said—
Y'all.
This is art, not photography class.
Are any of us holding cameras?
No...
That's right.
You think I'm gonna waste this opportunity and not look **majestic**?
Speak it to believe it!
I've always said you're a genius, Alisha.

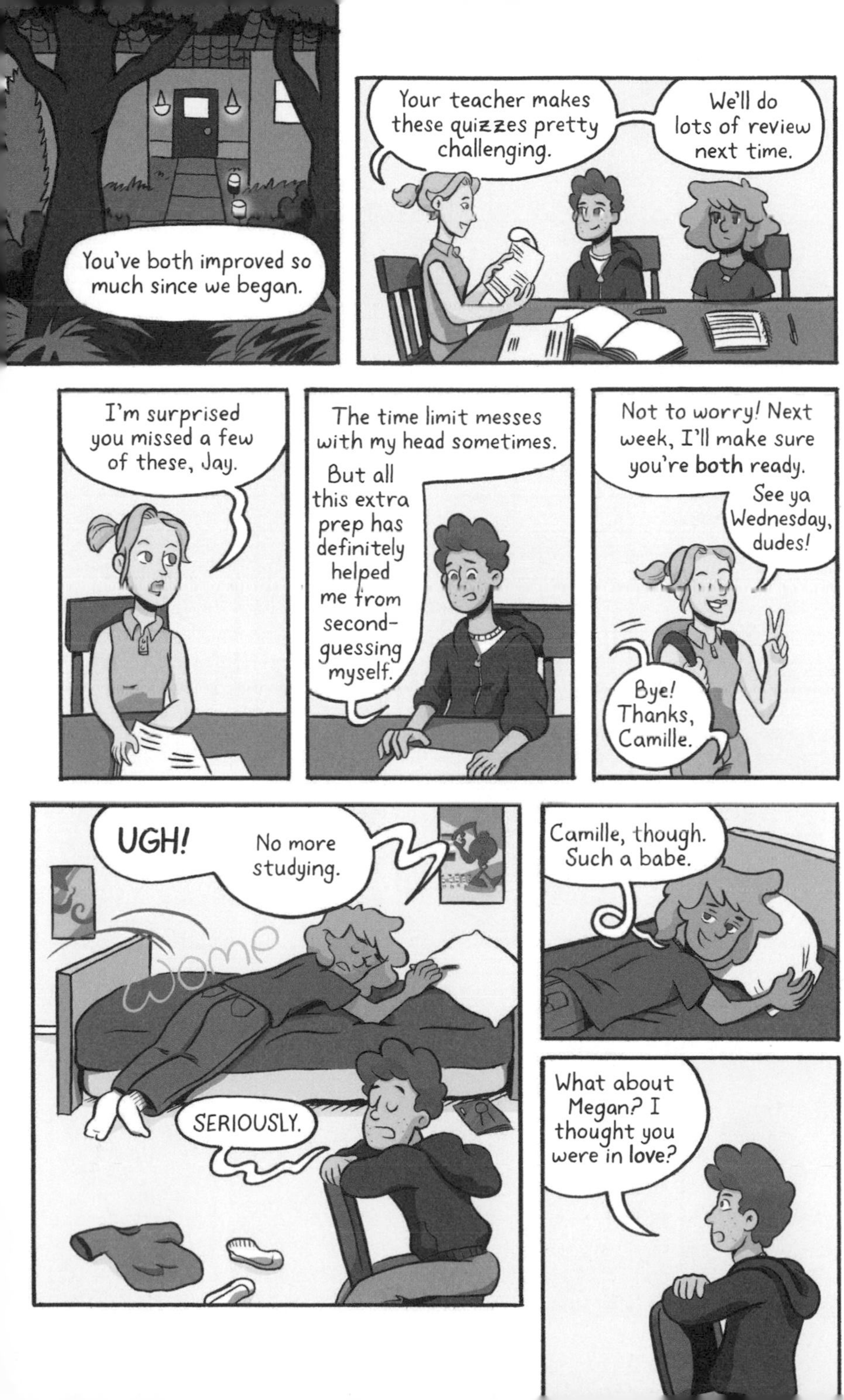
You've both improved so much since we began.
Your teacher makes these quizzes pretty challenging.
We'll do lots of review next time.
I'm surprised you missed a few of these, Jay.
The time limit messes with my head sometimes.
But all this extra prep has definitely helped me from second-guessing myself.
Not to worry! Next week, I'll make sure you're **both** ready.
See ya Wednesday, dudes!
Bye! Thanks, Camille.
UGH!
No more studying.
WOMP
SERIOUSLY.
Camille, though. Such a babe.
What about Megan? I thought you were in **love**?

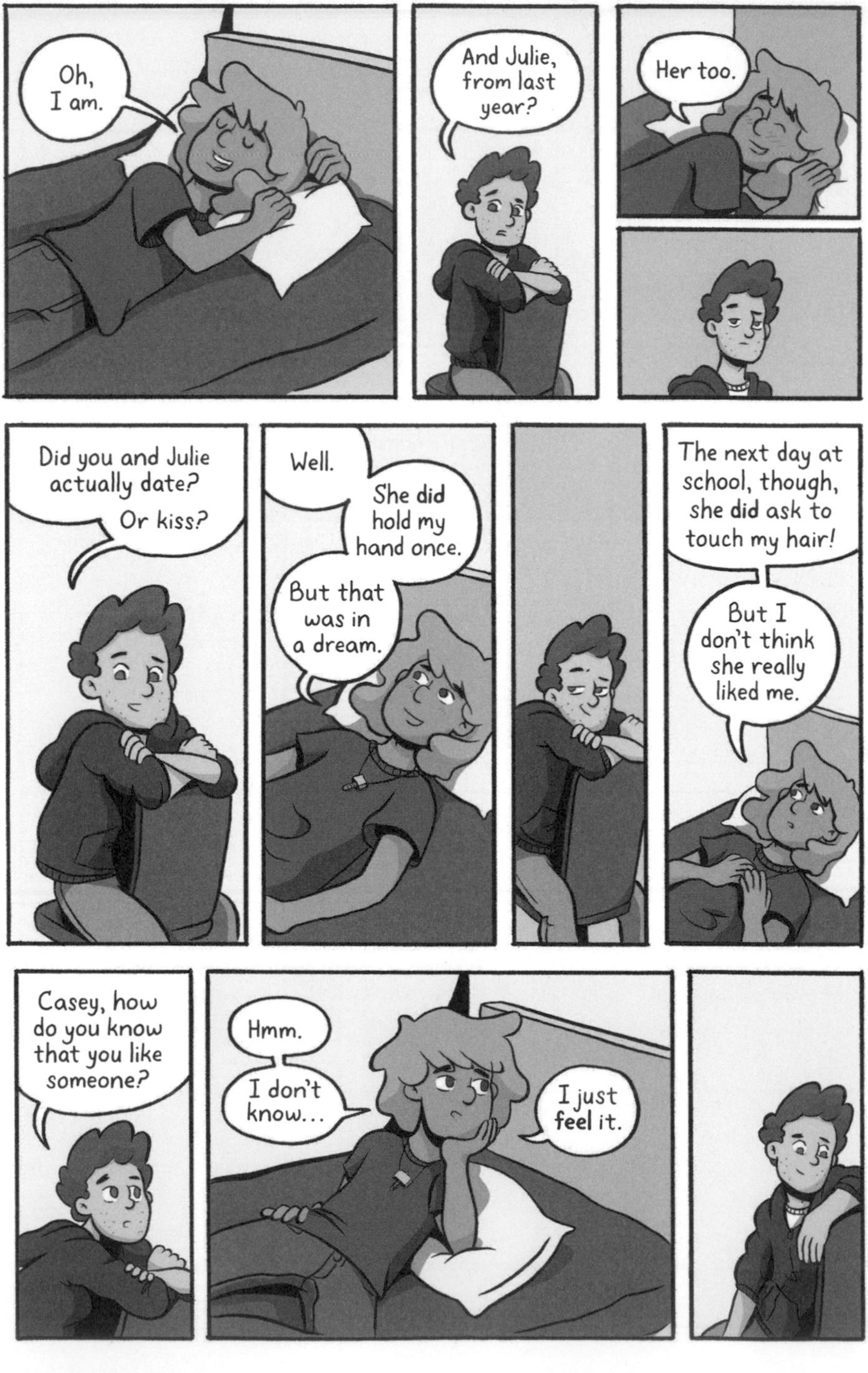
Oh, I am.
And Julie, from last year?
Her too.
Did you and Julie actually date?
Or kiss?
Well.
She **did** hold my hand once.
But that was in a dream.
The next day at school, though, she **did** ask to touch my hair!
But I don't think she really liked me.
Casey, how do you know that you like someone?
Hmm.
I don't know...
I just **feel** it.

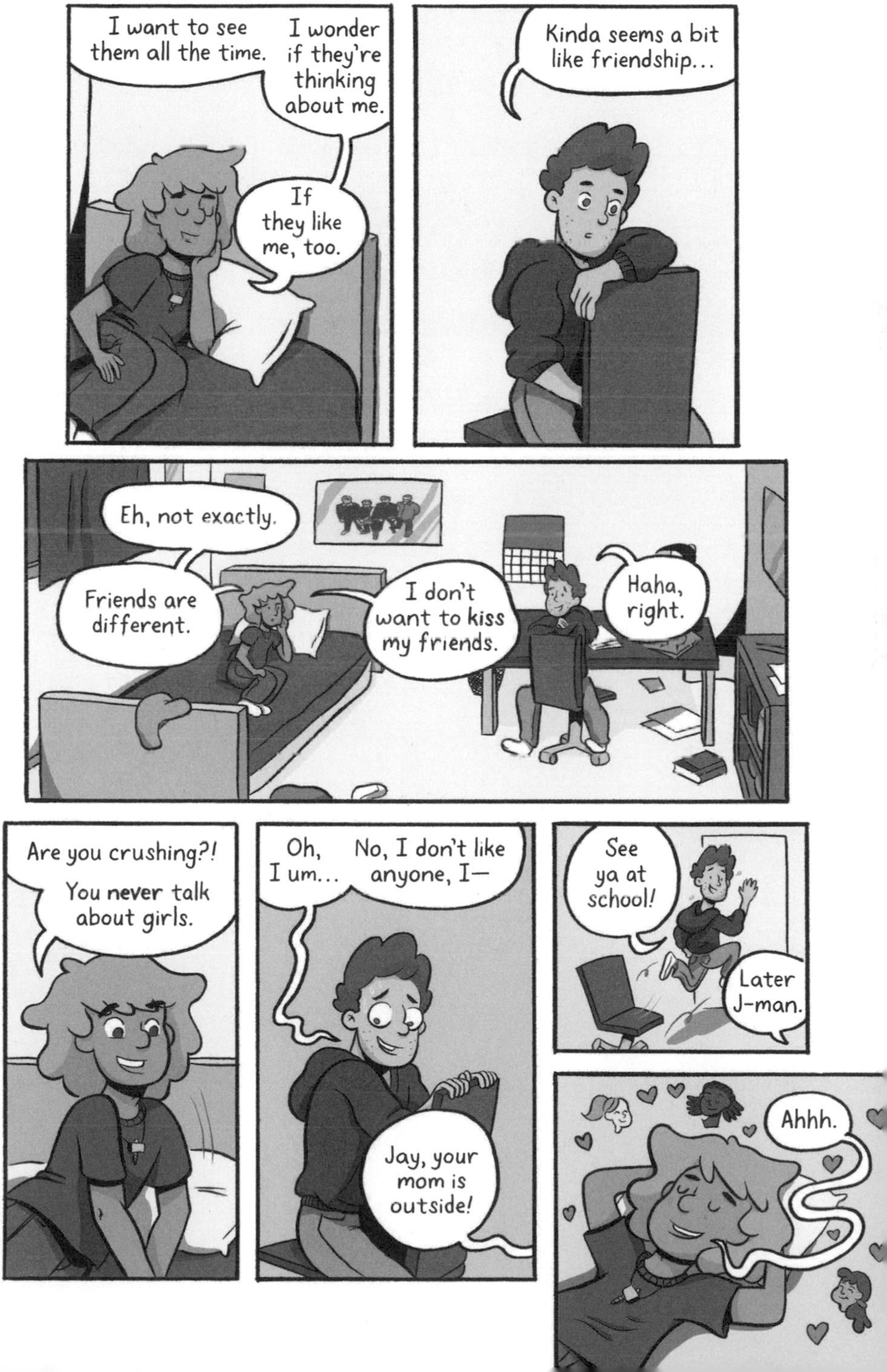
I want to see them all the time.
I wonder if they're thinking about me.
If they like me, too.
Kinda seems a bit like friendship...
Eh, not exactly.
Friends are different.
I don't want to kiss my friends.
Haha, right.
Are you crushing?!
You never talk about girls.
Oh, I um...
No, I don't like anyone, I—
Jay, your mom is outside!
See ya at school!
Later J-man.
Ahhh.

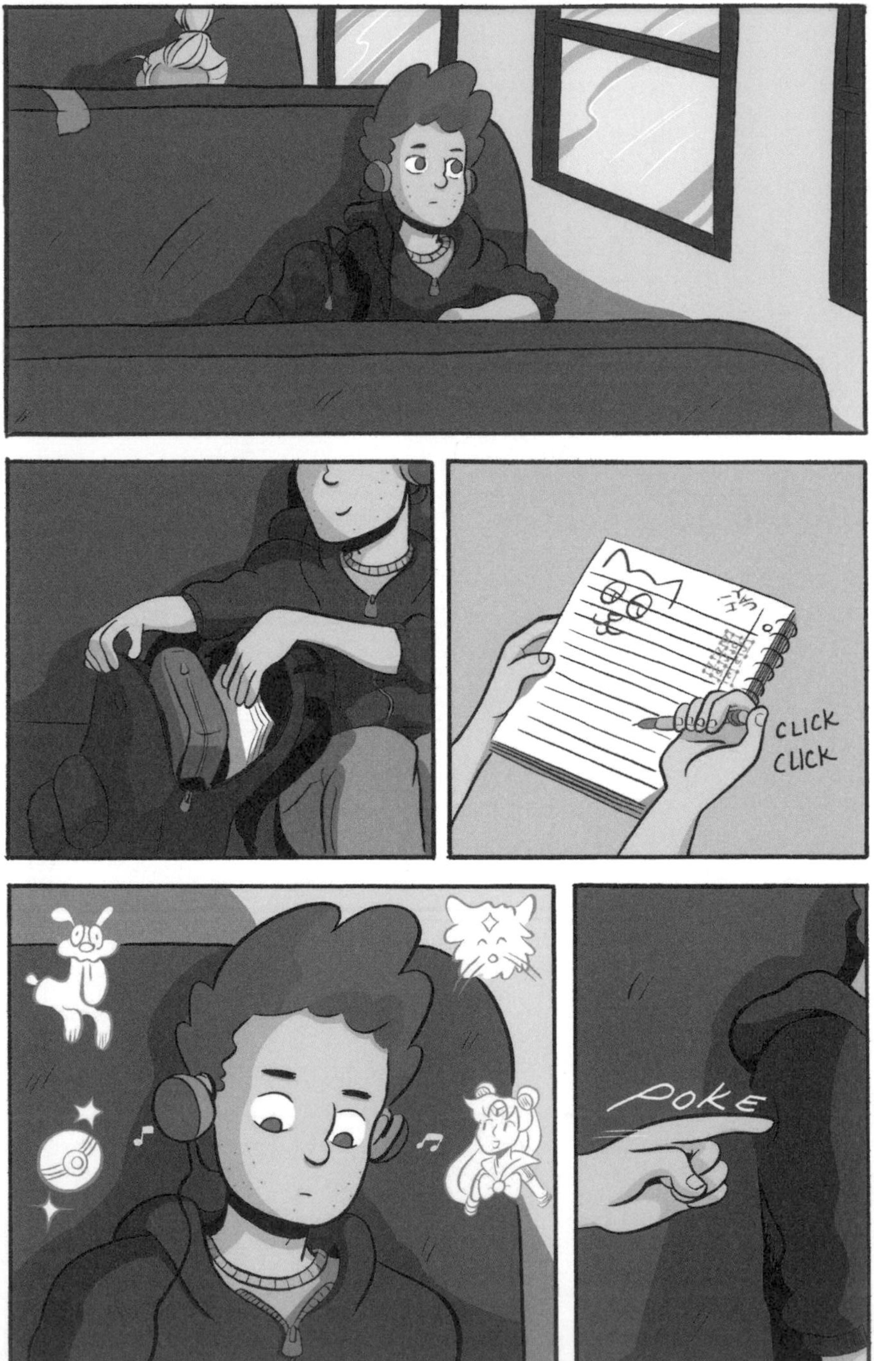
SAY HI!
CLICK
CLICK
POKE

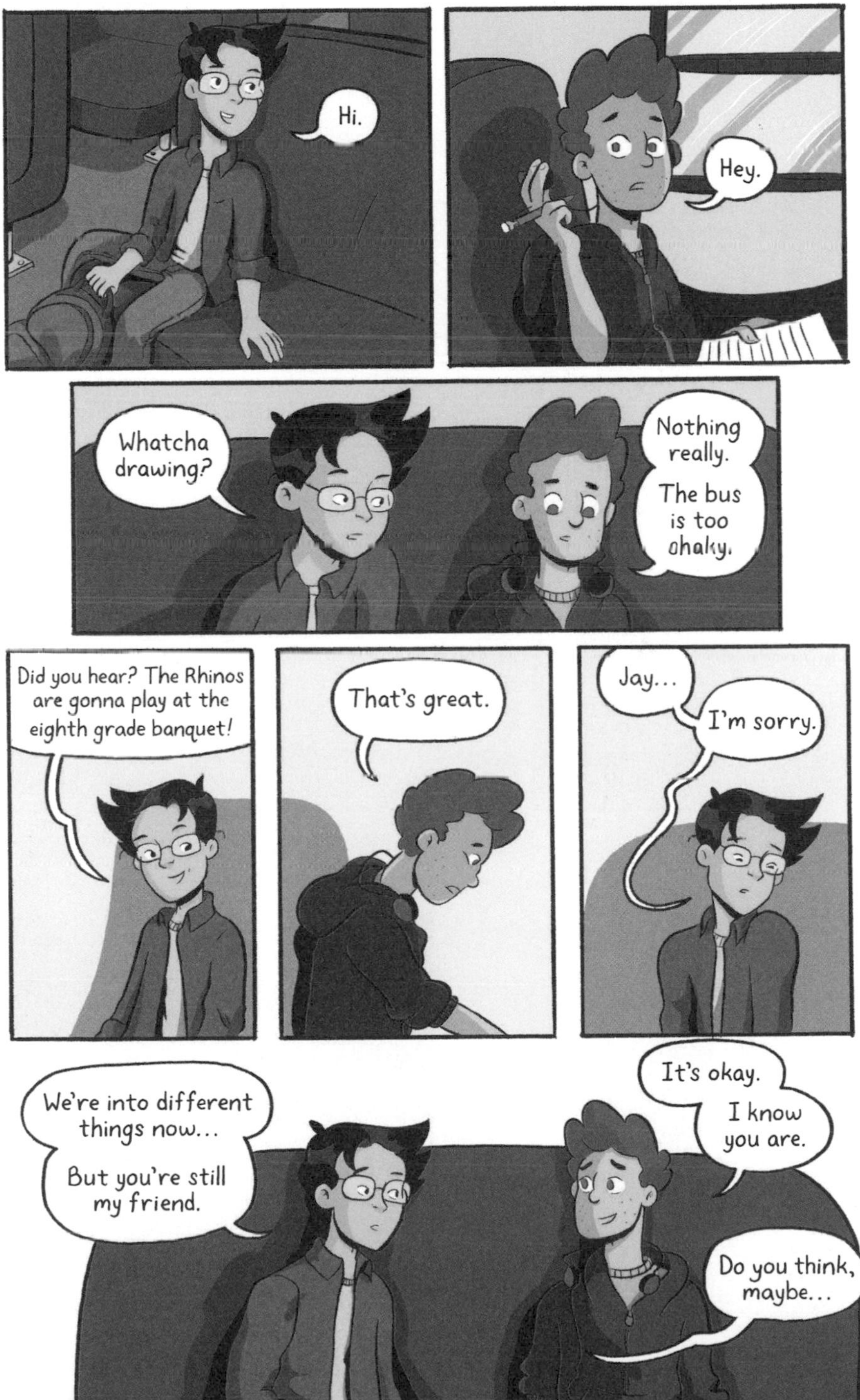
Hi.
Hey.
Whatcha drawing?
Nothing really.
The bus is too shaky.
Did you hear? The Rhinos are gonna play at the eighth grade banquet!
That's great.
Jay...
I'm sorry.
We're into different things now...
But you're still my friend.
It's okay.
I know you are.
Do you think, maybe...

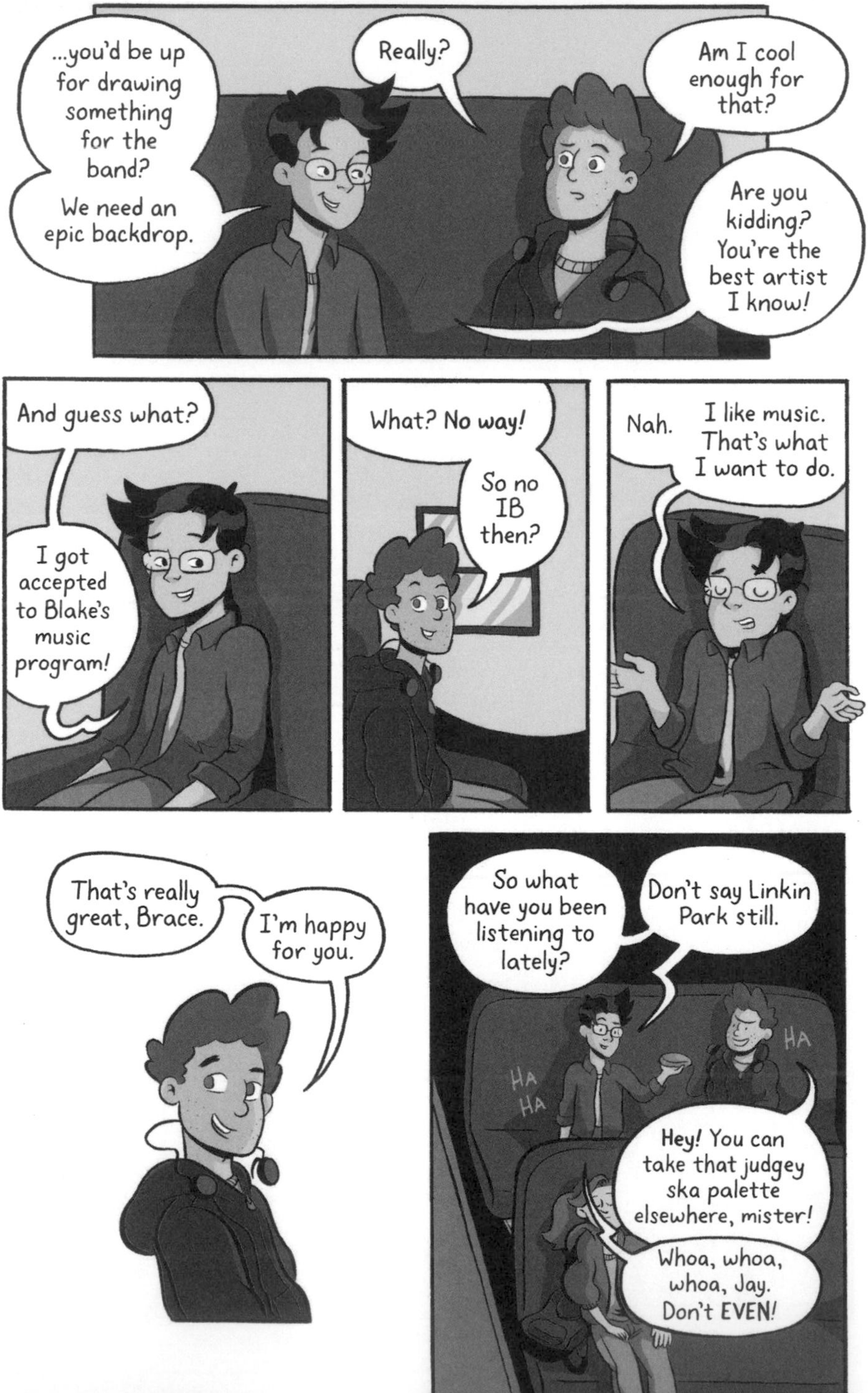
...you'd be up for drawing something for the band?
We need an epic backdrop.
Really?
Am I cool enough for that?
Are you kidding? You're the best artist I know!
And guess what?
I got accepted to Blake's music program!
What? No way!
So no IB then?
Nah.
I like music. That's what I want to do.
That's really great, Brace.
I'm happy for you.
So what have you been listening to lately?
Don't say Linkin Park still.
HA HA
HA
Hey! You can take that judgey ska palette elsewhere, mister!
Whoa, whoa, whoa, Jay. Don't EVEN!

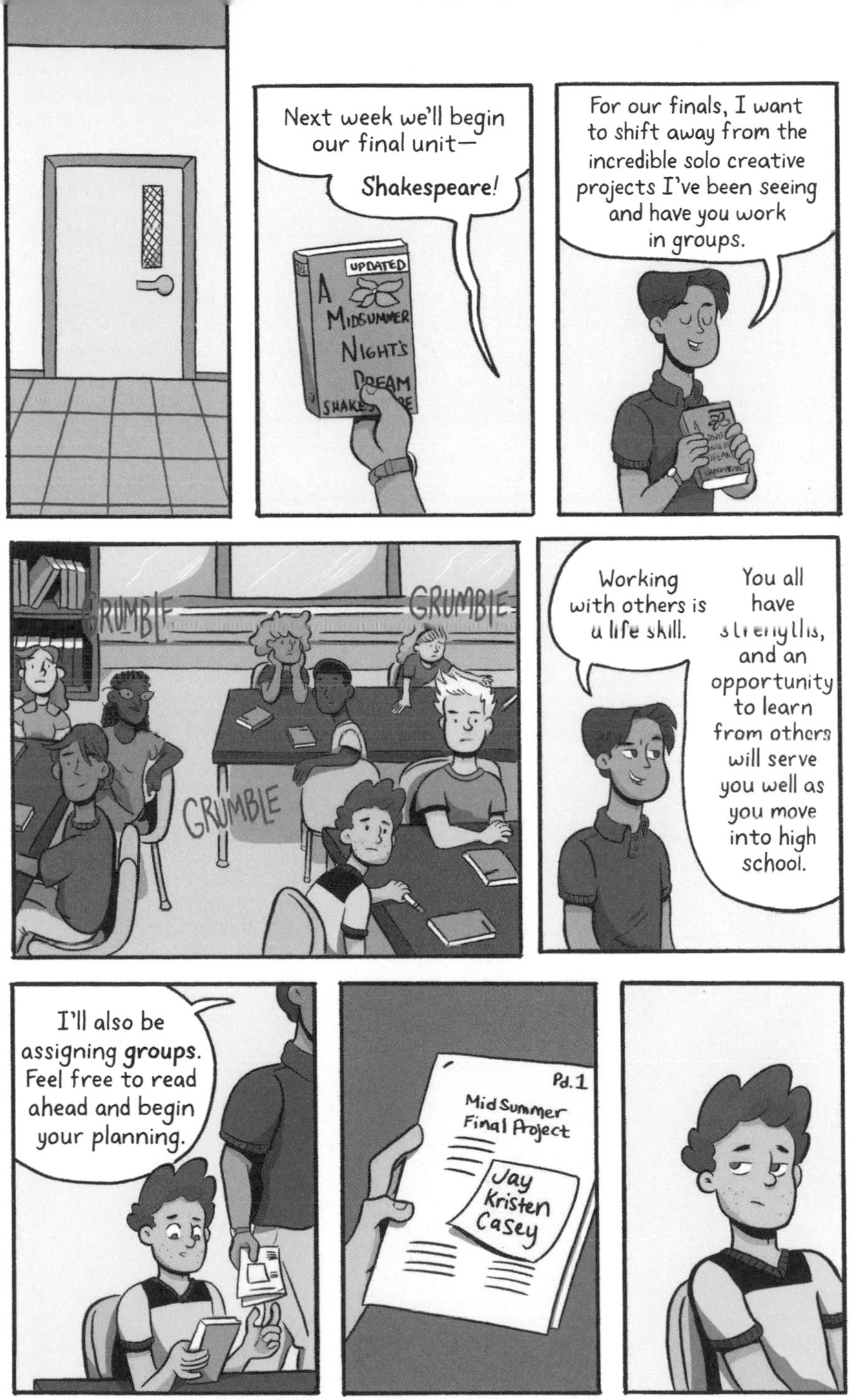

Next week we'll begin our final unit—
Shakespeare!
UPDATED
A MIDSUMMER NIGHT'S DREAM
For our finals, I want to shift away from the incredible solo creative projects I've been seeing and have you work in groups.
GRUMBLE
GRUMBLE
GRUMBLE
Working with others is a life skill.
You all have strengths, and an opportunity to learn from others will serve you well as you move into high school.
I'll also be assigning groups. Feel free to read ahead and begin your planning.
Pd. 1
MidSummer Final Project
Jay
Kristen
Casey

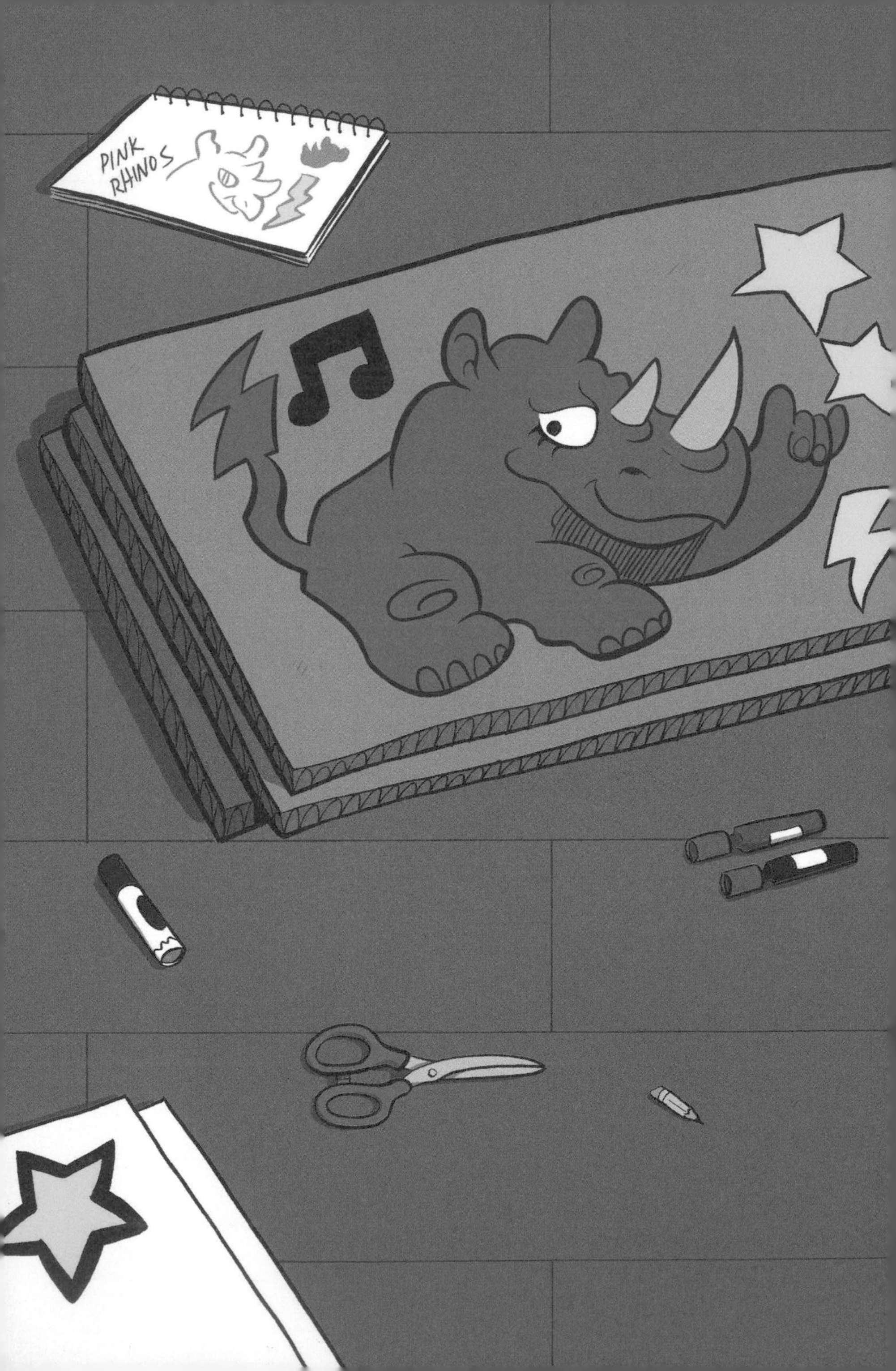
PINK RHINOS

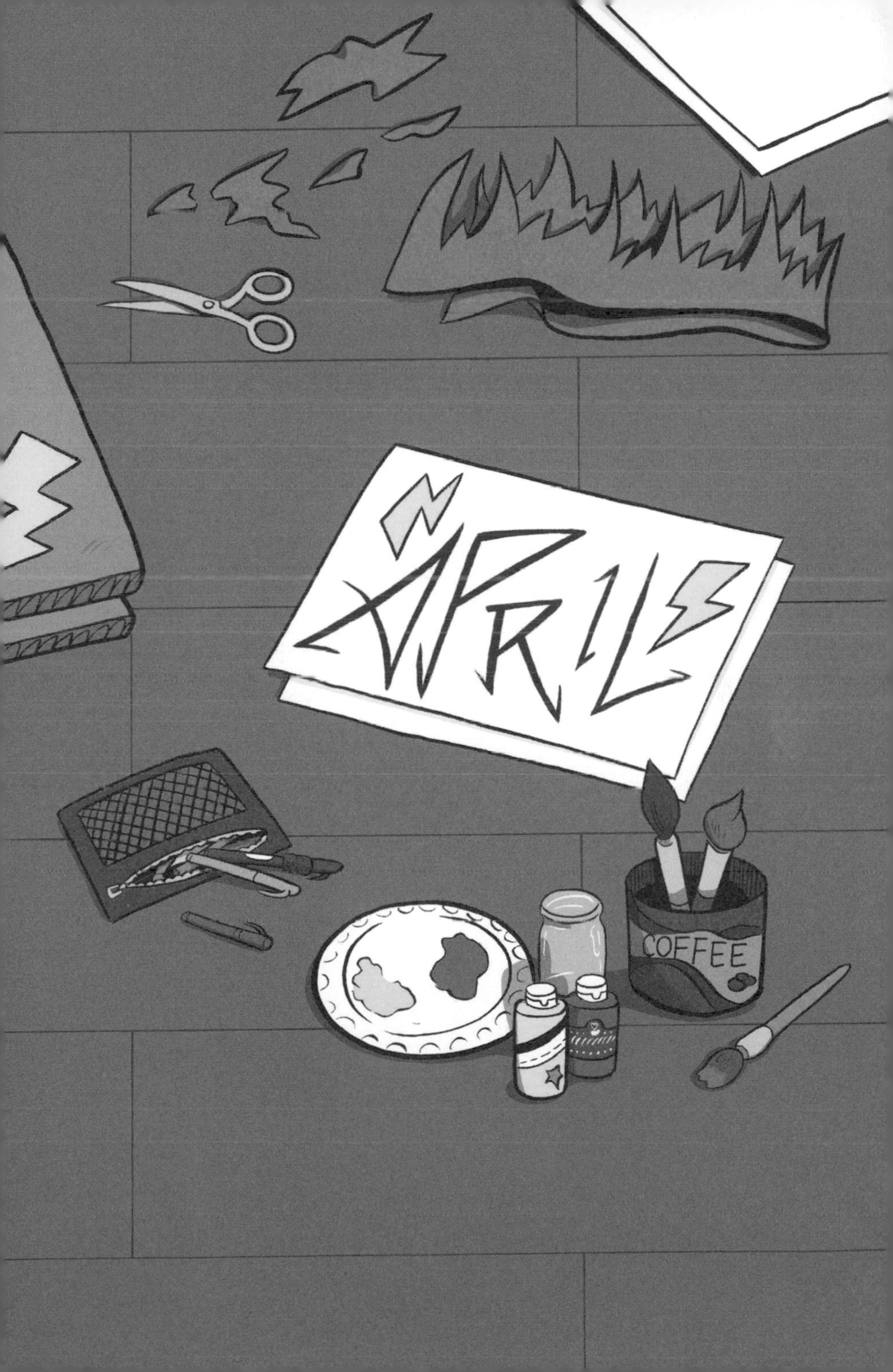
APRIL
COFFEE

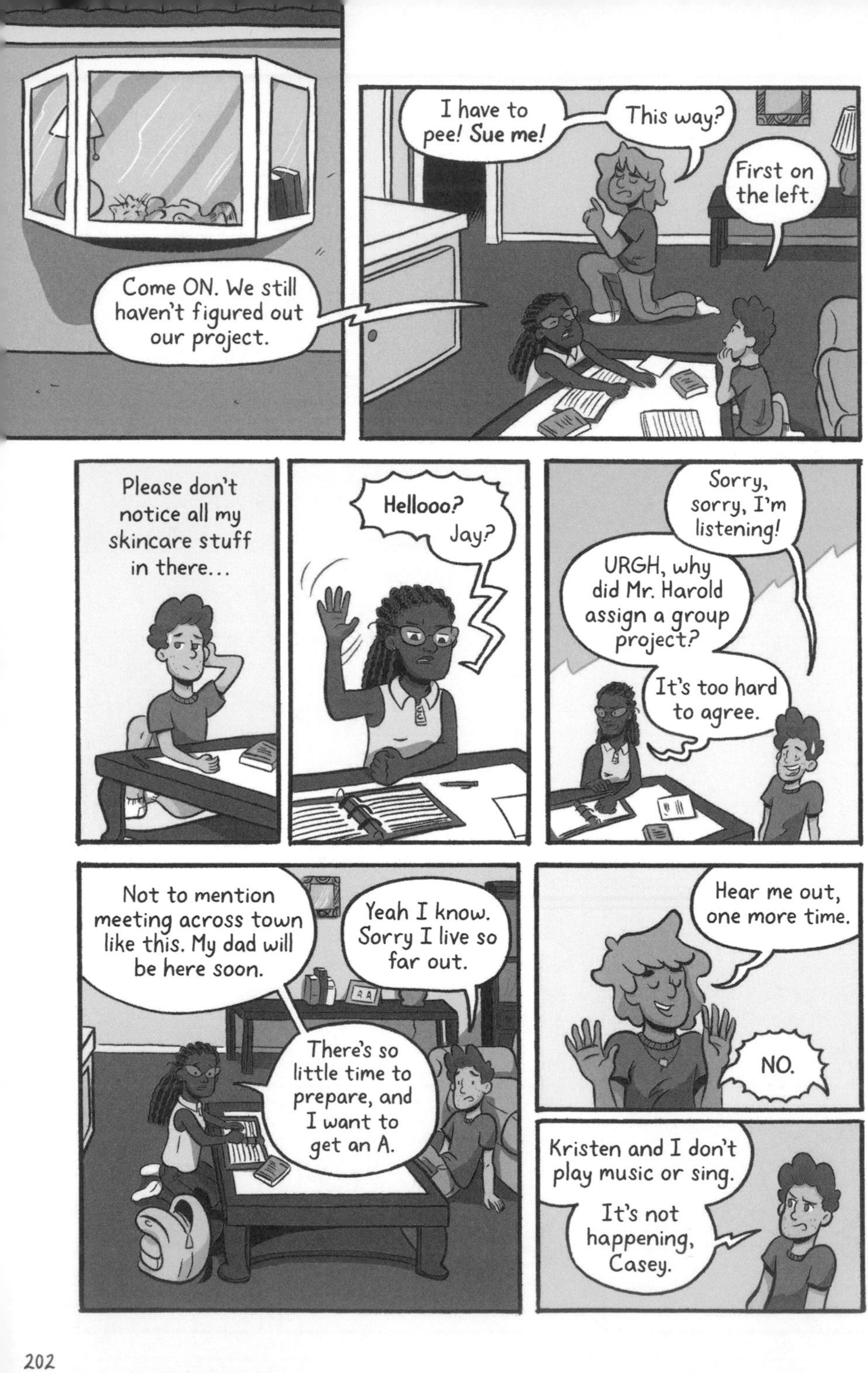
Come ON. We still haven't figured out our project.
I have to pee! Sue me!
This way?
First on the left.
Please don't notice all my skincare stuff in there...
Hellooo? Jay?
Sorry, sorry, I'm listening!
URGH, why did Mr. Harold assign a group project?
It's too hard to agree.
Not to mention meeting across town like this. My dad will be here soon.
Yeah I know. Sorry I live so far out.
There's so little time to prepare, and I want to get an A.
Hear me out, one more time.
NO.
Kristen and I don't play music or sing.
It's not happening, Casey.

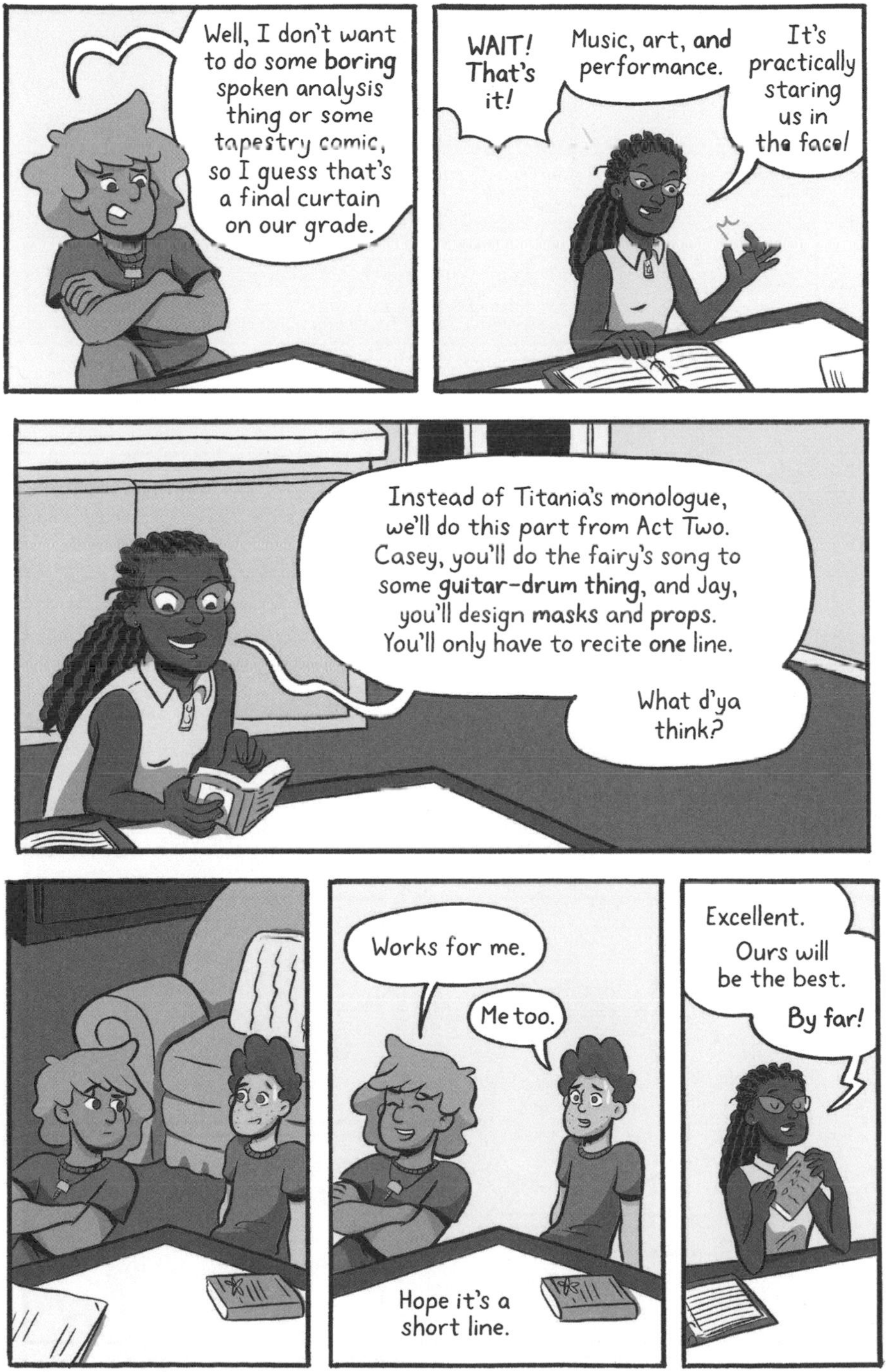
Well, I don't want to do some boring spoken analysis thing or some tapestry comic, so I guess that's a final curtain on our grade.
WAIT! That's it!
Music, art, and performance.
It's practically staring us in the face!
Instead of Titania's monologue, we'll do this part from Act Two. Casey, you'll do the fairy's song to some guitar-drum thing, and Jay, you'll design masks and props. You'll only have to recite one line.
What d'ya think?
Works for me.
Me too.
Hope it's a short line.
Excellent.
Ours will be the best.
By far!

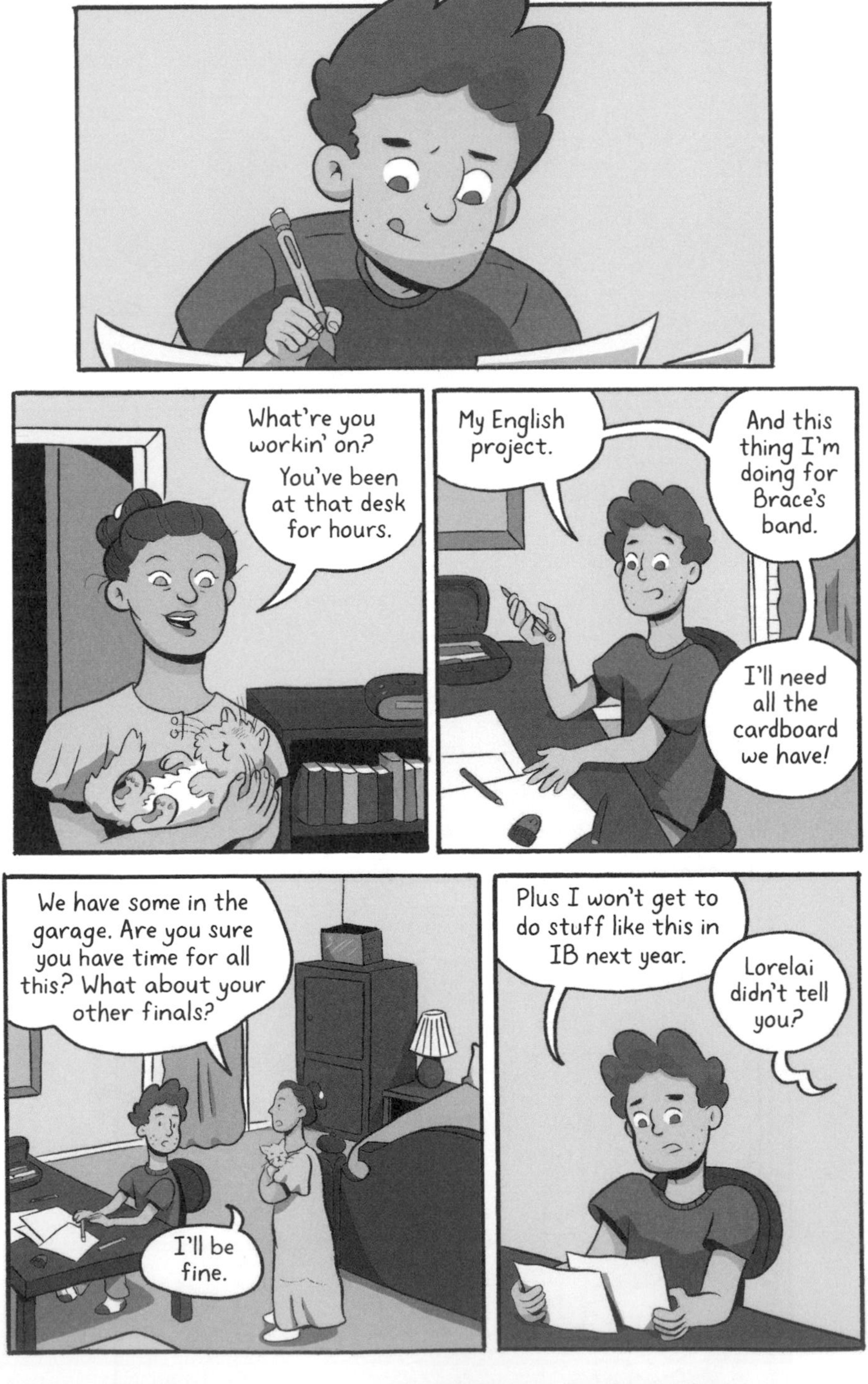
What're you workin' on?
You've been at that desk for hours.
My English project.
And this thing I'm doing for Brace's band.
I'll need all the cardboard we have!
We have some in the garage. Are you sure you have time for all this? What about your other finals?
I'll be fine.
Plus I won't get to do stuff like this in IB next year.
Lorelai didn't tell you?

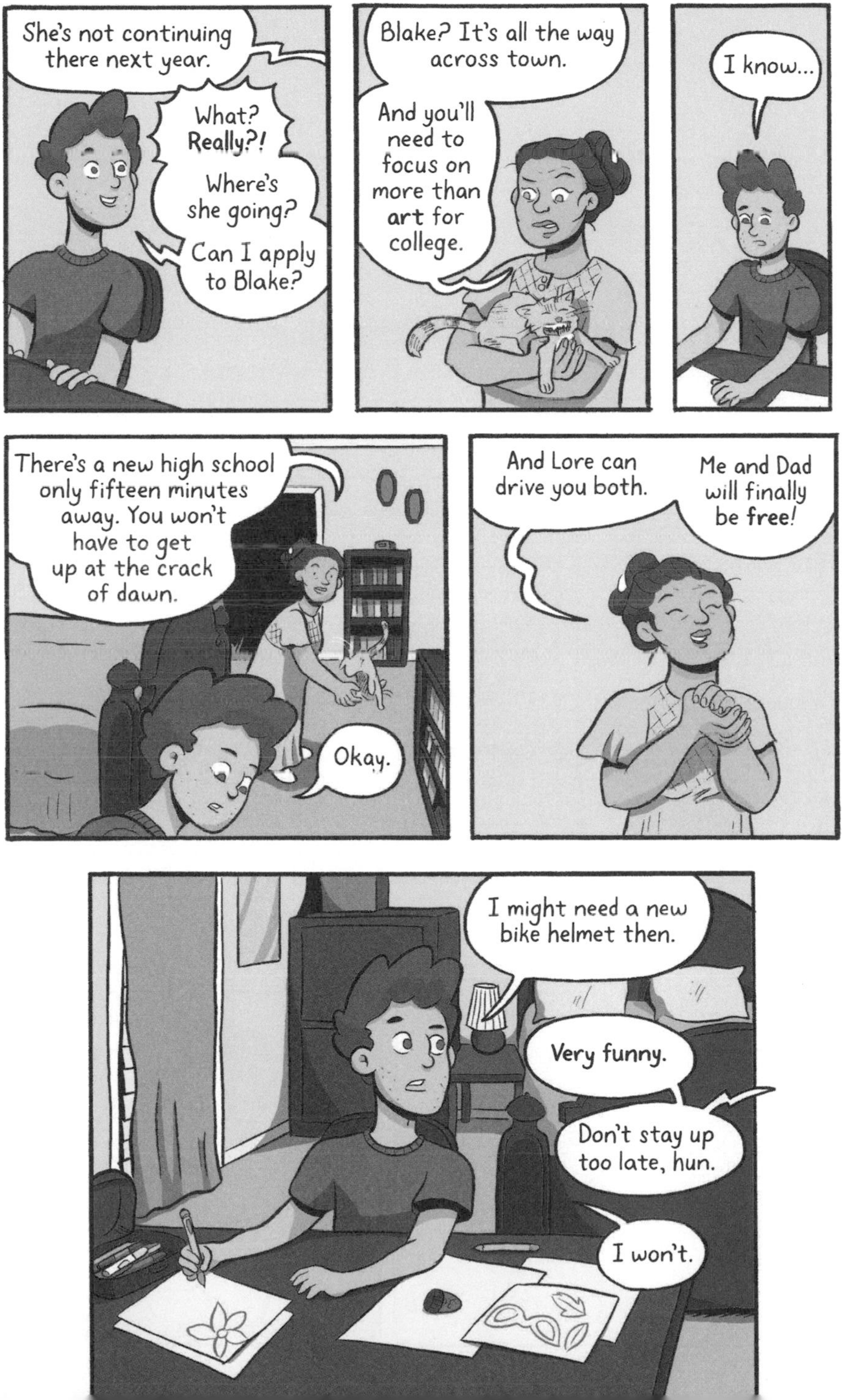
She's not continuing there next year.
What? Really?!
Where's she going?
Can I apply to Blake?
Blake? It's all the way across town.
And you'll need to focus on more than **art** for college.
I know...
There's a new high school only fifteen minutes away. You won't have to get up at the crack of dawn.
Okay.
And Lore can drive you both.
Me and Dad will finally be **free**!
I might need a new bike helmet then.
Very funny.
Don't stay up too late, hun.
I won't.

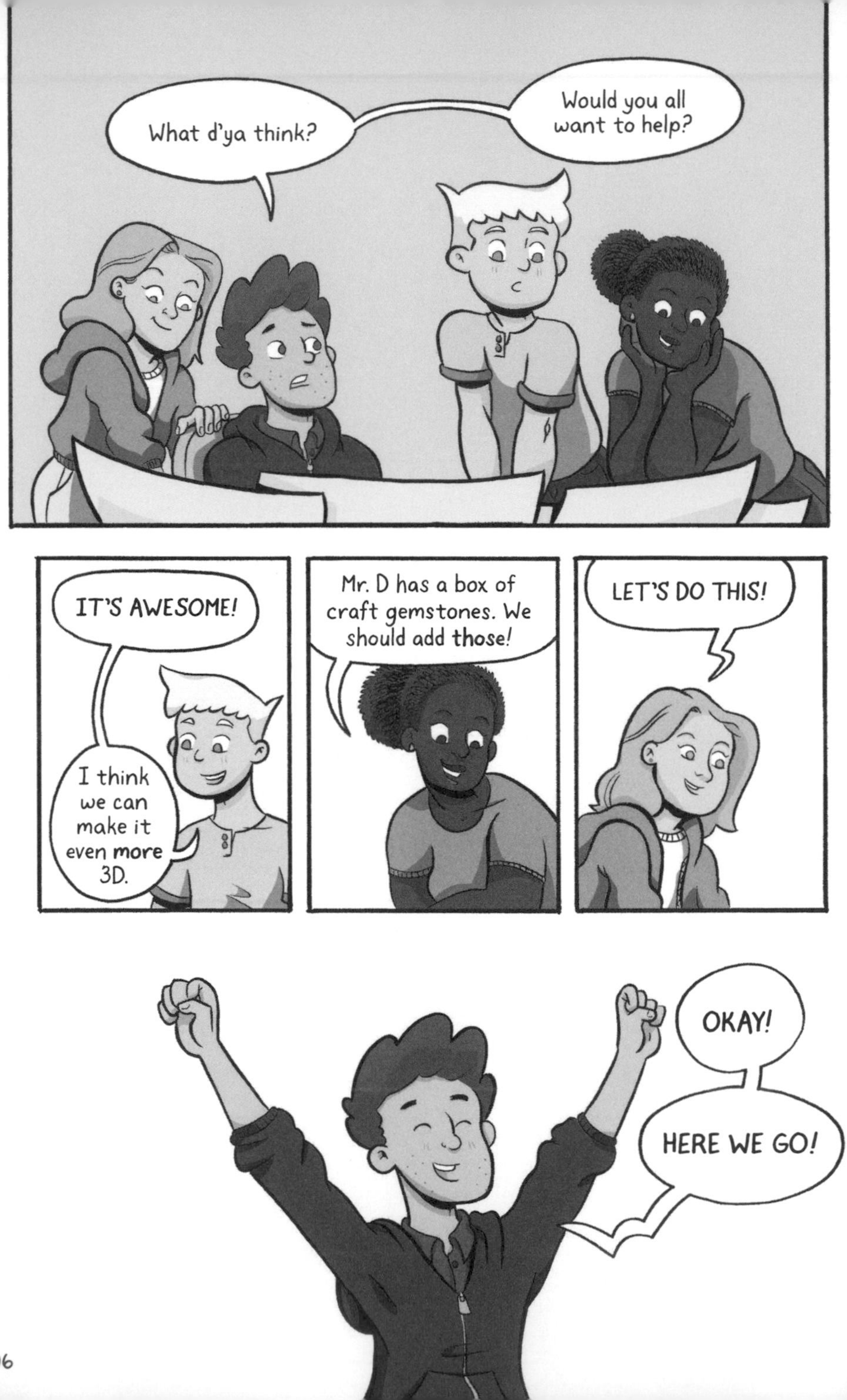
What d'ya think?
Would you all want to help?
IT'S AWESOME!
I think we can make it even more 3D.
Mr. D has a box of craft gemstones. We should add those!
LET'S DO THIS!
OKAY!
HERE WE GO!

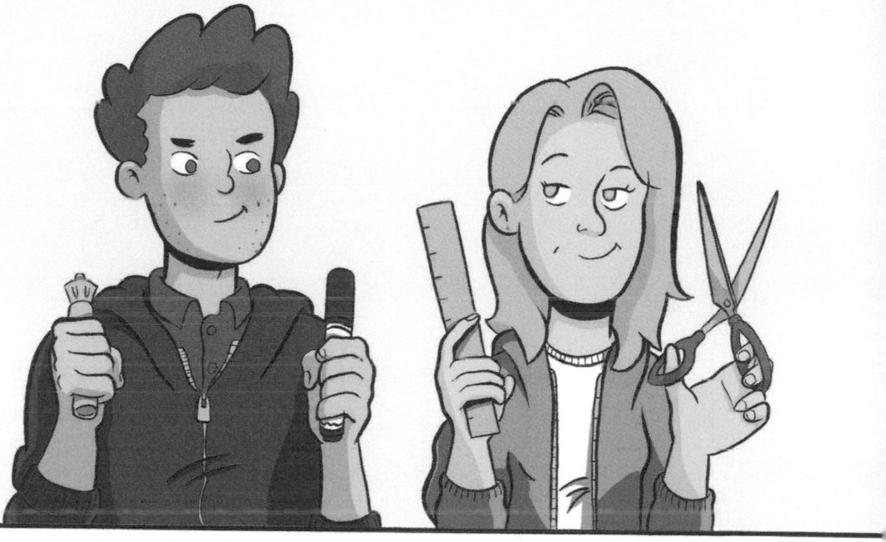

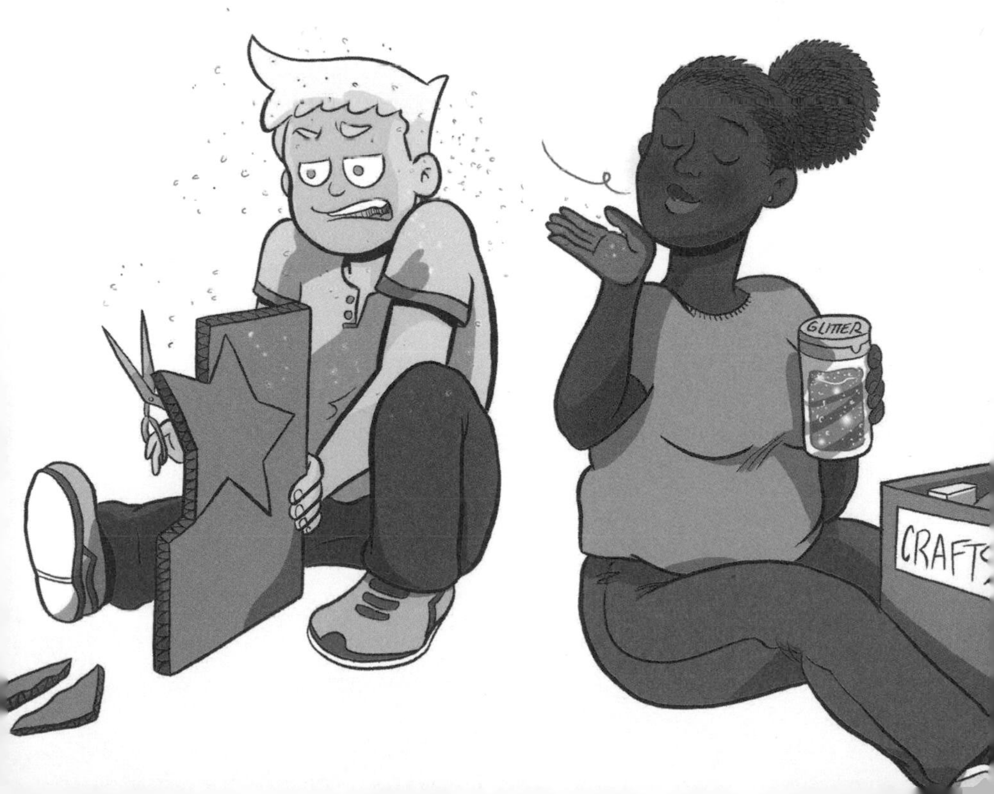
GLITTER
CRAFTS

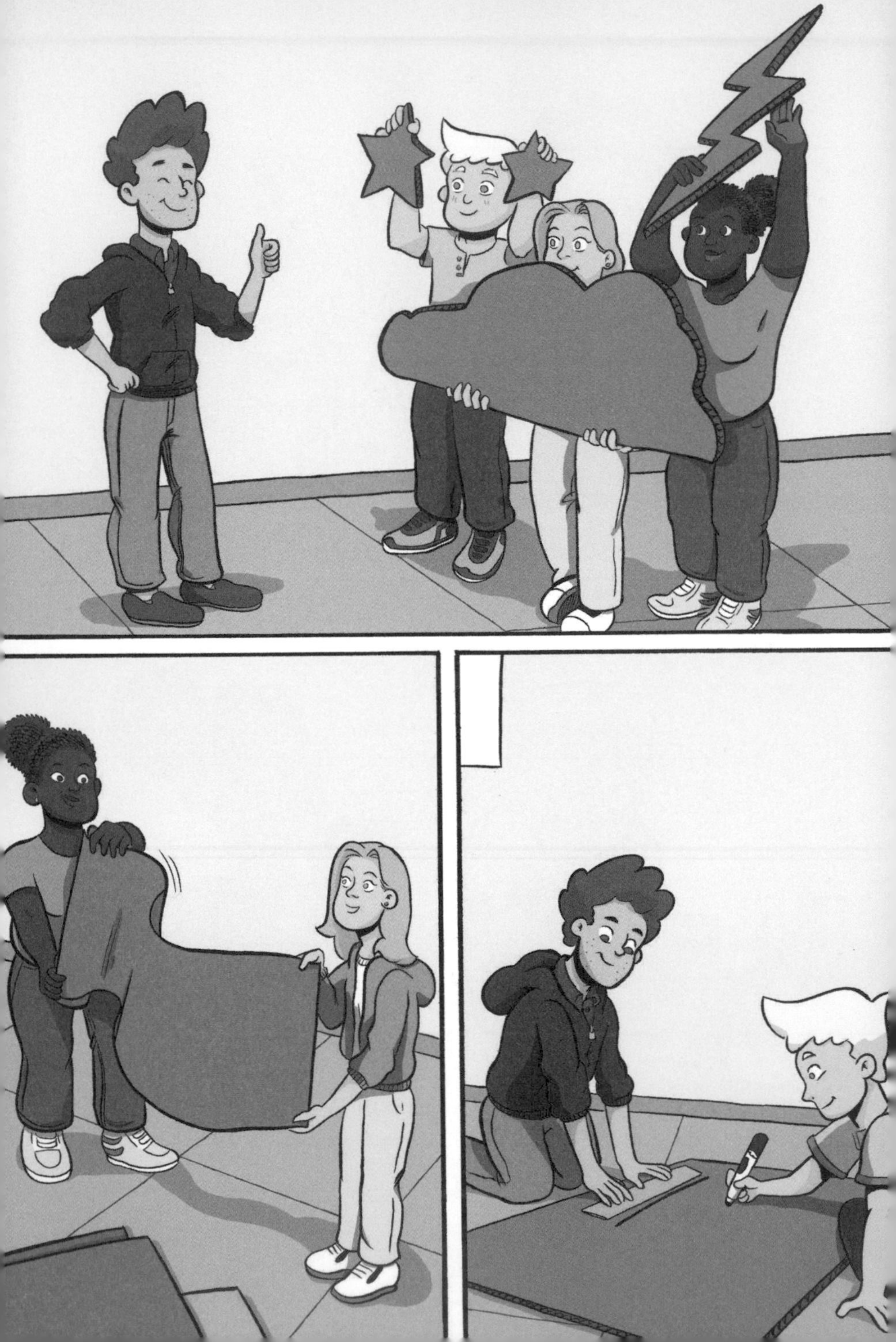

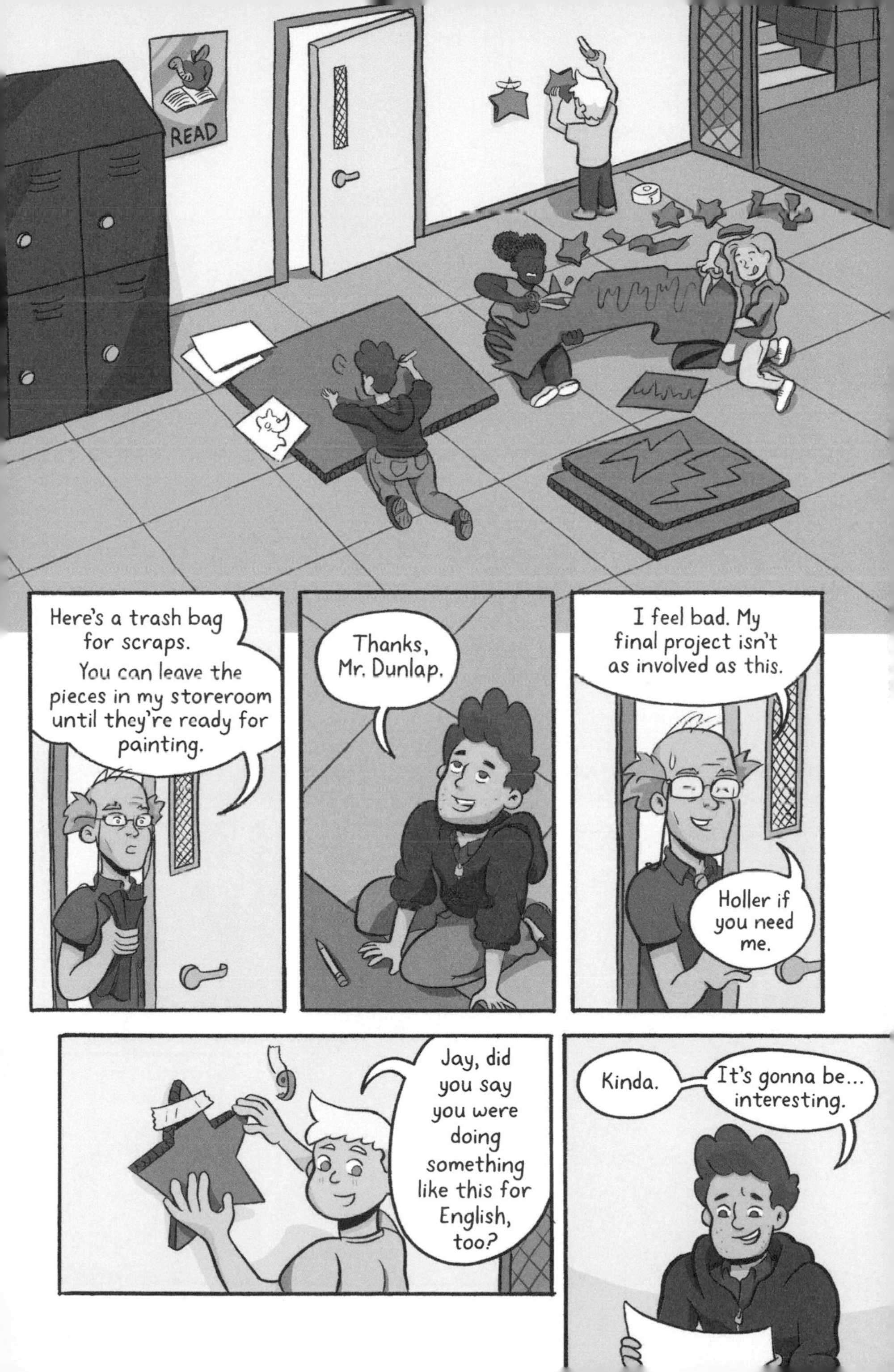
READ
Here's a trash bag for scraps.
You can leave the pieces in my storeroom until they're ready for painting.
Thanks, Mr. Dunlap.
I feel bad. My final project isn't as involved as this.
Holler if you need me.
Jay, did you say you were doing something like this for English, too?
Kinda.
It's gonna be... interesting.

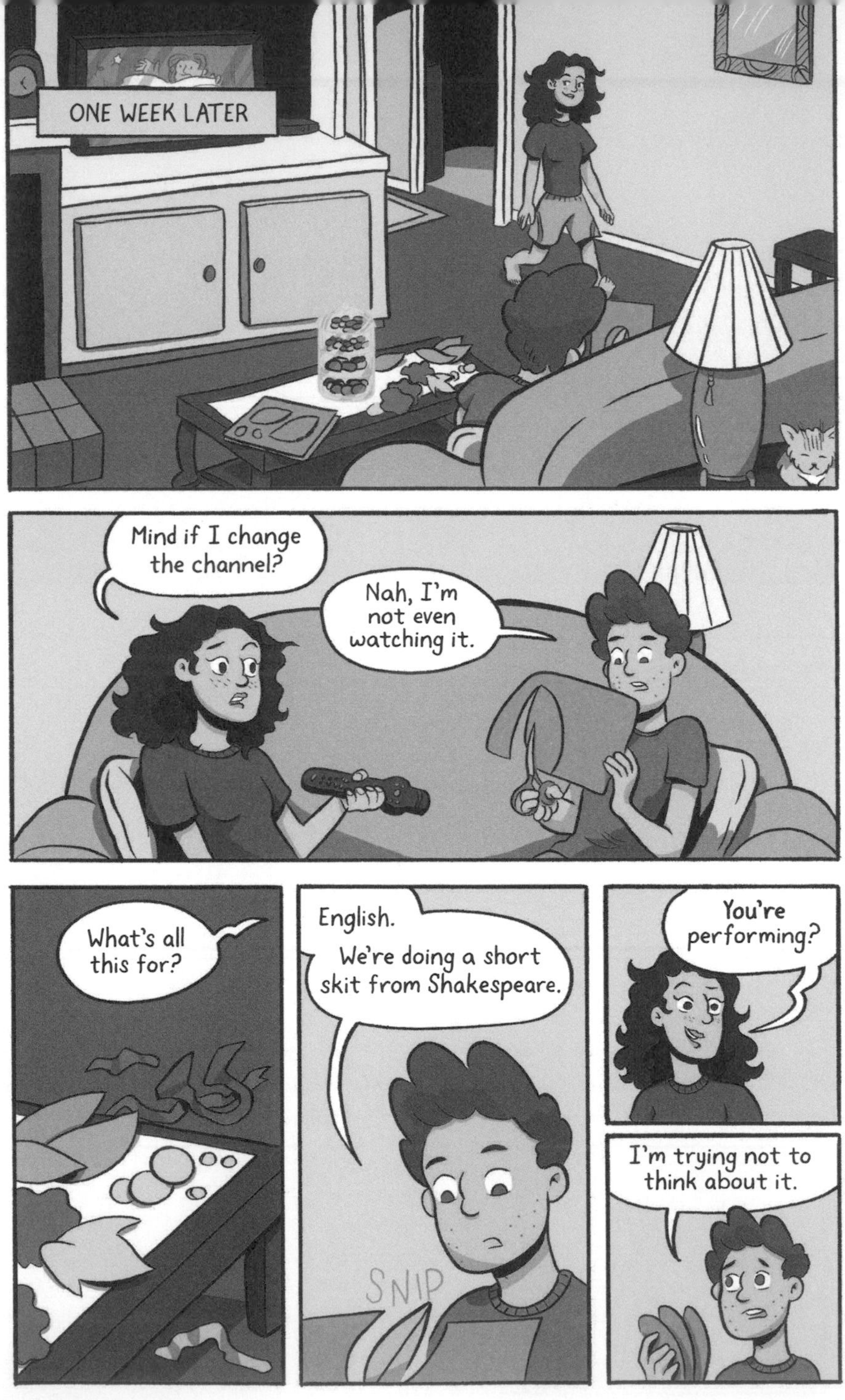
ONE WEEK LATER
Mind if I change the channel?
Nah, I'm not even watching it.
What's all this for?
English.
We're doing a short skit from Shakespeare.
SNIP
You're performing?
I'm trying not to think about it.

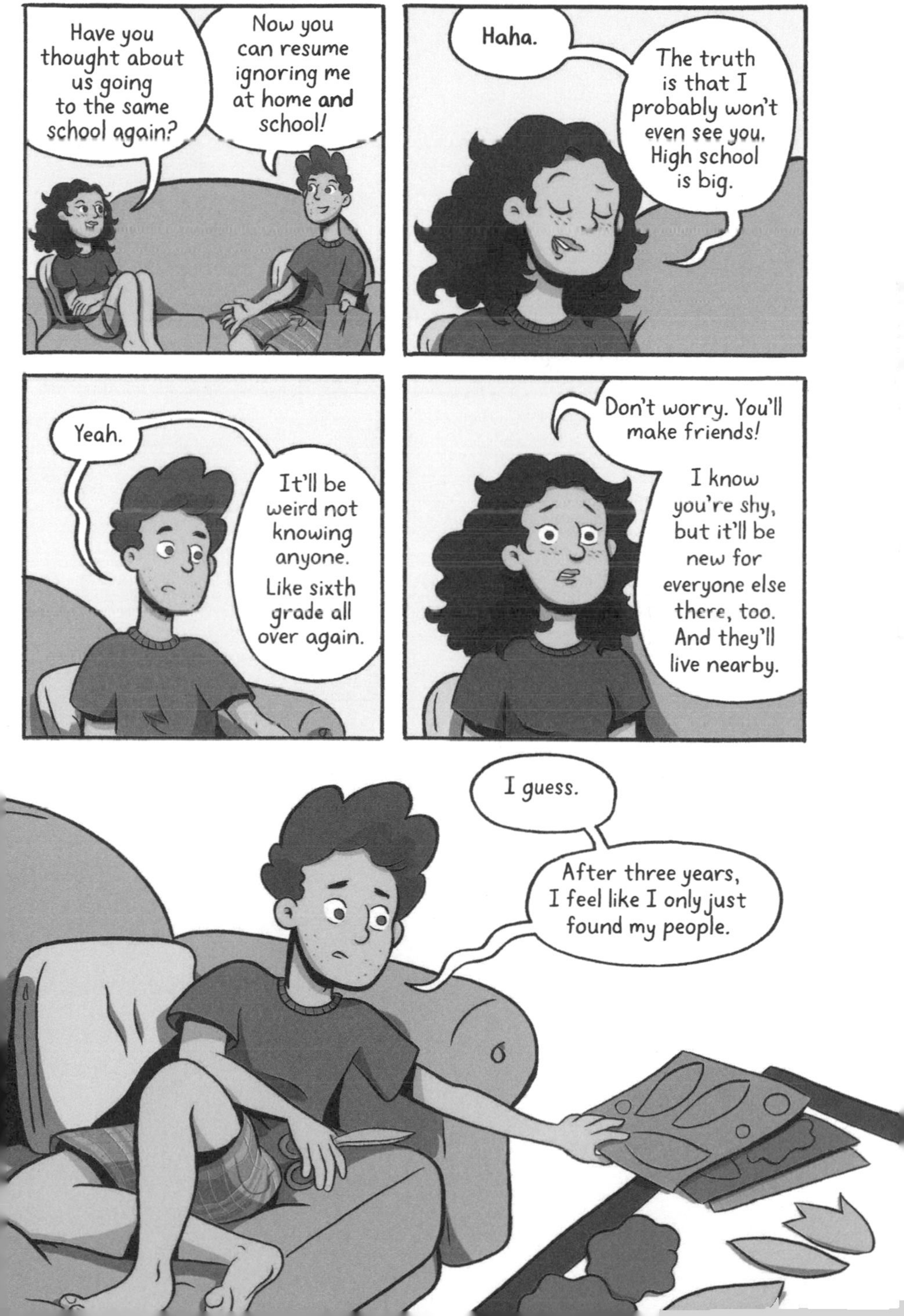
Have you thought about us going to the same school again?
Now you can resume ignoring me at home and school!
Haha.
The truth is that I probably won't even see you. High school is big.
Yeah.
It'll be weird not knowing anyone.
Like sixth grade all over again.
Don't worry. You'll make friends!
I know you're shy, but it'll be new for everyone else there, too. And they'll live nearby.
I guess.
After three years, I feel like I only just found my people.

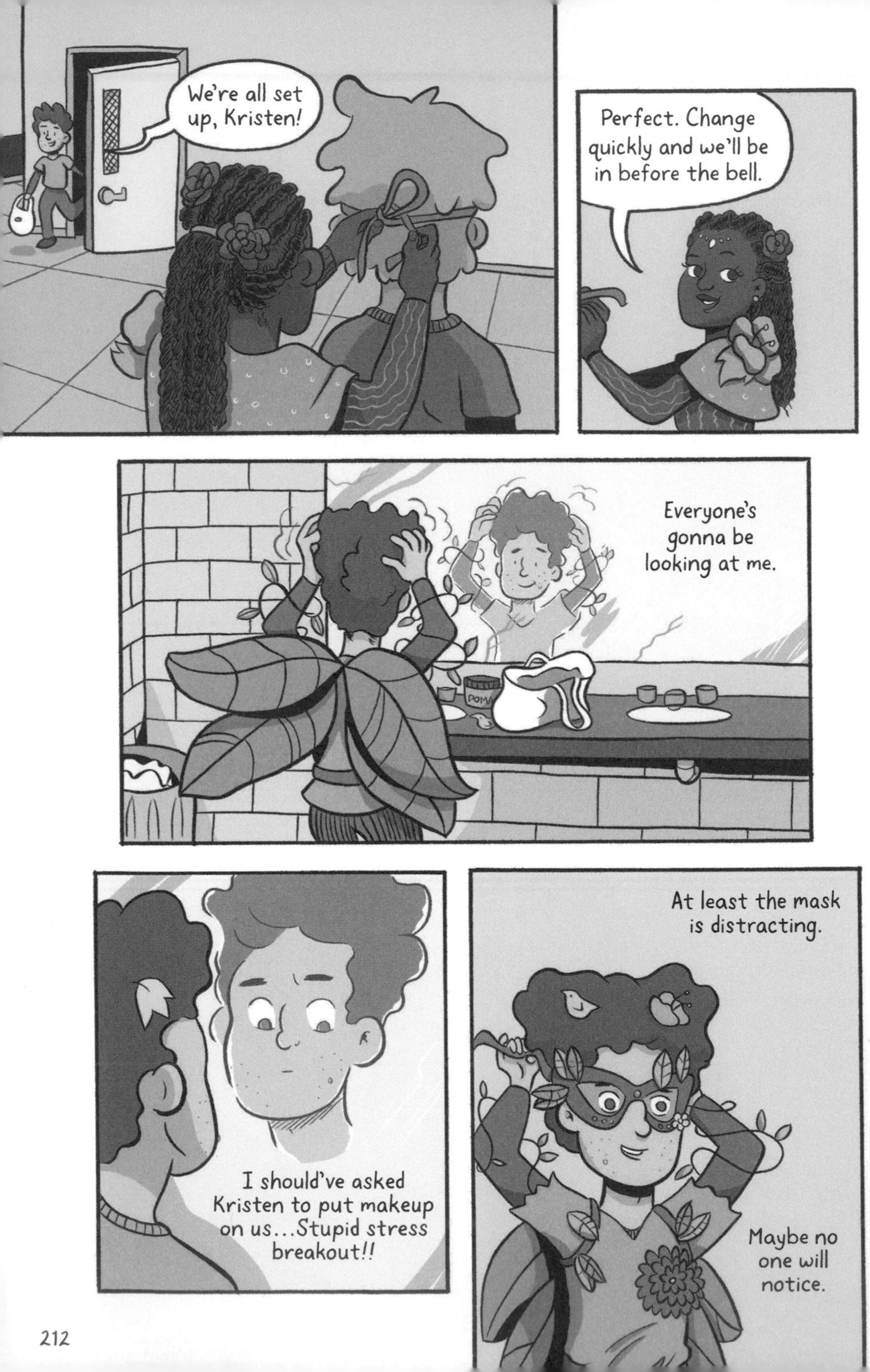
We're all set up, Kristen!
Perfect. Change quickly and we'll be in before the bell.
Everyone's gonna be looking at me.
I should've asked Kristen to put makeup on us...Stupid stress breakout!!
At least the mask is distracting.
Maybe no one will notice.

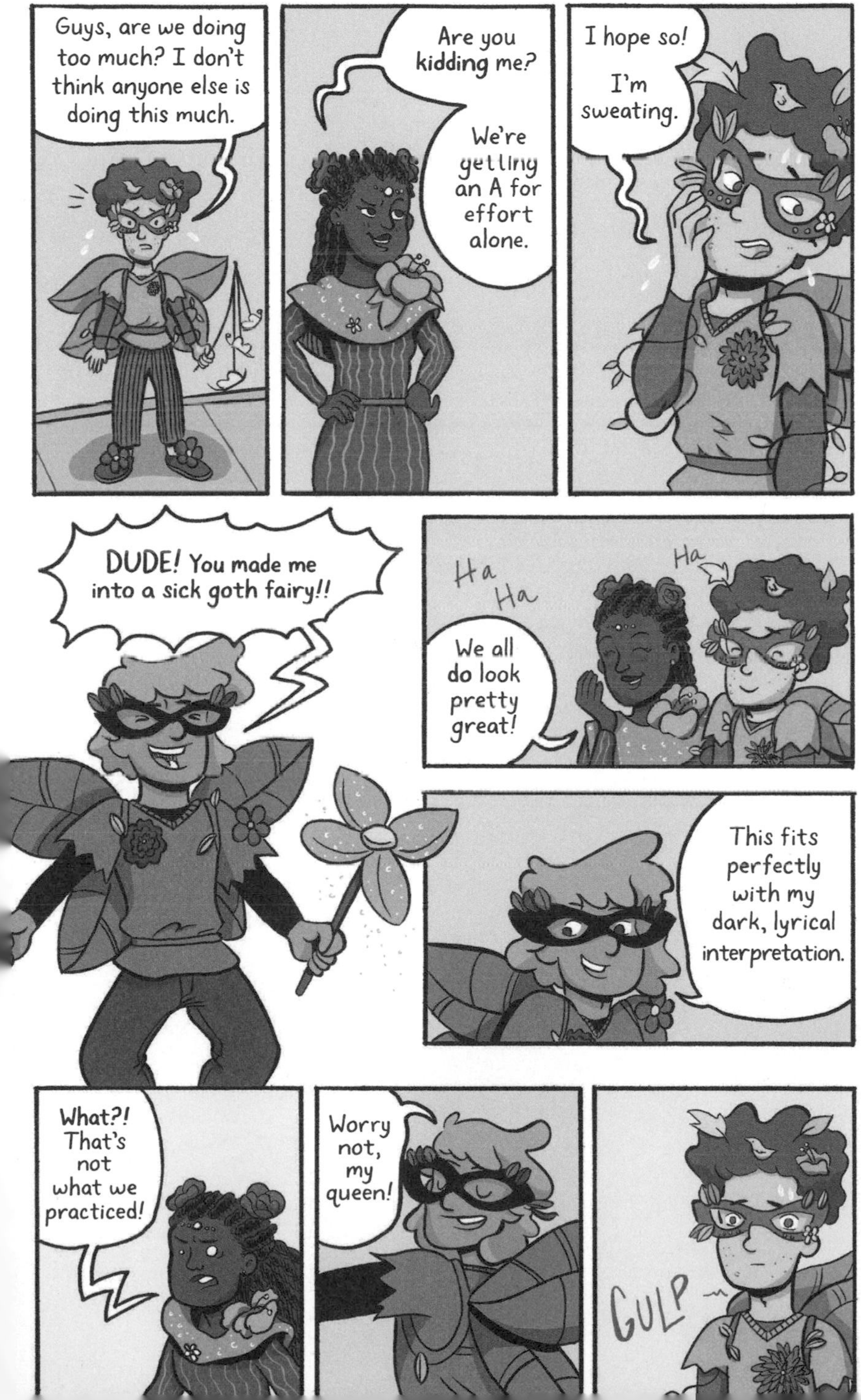
Guys, are we doing too much? I don't think anyone else is doing this much.
Are you kidding me?
We're getting an A for effort alone.
I hope so!
I'm sweating.
DUDE! You made me into a sick goth fairy!!
Ha
Ha
Ha
We all do look pretty great!
This fits perfectly with my dark, lyrical interpretation.
What?! That's not what we practiced!
Worry not, my queen!
GULP

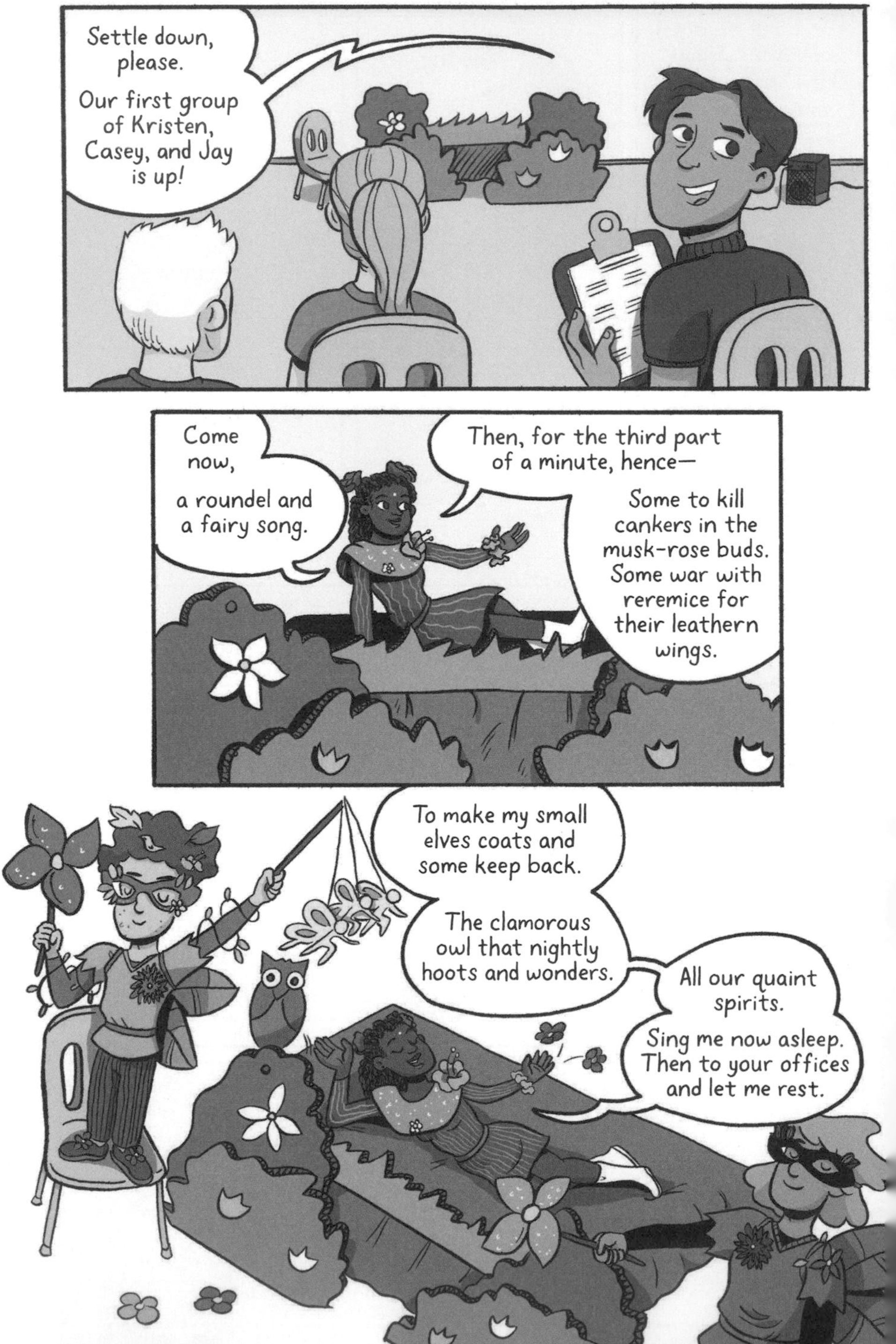
Settle down, please.
Our first group of Kristen, Casey, and Jay is up!
Come now,
a roundel and a fairy song.
Then, for the third part of a minute, hence—
Some to kill cankers in the musk-rose buds. Some war with reremice for their leathern wings.
To make my small elves coats and some keep back.
The clamorous owl that nightly hoots and wonders.
All our quaint spirits.
Sing me now asleep. Then to your offices and let me rest.

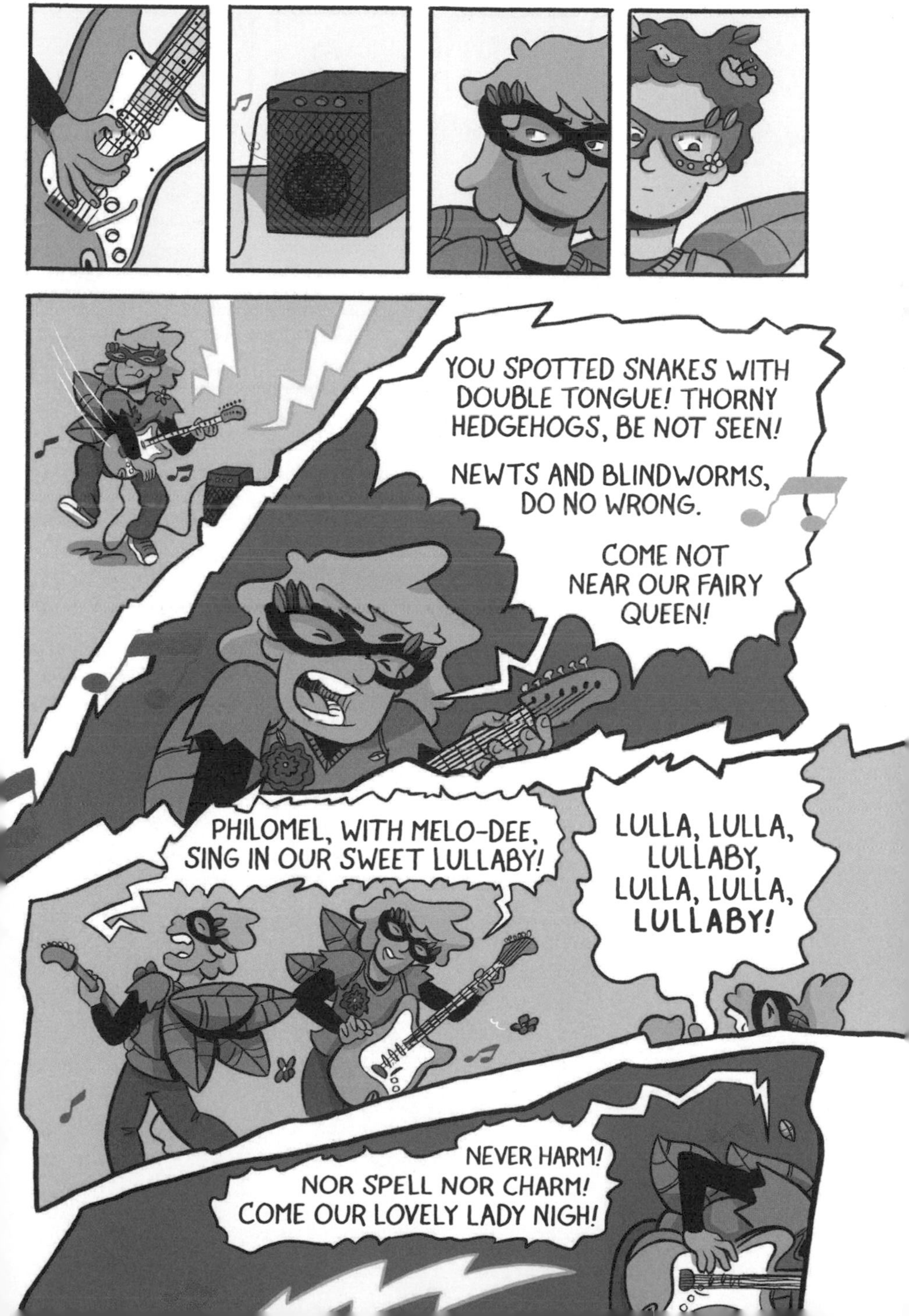
YOU SPOTTED SNAKES WITH DOUBLE TONGUE! THORNY HEDGEHOGS, BE NOT SEEN!
NEWTS AND BLINDWORMS, DO NO WRONG.
COME NOT NEAR OUR FAIRY QUEEN!
PHILOMEL, WITH MELO-DEE, SING IN OUR SWEET LULLABY!
LULLA, LULLA, LULLABY, LULLA, LULLA, LULLABY!
NEVER HARM! NOR SPELL NOR CHARM! COME OUR LOVELY LADY NIGH!

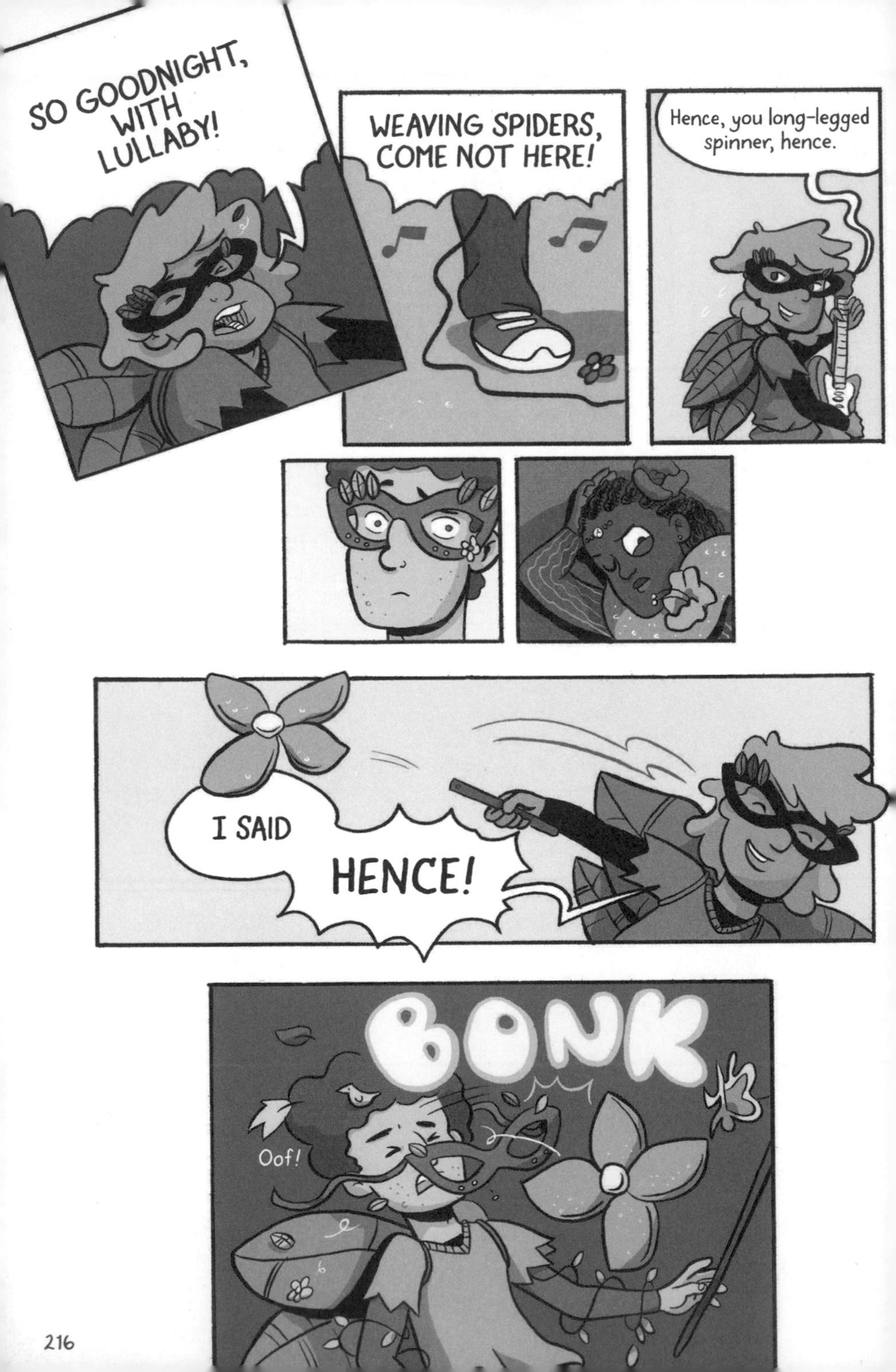
SO GOODNIGHT, WITH LULLABY!
WEAVING SPIDERS, COME NOT HERE!
Hence, you long-legged spinner, hence.
I SAID
HENCE!
BONK
Oof!

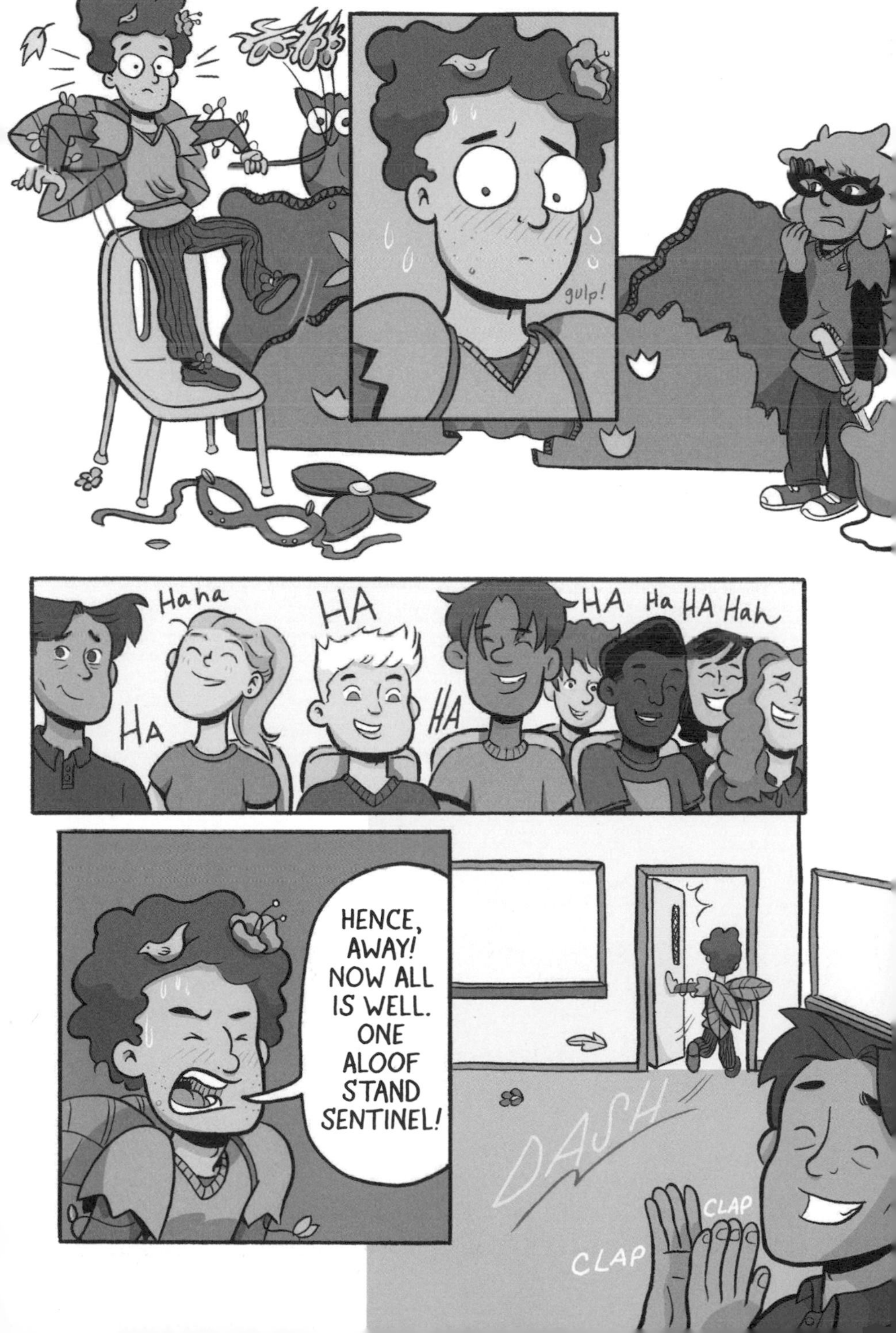
gulp!
Haha
HA
HA Ha HA Hah
Ha
HA
HENCE, AWAY! NOW ALL IS WELL. ONE ALOOF STAND SENTINEL!
DASH
CLAP
CLAP

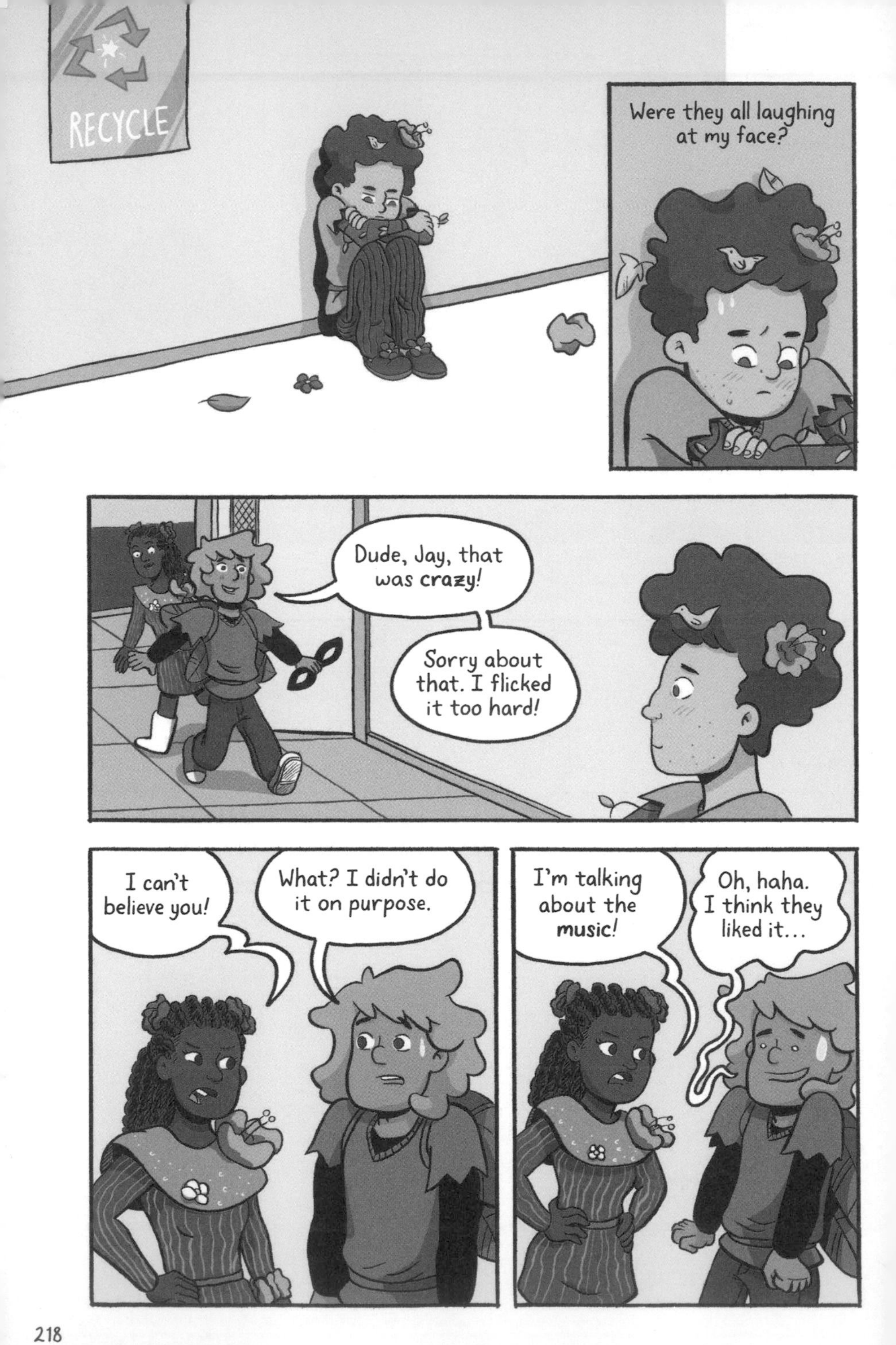
RECYCLE
Were they all laughing at my face?
Dude, Jay, that was crazy!
Sorry about that. I flicked it too hard!
I can't believe you!
What? I didn't do it on purpose.
I'm talking about the music!
Oh, haha. I think they liked it...

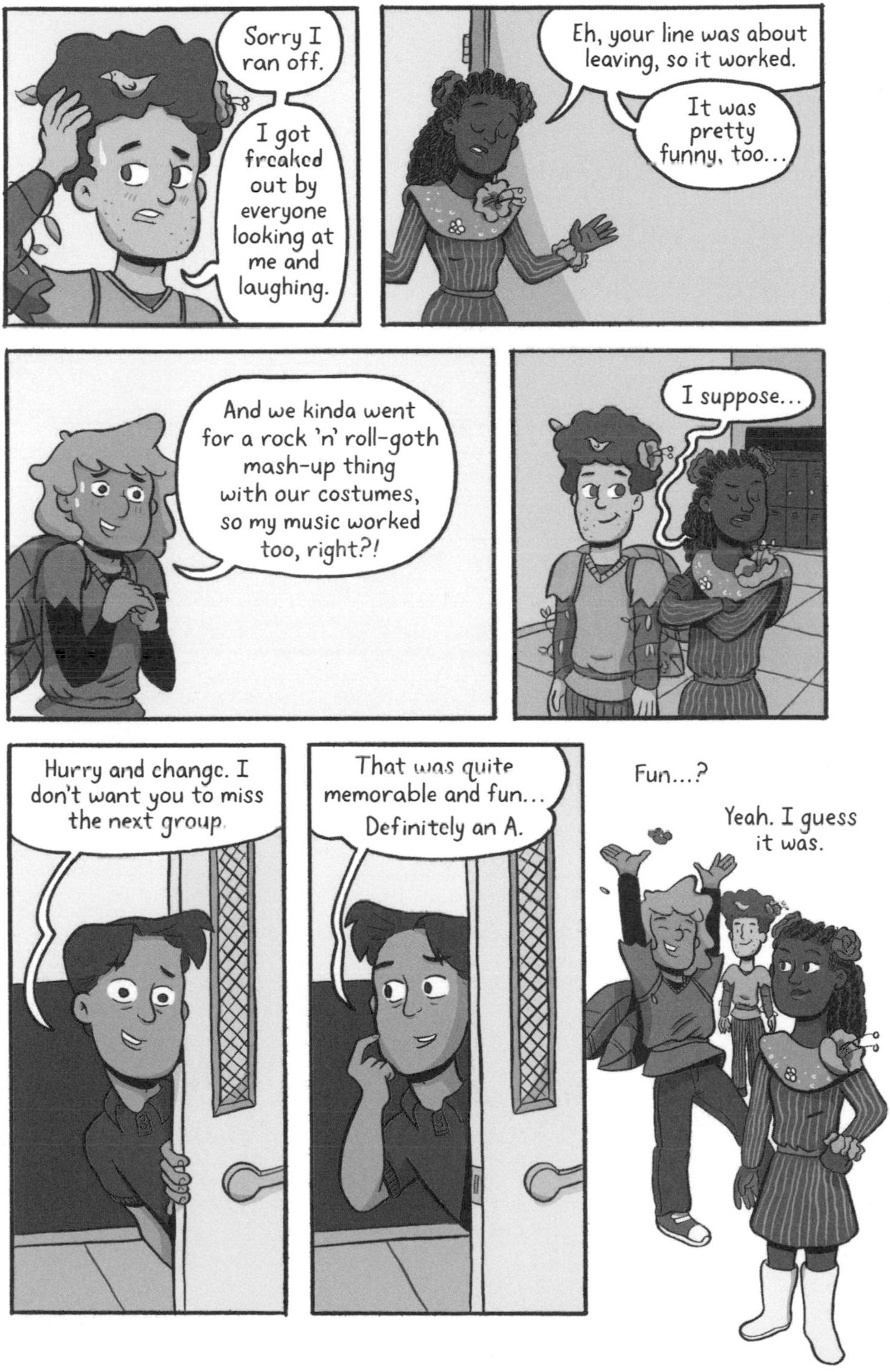
Sorry I ran off.
I got freaked out by everyone looking at me and laughing.
Eh, your line was about leaving, so it worked.
It was pretty funny, too...
And we kinda went for a rock 'n' roll-goth mash-up thing with our costumes, so my music worked too, right?!
I suppose...
Hurry and change. I don't want you to miss the next group.
That was quite memorable and fun...
Definitely an A.
Fun...?
Yeah. I guess it was.

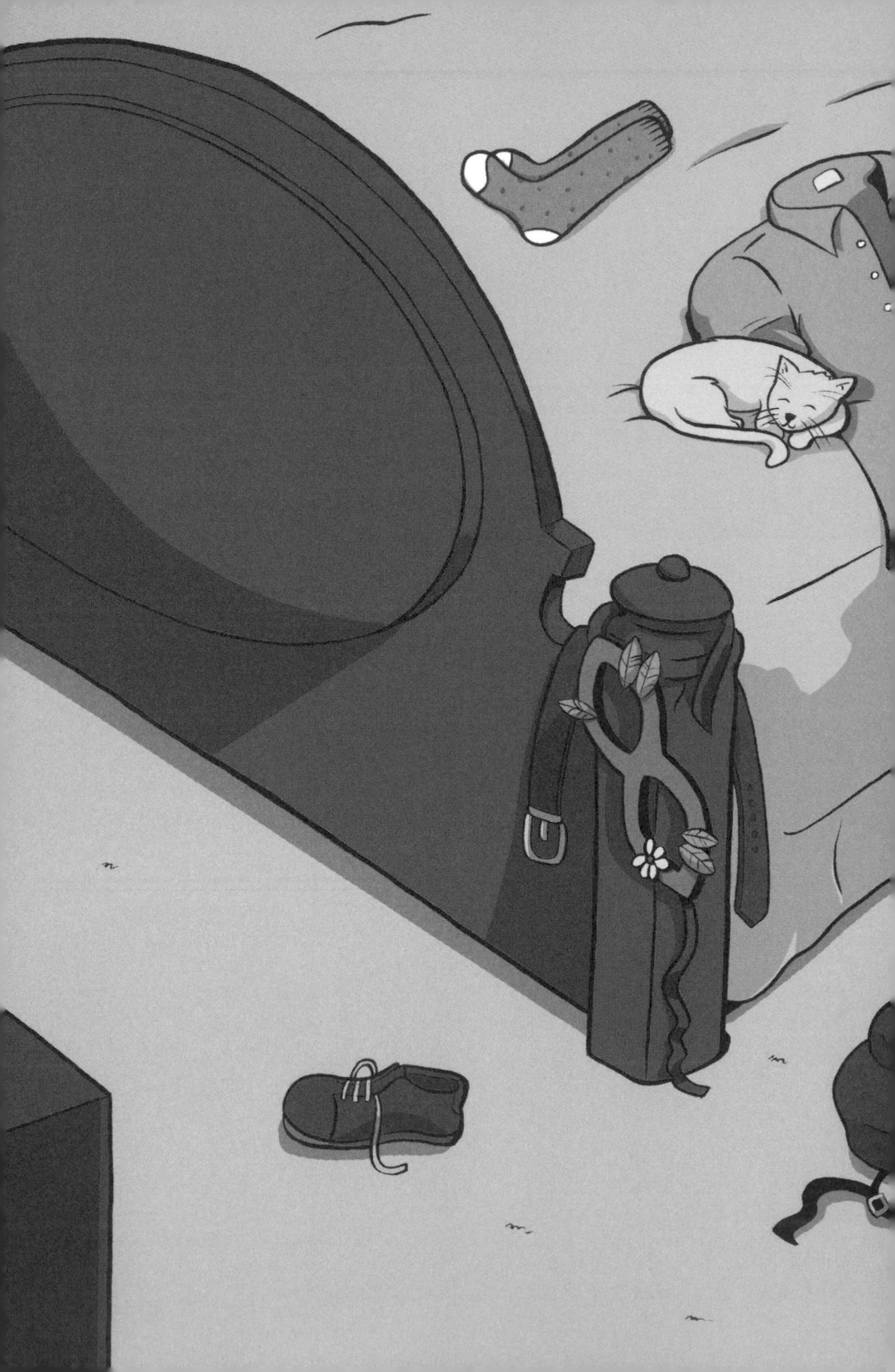

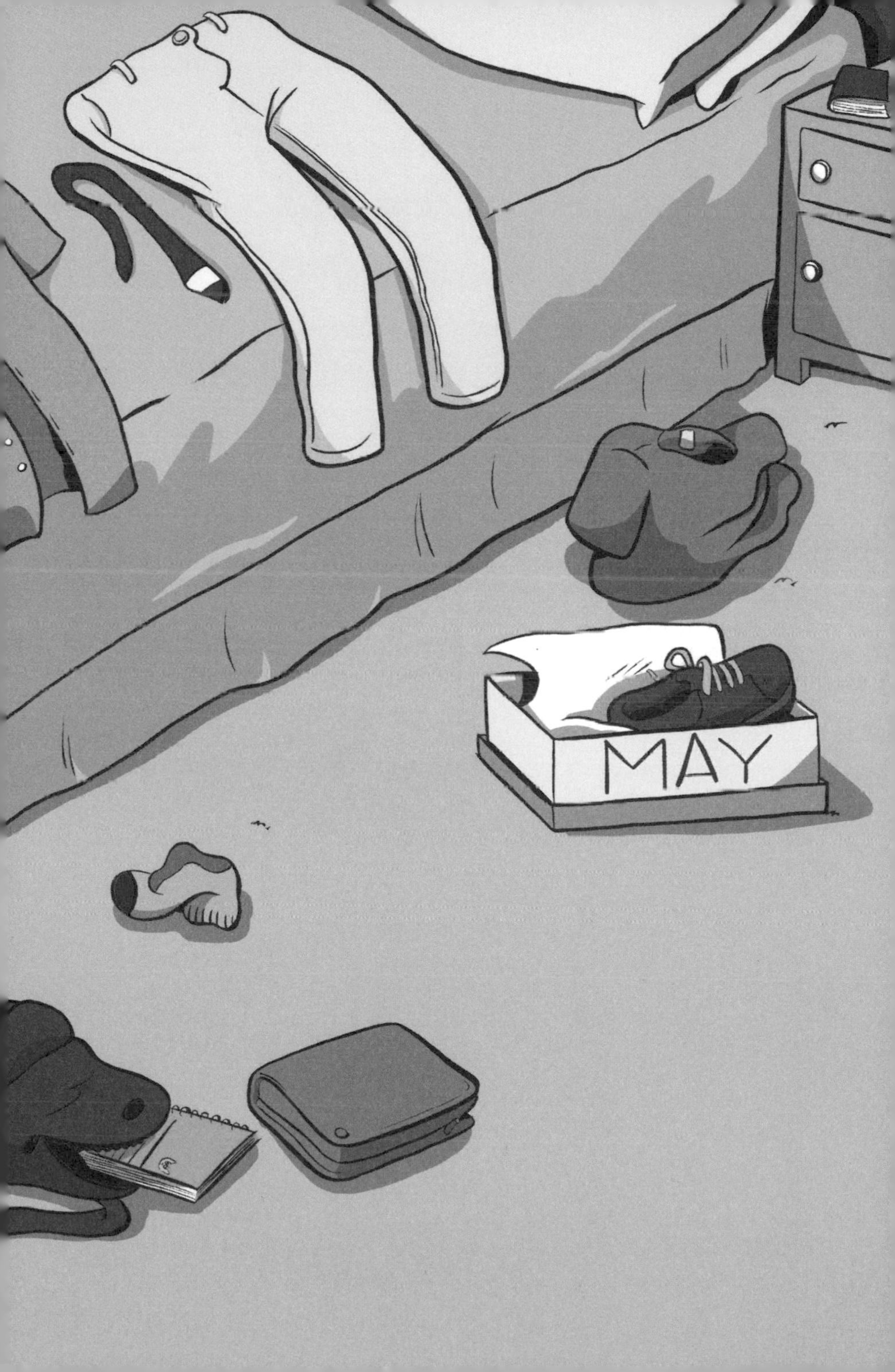
MAY

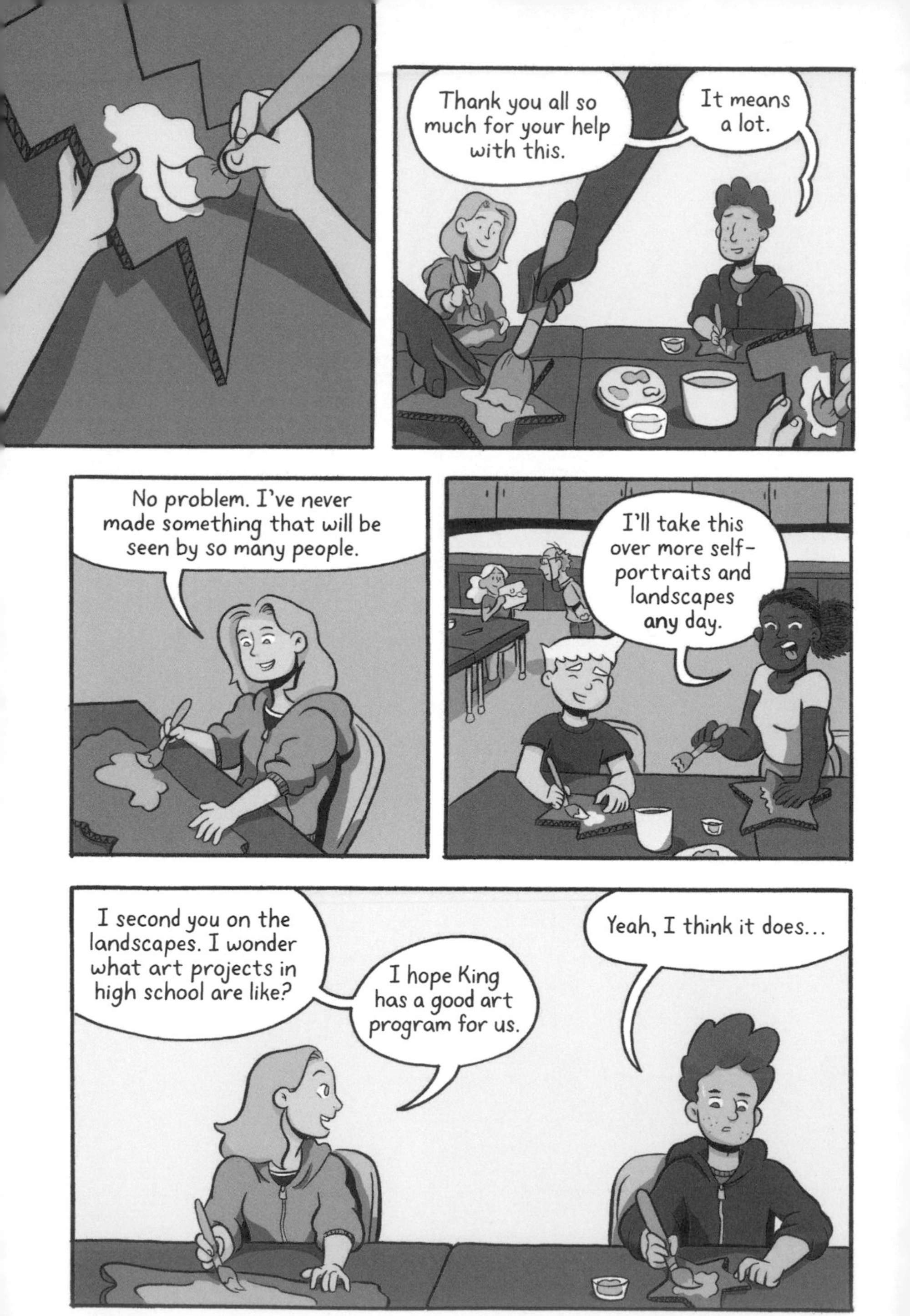
Thank you all so much for your help with this.
It means a lot.
No problem. I've never made something that will be seen by so many people.
I'll take this over more self-portraits and landscapes any day.
I second you on the landscapes. I wonder what art projects in high school are like?
I hope King has a good art program for us.
Yeah, I think it does...

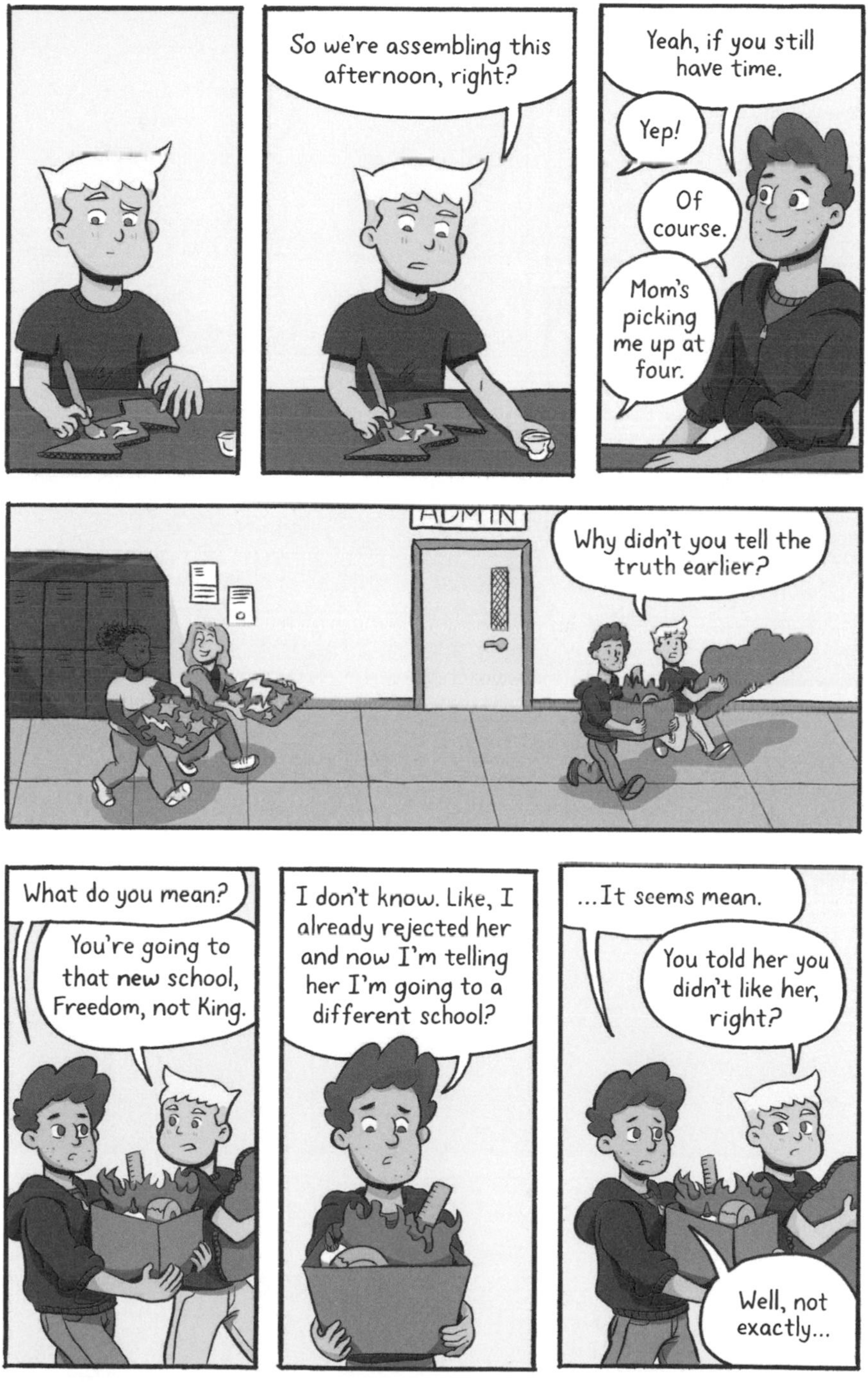
So we're assembling this afternoon, right?
Yeah, if you still have time.
Yep!
Of course.
Mom's picking me up at four.
ADMIN
Why didn't you tell the truth earlier?
What do you mean?
You're going to that **new** school, Freedom, not King.
I don't know. Like, I already rejected her and now I'm telling her I'm going to a different school?
...It seems mean.
You told her you didn't like her, right?
Well, not exactly...

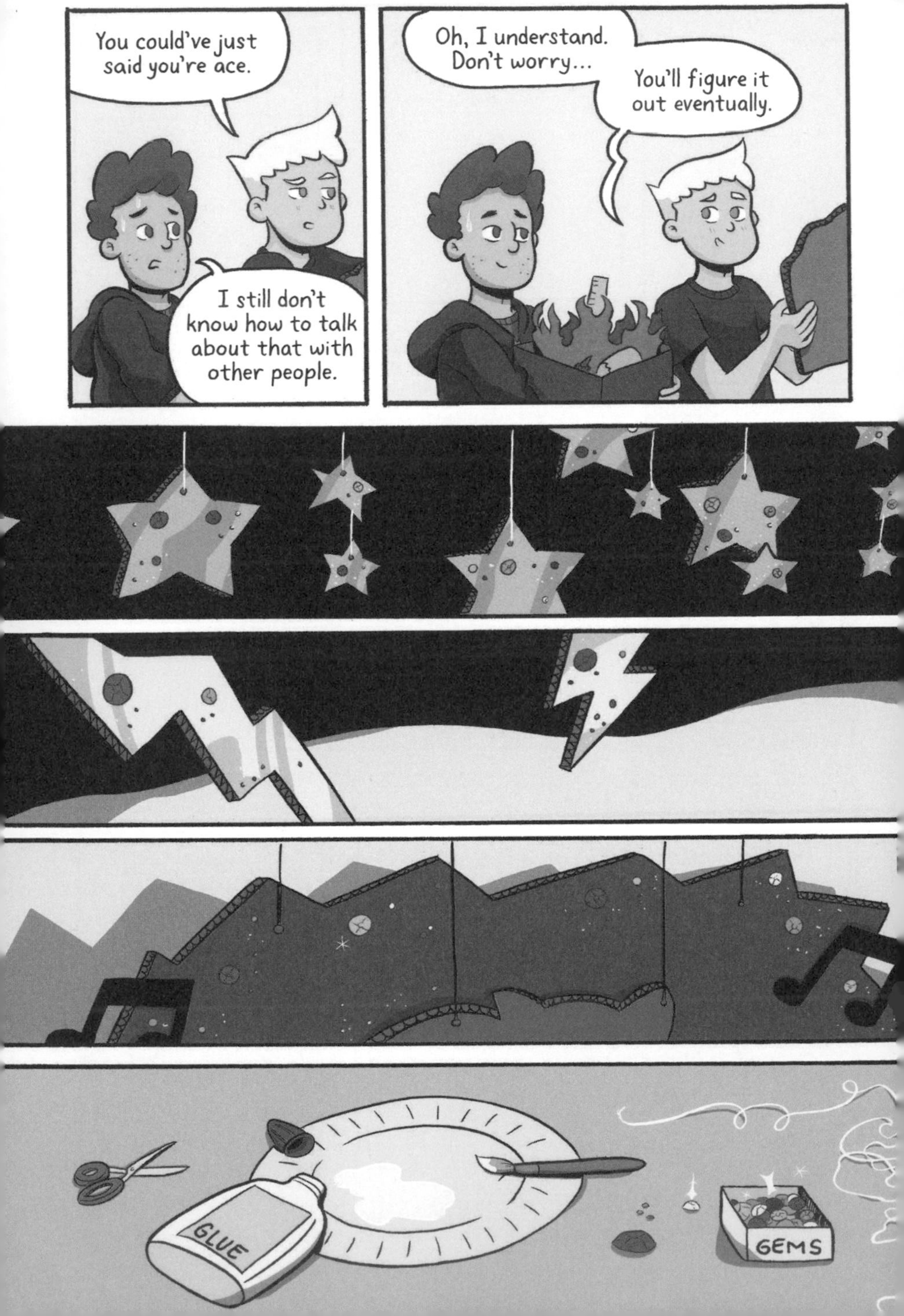
You could've just said you're ace.
I still don't know how to talk about that with other people.
Oh, I understand. Don't worry...
You'll figure it out eventually.
GLUE
GEMS

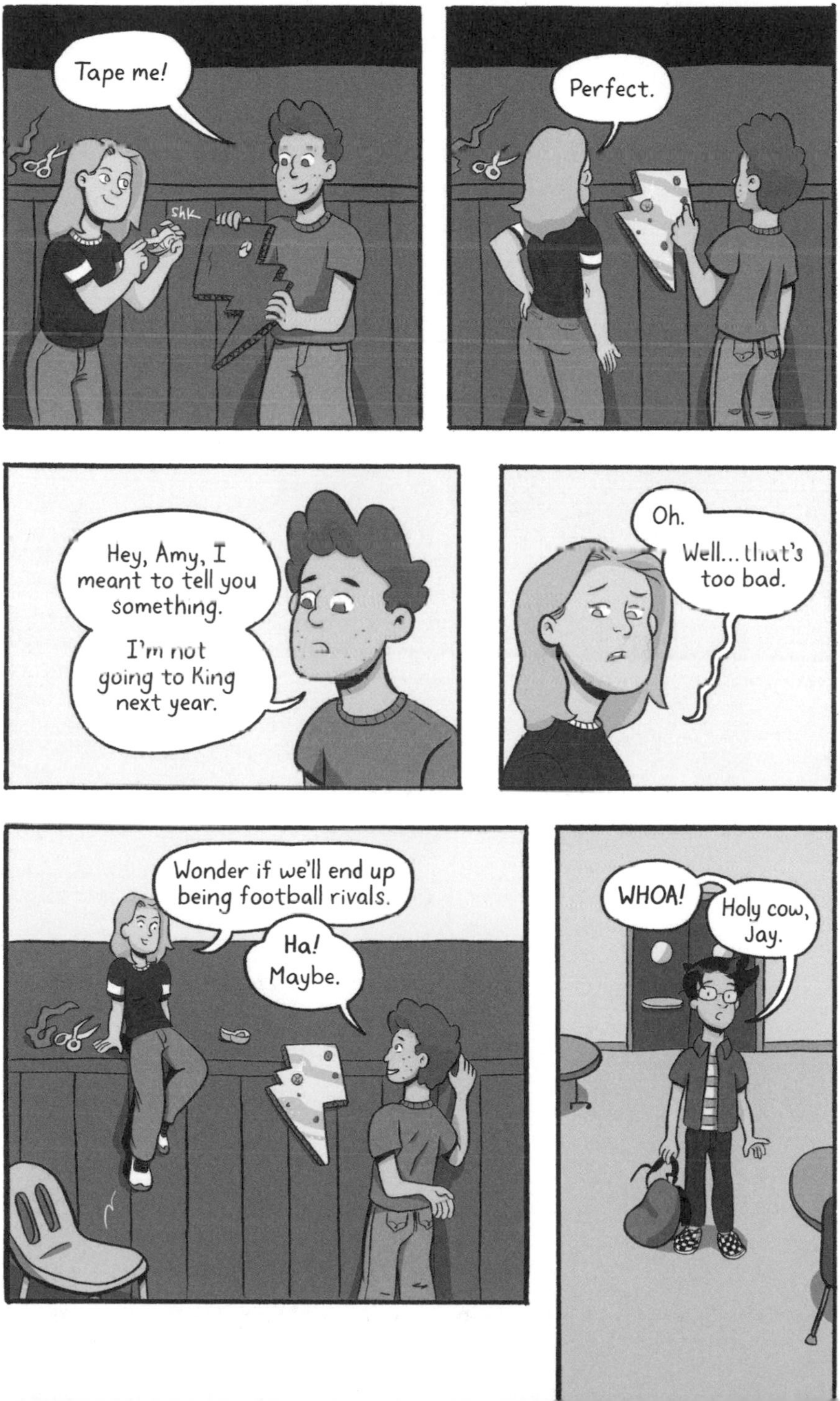
Tape me!
SHK
Perfect.
Hey, Amy, I meant to tell you something.
I'm not going to King next year.
Oh.
Well... that's too bad.
Wonder if we'll end up being football rivals.
Ha! Maybe.
WHOA!
Holy cow, Jay.

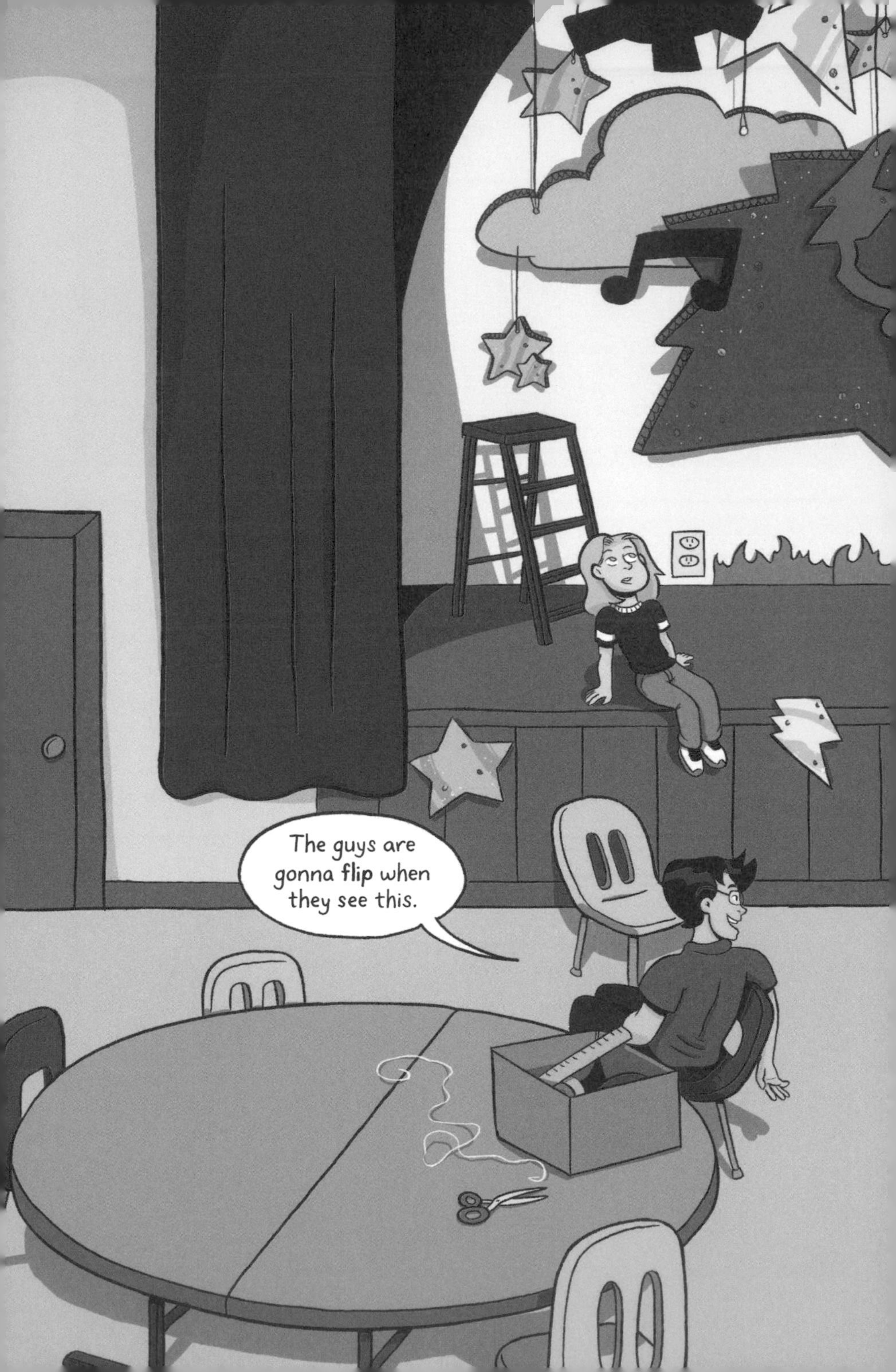
The guys are gonna flip when they see this.

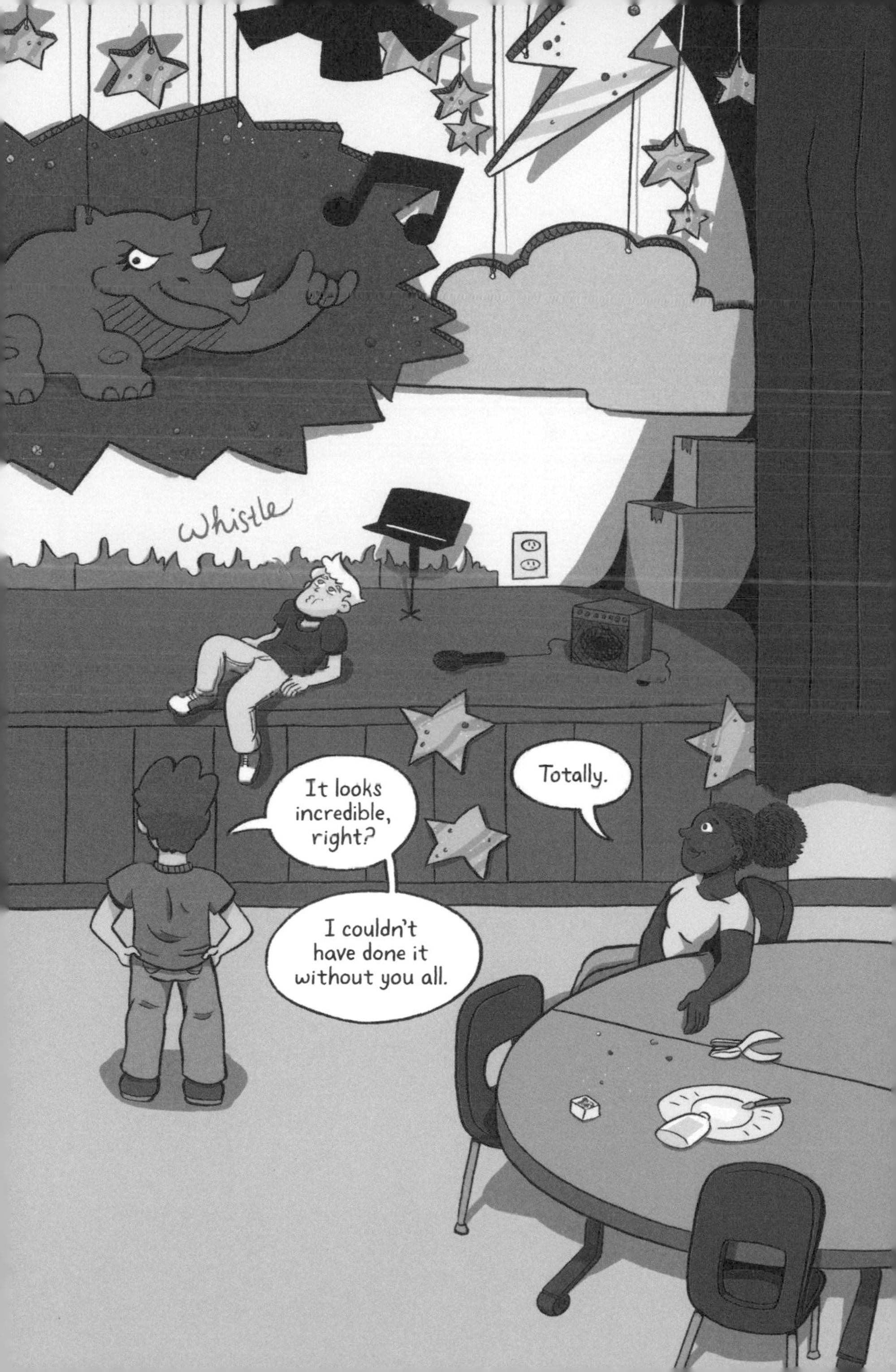
Whistle
It looks incredible, right?
I couldn't have done it without you all.
Totally.

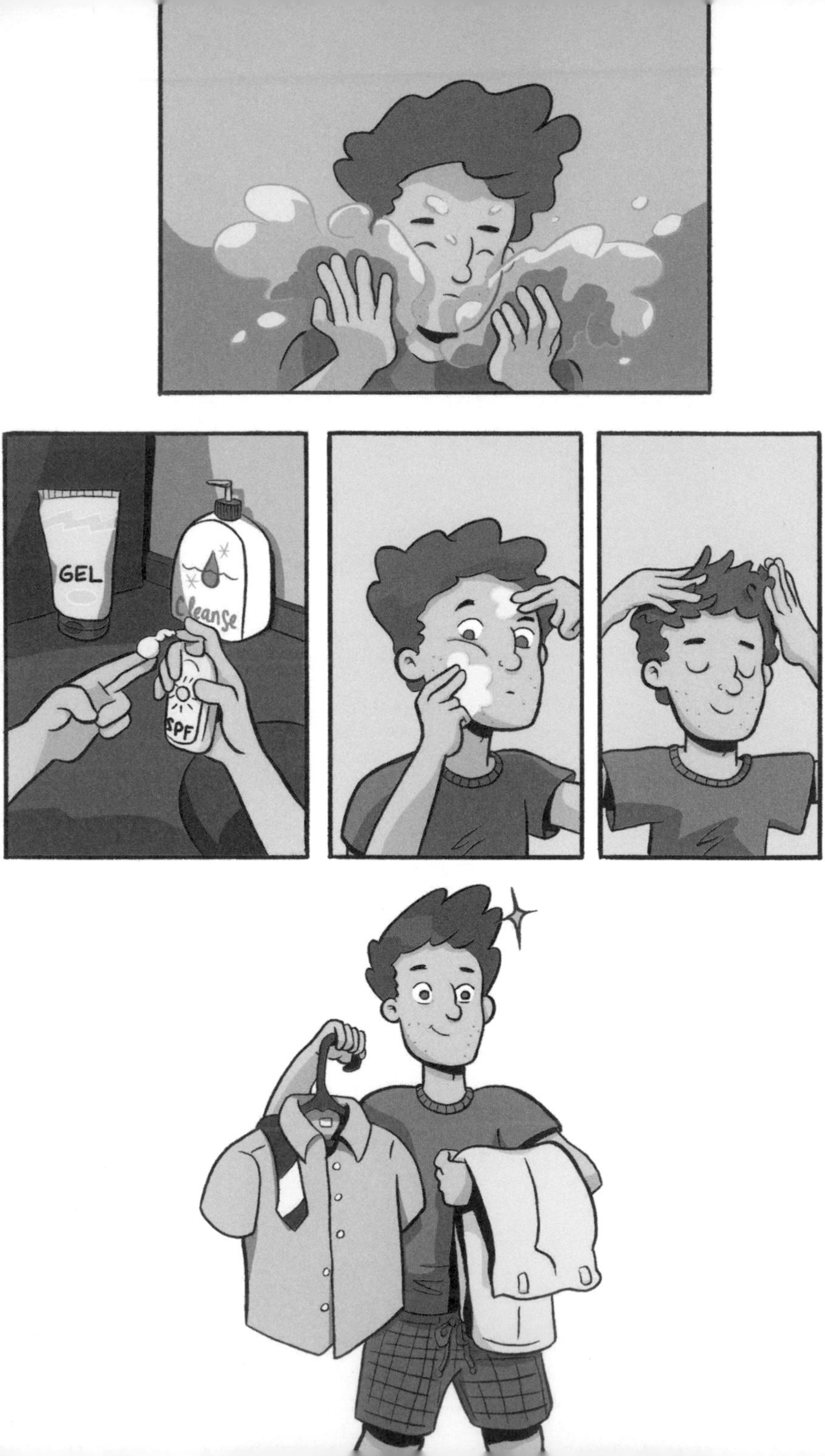
GEL
Cleanse
SPF

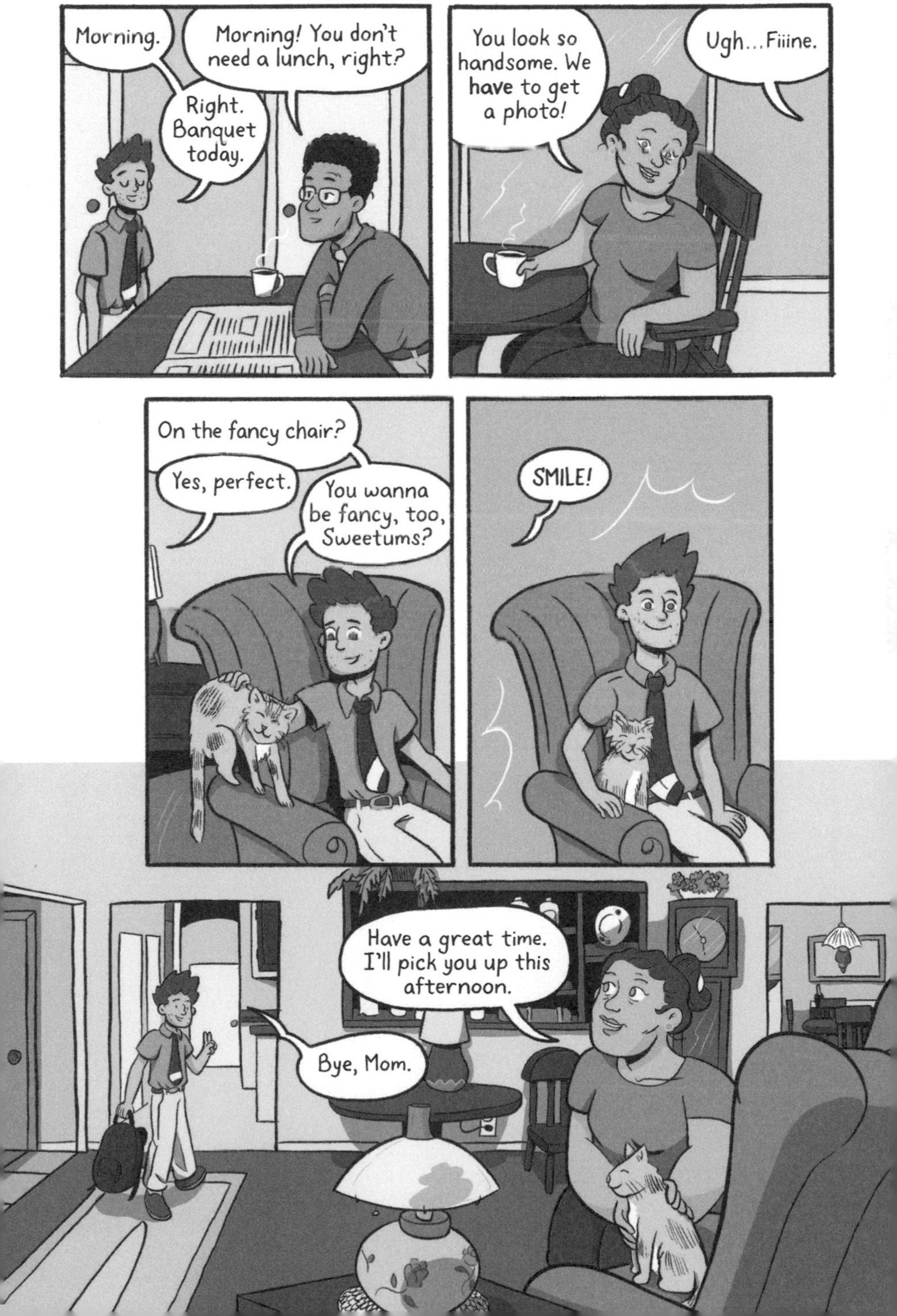
Morning.
Morning! You don't need a lunch, right?
Right. Banquet today.
You look so handsome. We **have** to get a photo!
Ugh...Fiiine.
On the fancy chair?
Yes, perfect.
You wanna be fancy, too, Sweetums?
SMILE!
Have a great time. I'll pick you up this afternoon.
Bye, Mom.

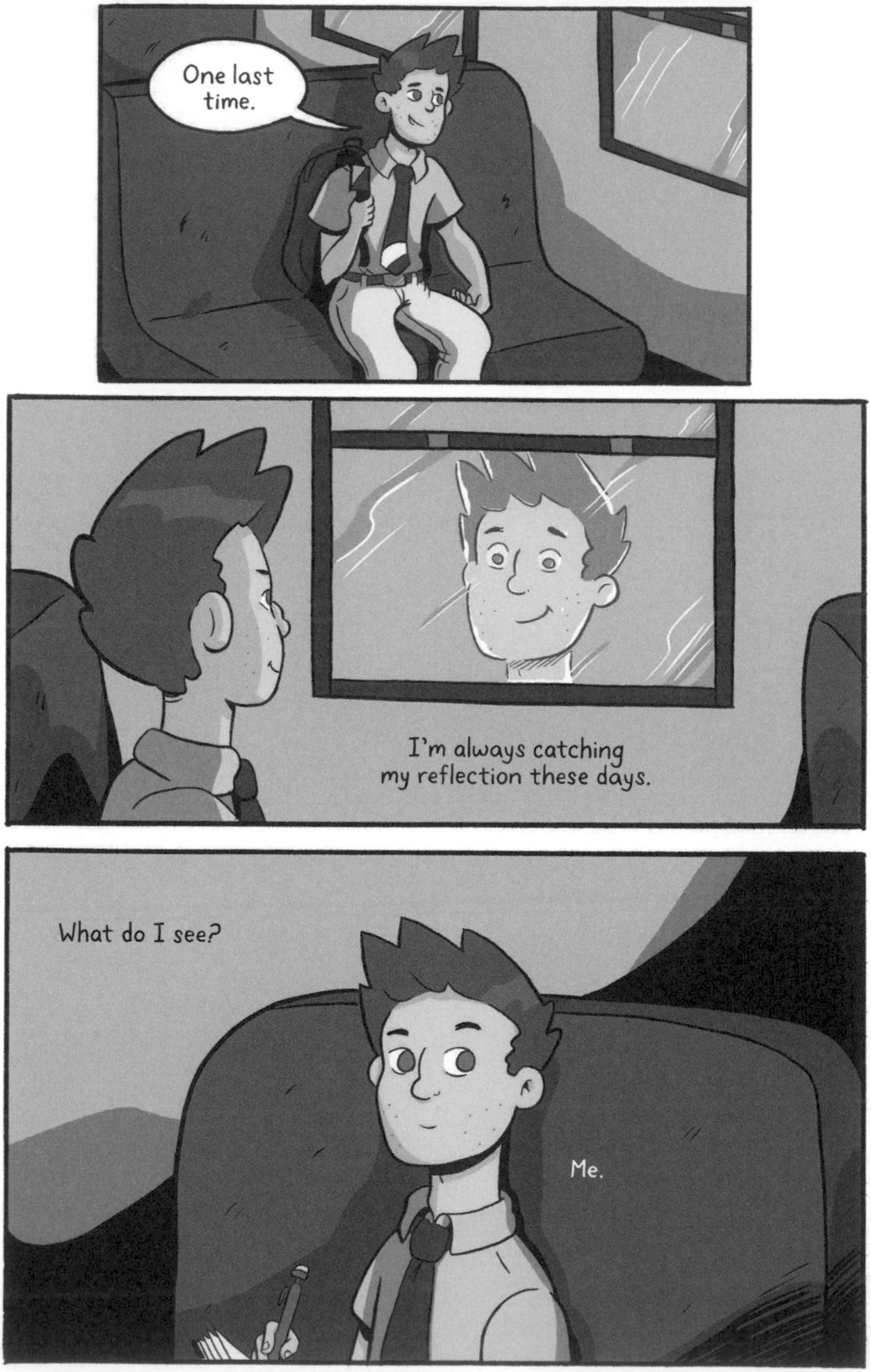
One last time.
I'm always catching my reflection these days.
What do I see?
Me.

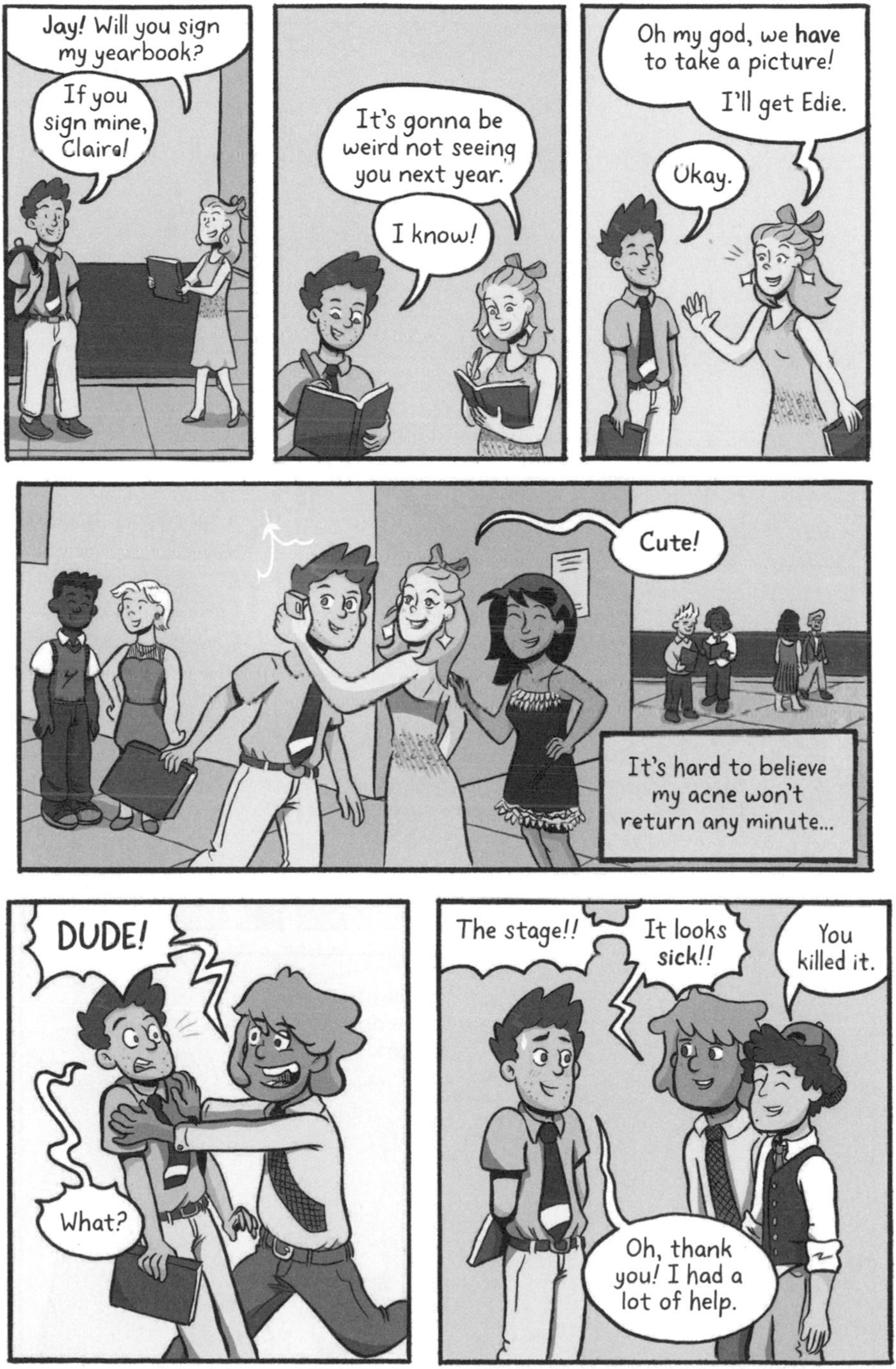
Jay! Will you sign my yearbook?
If you sign mine, Claire!
It's gonna be weird not seeing you next year.
I know!
Oh my god, we have to take a picture!
I'll get Edie.
Okay.
Cute!
It's hard to believe my acne won't return any minute...
DUDE!
What?
The stage!!
It looks sick!!
You killed it.
Oh, thank you! I had a lot of help.

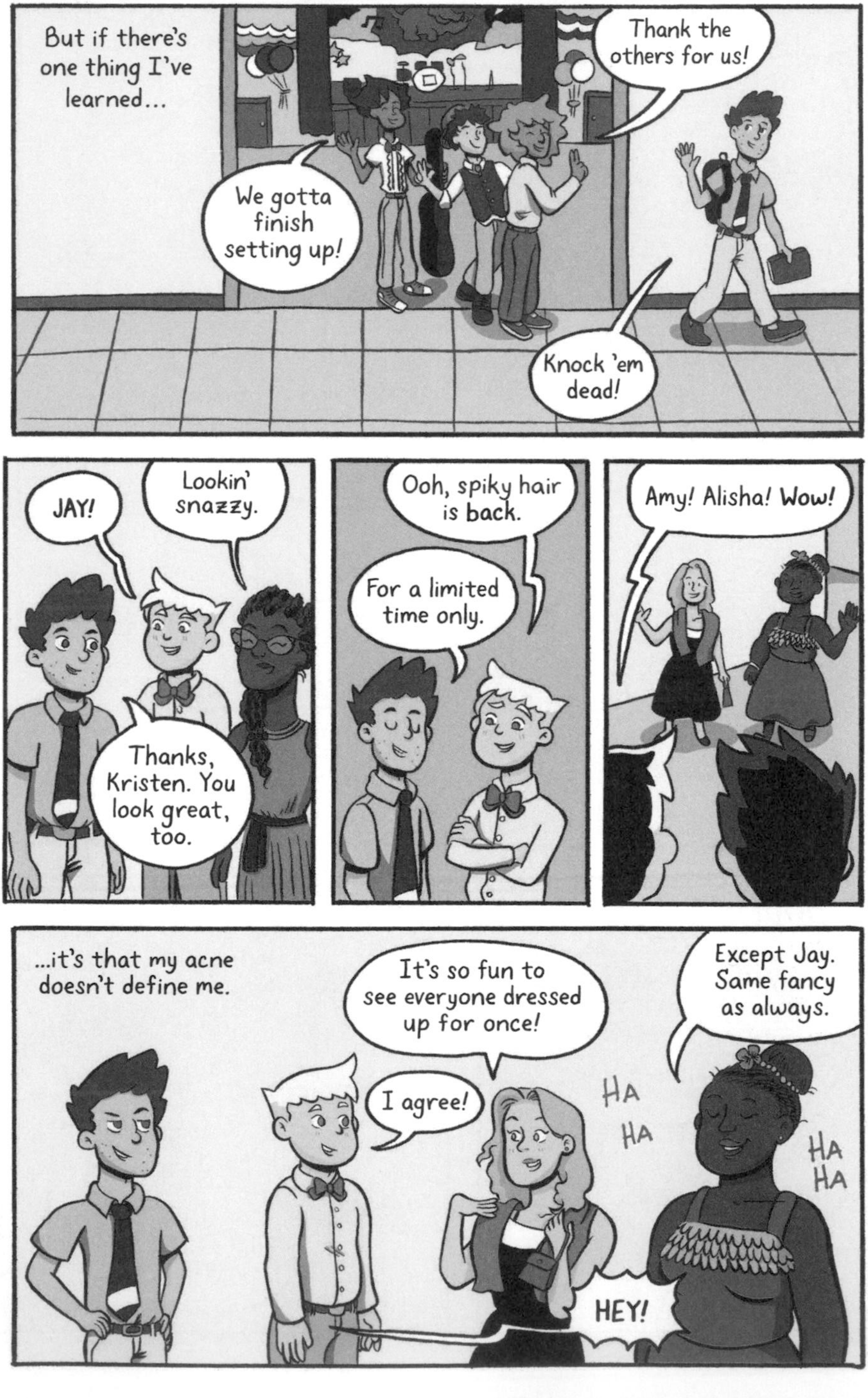
But if there's one thing I've learned...
Thank the others for us!
We gotta finish setting up!
Knock 'em dead!
JAY!
Lookin' snazzy.
Thanks, Kristen. You look great, too.
Ooh, spiky hair is **back**.
For a limited time only.
Amy! Alisha! **Wow!**
...it's that my acne doesn't define me.
It's so fun to see everyone dressed up for once!
Except Jay. Same fancy as always.
I agree!
HA HA
HA HA
HEY!

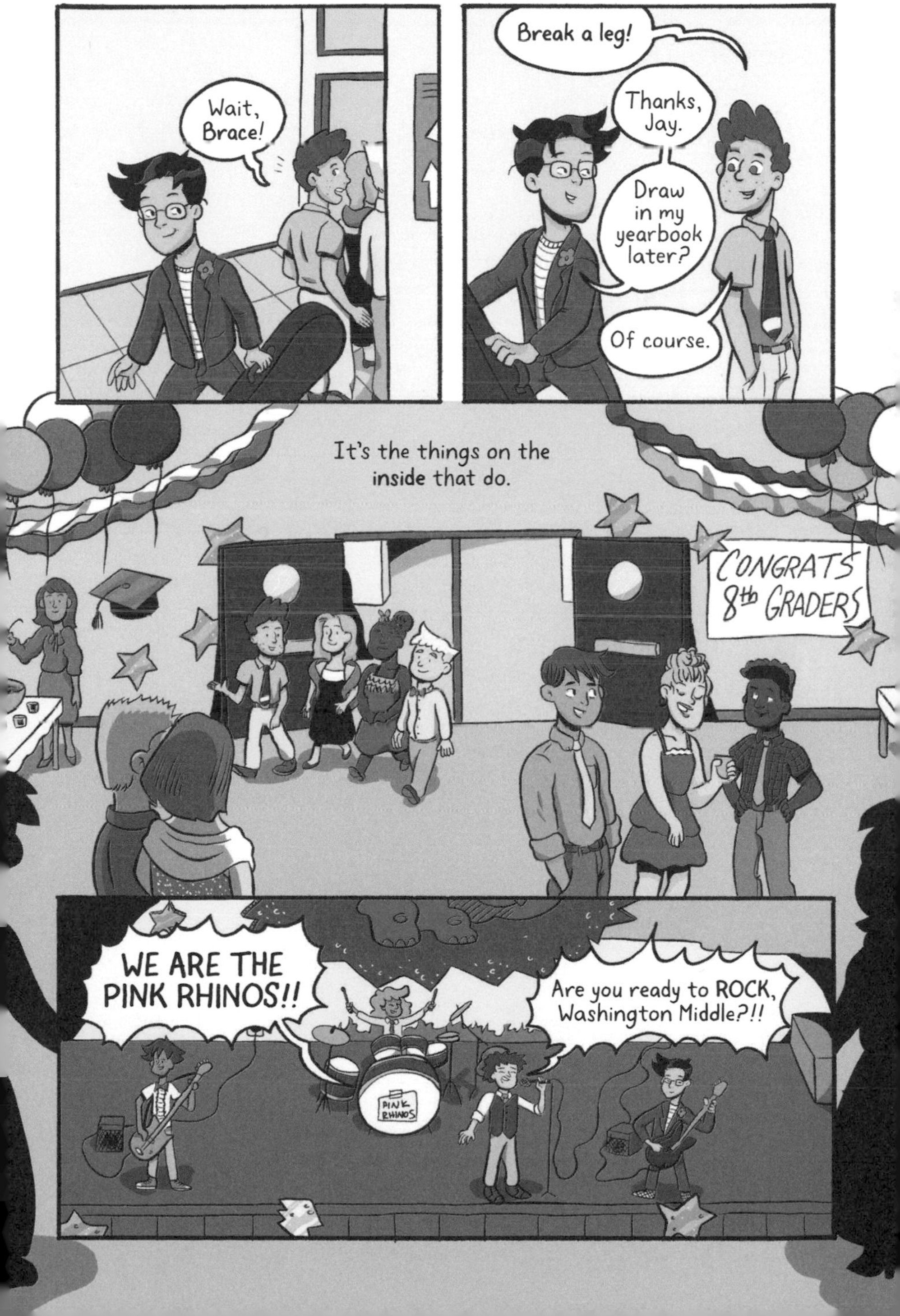

Wait, Brace!
Break a leg!
Thanks, Jay.
Draw in my yearbook later?
Of course.
It's the things on the inside that do.
CONGRATS 8th GRADERS
WE ARE THE PINK RHINOS!!
Are you ready to ROCK, Washington Middle?!!
PINK RHINOS

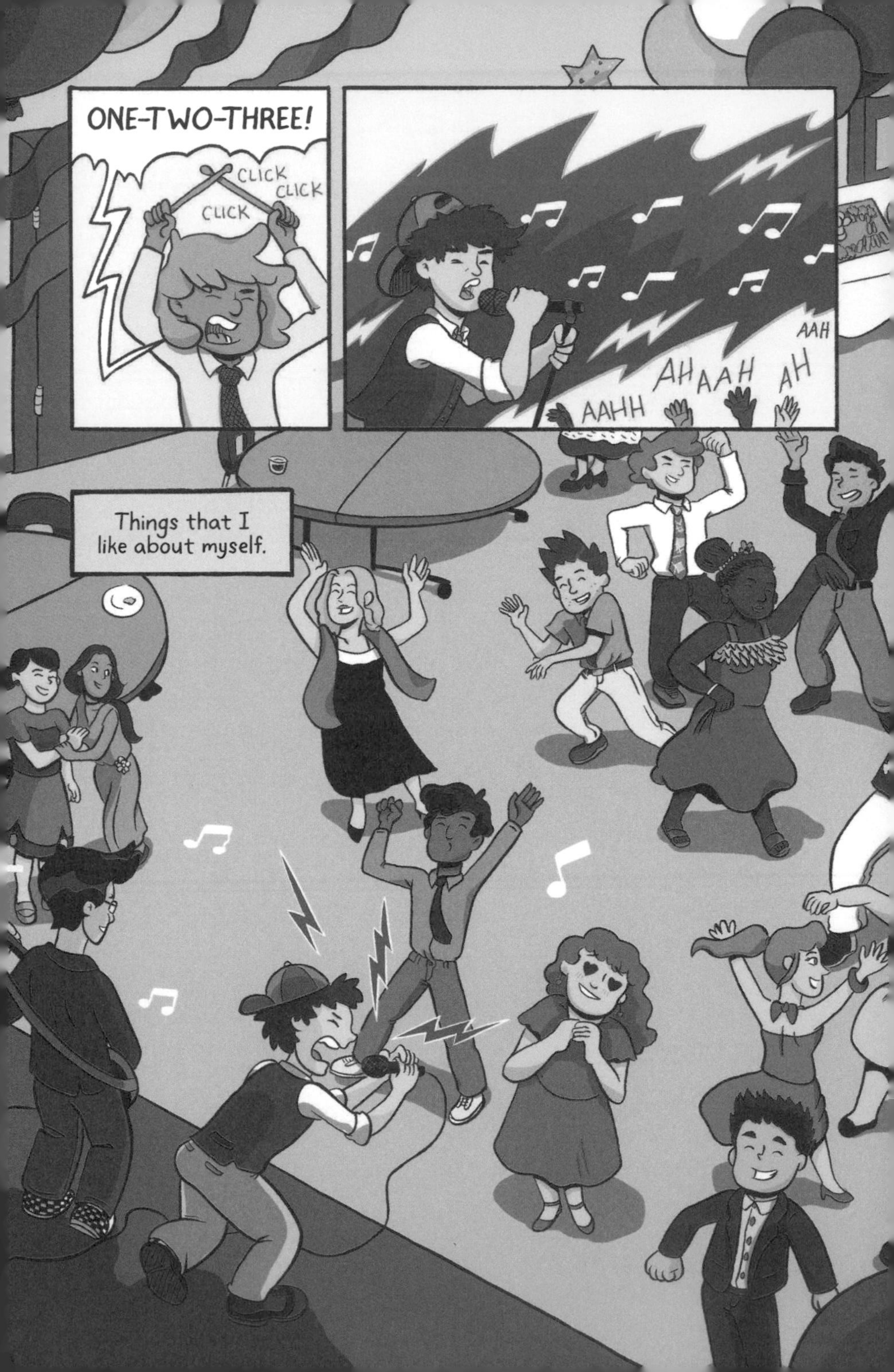
ONE-TWO-THREE!
CLICK
CLICK
CLICK
AAH
AH
AAAH
AH
AAHH
Things that I like about myself.

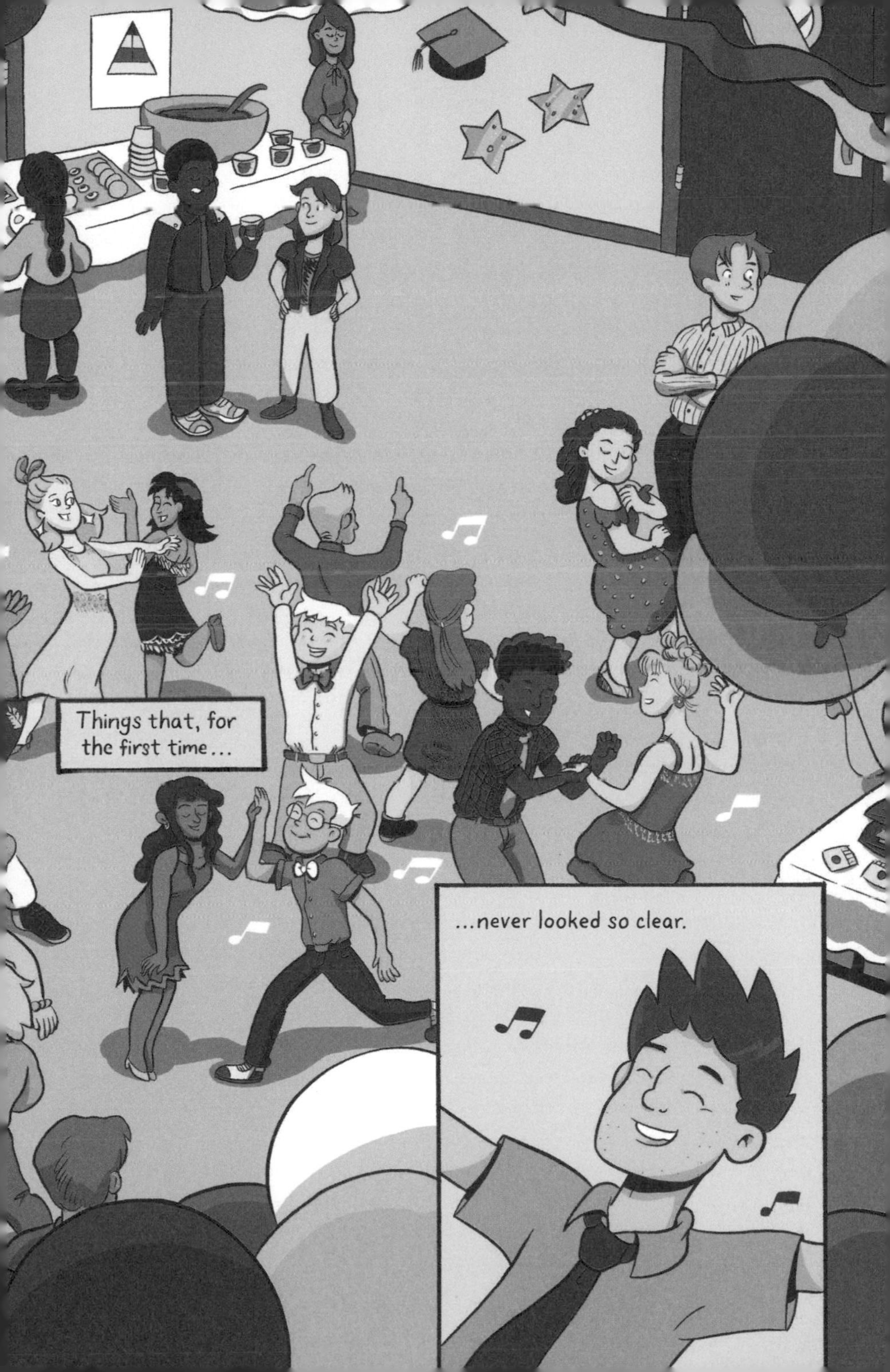
Things that, for the first time...
...never looked so clear.

Author's Note

This book is heavily based on my personal experiences; I think it still feels true, even without being "The Truth."

When it comes to my face, I'm very sensitive. I try not to let perceived vanity keep me from taking care of it, since there is a lot of shame that comes with being concerned over your appearance. In middle school, I was somehow blessed to not be afflicted with acne the way so many of my friends were. But, even as a shy, well-behaved, good student, my peers still found a way to tease me: for my nice handwriting, for gelling my hair, for occasionally wearing a nice shirt, and even for having nice skin by calling me a porcelain doll.

All of my skin troubles began during my senior year of high school, and again at the end of my senior year of college, lasting throughout my mid-twenties. While those may have been less common time periods to experience these ailments, I can assure you that having acne at any age absolutely sucks. Countless ointments, medications, doctor's appointments, and isotretinoin with all its blood work and side effects; I wouldn't wish it on my greatest enemy. All I wanted was to look in the mirror and see myself again. My self-worth and confidence took a major hit during these periods.

At job interviews and places I worked, I thought my acne was perceived as juvenile, and in turn they didn't take me seriously. My inner voice of judgment was hard to suppress when meeting new people, assuming they wouldn't want an acne-afflicted friend. I stopped auditioning for theater and local indie films since I couldn't imagine any director picking me for his leading man with a face like mine. Using clothes as a distraction helped—at least it seemed that way—if someone commented on my outfit, it meant they weren't looking at my bad acne flare-up. But I had flattened myself into one dimension and in my head, acne was my only defining characteristic. I'm immensely grateful to my handful of close friends, who always saw beyond the surface and liked me for myself, acne or not.

Eventually, with the help of a great dermatologist, a second, unpleasant round of isotretinoin, and an enormous amount of patience, my acne troubles did go away. It sounds so simple, but I know it isn't. And what worked for me, won't work for everyone. Even now at thirty-two, I still get breakouts if I don't stay vigilant with my skincare regimen.

This book is also about asexuality, something I wasn't sure I knew how to write about, since it's something I haven't spoken much about in my real life. I didn't even know that word until I was twenty-four, when I heard a character in a TV show use it to casually describe himself. At that moment, something clicked in my head. I immediately opened up a tab on my computer and searched for a definition. I thought I knew what it meant, but I had to verify. And there it was: a clear description of how I'd been my whole life.

Of course, as with any label, these things are fluid, and as time goes on I find that most days it still fits and other days it isn't quite right. But being honest with myself, without anyone else's opinion, is a kind of freedom that I cherish.

I did my best to pull a few threads out of a tapestry to weave a new tapestry, but is it ever possible to say everything in one book? Probably not. Just like one physical attribute or one label can't completely define any one person. And that seems a-okay to me.

Jarad

May 2021

Acknowledgments

Andrew Arnold, for championing me and my story and all of our unexpected life parallels. And for unwavering patience as we made this book during the pandemic.

Kelly Sonnack, for asking me all the right questions and believing in my leap of faith.

Tillie Walden, for encouraging me to be brave.

My family, for letting me sit in my room and draw and for always joking that every incident "is gonna be another chapter in Jarad's book one day." This is for all those times you paged me over the Barnes and Noble intercom. 😊

The amazing team at Harper who all helped *A-Okay* in different ways: Rose Pleuler, Barb Fitzsimmons, Martha Maynard, and Andrew Eliopulos.

My wonderful color flatting assistants: Madi Baker, Sam Bennett, Mercedes Campos-Lopez, Reilly Hadden, Leise Hook, Steve Thueson, and Masha Zhdanova; I couldn't have made this book without all your help. And Shelli Paroline for advice and encouragement when I really needed it.

My friends Katie Cawley, Robyn-Brooke Smith, Steve Thueson, Dan Nott, Daryl Seitchik, Cuyler Hedlund, Ashley Poston, Emma Hunsinger, Natalie Wardlaw, Coco Fox, Chris Crawford, Dave Lloyd, Michelle Ollie, Rachel Tillman, and James Sturm.

And Dr. B for helping me find clarity and teaching me how to take care of my skin. It takes a village. Thank you all so much!!

For anyone in search of their reflection

HarperAlley is an imprint of HarperCollins Publishers.

A-Okay
Copyright © 2021 by Jarad Greene
For information address HarperCollins Children's Books, a division of
HarperCollins Publishers, 195 Broadway, New York, NY 10007.
www.harperalley.com

Library of Congress Control Number: 2021938242
ISBN 978-0-06-303284-2 (pbk.) — ISBN 978-0-06-303285-9

21 22 23 24 25   EP   10 9 8 7 6 5 4 3 2 1
❖
First Edition